S0-AIX-804

*The Washington Story*

ALSO BY ADAM LANGER

*Crossing California*

# The Washington Story

*A Novel in Five Spheres*

----

# ADAM LANGER

RIVERHEAD BOOKS

*a member of Penguin Group (USA) Inc.*

*New York   2005*

RIVERHEAD BOOKS

Published by the Penguin Group

Penguin Group (USA) Inc., 375 Hudson Street, New York, New York 10014, USA • Penguin Group (Canada), 90 Eglinton Avenue East, Suite 700, Toronto, Ontario M4P 2Y3, Canada (a division of Pearson Penguin Canada Inc.) • Penguin Books Ltd, 80 Strand, London WC2R 0RL, England • Penguin Ireland, 25 St Stephen's Green, Dublin 2, Ireland (a division of Penguin Books Ltd) • Penguin Group (Australia), 250 Camberwell Road, Camberwell, Victoria 3124, Australia (a division of Pearson Australia Group Pty Ltd) • Penguin Books India Pvt Ltd, 11 Community Centre, Panchsheel Park, New Delhi–110 017, India • Penguin Group (NZ), Cnr Airborne and Rosedale Roads, Albany, Auckland 1310, New Zealand (a division of Pearson New Zealand Ltd) • Penguin Books (South Africa) (Pty) Ltd, 24 Sturdee Avenue, Rosebank, Johannesburg 2196, South Africa

Penguin Books Ltd, Registered Offices:
80 Strand, London WC2R 0RL, England

Copyright © 2005 by Adam Langer

All rights reserved. No part of this book may be reproduced, scanned, or distributed in any printed or electronic form without permission. Please do not participate in or encourage piracy of copyrighted materials in violation of the author's rights. Purchase only authorized editions.

Published simultaneously in Canada

Library of Congress Cataloging-in-Publication Data

Langer, Adam.
The Washington story : a novel in five spheres / by Adam Langer.
p.   cm.
ISBN 1-57322-324-7
1. Jews—Illinois—Chicago—Fiction.   2. Jewish families—Fiction.   3. Chicago (Ill.)—Fiction.
4. Jewish youth—Fiction.   I. Title.
PS3612.A57W37      2005                          2005046483
813'.6—dc22

Printed in the United States of America
1   3   5   7   9   10   8   6   4   2

Book design by Stephanie Huntwork

This is a work of fiction. Names, characters, places, and incidents either are the product of the author's imagination or are used fictitiously, and any resemblance to actual persons, living or dead, businesses, companies, events, or locales is entirely coincidental.

While the author has made every effort to provide accurate telephone numbers and Internet addresses at the time of publication, neither the publisher nor the author assumes any responsibility for errors, or for changes that occur after publication. Further, the publisher does not have any control over and does not assume any responsibility for author or third-party websites or their content.

*To Beate,*
*to my parents,*
*and in memory of*
*Abe & Sylvia Herstein and*
*Rebecca & Sam Langer*

# Contents

I

*Eruv*

Jill and Muley's Book of Boundaries (1982–83)

*1*

II

*Breirot*

Mel and Michelle's Book of Choices (1983–84)

*101*

III

*Yetziyat Mitzrayim*

Jill and Becky's Book of Exodus (1984–85)

*193*

IV

*Kaddish*

Muley and Hillel's Book of Mourning (1985–87)

*285*

V

*Aliyah*

Jill and Rachel's Book of Homecoming (November 25, 1987)

*355*

*Glossary of Selected Terms*

*379*

*Appendices*

*395*

*Acknowledgments*

*400*

*Thus the Lord scattered them from there over the face of the whole Earth:*
*And they stopped building the city.*

—GENESIS 11:8

# I

# *Eruv*

*Jill and Muley's Book of Boundaries*

*(1982–83)*

— — —

(A STORY OF WEST ROGERS PARK)

*Chicago is a city divided.*

—HAROLD WASHINGTON, NOVEMBER 10, 1982

Jill Wasserstrom, cub reporter for her high school newspaper, the *Lane Leader,* was a great believer in fate, so it was not surprising that she would read great meaning into the fact that, in 1982, during the second week of November, three historically significant incidents would occur within one twelve-hour period. On Wednesday evening, she and *Lane Leader* editor William Eamon Sullivan Jr. had stood in the ballroom of the Hyde Park Hilton to hear Illinois congressman Harold Washington announce that he would seek to become Chicago's first black mayor. And the next morning, she would hear WBBM reporter John Cody report both the death of Soviet president Leonid Brezhnev and the liftoff of the space shuttle *Columbia.* And yet, she didn't read meaning into the coincidence of all these events themselves as much as the fact that they all had taken place while she'd been thinking of Wes. Still, on that second Wednesday of November, as she rode in the passenger seat of Wes's pale orange BMW 2002, Jill determined that it was foolish to think that anything would ever happen between herself and Wes Sullivan; after all, Wes was a senior and dating Rae-Ann Warner, while Jill was a junior dating Muley Scott Wills. And besides, nothing interesting happened in West Rogers Park anyway.

The neighborhood of West Rogers Park, on the northwest side of Chicago, is the only Chicago neighborhood where synagogues outnumber churches, kosher pizza joints outnumber fast-food restaurants, and *kichel*s outnumber doughnuts. Throughout its history, the rest of Chicago has all but ignored it; during the blizzards of 1967 and 1979, the city's snowplows never once touched its side streets. West Rogers Park's dimensions had not changed during Jill's lifetime, yet to her, it was slowly yet inexorably shrinking, so much so that she often felt as though she were living in two separate and completely distinct worlds.

On North Shore Avenue, Jill lived with her father, Charlie, associate publisher and lifestyle columnist for the Schiffler Neighborhood Newspapers; her stepmother, Gail, publisher and heir to the Schiffler newspaper fortune; and their voluble infant daughter, Rachel. They lived in the imitation Frank Lloyd Wright home that Charlie and his first wife, Becky, had once called the Funny House. In West Rogers Park, Jill would study, walk Fidel, her brown-splotched, white mutt, or lounge on the beanbags in her bedroom with Muley Wills watching faded 16 mm films checked out from the Nortown branch of the Chicago Public Library.

In telephone conversations with her sister Michelle, a second-year theater major at New York University, Jill referred to West Rogers Park as "The Land That Time Forgot." Recently, a group of Orthodox Jews had petitioned the city to request that a border made of fishing wire, or an *eruv,* as it was called in Hebrew, be hung from the lampposts of West Rogers Park, encircling the neighborhood, thus creating the boundaries for a small community in which residents were allowed to perform certain activities otherwise forbidden on the Sabbath, such as pushing strollers to *shul.* To the Wasserstroms, the *eruv* was largely inoffensive; Charlie signed the petition for it and Gail wrote an op-ed piece supporting it. But to Jill, it was symbolic of the sameness of the neighborhood, its provincialism and insularity.

And in both Jill's moments of greatest rage, such as when her father had written a facile column titled "Ebony Bagels, Ivory Cream Cheese," about how blacks and Jews had a lot more in common than they thought (easy for Charlie to say, Jill said, seeing that his neighborhood had no blacks in it as far as she knew, aside from Muley and his mother), and in her moments of greatest contentment, reading revolutionary tracts in Muley's room while he drew flip books and short animated films, Jill had a sense that Life was something that was happening elsewhere. It was happening on the streets of New York, from which Michelle wrote letters home, addressed to "The Wasserstroms, 2847 W. North Shore Avenue, The Black Hole, 60645." It was happening in the corridors of Lane Tech and in the offices of the *Lane Leader,* where Jill was one of the only non-seniors on staff. It was happening in Moscow, in Cape Canaveral, Florida, on the south side of Chicago, in West Berlin. Life was what happened on subways and buses, not in the big, lumbering Cutlasses and Lincoln Continentals of North Shore Avenue, not in the kosher bakeries or the Judaica bookstores of Devon Avenue, not in West Rogers Park at all.

Nevertheless, on that night, November 10, 1982, Jill was brimming over with excitement the moment she arrived home, her hands full of notepads, cassette tapes, and a tape recorder whose microphone scraped the ground as she held her house keys with her teeth and pushed open the front door with an elbow. But her father, seated at the kitchen table with a pencil, spiral notebook, and can of Diet Chocolate Fudge Soda, was one of several people whom she could not inform of her delight. He'd appreciate her bright mood, that was certain—she had often found her father to be a slightly distorted mirror of her own emotions; when she smiled, he smiled, when she frowned, he frowned, and whenever she was angry, he'd gaze blankly at her and ask what was wrong. But there was no way he would comprehend the thrill she had felt after having gone out on a legitimate newspaper assignment. Not for a real paper, it was true. And no, it hadn't even been her assignment; she had merely accompanied Wes Sullivan as he covered Harold Washington's first campaign speech. Normally, when Wes reported stories, he brought Rae-Ann. But faculty advisor Louis Benson had insisted that this time he take one of the junior staffers.

Jill knew that Charlie would not be able to fathom why she had been so thrilled to stand in the Hilton ballroom, just a few feet away from the Reverend Jesse Jackson, next to the radio and TV reporters with their outstretched microphones, the daily newsmen with their notepads, scribbling and barking out questions, to listen to Washington declare his intention to destroy the Democratic political machine and "create a city in which every individual will receive his or her full measure of dignity," to stand so close to Washington that, as he brushed past her and stepped into a waiting black limousine, she could sniff the Manny's Deli pastrami sandwich he'd had for lunch. Washington's words filled her with an overwhelming gust of optimism as he positioned himself against the corruption of the old Chicago Democratic machine personified by his opponents, Mayor Jane Byrne and State's Attorney Richard M. Daley, son of the late Mayor Richard J. Daley, who had ruled Chicago for more than twenty years. But there was no point in discussing any of this with Charlie, who was leery of a black mayor—look at what they did to Martin Luther King; who knew what some nut with a gun might do?—and who never contradicted his wife, who called herself a Libertarian and had her own reservations about minorities in positions of power.

Muley Wills might have enjoyed hearing Jill's enthusiastic summary of Washington's speech. But he was spending the week with his lab partner, Connie Sherman, and his Life Sciences teacher, Sam Singer, in Cape Canaveral, Florida, where they had won a contest to have an experiment performed on the space shuttle *Columbia*. Furthermore, Jill's excitement was only partially related to Washington's announcement; she couldn't confide in Muley that the reason her cheeks were flushed and her eyes were sparkling was that she had spent the entire evening with Wes Sullivan.

On the drive to Hyde Park, Wes had told Jill that the one thing he liked about his name was that it was infinitely malleable. To his father, an executive editor at the *Chicago Tribune,* he was "Will Junior." To his German mother, whom his father had met while stationed in Bremerhaven, he was "*Wilhelm.*" To his sisters, he was "Willie." To his younger brother, Casey, who was developmentally disabled, he was "Willum." To the whites on the basketball courts, he was "Sully"; to the blacks, he was "Big Bee-yill." When his girlfriend, Rae-Ann, was mad at him—which was often—he became "William Darn-it!" To *Lane Leader* cartoonist Hillel Levy, he was "Willie Aames." But the name he liked best, the one he invited Jill to call him, was "Wes."

Until this night, however, Wes had never once called Jill by her first name. When she'd first started writing for the paper, he'd called her "Sixty-One," because she was sixty-one inches tall; after she'd turned in her first reported piece, an article about street gangs for which she'd interviewed members of the Folks and the Latin Kings, several of whose girlfriends complimented her during Flag Football on her balanced reporting, Wes had started admiringly referring to her as "Woodstein," a nickname that *Washington Post* editor Ben Bradlee had given to Watergate reporters Bob Woodward and Carl Bernstein. But tonight, as Jill and Wes discussed everything from movies (Wes said that he was "totally pissed" because he'd wanted to see the German New Wave double bill at The Parkway, but Rae-Ann had threatened to dump him if they missed *An Officer and a Gentleman* again) to his brother Casey's mental disability (Wes said that he'd recently told Casey's counselor in an "adaptive learning program" to "stop treating everybody like a fucking moron") to Harold Washington's speech ("That dude's one erudite motherfucker"), Wes had started calling her "Jill."

"You know something, Jill?" he had said as they walked from his car to the Hilton lobby, passing two dozen people waving hand-lettered RUN HAROLD RUN! posters. "You'd be cool to date 'cause you wouldn't put expectations on your boyfriend." But before Jill could respond, Wes, in his army pants and his ripped, gray, mud-stained "Property of Alcatraz" T-shirt—even in the dead of winter, he nearly always wore short sleeves—jogged toward the ballroom, muscling past reporters, photographers, Washington supporters, and University of Chicago parents and alumni disturbed by the sight of so many black people in their hotel.

While driving home, Wes said that it would be "pretty fucking hilarious" if he walked out on Rae-Ann in the middle of *An Officer and a Gentleman,* then picked up Jill so the two of them could see "a real movie." As he drove, Wes kept pointing out Clark Street restaurants, such as Happy Sushi and Tenkatsu; man, he loved trying ethnic food, but Rae-Ann only liked quesadillas, pizza, and Wolfy's hot dogs with ketchup. She was so suburban; she never let him listen to his tapes—the Boomtown Rats were too depressing, Prince was too dirty, and Sting "tried too hard to sound Hispanic"—so Wes had to listen to her Romeo Void cassettes every time they drove to Pepe's Tacos yet again, with Rae-Ann singing, *"might like you better if we slept together,"* even though she was still withholding sex from him. Jill told Wes that she would be happy to try any of the restaurants he had mentioned, but then Wes eyed his car clock and said that it was getting late. And when he dropped Jill off at her house, reminding her that her Washington notes were due first thing in the morning, he was calling her "Woodstein" again.

When Jill arrived home, she asked her father if Muley had called. No, Charlie said, and Jill felt thankful—had Muley called, she might have felt guilty about being out with Wes. Jill and Charlie chatted briefly—about Charlie's phone conversation with Michelle, who would be coming home for Chanukah and seeing her new sister for the first time ("I miss her so much," Charlie said of Michelle), about Gail and Rachel's trip to see Gail's retired parents in Florida ("I miss them too," Charlie said, even though Gail and Rachel's entire trip would last only thirty-six hours). And then, since there was no human with whom Jill could discuss her evening with Wes, Jill decided to walk to the lake and discuss it with Fidel.

Jill frequently discussed critical matters with her dog—the political situation in Nicaragua, *Lane Leader* politics, Gail's refusal to let her hold Rachel for more than ten seconds without criticizing her ("Jill, honey, she gets hungry when you hold her like that; she thinks you're going to nurse"). Jill's conversations with Fidel were never conducted aloud, and the fact that the dog couldn't talk back made her more comfortable discussing her rapidly developing crush on Wes. Even though, Jill thought as she led Fidel over the border between West and East Rogers Park toward Lake Michigan, the aforementioned crush was moot anyway since Wes was a foot taller than her, two years older, and already had a girlfriend who was also taller and older, though not necessarily smarter.

What irked Jill, though, later that night, as she sat in a lifeguard's chair on the beach and watched Fidel frolic in Lake Michigan, the nearly full moon shimmering on the black water, was that even if Wes were two years younger and a half-foot shorter and even if he weren't dating Rae-Ann, whom Jill loathed because she introduced every sentence with "It's like," and modified each adjective with "totally" since someone had once complimented her by saying that she talked just like a "Valley Girl," Jill still couldn't date Wes because Muley—who was so progressive in his imagination yet so conservative in reality—would get upset.

And what irked her even more was that she was even bothering to think about Wes at all, that when she should have been typing up her Washington notes or saving the beleaguered fruit flies that were threatening to sabotage her Accelerated Sciences drosophila experiment and send her grade plummeting to an A minus, she was thinking about some guy who could be dating any girl at Lane, and who, this time next year, would be gone anyway, attending Reed or Deep Springs, the only schools Wes termed "cool enough" to let him "do his own thing."

There was really no point in thinking about any of this, so Jill resolved to stop. Which she did until the next morning when, after briefly listening to the news on WBBM, she surreptitiously burrowed into Michelle's old theater makeup kit, rapidly applied light blue eye shadow, maroon lipstick, and a few pumps of Chanel No. 5 behind her ears, and arrived early at the offices of the *Lane Leader* in a black turtleneck, a black skirt, and black tennis shoes. Wes was already in the *Leader* office, wearing the same ratty T-shirt and army pants as the previous evening; he sported a black armband. He was clacking away at a manual typewriter when Jill entered and placed her notes in his mailbox. "Right on time again, Woodstein," Wes said, but when he got a closer look at Jill, he sneered. God, he wondered aloud, why did women wear makeup; that was so fucking stupid.

Jill was too busy holding back the tears that had come geysering to her eyes to devise an appropriate response. Her lips opened, then closed, but no sound came. Wes, who had sisters and knew when he had offended them, began to say something conciliatory, but then noticed Jill's black turtleneck, the shoes, the skirt. He then glanced demonstratively down at his own black armband. Why was she wearing black, he wanted to know, was she honoring Brezhnev too? And now the tears Jill felt were no longer tears of shame; they were tears of happiness, for Jill felt as if she had found someone who understood her completely. Yes, she said, she had just heard the news about the general secretary of the Communist Party. Wes regarded her with a somber smile full of squints and dimples. She was so cool, he said.

M uley Scott Wills had entered the NSEC (NASA Space Experiment Competition) each year at Lane Tech, but only this year, in which he had spent a grand total of forty-five minutes on his project, had he been named one of eight finalists and invited to the Kennedy Space Center in Cape Canaveral. His freshman year, he'd proposed an elaborate projection system that would use the surface of the moon as a screen upon which everyone in the world could watch free movies on full moon nights. That proposal had netted him a form letter from NASA and an admonition from his Astronomy teacher not to waste his time on unworkable ideas. The following year's experiment would have tested the effect of a zero-gravity environment on human emotions; in earlier years, he'd heard his deeply depressed mother say that the world was weighing her down and he wondered if a weightless environment might cure her. NSEC responded with another form letter. This year, the winning experiment he'd devised with his lab partner, Connie Sherman, a sophomore who was taking the class largely so she could sit next to Muley, involved growing peas. Ten pea plants would be grown in a greenhouse on Earth, ten others aboard the shuttle.

Though Muley had been eager to tour the space center and film the shuttle liftoff with an 8 mm camera, he had been dreading the rest of the trip, in part because he would have to spend five days apart from Jill, with his Life Sciences teacher, the recently divorced Dr. Singer, who drove a convertible red Alfa Romeo with "COSMOS" plates, sported a satanic beard, and fancied himself a swinger. The exceedingly flirtatious Connie—who often told Singer that she'd dated men older than him—was the other reason for Muley's dread. Connie, whom Muley had known since fifth grade at Boone Elementary when she and her mother had moved from an apartment in Budlong Woods to a town house on Touhy Avenue, was a Bubblicious-popping, Camel-smoking young woman who wore torn jeans and tight concert shirts, mostly to annoy her Ford-dealing stepfather, who once told her that she "oozed too much sexuality." When Dr. Singer announced that she and Muley had been named NSEC finalists, she kept saying to Muley, "Five whole days; think of what we can do for five whole days."

They'd driven the whole way down with Dr. Singer and Connie up front and Muley crammed into the backseat, stopping only for gas, pee breaks, and hamburgers. For most of the ride, Muley remained silent while Dr. Singer cranked Boz Scaggs tapes and complained about his ex-wife, who had full custody of their two children, and Connie discussed her boyfriend, Britt Hurd, a Lane senior whose mother was trying to talk him out of dropping out of high school, joining the Marines—where he could get paid for his favorite pastimes: "ass-whoopin'" and "blowin' shit up"—and marrying Connie. "Don't get married," Dr. Singer told Connie. "Enjoy your youth." Connie looked back at Muley and winked.

They arrived at the Space Coast Inn shortly after ten on Wednesday night. Muley had been planning to call Jill from the motel, but Dr. Singer said that he and Connie only had ten minutes to "freshen up" before they were to meet him in the lounge, where he would buy them highballs from a "sexy singer" who, he was certain, had been "giving [him] the eye" when they had checked in. In the half-empty lounge, as the aforementioned singer crooned "Rocket Man," Muley sipped from his highball glass, assuming that once Dr. Singer and Connie were on their second drink, neither would notice him sneak away. But once he was in his room, the moment after he had stepped out of his shower and changed into a faded red Chicago Black Hawks T-shirt and a pair of black nylon shorts, someone was slapping loudly on his door and when Muley asked who was there, Connie said it was the hotel detective and wasn't Muley too young to be alone in a single room. Muley opened the door a crack, but Connie pushed it open the rest of the way, entered, then sat down on a bed. *God,* she said, she thought she'd never be able to get away—why did Muley leave her with that creep? Muley apologized, saying that he thought that he was the only one who thought Singer was a creep, but added that the drive had tired him out and that they had to be up by six the next morning to catch the tour bus. Connie said that was seven hours away; was he going to sleep through his whole vacation? No, Muley said, actually he'd been planning to call his girlfriend. Cool, Connie said, go right ahead; did he mind if she watched TV—she didn't feel like going back to her room; there was something sad about being alone in a room with two beds in it. She didn't understand why they couldn't have just roomed together—why did everyone think that if a sixteen-year-old guy and a fifteen-year-old girl shared a room they'd wind up having sex? It was just stupid. Go on, she said, call Jill and pretend I'm not here.

Connie grabbed the remote control, turned on the TV, and flipped channels, settling on a hotel station broadcasting an X-rated film—a buxom blonde was lounging in a hot tub, a champagne flute in her hand as a burly workman with a toolkit asked her if anything else needed fixing. Connie laughed hysterically, covered her mouth, apologized, then snorted and laughed again. She asked Muley if he'd ever seen one of these movies before. No, he said, but they were unpleasant to watch because they were shot on cheap film stock. Maybe, Connie said, but they sure were funny. She couldn't believe that Britt often asked her to say things that the women in these movies said. Sometimes, she wished that she had the guts to dump him, but who else would want someone like her? What did she mean "someone like her," Muley asked. Someone with as much "mileage" as her, Connie said. Muley said he didn't understand. Well, put it this way, Connie said, how many times had he had sex with his girlfriend? If he added at least two zeroes to that number, then maybe he'd get the idea. Muley muttered that some numbers stayed the same no matter how many zeroes you added. "That's cute," Connie said. "You're a good kid, aren't you?" She asked what Muley and Jill did on their dates. Muley said that sometimes they watched movies, sometimes they listened to old radio shows on WNIB, and sometimes they just talked.

"And?" Connie asked. And sometimes they danced, said Muley. No offense, Connie said, but didn't that get dull? Not really, Muley said, he was only sixteen. So what, Connie snapped, did he think something was wrong with her because she did things with Britt other than talking and listening to *Fibber McGee*? No, Muley said, then asked why his relationship with Jill was so important—Muley liked watching movies with Jill, Connie liked having sex with Britt; so what? No, Connie said, she didn't like having sex with Britt; she just couldn't think of anything better to do. Come on, Muley said, plenty of people would date her. "But *you* wouldn't," Connie said. That was different, Muley said, he was dating Jill. That was exactly the point, said Connie, all the good people were taken; here she was willing to do anything Muley wanted and he'd rather watch movies with some girl who wouldn't even let him touch her. Jill let him touch her sometimes, Muley said. *Jesus Christ, Muley,* Connie said and told him to give her a break. On her way out, she changed the TV channel to one broadcasting a Pepé Le Pew cartoon.

Now it was too late for Muley to call Jill. At this hour, Gail always answered the phone, then sighed when she heard Muley's voice. He sat on his bed and tried doodling, but he couldn't concentrate. He shut off his lights, wondering whether the relationship he had with Jill where all they did was talk, watch movies, and once in a while hold hands, and once in a longer while kiss was what true love was supposed to be. Every time he had suggested to Jill that they do something more, Jill resisted—she wasn't a prude, she said, but she still didn't want to do "anything slutty" with him. Now, he wondered what good an artist could be if all he knew of love had come from the classic novels his mother had described to him, books in which love was a forbidden kiss in a rowboat, a hand-in-hand stroll into a dark wood where fever overwhelmed those who dared succumb to passion. Maybe there were two kinds of love—the kind he had with Jill and the kind he could have with Connie. He wondered if she was still awake, but the moment he turned his bedside lamp back on, there was a knock at the door.

"Mules," he heard Connie whisper loudly. He stood up and opened the door. Connie stood in the hallway. Her hair was wet and pungent with jojoba shampoo that smelled like Dr Pepper. The hallway was silent save for the whir and *kuh-clunk* of the ice machine. Connie apologized, then asked if Muley was still speaking to her. Sure, Muley said, did she want to come in? No, Connie said, but could he do her a favor? She knew that this would sound really stupid, but she could never fall asleep without someone else in the room—would Muley mind staying with her until she was sleeping?

Muley hadn't really believed Connie, had immediately assumed that when they got to her room, she would throw her arms around him, touch his hand, his neck, his shoulder, that she would press her lips to his cheek, his lips, his eyes. And he felt somewhat deflated when all she did was curl up under the covers and ask him to tell her a story. Muley began describing a movie he might make, something he frequently discussed with Jill. He spoke of a film that would begin and end with the space shuttle blazing across the sky, but moments later, he sensed Connie tiring of his monologue, and then it was Muley touching Connie's cheek, her neck, her hand, her shoulder, it was Muley pressing his lips to hers. And then, as Muley had imagined she would, she did kiss his neck as he touched her cheek, but then, she turned away and pulled his arm across her body. Muley could feel her damp hair against his cheeks, his lungs filling with Dr Pepper shampoo. He stayed awake the entire night, feeling Connie breathing against him, her back against his chest, filling his arms, then seeming to slip out, then filling them again, like the calm summer waves of Lake Michigan flowing in, then out.

The next morning, they stood beside each other on Playalinda Beach with a good view of the Canaveral launch pad and they could feel the rumble of the shuttle's engines, feel it in their chests, in their quivering knees as mushrooms of gray-white smoke billowed out from *Columbia,* the body of the craft and its booster rockets perpendicular to the ground as Muley filmed it rising slowly, just an inch at a time it seemed, before it surged upward, rocketing above a pale gray water tower, then into the perfect blue sky.

After they'd toured the space center, inspected lunar rovers, walked through the Rocket Garden ("I've never seen so many phallic symbols in one place," Connie said), dined on 75-cent hot dogs with bright yellow mustard and atomic green relish in the Carousel Cafeteria, after they'd reboarded the red, white, and blue tour bus with the other finalists and their teachers, after the NASA publicity flak had informed Muley and Connie that turbulence aboard the shuttle had upset the dirt in their pea plant plots, thus disqualifying their experiment, after Dr. Singer had treated them and "Malynie," the Space Coast Inn lounge singer, to dinner at Paul's Seafood in Titusville, then wished them good night, Muley didn't even think to return to his room and call Jill. And once he was in Connie's bed, he felt the skin beneath her shirt and, though he did tense slightly when she unzipped his pants, once they were off, everything was smooth and warm and easier than he had ever imagined. He stopped for a moment, apologized for moving too quickly, but Connie told him not to worry, to keep going, then said something about the pill and to keep going, and for a brief space of time as he kept going, his breathing heavy, his heartbeat fast, his mind was free of thoughts of films, of Jill, of West Rogers Park, of Chicago, until suddenly, he could go no longer. He gasped and closed his eyes, his mind settling upon the moment the last frame of film passes through a projector and all that remains on the screen is a bright white light even as the projector keeps going.

In Muley's bed, on their last night in the Space Coast Inn, Connie asked him what he would tell Jill. Muley said he didn't know. To him, it had seemed that time had stopped in Florida, but now he could feel it moving again. The clock read 5:15 and a silvery blue stripe of dawn was peeking under the blinds. Muley asked Connie what she would tell Britt. Was he crazy, Connie asked. She wouldn't tell Britt anything; she wondered whom he'd kill first, her or Muley. Then she decided that Britt wouldn't kill either of them; he'd tell her stepfather so that he'd kill her and Muley. The best thing, she said, would be to find someone to seduce Britt so he would break up with her. Then they could find Jill a good boyfriend. Muley flinched. He hadn't even considered that Connie might want to see him after they returned—why would someone with so much mileage want someone with so little, he wondered as Connie began proposing and ruling out various suitors for Jill. The guys she knew in Auto Shop weren't smart enough for Jill, she mused; in her gym class, they weren't short enough; in Life Sciences, they weren't cute enough, save for Hillel Levy, but he was too rowdy; he'd served three detentions after entering the space shuttle contest by proposing to measure the effect of a weightless environment on the speed, consistency, and trajectory of ejaculate—his semen would be the control; Captain Vance Brand's would be the experimental. Maybe they should run away, Connie said. She asked Muley where he would live if he could choose any city in the world. Muley said he lived in Chicago. Yeah, Connie said, but what if he couldn't live in Chicago?

When Muley didn't respond, Connie said that if she had her choice, she'd go someplace warm like Puerto Rico, where clothes were cheap and you didn't need too many of them; didn't he think that they could be happy there? Why couldn't they be happy in Chicago, Muley asked. Because they couldn't be together in Chicago, Connie said—what was the matter with him, why was she making all the plans? He was supposed to be the guy with all the big ideas. Muley said he didn't like saying things that weren't true. Oh, Connie said, so "all this" was a lie. She swept her hand grandly, as if hoping in her gesture to encompass the bed, the room, the hotel, Florida, and everything else in the world. She snorted, then began searching for her underwear, found it, put it on, and threw on her Journey concert jersey. Muley started to speak, but before he could, Connie told him that she didn't need his bullshit; he'd gotten what he wanted, and now their time together was over. Come Monday, she'd be back drinking bourbon with Britt and his buddies atop the Skokie water tower and Muley would be back watching Bugs Bunny with Jill. She walked out, carrying her socks and shoes.

On the drive back home, Muley and Connie sat scrunched in the backseat of Dr. Singer's sports car while Malynie, who had quit her motel gig to pursue an acting career in Chicago, sat up front, sang along to "Lido Shuffle," and laughed at every one of Dr. Singer's purportedly witty jibes. Every so often, Muley would try to engage Connie in a discussion of movies, but Connie would either say, "I'm sorry; I wasn't listening" or "That sounds boring. Who'd want to see a movie about that?" then pretend to sleep. At one point, she opened her eyes groggily, looked up at Muley, and cooed sweetly, "Oh, Britt," then pretended to recognize Muley and snapped, "You're not Britt!" before closing her eyes again. Once they were back in Chicago, Muley suggested that Dr. Singer drop Connie off first. "Great," Connie said, and rolled her eyes. "Just drop me." She then instructed Dr. Singer to drop both of them off at her house; Muley could walk home from there.

In front of the Shermans' Touhy Avenue town house with its bone-colored vinyl siding, Muley—suitcase in one hand, camera case in the other—said that he was heading home. Connie gaped at him; after the time they'd spent together, he wasn't even going to come in? Muley said he figured he wasn't welcome this late. "Like anyone's even going to know you're here," Connie said, adding that even if anyone heard them, they would just assume he was Britt, and her stepdad had learned the hard way never to mess with Britt.

Inside Connie's house, the living room TV was on, illuminating slumped figures on a yellow couch with a ripped plastic cover. There were muffled voices and canned laughter. Connie dropped her suitcases in the front hallway, reached a hand out to Muley, and led him upstairs to her room, where there were dirty clothes all over the floor—dresses, skirts, underwear—dusty Tommy Tutone and Greg Kihn LPs out of their sleeves stacked beside a record player, posters of Rod Stewart and Al Pacino Scotch-taped to the wall. The room smelled of perfume, stale cigarettes, and grape chewing gum, and there seemed to be no way of walking without stepping on something: a pack of gum, an overdue library book, a cat—"Hasn't anybody fed you, Mosheleh?" Connie asked and picked up the tabby. She took a tin of cat food from her dresser, already half-opened, and poured it into a yellow plastic bowl.

Connie sat down on her unmade bed, and invited Muley to sit beside her. But Muley feared what would happen if he sat on her bed, so instead he sat on a small, wobbly chair at her desk. On it, there was a framed photo of a boy, about fourteen, posing on one knee in a Mather Rangers football uniform. Hanging off the photo, a blue-and-white graduation tassel. Muley looked at the boy in the picture—red cheeks, blond hair parted down the middle—then picked up a worn stuffed panther from Connie's desk. "That's me," Connie said with a contemplative chuckle,

"I'm a panther." That's what Britt said about her, she added—she was gentle with her friends, deadly if you crossed her. She then proceeded to discuss people she knew and assign the characteristics of animals to them. Britt was a panther, too; her mother was a parrot—loud and vain; her stepdad was a rhinoceros—plodding yet dangerous. Muley asked what sort of animal he was, was he a panther, too, he asked hopefully. Connie shook her head. A penguin, she said—he was quiet and thoughtful. She began to say, "monogamous," but stopped.

Muley studied the picture of the boy on Connie's desk. "So, that's what a panther looks like," he said. No, Connie said, a unicorn. Muley said he'd thought she'd said that Britt was a panther. Yeah, Connie said, but that wasn't Britt; it was her brother, Andy. The way she said it—her distant eyes, the sound that nearly echoed in the back of her throat—made Muley understand immediately that Andy was dead. It was a long story, Connie said—there'd been a girl at the U of I who'd broken up with him, but that really had so little to do with it.

"He would've really liked you," Connie said, then asked if Muley would stay with her until she fell asleep. Muley nodded. He wouldn't have sex with her, though, couldn't have sex with her, no matter how much he might have wanted to. In Florida, he could justify it, but not here in West Rogers Park. He watched Connie sleep, her cat purring beside her; then, he stared into the eyes of Andy Sherman. He wondered how he could leave, knowing how hard it was for Connie to be alone; then, he wondered how he could be here while Jill was lying alone in her house on North Shore Avenue—he thought of how Jill had told him how her late mother Becky had always loved that house, but had never had a chance to live there. And Muley wondered why he always felt drawn to people who he would later learn had lost someone. And then he wondered what he himself might have lost, but it seemed selfish to think of that, so instead he thought of a movie he might make, a movie about a young man with a useful ability to split himself in two.

Jill had agreed via notes passed back and forth with Muley in study hall to spend their Friday movie night downtown at the Carnegie Theater, where *Hammett* was playing, but she vetoed Muley's suggestion of Chinese food afterward. Instead, she suggested Nuevo Leon in Pilsen, one of the restaurants Wes's girlfriend Rae-Ann hated because she was afraid of the neighborhood. For

Muley, the week had gone surprisingly well. Jill had expressed little interest in his Florida trip, only nodding at her locker when Muley informed her of the pea plant fiasco. And Connie hadn't shown up at school for the entire week. On Thursday in Life Sciences, Dr. Singer asked Muley if he'd heard from Connie, if everything was O.K.—"Sure she's O.K.," Hillel Levy had quipped. "She's probably just banging the gardener again"—and if Muley could bring her a reading packet. But that night, by Chippewa Park, across the street from her house, before Muley could leave the packet in her mailbox, he saw her bound down her front steps toward a waiting white El Camino with green trim, its motor gunning, its muffler barely muting the engine's rumble. Once Connie got in the car, the El Camino peeled into a 180-degree turn, swerving around on Touhy, heading east. Muley could see Connie's hand unwrap a cigarette package and toss the cellophane out the window, while Nazareth's "Hair of the Dog" blasted and Britt Hurd ran the red light on Sacramento Avenue.

On Friday, Jill didn't arrive at the Wills apartment until 6:15 and she seemed remarkably unconcerned when Muley said that they might miss the seven o'clock movie; there was a nine o'clock show, too, she said as she dawdled in Muley's front room, discussing Dashiell Hammett's stand against McCarthyism with Muley's mother, Deirdre, and her boyfriend, Mel. By the time that they finally left, it was half-past seven, and they had to rush to make the nine o'clock movie. Jill's relaxed attitude seemed strange to Muley, though he worried that he might be ascribing aberrant behavior to Jill when it was his Florida weekend with Connie that was creating tension. For, just as on any other Friday night, they walked together, sometimes hand in hand, sometimes not, shared a medium popcorn in the front row of the theater, whispered to each other during the coming attractions, agreeing that *Time Stands Still* looked interesting and *Quest for Fire* looked dumb. It did, however, seem particularly odd to Muley that Jill kept squirming in her seat and looking around until the movie started; and as soon as the final credits began rolling, she jumped up, bolted for the exit, then crouched down in front of the theater and spent a long time tying and retying her shoes.

When Muley caught up with her, Jill said, "All right, let's go," but stopped briefly to contemplate. What would be better, she asked—walking west to Halsted and catching a bus or taking the subway? Muley was about to answer when someone shouted, "Hey, Woodstein!" Wes Sullivan was exiting the theater, wearing a sleeveless black Effigies T-shirt, a long arm dangling over the shoulder of

Rae-Ann, who wore a ribbed pink sweater and a string of pearls. Wes patted Jill on the shoulder and shook Muley's hand. "Good to see you," he said, then revealed that the movie had blown him away—man, he loved German New Wave directors; even in Hollywood, they didn't compromise their frickin' style. He said that he and Rae-Ann were starving—did they want to get some grub? Jill said that she and Muley were going to Nuevo Leon. "Let's do it," Wes said, confidently leading the way to his BMW, then asking Rae-Ann, "O.K., honey?" Rae-Ann sneered.

Halfway to Nuevo Leon, Muley and Wes were officially introduced. But for the rest of the ride, Wes kept mispronouncing Muley's name with a deliberate and oversensitive inflection, seeming to think that it was some sort of African name. "I'll tell you something, Myoo-Lay," he would say, or "Where did you get your name, Moo-Lie?"

As the four of them sat at a table by the Nuevo Leon jukebox, it became clear to Muley that Jill was infatuated with Wes. And he nearly convinced himself that what Jill was doing—smiling at his jokes, gazing longingly when he discussed books or movies or city politics—was somehow worse than anything he had done with Connie. At one point, Wes mentioned *Hammett*'s director, Wim Wenders. He said wouldn't it be cool to make movies where you could "invent your own freakin' world" and make it subject to "whatever freakin' rules you wanted," and Jill—who had noticed Muley's continuing silence—interjected, "Muley makes movies." Wes nodded, impressed, then asked Myoo-Lay what kinds of movies he made. "Well, they're not really movies," Jill said before Muley could answer. "They're more like cartoons." Wes smirked. "Oh, cartoons," he said, then switched topics: How about that tax increase that Harold Washington was proposing—neither of his opponents "had the stones" to suggest something so bold while running for office.

Initially, Wes solicited Muley's opinions ("What do you think about tax hikes, Myoo-Lay—you pretty jonesed about that?"), but later excluded Muley in much the same way as he did Rae-Ann, who endured the conversation with all the joy of an ex-wife trying to be civil for the sake of the children. At several points, Muley tried to demonstratively ask Rae-Ann for her opinions on whatever Wes was discussing, but she would just shrug, pop her gum, then turn to stare at Jill.

Muley couldn't understand what Jill saw in Wes, who seemed to feel a need to explain everything to Rae-Ann. "See," Wes would say to her, "in a Chicago election, they have something they call a 'primary,'" or "You should know that every magazine has a particular political slant." Muley secretly hoped that Jill was humoring Wes and that, once he was gone, they would laugh about him.

But later that night, atop the Belmont el platform, Jill just discussed how "refreshing" it was to talk with someone about "actual things" that "actually matter." Muley quietly observed that Wes seemed more concerned with appearing *as if* he cared than actually caring. So what was Muley suggesting, Jill snapped, that it was better to take his approach and not talk at all? Muley said it was true that he didn't talk much to people who didn't really care what he said, and by the way, didn't Jill think it was weird that Wes kept explaining everything to his girlfriend? Jill said that Rae-Ann needed things explained to her; she was dumb, she didn't understand that *Valley Girl* was a parody, she probably thought that *E.T.* was a documentary, and besides, she had kept calling her "Sixty-One" even after Wes had told her to stop. Muley said that Rae-Ann was in his Honors Filmmaking class and didn't seem particularly dumb, and if she was, then why was Wes dating her? Jill said that sometimes people got stuck in relationships even after they'd outgrown them.

Muley didn't respond to that last statement. The el train arrived, and its doors swished open. As the train wheels whined shrilly and the train curved past the Sheridan el stop, the seemingly infinite expanse of Graceland Cemetery below, Muley told Jill that he didn't dislike Wes personally; he just disliked how he hadn't let Jill finish her sentences. Jill said, of course, that's how arguments worked when people felt passionately about issues; they constantly interrupted each other—at least Wes didn't treat her like she was some precious object to be worshipped from afar. Is that what she thought he did, Muley asked, were there things that she wanted to say to him but hadn't? Not really, Jill said, what did he have in mind? *Like*—Muley felt his left hand quivering slightly—did she want to date Wes? What was he talking about, Jill asked, Wes was dating Rae-Ann. But hypothetically, Muley said. Jill said that she didn't like thinking hypothetically; hypothetically, anything could happen, hypothetically they could all be dead tomorrow, hypothetically she could become a lesbian at any moment. What about him *hypothetically,* she asked, would he date other people? Like who, Muley asked. "Connie Sherman," Jill proposed.

As they exited the Loyola train station and began walking south toward Devon, Muley asked Jill why she had mentioned Connie. Well, Jill said, (a) because Connie had a crush on Muley and (b) Connie was about as different from herself as she could imagine. Why would he want someone different, Muley asked. Why would he want someone the same, asked Jill. No one was the same, said Muley. Jill said she doubted that; plenty of people were just like her; when it came right down to it, little separated any human being from apes, let alone other people—didn't he ever get sick of her sometimes, Jill asked. Never, Muley said, why, did she ever get sick of him? Of course, said Jill, she got sick of everybody from time to time; she found it strange that he didn't get sick of people. Why would he get sick of her, Muley asked; he loved her.

Continuing west on Devon, Jill soon felt a chilly fear solidify in her, a sense that she had said too much. She had never had a boyfriend other than Muley, not really, although Shmuel Weinberg had once kissed her by the duck pond at Indian Boundary Park, although she had kissed Hillel Levy during the champagne snowball at her Bat Mitzvah and he had shouted, "More tongue, damn it, lady!" She had never felt as comfortable with anyone as she did with Muley, and breaking up with him would mean the end to so many other things, the end to dinners at the Wills household, the end to watching movies together and riding trains and buses and walking the dog, the dog that Muley had found for her one January night. There had been a time, not long after her mother's death, when Jill had decided never to love anyone, because the risk was too great—of late, she had modified that position. But now she wondered if she hadn't been right in the first place. She could easily imagine falling in love with Wes, but couldn't imagine him ever falling in love with her. Yet, the oddest thing was that if, by some strange twist of fate, Wes did fall in love with her, if they walked hand in hand clutching U.S. OUT OF NICARAGUA signs, then huddled in each other's arms in the back of a paddy wagon, she couldn't imagine anyone else she'd rather discuss it with than Muley.

As he walked beside Jill, Muley tried to purge his mind of Connie Sherman. He wondered if someone had told Jill about Florida. He wondered if something about him looked different, smelled different, if he seemed more confident now, or less so. He contemplated a life without Jill, without seeing her on Friday movie nights, visiting her at the Funny House on North Shore, greeting her gregarious dad and suspicious stepmom, then going downstairs to her room to watch movies that had turned pink with age, without walking Fidel to the beach, without lifting little Rachel, who giggled whenever he picked her up, then screamed when Jill tried to hold her. The strangest thing about the time that he had spent with Connie, the thing that ached the most was the fact that Jill was just about the only person with whom he would have wanted to discuss it.

When they reached Muley's apartment building on California, Muley assumed that Jill would say good-bye with her quick peck on the cheek or even quicker peck on the lips. But then Jill asked Muley if she could come in. Muley nervously wondered if Jill had some hidden agenda, some topic to discuss in private. This idea filled Muley with so much anxiety that what he first said to Jill as they lay side by side on his bed, looking up at the phosphorescent Milky Way he'd painted on the ceiling, was that he needed to confess; in Florida, he'd spent the night in Connie's room; they'd "kissed a little bit," then they had "gone a little further." He said he hoped that Jill wasn't angry. Jill lay in the dark, silent for a moment, then said that she herself hadn't had any "steamy evenings" while Muley was out of town, but she had, for three nights straight, fantasized about such an evening with Wes. She couldn't help thinking about what would happen if he broke up with Rae-Ann because she had, say, misspelled one word too many or he had heard her say "awesome," "cool beans," or "tubular" one too many times. She knew it was foolish to consider, but still, what did it mean that Muley was supposed to be her boyfriend and she was thinking about Wes? Were they supposed to break up, or was that just what happened to couples? She asked Muley if he knew; he said that he didn't.

Only an inch separated Jill and Muley as they lay on his bed. But Jill felt so far away now that Muley wondered if she would be leaving soon; in truth, it felt as if she had already left. But at that moment when Muley was envisioning a movie in which a man would reach out and grab time, extend his arms so far that he could grab both ends of it, then bend one end so that it would meet the other and become a circle and the universe would never end, just go around and around and always stop on a moment of happiness, Muley felt Jill stir; she reached out to touch Muley's hand, then brushed her hand against his cheek, pressed her lips to his. Muley stroked Jill's hair, held her close so he could feel her breath against him. They lay there for a moment, their bodies pressed up against each other's. Jill pulled Muley on top of her, drew her arms around him, but then they heard the sound of breaking glass, and something clunking against the bedroom floor.

Jill jumped up and switched on the light, and then she and Muley both heard someone flooring a car with a bad muffler, tires screeching, Nazareth music playing loud; there was a saucer-sized hole in the window through which a strong wind blew, carrying a misty rain with it. A jagged hunk of granite was on Muley's bedroom carpet, shards of glass all around, and Jill wondered if fate might have intervened on her behalf.

The Lane Tech newspaper, the *Lane Leader*, had taken its name from the *Nortown Leader*, part of the chain of Schiffler Neighborhood Newspapers that employed both Jill's father and stepmother. The Schiffler papers were in dire financial straits and seeking a buyer, while the Lane publication was one of the city's most respected high school newspapers. The *Leader*'s reputation was due in large part to faculty advisor Louis Benson, who had been fired by the *Chicago Tribune* in 1956 at the age of twenty-eight for drinking on the job; he'd been driving his supervising editor's Thunderbird at the time. Benson was so incensed by his dismissal that he sought to prove that a bunch of teenagers could run a paper better than the *Tribune*.

The *Lane Leader* was midway between extracurricular activity and cult; its students arrived early, worked late, ate lunch in the newsroom, and flashed press credentials, which granted them safe passage through school hallways when classes were in session. Benson's students frequently suffered ignominious fates, for he instilled in them such a sense of superiority that they would be fired for insubordination in their future jobs. In high school, though, they were among the city's best journalists, and one of the best was this year's editor, William Eamon Sullivan Jr., never mind that his father, William Eamon Sullivan Sr., had fired Louis Benson in 1956 for totaling his car.

Benson's animosity toward the *Tribune* had only grown over the years, and he delighted in the opportunity to teach Sullivan Sr.'s son; sometimes, he drunkenly fantasized about turning him against the old man. In class, he skewered the *Trib,* which he referred to as "Sullivan's dad's rag." Strutting about the office with his vest, pince-nez, and Van Dyke beard, Benson would bark out the surnames of staff members he respected, such as "Sullivan" and "Wasserstrom," and refer to the others in descending order of respect as "You," "Her," and, in the case of Hillel Levy, "You with the Earring." Every Friday, when the paper came out, Benson would post all the pages on an office wall with his editorial remarks, usually eviscerating the articles ("Criminally undersourced," he wrote of Rae-Ann Warner's

hot dog stand survey). But legend had it that in 1963, on one particular investigative piece, written by Isaac Abner Mallen, Benson had written, "It appears
that Mr. Mallen may have a future in journalism after all."

Wes frequently said that he had no need for Benson's praise, but the man's
name kept cropping up in Wes's conversations. And Wes would work late evening
and weekend hours at the *Leader,* report on community meetings and political rallies, all in the unstated hope that one of his articles would merit Benson's comment, "It appears that Mr. Sullivan may have a future in journalism after all."

Early in the semester, Benson had instructed the *Leader* staff to write about issues of true importance to students. Wes had first written about the poor quality
of Lane washrooms—the lack of stall doors, the abrasiveness of cheap paper—
but Benson derided the piece ("Administration Stall-ing on Restrooms") as
"griping about wiping." Benson had said that the paper needed more political
coverage, but Wes's op-ed applauding the radical Puerto Rican independence
group, the FALN, was labeled "inflammatory, uninformed, and worst of all, un-
interesting." Until Jill had described the acts of vandalism and harassment directed toward the junior whom Wes frequently greeted with high-fives and
"Mue-Lie, Mue-Lie," Wes had not found the article that could win Benson's praise.

Jill had told Wes that, after Britt Hurd had learned that Muley had "fooled
around" with Connie Sherman in Florida, not only had he hurled a rock through
Muley's window, not only had his pals ransacked Muley's locker, but senior
Reuben Sorkin told Muley in Team Handball class that soon Britt would "get
him real good." Jill hadn't anticipated that Wes would see this story as fodder for
a series of articles about race relations.

Wes had stopped by Jill's house late one Monday. Jill didn't spend Monday
evenings with Muley—who had been cattily told by Connie just days after the
rock-throwing incident that her relationship with Britt had improved markedly,
that he'd been so afraid of losing her that he drank a half-bottle of Jim Beam and
started puking and shitting blood, then called her on the phone and sang "Love
Hurts." On Mondays, Muley worked as a projectionist for Ajay Patel at the Nortown Theater, where *E.T.* had been showing for weeks now, and Rae-Ann attended New Centurions Christian youth group meetings, so Wes would often
drive to Jill's house, do his homework, and watch the TV news in the Wasserstrom living room. He'd join her for dog walks, discuss the possibility of volun-

teering for the Washington campaign, then before he'd say good-bye, complain about Rae-Ann and all her "Bible-thumping friends."

On this particular Monday in the Wasserstrom living room, Wes revealed that he and Rae-Ann had fought once again, this time because he hadn't said grace over the nasty-ass olive-and-onion sandwiches her mother had made for them. Rae-Ann had refused to give him his sandwich until he thanked the Lord for this "bountiful feast"; he'd snatched the sandwich out of her hand and Rae-Ann had started crying. Jill agreed that relationships were difficult, and that she too felt stifled around Muley, but in light of recent events, she felt she had to be supportive.

The fact was that Muley hadn't sought Jill's support, but given that he had been frustrated by his Honors Filmmaking final project, he did welcome the uncharacteristic indulgence that Jill had begun showing him since he had become subject to Britt's wrath. Sometimes, he even pretended that the threats, the locker vandalism, the sinister remarks from Britt's henchmen, were taking their toll. But the only time that the situation truly irritated him was when Jill invited Wes to one of their movie evenings, and Wes brought along a tape recorder.

Over fried mushrooms, soup, and grilled cheese sandwiches at the Seminary Diner on Lincoln Avenue, Wes turned on his recorder and quizzed Muley about Britt and Connie. As Wes spoke, Muley avoided his gaze, just looked at Jill with an expression of vague reproach, while Jill, divided between loyalty to Muley and affection for Wes, between a sense that what Wes was asking was none of his business and a belief that it was a journalist's prerogative to get the best story, between sympathy for Muley and a gnawing satisfaction derived from the feeling that Muley shouldn't have fooled around with Connie, stared intently at her sandwich as Wes began every question with "How does it feel?"

After the fifth time Muley said "I don't know," "I never thought about it," or "I thought we were going to talk about the Saura movie we just saw at Facets," Wes became frustrated. How come Mue-Lie wasn't angry with Britt for disrupting his life, he asked. Muley said that he saw Britt's point of view—you didn't mess around with someone's girlfriend and expect him to accept it. What about the "role of race"? Wes finally asked. He asked Muley if he thought that Britt would act differently if he were "a honky." Muley got up from the table, ostensibly to use the washroom. Jill was about to tell Wes that he'd asked enough questions, but after Wes kissed her, telling her that he really shouldn't be doing this but he'd wanted to forever, Jill lost her bearings. When Wes kissed her again, she did have the where-withal to tell him to stop, that Muley would be back any second. But Muley had already slipped out the back of the restaurant, feeling somewhat guilty that he had not paid for his meal, yet so free that it almost didn't matter.

There was only room enough in one's brain, Muley thought as he walked through the alley behind Lincoln Avenue, to consider a finite number of topics. He rarely thought long about the fact that his mother was black, that his estranged father was Jewish, that his uncle was a born-again Christian. Religion, race, and class were not categories he found interesting. Muley's sudden departure was less a result of Wes forcing him to confront long-suppressed feelings of disenfranchisement than of frustration at being unable to convince Wes that he was telling the truth. And beyond that, he could not bear to watch Jill continue to succumb to the charms of William Eamon Sullivan Jr.

Muley preferred to consider other matters: films, for one. Ever since Jill had casually dismissed his "cartoons," he had become increasingly dissatisfied with the limitations of two-dimensional images. Now the monotony of the flat screen troubled him. Fine artists worked with frames of all shapes and sizes, on a grand scale and in miniature. But whatever Muley drew would, by necessity, wind up projected on a stationary white rectangle, like the one he saw every Monday at the Nortown as he listened over and over to that Speak & Spell voice ("*Hoooome. Phone hooooome*"). He felt his art stagnating, much like his relationship with Jill. As he walked through the alley, he thought of projecting films onto circles and triangles, onto the sides of buildings, onto windows, mirrors. He was still considering alternative screens when he glimpsed Wes's BMW moving slowly toward him, highway lights glaring in his eyes, its horn toot-tooting away. He walked straight past the car, kept walking until he reached the Fullerton Avenue el stop, paid his fare, and climbed the stairs. From the top of the deserted el platform, Muley could see Wes's car turning onto Fullerton, then heading west toward Ashland. And, though he could not see clearly that far down, Muley could almost envision the scene inside the BMW—Wes placing a hand atop Jill's, Wes kissing her. He could nearly imagine Wes telling Jill not to say anything about the kiss—not until he had "sorted out" his relationship with Rae-Ann. And, though Muley could neither see nor hear inside Wes's car, the empty space he felt in his gut was almost the same as if he had.

— — — —

Before Wes's article was published in the *Lane Leader* bearing the headline "Is She Really Goin' Out with Him: Love and Race at Tech, Part I," and featuring two paragraphs about Muley's dalliance with Connie ("Nearly a month after it happened, Muley Wills still doesn't want to talk about it."), the harassment campaign against Muley had more or less subsided. Britt Hurd had magnanimously considered putting the past behind him and taking Muley out for a steak dinner at the Angus since Connie had promised to marry him once she was out of high school. But now, as Connie had somewhat too gleefully told Muley before Life Sciences, Britt would not stop at mere vandalism or threats; he wanted to "settle things with his fists." What pissed Britt off most, Connie had said, was the assertion in Wes's article that he was racist—he didn't give a shit what color people were; he was "an equal-opportunity ass-kicker." Connie told Muley that Britt would meet him in the Hero's Submarines parking lot on the corner of Western and Addison after school on the following Friday at 4 P.M.

Muley had never been in a fight. At Boone Elementary School, there had been at least four fights a day. Boys on the playground would pummel each other into headlocks, rip off balaclavas, pelt kindergartners with crab apples and stones; in gym, it would start off as a game—a hard foul, a ball whipped in frustration, a mischievous grundy, and soon there would be bloody noses, black eyes. But Muley kept to himself during gym class. In track, he was neither so fast that he inspired jealousy nor so slow that he provoked ridicule. In recess, he would sit atop the jungle gym with Jill and watch kids playing freeze tag, Red Rover, and fast pitch, but when there was a fight, he looked away.

At Lane, fights were less frequent but, when they occurred, far more brutal. Certain surnames became notorious: "Hurd and O'Toole got picked up by the fuzz again," "Don't mess with him; he's one of the Sorkins." Almost every Monday in the cafeteria, someone would wander in carrying a lunch tray with one hand, the other arm in a sling, and the story would be whispered from table to table—that was Duncan Kirby; he'd said some racial shit to a little black kid and the kid's brothers had beaten the crap out of him with two-by-fours; there was Pablo de la Fuente; he'd scraped a gangbanger's Plymouth near Church's Fried Chicken and when he apologized, they'd told him, "Man, you shoulda thoughta that before." At the start of the school year, after a school assembly on racial understanding, a pair of black girls had seen Hillel Levy snickering about something. "Smart-ass white boy," one girl had said and punched him in the nose.

Muley hadn't mentioned the fight to anyone, but by week's end, everyone was aware of it and had advice to offer. Jill had suggested that the two of them head downtown to the Art Institute right at 3:30—*The State of Things* was showing. His mother's boyfriend, Mel Coleman, offered a crash course in karate; Muley's friend Gareth Overgaard, from the University of Chicago, suggested emigrating to a country less obsessed with physical violence—Iceland, for example; Hillel Levy proposed sneaking into the chemistry lab, stealing a beaker full of silver nitrate, adding a package of Pop Rocks, then dipping Britt's dick into it.

Friday at 3:30, Muley put on his jacket, packed up his books, sauntered down the Lane hallway and out the door. He walked purposefully across the front lawn, neither eager nor anxious. At Hero's, he ordered an American sub with extra dressing and a Hawaiian Punch, then sat alone at a back table and consumed his meal as the rest of the Lane crowd entered—the football players, their team jackets just a bit too large for their gum-snapping girlfriends; the punks, aggressively quoting Clash lyrics in Brixton accents; the pregnant girls eating subs, one advising another to consume her entire sandwich ("Finish, girl; you're eating for two now"). The editor-in-chief of the *Lane Leader* was there too, with his pen, his tape recorder, and his reporter's notebook.

Just before 4 P.M., Britt Hurd's El Camino rumbled into Hero's parking lot with "Go Down Fighting" blasting from its speakers. Muley took a sip from his cup of punch, swung his backpack over one shoulder, and walked outside. He sat down on a concrete block in the parking lot as Britt Hurd and Denny O'Toole hoisted themselves out of the car windows, and Reuben and Eli Sorkin leapt out of the cab. Connie remained in the car and turned up the Nazareth song. Muley stared straight ahead as Reuben Sorkin—who had only recently made the transition from fat kid to big guy and was relishing the authority that transformation had provided him—grabbed the cup of punch out of Muley's hands, took a sip, spat it out, and asked what that shit was, Jonestown Kool-Aid? "Never can tell," Muley said as Denny O'Toole, hands in the pockets of his tan down vest, advised Reuben not to drink that shit; he might get herpes. Yeah, that was right, Reuben said and spat a few more times, then wiped his tongue with the sleeve of his jeans jacket. The two of them sat on the concrete block, one on either side of Muley as Britt and Eli smoked cigarettes and leaned against the hood of Britt's car. Denny told Muley that Britt wasn't a bad guy—all he wanted was an apology and a case of Stroh's and they could forget what had happened.

Muley said that he didn't believe in apologies; whatever he'd done with Connie wasn't anything he could take back. Denny laughed and Reuben snorted, then asked Muley if he thought that he was some kind of hero. This guy was something else, Reuben said—they were offering him a way out, and he was basically saying fuck you. Reuben asked what Muley was—some kind of Christian? No, Muley said, he wasn't anything. Denny and Reuben walked back to the El Camino as Muley drained his punch, tilted the cup, and sucked on the ice.

Britt was wearing his "ass-kicking outfit"—faded black jeans, boots, sunglasses, and a black mesh Pittsburgh Steelers half-jersey with the number 20 on the front and the name BLEIER on the back. He told his buddies to "hang back" and Connie to stay in the car—he tossed his cigarette down on the asphalt, flipping his hair out of his eyes with reverse nods as he walked toward Muley. Britt told him to get his ass up. Muley stood and stared directly into Britt's eyes—the two of them were about the same height. Britt asked Muley what he had to say for himself. Not much, Muley said, what did he have in mind? That was right, Britt retorted, there wasn't much to say, was there? He asked if Muley was "queer." He made a limp-wristed gesture and looked back at his buddies; they sniggered. No more than Britt was, Muley said. What was that, Britt wanted to know, was he calling him queer? No, said Muley. That was funny, Britt said, he thought he'd suggested he was queer; was Muley calling him a liar? He told Muley to take a swing at him; he never hit someone first.

Wes was sitting cross-legged on the hood of his BMW, taking notes. There was "a hushed anticipation in the air," he wrote, puzzled and at the same time fascinated by the apparent acquiescence of the crowd that had gathered in the parking lot—any one of them could have called the police or stepped between Muley and Britt, who was now licking his thumbs one after the other. "C'mon," Britt said as he licked a thumb, then snapped his fingers in front of Muley's eyes as if trying to wake him out of a trance. "C'mon, take a swing."

"Hit him now, Mue-lie," Wes shouted. "Hit that slack-jawed fucker."

Britt stopped snapping and turned toward the BMW. What was that, he wanted to know? Wes scribbled on his notepad. "You, *deaf boy*," Britt said, pointing at Wes. He scuffed across the parking lot toward Wes, kicking pebbles along the way. "I'm talking to you," Britt said, then asked Wes what he was doing. Minding his own business, said Wes. Yeah, Britt said, that was wise, what kind of shit was he writing? Nothing, said Wes. "Oh yeah?" Britt asked. He ripped the notebook out of Wes's hands, at which point Reuben Sorkin reached into the cab of the El Camino and pulled out a baseball bat to stop Muley, who was walking out of the parking lot. Reuben tapped the bat against a meaty palm and asked Muley where he was going. "Let him go," Britt said.

"Go on, get out of here," Reuben told Muley with a smirk as Britt opined that there was no point in fighting a pussy who wouldn't fight back; besides, he could only deal with one pussy at a time, and right now he was dealing with this pussy over here who had called him a—what had he called him, he asked, he couldn't quite recall—oh yeah, now he recalled, he said, a *fucker,* wasn't that it? Yeah, said Wes. Britt told Wes that he was actually right, he *was* a fucker; he fucked a lot, but he didn't like being *called* a fucker; Wes would have to call him "Mr. Fucker" or else he wouldn't be showing proper respect. He asked Wes for his name. "William Eamon Sullivan Jr.," Wes said. Britt's smile faded—was he the same Sullivan jagoff who'd written that shit in the paper? "You're lookin' at him, boy," Wes said, and in one smooth motion slid off the hood of the car and threw a punch at Britt's jaw, then another in Britt's gut before Britt was on him and the two of them had fallen to the ground. Wes's glasses skittered across the asphalt as Muley walked north on Western wondering if Jill would still want to go to the movies tonight if she knew that Wes had fought instead of him, if she knew that he didn't much care what happened to Wes.

Wes pinned Britt's arms to the ground, the crotch of his jeans right up against Britt's face. Britt asked if Wes was trying to fight him or fuck him. Wes pushed down harder, his blue jeans zipper slicing into Britt's cheek, a pearl of dark red blood just under Britt's eye as Britt yelled to his buddies to get this cocksucker off him. And then they were all on Wes, shoving him back onto the hood of the BMW. Reuben held down Wes's legs with his baseball bat while Britt wiped blood off of his face with the back of a hand and watched Eli throw punches into Wes's face, his stomach, his groin. At the sound of police sirens, the crowd scattered, some for the bus stop, some for Addison Street, some back into Hero's Subs. Reuben, Britt, and Eli ran to the El Camino and jumped inside. Britt started the motor, gunned it, careened onto Western, then backed up fast into the parking lot after it occurred to him that Connie wasn't in his car anymore. She was standing over Wes, who was lying across the hood of his car—bright red bruises were on his face, his jacket and shirt were torn, and there was a hole in the right knee of his jeans, blood oozing out. His hands were cupping his crotch. "Fuck," he kept saying, "fuh-huh-uhh-uhhck."

"Hey," Connie said. She held both halves of Wes's glasses and handed them to him. They hadn't gotten banged up too badly, she said, some superglue would do the trick, how was he feeling? Just great, Wes said and barked out a laugh, but the laugh hurt his stomach. Connie asked if he needed to go to the hospital. Nah, Wes said, those guys hadn't hit too hard; he knew guys who hit harder.

"Come on, Connie, let's go," Britt shouted as he pumped the gas of the El Camino. Wes asked Connie why she hung around with those assholes; she could do a lot better. Connie laughed, patted Wes's cheek, then said that she had to go. Wes's facial expression turned bitter. Fine, he said, go back to your friends; *they're waiting for you.*

Britt spent four hours in the Ridge Avenue lockup, discussing explosives with a couple of other Nazareth fans who'd been picked up for drunk and disorderly conduct. He got out just in time to meet his buddies to drink bourbon atop the Skokie water tower. Wes hadn't intended to call the police, but his father had insisted he do so, and Wes knew that once his first-person account of the incident ("Love and Race at Tech, Part II") was published, cops would ask questions. Wes hadn't intended to go to the hospital either, but his father had insisted on that too. Which was how Muley found himself at Weiss Memorial with Jill early Friday evening. They could see *The State of Things* some other time, Jill had said.

When Muley and Jill entered Wes's room, Wes was recounting the day's events to his mother, Dorothea, his younger brother, Casey, and Rae-Ann, all of whom were standing around his bed, rapt. Wes said that he anticipated that his life would get a whole lot worse before it got better and there would probably be more confrontations—that's what happened to war correspondents; true, this wasn't Vietnam, where his uncle Eamon had served, not Korea, where his father had begun his journalism career, but this was an election year, and there was a war going on in Chicago, and Lane Tech was right on the front lines.

Jill had brought Wes a small get-well gift—a miniature edition of *The Communist Manifesto*—but when she saw Rae-Ann eyeing her with apparent jealousy, she stuffed it all the way down in her jeans pocket. Wes shook both Jill and Muley's hands, telling Muley that he hoped Britt hadn't gotten him too bad; there was no need for two people to get rolled for nothing. He asked Jill if she had seen the fight. Jill said that she didn't like fights. Wes said that he found beauty in boxing, in the balletic matches of Sugar Ray Leonard and Roberto Duran, not in the graceless brawls in which Britt and his ilk partook. Though, he allowed, pointing a finger at Casey, if he ever saw him fighting, he'd let him have it. He grabbed Casey and pulled him into a headlock; the boy giggled until he became short of breath and started coughing.

Rae-Ann asked if Jill wanted to accompany her to the cafeteria to get some Jell-O. And Jill, thrown off guard by the fact that Rae-Ann had deigned to speak to her, and terrified that Rae-Ann would ask if she'd ever kissed Wes, neglected to ask Muley to come with them. He stood by the door, hands in his pockets, wondering if it was only Jill's fondness for Wes that made him feel the disdain that he couldn't recall ever feeling for anyone else.

While Rae-Ann and Jill rode one elevator down to the first floor—Rae-Ann told Jill that she really didn't know whether she and Wes would stay together because Wes had only applied to West Coast schools and she had only applied in the Midwest—Connie Sherman was taking another elevator up. She was clutching a pink rose. When she arrived in Wes's hospital room, Casey and Wes were seated side by side on Wes's bed, watching a Chicago Bulls game, while Muley sat on the radiator by the window next to Wes's mother. Reggie Theus was hurting the Bulls by taking too many shots, Wes said, adding that teamwork was the most important thing in sports. "Teamwork and loyalty," Wes said, then shot a disdainful glance at Connie, who was kissing Muley on the cheek; Muley made as if to return the kiss, then noticed Wes looking at them and turned to gaze out the window at the lake. Wes's mother embraced Connie, then noticed her low-cut violet leotard top, and held her at arm's length. She then said that it was time for everyone to go; Wes needed to *schlafen.*

Once Wes's mother and brother had gone, Connie—whom Wes had not yet greeted—told him how sweet he was to be so patient with his little brother. She placed the rose beside him on the bed. Wes blinked twice as if trying to use his eyes to change the TV channel broadcasting Connie into his room. What did that mean, he asked, that he was to be commended for being nice to a "retard"? Connie said that she hadn't meant it that way at all; it was just obvious that he was a good older brother and it was nice to have good older brothers. Fan-fucking-tastic, Wes said, he was glad to have Connie's approval; it meant a lot coming from someone as loyal as her. What was his problem, Connie asked, she just wanted to see if he was O.K. Wes suggested that she ask her boyfriend, if he was out of jail. Connie said that Britt regretted what he had done; as long as Wes didn't write anything else, he wouldn't mess with him—once he'd beaten guys up, he liked buying them strip steaks afterward. And he really respected Muley for not backing down, she said.

Well, Wes said, she could tell Britt that he wouldn't stop writing his articles. Then she was sorry for what would happen to him, Connie snapped. *And you too,* she said, pointing a finger at Muley before storming out of the room. Go on, Wes said, *and take your fucking rose, too.* He whipped the flower at the door, then grabbed the remote control and turned up the volume of the Bulls game. He asked Muley if he liked basketball. Not much, said Muley. Wes apologized—he said he hadn't asked Muley about basketball because he was black; he hoped that Muley hadn't taken it that way. Muley said no, he hadn't taken it that way.

After one of the longest half hours in his memory, when Muley thought that Jill might have already left the hospital, she and Rae-Ann returned, having spent their time in the cafeteria consuming Jell-O and discussing Rae-Ann's "righteous" Christian youth group, Rae-Ann's "adorable" nieces, Rae-Ann's sister's "gorgeous" wedding, Rae-Ann's "bitchin'" college application essay ("It's Not Bad to Be Good!"), and briefly, Connie Sherman ("that little fucking tart"), whom they had seen walking tearfully past the cafeteria. "What was she doing here?" Rae-Ann asked Wes, knowing—but not revealing, for Wes had never told her—that Wes had lost his virginity to Connie, who had been fighting with Britt at the time, and that Connie had briefly stopped speaking to Wes after she discovered that he had been snooping through her diaries. (Rae-Ann had never addressed any of these subjects directly with Wes for fear they might make her subject to questions about her own virginity, which she cherished greatly, though the previous summer she had, in fact, enjoyed experimenting with fellow counselor Julie Ying during two weekends at youth camp.) Wes said that he'd explain later.

When the basketball game was over, it was too late for Muley and Jill to see their movie, so they all stayed in Wes's hospital room watching the news on Channel 9, where Harold Washington was speaking about how he would "heal Chicago—reach out to all areas and bring it together." Jill had told everyone to quiet down so they could listen, but before the report was over, Wes's and Muley's thoughts had moved on to more pressing matters; each was thinking about how to skillfully avoid the topic of Connie, while Rae-Ann was wondering whether Jill would ever consider experimenting with her. And soon, just as Jill had started to wonder with whom she could discuss having kissed Wes in his car, a nurse arrived to say that visiting hours were over.

"Call me sometime; we'll go shopping, Miss Sixty-One," Rae-Ann happily shouted to Jill from her mother's Cutlass as Muley and Jill waited for a north-bound bus.

Despite the once-crimson, now-indigo bruises on Wes's flanks, his neck, and his back, his *Lane Leader* articles continued unabated. With each, he grew bolder, referring to Britt and his cronies as "that Hurd of illiterate, racist thugs," hoping that soon Louis Benson would write, "It appears that Mr. Sulli-van may have a future in journalism, after all," though Benson's most positive re-mark to date was "Could be less didactic." Yet Britt maintained a low profile after his arrest; some unsigned, threatening notes arrived at the *Leader* office tar-geting Wes specifically and the *Leader* in general, leading Louis Benson to ask his friends on the police force to make additional sweeps of the high school, but as of finals week, no one at Lane had seen Britt, and even if Connie never said so, the rumor was that Britt had dropped out.

The *Lane Leader*'s holiday issue featured Jill's op-ed piece calling for mayoral debates ("Not entirely worthless," Benson had commented), a roundup of break-dancing movies ("Deadly dull, Miss Warner. Deadly dull."), and Wes's most in-flammatory article to date. It was not traditional journalism, he had explained in a staff meeting, so much as a call to action. The article covered much of the ground of previous pieces, but formed them into a disturbing narrative—it began with "a stolen kiss between teenagers," continued with a rock thrown through a window, a rumble in a sub sandwich shop parking lot, and threats in a hospital bedroom, and concluded with the unsigned notes that the *Leader* had received. Benson had termed the article "more risible than readable," and com-mented that, "given the material," it was "surprisingly uncompelling."

Muley himself did not read the article, and though Jill had noted that Muley had become increasingly distant, even to her, his moodiness had nothing to do with Britt or Connie and little to do with the fact that Jill now worked late at the

*Leader* every night when she wasn't stuffing envelopes or Xeroxing position papers at Harold Washington's Lawrence Avenue office, which just happened to be within walking distance of Wes's house, even though Wes had never shown up to volunteer. Muley's ill humor stemmed mostly from the fact that, on the last week of classes, his final project was due for Honors Filmmaking.

Held in the auditorium, this was a gut class, one of the easiest A's at Lane, taught by an Israeli woman named Irit Ben-Amar, who insisted that all students call her by her first name. She taught in tank tops and bare feet, and spent one class a week screening her own plotless films: In one (*Gymnopédie pour des poissons*), a goldfish swam back and forth in a tank to Erik Satie music; in another (*Aye, No, Know, Eye*), Irit contemplated her face in a mirror and repeated the phrase "I am not I. You are not you." *We Are Naked* began with a close-up of Irit's lips as she whispered, "I am naked." In one slow, continuous take, the camera pulled back to reveal Irit and her boyfriend Ephraim Tekulve—a heavily bearded carpenter—seated on a couch, fully clothed. Irit and Ephraim took turns whispering "I am naked," then "You are naked," then "We are naked," at which point the film faded to black. Irit encouraged students to express themselves fully, thus Hillel Levy's film *Condomplation*, in which a deaf mute went to a drugstore to buy condoms and found a blind shopkeeper unable to fulfill his request, received an A, as did Rae-Ann's *Connie Game*, in which a slut got her comeuppance.

Muley knew that all he had to do was film anything, slap his name on the front and "The End" at the end, and he would get an A, but he didn't want to make "just cartoons" anymore, and the flat screen still vexed him. He'd think about the scratches on a length of banged-up film and wonder if the scratches themselves could tell a story. He thought of the vertical orange stripe of leader that appeared before the first images of an 8 mm film, wondered if he could create a thin, vertical, orange movie with images falling down the screen rather than across it.

One week before the due date, Muley sat in his bedroom and jotted down ideas. "A boy sits in the audience of a movie theater," he wrote. "He stares up at a blank screen. On the screen, he sees an image—a boy sitting in the audience of a movie theater." He could see the image repeating itself as in a perpetual mirror, the boy watching the boy watching the boy, an endless procession of realms or spheres. And then he wondered what purpose any of the images served.

Stumped, he whipped off a short animated sequence about an earthbound kangaroo in a zero-gravity environment. He found the title uninspired (*Being and Boing*), the denouement hokey (a cub in the kangaroo's pouch helps his mother to bounce again), but the film was adequate.

At the beginning of the final class, Muley handed Irit his film reel, then slunk down in a front-row seat, almost too embarrassed to watch. A chemical odor permeated the auditorium, alcohol or acetone mingling with the usual scent of sweat and wet carpet. Muley watched the room grow dark, the projector lamp illuminate the screen, the vertical orange stripe, and then the purple kangaroo—who wore yellow gym shoes that seemed stuck to the ground with wads of chewing gum as she tried bouncing, while children, buildings, and cars floated around her. Appreciative giggles were heard as a dream sequence began—the kangaroo imagining a world where she could fly and everyone else was moored to the ground.

And then something soared across the auditorium, something fast and orange, reminiscent of that vertical stripe at the beginning of the film. A small *thuhmp* was heard, and the screen shuddered. At the center of the screen, in the middle of Muley's floating cityscape, a small hole appeared. The hole was no bigger than the diameter of a cigarette, but soon it expanded, spread out, erasing, melting, blackening the hastily colored flying skyscrapers, seeming to send the purple kangaroo scurrying to a corner of the screen, as the audience's initial awe suddenly transformed into panicked realization; the screen was on fire. The air was suddenly thick with smoke, the smell of melting plastic. And soon, students were scrambling, stumbling over each other, running, falling, picking themselves up, climbing over seats, into the aisles and out the exits. Someone hit the fire alarm, and a low insistent honking sounded simultaneously with the incessant blinking of red fire-alert lamps, which turned the burning screen red then black, red then black. Black feathers of screen somersaulted in the projector's glare, the ring of fire pushed outward until the screen was just one giant hole, the white projector light illuminating the brick wall behind it and the gray steel emergency exit door, white then red, white then red.

When the firefighters came, two trucks' worth, the lights were on in the auditorium and a gray fog hung in the air. The floor was carpeted with ash and flaky black jigsaw pieces. Muley was inspecting the world behind the movie screen. He had been the only student to remain after the fire had started. He had watched, transfixed by a movie that had truly existed in three dimensions, a movie with a smell, a taste, and a heat coming off of it, that existed not forever but for a moment, exploding, then reducing itself to ash, beautiful while it lasted, impossible to reproduce.

Outside of the high school, fire trucks were stalled on Western and traffic was stacked up for blocks in either direction. There were about a half-dozen squad cars too, blue lights rolling, sirens wailing. Britt's El Camino was parked in a loading zone, motor still running. Two police officers were questioning Britt as he leaned against his car, smoking a Marlboro. It was nearly freezing outside, but he wore only blue jeans, boots, and a black T-shirt on which was written "I've Got Tough Nuts!" There he is, Britt said sarcastically as Muley walked across the front lawn of the school. Tell them, Britt said, tell them how I've been harassing you. But when Muley approached him, all he did was hold out his hand. Britt didn't shake it at first, just looked at it. What the fuck was that for, he wanted to know. He just wanted to thank him, Muley said. What was this, asked Britt, "some kind of 'Jesus love thy neighbor' shit?" That fucker was crazy, Britt told the cops, shaking Muley's hand with mock enthusiasm and an exaggerated smile. Come on, one of the cops said and opened the back door to the squad, let's go. Muley said that he hoped to talk to Britt sometime. Britt asked if Muley had seen the fire; that's all he had to say to him and his little boyfriend, Wes. Muley said that he just wanted to know which chemicals Britt had used. This was entrapment, Britt said, he wasn't that frickin' stupid. Muley began to walk away, but then Britt said wait a second, why did Muley want to know? Because it looked cool, Muley said. Yeah, Britt said with a smile, didn't it?

## WINTER BREAK 1982-83

Michelle Wasserstrom had been riding the Amtrak Broadway Limited for nearly an entire day when she arrived at Chicago's Union Station with her hair sopping wet and saw her sister Jill accompanied by two people she didn't know—a tall, skinny dork with half a beard, sandals, and a raggedy "Property of Alcatraz" T-shirt, and some dykey-looking chick who, Michelle assumed, was dressing up like a preppie to conceal her sexual orientation. That Jill was traveling with some sweater-wearing lesbian and her beard seemed odd, but then again, her entire train journey had been exceedingly odd, particularly the fact that her own ex-sort-of-boyfriend, whom she thought she had shaken long ago, was now jogging behind her, calling her name.

It had been more than four months since Michelle had been in Chicago, four months since she had been home, whatever that word meant now, and had it not been for her father telling her a gazillion times that he missed her, she might well have made it four years before returning, or at least until she had become famous, whichever came first. Michelle knew it was somewhat peculiar that just a few weeks after Gail had asked her and Jill how they would feel about a new little brother or sister in the house ("Depends who the mother is," Michelle had said), she had decided to transfer from the U of I to NYU. But, as she had assured her father, there was no correlation whatsoever (or practically no correlation, as she had admitted in a letter to Gareth Overgaard, with whom she had attended Mather High) between news of the latest entry into the Schiffler-Wasserstrom family and Michelle's decision to spend as much of the rest of her life as possible in New York City. Or Los Angeles. Or wherever.

Until her father had told her how much he missed her, Michelle had had no intention of spending winter break in Chicago. She'd already picked up an application for a holiday sales job at Macy's. But there was no chance to rescind the foolish offer she'd made to her father, not after Charlie had already started giddily discussing a "Welcome Home" dinner at Myron & Phil's restaurant, not after he had told her about his plans for the "whole family" to go to Brookfield Zoo so that "little Rachel" could hear people carol to the animals, not after he had offered to buy Michelle's train ticket—Michelle said that plane rides were far too quick; she would need the whole twenty-three–hour rail journey to "decompress."

During her first month at Champaign the previous year, she'd taken the bus to Chicago nearly every other weekend—that, at first, had been necessary to combat the claustrophobia she experienced crammed with two other girls into what had been euphemistically billed as a "one-room triple." Which might have been tolerable had her roommates not been Charlene Rosen from Highland Park and Bettina Wright from Urbana—a pair of mean, gossiping virgins who tried desperately to act tough and talk dirty. Though Charlene had never been south of Evanston, and though Bettina had never been north of Rantoul, the two college freshwomen were united in their disdain for Michelle, who had declined to do

Jägermeister shots with the offensive linemen downstairs (Bettina's idea) and had also passed up the opportunity to join the other drunk girls in the bathroom to watch how each other peed (Charlene's).

In October, Michelle's request for a dorm change was granted and she was placed with three Asian students, two of whom spoke disparagingly of Michelle as "the white ghost," and one of whom stopped talking to Michelle shortly after Michelle had asked her to teach her some good swear words. Once second semester had rolled around, Michelle had developed friendships with some of her fellow Theater students, but by that point, Charlie had announced Gail's pregnancy, and Michelle had completed her auditions and sent out her transfer applications.

The Broadway Limited had just pulled out of Altoona, and Michelle had already been riding the train for twelve hours; though it was two in the morning, she felt wired. She'd been seated next to two West German backpackers who tried to engage her in conversation from the moment they entered the train. At first, she'd answered their questions politely—yes, she was an actress, no, she'd never thought of modeling, no, she'd never been to Germany, yes, she was Jewish, no, she didn't hold them responsible for the crimes of their grandparents, but no, she wouldn't join them for a beer or a "*sandvich*." Later when she ignored them, pretending to be too engrossed by her Stanislavski reading, they switched off her reading light, and giggled. "*Ziss* is no reading zone," one said. Later, when they had finally fallen asleep and the taller one had begun to snore, Michelle could stand their presence no more. "*Ziss* is no drooling zone," she said before whomping him with her book.

The lounge car smelled ever-so-slightly of urine and ever-so-strongly of cigarettes. Michelle purchased a can of Pabst (a brand she referred to as "Pabst Smear"), then looked for an open seat. She chose a table near the back of the car, the one located nearest the restroom, which was why she presumed only one person was seated at it. And, thankfully, that person appeared to be passed out or sleeping, head plunked down on folded arms, mop of hair spread out over the mustard-yellow vinyl tabletop. Michelle popped her beer, opened her book, glanced at the creature opposite her to make sure that it was asleep, saw the creature lift its head, recognized the face, looked back down at her book, then snapped her head back up. "Holy fucking shit," she said.

She couldn't remember when she had last seen Larry Rovner, the self-proclaimed Zionist "Jerusarock jock" majoring in Econ at Brandeis—possibly a concert in some godawful suburb near O'Hare where he and his old band Rovner! had been shouted off the stage by a bunch of bikers in Judas Priest shirts? No, later than that, at a Chanukah party at his dad's new house in Evanston, where she'd drunk too much grain alcohol punch, and she'd said something she'd intended to be innocuous to Larry's girlfriend, something like "Yeah, I'd wear a *ch'ai* too, but I wouldn't want to draw so much attention to my tits." Then the girlfriend—Hannah or Shoshana, Michelle couldn't quite remember—blurted out some crazy shit about Michelle being a self-hating Jew. Hannah or Shoshana insisted that she wanted men to "ogle her bosom" (she pronounced it *bozz-um*), so that they could learn something about Judaism. What would people learn by looking at her *ch'ai,* Michelle asked, that Jewish girls had big boobies? Well, apparently that's not true, Hannah or Shoshana had said, eyeing Michelle's chest. As Michelle made her way to the door, she nearly slammed into Larry, who called Hannah to his side—he said that he wanted to introduce his new girlfriend to his old one. "We've met," Hannah said curtly.

And now she was sitting across from Larry, who said he was taking Amtrak because planes reminded him too much of Buddy Holly and the Big Bopper. He blearily told Michelle that he was glad to see her; she looked good—had she lost weight? No, Michelle said, she'd actually put on ten pounds at NYU. Really, Larry said, she looked skinnier. That was probably because he had a big girlfriend, said Michelle. Larry said that Hannah wasn't his girlfriend anymore; she was his fiancée. Michelle tried to hold in her laughter by taking a sip of beer, but it went down the wrong way and she started hacking and sprayed Pabst on the window. She wiped it off with her sleeve.

"Fiancée?" Michelle asked. Larry nodded sheepishly. Go ahead, Larry said, make fun of him. But Michelle said that she wouldn't mock Larry for being engaged, not because she couldn't come up with a good enough joke, but because she could come up with too many. Marriage. She shivered at the thought. Marriage meant houses; houses meant children; children meant posterity; posterity meant death. She wondered who but Larry Rovner would even consider marriage before the age of thirty, let alone follow through on the mad plan. She noted that Larry wasn't wearing his yarmulke.

Larry sneered with self-reproach. "She can't control everything I do," he said.

Wow, Michelle said, it sounded like he was looking forward to married life. Larry said he wasn't positive that he would actually go through with it; he was still looking for a way out. The truth of it was, after his parents' divorce, he'd stopped believing in marriage. Now on Wife No. 2, his father had channeled his pornography addiction into the more socially acceptable practice of reading sexual self-help books, such as *How to Make Love Like an Animal,* which featured pictures and diagrams more lurid than any issue of *Gallery* Larry had ever perused. Michael Rovner now proudly displayed these books next to his volumes of military and maritime history. Larry's mother, Ellen Leventhal, had just blown off the family when she'd decided that it had no redeeming value. When Larry and Hannah had visited the Midwest for the Fourth of July, Larry's father and stepmom had hosted a barbecue, bought them tickets to *A Chorus Line,* saved seats for them at Grant Park for the fireworks; when they had visited Larry's mom in Lake Geneva, she had tossed them the keys to the bicycle locks, then said that she was leaving for a road trip. And yet, Hannah had told Larry that she preferred his mother: "She's so much cooler than your dad," she'd said, and he'd had to agree.

After the Amtrak club car attendant announced last call and Michelle had purchased two more cans of Pabst, Larry explained his engagement. For a long time, he had been uncomfortable with the fact that Hannah—a Brandeis Playwriting major from Manhattan—seemed to be running his life. When he had a gig at a club, she'd tell him which songs not to play. They always ate on Main Street, where she charged *sag paneer* or sushi combinations to her parents' credit cards. She consistently indicated that her parents' wealth made her family a greater priority than his; when his dad or sister called, Hannah blasted her stereo and danced, but when she talked to her parents, if he so much as strummed his guitar, she would fiercely snap, "I cannot hear one word, Lawrence!" Earlier in the month, Hannah had contracted mono and had gone to her parents' apartment to recuperate and it had been Larry's best two weeks in years—"maybe since you and me were together," he told Michelle, who gave him the finger. He aced all his tests, drank Long Island iced teas, and smoked hash with his musician pal Nate Yau, bassist in the punk band Too Much Johnson, who advised him to find a new girlfriend before he turned into a "Jewish pod person." He ate crap food in the cafeteria, masturbated at times and places of his choosing. But when

Hannah returned, they'd only had sex, arguments, and "serious talks." After one such talk, she told him that they should just call off their relationship. Larry was so terrified of being alone that he proposed marriage. And now her parents knew, her sister Liesel knew, everyone in the Hillel Society knew, and that was hardly the worst of it.

Three cars down was the slumber coach. It was dark, smelled vaguely of drool, and vibrated with the sounds of elderly couples snoring. The train was rattling slowly through Pennsylvania, passing auto graveyards, shuttered Texaco stations, lonely little bungalows with porch lights on. Larry slid open the door to his room; two maroon cushioned seats were positioned opposite each other, one beside a toilet. Larry stepped on the toilet, pulled down a duffel bag, unzipped it, removed a Walkman, handed it to Michelle, and sat down. What was this, Michelle asked. The worst birthday gift in the history of the Jewish people, Larry said. He told her to put on the headphones.

Even in the moments when she'd resented Larry—when he'd dumped her for Hannah—even when she'd found him most ridiculous—prancing about onstage like a Semitic Mick Jagger with an Israeli flag cape instead of a Union Jack—Michelle had almost always admired his songs. Not the lyrics so much, not the Zionist anthems he bellowed, the electric *brachas* he wailed, but the drumming and the aggressive pop hooks. Even now, two and a half years after their break-up, she still remembered the songs that played on his Walkman. And though she didn't recognize the voice singing, *"It's almost sundown, baby / Maybe I should take you home,"* she did recall the song: "(My Lovin' Ain't) Always Orthodox." It didn't sound like a rock song, though; it was full of synthesized strings and ping-ponging electronic drums. Plus, the lyrics were different. Michelle remembered one line—*"Take a walk with me, Zipporah / I'll show you something you won't find in your Torah."* But now it was *"Take a walk with me, Zipporah / Let's stay up all night reading Torah."* Michelle pushed Stop, and searched for a word to describe the music. "Emasculated," Larry said.

Larry and Hannah had been having the same argument ever since she had first heard his music—whether his songs would be better as straight-ahead rock anthems or show tunes in the context of a Broadway musical. "Just think," Hannah would often say, "our names in lights." She said "our," because in her fantasy, her parents would produce and she would write the book for an update of *The Jazz Singer.* For his birthday, Hannah had given Larry a Star of David sweater and, in a Tiffany jewelry box, a cassette tape, on which she had printed "The NEW Jazz Singer, by Lawrence Elliot Rovner." There were hand-lettered quotes from fake reviews all over it—"Rovner Takes Broadway by Storm," "Look Out, Jerry Herman: Here Comes Larry Rovner." Apparently, she'd paid a music composition graduate student to arrange a half-dozen of Larry's songs and record them with singers from the music department. And what could Larry tell her, knowing how much time and energy she had spent on the tape? What could Larry tell her, once she invited everyone from the Hillel Society to listen, then sent copies of his songs to all of her friends' grandparents?

Throughout the first weeks of December, he'd brooded about the marriage, and the tape Hannah always insisted on blasting, angelic choir voices destroying the anthems of his angst-ridden youth. Who was that guy with the falsetto singing, "Almost Cut My Isro (But I Felt Like Lettin' My Jew Flag Fly)"? he would wonder. Why was some warbling Barbra Streisand turning his tortured ballad of adolescent voyeurism, "Let's All Go to the Mikvah (And See What We Can See)," into a paean to Jewish bathing rituals: "Let's All Go to the Mikvah (And Get Ourselves Clean)"?

Larry was so glad to have three weeks away from Hannah, three weeks to vegetate at his father's house and contemplate whether or not to embrace her parents' wealth and sell his soul. He asked Michelle what she would do. Michelle asked if Hannah's parents were loaded. Yeah, Larry said. Michelle asked if the musical had a good part for an NYU sophomore with some damn fine stage presence. "But Hannah hates you," Larry said, then stopped. Well, he agreed, at least that would be one way to make workshopping the musical less of a drag.

That morning, when Michelle and Larry had sex in his tiny, sweaty slumber coach ("I'll try anything once," Michelle had said), their minds were far away from the blue-gray midwestern dawn breaking outside their window. Larry was thinking how cruel and devilish he was for having sex with an old flame while his fiancée, *oy gevalt,* his *fiancée,* was on board a Cunard ocean liner for the annual Goodman family trip. Meanwhile, Michelle was thinking about her father's house on North Shore, thinking about the infant stepsister she would soon meet, thinking also about the insane theater exercises she'd performed three mornings a week at NYU, crawling around the floor and pretending to be an alligator, learning how to breathe through her anus, repeating Shakespeare soliloquies using only consonants: "Tb r nt tb tht s th qstn." She was thinking about all this to keep from laughing at Larry's sexual performance, and how much he had changed since those first bumbling encounters in his parents' basement. Now his muscles were toned, his stomach hard, his legs slender but powerful, his technique utterly hysterical: the way he switched positions without changing his workmanlike facial expression, his aerobic instructor's grunts of encouragement— "Yeah, baby, all right, baby, that's the way, baby." Unable to keep a straight face, Michelle slid out from under him and asked him if he had ever heard of just fucking instead of doing the whole *Jane Fonda Workout* video. Larry smiled. Sure, he said, sometimes he wished it could be fun again. Moments later, Larry was conked out. Michelle crept out of his coach, through the club car—opening for business once again, the smell of Sara Lee sweet rolls and coffee not quite disguising the scent of piss—and back to her seat, where both German backpackers were snoring now; their breath fogged the view of silos, Kmarts, and farmhouses.

The train was scheduled to arrive in Chicago at 1:25 in the afternoon, but an unseasonably warm winter rain slowed rail traffic and the car proceeded north at a clip of ten miles per hour, creeping past the Indiana steel mills as a sick, industrial odor seeped through windows that only appeared airtight. Michelle found three empty seats and lay down, feeling gross—sticky, sweaty, in need of a shower. There had been a time when she could just have sex, then go about her day; she had often thought all this fuss of douches, showers, and bidets was part of an industry based on the creation of shame, and she had never viewed sex as shameful. To her, it was midway between athletic activity and improvisational comedy, a method by which she could understand the behaviors of those around her, something that was required of an actress, a profession she had embraced, not because it provided an escape from herself, but because it made her feel more like herself than anything else she'd ever tried. There was no sense of self-loathing in sex; no love either, though. Michelle's high school pal Myra Tuchbaum, who had become insufferable now that she was no longer drinking, smoking, or threatening suicide, relished writing letters from SIU in which she told Michelle that the reason why Michelle had never fallen in love was because she was afraid of people getting too close to her, that ever since her mother had died, she couldn't bear the thought of opening up to anyone. Maybe so, Michelle thought, but if Larry Rovner was anything to go by, love was hardly a bargain.

Nevertheless, lying on her back, a rucksack underneath her head as she watched the Chicago skyline upside down through gray, rain-soaked windows, she did feel just a tad unclean. She wondered if there were showers at Union Station; the idea of taking one there sounded so disgusting that it seemed like the appropriate thing to do, something that would be good material to draw upon when she was playing some bag lady or hooker—at some point, every great actress played a hooker. That's how you paid your dues in Hollywood: you broke in playing a hooker; you got nominated for an Oscar when you played a bag lady.

But there were no showers in Union Station, so upon her arrival, she stuck her head under a faucet in the ladies' room, swished her head from side to side, and splattered the mirrors. Emerging from the washroom, she spotted Jill and her cohorts standing near suitcases rotating on a creaking metal carousel in the baggage claim. Michelle hadn't wanted Jill's friends to drive her home. She didn't like the idea that Jill was now old enough to have friends who drove cars. She didn't like that Jill waved when their eyes met; Jill should never wave, she thought, she should always roll her eyes, shrug, say something caustic; she didn't like when Jill hugged her; Jill should always squirm out of a hug, shudder if anyone so much as touched her. She was thankful that as she and Jill were walking hand in hand—that was weird, too, by the way—Larry dashed up to them, breathless, tapped Michelle on the shoulder, and asked her to write down her phone number. Michelle scribbled it on a crumpled Amtrak napkin, and Larry said that he hoped he could see her during his spring break when he'd be in New York with Hannah and "her fuckin' family." He kissed Michelle on the cheek, greeted Jill, calling her "Jane," then ran off, duffel bag over a shoulder, guitar on his back, a Glad bag filled with laundry in one hand, to meet his father, his stepmom, and his sister Lana, who had grown at least six inches since Michelle had last seen her, whose hair was now short, feathered, and frosted nearly blond, like an Olympic ice skater's. Michelle asked if Jill wanted to say hi to Lana, with whom Jill had attended Hebrew school; Jill said no, she was sure that they could find better ways to occupy themselves. Michelle breathed a sigh of relief; it was comforting to know that Jill hadn't changed completely.

Still, riding north in Wes's car, Michelle could not shake the feeling that she no longer belonged in Chicago, that in her absence, the tectonic plates of her former universe had shifted. Even though she sat up front with Wes, it only took the length of the ride under Wacker Drive for her to drift from the center of

attention—chattering nonstop about the *ghastly* train ride, the *hellish* NYU production of *An Enemy of the People* she'd stage-managed—to a spot barely along
its periphery. When even her tales of Larry Rovner's newfound sexual prowess
failed to raise a peep out of Jill or Rae-Ann and only inspired Wes to comment
superfluously, "He's probably been working out," Michelle retreated further into
the world of her thoughts. She thought that three weeks in Chicago could just as
well be forever, as Jill suggested they stop for cheese fries at The Wiener Circle—
Jill had to be possessed by some sort of demon; the tofu-snarfing vegetarian was
suggesting *cheese fries*.

In the past, when she had taken Jill to Rovner! concerts, to visit Gareth in
Hyde Park, Michelle had set the agenda. Now she was the one feigning interest
in the conversation. When the rain had stopped, they sat outside in the surreal
December warmth on red picnic benches, discussing *politics*; well, Jill and Wes
discussed politics while Rae-Ann didn't say much of anything, just smiled with
pursed, disapproving lips, only interjecting to ask Jill when the two of them
would go shopping together. And, to Michelle's astonishment, Jill actually
seemed excited by the idea. Now and again, Wes would try to include Michelle
in the conversation—had she already decided how she would be voting in the
mayoral primary or would she wait until after the debates? Michelle said that she
wasn't registered; her only opinion about Chicago politics was that it was cool
that Chicago's mayor, Jane Byrne, liked singing "Take Me Out to the Ballgame,"
even though she couldn't carry a tune. Beyond that, she couldn't imagine why
anyone gave a shit. At one point, Michelle asked Jill, "How's Muley doing?" since
Jill's letters had of late been completely devoid of any mention of him, but Jill
flashed her a look of death and said that this was not a topic for public discussion.

After they had left The Wiener Circle, Wes drove north on Clark Street, keeping up a running commentary as he blasted WXRT, making up details and getting a fair number of them wrong: "This is Elvis Costello; he writes all the songs
for Squeeze." He pointed out sights to Michelle, as if she were a tourist. There
was Wrigley Field, that was where WLUP had held Disco Demolition; this was
Andersonville—all the Swedish lesbians lived here; this was Ridge Avenue, it was
a diagonal street; all diagonal streets had once been Indian trails. Michelle said
that didn't make much sense; the Pottawattomies spent all their time walking diagonally until honkies invented right angles? Wes said he wasn't sure that the
story was true; it was just something he'd heard once. Michelle said it didn't mat-

ter if he'd heard it before; the idea was still retarded. Jill's face reddened—Wes's brother had a mental disability, she said.

Once Wes had dropped Michelle and Jill off, Michelle lugged her bags toward the front door of the Funny House and said that she hoped that she and Jill weren't fighting. No, Jill said, she had come to expect such rude behavior from Michelle. What was she talking about, Michelle asked, how the hell was she supposed to know that guy's brother was a retard? The point, Jill said, was that Michelle shouldn't have been using the word in the first place. Why, Michelle asked, because it would offend the retard driving the car? No, Jill said, because it offended *her*. Why, Michelle asked, because she had a crush on the retard driving the car? Was she boning that guy? Not everything was about sex, Jill said. Of course everything was about sex, said Michelle, hadn't Jill learned that yet? Come on, she said as Jill stood in front of the house, arms folded, she wouldn't go inside if Jill was still pissed; how about a reassuring hug? Fine, said Jill, reluctantly embracing Michelle. That was better, Michelle said, now tell her, was she fucking that guy? No, Jill said. But she wanted to fuck that guy, right? No, Jill said, then blushed; he had kissed her a couple of times, she said. "Ooh you little skank, tongue or no tongue?" Michelle asked. Jill said that it had happened so fast, she didn't know. That was fucking disgusting, Michelle said; that guy was gross.

Michelle had hoped that her father, Gail, and Rachel would be asleep when she arrived. That way she could play with the dog, inspect the crib, coo if the baby was cute or make an inappropriate joke if she was fat. She didn't want Gail to judge her reaction, to say that she wasn't effusive enough, or that she was too effusive—*Stop being so effusive! You're scaring the baby!* She was good with kids, had been a good babysitter; the worst thing she had ever done was to buy a kid a copy of *Juggs* magazine, but that had only been to shut that Hillel Levy kid up.

But alas, no one was asleep in the house that Gail no longer allowed to be called the Funny House; it was the Schiffler-Wasserstrom House, thank you very much, and there was nothing funny about it. And, truth be told, the Funny House deserved a different name, for it bore only the slightest resemblance to the house that Michelle remembered. She saw a new island kitchen with lemon-yellow walls and glass cupboards. The screened-in porch was now a bricked-in playroom. She saw framed photographs of Charlie, Gail, and Rachel on a mantel, and strange appliances—blenders, pasta makers, Ginsu knives. Chanukah presents were piled on the dining room table, around which the rest of the family was seated, the rest of the family save for the dog, who, Gail explained, was in Jill's bedroom with the door closed because he always got too excited about packages and broke things. Jill stated exasperatedly that the only reason Fidel got excited was that he was starved for human contact. She demonstratively bounded downstairs to liberate the beast.

Michelle noted a great many changes in the brief moments that she'd had to survey the house. But the greatest transformation was that of Charlie and Gail. Both had lost weight; Gail's hair was lighter, longer; Charlie was clean-shaven, red-cheeked instead of pale. And when she sidled into the dining room and hugged and kissed her father, who smelled like some poisonous designer aftershave instead of the foul-smelling lime potion she had always loved, and when Gail affectionately rubbed her shoulder and called her "kiddo," Michelle noted the most important change of all: she was here.

In Michelle's absence, the Funny House had become a home, one in which, even as she held Rachel and sat at the table bouncing the child on her lap and telling Charlie that Rachel had her father's hair but the nose was definitely Gail's, she was only a guest. For the idea of home itself, a place where people sat around tables, consumed meals together, and told stories about their days, was something that existed only in the distant past, in the life of someone else, another character she had played, back when she'd been a loving daughter, a somewhat dutiful sister. There were times when Michelle had longed for the family outings of old, sitting on the hood of Charlie's Thunderbird watching *Paint Your Wagon* at the Sky-Hi drive-in on McCormick Boulevard, strawberry-picking in Kenosha County, Wisconsin, Becky listening to "Music from Broadway" on WXFM and singing along, riding the train to Poughkeepsie to visit Becky's parents. Everywhere Michelle had lived after Becky's death seemed temporary.

Gail was now treating Michelle as if she were not her stepdaughter but an old girlfriend or a particularly cherished boarder, one known for her way with children and her promptness in paying the rent. Her Chanukah gifts to Michelle were generous yet devoid of sentiment: cloth hangers, wool socks, a McDade's gift certificate. While Charlie put Rachel to bed and Jill walked Fidel, Gail sat at the dining room table, lit a cigarette, offered one to Michelle, and discussed boring things with her: the alterations to the house, Rachel's eating schedule. She showed Michelle seed catalogues and asked whether she should grow forsythias or hydrangeas. She discussed the financial predicament of Schiffler Newspapers, the impending bankruptcy that she hadn't yet mentioned to Charlie because "your dad always gets so sad when he hears bad news."

Finally, Gail asked Michelle when she would be going back to New York. Michelle's return ticket date was more than three weeks away, but as she took a drag on her cigarette, the first words that came out of her mouth were "As soon as I possibly can."

M ichelle spent New Year's Eve atop the West Rogers Park toboggan hill known as Mount Warren with Gareth Overgaard, who, Michelle noted, still hadn't outgrown the habit of wearing only black and olive green ("Is that supposed to be radical, Overgaard?" she'd asked him). Gareth told Michelle that he was sorry to hear of her family's financial situation, but the Schiffler papers were "shit rags—no offense." Michelle agreed, although she enjoyed her father's "Life of Charlie" lifestyle column (largely because her name frequently appeared in it) and the Police Blotter, which reported neighborhood crimes labeled with Gail's inappropriately flippant headlines, such as the one Gail wrote for retired bakery proprietor Bess Vaysberg's harrowing encounter with a thug who Maced her, then grabbed her purse ("Papa's Got a Brand-New Bag!").

Three years earlier, on December 31, 1979, Michelle and Gareth had vowed— well, Michelle had vowed and Gareth had grudgingly voiced his consent—to spend every New Year's in Warren Park. But now Michelle had no idea when she would return here, particularly given the fact that Gareth, her only good friend left in the city, would be graduating early from the U of C, after which he would join the Peace Corps, even though Michelle said that he was "too husky" to have the stamina required for "digging shitters." To accentuate this point, she lifted a shovel and plunged it into the ground. Usually, Michelle and Gareth brought beer to Mount Warren; on a great many occasions, they brought pot; not infrequently, they brought Myra Tuchbaum. This year, they brought beer and a dime bag, but also the shovel and Charlie Wasserstrom's cloth Bernard Horwich JCC bowling bag.

Michelle unzipped the bag and pulled out a series of items: an empty flask of Wild Turkey, a joint, a paperback copy of *Our Town,* a cassette tape with *Flirtin' with Disaster* on one side and *Bebe Le Strange* on the other, an old diaphragm that she called her "rubber yarmulke," rejection letters from Harvard and Yale, acceptance letters from U of I and NYU. She then returned each item to the bag, solemnly observed, "On this night, we bury our sins," then asked Gareth what he had brought. Gareth hadn't brought anything; he said that he was an atheist and, thusly, thought rituals were dumb. True, Michelle said, but only because people conformed to rituals that had no meaning in their own lives; this ritual, however, was profound—they were burying their past so that, centuries from now, archaeologists could dig up Mount Warren and learn that the youth of America had spent the latter part of the twentieth century smoking weed, listening to bombastic rock, and being barred from overrated institutions of higher learning. What would Gareth bury, she asked, what would future generations learn from him?

"Jesus, you're irritating," Gareth said and reached into his jacket. He found pocket lint, a paper clip, loose change, a ticket stub for *The Battle of Algiers,* a stick of frankfurter-shaped bubblegum from Fluky's Red Hots, and a crumpled flyer from the Youth Spartacist League. Michelle said she couldn't believe that was the most interesting shit in his pockets. "Put them in the bag," she said with a sigh. Smirking, Gareth put everything into the bag except for the change. "Put it in," Michelle insisted. Gareth said that he needed the change for laundry. No he didn't, Michelle said, he came home on weekends and his mother did his laundry. She handed the shovel to him.

Gareth dropped the shovel—why was digging his job? Look, Michelle said, first of all, he was a lard-ass and needed to get in shape to dig toilets in Burundi; second of all, since he hadn't brought any artifacts, it was his duty to pitch in; she didn't understand the idea of committing halfway to a plan, agreeing to bury a time capsule, but bringing only lint, coins, and ticket stubs. She couldn't believe that someone who never did laundry didn't have anything more interesting in his pockets. She reached a hand into his left jacket pocket. "Get the fuck out of my pockets, Wasserstrom," Gareth said. She reached for the other pocket, but Gareth grabbed her hand. "Be cool," he said—you didn't just reach into people's pockets. He stepped toward Michelle and asked if she knew what her problem was. No, Michelle said. Gareth said that she didn't have any appreciation for people's privacy. Yeah, well, did Gareth know what his problem was, Michelle asked. What, asked Gareth. Michelle said it was that when he got into an argument, he became so focused on impressing people with his intellect that he forgot to guard his pockets. She plunged a hand into his right jacket pocket and withdrew a package of condoms. "Oh my God," she gasped, then laughed. "Who's the lucky guy?"

"Can I have those back, please?" Gareth asked stonily. Why, Michelle asked, was he planning to use them this evening? She requested that he please be gentle with her.

"I'd like to have those back," he said. Michelle handed them to him, and he started walking down the hill. Where was he going, Michelle asked, there was serious manual labor to be done. Gareth kept walking. Come on, Michelle shouted, stop acting like some big fat queen. Gareth stopped halfway down the hill. Yeah, that's exactly what he was, he shouted—a big fat queen, now was she satisfied? Christ, Michelle yelled back, she'd known that for about a century; she'd known it longer than he had.

"Fuck you, Wasserstrom," said Gareth as he made his way down the hill. He told Michelle not to follow him.

The digging, as it turned out, was easy. Michelle enjoyed physical labor— during her NYU drama department servitude, she liked constructing sets, operating powerful electric saws and sanders, wearing a sweat-stained bandana and cut-offs, painting bulky wooden flats. After twenty minutes, her hole went down a foot and a half. She rested her hands on the shovel and gazed into the abyss. She knelt down, grabbed a handful of cold, wet dirt, and let it sift through her fingers. She thought briefly about her mother's funeral, about how she'd been the only person who hadn't cried, save for Jill, who had stayed away altogether. She thought about how, later that night, she had cried, but only because she was thinking about how she'd been the only one not to cry. She thought about Jill in the next bed telling her to stop crying, there wasn't any point. Michelle had said nothing more the rest of the night, except for a prayer she'd learned at K.I.N.S. But now she couldn't remember that prayer, so instead she sang a John Lennon song, "Watching the Wheels," figuring that the next best thing to a prayer for the dead was a song by a dead person.

When she was through singing, she dropped the bowling bag in the hole and shoveled the dirt over it, chanting "Volga boatmen! *Huh!*" She filled the hole, smoothed over the top, sat on the burial mound, lit a joint, and watched the traffic below on Western Avenue. But soon, footsteps and voices approaching Mount Warren disturbed her beatific contentment—a new generation of burnouts had no doubt appropriated the hill as their base of operations. Michelle didn't like the idea that anyone else came here; she thought that it should be preserved as a monument to her youth, that it should be renamed Mount Saint Michelle. She stubbed out the joint, stood up, wiped the dirt off her hands, ready to descend, when Jill's dog, Fidel, suddenly leapt upon her, practically knocking her back down, then licked her nose.

Michelle stood for a moment, watching Fidel encircle the mound she had just created, sniff, then start digging furiously. "Stop it," Michelle hissed. The animal sat, tail wagging, panting in Michelle's face as she leaned over to pet him. She considered waiting a moment for Jill—perhaps Muley would be with her. But once she heard someone strumming an out-of-tune guitar and a few voices, less drunk than they were trying to seem, singing "American Pie," she started to descend. She could see Jill—a person whom she hardly seemed to know at all now—walking up the hill followed by some staffers from the *Lane Leader:* Wes Sullivan swigged from a bottle of champagne and passed it to Rae-Ann Warner as Hillel Levy sang, "Drove my Chevy up her levee, but Hillel Levy was dry."

After 1982 had turned into 1983 and Wes had sloppily kissed Rae-Ann, then hugged Jill, whispering in her ear, "Next year I hope it's you," and Rae-Ann had told Jill that one of her resolutions was to spend more time shopping with her, and Hillel had kissed everyone on the lips and said, "Just 'cause I like kissing guys on the lips, that doesn't mean I'm gay, right?" then, later, "Just 'cause I like going down on guys and squeezing their nuts, doesn't make me gay, right?" Michelle, a shovel over one shoulder, had reached the foot of the hill and started heading west.

On Albion near Fairfield, Michelle turned north and walked through the alley. She had fond memories of this alley, of sneaking out of recess during *dalet* to smoke with *Shiffra* Tuchbaum and *Avram* Sherman, after which everything in Hebrew school would seem funnier—Rabbi Grossman making them write "I must not laugh at Maimonides" a hundred times; *Yehuda* Rovner shushing them during the *ash'rai*; everything was funnier, save for the weekly Jewish humor filmstrip featuring Henny Youngman and Shecky Greene's comedy routines. The filmstrips were titled *You Don't Hafta Be Jewish*. But you *do* hafta to be ninety, Michelle had observed.

As she walked, Michelle could see a low purple fog illuminated by a pair of headlights. The air was thick with a sweet chemical odor and a hint of something burning. Nazareth music was playing, getting louder as Michelle walked on, wondering why there was so much smoke, wondering why anybody still listened to Nazareth. Michelle walked toward the fog.

"Muley?" she suddenly asked.

Michelle had always liked Muley, always thought that her sister took him for granted, had long wondered what he saw in Jill. Whenever Jill described him in her letters, he seemed distant, desperate, moonstruck, as if love had lobotomized him. She wondered what the point of love was when the people she knew almost always seemed so much more alive and confident without it.

Now she could see him kneeling in the headlights' glare, a movie camera perched on his shoulder as he filmed the fog. With his free hand, he held up two fingers. "Now?" she heard a voice asking. "One second," said Muley. He adjusted his position, took the camera off his shoulder, then lifted it back up. "Now," he said. A match was struck, someone pumped Nazareth up louder. And then, as the purple fog descended, a ball of orange smoke rose in the air, illuminating the El Camino below it, and then two more smoke balls, all of them casting a glow upon the carpet of purple smoke, which spread across the alley, enveloping Michelle's gym shoes. "Now," Muley called—another match was struck, a wick lit, a pinpoint of yellow light shot upward, piercing the floating smoke pumpkins. Muley filmed, leaning backward as an explosion rumbled in the sky.

"That's all we got," someone shouted. "Except for the bottle rockets. Wanna see those?"

"Not much," said Muley. He turned to face Michelle.

"Hey," she said. She waved—a half-sweeping gesture, like wiping a window.

"Hey," said Muley. He smiled and kissed her cheek, self-assured yet unassuming, as if he'd spent the past year attending a finishing school. He was taller than Michelle remembered, taller than her now. "You see all that?" he asked.

Before Michelle could respond, a woman leaned out of a third-floor apartment window. "I heard it," she said, "and my dishes are still rattling." At this, Britt Hurd leapt out of the cab of his El Camino, as if dismounting a pommel horse. Hey, he shouted, why didn't he come up there and rattle the rest of her damn china? Muley recognized the woman and told Britt to take it easy. "Sorry, Ms. Bernstein," Muley said. "We were just shooting some film." Boone P.E. teacher Aviva Bernstein said she didn't care what they were shooting; she was calling the cops. "Fuck that," Britt said. He ran to the El Camino, grabbed a fistful of bottle rockets, and fished a lighter out of his blue jeans. Britt's pals walked toward him: the Sorkin brothers, hands in the pockets of their denim vests; Denny O'Toole, wearing mittens with the fingers cut off as he finished a joint; Connie in a fake raccoon jacket. "I remember you," Connie said, pointing a little finger at Michelle. "You're Jill Wasserstrom's sister." She asked if Muley was dating the entire Wasserstrom clan. Michelle said that she remembered Connie, too; hadn't she deep-throated everyone at Jill's Bat Mitzvah? Britt flicked his lighter and brought it close to the tip of his bottle rocket bouquet as Connie said that maybe they ought to split; Ms. Bernstein probably would call the cops. Britt said he didn't give a shit who she called; as long as he was still legally a juvenile, the cops wouldn't do jack. But then Muley said that they should go; he didn't want trouble. At this, Britt suddenly relented. "Really, Wills?" he asked. "You think we should head out?" That was cool, Britt said, he'd wanted to check out a couple of parties anyway. He asked if Muley wanted to come. Muley shook his head and asked Britt if he'd remembered to write down the names of the chemicals he'd used for the explosions. Britt handed a folded piece of paper to Muley, then strutted back to his car. As he revved the engine, he said he hoped that everyone would make it safely to 1984, save, perhaps, for that Wes Sullivan motherfucker. Connie hopped in the front seat and blew Muley a kiss; Denny, Reuben, and Eli climbed in the cab. Bottle rockets flew in all directions as Britt floored the car, cranked the stereo, and screeched onto North Shore.

After they had gone, Michelle said that she didn't like Muley hanging around with burnouts and ruffians; she was the only burnout or ruffian with whom he was allowed to socialize. Muley said that those people weren't so bad. Michelle said wasn't that particularly dumb-looking, slack-jawed guy Britt Turd? That guy was a "foaming erection." Muley said that he didn't like dividing people into those who were "erections," and those who weren't. What about Wes Sullivan, Michelle asked. "No comment," said Muley, but when Michelle made a *boing-boing-boing* erection sound effect, Muley stifled a laugh.

From the alley, they walked north to Barnaby's Pizza, and Michelle continued to criticize Muley's choice of friends: Britt was a thug and that Connie creature was a skank. Sure, Michelle said, she herself had once had a skanky reputation, but Connie was a *serious* skank. What did she have against skanks, Muley asked. Michelle said that there was plenty of middle ground between her sister and skanks like Connie; she sincerely hoped that Muley hadn't boned that skank. But when Muley broke into a grin, then turned away, Michelle whooped and pounded him on the back. "Dude!" she exclaimed. It wasn't that big of a deal, Muley said. "Dude," Michelle said again, and because she couldn't think of anything else to say, she kept saying it: "Dude, dude, dude!" She asked him how it had been, had it been his first time, had he worn a "hat"? She said that they had to celebrate; she was buying the first pitcher.

Over that first pitcher, Michelle and Muley reminisced about the times when they had acted together on children's radio shows; over the second, they discussed Muley's relationship with Jill—they were still dating, but they might start "seeing other people," Muley said, to which Michelle snapped that she hoped her sister hadn't used that "totally gay language." Over the third pitcher, Michelle stopped mentioning Jill and started flirting with Muley—when Muley asked why she had brought a shovel, she said that she was "prospecting," then told Muley that he had to visit New York. But on pitcher number four, Michelle decided that flirting with Muley was too much like incest, so why didn't they just go home. Near dawn, as they parted at North Shore and California, Michelle advised Muley never to act too infatuated with her sister; Jill only wanted things she wasn't sure she could have—let her spend all the time she wanted "wanking off Wes," and soon enough, she'd come back to Muley. Muley observed that Michelle was making Jill sound downright skanky. In her dreams, Michelle said, and wished him Happy New Year. Then Muley turned east and Michelle walked west, wondering how Chicago would change if she stayed away for another year or more. Her ex-boyfriend was engaged; her asexual best friend was gay; her father had a baby daughter; his wife was acting nice to her; her sister was hanging out with a pack of ghouls; and she was walking west alone.

Michelle was cooking ham and eggs for Gareth in her father's kitchen when the phone rang; she picked up and heard Muley's voice on the other end. Cooking breakfast was one of several acts of penance she had offered to perform after Gareth had agreed to speak to her following their New Year's Eve argument. Gareth had not returned Michelle's phone call, but later, when she had arrived on his parents' doorstep bearing several Barbra Streisand albums, a 1940 *Look* magazine with Judy Garland on the cover, and a photo of

Bette Davis ("Get this bullshit out of my face, Wasserstrom," he had said), he accepted Michelle's offer to do his laundry and cook him a meal.

Michelle asked Muley if he was calling for Jill, and hadn't she fricking told him to stop acting desperate? But Muley said that he was actually calling on behalf of his mother's boyfriend, Mel, who was directing an industrial video—Mel had fired an actress and needed a replacement. "I'm there," Michelle told Muley. One day later, Michelle was auditioning for Mel. One day after that, she was meeting him for lunch at Catfish Digby's. Twenty-four hours later, she was lying in bed as he filmed her.

The plan had been for Mel's feature film debut, the 1920s drama *The God-fathers of Soul,* about the rise and fall of fictional gangster Tiny Walker—whose exploits were based loosely on those of contemporary incarcerated underworld figure Tiny Cubbins—to have begun shooting the previous autumn, but the film's executive producer, Muley's estranged birth father, Carl Slappit Silverman, hadn't wanted to rush. Mel, who was easily distracted and had always had trouble finishing projects since they never matched up to his dreams, hadn't wanted to rush either. Both Carl and Mel were new to the movie business—Mel's experience was limited to audio production; Carl, founder of the music label Slappit Records, had made most of his money in pop music.

When Carl had sold his record company and moved his operations back to Chicago, where he could be closer to the gritty black underworld of which Mel had written in *Godfathers,* and where he could also hatch a plot to win Deirdre Wills back from Mel and reunite with his son, he leased a long-abandoned firehouse from the city, just south of Cermak Road on Michigan Avenue, and spent more than $2 million rehabbing it into Bronzeville Studios; there would be a soundstage on the first floor, editing facilities and administrative offices on the second and third, a screening facility on top.

During the first half of the twentieth century, the neighborhood just a few blocks south of the Bronzeville Studios building had been known as both Bronzeville and Black Metropolis. Louis Armstrong and Count Basie performed in the nightclubs near 31st and State; movie houses screened silent features by Oscar Micheaux; during Prohibition, there were speakeasies, dice joints. In Mel Coleman's script, Cermak Road marked the dividing line between the white and black underworlds.

While the soundstage and studios were being built, Mel maintained an editing suite in West Rogers Park's Devon Building. In order to learn as much about filmmaking as possible, Mel had volunteered to make a training video for his eldest brother, Roy, who owned three Speed Freak printing shops and who grudgingly granted Mel access to his Western Avenue store. Three weeks later, Mel had returned to Roy's Speed Freak with a crude ten-minute video titled *A Stupid Mofo's Guide to Working at Speed Freak.* Though Roy forced a chuckle or two at Mel's film, which detailed the dos and don'ts of operating copying machines, he told Mel that he had wasted his time. He asked Mel to rewind the video and play it again so he could show him exactly what was wrong with it. But after the video started up again, the phone rang and Roy left the room. While Roy was on the phone, a vice president of Speed Freak International arrived unannounced to survey the premises, then sat down and watched the video. When it was over, he found Roy, congratulated him, and said that he wanted to make Mel's video available to all Speed Freak franchises. And though Roy Coleman didn't buy his brother's video, many Midwest Speed Freaks did. The video served as Mel's calling card. Within six months, he had made such films as *Shake This,* which instructed Wolfy's Hot Dogs' employees to safely operate milkshake machines, and *Thou Shalt Not Steal . . . Anymore,* a video that the Hank Schiffler Ford dealership had been required to make as part of a settlement with the attorney general's office.

The motel housekeeping staff training video in which Mel had cast Michelle was called *Talkin' a Whole Lot of Sheet,* and would be the first project actually filmed in Bronzeville Studios. Michelle's lines ("Just because they're in a one-star motel doesn't mean your customers aren't entitled to five-star service") were easy to master. And though it took some practice to make a bed in the thirty seconds indicated in Mel's script, by the time that Mel arrived at the studio wearing a burnt-orange leather coat and wraparound sunglasses and asked Michelle if she was "the talent," she could do it in twenty-five.

Michelle had had several previous encounters with Mel. She had drunkenly asked him if he wanted to get laid at her sister's Bat Mitzvah, and she had sung backup on a demo that Larry had recorded at Mel's old studio. The last time she had seen him, she had read the part of Al Capone's mistress, Jasmine Huggins, in an early draft of Mel's screenplay, and his approach to his work had changed significantly. In that first reading, he had been self-effacing, calling his script "some bullshit I wrote when I was drunk off my ass." Now, even though he was direct-ing a mere training video, and even though he had written the script longhand on notebook paper, he insisted that every line be spoken exactly as written. He told Michelle that he'd grown tired of actors who questioned him; they were like wild animals, he said—they smelled weakness. The only way to get them to obey you was for them to respect or fear you—respect took time; fear was quicker. He told Michelle that she seemed to "have her shit together"—actresses weren't sup-posed to have their shit together; that was one of the two reasons he didn't date actresses. And the other reason? Michelle asked. Because he "already had a lady friend," said Mel. Yeah, Michelle said, she knew that he was dating Muley's mother—that must be a rockin' party every night, she said, recalling Deirdre Wills as a stern and exacting substitute teacher at Mather High. Yeah, said Mel, something like that.

After the filming, their conversation continued over vegetable lo mein and Bring Your Own Budweiser at Three Happiness in Chinatown, where Mel bought Michelle dinner. There was an ease to Mel and Michelle's rapport—they laughed at each other's jokes, poked fun at each other's ambitions, snickered as they read fortune cookies, and added the words *in bed*—"In the future, you will create a masterpiece in bed." Three times during the course of their meal, Mel asked Michelle how old she was, but each time interrupted her. "I don't even want to know," he'd say.

Driving Michelle back to West Rogers Park, Mel made no further mention of his "lady friend." He asked Michelle if she would be free the next weekend and if she would be interested in starring in *No Quarter,* a training video about re-pairing jammed change slots in washing machines, and maybe they could go out for a bite afterward. When Michelle said that she would be back in New York by then, Mel asked if she needed a ride to the train station. Michelle thanked him but said that Jill and her "gaggle of weird friends" would be driving her.

Michelle was packing her bags for New York when Mel called to ask for her address, ostensibly so he could send her a copy of the video. And though he said, "Well, that's the only reason I was calling," he kept her on the phone for nearly an hour, then asked once more if she was sure that she didn't need a ride to Union Station. This time, she said she did; her sister's friends had crapped out on her at the last minute. Mel excitedly told Michelle that he'd pick her up immediately so that they could grab lunch; Amtrak food, he proclaimed, was some nasty shit.

What Mel missed most by being in a committed relationship with Deirdre Wills, whom he'd been dating seriously for more than a year, was not the thrill that came from having sex with multiple women. Whatever pleasures he had experienced in his promiscuous teens and twenties were more than compensated for by his celibate early thirties, an age when paychecks began to matter more than looks and charm. What he missed was the anticipation and the mystery of new partners. He liked how Deirdre made him feel about himself—with her, he felt intelligent, reputable, and mature, and he didn't know what he wanted with this young white girl with her sassy mouth and her pert but smaller-than-medium-sized boobs. He didn't know what he liked about Michelle other than that she was easy to talk to and that she was safe, in that she was leaving for New York and not coming back anytime soon. His hope for their breakfast at Lou Mitchell's diner was that during the course of the conversation, she would signal her interest in him, give him an opportunity to feel good about himself, and he would chuckle with regret at unfulfilled desire and say, "Maybe if you lived in Chicago things might be different."

But on that Friday, Michelle would not give him any such satisfaction. She too planned to flirt with Mel, to trick him into making some unguarded statement of desire, at which point she could look deeply into his eyes and say, "Well, Melvin, maybe if I were in Chicago things might be different, but I've gotta board a train." At breakfast, Mel and Michelle each tried to get the other to make a misstep, Mel hoping that Michelle would reveal herself to have something in common with the girls he'd dated at Roosevelt University, the ones who brought him back to their dorms as a trophy; Michelle hoping that Mel would say something lecherous, thus revealing himself to have something in common with the drama directors who'd hit on her, the dormitory RAs who'd try to win her trust by warning her about Don Juans who preyed upon new girls; both Michelle and Mel hoping to avoid the terribly inconvenient situation of actually liking another human being when one of them was in a serious relationship and they lived eight hundred miles apart.

At Union Station, as Michelle and Mel stood at the gate, the unspoken question arose as to whether the two should hug, shake hands, or kiss. They stood face-to-face, like wrestlers squaring off on a mat. But all Michelle said was "Check you later, Melvin," then Mel said, "Peace," and less than a half hour later, Michelle was sitting in Economy class, her Walkman blasting Joni Mitchell's "Blue" as she watched snow swirling before the shrinking Chicago skyline, thinking for the first time that she was sorry to see that skyline fading in the distance; while Jill, who had been unable to arrange Michelle's ride to the train station, was standing in the bedroom of Wes Sullivan, whose cheeks were red, whose eyes were bloodshot.


W hen she had pictured Wes's bedroom on Bittersweet Place, Jill Wasserstrom—though of course she usually had more important issues on her mind than Wes's bedroom—had assumed that it would resemble the interior of his BMW. She imagined dog-eared copies of Marx, campaign posters and buttons, a desk defaced with bumper stickers, shoeboxes full of Pete Seeger and Fela Kuti tapes. But even if Wes himself was a rumpled mess with too many creases on the left side of his face, as if he'd spent the past week with his head jammed into a pillow, his room looked like a furniture store's designer showroom. His well-thumbed revolutionary volumes were arranged alphabetically on three waist-high bookshelves; his record albums were encased in plastic slipcovers on a built-in shelving unit with a ladder on wheels to access the topmost LPs. His ripped T-shirts and jeans were folded neatly in a mahogany armoire that had once belonged to his great-grandfather John Harper Sullivan, who had arrived penniless in Chicago in 1881, made his fortune in textiles, and was now buried in Graceland Cemetery. There were no posters on the walls, just framed black-and-white photographs of John Harper Sullivan and his family posing in front of Sullivan's Textiles on South Halsted Street, of Great-uncle Francis Sullivan in his Chicago White Stockings uniform, left leg kicked high in the air, of Eamon Sullivan, Wes's father's favorite brother, smiling with his Air Force unit, only days before his plane was lost.

When Jill arrived, Wes said that it was good of her to come on such short notice. He was flicking the ashes of a cigarette into a green blown-glass bowl that he held in his palm as Jill studied his pictures, remarking upon how unaware she was of her own family's history. Her grandfather on her father's side had owned a soda pop factory, but she had never even seen a pop bottle from the factory, never seen a picture of it, nor of her father's only friends at the factory—a trucker named Lloyd Cubbins with whom he played catch, and a German shepherd named Holler who had been shot to death when the factory had been burglarized. While Jill's mother had been alive, Charlie had taken home movies of Becky and the kids at Lunt Avenue Beach, made reel-to-reel tapes of Jill and Michelle singing with their mother, of Michelle pretending to host *The Tonight Show.* All these had disappeared. Jill was wondering what it might have been like to grow up in a house surrounded by her own history when her eyes settled on the only color photos in Wes's room.

Three pictures were encased in pewter frames on a rolltop desk. In the left photo, a younger, clean-shaven Wes was sternly drawing a bow across a violin. At right, Wes was hugging his brother Casey in front of a snowman. In the center photo, Wes and Rae-Ann were dressed in formal attire, but the moment Jill saw that picture, Wes turned it facedown. He said that he couldn't look at Rae-Ann anymore, knowing he'd been cuckolded. He opened a desk drawer and pulled out a pink notebook with Garfield stickers on it, then asked Jill if she'd noticed anything different about Rae-Ann when the two of them had gone shopping downtown. No, Jill said nervously, why? Wes opened the notebook and thrust it in front of Jill; her hands trembled as she glanced down at Rae-Ann's bubbly script—what was it, she asked, still wary. Wes said that he'd found it in Rae-Ann's bedroom; he asked her to read it. Jill said that she didn't want to read anything personal. Wes said that it wasn't personal; he just wanted her opinion. Jill skimmed a page—there was a poem titled "How Can I Tell?"—"How can I tell how I feel about you / How can I tell how I feel when you're there / How can I tell you that this love is true / How can I tell that the world isn't fair?" Wes asked Jill what she thought. Jill said that she didn't know much about poetry but didn't think that good poetry was supposed to rhyme. Wes said that the next poem didn't rhyme, why didn't she read it? It was called "My Secret Lover."

Jill said that this really wasn't any of her business, couldn't they discuss something else? Wes said that he wished he could talk about anything else, but he hadn't slept since he'd found this notebook. He'd been at Rae-Ann's house and she'd asked him to choose a record from her room, and the notebook had been right there on her dresser, almost as if she'd wanted him to find it. He'd started reading, and when Rae-Ann called up to ask what was taking so gosh-darn long, he'd stuffed the notebook into his pants and grabbed the first record he could find—"Just Gaga for the Gospel." Rae-Ann had been thrilled by the album choice, thought he was finally embracing religion; Mr. and Mrs. Warner had entered their living room, beaming approvingly as Rae-Ann told them who had picked out the album—"It wasn't me; it was totally Wes." All three of them grinned while Wes was quietly seething, wondering about the identity of Rae-Ann's "secret lover." He had considered everyone he knew and determined that it had to be some Jesus freak in Rae-Ann's church group, but when he deviously asked whether he could join her at the next New Centurions meeting, she hadn't blushed or turned pale; she said that it was an awesome idea, and he had attended three meetings in a row, wasting precious time he could have spent volunteering for the Washington campaign with Jill leading singalongs of "Old Man Jesus (Where Can You Be Now?)" at a Wheaton elder care center, consuming a box lunch while watching an indoor soccer game between the Chicago Sting and the Baltimore Blast, practicing traditional African dances, such as the juba, as part of a church exchange. Wes asked Jill if Rae-Ann had ever mentioned any guys she might have liked. No, Jill said quickly, she had never heard Rae-Ann say that she liked any guy other than Wes.

The statement was technically true—Jill hadn't lied. Jill was, though, as yet uncertain how to process Rae-Ann's recent confession in a women's dressing room of Marshall Field's. For forty-five minutes, Jill had watched Rae-Ann model cocktail dresses for Spring Cotillion, then, at Rae-Ann's urging had tried on a series of unflattering pink and lavender dresses. Though the dresses all hung loosely, Rae-Ann kept saying that Jill looked "elegant" and "foxy," words Jill did not associate with herself. She had never found her looks bad, per se, just not so striking that anyone but a romantic like Muley would ever comment upon them. Everyone at Lane said that girls looked like this or that celebrity; no one ever said that about Jill, save for Hillel Levy, who once remarked that Jill resembled Robert De Niro wearing a wig. In the dressing room, Rae-Ann said that Wes would really like the dress Jill was wearing. Jill asked Rae-Ann why she was mentioning Wes—he was Rae-Ann's boyfriend, not hers. "I know that," Rae-Ann said, but added that it didn't matter; she liked girls more than guys anyway.

As Rae-Ann twirled in a cocktail dress, Jill responded that she tended to like girls more than guys, too; most guys were immature, sex-obsessed, and prejudiced, but there were exceptions, such as Wes and Muley and Daniel Ortega. Yeah, Rae-Ann had agreed, but she *really* liked girls more than guys—she asked

Jill if she ever found girls attractive. Jill said that she was more impressed by intellect than looks. Rae-Ann asked Jill which women she found intellectually attractive. Jill listed Virginia Woolf, Barbara Jordan, Bernardine Dohrn, Linda Ellerbee, and Simone de Beauvoir, then asked Rae-Ann whom she liked. Rae-Ann said she didn't know who was "intellectually attractive," but she knew who was hot: Amy Grant, Linda Fratianne, Tai Babilonia, and Chris Evert. Oh, and one other person, she said, and kissed Jill on the lips.

At first, Jill was not certain what was happening. Jill had never once considered that Rae-Ann might be a lesbian. For, unlike Rae-Ann, lesbians were cool; lesbians were *interesting.* Though Jill had not yet experienced any strong desire for a woman, she still entertained the notion that one day she might wake up a lesbian. She delighted in raising the specter of her potential lesbianism, telling her uncle Dave that no, she wouldn't go to Homecoming, such events were not welcoming to *lesbians*; or declaring to Gail, when she'd say that a particular pantsuit would be nice to wear to Michelle's or Jill's wedding, "not if we turn out to be lesbians," hoping that if she said it often enough, it might turn out to be true.

And though Jill did not enjoy the experience of Rae-Ann kissing her, she did find it *interesting* that Rae-Ann was kissing her and she wondered if she would be small-minded or Republican to object. She considered her options—how to stop without seeming prudish, whether to tell Rae-Ann that, even if someday she did become a lesbian, she still wouldn't feel attracted to Rae-Ann. Jill's indecisiveness lasted long enough for Rae-Ann herself to break away. "Wow, you sure like to kiss," she said.

Since that incident, Jill had seen little of Rae-Ann. She had fielded a phone call the next morning during which Rae-Ann suggested that they "take it slow," lest Wes suspect something was amiss. There had been a pink Hallmark card with cupids on it, but nothing more, and as winter break neared its conclusion, Jill had presumed that the Rae-Ann Warner episode would too. But now a distraught Wes, who, Jill noted, looked even cuter when his eyes were watery and his cheeks were flushed, was asking Jill if he should break up with Rae-Ann immediately or "roll" whichever "Christian cretin" had inspired her doggerel and would take the virginity of which he had been so respectful. He bit his lip, steeling himself for the answer. Jill asked if she could take another look at Rae-Ann's notebook, then said she doubted that Rae-Ann had a "secret lover" in the sense that Wes assumed. What other sense, Wes asked—what did "secret lover" mean if not another guy? Maybe another guy, but not anybody Wes should be jealous of, Jill said. What guy, Wes asked. Jesus, said Jill.

At first, Wes looked skeptical; then he smiled and flipped through Rae-Ann's notebook. He skimmed each poem, nodding with relief. He pulled Jill close and told her that he didn't know how to repay her for saving his relationship. He asked her to take a good look around his room; if she liked any of his stuff, she could take it. But since Jill didn't ask for anything, Wes asked Jill if she would do him a favor instead. Could she visit Rae-Ann on some random pretext and return the notebook he had taken? Jill asked why he couldn't bring it back himself. Wes said he couldn't risk it—Rae-Ann had gotten pissed at him before for snooping through her diaries.

Jill found Wes's request presumptuous, but she nevertheless consented. She went back home and changed into an outfit that she figured Rae-Ann would find unattractive—wrinkled, gray jeans, an old "Best Dad" sweatshirt of her father's, and, pinned to her backpack, a HONKIES FOR HAROLD button. She rang Muley's doorbell to see if he would accompany her to Rae-Ann's house, but Muley wasn't home; Mel was—he said that Muley was at Angel Guardian, then asked, oh, by the way, had Michelle mentioned him recently?

On the grounds of Angel Guardian Church, Ephraim Tekulve, boyfriend of Irit Ben-Amar, kept a large, dank shed that smelled of sawdust and turpentine. Tekulve had lived for ten years as a squatter on Maxwell Street and tried valiantly to live without being tainted by money. He recycled wood; he scavenged Dumpsters behind supermarkets; for a time, he had composted his own waste. When Angel Guardian hired him as staff carpenter, he had refused payment and instead asked if he could work rent-free in the church's shed. Here, Irit invited Muley to work on his film projects.

An El Camino was parked in the Angel Guardian lot when Jill entered the shed. Muley was operating a table saw, and Britt Hurd, who was spending the last days of Christmas break in Chicago before he would attend military school in Florida, was taking a blowtorch to a movie screen. Both Britt and Muley wore goggles, but when Jill entered, Muley removed his and switched off the table saw. He kissed Jill on the cheek, then asked her if she had met Britt. Noticing Jill, Britt shut off the blowtorch, stood up, and offered his hand, but Jill stared at it, feeling her eyes burn. "Fine," Britt said, "don't shake my hand, I don't give a shit." He glanced at Jill's button and said, "Honkies for Harold? Who the fuck's

Harold?" Jill angrily made for the door. Muley told her to hold on for a second, but she was gone. "Women," Britt snorted.

As she walked through the snow that had collected in the parking lot, Jill felt that she had been betrayed; it hardly seemed accidental that Muley was associating with the thug who had put Wes in the hospital. When Muley caught up to her on Ridge, Jill told him that she knew he didn't like Wes, but that didn't mean he had to hang out with Britt. Muley explained that he was working on a project and Britt knew a lot about chemicals and explosives. Jill said that Britt was also a criminal, an arsonist, and a bigot. Why, Muley asked, because Wes said so? That was low, Jill said, then in a fit of rage boldly revealed that she'd betrayed Muley; she'd made out with someone else. Here it came, Muley thought—his punishment for his nights with Connie in Florida. Muley swallowed. "With who?" he asked. "Wes?" Jill said that Muley's imagination was surprisingly limited—why did he assume that she would only make out with guys? In fact, she said, she had been making out with Rae-Ann. She whipped off her backpack, unzipped it, pulled out Rae-Ann's notebook, and showed him "My Secret Lover." Muley glanced at it; Jill's story seemed dubious—Rae-Ann didn't seem interesting enough to be a lesbian, he thought. "Are you sure it's about you?" he asked. "It sounds like it's about Jesus."

Jill snatched back the book, stuffed it into her backpack, and sprinted toward a bus that was standing at Ridge Avenue and Devon, her HONKIES FOR HAROLD button bouncing up and down as she ran. Muley began to follow, but once the bus had crossed into East Rogers Park underneath the *eruv* strung from the lampposts of Ridge, he stopped. He looked at the bus as it sped farther away from West Rogers Park, then up at the border made of fishing wire. Then he looked back at the steeple of Angel Guardian. He turned around and began to walk back toward his art project.

When Jill arrived at the Warners' house, Rae-Ann told Jill that she was wearing a "hot outfit," but didn't let her into the house. "We have people over," she said, adding that Jill really should have called first; though she knew that Jill was anxious to see her, she'd have to be patient. But when Jill unzipped her backpack and produced the notebook, Rae-Ann's eyes lit up. *Oh my God, thanks so much,* she said—she'd been looking for it everywhere, where had Jill found it? Jill tried to think of a lie, but couldn't. It was in my backpack, she said, which was essentially true. Rae-Ann winked at Jill and said that she must have subconsciously wanted Jill to find it; she asked if Jill had read any of her poems. Jill said that they looked personal. Not really, Rae-Ann said, they were just her Jesus poems.

When Jill got home that night, the snow had stopped falling and the temperature was hovering near zero. Muley was sitting on the front steps of her house, wearing a navy blue parka with the hood up. He was blowing on his hands; a sketchpad lay on his lap; Fidel sat beside him. Jill was too cold and tired to be angry anymore; she asked Muley whether Charlie and Gail knew that he was out here. Muley said yeah, Charlie had invited him in for cocoa, but he had wanted to stay outside; he asked Jill if she wanted to go in. Yes, Jill said, she was tired; she wanted to go in and warm up. No, Muley said, she hadn't understood him; he hadn't been asking if she wanted to go inside the house, he was asking if she wanted to go inside *there*. He nodded over to the lawn. Although all the other lawns on North Shore were white with snow, the Wasserstroms' was just about bare. In the middle of it, Muley had built an igloo; a soft orange glow emanated from its rounded entryway.

Once they were inside the igloo, sharing a cup of well-sugared coffee that Muley had brought in a thermos, Muley showed Jill sketches for an art project. What he didn't like about movie screens, he said, was that they represented barriers. He didn't like how they always remained white at the end of a film, that no matter what had been projected, they remained unsullied. He wanted to create screens that would show the effect of whatever was being projected upon them. He no longer liked the idea of art that was permanent, because permanence was a lie. He took a candle and held it to the igloo's roof. Soon, the snow began to melt, and water dripped down.

After Muley had melted enough snow to make a small hole in the roof, he and Jill lay in the snow and watched airplanes and stars. Muley said that soon they would both be in college; he could already feel the world expanding and pulling them away from each other, and who knew how long they would stay together then? He asked Jill if they could make a deal; here in West Rogers Park, from Howard to Peterson, from Ridge to Kedzie, they would always be together. But once they traveled beyond those boundaries, there would be no rules.

Jill took a breath, and then she held Muley's hand. "All right," she said.

On the first day of school following winter break, Louis Benson called a special meeting of the *Lane Leader* staff to discuss a new batch of threatening letters. The ones that had arrived at the *Leader* office before break had all been vague. But now each staffer had received the same note with a hand-printed message: "On 2/22, Harold's going down. And so will you!" Though many felt frightened, and Rae-Ann's parents would soon insist on driving her to and from school, thus allowing Wes to drive Jill home every day, Benson relished the attention. He thrived on controversy. When the paper had run an investigative series on street gangs, he had faced down some Vice Lords on his front lawn with a loaded rifle; when he had approved a scathing review of the student musical *Anything Goes,* he hid in the bushes in front of his house and waited for the few disgruntled cast members who had plotted to blow up his mailbox, then ran after them with a hammer. Now, for one of the first times since the *Tribune* had fired him, he felt that he was involved with something that mattered.

Benson had initially viewed this high school job as an interim measure. But when, after two years with the *Leader,* he was offered a reporting job on the *Chicago Daily News,* he turned it down. The high school job came with more security, more vacation, more money, more time for his own writing, and perhaps most important, more opportunity to avoid journalism, a profession that had begun to terrify him. One of the main reasons he had quaffed three Rob Roys on the night that he'd crashed William Sullivan Sr.'s Thunderbird en route to interview Adlai Stevenson was that he had grown more and more afraid of interviews; in the presence of politicians, he felt ignorant; with police chiefs, unmanly; with athletes, weak; with criminals, naïve; and with his editors, all of the previous four.

His plans to write soon fell by the wayside. He would dictate blistering op-ed pieces about the corruption of Richard J. Daley's machine to his wife, but would wake up in the morning and find his writing flat, his opinions pedestrian. His all-time best student, Isaac Mallen, became an editor at Spofford & Quimby Publishers and sent letters to Benson every six months or so, always encouraging him to propose a book. But Mallen rejected Benson's only suggestion—*A Teacher*

*Remembers,* which would detail his most successful students' accomplishments, interspersed with Benson's recollections of them—on the grounds that none of his students were noteworthy enough, not even Isaac Mallen.

Every year, Benson lectured about the importance of high school journalism; his students usually believed him, but he rarely believed himself. Every year, he spoke loftily of the statewide Front Page journalism awards, but even though he threw fits on the rare occasions that the *Leader* failed to win the "Editorial Excellence" trophy, he never felt satisfied when the paper did win. Several years earlier, when a vice principal told him that the school had run out of room for all the *Leader's* trophies, and did he perhaps want to take some home, he'd declined, then told a janitor to haul them out to the Dumpsters.

But the *Leader's* series on race, spearheaded by Wes Sullivan, was having an impact beyond any Benson could recall. The threats were only part of it. Teachers were cornering him in the hallway. The right people were praising the *Leader;* the right people were lambasting it. Pep Club supervisor Martha Mayhew may have plunked her tray down next to Benson's at the faculty cafeteria and sternly lectured him about "the perils of undermining school spirit," but Track coach Marvin "Quick" Mix, a beloved former Lane athlete who had faltered in college, where his nickname became "Quick Six" for his ability to chug-a-lug a six-pack, thanked Benson for "telling it like it is."

And though the most recent remark Benson had written about a Wes Sullivan article was "This isn't altogether awful," during this first editorial meeting of 1983, Benson said he thought that all the controversy might well result in a book Isaac Mallen would publish. He envisioned a collection of *Leader* articles, accompanied by his own observations about the state of race relations in Chicago. But for that to happen, he said, every editor would have to double his or her workload. He wanted hard-hitting political cartoons, he told Hillel Levy; no more big-bosomed waitresses serving cigar-chomping school administrators blubbering, "Come to think of it, I'll take two." If Wes delivered as good an issue as he was capable of, Benson would nominate it not only for the Front Page trophy but also for a John Fink Chicago journalism award. He didn't care if high school papers weren't qualified; he wanted to see the judge who could say that the *Sun-Times* or, he said, looking at Wes, "that rag your dad works for" could do better.

At the end of the meeting, Benson dismissed everyone except Jill and Wes.

He sat atop a wobbly table between two typewriters, hands in his vest pockets, his gleaming black shoes on a yellow plastic chair below him. He said that he was relying particularly upon the two of them; he wouldn't accept Wes's innuendoes or anonymous quotes anymore, and Jill, as chief researcher, would have to dutifully fact-check every assertion that Wes made. But if the two of them did their best, he might just be able to say that Jill would be editor-in-chief her senior year and that Mr. Sullivan "had a future in journalism after all."

Though Wes smiled when Benson uttered that phrase, afterward in his car when he and Jill discussed the meeting, he turned surly. Wasn't that just like Benson, he said, to turn all concerned when he saw something in it for him; now he was "Mr. Rah-Rah Boy Scout Troop Leader" telling them to "win one for the team" just because he thought he might get a book out of it, even though he hadn't done any research, hadn't gotten rolled at Hero's Subs. He'd always thought that Benson was tough, but you know what? He was just a small, pathetic little man afraid of death. Why was he supposed to risk his ass for Benson? Why should he subject himself to more of Britt Hurd's threats? He said that he had half a mind to quit and let Benson face the threats and Britt on his own.

As Wes drove up Western, Jill said that she actually wanted to discuss those threats—she had been thinking about Muley spending time with Britt, couldn't believe he was doing it only out of spite. She asked if Wes thought that Britt had actually sent the notes. Of course he had, Wes said, what made her suspect otherwise? Well, Jill said, it seemed strange that the most recent note had read, "Harold's going down. And so will you," but when she had talked with Britt, he seemed to have no idea who Harold Washington was. When had she talked to Britt, Wes asked. Jill said that Muley had been working with him on a project. Wes laughed ruefully but said nothing.

In fact, Wes didn't speak again for more than a minute. Jill asked what he was thinking about. Keldrick Burden getting kicked in the nuts, Wes said. Keldrick Burden, Wes explained, had been in his sixth grade class at Ogden; he'd been one of the only black kids, and everybody had teased him. Except for Keldrick's older sister, Cissy, Wes was Keldrick's only friend. Keldrick had buckteeth and some of the kids, Duncan Kirby for example, would put chopsticks under their upper lips to imitate those long, lapine front teeth.

The worst of it had come when Duncan returned from a trip to visit his grandparents in Houston. He was wearing a Western outfit complete with lasso, cowboy hat, and boots. Duncan wanted to demonstrate the strength of his new boots, so two of his buddies pinned Keldrick to the ground and he had kicked Keldrick hard in the nuts and sung "We Are the Champions." Wes went after Duncan, tackled him on the playground, and beat the crap out of him until a teacher pulled Wes off and dragged him to the principal's office. And while Duncan went to the nurse's station and received a handful of cream soda–flavored Dum-Dum suckers, Wes was suspended for a week. When he returned, none of his classmates would talk to him, not even Keldrick, who, when Wes saw him again, was laughing and playing I-Spy with Duncan and his buddies. And on the school bus, Cissy Burden told Wes to find another charity; her brother could take care of himself.

Whenever Wes did the right thing, he said, he was resented. When he played pickup basketball and sacrificed his body, taking the charges of bigger players, his teammates told him that he took the game too seriously. When he cracked an egg over the head of Eli Sorkin, who'd egged his brother Casey on Halloween, his father told him, "Don't fight your brother's battles." Now he'd put his ass on the line to defend Moolai Wills from Britt and here Moolai and Jill were, hanging out with the bastard, and all the great Louis Benson wanted was to steal his ideas. Sometimes, he said, he felt like giving up, becoming a Republican, letting every Keldrick Burden get kicked in the nuts; what was the point of trying to do the right thing when it only pissed everyone off?

Tears welled up in Wes's eyes as he drove north, passing a pale green statue of Abraham Lincoln at Lawrence Avenue. Then he blinked and swallowed. He told Jill that he didn't blame her or Muley; he knew that all this was his own fault. He knew that Jill and Muley were decent people, and he himself was not. Not really. He was jealous, mendacious, competitive, vain, made shit up and got pissed when people called him on it. The hardest part of being Casey's older brother was not looking after him because he was disabled, not compensating for his father's neglect or his mother's denial; it was the look Casey had in his eyes when he saw him, as if he were some sort of hero. Sometimes, he wished he could just fuck up, get a B in a class, maybe even fail one; then he could stop pretending.

Jill reached a hand toward Wes's cheek, but stopped. Her hand hovered just above the gearshift as she contemplated whether to touch his cheek or his hand or whether he would even want her to touch him at all. She raised her hand another inch, then stopped again, knowing that she had never kissed anybody—well, kissed, yes, but never initiated; she'd always let Muley make the first move, then stopped him when he made the second one. She knew what people thought of her, that she was too intellectual, that all she cared about was homework and politics, that she had no deep passions, and here she was in a car seated beside someone she loved, or maybe she didn't love him, maybe she just liked him a lot, Jill didn't know, how could she know with her hand floating in the air, not even daring to move it another inch. Fine, she thought, what could she lose, she could just touch his cheek. She reached her hand farther toward him, but then she looked up to see the green traffic light of Peterson Avenue, the southern border of West Rogers Park approaching, and she felt her inhibitions returning. She quickly put her hand back in her lap, remembering the vow that Muley had asked her to take, that they would remain faithful within these borders, constructing an invisible *eruv* around themselves. But Jill didn't know what to do when Wes sped past the Nortown Theater—*Timerider* was on the marquee—and grasped her hand.

That was all right, Jill thought nervously—Wes's hand touching hers; that was only a friendly gesture. Friends held hands in many countries; there was nothing inappropriate about it. It would be xenophobic and ethnocentric to think otherwise. As Wes stopped at the Devon traffic light and ran his fingers through Jill's hair, she tensed again, then relaxed. Though this action occurred within Jill and Muley's carefully delineated boundaries, here, too, there was room for interpretation. For example, Jill thought, had Wes noticed a wasp near her face, he could have inadvertently touched her hair while swatting it away. But she didn't know how she could justify to either Muley or herself the fact that Wes, after pulling into the Warren Park lot and turning off the ignition, was covering her neck and her cheeks with kisses. She flung open the car door, then started running for the park.

Jill could hear Wes yelling for her to stop. But she kept running with her coat unzipped, over a thin layer of snow that glowed pink under the park lights. She ran around Mount Warren, over the icy soccer fields and bike trails, past the chess tables, through a lonely playground, ice upon the chains of the swings, around the golf course and out onto the Pratt Avenue sidewalk. She did not stop running until she had crossed Ridge. Then she stopped, caught her breath, and waited for Wes.

Wes said that he didn't know what had come over him; could she forgive him? Jill told Wes to stop apologizing, and then she kissed him. And when they reached Clark Street, she kissed him again. They held hands all the way to the lake, where they kissed on hills of frozen sand, for they were in East Rogers Park and the rules under which Jill had operated in Warren Park no longer applied. She could feel Wes's breath in her ear as he wrapped his scarf around her, and she didn't know what made her happier—that she was in Wes's arms or that she was so bundled up that Muley could not have recognized her.

Later that night, while Wes was skipping stones across the frozen lake, watching them hop before skidding off toward the black horizon, he asked Jill, if it so happened that he ever broke up with Rae-Ann, and if it so happened that Jill was no longer dating "Myoolai," would she ever consider dating him? On the one hand, he couldn't imagine life without Rae-Ann. But he knew that someday they would have to break up, though he hated the idea of hurting her. Just the other day, he and Rae-Ann had attended church, and she had told him something so touching—that he was the only guy with whom she could ever see herself.

Wes began to fantasize aloud about what he and Jill might do as a couple. They could go to Central America—did Jill know where Rae-Ann wanted to spend her ultimate fantasy vacation? Wimbledon, to watch Chris Evert play tennis. He asked Jill about her fantasies. Jill was about to tell Wes that she did not indulge in fantasies, but that wasn't true. Of course she had fantasies; most involved universal nuclear disarmament, some involved the reincarnation of specific people—well, one specific person, whom she hadn't seen since she was nine—and many involved being with Wes—lounging with Wes in a hot tub while having a deep, penetrating conversation about the disintegration of the Democratic political machine, walking with Wes on a desert island, passionately debating wage and price controls. But what Wes was really asking was whether she fantasized about the real him. Did she imagine going to the prom with Wes, making out during the midnight creature feature at the 400 Theater, ordering french fries at Wolfy's, sharing each other's ketchup? To which the answer, of course, was yes, but she couldn't tell him; she merely said well, she had no idea where the future might lead her; she would leave the matter up to fate. "Fate," Wes said— he stumbled over the word. Yes, Jill said, she was a great believer in it. Wes said that he wished that he was a great believer in anything, then kissed her once more before they walked back to his car.

Wes drove Jill home, silently ruminating for the first mile. Then he asked Jill what she was thinking. "You first," Jill said. Wes took a breath and said that he was actually thinking about what Jill had said earlier, which had made him so upset. About Britt? Jill asked. Yes, Wes said, her suggestion that Britt might not have written those notes, that she had seen Britt with Moo-lai. He asked if Jill knew why he had gotten so upset. Jill asked if it was because he was now wondering if Britt had written the notes at all. Wes smiled. No, he said, it was because he knew that Britt had done exactly what he had suspected him of, but he also knew that if he wrote the balanced article that Louis Benson wanted, readers might sympathize with Britt and not see him as the vicious s.o.b. Wes knew him to be. That's why he was really considering quitting the paper, forgetting the Front Page trophy and that bullshit about the John Fink award.

Jill said he didn't know where his reporting might lead, but Wes said that wasn't true; he already knew exactly where it led. He'd already done the research, had already written up his notes, but Jill was the first person he was telling. He'd begun to tell Rae-Ann that he was considering confronting Britt at his house without his "bodyguards," but she'd been so opposed to his going, he still hadn't told her that he had actually gone. Jill asked what he had said to Britt. Wes said that Britt hadn't been home; he was already on his way to the Nordhagen Military School in Florida.

While he drove west, Wes described his trip to the Hurd residence on Leavitt Street, adding details as he went along. Jill listened, captivated. Wes said that he'd found the Hurd house to be surprisingly well maintained. The evergreens were trimmed, the shutters recently painted, no KKK literature in sight. Wes had rung the doorbell, Mrs. Hurd had answered, and to his surprise, she wasn't a hillbilly. What was she like, Jill asked. Vietnamese, said Wes. She invited him in and poured him a Pepsi in a Speedy Gonzalez glass and offered him a plate of Hydrox chocolate cookies. And, while Wes had nibbled on the cookies and sipped on his Pepsi, Mrs. Hurd said that Wes seemed like a good boy and she hoped that he could help her son—Britt had a good heart, but a "very bad temper." Wes asked what had made Britt so mad. "Me," said Mrs. Hurd.

Wes told Jill about how Mrs. Hurd had taken him upstairs to Britt's room, which reminded him of his own bedroom. On the dresser were framed photographs of a man in a military uniform. Two of the photos had medals dangling over them. The man in the photo was Britt's father, Mrs. Hurd told Wes, who said that her husband looked very handsome. "Yes," Mrs. Hurd said, but he had died eight and a half years earlier; he had gone to the North Woods for a hunting trip with some Army buddies and one of his friends' rifles had accidentally discharged. She said the word *accidentally* bitterly, but when Wes asked her to elaborate, she said that she was tired of talking about it; she couldn't live in the past forever, even if Britt tried to make her. Jill asked what Mrs. Hurd had meant; had she remarried? Yes, said Wes, five years after her husband's death, she had married the office manager of her travel agency. She didn't tell Wes much about him, but she showed him a picture. He was Jamaican, Wes said.

Jill rolled all this around in her head. It was an interesting story, she said, more interesting, in fact, than anything that they had published in the *Leader* thus far, and Wes had such a phenomenal memory for details; he had to write it up. Yes, Wes said with a sigh, he knew he did, but it still wouldn't explain anything. If he published it, though, everyone would think that it did; he'd probably win a Front Page trophy, Benson would get a great story for free, and everyone who read it would think that they understood Britt. Sure, it was tragic that Britt's father was dead; yes, it was unfortunate that his stepfather, who happened to be black, disciplined him harshly, but Britt's sob story was nothing more than a distraction from the simple fact that Britt was a bigot and a bastard. And who really cared what made him that way?

After Wes had passed through the intersection of Pratt and California, he tried to kiss Jill once more, but since it was late, since she was within the *eruv,* and since Muley's igloo hadn't completely melted, she offered her cheek and a handshake. Then she said good night, jumped out of the car, and ran like hell to her house, thus avoiding any further temptation.

## SPRING 1983

Jill took to her new *Lane Leader* responsibilities with fervor. Despite the fact that the Democratic primary was approaching, and polls showed that any of the three candidates could win, she resigned her envelope-stuffing position in the Washington campaign, thinking that it might compromise her journalistic integrity, and took her Washington buttons to the city's new recycling center downtown. She worked every night at the Hild Library, where Benson had temporarily moved the *Leader* offices in response to the threats against his staff. Here, she would check Wes's hastily scribbled transcripts, mark up his drafts requesting clarifications, and insist that he remain focused on his work whenever he tried to lure her into a kiss or bitch about Rae-Ann. All that could wait, Jill said—their work was more important.

Jill and Rae-Ann's exchanges grew noticeably less cordial—whenever Jill marked her spelling errors in red, Rae-Ann interpreted Jill's behavior as payback for not spending more time alone with her. More often than not, Jill would spend her Fridays after school working, canceling movie nights with Muley, who was spending nearly every evening at Angel Guardian, experimenting with films, projectors, and screens.

On the night of the primary, Jill locked the door to her room on North Shore and tuned her radio to WBBM, brushing Fidel, listening intently until Harold Washington had spoken at 2:35 A.M. and his supporters had sung "We Shall Overcome." Washington's surprise victory over both Mayor Byrne and Richie Daley proved a boon, not only to Jill, who, immediately after Washington had finished speaking, cranked up E.L.O.'s *Discovery,* an album her sister had long since relegated to her "unlistenable dustbin," and danced alone in her Greenpeace T-shirt and underwear to "Don't Bring Me Down," while Fidel barked along; not only to Louis Benson, who stayed all night at the *Leader* offices with his rifle, ready to face down any miscreant who threatened his editors—he was disappointed to find no intruders other than a few stray rats and a slow-moving raccoon; but also to Schiffler Newspapers, whose finances had been in such a dreadful state that Gail had considered shutting them down altogether and turning full attention to selling the land upon which their offices stood, her only reservation having been how she would tell her husband.

Although most city newspapers took an optimistic approach to Washington's victory, the Schiffler papers immediately shifted their focus to his general election opponent, a well-intentioned, moderate Republican state legislator named Bernard Epton who, as Gail's front-page editorial noted, could become *Chicago's First Jewish Mayor.* The first postprimary issue saw Schiffler Newspapers' circulation triple, thanks in no small part to interest in Epton's candidacy in West Rogers Park. The following week's papers—in which Charlie's column discussed Jewish-American heroes such as boxer Mike Rossman, who fought with a Star of David emblazoned on his shorts, and baseball players Rod Carew, who wore a *ch'ai* as a tribute to his wife, and Dave Parker, who wore a Star of David, not because he was Jewish, but because his name was David and he was a star—saw their ad sales reach their highest numbers ever.

The imminent April general election was so much a part of the city's consciousness that even at Lane, where only a handful of students were of legal voting age, it dominated the curriculum. HONKIES FOR HAROLD buttons were popular, but so were ones emblazoned with ANTI-SEMITES FOR EPTON. In Jill's Debate class, she endured a dozen speeches from students speaking on behalf of either candidate; more than a half-dozen were titled "It's Our Turn!"

Though the threats to the *Lane Leader* did not materialize on February 22 (according to Wes, this was because Britt was at military school; according to Louis Benson, it was because he was heavily armed), the Sullivan-edited series on racism created the school's most popular editions since 1958, when the school had celebrated its fiftieth anniversary. The series would culminate with a post-election wrap-up, published just in time for entry into the Front Page and John Fink competitions, and would feature Wes's latest article about Britt, which took its headline from a controversial quote attributed to Democratic Party chairman Ed Vrdolyak: "It's a Racial Thing."

Five days before the general election, the Wasserstroms were hosting Passover seder. Gail, heartened by the fact that she hadn't seen Muley around the house lately—biracial relationships, she told Jill, were "dreadful for the offspring"—encouraged Jill to invite a more suitable date. Jill's fury at Gail's statement was only partially offset by the glee she felt when she decided to invite Rae-Ann. Making out with Rae-Ann seemed less intriguing than ever, but doing it in her bedroom with the door closed only partway while everyone hunted for the *afikoman* seemed irresistible. And, though she didn't like the idea of being naked or even in her underwear with Rae-Ann, even less so since their last outing together during spring break, when Rae-Ann had manhandled her breasts in the changing room of TJ Maxx, ostensibly to show her how a bra was supposed to fit, she was intrigued by the idea of having Rae-Ann sitting on her bed in her peach bra and panties right when Gail would barge in and say, "Ladies, come on up, we're serving fruit compote." Unfortunately, Passover fell within a few days of Easter Sunday, when Rae-Ann would be visiting her grandparents in Whiteland, Indiana. Jill then invited Muley, if only to spite Gail, but he also declined, citing a field trip to the

Doane Observatory of the Adler Planetarium to observe the space shuttle passing through the sky on the night of the first seder. It was the first time that he had ever said no to one of Jill's invitations, and she felt strangely hurt.

Asking Wes hadn't occurred to Jill, or rather, had occurred to her but seemed too daunting until he himself called to invite her for his family's Easter brunch since Rae-Ann would be "visiting the Klansmen and faith healers in Whiteland." Jill, in turn, invited Wes to Passover. Wes said that an ecumenical atheist's weekend sounded great; they could celebrate the upcoming week when college admissions departments would announce their decisions, the mayoral election would be decided, and, perhaps, various issues regarding their relationship could be revisited.

On that first Passover evening, as Jill waited for Wes to arrive, Muley and Connie joined Dr. Sam Singer and his new wife, Malynie, on the coast of Lake Michigan to see if they could catch the slightest glimpse of the space shuttle *Challenger,* which was making its inaugural flight. Muley had brought a movie camera with a powerful zoom lens, and Connie, who had become noticeably more flirtatious with Muley ever since Britt had left Chicago for military school, had brought a Native American blanket, pocked with cigarette holes. The entire Life Sciences class had been invited, but the trip was optional, and the only students in attendance were Muley, Connie, and Hillel Levy—who wasn't interested in astronomy but planned to spend the evening peeping through fogged-up car windows to see if he could espy anyone "eating some choice poontang" since the planetarium parking lot was a well-known makeout spot. Once Muley had screwed his camera onto his tripod ("Tripods ain't the only things with three legs, Mr. Wills," Hillel had sniggered), Connie invited him to join her under her blanket; maybe after he'd set up his camera, Muley said.

The docks of Lake Michigan were empty—orange buoys bobbed in the ice-cold water. Occasionally, a small plane from nearby Meigs Field would streak by and the water would ripple in its wake. Connie was sitting on the sloped grass alongside the observatory as a line of people stood waiting to look through the observatory's telescope. Dr. Singer and Malynie kissed on a patch of the shadowed lawn while Connie shifted underneath her blanket. Hillel, standing with his hands in the pockets of his Mighty Mac, asked if it was warm enough under the blanket—maybe she needed someone to make it warmer. Connie flung the blanket at him and said just take the goddamn thing. She skipped over to Muley, who was adjusting his viewfinder. She took one of his hands, said it was cold, and asked what he was doing. Muley gently extracted his hand and said that he wanted to film the *Challenger's* path. Connie asked who would want to see a little speck moving across the sky—it wouldn't look like anything. Muley said that he wanted to show how even the smallest objects could create a great impact. He would make a short film, he said, in which a tiny pinpoint of light—the shuttle—would slice across a movie screen that would burst into flames, then split into two.

That made no sense, Connie said; why go through all the trouble of making a movie if you knew you would set fire to the screen? She told Muley that he was clever, but someday he'd have to be more realistic about his future. Muley, swabbing his lens with his shirttail, asked what exciting things she might be doing with her future. Connie cheerfully said that she didn't think about it much because she knew that she wouldn't live long, not if she spent her life with Britt. She asked Muley to sit beside her on the grass, but Muley said that he didn't want to miss the shuttle—he asked Dr. Singer how much time they had. Dr. Singer told Muley to check the assignment sheet, then continued making out with his wife. *You see,* Connie said, he doesn't care if we watch it or not. *God,* she said, why did Muley hate her so much, why was a little speck in the sky more interesting than her? She said she'd bet she could start humping Hillel, and Muley wouldn't even care. She walked briskly over to Hillel, who was wandering along the sidewalk, casting glances into the back windows of cars.

"Hey, Levy," she shouted. Hillel turned around with a start. "Golldarn it, lady," he said—right when he was about to see some action, she'd shouted at him and now this guy had stopped eating out his girlfriend. Connie, imitating Violet Bick in *It's a Wonderful Life,* asked Hillel if he ever got tired of just watching things. No no, Hillel said, no way—he didn't want Britt jumping out from the bushes, kicking his ass, then chopping off his dick. Britt wouldn't do anything, Connie said, he was in Florida.

"Well," Hillel said, cracking his knuckles as he spoke in a Three Stooges voice, "why didn'tcha say so in the *foist* place?" Connie grabbed his hand and led him back down to the slope of grass where Muley was slowly pivoting his camera toward the southeastern sky. Hillel suggested a more secluded area—he pointed to some bushes surrounding the Meigs landing strip and chanted, "Push, push in the bush." No, Connie said, she *wanted* people to see. "Hey," she said to Muley, she and Hillel would be screwing over there—she pointed vaguely south. If Muley wanted to focus his camera on something more interesting than specks of light, he was welcome to film them. She pulled Hillel down into the stiff, frozen grass and started unzipping his Mighty Mac, while space shuttle *Challenger* slowly traced a faint white arc across the black Chicago sky.

The Wasserstrom seder was called for 7:00, but at 7:30, only twelve of the thirteen invited guests had arrived. Nevertheless, it was Charlie Wasserstrom's twin brother Dave's opinion that it was time to "get this show on the road." With the exception of Dave's wife, Peppy, who was in the kitchen with Gail forming matzo balls and plopping them into a cauldron of bubbling chicken soup, all the guests were gathered around the dining room table, the pauses in their conversations punctuated by the boisterous wails of a seemingly inconsolable eight-month-old Rachel Wasserstrom.

Charlie, in a dark blue suitcoat, white shirt, red tie, black suspenders, and white yarmulke, was seated at the head of the table, bouncing Rachel on his knee to little effect, thumbing through the Haggadah, and preparing to host a seder for the first time in his life; even when Becky had been alive, seders were always held at Dave and Peppy's house in Elmhurst. Seated around the dinner table were Dave's friend and business partner, Artie Schumer, tan muscles rippling out from under his black polo shirt; his wife, Shorty; and their children—Donnie, manager of an auto body shop and a fleet of tow trucks in Villa Park; his wife, Penny, pregnant with their first child; Bobbie, a Chicago Stadium beer vendor studying real estate at Triton College; Rickie, starting left guard on the York High football team; and Pammie, an eighth grader at Bryan Middle School who dreamed of being a dancer despite the fact that her father had told her, "Not with that *tuchus* you won't." Topics of conversation ranged from time-shares in Phoenix to package deals to Aruba.

Dave Wasserstrom sat opposite Charlie, his hands caressing the arms of his chair—this house was not as big as his house, he thought, nor was it as new. His children had rarely cried as much as Rachel, and when they had, he'd given them a good whack. His younger son, Manny, who had been cut from umpire school in Florida and was now working as a night watchman at the Grant Park garage, was seated to his immediate right. Manny's brother, Arthur, finishing up at John Marshall Law School, sat next to his wife, Debby, a dental hygienist and a devout convert to Judaism. Her hair was in a babushka and a pair of bifocals was perched on her nose as she underlined Haggadah passages with pencil. Next to Debby, there were four empty seats, which were to be occupied by Peppy, Gail, Wes Sullivan, and Jill, who was sitting in her bedroom beside her dog, staring at the phone, asking Fidel why Wes was so late.

It had only been two days since Wes and Jill had discussed the seder; he had asked whether to bring a side dish or a flourless dessert, then said that he would go to the library and Xerox *kugel* recipes. Jill watched her Felix the Cat wall clock inch toward 7:40, the shifting eyes ticking off seconds. She wondered if she should call Wes's house to ask if he was on his way; maybe Rae-Ann had learned that Wes was coming for Passover, had canceled her Whiteland trip, and was now confronting him and revealing everything about changing rooms and Marshall Field's. Trepidatiously, Jill dialed Wes's number.

The phone rang only once.

"Oh, so now you're calling back?" Wes asked without saying hello.

Jill quickly hung up, then sat frozen on her bed. She tried to process what Wes had just said. Was that Wes, she wondered; how could he have known that she was calling? Had he expected to hear from someone else? Well, maybe it wasn't him, she thought, maybe it was his father, maybe they had similar voices. She had to call back to see for sure. She picked up the receiver again, then put it back down. No, not immediately, she couldn't dial immediately, couldn't face that brusque, Wessian voice dismissing her again. She took a breath. No, she would go to the table and help her father read the *kiddush*. Then she would call. When she reached the dining room, she saw Rachel's face pressed into her father's shoulder, her cheeks red and wet as Charlie feebly *shh*'ed her. Peppy and Gail were walking daintily, one behind the other, carrying steaming bowls of matzo ball soup as Uncle Dave hollered that they should skip the ritual of washing the hands since he assumed that everyone had already done that "in the can."

"Soup's here," Gail said. "Who wants soup?" Charlie said he thought that they weren't supposed to eat the festival meal at least until they had recited the blessings and the plagues. Dave said that this wasn't the festival meal, this was just soup; he turned to Jill and asked where her "imaginary date" was.

"What?" Jill asked.

Uncle Dave repeated his question, but Jill did not respond, fearing that if she actually spoke, she would risk ruining the seder that her father had been so eager to host, thus precipitating an eternity of seders at Uncle Dave's house, where the men and boys habitually retired to the living room to pontificate, flatulate, and watch NCAA buckets while the women cleared the table and washed dishes. Dave wondered aloud if Jill's absent date was the prophet Elijah, for whom a goblet was traditionally placed on the seder table.

"Elijah Jefferson?" Artie Schumer quipped, mocking Jill's displeasure with his and Dave's bigotry by uttering a purportedly Afro-American–sounding name.

"Elijah Jefferson of the Harold Washington election committee," Uncle Dave said with a laugh, then opined that the only reason he was sorry that he didn't live in Chicago was that he couldn't cast a vote for "Ol' Bernie Epton," now there was a real *mensch*. Jill told her father that she was going to her bedroom to make another call. Dave asked if Elijah would mind if he ate his soup, and Rachel shrieked even louder.

Jill could hear peals of laughter as she returned to her room and shut the door. Her approach to her uncle Dave and Artie Schumer had always been to remain silent, for the few times she'd actually confronted them about their sexist and racist remarks, matters had only gotten worse. She considered what Wes would say if he heard Uncle Dave discuss the *schwarzer* who swept up his stores, imagined Wes asking Artie to step outside after he spoke of getting *gypped* or *shanghaied* down in *Browntown*. But Wes, alas, was not here. And though she was still unsure whether that had, indeed, been Wes on the line when she had called minutes earlier, she needed to learn why he had been so curt with her.

Jill sat on Fidel's pillow; Fidel sat on her bed. Jill gnawed on the end of a pencil; the animal chewed on his bone. Then, in one frantic motion, Jill grabbed the phone and dialed Wes's number so fast that, before she could even decide whether or not calling Wes was prudent and practical or jealous and clingy, the phone was ringing. One ring, two rings, three rings, four. She was about to hang up when someone picked up the phone. There was a long silence, then the sound of someone dialing. Jill said hello, but all she could hear was the scrape of the dial unwinding once, twice, three times. "Hello?" she said. Another long silence. Then Wes asked who the hell was on the phone. "It's me," Jill said. "Oh shit," said Wes.

"Oh shit?" Jill asked.

"Wait," Wes said groggily. "Wait wait wait."

Oh shit? That was the net result of months of foreign films and stolen kisses, of bull sessions about Harold Washington, Leonid Brezhnev, and Yuri Andropov, of trips to the New Wave section of Rose Records, of Sundays doing paste-up for the *Lane Leader,* late nights eating ice cream sandwiches and trading drafts back and forth in the Hild Library conference room? *Oh shit?* For a moment, she considered that the past months of flirting with Wes and being mauled by Rae-Ann had been some horrific practical joke that Wes had cooked up, one that would culminate at the prom with her dress covered in pig's blood and demonic voices hissing, *"They're all gonna laugh at you."* Oh shit. She wondered if this phrase would come to characterize all the most eagerly anticipated events of her life ("Ms. Wasserstrom, the Nobel Peace Prize committee has the following message for you: *'Oh shit.'* Simone de Beauvoir respectfully declines your interview request with this note: *'Oh shit.'* 'And you, Wes Sullivan, do you take this woman to be your lawful wedded wife?' *'Oh shit.'*"). Jill hung up and ran upstairs to the seder table, and when she heard the phone ringing, she told Gail to say that she couldn't come to the phone. She sat and consumed her soup warily, listening to the *Pesach* cacophony—Rachel wailing, Artie making fat jokes, the Schumer boys slurping soup, Shorty and Peppy discussing shopping in Reno, Charlie flipping pages in the Haggadah. She waited for more questions from Uncle Dave about whether Elijah would be arriving soon.

But no such questions came. Dave was now too busy plotting methods by which he could continue to postpone the Haggadah reading; if the Haggadot had not been opened by the time the brisket and orange chicken were served, it would be that much easier to discard the reading altogether, thus ensuring an arrival time in Elmhurst by midnight so he could get six hours of sleep. Why didn't they serve the gefilte fish before the blessing over the parsley, he suggested, winking at Artie's youngest son Rickie, a co-conspirator in the plot. Yeah, Rickie said, that idea was kick-ass, he was *starving* for gefilte fish, even though the only time he'd tried it (twelve years prior when Becky Wasserstrom had made it), he had spat it onto the rug.

Jill held her soup spoon in one hand, her Haggadah in the other. Over the din, she could hear Gail in the kitchen saying, "Who shall I say is calling?" Jill studied her book intently, the black ink sketches of the egg, the bitter herbs, the parsley. She wondered if G-d would find it sacrilegious that she had placed one of Fidel's marrow bones on the seder plate, as she tried to ignore Gail's voice saying, "Let me see if she's available." She turned to see Gail, telephone in hand, its putty-colored cord dragging behind her like a tail. "It's for you," Gail said, then added in a whisper louder than any scream, *"I think it's Wes."*

"So, how about that alleged gefilte fish?" Uncle Dave said; his daughter-in-law, Debby, glared at him but said nothing. Gail handed the phone to Jill and took Rachel in her arms in a futile attempt to stop the infant from crying.

Jill walked back to the kitchen. Aunt Peppy slipped past her and began spooning portions of gefilte fish on saucers, dollops of beet-colored horseradish beside them. "Who is this?" Jill asked, placing a hand over an ear. The voice on the other end said nothing for a moment or two. "Hello?" Jill asked tersely. She could hear her father in the dining room suggesting that they start the service after the gefilte fish. Dave told Charlie to "hold his horses."

"Hello?" Jill said again. But no hello came in return. All Wes said was "It's so fucked up."

He sounded exhausted. Jill asked if he was stoned. Wes said that it would be better if he were. He was sorry; he had fucked everything up. Jill asked hopefully if he wanted her to leave the seder and come over. At this suggestion, Wes suddenly turned lucid. "Oh no," he said, "no no no." Jill asked if he had spoken to Rae-Ann recently, and Wes spat out a laugh. "Yeah," he said, he'd talked to that Jesus freak and he didn't assume that he'd be talking to her again anytime soon; that relationship was "toast."

"Fuck it, man," he said, he couldn't talk about this right now; he asked what time the seder was starting. Jill said that it had already begun. *Fuck,* Wes said. He asked if it would be O.K. if he showed up around ten. Jill said that the seder would be over by then, particularly if Uncle Dave had his way. Wes said that he didn't think he'd be very good company tonight anyway—could they discuss all this on Easter? Oh, Jill said, he still wanted her to come? Of course, Wes said, she was the only reason why he might be able to survive the whole ordeal.

After she hung up, Jill resolved not to think about Wes for the remainder of the evening. Though she had been looking forward to his arrival, the fact that he had apparently broken up with Rae-Ann meant that their next time together would take on added significance. Her relationship with Muley would have to be reassessed, most likely discarded. The borders between West Rogers Park and the rest of the world would have to be erased. In her life, there would be no more *eruv.* She would not be someone who lived here but also there, who was a child here and a grown-up there, who loved Muley here but loved Wes there. Everything would be here; there would be no more there. She felt terrified, yet exhilarated too.

Once Jill entered the dining room, where the decibel level seemed to have crept up yet another notch, she noticed that everyone had finished their gefilte fish. And now, since they were already well into the festival meal, Dave pointed out, there was no reason why they shouldn't move on to the main courses. The chicken smelled good, he said, and if it cooked any longer, it might get too tough.

Jill looked around the table, her eyes settling upon her uncle. Whenever she secretly rolled her eyes at her father, whenever she angrily pitched into the trash another one of his aphorism-ridden newspaper columns, she would console herself by recalling that her predicament was nowhere near as dire as it might have been had Dave and Peppy made good on their offer, after Becky had died, to adopt her and her sister. She could be living with them in their monstrous house in Elmhurst with fountains and pillars, blasting the *Big Chill* sound track to drown out the sounds of Bears games on TV, hiding in her room from the Schumer kids across the way.

At the seder table, there was now a general clamor for brisket, a general appeal for orange chicken to be served *immediately,* not after the recitation of the Haggadah. It appeared that Dave had lined up the votes to officially veto the performance of the Passover ritual altogether. Jill didn't understand why her father always ceded authority to his brother, why her uncle always intimidated him into adopting whatever scheme he devised. Years earlier, he had talked Charlie into investing in Artie Schumer's doomed real-estate venture, in which Dave himself had chosen not to invest; when Charlie went out with Dave and Peppy, Dave always chose the movie—Mel Brooks's comedies, whose crude humor Charlie despised; Charles Bronson action pictures, whose violence Charlie abhorred; and one time, the X-rated film *Emmanuelle*—Charlie had stood in the lobby of the Lincoln Village Theater for most of the film with Peppy, who had denounced it as *"tuchus auf den tisch."* Yet Charlie never said a bad word about his brother. No matter what cutting remarks Dave would make, Charlie would smile and smile and smile. The brisket would be served, the orange chicken, the fruit compote. Then the flourless chocolate cake would arrive, accompanied by Joyva fruit jells and macaroons. Everyone would wolf down their desserts, and Dave would yawn and say that he and the Schumers had a long ride ahead of them. And once the guests were gone, and Jill, Gail, Charlie, and Fidel had cleaned up, Charlie would say how disappointed he was that they hadn't had a chance to recite the Haggadah.

But this night was different from all other nights, for on this night, Jill, whose anticipation of her new life with Wes had given her a new strength and sense of responsibility, would not allow Uncle Dave to win. She picked up her Haggadah, took a sheet of matzo, and broke it in half. "This is the bread of affliction which our ancestors ate in the land of Egypt," she said, looking icily at her uncle. "All who are hungry—let them come and eat. All who are needy—let them celebrate Passover with us. Now we are here; next year may we be in the Land of Israel." She spread some schmaltz from the gefilte fish onto the matzo so that Fidel would be able to find it when it came time to hunt for the *afikoman,* then asked Pammie to read the Four Questions.

"How is this night different," Pammie asked slowly, "from all other nights?"

"Because tonight we eat brisket and orange chicken," Dave offered, but by then, it was too late. Charlie and Gail thumbed through their Haggadot to find the right page; Peppy ran to the kitchen to turn down the temperature of the oven. Artie began to help his daughter sound out words. Jill held back a smile as she saw her uncle fumbling in his shirt pocket for his bifocals so he could follow along. Even Rachel, still in her mother's arms, had stopped crying.

"Charlie?" Gail said, nudging her husband to read.

"'We were slaves of Pharaoh in Egypt,'" Charlie read, "'and the Lord our God brought us forth with a strong hand and an outstretched arm.'"

The reading proceeded, even as the brisket grew gray, even as the orange chicken became tough. The wine was drunk, drops of it spilled, one drop for every plague: blood, frogs, vermin, wild beasts, Artie Schumer, pestilence, boils, hail, Uncle Dave, used-car salesmen, locusts, darkness, people who say *schwarzers,* the slaying of the firstborn.

"'In every generation,'" Debby read, "'one must see oneself as having personally come forth from Egypt.'"

Jill sat at the seder table, listening to the Passover story and the Psalms of Praise. Now I am Muley Wills's girlfriend, she thought; next year may I be Wes Sullivan's lover; now I am a high school junior, next year may I get into a good college far away from Chicago; now Chicago is ruled by Jane Byrne's administration, next year may the mayor be Harold Washington; now I'm sitting with Uncle Dave, Aunt Peppy, and the Schumers. Next year, may I please have something better to do.

"So," Dave asked, "is it time to eat yet?"

*Now we are slaves,* Jill thought. *Next year may we be free.*

The front door to the Sullivan house was already partly open when Jill arrived at Bittersweet Place on a rainy Easter afternoon. She had not heard from Wes since Passover; neither he nor Rae-Ann had attended school on Good Friday, when the crowning issue of the *Lane Leader* was published. Jill hadn't called Wes, fearing that he might tell her not to come over for Easter after all. She stood in the rain, wondering who would answer the door, hoping it would be either Wes or his frazzled but gracious German mother—she had never met Wes's father and Wes said that he always engaged guests in discussions of hunting, fishing, and Reaganomics. But nobody came to the door as rain smacked the back of Jill's neck. The idea again asserted itself—that this was a practical joke.

She had walked down the front staircase, then three steps in the direction of the 7-Eleven to buy paper so that she could write a quick note to Wes, when she heard a rapping sound above her. She looked up to see Wes in a second floor window—his hair a mess, his beard unkempt, his T-shirt ripped by the shoulder. Why was he wearing a T-shirt on Easter, Jill wondered. She had spent more time than she would have cared to admit planning her own outfit—a crisp white shirt, black loafers, tuxedo pants, and a thin black tie. Wes was motioning madly with both hands, directing her to come in. He looked befuddled, as if he couldn't understand why she was so stupid that she hadn't known to enter in the first place. She walked back to the door and pushed it open.

The house was immaculate, yet empty; the dining room table looked sleek yet untouched, as if there had never been any Easter brunch, as if there had never been any sort of meal consumed here, as if meals were only eaten in the cellar or the maid's quarters. Jill slipped off her loafers, placed them by the door, and walked cautiously upstairs.

Wes was hunched over a backpack when Jill entered his room; he was punching down the contents of his backpack—folded shirts and jeans were piled on the bed; a full duffel bag and a sleeping bag lay on the floor. Wes asked Jill if she needed some shirts; he couldn't take all of them. Where was he going, asked Jill. Wes laughed cynically. Don't ask, he said. He invited her to sit on the bed, but Jill remained standing; she watched him pack, then asked if Easter brunch had been canceled. No, Wes said, it was still happening—at his cousins' house in Hinsdale. So, Jill asked, were they going? Wes said that she was welcome to go. Jill asked if he would be coming, too. No way, man, Wes said, he had to get the fuck out of this shithole; he only had two hours before they all came back. Jill could go to Easter brunch without him; that might make everything easier.

Jill asked Wes what he was talking about—she wouldn't go to his family's brunch alone. Wes said that she might have a good time, and the food would be good. And while she was there, she could give a note to his folks. He went to his desk and picked up three envelopes—one addressed to his parents, one to Louis Benson in care of the *Lane Leader,* and one to the *Leader* staff. Jill said that she wouldn't do anything until she knew what Wes was doing.

All right, Wes said. He sat on the floor, his hands folded between his legs. She would hear all about this on Tuesday, so she might as well hear his side. Jill sat across from him, her back against the door. She looked straight at Wes, but he gazed past her. Well, Wes said, Benson had fired him from the *Leader.* Why, asked Jill, what had Wes done? Great, Wes said, he was glad that after all the time they'd spent together, she was so supportive; why did everyone immediately assume that he had done something wrong and not that Benson had some vendetta against him? So, Jill asked, confused, Benson had fired Wes for no reason? Not exactly, Wes said, but Benson was full of shit anyway; he was contending that Wes had invented his whole story about Britt, the one that Benson had set him up to write in the first place. And not only that, Benson accused him of forging the threatening letters to the *Leader* offices to make a more compelling story, an allegation that was based on nothing more than conjecture. And Benson hadn't just fired Wes from the *Leader;* he had written letters to the principal of Lane and to all the colleges to which Wes had applied. Basically, he said, Benson was trying to crucify him to settle some grudge against his dad. High school was such bullshit, Wes said, it was all fake. That's what he was trying to prove in his own admittedly twisted way, by writing that story about Britt, that he could write whatever he wanted, make up shit, and it wouldn't matter to anyone outside of high school.

Wait, Jill said, she wasn't following—what had he written that was made up, was he talking about the quotes, because she'd checked all of Wes's interview transcripts. Wes said the point was that it didn't matter what was made up and what wasn't; Benson was pretending that he ran a real newspaper when he was just a drunk who couldn't hold a real job. The fact that Benson was trying to hold him up as an example only showed how pitiful the man was—he wasn't even eighteen, and here was some sixty-year-old asshole getting his rocks off by trying to ruin his life. Jill said that Wes was speaking too quickly; she wanted to know how much of the story that Wes had written was invented. Wes said that he didn't think she understood his point; he thought that she was the one who understood him. Sure, Jill said, but that still didn't mean she knew what was true and what wasn't—some of the story he'd written about meeting Britt had to be true, she said, she'd checked the notes word for word. *Unless,* Jill said—she suddenly felt ill, her hands icy, her fingers red and small, in her stomach a feeling of churning emptiness—unless he had made *everything* up, even the story about Britt's mother that he'd told her in his car. There was no such thing as objective truth, Wes observed, that was all bullshit, he could take a set of quotes and make them mean anything he wanted by the context in which he placed them.

"Wes," Jill said, feeling her hands tremble as she spoke, how much of his article had he made up—all of it? Wes was silent for a moment. Then he said that Benson would have fucked him over even if he hadn't, that Benson had planned it all out from the beginning, and he had fallen into Benson's trap. Every time he'd written something true, Benson had said that it wasn't good enough; it was "readable," it "wasn't altogether awful." He didn't know what was "true" and what wasn't anymore. Some of it was stuff he'd observed, some of it was based on what Connie had written in diaries he'd read once, some of it was taken from conversations he'd overheard; in other places, he'd "extrapolated" based on what he'd assumed to be true. That's what journalism was—*gonzo* journalism, the kind that Tom Wolfe wrote, Hunter Thompson. Everything else was just hackwork, the kind that Benson had written before the *Trib* had canned his sorry ass.

And the letters, Jill asked, the letters that threatened the *Leader* editors, had he written those as well? Wes said nothing. His facial expression slowly transformed from defiance to desperation. And though Jill felt that she should be angry, she now felt only a deep sadness, and an odd affection, as if by revealing his crime, Wes had suddenly become more human, more attainable. "But why?" she asked him. Why, when there was already so much hatred in the city, would Wes do something that could damage the causes in which he believed? Because he was tired of being the golden boy, Wes said. He rattled off a litany of explanations, none of which Jill found persuasive. He said that he was sick of people worshipping him and this was his way of making them stop. He said that he was sick of being compared to his father. He said that Britt had put him in the hospital and he wanted to pay him back. He said that what he had written was truer than any supposed "fact," that he was creating a portrait of Britt that was more real than the purported truth. Every time he'd told the truth, no one gave a shit, but when he'd start adding little bullshit details, everyone had complimented him, even Jill. And then, finally, he said that he had really wanted to win the Front Page trophy, and didn't think he had the talent to win it outright, that the only way he could get it was by making shit up. He said that he wanted to come back from the awards ceremony with his trophy, whip it at his father, and say, hey, maybe he had a future after all. Christ, Wes said, he didn't know why he'd done it; maybe the truth was that he was just a stupid asshole, and there was nothing more to it.

There were tears in Jill's eyes as Wes spoke, but when she saw the tears trickling down Wes's cheeks, she blinked hers away. "What are we going to do?" she asked. Wes said that *we* weren't going to do anything. He'd had enough of school, enough of Chicago. He'd told Rae-Ann everything, and she'd broken up with him, hadn't even let him explain his side. He had some money his grandmother had left him, and now he was hitting the road. He had his clothes and his books— some Kerouac, some Vonnegut, that was all he needed. He said he might head down to Mississippi for a while, try community organizing; he had a West German passport—maybe he could hang out there. Couldn't he just apologize and make some compromise? Jill asked. Wes touched Jill's cheek and told her that it was sweet of her to worry; the only problem was that he wasn't sorry. He supposed that made him a shitty person, but he wouldn't lie; he'd lied enough already.

Wes touched Jill's hand; his black eyes gazed meaningfully into hers. "The only thing I'm sorry for is what I did to you, kid," he said. Jill blinked, felt a strange warmth begin to envelop her, then shook it off—if Benson hadn't challenged him, Wes would've gone down to Normal, Illinois, collected his trophy, and continued lying—how could he be so arrogant? She started to wonder aloud whether all egotism was just a cover for deep insecurity. But Jill could not finish her sentence; the moment she tried, Wes kissed her.

It was an absolutely egotistical gesture; Wes was not so much trying to seduce her as to shut her up. It was insulting, crass, patronizing, controlling, simplistic, just plain obnoxious, but Wes's lips tasted so sweet to her, and she felt embarrassed by the chill racing up her spine, the quickening of her heartbeat, for she knew that she meant nothing to Wes. She wondered how long he would keep kissing her, her cheeks, her eyes, her neck, then her lips again, how long he would touch her as his hands ventured underneath her blouse, how long she would continue to touch him as she felt his back beneath his T-shirt.

She had heard her classmates discuss experiences such as this one in the Lane cafeteria, had once heard Connie Sherman and Devorah Kerbis read questions aloud from a sex quiz featured in "Ask Ann Landers," heard one ask the other, "Have you ever been *parked* for more than an hour?" *Parked*? Jill had asked, what did that mean? Devorah had laughed, but Connie, who often took on a mentoring role toward those less experienced than her, explained that what Ann Landers was asking was whether she had ever made out for more than an hour, in a *parked car,* in this instance. *God,* Jill had said, that sounded *boring.* Again, Devorah laughed, but Connie said that Jill was right. In many cases, parking *was* exceedingly dull. But, Connie added, when you were with someone who knew what he was doing, hours could pass and you wouldn't even notice; next thing you knew, his mom would be knocking on the door and telling you to "Get home, you skanky tramp." Jill had nodded, affecting worldly wisdom, but dismissed the notion. She was aware on an intellectual level of sexuality, felt a sense of warmth and contentment during her cuddling sessions with Muley, had experienced a pleasurable, tingling sensation when Frau Messersmith made her PE students shinny up and down a rope in the Lane gym. But until this moment with Wes, she had been more theorist than practitioner.

Right now, it didn't matter that Wes was a liar and a coward, that despite his professed politics he was an arrogant chauvinist. When Wes held Jill's hands and asked what she was thinking, she didn't want to respond for fear of sounding foolish. The only words that came to mind were sappy song lyrics—"I don't know how to love him," "Good girls don't (but I had to)," "I wanna soar, but I feel so sore." She asked Wes what he was thinking. Wes opened his mouth, shut it, bit his lip, and shook his head. "What?" Jill asked. He laughed nervously, looked up as if trying to summon strength. "I want to make love to you," he said.

Jill swallowed hard. Her hands trembled, her heartbeat quickened. She felt small, cold, young, afraid. She took a breath, held it in. She felt happy, flattered, giddy, foolish. She let the breath out. She felt like an impostor. "Well, aren't you going to at least say *something*?" Wes asked. But Jill said nothing. "Do you want to make love to me?" Wes finally asked. Jill knew that she had to respond, but her thoughts were blank. Sentences formed in her brain, then floated about, unfinished. "Do you?" Wes asked. And, for Jill, the answer to that heretofore unfinished sentence was, simply, no. No, she wouldn't make love to William Eamon Sullivan Jr. Not because she didn't want to—she probably would have said yes to Muley if it hadn't always seemed to mean so much to him. Not because she maintained some sanctified vision of her virginity—that was just Moral Majority propaganda. Not because she was too young, either. Not even because she quivered at the words *make love,* a phrase that Michelle had often warned her about ("If any guy ever says he wants to 'make love to you,' reach for your track shoes," Michelle had said). No, the reason she would not make love to Wes was that she objected to his presumption that because she had been kissing him, she would automatically *make love* to him. No, she did not want to make love to Wes, she thought, but then she was kissing him all over again, her hands in his hair, how soft it was, how smooth, the feeling of his breath against her neck, how it chilled and warmed her all the same. Yes, she thought now, yes, she would make love to Wes, for though he was a liar, his touch, his kiss, his breath, all felt indisputably true. "Yes," she said. "Yes."

"Thank you," said Wes. Jill leaned upward to kiss him again, but he just pecked her on the lips, then on the cheek. He smiled, shook his head wistfully, as if contemplating what might have been. "I just can't do it, Woodstein," he said, then added, quoting Jill with a smile, "Maybe someday if it's fated to be." He cupped Jill's shoulder, stood, then thanked her again and said that she didn't know how much he had needed to hear someone say that they wanted to make love to him. There was nothing quite like it.

"'Someone?'" Jill repeated. She blinked, cocked her head to one side, then the other, as Wes stood and retrieved his letters. He asked if Jill would deliver them for him, and if she'd walk him to his car.

"'Someone?'" Jill repeated, but this time so quietly that Wes didn't hear. She watched as he took the last remaining shirt out of his closet—denim with snaps; he wore it unbuttoned over his T-shirt. Then he grabbed a beat-up black Chicago Police Department jacket, put it on, and zipped up his bags.

"Time for me to make wheels," he said and walked out of his bedroom. Jill trailed behind him, the word *someone* ping-ponging off the walls of her brain.

Wes's BMW was parked halfway down Bittersweet and, as Jill followed Wes, she had the sensation that she was watching herself from a great distance and that both she and Wes were very small. She watched herself hugging him good-bye, heard herself telling him to write her when he reached his destination, watched herself watching Wes get into the car, start it up, and skid through rain-filled pot-holes as he hooked a left onto Sheridan, then sped out of sight.

Jill walked alone through the thinning rainfall toward the Wilson el stop in the prematurely dark gray afternoon, catching glimpses of her reflection in the rain-soaked windows of pawnshops. *Someone,* she thought. *Someone* meant *any-one. Anyone* meant *no one,* which was how she felt on the train ride home: like no one. Jill was so glad to hear Fidel's two welcoming barks when she returned home, was so happy to feel his hot breath upon her cheek. And, though Fidel usually slept on a pillow below her, that night when Jill went to bed, he slept be-side her, his head on her pillow, her hand feeling the warm beats of his heart.


# ELECTION NIGHT 1983


On a warm April night, a good while before Harold Washington would officially declare victory, defeating Bernard Epton by a mere fifty thou-sand votes, only about twelve percent of them from whites, a desperate and con-fused Jill Wasserstrom walked to Muley's apartment to seek advice, only to be informed again by Mel that Muley was at Angel Guardian. Mel invited Jill to watch the election returns with him and Deirdre. Jill thanked him and said that she had been planning to go downtown to Donnelly Hall to see if she could get into Washington's headquarters. But first, she needed to consult Muley on a per-sonal matter. Mel said that his advice was better than Muley's, adding that he wanted to ask Jill some questions about her sister.

"You realize," Mel told Jill with a smile, "it might be your last opportunity to talk to me." If that "Epton mofo" won the election, he explained, he just might not be in the mood to converse with any white folks anytime soon. Jill said that she appreciated the offer, and understood what Mel meant, but still, she had to find Muley.

Jill stopped quickly at her house, pocketed a transistor radio, pumped air into the tires of her bicycle, then rolled it through the front hallway toward the door. Charlie and Gail were in the living room watching the early returns, Charlie drinking a Diet Rite, Fidel on a pillow in front of him. Gail was standing and rocking on the balls of her feet as she bounced an uncharacteristically quiet Rachel in her arms and narrated the election returns, using the term *we* when referring to the Republican candidate—"We're doing well in the lakefront wards, sweetie pie," she said. "We got a real good turnout at the polls, snooky-snooks." Jill said that she was biking to Angel Guardian to find Muley. "I thought that was through," Gail said. "What about Wes?" As Jill wheeled her bike out the door, she could hear Rachel starting to cry again.

Muley was not necessarily the best source of advice on matters involving Wes, but he was the best that Jill could do—her sister, whom Jill generally never called, had been distracted when they had spoken on the phone. In the background, Jill heard giggling and a male voice singing, *"Come over here, Zipporah; I won't dance unless it's the whore-a,"* at which point Jill got off the phone as quickly as possible. It would be reasonable to consult Muley in this instance, she thought, tuning in WBBM on her radio, inserting her earphone, pedaling east on North Shore, then curving onto California, heading south; Wes had left town anyway, and even now, Muley was still the only person she could trust.

Jill had been dreading this afternoon's editorial meeting, the first since Wes's departure. Before the meeting had even begun, Rae-Ann, her cheeks streaked with mascara, dragged Jill into the girls' bathroom and asked her how much she had known, *damn it,* then accused Jill of plotting Wes's demise so that Jill could have her all to herself. She then collapsed into Jill's arms, kissed her on the throat, then pushed her away, saying that she couldn't believe that they were doing this so soon after she had broken up with Wes, and why didn't Jill leave her alone for once; she'd been a good, devout girl before Jill had corrupted her. At the meeting, Benson had silently read the note from Wes that Jill had given to him, then took a seat atop a long wooden desk. He put his thumbs in the pockets of his vest. Under normal circumstances, the current issue of the *Leader* would be tacked to the wall behind him with his remarks scrawled in red, but this week, there was only a piece of white posterboard on which he had written INTEGRITY.

"That's all we have, ladies and gentleman," Benson said, then invited the editors to contemplate the word silently before he spoke further. And though Benson had begun to appreciate Hillel Levy's ribald comments, this time when Hillel quipped, "That's not all *I* have, boys and girls," then pointed down to his groin, Benson snapped, "Shut it, Levy." After the silence, Benson read Wes's letter aloud, his voice dripping with sarcasm.

The letter was eloquent. In it, Wes took full responsibility for his "fatal weakness," apologized for "violating the integrity" of a "hallowed institution," made a glancing reference to the "satanic temptations" offered by an "unprincipled faculty advisor," then exhorted the other staffers to fight for the equality and honesty that he never had the courage to live up to himself. Benson thanked Jill for delivering Wes's letter, then told her that the two of them would have a "tête-à-tête" after the meeting.

When Benson invited her into his cramped office with artifacts that marked his transformation from sixties peacenik to eighties libertarian, from Eugene McCarthy buttons to John Anderson posters, Jill assumed that he would ask her to resign. Instead, he told Jill that he would be appointing her acting editor in chief. Jill considered the matter briefly, then said that several seniors on staff were more deserving. After all, she had been in charge of fact-checking and was responsible for the fact that Wes's lies had been published. Benson said that Jill's naïveté was a sign of her fundamental decency. He asked her to accept the position. He had faith in her, he said—though her writing suffered, at times, from a flat earnestness, he had little doubt about the reporting skill she could bring to her first assignment as editor in chief: writing the next cover story. Jill said that she and Wes had discussed devoting their final issue to student reaction to the mayoral election. Benson said that wasn't page-one material; the topic of the next cover story would be Wes Sullivan's fall from grace. Done properly, it was the sort of article that could win a Front Page trophy, maybe even a John Fink.

As she pedaled fast on California, then swung a left onto Devon, Jill realized that if she had half the integrity with which Benson credited her, she would have rejected the assignment outright. She was too close to the story; she could never be objective. But she was greedy—she despised herself for her avarice, but couldn't deny feeling it. She wanted to be editor in chief, wanted to exert influence over political discourse in Lane's hallways. Instead of politely declining, she asked Benson if they could discuss this matter the following morning.

As she reached the Angel Guardian shed, Jill hoped that Muley would offer sensible advice. Except Muley wasn't there. He had just left, said Irit Ben-Amar, who was focusing her camera on a naked Ephraim Tekulve, seated in the lotus position on a blue gymnasium mat. He flashed Jill a peace sign and asked, "What it is?" Jill asked Irit if she might know where Muley was, at which point Tekulve reported that "a ravishing young lady" had burst in, very upset, and Muley had chased after her. Jill asked where they had gone. The Skokie water tower, said Tekulve.

Jill remounted her bike and pedaled north; at Howard Street, the northern border that separated Chicago from Evanston, she turned west. She listened to John Cody on WBBM; he was at Washington headquarters, and he said that the mood was "cautiously upbeat." Craig Dellimore at Epton headquarters said much the same thing. Jill biked past strip malls and restaurants—Chicken Unlimited, the Fish Keg, IHOP—as she headed west toward Skokie.

West of West Rogers Park, west of the Winston Towers condominiums, over the Chicago drainage canal but before the suburbs truly began, there was a thin strip of industry and desolation stretching all the way from the north side of Chicago to Evanston. Here were auto body shops, a Bell + Howell plant, Klein Tools, General Automation, the overgrown lot of what had once been the Sky-Hi drive-in, an outdoor garden center where one could dig up and haul away manure, and, underneath it all, the multimillion-dollar Deep Tunnel that was being built to address frequent flooding. Neighborhood conspiracy theorists wrote long, handwritten letters to the Schiffler Newspapers, hypothesizing that the Deep Tunnel was so expensive and fraught with difficulties that it must have some nefarious alternative use—perhaps the U.S. military was housing MX missiles in it.

Over the tunnel, Jill followed a crude, muddy bike trail as she sped toward the water tower just west of McCormick Boulevard. To get to the tower, she navigated a path of weeds, broken glass, crushed cans, and a set of abandoned train tracks. The tower was pale and grayish-white and stood nearly two hundred feet high. The paint at its base was chipped and peeling and the mushroomlike receptacle at its apex was covered with graffiti: BRITT 'N' CONNIE FOREVER, SHMUEL 'N' BIBI FOREVER, ROVNER! SUCKS!!

When she reached Oakton Avenue, Jill dismounted her bicycle, turned off her radio, and wheeled the bike over the rubble. There was an odd scent in the air—vaguely sweet, vaguely rotten, like the inside of an old refrigerator. Muley was standing at the base of the tower, his hands clutching one of its metal legs as he looked up; Connie Sherman was climbing. Jill stood amid barberry bushes, listening to Connie laugh as Muley shouted for her to come down. "Catch me," Jill heard Connie say. Her voice sounded dishonestly cheerful, glee disguising desperation. Jill stood still, unsure whether to step forward—she didn't know which rules applied here; she wasn't in West Rogers Park, she wasn't really in Skokie or Evanston; this was uncharted territory. But the moment when Jill was about to leave, to ride back to the city whose rules she understood, Muley turned to her. They'd barely spoken in weeks—quick hellos and cheek kisses in the Lane hallway, rushed conversations postponing Friday movie nights. What was going on, Jill asked. Muley shook his head.

Connie was two-thirds of the way up the water tower, silhouetted by the light of the haloed gibbous moon. She sat on a rung and lit a cigarette, her legs kicking back and forth, as if she were sitting at the edge of a swimming pool. She asked Muley who was down there with him—the cops? No, Muley said; it was just Jill Wasserstrom. "Hey, Jilly-girl," Connie shouted, and suggested that they join her up there; the view was great, though it would go better with bourbon. She asked if Jill wanted to get some. She flung down her wallet, which landed at Jill's feet. Connie told Jill to take ten bucks, then buy a bottle. Muley suggested that she climb down and buy it herself. "Nice try, Mules," Connie said. From the foot of the tower, Jill could see the orange glow of Connie's cigarette, its smoke trailing up toward the moon. Jill asked Muley if she should call the police, but before Muley could answer, Connie shouted, "And don't even think about calling the cops."

Jill asked Muley how long Connie had been up there. About twenty minutes, he said. He'd been working at Angel Guardian when Connie had walked in. She was crying and yelling at the same time, then she had seen Irit filming a naked Ephraim Tekulve and asked Muley why he was hanging out with naked people. She ran out of the shed, mumbling something about the water tower. Following her out to her father's black dealer LTD, Muley asked her to slow down; she was talking too fast. Once she was in the car and had started it up, she rolled down the window and told Muley that Britt Hurd was dead.

Connie said that Britt had been down in Jacksonville at the Nordhagen Academy. For a while, he had been miserable, called her late at night, sometimes screaming, sometimes bawling, all of which had culminated with two frantic calls—one before he had stolen the sergeant's car, one from a Jacksonville police station after he had been caught. But afterward, little by little, he had grown accustomed to the school. He would call Connie every night, then only every other night, and then, most recently, on Friday, when Wes's article about Britt had been published in the *Lane Leader.*

Connie had read the article thinking at first that it was an April Fool's joke, but the more she read, the more confused she became. She had called Britt, mentioning the topic casually because she knew his temper. Unfortunately, there was no way to nonchalantly tell Britt that an article about him titled "It's a Racial Thing" had been making the rounds of the Lane cafeteria. Parts of Wes's article were surprisingly accurate; he had used writings from Connie's old diaries, details about Britt that no one knew other than her. Once he had stopped swearing, Britt asked Connie who had written the article, and when Connie told him, he said that he was coming back. Connie told him that he would never be allowed out of Nordhagen. Britt said *Shit, Connie,* it sounded like she didn't even want to see him. He told her that he loved her, then hung up.

That was the last Connie had heard from Britt. Doing eighty miles an hour on the Dan Ryan Expressway in a stolen Plymouth Volaré, he had attracted the attention of the Illinois State Police. They gave chase and Britt slid across three lanes of traffic. The car had hit a retaining wall, flipped over, spun on its roof, then finally stopped on 31st Street. Britt's mother had called from her travel agency to tell Connie the news.

After Connie had told Muley this story, she pulled her father's car into Drive and skidded out of the Angel Guardian lot. Muley asked Irit if he could borrow the keys to her and Ephraim's pickup truck, and though he had never actually driven a car, moments later he was in pursuit of the Shermans' LTD. When he reached the tower, Connie had already started to climb—was he going to join her, she'd asked, or was he chicken?

Connie was moving again, climbing farther up. She was carrying something in her right hand. "Damn," Muley said, took off his jacket, and placed it on the ground. He gritted his teeth, took a breath, and grabbed a chipped metal rung at the bottom of the tower. Wait a minute, Jill said, where was he going? Well, he couldn't just stand there, Muley said, as Connie declared that they really had to come up for the view—she was holding on to the uppermost rung with one hand, spinning on the heel of her gym shoe. "Whoa," she said, slipped, caught herself, forced a laugh, then spun back and hoisted herself onto the catwalk. She held on to the railing with her left hand; with her right, she shook a can of spray paint, then began to tag the top of the tower.

Jill asked Muley what he was doing as he began to climb. Muley asked what was he supposed to do—just let her fall? Yes, Jill said, it was presumptuous for him to interfere. People shouldn't be saved—the very idea of asking someone to save you was egotistical. Probably so, Muley said, but he had to go up. Atop the tower, Connie had spray-painted BRITT and she was continuing to write. Her sneakers squeaked on the rusted rungs as she inched her way around. Well, Jill said, Muley shouldn't expect her to watch him kill himself. He was almost fifteen feet above the ground, still climbing.

Jill turned to leave, but she could only move a few yards. She tried to look away, but couldn't stop staring at the tower. All her life, at least since her mother had died, she had felt surrounded by death, feared it, did everything within her power to avoid thinking about it, which was the same as thinking about it always. She had never actually seen somebody die, though, never seen anyone dead. And now she felt as if she were fated to watch the two of them tumbling downward, Connie, then Muley. She turned on her radio, hoping that the noise would soothe her, but she couldn't hear or understand a word. Atop the tower, Connie had spray-painted CONNIE 'N' BRITT.

Muley already felt his arms growing weary. He had hardly slept these past few weeks, throwing every part of himself into his films and his screens. As he looked down, Jill appeared to be barely more than a shadow in the moonlight. He felt himself growing woozy, the ground below not quite spinning, just slightly askew, though he was not even one-third of the way up. The rungs of the tower were rough on his skin; smears of rust rubbed off on his palms. The lake was to the east, Chicago to the south, but he was facing west and as he climbed all he could see was an endless expanse of flat dark land, occasionally interrupted by head-lights on distant highways. With each step, it looked as if the land below were rolling away, as if he were looking through the zoom lens of a camera and someone was violently twisting the lens back, then forth. He resolved to focus on only one rung at a time, to look neither up nor down, to listen neither to Jill below telling him to stop nor up to Connie, who had finished spray-painting CONNIE 'N' BRITT R.I.P., and was now spraying something else.

From down below, it all looked so graceful—Muley climbing, Connie standing at the very top, spray-paint can in her hand, shaking, then spraying, then shaking again. But Jill figured that from down here, falling would look graceful and easy, too. She watched Muley clutching one rung, watched Connie spraying MULEY in black on the pale white tower. She couldn't feel Connie's exhilaration or desperation, couldn't feel that Muley's hands were starting to hurt, that his arms were starting to ache, that he was growing short of breath.

Muley felt as if he could climb no farther. The rung six inches above his head seemed too high to grab. The rung just below was too far down; if he stretched his foot toward it, he thought that he might slip. When he looked up, the moon spun; when he looked down, the earth receded; and when he stared straight ahead, his body ached. Jill was gripping the handlebars of her bicycle as Connie spray-painted an L. Muley had seen Connie sit atop one of these rungs, had seen her dangle her feet—he had no idea how she had done it, how she could have turned around without losing her balance. He reached up, but when he did, a pain shot through his shoulder. He wondered if he had pulled a muscle. He looked up, looked down, looked ahead, none of it was good—he closed his eyes.

Connie had just finished writing MULEY and LOVES and had just started to spray-paint CONNIE when she looked down to see Muley. His eyes were shut, and his hands were gripping the rungs of the water tower. He was wishing that he could erase everything from his mind; sometimes, reality just hurt too much. His arm ached as he lifted it, but he could do it slowly now, an inch at a time. He held onto a rung to steady himself, then reached up again—his legs were shaking, he could hear his heart thumping in his eardrums. He reached up one more time, expecting to touch metal, but instead, he felt Connie's hand. She was standing just above him, her eyes red—she wiped them with the back of a hand before stepping down toward him.

And, with his eyes open and Connie's staring back into his, he had suddenly reentered a sphere where different things mattered; not whether he would live past this night, but how Jill would feel about the fact that he and Connie were kissing, then descending together, what Connie would say to Jill when they reached the ground. But when Muley felt the solid and trustworthy earth underneath his sneakers and Connie holding him close, Jill was already gone.

Jill was pedaling fast along the bike trail. On her transistor radio, she could hear John Cody of WBBM say that Big Jim Thompson had spoken with him, and when asked about whether the remaining votes would go to Washington or Epton, Thompson had soberly said, "They're Harold's." But though the news was thrilling, Jill had other reasons for biking fast. Not because of the kiss that she had seen Muley and Connie share near the top of the water tower, or at least not entirely because of that. She had seen it happen, yes, and though she had convinced herself that she wasn't really watching it happen, was only watching herself watching it, that didn't stop it from smarting. Nevertheless, as she rode past the factories on McCormick and the Kedzie Avenue body shops, she was thinking about the article she would write, the article about the unforeseeable consequences of seemingly unremarkable acts, the article about William Eamon Sullivan Jr.

Standing at the podium of Donnelly Hall, Harold Washington was addressing the crowd. "This has truly been a pilgrimage," he said. But Jill didn't have time to ride south for the victory celebration; she needed to start writing immediately. As she rode, Connie and Muley were walking back toward Oakton Avenue. Looming above them in the pale moonlight was the Skokie water tower and the message that Connie had failed to finish writing; it now read simply, MULEY LOVES. Jill turned east on Howard and pedaled back toward West Rogers Park, the *eruv* above her, her home only a little more than a mile away.

# II

# *Breirot*

*Mel and Michelle's Book of Choices*

*(1983–84)*

----

(A STORY OF WEST ROGERS PARK
AND THE REST OF CHICAGO)

*Maybe too much is made of one play.*
—JERRY DYBZINSKI, SECOND BASEMAN,
CHICAGO WHITE SOX, OCTOBER 8, 1983

*I'm sorry it happened. I'm sorry it started something.*
—LEON DURHAM, FIRST BASEMAN,
CHICAGO CUBS, OCTOBER 7, 1984

*Chicago is not an island unto itself.*
—MAYOR HAROLD WASHINGTON, 1983

Michelle Wasserstrom was sitting in the back of a taxicab en route to La Guardia Airport, where she was to meet her father, whom she had barely seen in a year, when she paused to once again consider a bit of advice that Gareth Overgaard had provided in his most recent letter to her. Gareth's letter had come to mind shortly after Michelle had bolted out of the Question and Answer session of an NYU guest lecture, delivered by a sweaty, diminutive, name-dropping New York film director. Michelle, seated in the audience, wearing her hair in a bun and catgirl glasses that she did not need, raised her hand and said that she was "in the throes of a dilemma." She had come to NYU wanting to be exclusively a stage actress, but her fellow classmates in the Experimental Theater Wing had "irritated the living bejeezus out of her," so she had asked for permission to take classes outside her discipline, including Acting for Film, which she "hadn't completely hated." She was also still considering musical theater. She asked whether she had to choose right away, or dabble in each and see where she found the most success. The director regarded Michelle with a pained expression, as if she had just demanded that he cast her in his next gritty Manhattan police procedural. He rubbed his freckled scalp, sighed, then stressed that one had to choose—that's what he'd told Martin Balsam more than thirty years earlier; the more options you tried, the more likely it was that you would succeed at nothing.

As her taxi inched through the Midtown Tunnel, Michelle puzzled over how she—a mere lass of twenty—could limit her choices. She felt as if she were in a satellite country of the Soviet Union, where, at the age of six, she was already training for the biathlon team. And yet, she suspected that the reason why she wasn't famous yet was that she had difficulty saying no to any opportunity. Larry

Rovner had asked her to workshop the lead female role in the Goodman family production of *The New Jazz Singer* at the Delancey Street Project. A grad student wanted her for a pantomime adaptation of *A Midsummer Night's Dream*. Mel Coleman was flying into New York this week to audition her for the role of Jasmine Huggins in his long-delayed film *Godfathers of Soul*. She'd agreed to everything, even though auditions had not yet been held for spring Mainstage productions in which she'd be required to act most probably as a Lady-in-Fricking-Waiting, while some big-shot director like Robert Wilson or Richard Foreman or Ulu Grosbard or whoever would cast his pals in lead roles, leaving aside the fact that she was working her ass off every Tuesday and Thursday afternoon, selling subscriptions to *Ebony, Newlook,* and *Omni* magazines over the phone, and getting paid in cash by the office manager, who'd told Michelle that he'd marry her if she gave up her acting career.

Maybe the director was right, she thought, maybe she did have to choose. Maybe bad decisions were better than no decisions at all. Gareth had written that the previous year, he'd been wavering between declaring his major as Political Science or Economics. He'd even consulted his parents, both of whom were professors and therefore "useless." His idealistic but hapless father had voted for Poli Sci; his decisive yet uninformed mother had said Econ. At which point, Gareth wrote, he'd made his decision: "Fuck it—I'm majoring in Education." When you're stuck between two choices, don't choose either, Gareth wrote, *always choose the third.*

No, Michelle finally decided as she began scribbling a letter to Gareth in the back of the cab. "You're wrong, Dr. Brewster," she wrote, quoting a line from *Tootsie* that she'd adopted as one of her signature phrases, you needed to choose *all three.*

The previous semester, Michelle had moved out of her squalid Rubin Hall dorm room and into an illegal three-bedroom conversion on 13th Street, where she had initially feuded with one of her new apartment-mates, Bert Liu, a long-haired and self-assured French horn player, whose quiet confidence had an oddly aphrodisiacal effect on ten percent of the dozens of women he attempted to seduce. While they'd been sharing a bong and waiting for their other roommate to arrive, Bert had told Michelle that sooner or later they'd wind up having sex, so they might as well just get it over with. Michelle had not commented; she'd merely looked up from the bong to the framed poster above Bert's bed. On it were three photographs: a Ferrari, a reclining woman in a bikini, a bottle of Dom Pérignon. Underneath the photographs, in red script, the word *Choices*. Michelle looked at it and snorted. She said that she'd seen this poster before in other guys' bedrooms and it always seemed to be missing one key photo. Which photo, Bert asked. The one of a sock and a jar of Vaseline, Michelle said. She leaned toward the bong, but Bert pulled it away from her; he told her to get out of his room.

"No, you're wrong Dr. Overgaard," Michelle now wrote as the airport became visible through the taxi's windshield. Choices were only for unimaginative people like Bert Liu. There were twenty-four hours in a day, 365 days in a year, she was only twenty ("not a wizened man of twenty-one," she wrote); there was plenty of time to do everything she goddamn pleased.

O n that same afternoon in 1983, on the playing field of Comiskey Park, Chicago White Sox second baseman Jerry Dybzinski made a critical base-running error, thus all but assuring the victory of the Baltimore Orioles and the continuation of the period of futility that had marked Chicago baseball ever since the last Sox World Series victory in 1917. But, four miles above the ground in an American Airlines 747 bound for La Guardia, Mel Coleman remained blissfully ignorant of his team's fortunes.

Mel had been discussing the Sox with Charlie Wasserstrom, who was seated next to him. He had been scribbling on the most recent draft of *Godfathers of Soul* when he looked up to see Charlie sitting across the aisle, studying the *Tribune* sports section. Mel debated whether or not to acknowledge the man, but finally reintroduced himself, then asked if Charlie was hoping the Sox would "tank it," just as they seemed to every year. Charlie said no, he'd been a Sox fan ever since he'd been a boy. Mel said "Excuse my mistake," adding that he'd taken Charlie for a Cubs fan. Yes, Charlie said, but he liked both teams. Mel raised an eyebrow; you couldn't root for both teams, he said—this was Chicago; you had to choose.

Now that Harold Washington had been in office for half a year, the city's divisions were starker than ever. A coalition composed largely of white aldermen had formed upon Washington's election and voted in opposition to the mayor on nearly every issue, 29 to 21. The city was divided between black and white, between Washington and the establishment. Baseball may have crossed some racial lines, but divisions were there, too, between the cuddly north side Cubs and the scrappy south side Sox. The crowds at Comiskey Park may have often shouted "Ha-rold! Ha-rold!" but those cheers were for Sox outfielder Harold Baines.

Mel took the empty seat beside Charlie, offered his hand, and told him that he was "casting a feature" in New York, then asked Charlie why he was traveling. Charlie said that he was visiting his daughter Michelle in New York, where he also had a meeting with a "publishing guy" about a "book thing" that "probably wouldn't turn out."

In fact, Charlie had already been offered a sizeable sum for the "book thing," but he remained suspicious of anyone who would suggest that he be paid for something at which he still felt he lacked any skill. When Schiffler Newspapers folded shortly after Harold Washington's inauguration, and Gail had sold the Schiffler Building and its surrounding land to a commercial developer, Charlie assumed that Gail would quickly find work at the *Tribune* and he would leave behind his career as a columnist and return to managing restaurants—it was the industry that he knew and he missed the energy and excitement of it. He was therefore stunned when Gail returned early from a meeting with *Tribune* executive editor William Eamon Sullivan Sr., who had been surprisingly brusque, perhaps in part the result of a still-smoldering scandal involving his son, who had recently returned William Sr.'s check in an envelope postmarked West Germany.

Charlie had rubbed Gail's shoulders as she sat on their living room couch; he told her that their luck would change soon—maybe she should send Sullivan some more of her article clips. No, Gail said, maybe *he* should do it himself. "It's you he wants," she explained, then apologized for having snapped at Charlie. It was just that she had been pursuing journalism since high school, yet Charlie, whom she loved dearly but who was clearly not a *writer,* was being courted by the city's biggest paper.

Charlie met with Sullivan, who, over hamburgers at the Billy Goat Tavern, offered him a four-day-a-week column where he could "do what he did best" at a salary far higher than the one he'd enjoyed at the Schiffler papers. And when word of Sullivan's offer was leaked to the *Sun-Times* gossip columnist, Irv Kupcinet, Andrea Levy, senior editor of *City Times* magazine, made Charlie a better offer, telling him that his homespun columns about family and fatherhood would fit well alongside *City Times*'s true-crime reports, profiles of local athletes, and full-color fashion section.

The money that *City Times* offered Charlie to write a monthly column was somewhat smaller than the amount Charlie had discussed with William Sullivan, but he accepted the job, partly because *City Times* would allow him to spend three days at home with Rachel, who had become increasingly moody and vocal whenever Charlie or Gail would leave the house, and partly because he would only have to write twelve columns a year instead of more than two hundred. He worried that *City Times* readers would soon tire of what Jill called his "quotidian observations." But after his first column, in which he discussed his joy at Rachel's birth, attracted a record number of children's clothing advertisers, he received a call from New York agent Naomi Boldirev, who suggested he turn his column into a book. Charlie told her that a book sounded like an awful lot of work, and didn't expect to hear from her again; he played down the whole phone conversation when he discussed it with Gail, because he knew that every Chicago publishing house had rejected Gail's book proposal for *Steer Clear: A Guide to Chicago's Worst Tourist Attractions,* leading her to settle for a job doing PR for Orange You Hungry?, a chain of trendy Chicagoland restaurants, each of which was named with a culinary pun, such as Claim Your Steak!, Just for the Halibut!, and Clam Kadiddlehopper's.

Nevertheless, Boldirev took only a week to find a publisher for Charlie's fatherhood memoir: Spofford & Quimby Ltd., whose editor, Isaac Abner Mallen, was flying Charlie to New York. Charlie told Mel that he didn't care that much about the book or the money, but he couldn't pass up the opportunity for an all-expenses-paid trip to see his daughter, who came home less and less; it frightened him to think that she would no longer regard his home as hers. He had only seen her briefly in June when she and her "oldest pal Larry" had picked up Jill, who had left Chicago to room with Michelle in Manhattan for the summer, not long after she had won a Front Page trophy for her article about Wes Sullivan.

Charlie took his frayed and overstuffed brown wallet out of his back pocket and showed Mel his pictures. There was Rachel, he said, showing a photo of an infant glaring into the camera from her playpen. And there was Jill, he said—she was standing in front of K.I.N.S. in an overcoat, a BETTER RED THAN DEAD button pinned over her heart. And here, Charlie said, displaying a picture of Michelle in the role of Anne Frank, "this is my oldest." It was only when he saw this picture that Mel began feeling guilty.

Mel was on a business trip. He had been clear about that. He had told Deirdre and his producer, Carl Slappit Silverman, that he was going to New York to complete casting for *Godfathers of Soul.* He had cast all the major roles, including Al Capone, Richard J. Daley, and Buddy Bradford, with Chicago talent. Chicago actors were hungry; they had a blue-collar work ethic, he frequently said. In the role of Jewish gangster Meyer Lansky, Mel had cast Lennie Kidd, his old colleague from his public radio days. Lennie was a recent convert to a "neo-Buddhist" sect; he worked as a radio announcer for a public radio show called *Bunny Day* and as a stand-up comedian, perhaps best known for his lewd parodies of Irish songs, such as the ballad "Mary Ann" (*"By the banks of the Liffey / I sprang a great stiffy / As I thought about Mary Ann / Her eyes were black as coal / And her skin soft as sand / And I knew her as well as the palm of my hand"*). But Mel still hadn't found someone to play the fictional character of Al Capone's mistress, Jasmine Huggins.

Dozens of actresses had auditioned—white actresses, black actresses, Asian ("Huggins don't matter," Mel had observed. "If it's the right lady, she'll be Jasmine Chang"). On one occasion, Carl Silverman slouched in a director's chair during auditions and muttered that all of the actresses he'd seen had seemed "pretty fly" and why didn't they just settle for one of them. Mel said that not one of the actresses who'd auditioned could compete with one particular "New York actress." Carl, with a peculiar glint in his eye, urged Mel to fly to New York to see if he could lure that actress into taking the role.

Mel had talked himself into thinking that his intentions vis-à-vis Michelle were completely honorable; he truly felt that she was the only actress who had the seductive qualities necessary to make the character of Jasmine Huggins seem like an actual human being as opposed to the "pubescent fantasy girl" Deirdre had called her when she had helped Mel edit his script. But, Mel asked himself as he passed Charlie's pictures back and told him that he had a beautiful family, one that he'd be proud to have himself, if his intentions were so honorable, why had he told Deirdre that he would be auditioning dozens of actors instead of just one? If his intentions were so honorable, why had he asked Michelle not to tell either her sister or Muley that he would be coming through town? And finally, if Mel's trip was one of honorable intentions, why, when he saw Michelle at the La Guardia baggage claim, running into Charlie's arms, did he feign no knowledge of her whatsoever and just tip his tam-o'-shanter in Charlie's direction, and say "Go Sox" before heading to the taxi stand?

There were two beds in Mel's hotel room at the Helmsley Middletowne. A bellhop asked Mr. Coleman if someone might be joining him. "My brother might," Mel had said, handed the man a twenty-dollar tip, then placed a DO NOT DISTURB sign on the door. He opened the drapes, gazed down on an airshaft, slipped off his shoes, sat on the bed, and flipped on the TV, watching long enough to determine that the Sox had been eliminated from the play-offs. A downcast Harold Washington, wearing a Sox cap, was being interviewed—"I thought this was the year we'd finally do it," he said.

Mel turned off the TV. He had two days before he would meet Michelle at the Morrison Studio on 10th Street, two days before he would ask her if she would want to have dinner afterward. He had no other events planned, even though he'd reserved the hotel room for a week. As he took a long hot shower, he briefly considered whether his entire journey was one of folly. He had an intelligent, beautiful lady friend in Chicago, one he was considering asking to marry him. Deirdre was smarter than he was, something he found sexy. He liked that she nearly always called him on his bullshit, liked that it had taken so long for him to woo her—every night he spent in her bed felt like a testament to his intellect and his seductive skill.

There had been a time when Mel had thought that, once his parents were gone, he would become the freewheeling, amoral playboy of his fantasies, the guise he had assumed while writing a now out-of-print book of grooming and dating tips, titled *Mel's Manual for Men*—all-night lovefests, three girls at a time, champagne, caviar. There would be no home anymore, no family to tie him down, he would be free. No longer would he be thwarted by his father, the deacon at Church of Our Savior, who, despite his occasional philanderings, had impressed upon Mel the necessity of being a man of one's word. No longer would he feel guilty under the watch of his mother, who had quietly accepted her husband's infidelity.

But the effect of his parents' demise was exactly the opposite. His father no longer presided over his Pitner Street manor, it was true; and no, his mother did not live above Mel's two-bedroom Clarendon Avenue apartment as she had after her husband had died. Instead, Eugene and Oneida Coleman were now everywhere, supervising all of Mel's movements. They were in his head, chastising him for leaving Deirdre in Chicago and not telling her about Michelle. There was his father telling him that he was thirty-six years old; it was time to build a family. And now as he stood naked in front of the bathroom mirror, using tweezers to pull out the one silver whisker on his chin, there was his mother telling him not to stare at himself; narcissism was sinful.

There were at least two conceivable paths Mel's life could follow, and as he grabbed a towel, he thought about each. He could marry Deirdre if she would have him, move in with her and Muley, whom Mel counted among his best friends. Deirdre was still young enough to have more children. They could build a life for themselves, something permanent. He liked the idea of being a family man, of standing side by side with a mature, intelligent, and outspoken lady. He liked the nods of respect that he received when he accompanied Deirdre to Marshall High faculty events, liked the idea of being one of those classy Hollywood directors who didn't marry any old starlet.

Or, Mel thought as he applied cologne and antiperspirant, he could pursue a white girl more than fifteen years younger than he was, thus incurring the wrath of his future fan base—black audiences would call him a traitor; liberal whites would call him a sellout. All that for an affair that could never last. Girls didn't date men fifteen years their senior for love—only in Woody Allen movies. White girls didn't date black men for love—only if the guy was Billy Dee Williams.

With Deirdre, he thought that he might have left his youthful, hormonally addled days behind. Three years earlier, she had refused his invitations for dinners, movies, and "good conversations," said she wasn't interested in having him prepare his special "Flaming Coleman" dessert for her, had been appalled when she learned that, without asking permission, he had based some of his film script on the criminal exploits of his old WBOE pal Lloyd Cubbins's incarcerated son, Tiny. But when Lloyd Cubbins had hardly blinked at Mel's script, and the gangster Tiny himself, whom Deirdre visited weekly at the Joliet Correctional Center, said he didn't care, Deirdre ultimately relented.

Once it began, theirs quickly became a mature relationship—or at least the sort of relationship that Mel assumed mature people were supposed to have. They sat on armchairs, sipped wine, discussed books. At Deirdre's side, he saw himself as the husband she should have had, the husband his father should have been to his mother. He had thought that acting so mature would mean that he would stop having the same thoughts he had had in his youth. But instead, it seemed only to mean that he would not act on them.

That first night in New York, after he had grown weary of editing his script, Mel decided to go out for the evening to get his mind off of Deirdre and Michelle.

But the title of practically every movie and play he considered filled him with more guilt and anxiety. He couldn't see *Risky Business* and he couldn't see *Romantic Comedy,* couldn't see *Fool for Love* or *My One and Only,* and he certainly couldn't go to the West Bank Café, for it was premiering a show called *Dick Deterred.* He wound up at *Fanny and Alexander* at the Loews 83rd Street, fell asleep for two hours, and still managed to catch the last half. And the next morning, though he was not a religious man, he spent a good chunk of time in church.

On the Saturday evening that she returned home to her 13th Street apartment, the worst thing that Michelle could say about her time with Mel was that he had been a perfect gentleman. She had first spent two days with her father—seeing shows such as *Fool for Love* and *Dick Deterred,* eating steak and lobster to celebrate Charlie's book contract for his memoir, *In Her Footsteps: A Father's Journey,* and fending off the same forlorn question that Charlie asked a dozen times in a dozen different ways: "Do you think you'll come back to Chicago after you graduate?" "Do you like New York as much as Chicago?" The last time he asked, Michelle was walking him to his gate at La Guardia. "Should I tell Gail to leave your room just the way it is for when you come back?" Charlie asked.

"No, Dad," Michelle said as she kissed her father on the cheek, "she can do what she wants." And once he had boarded the plane, Michelle sprinted for the taxi stand so that she could keep her appointment with Mel.

When Michelle opened the door to the audition studio, Mel was seated on a folding chair in a room full of mirrors. He was dressed all in black, except for the white stitching on his Western boots and his turquoise bolo tie. On his lap, he had a script in an open three-ring binder. He chomped an unlit cigar. Michelle sashayed into the studio in her jeans jacket and faded black *Moose Murders* T-shirt, while Mel, trying to cultivate an air of professionalism, didn't look up from his script, just told her he'd be with her shortly. Michelle plopped her jacket on the floor, waltzed over to Mel, peered over his shoulder, and read the words *Jasmine Huggins smokes a cigarette—her silk kimono is slightly open.* Michelle told Mel that she had left her kimono at home; would he prefer for her to perform "in the nude"? She affected a contemplative expression and told Mel that she had no problem with full frontal nudity "as long as the role calls for it," a phrase she'd heard others use in class and one she roundly mocked in letters home to Gareth. Mel didn't crack a smile; he handed her some pages, told her to study them, then added that yes, nudity might be required, but they could discuss the matter if and when she was cast. Michelle snatched the pages, took them to a corner of the room, and sat on the floor. She studied her lines; Mel studied his script—each tried to avoid eye contact with the other. As she read, Michelle wondered if Mel knew that she didn't really give a damn about his movie.

The scene was a minute long and most of the lines were Al Capone's. In it, Jasmine Huggins—who has arranged for Capone's murder on the Ides of March—has second thoughts and urges him to stay home. It began with the line "I been thinkin'" and concluded with "Fuck you, Al Capone, fuck you." Michelle figured that this audition would last about ten minutes max, after which she and Mel could go out for food. But Mel continually made her repeat the same lines, asking for minor, nearly indistinguishable variations—"All right, good, but now do it more pissed off," "O.K., now do it looking at me," "Don't emphasize the word *you,* emphasize the word *fuck,* and the last syllable of Capone, really draw it out." He took the script and demonstrated: "*Fokk* you, Al Ca-*po-o-one,*" he read, "*Fokk* you." He handed back the script. "Do you see how that works?" he asked.

This was one of Michelle's least favorite phrases. She had heard it from her Pakistani coworkers when she'd worked the counter at the North Shore Kosher bakery—"Now you put every *babka* in a wax bag, do you see how that works?" She had heard it from Myra Tuchbaum, who had joined a "Just Say No" club at Southern Illinois—every time you said no to drugs or alcohol, you gave yourself a point. "Do you see how that works?" Myra asked.

Michelle tossed the pages to the floor, stood with her hands in her jeans pockets, and said, "Let's go, mofo." Mel told her to pick up her script, but Michelle said that they'd already read through it so many times, she had the shit memorized; if you read through a script eight zillion times, unless you were a retard, you could memorize it. "You see how that works?" she asked. Mel bit the inside of his lip hard, trying to look angry instead of amused, then called "Action!"

"I been thinkin'," Michelle snarled, reading her lines with an intensity that bordered on ferocity, and as Mel watched Michelle, he started believing that the little gangster flick he'd written could become something more: a serious epic that would be part *The Godfather,* part *Shaft,* the sort of project that would win him instant fame and a three-picture deal. He kept fantasizing about his film's potential right until Michelle delivered her last line: "*Fokk* you, Mel Co-o-ole-man. *Fokk* you." At which point, Mel burst out laughing, stood up, and placed a hand on Michelle's shoulder.

That was good, Mel said, that was real good, he liked the way that *soooouuuunded*—he drew out the vowels to demonstrate his enthusiasm—did she want the role? Not if he was going to tell her how to read every fucking line and make her do it twelve dozen times, Michelle said, but as she said it, she touched Mel's hand. They looked at each other for a moment, then Mel asked Michelle if she was hungry.

They ate at Charlie Mom, shared moo goo gai pan, egg rolls, and fortune cookies ("You will achieve eternal happiness in bed"), then walked all the way up to the Guild 50th Street, where they watched one of the worst films either had ever seen, *Staying Alive.* They laughed all the way through it, their hands grazing each other's as they shared popcorn and Junior Mints. Afterward, Michelle sang the theme song, "Far from Over," ran to the first pay phone she could find on a street corner, and imitated John Travolta in the film, elated to be cast in a Broadway show. "I got it?" she asked, then pumped her fist. "Way to go, Manero!"

Mel never asked Michelle to come back to his hotel room; Michelle never suggested that she spend the night there, but after the movie, there seemed to be little doubt about where they were going. Walking east on 50th, Michelle told Mel that she would happily act in his movie, but she couldn't miss any classes—she knew that sounded weird because she probably seemed like a skank and a fuckup ("my previous brilliant careers," she said), but it was, in fact, true. Mel said that if she took the role, he'd make sure that the shoot coincided with her winter vacation, and she wouldn't need to attend any rehearsals.

"Jesus, Melvin," Michelle asked. "Do you like me that much?"

Mel took a breath. "I just think you're that good," he said.

Michelle didn't return to her apartment until Saturday after Mel caught his flight. The first night in Mel's room, they ordered in pizza, watched *Sha Na Na,* talked until two in the morning, turned off the lights, and lay in separate beds, where they pretended to sleep. They saw bad movies and Broadway shows—Mel would laugh uproariously when Michelle imitated the performers they had seen, twirling herself around lampposts and singing "Strike Up the Band." They drank too much rum at overpriced hotel bars, went into museums and ran through them when they got bored. Mel even accompanied her to an NYU Legal Ethics lecture, where they sat in the back and passed notes.

When Michelle finally arrived home, she discovered with some dismay that she had lost out at "Orgasm Bingo," a game that she had been playing with her roommates since the beginning of the semester. She and Destry Valance—a pseudonym that directing student Desmond Valencia adopted in order to easily distinguish between men he'd met at Danceteria calling up for dates and relatives in Guam checking up on him—had designed three bingo cards, one for each roommate. In each square were written orgasmic exclamations, such as "Don't Stop!" "Oh God! Oh God! Oh Jesus! Oh God!" and "Thank you very much" in an Elvis Presley accent. Whenever one of the players' partners reached climax and cried out one of the phrases, the player could block out a square. Whoever got five in a row would collect five bucks each from the other players.

Destry, his arms folded, sat on the tea-stained, once-white couch in the living room, listening to "Doctor, Doctor" by the Thompson Twins on his boom box; he informed Michelle that Bert Liu had just declared victory. Bert kept a leather-bound *Sex Book* on his night table, which women signed as if it were a guest registry at a bed-and-breakfast: "Best night I've had this semester—Liesel Goodman, freshman." A few minutes earlier, Taylor Weiss had moaned, "Fuck, that's good," and Bert had emerged from his bedroom, a towel around his waist, presented his Bingo card to Destry, and collected his five dollars.

With a grin, Destry pointed out that Michelle's bingo card was blank; he asked what her excuse was—"Goin' Christian on us?" Michelle grunted, then sat down on the couch with her *Godfathers* script and asked Destry what he meant. Well, Destry said, she'd been out with a guy for a week, and her Orgasm Bingo card was blank—it all sounded pretty Christian to him. Yeah, Michelle said; maybe she'd found God. Or maybe, Destry began, the smile on his face was half-grin, half-leer. "Maybe what, asshole?" Michelle asked. Maybe she'd found love, Destry sang. Michelle flipped him off and kicked off her shoes. "Believe me," she said, "when I'm in love, you'll be the first to know." She cracked open her script and a note fell out, written on Helmsley stationery: "Maybe someday . . . Love, Mel."

"Love notes?" Destry asked.

Michelle used her right big toe to shut off Destry's boom box.

"Love this," she said.


A fter arriving at O'Hare Airport that Saturday night, Mel drove straight to the Wills residence on California Avenue. The West Rogers Park synagogues had just released their congregants. As Mel walked past K.I.N.S., one of seven temples within a six-block radius, he passed Orthodox mothers pushing strollers, old men with canes walking slowly out of *shul,* families getting into station wagons bound for the kosher pizzerias and falafel shops of Devon Avenue.

Mel had generally had good relationships with Jews, despite the fact that the minister at his father's church had often lambasted "merchants" and "moneylenders" in his sermons. As Mel continued south on California—troops of Hasidim taking up more than their share of the sidewalk—he was amused by the packs of men in black overcoats, black hats, and beards. But for their *payess* and *tsitsis,* they looked like feds from 1940s B-movies. For a moment, Mel considered inserting a scene in his movie in which the gangster Tiny Walker would think that he'd been caught by some G-men who, instead, would greet him by saying "Good *yontiff,*" then ask if he was Jewish and if he wanted to put on *tefillin* in a Mitzvah Mobile. "Ain't goin' in no goddamn Mitzvah Mobile," Tiny would say. Mel could reprise the scene toward the end of the film—Al Capone would be pursued by actual G-men whom he would mistake for Hasidim. "Good *yontiff,* boys," Capone would say, but then they'd cuff him.

It was a good idea for a scene, Mel thought as he entered the vestibule of Muley and Deirdre's apartment building. But now it seemed too flippant for the kind of movie that he was making. He wondered if it might offend Carl Slappit Silverman; more important, he wondered if it might offend Michelle. Not that Michelle's opinion concerned him—he already had a girlfriend, he continually reminded himself, one his own age, and the fact that he had not tried to cheat on her in New York was a testament either to his self-control or his insanity. It had almost been a game between Michelle and himself, as if they had secretly agreed to spend a week in a state of suspended desire, like some couple in one of the classic novels on Deirdre's shelves, forfeiting happiness in exchange for propriety. Someday, he'd see Michelle walking down the street—their spouses would be long dead. She would remove her chapeau and silver hair would spill down. Either that, or they would fuck the next time they saw each other.

Mel let himself into the Wills apartment, using the key that Deirdre had finally given him, the key that had both flattered and scared him, for it was accompanied by expectation and responsibility. The apartment was dark; the only light was coming from under Muley's door. Mel hoped that Muley wasn't entertaining that nymphomaniacal psychopath, Connie, the one about whom he'd warned Muley—"When a girl takes you to the top of the Sears Tower and says she'll jump unless you stop her, you know what you do?" Mel had recently asked Muley. "Let her jump."

But Muley was alone when Mel entered his bedroom. He was standing in his socks on a chair, excitedly sketching something in pencil on an enormous sheet of white paper that covered the entire north wall of his room. The sheet was divided into squares, each about one foot by one foot. On the first square, Muley had written in block letters, "Project for Film #1: The Exploding Screen." He had moved everything else in the room as far away from that wall as possible: his bed, his desk, his NHL Pro Street Hockey set, his bookcases, even the illuminated world globe that he had found in an alley behind the now-shuttered Hurd Travel Agency; his film projector and cameras were on his bed. "Hey, Michelangelo," Mel said, "what's all that bullshit on the wall?"

Muley put his pencil behind his ear and hopped down from the chair. He shook Mel's hand and they embraced. Muley said that most of the art schools to which he was applying wanted to see samples of his work; he had an idea for a film project, and was storyboarding it on the wall so he could see it all at once. Mel told Muley that he was one crazy motherfucker, then asked if he was alone. Yeah, Muley said. No naked Connie chick in the closet? Mel asked. Not since last time he'd checked, said Muley, adding that Connie was taking karate at the JCC. For weeks after Britt Hurd had died, Muley had urged Connie to see a counselor. She had finally agreed, but her stepfather said "Nothing doing"—he wasn't paying for that *mishigoss,* and Connie had started taking self-defense classes instead in preparation for the law enforcement career she now envisioned for herself. She was currently patrolling el platforms and subway cars for the Guardian Angels.

Mel asked Muley where his mother was. Muley said she'd gone to see *Zelig* at the 400 Theater; he'd recommended the film to his mother after having seen it with Jill. Though Muley had told both Jill and Connie that he wanted just to be friends with them because he thought that he might be gay, he still saw them regularly. The line about being gay had been the suggestion of Gareth Overgaard, who said that it would be a convenient way for Muley to avoid Connie's advances and maintain his friendship with Jill, who, Gareth had said, would become interested in Muley again shortly after she discovered that he was unavailable. Gareth, however, had not predicted Connie's initial tears when she hypothesized that she had "oozed too much sexuality," and had consequently "made Muley gay," nor had Gareth guessed that Connie would frequently try to "turn Muley straight again" by practicing kickboxing moves in his room, wearing her Guardian Angels jacket, beret, and nothing else. Gareth had also failed to predict the in-depth discussions in which Jill would engage Muley, suggesting that if he decided to come out, she would do a very tasteful profile in the *Lane Leader,* for which Jill was serving as editor in chief, even after *Leader* advisor Louis Benson had been dismissed for allowing Wes Sullivan's unsubstantiated article about Britt Hurd to be published.

Mel asked Muley if his mother had gone out alone. No, Muley said. Who was she with, Mel asked, some stud? "Hardly," said Muley; she was "with Slappit."

"Your father?" Mel asked.

"Slappit," Muley repeated.

Muley had peers who didn't talk to one parent or another, such as his Physics lab partner Hillel Levy, who often walked into Nagilah Israel when his father was on his break, and spat on his falafel balls. Muley understood Hillel's sentiments, but what he felt toward his birth father, Carl Silverman, who had moved to L.A. to become a recording mogul rather than fight for custody or try to reconcile with his mother when she had confronted him for underpaying her ailing father, blues singer Jimmy Wills, was not so much anger as confusion that had eventually transformed into indifference. Muley did not resent that Mel had gone into business with Carl; he was not angry that his mother—who had once vowed never to speak to Carl—now endured his calls on a semiweekly basis. Mel had pragmatic reasons for working with Carl. Deirdre had years of history with him. Muley had neither.

"Why's she spending time with your pop?" Mel asked.

Muley shrugged.

For a moment, Mel felt hurt, nearly offended. A moment later, he was intrigued, excited too. He wondered if Muley knew that he was now secretly hoping that Deirdre was spending all her free evenings with Carl just as he had spent the past week with Michelle. He wondered if Muley knew that he was considering storming out, saying well, if that's what happens when I'm out of town, maybe I'll start spending my nights with the lady of my choice.

"How often has she been out with him?" Mel asked.

"Just this once," said Muley—the Chicago teacher's union was on strike, and, save for trips to the library and the Joliet Correctional Center, his mother hadn't been out of the house much. Mel shrugged and said, "Damn," then went to the kitchen, grabbed a wheatgrass juice out of the fridge, and retired to the living room with a video of *Mean Streets,* one of the films he was studying to develop the visual style of *Godfathers of Soul.* As he watched the movie, he kept looking up at the clock, preparing to get more indignant with each minute that passed. But he couldn't work up the requisite anger, for ten minutes later, Deirdre walked in, then joined him briefly in the living room, where she asked if he was going to watch that crummy movie for the nineteenth time or were they going out for a drink? Mel said he thought that Deirdre didn't like drinking. No, Deirdre said, but after going out with Carl, she needed one.

On the drive to the Double Bubble, Mel asked Deirdre why Carl had been calling so much lately. Deirdre sighed and said that she thought that Carl was still in love with her, or at least thought that he was; she felt sorry for him—since he'd returned to Chicago, he had left behind all his California contacts, and he had so few people to talk to. Mel pretended to contemplate Deirdre's statement gravely, as if it contained surprising and dramatic information that would affect both of their lives instead of having been perfectly obvious ever since Carl had moved back into town. Mel asked Deirdre if she was falling in love with Carl again, but Deirdre told him that he was out of his mind. Why, she asked. Did Mel want her to be in love with Carl? He hadn't met some sexy actress when he'd been in New York, had he? Of course not, Mel said, he'd never dated actresses, they were all crazy anyway. He laughed, a bit too loudly it seemed to him. He wondered if the laugh sounded hollow to Deirdre too, for even as he put a hand on Deirdre's thigh, he was trying not to think of Michelle. And later, at a back table of the Double Bubble, where he and Deirdre were sharing a bottle of Chardonnay and discussing Flaubert, he tried not to think of Michelle. And that night, when he and Deirdre made love—silently, as always; in darkness, as always—he was still trying not to think about her.

Carl Slappit Silverman had been sitting in a seemingly interminable *Godfathers of Soul* production meeting at Bronzeville Studios when he heard a phone ringing down the hall and sprang up to answer it. Before he had sold his old record label to the Los Angeles company that renamed it Pico Records, Carl had always felt energized in meetings discussing rhythm tracks, vocals, overdubs. But he didn't understand how anyone could give a damn about aspect ratios, camera angles, or even tastefully done, soft-focus shower scenes, and though this meeting attended by Mel, cinematographer Ron Claxton, and their crew had lasted only forty-five minutes, Carl had already left the room four times—to use the john, to order out barbecue, to pump quarters into the parking meters, and now to pick up the phone in Mel's editing suite and hear Deirdre's harried voice on the other end. Carl told Deirdre that Mel was in a meeting and asked her if anything was wrong. And moments after she'd told him that her Fiat had stalled on the Stevenson Expressway en route to the Joliet Correctional Center for her weekly meeting with Tiny Cubbins, Carl was brushing the crumbs off the passenger seat of his cream-colored Cadillac DeVille and rummaging in his glove compartment for cologne as he drove toward Joliet to rescue the only woman he had ever really loved.

It was Carl's belief that anything in life could be achieved with a steadfast singularity of purpose. The trick, he thought as he sped west on the Stevenson, with "Snatch It Back and Hold It" cranked up all the way, was not to want too many things, and not to want more than one at a time. Carl's father, Mendel Siletsky, who had changed his name shortly after arriving in America, had been born in Chernovtsy, the second oldest of five children, and the only one to rebel against his father's authority. Ordered to wear a long black coat to *shul* as a teenager, he had taken a pair of shears and sliced off a foot and a half of material and wore the coat to town, frayed and tattered, while his father, a cantor, looked on with horror. Sent by his father to join the Russian army before he was even old enough to be eligible, he never reported to duty—he gathered the family's menorah and candleholders, and his late mother's jewelry, sold them in the town square, and rode a train to Germany, vowing never to speak to any member of his family again.

From Hamburg, Mendel sailed to Ellis Island. The ship was cramped, its floors slick, and it pitched and rolled with every wave on the Atlantic. Sometimes the stench of sweat and vomit would become so oppressive that Mendel would stand on deck for hours at a time, feeling the cold salt spray upon his cheeks. On board, he met a girl, Sadie Sadkowsky, who hadn't stopped crying during the entire first three days of the Atlantic crossing. Though they had lived less than a mile from each other in Chernovtsy, they had never met. When Mendel found the nerve to approach her and ask why she was crying, she told him that her parents had sent her to live with a family that she had met only once before; they had mailed her a picture of a man named Joseph Popko, whom she was supposed to marry. Mendel told her that she needn't marry anybody she didn't want to; in America, you could marry whomsoever you pleased.

For most of the rest of the journey, Mendel sat with Sadie and proposed fanciful visions of the future they could have together in America—a house on the shores of Lake Meshuggeh; servants and maids waiting upon them; gilded coaches whisking them to the Yiddish theater. When they had enough money they'd send it back to their families—or at least they could send money to the Sadkowskys; Mendel's family, he said, could go to hell. Sadie and Mendel kissed as they passed the Statue of Liberty, at which point Sadie said that she guessed this was good-bye—one week from now, she'd be married to Joseph Popko. And then it was Mendel who cried.

At the end of the day, after he'd been processed at Ellis Island, Mendel Silverman walked through the city, on his back a sack of clothes that barely qualified as rags. He slept crumpled up in the doorway of a butcher's shop. The next morning, he walked until he found the Popko residence and banged on the door until it opened.

"How did you find me?" Sadie asked.

Mendel asked her if she was ready to go.

The first years of Mendel and Sadie Silverman's life in Chicago—in a fifth floor walk-up on Douglas Boulevard—were blissful. In the summers, they would open their windows, turn the volume up all the way on their radio, and step out onto the roof, where they would dance all night long. When Sadie discovered that she was pregnant, all of Mendel's coworkers in the clarinet factory bought him vodka shots at Strulowitz's. Seven months later, the child, a girl, was stillborn. Mendel and Sadie spent much of their twenties avoiding discussion of the child, and much of their thirties discussing little else. They hardly ever had money to pay the rent—the clarinet factory closed, the egg factory had no further need for a candler; Sadie worked as a typist for a pop factory, where her salary barely covered groceries and streetcar fare.

One night, walking home from Manley High School, where he was working as a janitor, Mendel was mugged by two kids who couldn't have been more than sixteen; they took his Vulcan Cricket watch and the contents of his wallet: seven dollars that he'd hoped to spend on a present for Sadie's fortieth birthday. Mendel couldn't bear to come home. He sat for hours on a bench in Douglas Park waiting for someone else to mug him, to take him out of this pitiful existence. He would have been better off in Chernovtsy, he thought. Sadie would have been better off with Joseph Popko. Near dawn, when Sadie finally found him, he started to cry—he told her that he had no money. He knew it was her birthday and, as a present, he would give her freedom to her; she should leave him while she still had some of her youth. Sadie took Mendel's hand and told him to come home. For what, Mendel asked. *For what?* They walked back to their apartment building, climbed up to the roof, and Sadie turned on the radio, which was playing Glenn Miller—"Moonlight Becomes You." She held Mendel close. "For this," she said. She covered his eyes with her hands, and said the *Sh'ma Yisroel.* Soon after, when they learned that Sadie was pregnant again, they told no one, made no plans. And when Carl was born healthy, they had no money, no room, not even for a crib. Mendel attempted to make amends for his previous failures, but he was forty-three years old now. He found work, but it never paid well.

In 1947, when Carl was four, Mendel and Sadie saved enough to drive to Union Pier, Michigan, and stay overnight in a resort hotel, but their beat-up old Packard broke down on the highway. Even now, forty years later, looking at Deirdre's yellow Fiat with its hood up on the shoulder of I-55, Carl still remembered the sight of his father feebly waving his black felt hat at the smoke billowing out of the Packard's hood, his mother sitting on a mound of pebbles, her eyes sparkling with tiny rainbows—they'd been taking the trip for him, she'd said, they'd wanted to make up for all the expensive toys and vacations that they'd never been able to give him. At that moment, at that young age, Carl vowed that not only would he never want for anything, he would never want anything. He would always have enough money to buy whatever he wanted, but would never want what his money could buy.

When Carl started learning how to make money, he never spent much on himself, giving most of it to his parents, putting the rest in one measly checking account that he had opened after his Bar Mitzvah, which he'd helped to pay for with money from a paper route. He did his homework on the streetcar to and from the Loop, where he parked cars and made good tips. On weekends, he worked the cleanup crew on nonunion construction sites, sold the scrap wood he salvaged to furniture makers; during the summers, he shelved books at Kroch's and Brentano's on Wabash, where he became infatuated with eighteenth-century German philosophy and the writings of W. E. B. DuBois, Frederick Douglass, and Marcus Garvey. The knowledge he gained from the books helped him secure admission to the U of C. And, once he felt that he'd learned everything that school could teach him, he discovered his true life's calling at Teresa's Lounge, where he saw Muddy Waters singing "Sail On," acquiring the nickname Slappit when Waters's pianist saw him slapping his table with the beat.

Carl's first love, as a freshman at Manley High, had been Angela Napoletano, but she had passed him a note telling him that her brother Richie said that she wasn't allowed to date Jewish boys. After school, Carl had bicycled over to the Napoletano residence, a knife in his pocket. He stood in the alley below Angela's window and told her that he wouldn't allow any bully to keep them apart, and if Richie wanted to try to beat him up because he was Jewish and liked his sister, then that's the way it would have to be. Yeah, Angela had said, but there was one problem: She didn't like him. One week later, Angela was dating Marty Eisenstaedt, the older brother of Carl's best friend, Lou. Carl approached Angela in the Manley schoolyard and said he thought that she couldn't date Jewish boys. Angela told him that she only couldn't date *some* Jewish boys.

After that, there had been Deirdre, whom Carl had met at her father Jimmy Wills's apartment, shortly after he had signed him to Slappit Records. He had never known any woman as attractive and argumentative, but after their relationship had imploded, he had moved to L.A., focusing solely on his career. His experience with Angela had convinced him that he had no future with white women. He found them evasive and dishonest; they were always too fat or too thin; he didn't like their politics or their hair. Prejudicing black culture over white culture wasn't racism; it was logic. But the black women he met after

Deirdre generally didn't find him attractive. He had had high hopes for a successful relationship with Ronnie Wilbrough, an Oakland activist who enjoyed discussing civil disobedience, school lunch programs, and Odetta with him. Even though Ronnie was a lesbian, Carl suggested that they get married and maybe she'd change her mind. Ronnie proposed instead that Carl father her girlfriend Brenda's child, but on the appointed day, when Carl had rented a room at the Fairmont, he learned that Brenda was white and not only white but Jewish. That experience had scarred him to the point that he resolved to eliminate sex from his life. No more attempts to date up-and-coming R&B singers, no across-the-room leers at dancers from *Soul Train,* no slow cruises down Hollywood Boulevard calling out "Y'awl wanna spread it on some white bread, sistuh?" to hookers who flipped him off. The new antisex policy proved good for business and his mental health, up until the moment that he had heard his son's voice on an NPR kids' radio program and it had all come rushing back to him. He had soon decided to refocus his energy on returning to Chicago and regaining all that he had lost.

Throughout his life, Carl's successes were directly related to the fact that he had only one goal at a time; he had only stumbled when he had been unable to decide which he wanted: to run a lucrative record label or to live forever with Deirdre and Muley. Only recently had he realized that he'd made the wrong choice. It may have seemed that Carl was once again falling victim to the perils of desiring two things at once: becoming a motion picture mogul and rekindling his relationship with Deirdre. But in Carl's mind, everything he was doing would someday reunite him with Deirdre. He didn't give a damn about money anymore.

Carl had modeled his personal strategy for winning back Deirdre on the late-career technique of Muhammad Ali: the rope-a-dope. Fighting George Foreman in Zaire, Ali knew that he didn't have his opponent's strength, his youth, or his energy, so he let Foreman whale upon him for the first seven rounds, waiting for the boxer to tire himself out. Sure enough, come round eight, Foreman had nothing left. Carl knew that Mel was younger, hipper, better-looking; the object was not to compete with him but to be the only one left standing. If *Godfathers of Soul* proved successful, and Carl would spend all the money he could to make sure that happened, Mel would not remain in Chicago; he'd be off to L.A. within a year.

The rope-a-dope was a long-term strategy, one requiring patience and a reliance on small, manageable goals. The first had been to get Deirdre to speak with him. The next had been for her to tolerate his presence. Carl had achieved another goal when Deirdre had consented to join him for *gedempte fleisch* at What's Cooking? and *Zelig* at the Nortown. The fourth goal was for Deirdre to call him up of her own volition. Deirdre had actually been calling Mel when her car had stalled on the highway, but Carl counted the fact that she had not objected when he had offered to help her as another small victory.

And though Deirdre may have seen Carl's impolite, overbearing nature as a liability in virtually every social context, when he was dealing with auto mechanics and tow truck drivers, it was a godsend. Fifteen minutes after Deirdre had called, there he was on I-55, talking down the price of a tow. Fifteen minutes after that, he was at the service station bawling out the mechanics. And before even one hour had elapsed, he was driving behind Deirdre on the Stevenson, following her all the way to California Avenue to make sure that she got home safely. Deirdre asked Carl if he wanted to come in for a cup of tea; he thanked her, but said that he didn't have time—there was a fascinating production meeting going on at Bronzeville and he didn't want to miss another second of it. But, he said, if she wanted some company the next time she was driving to Joliet to meet Tiny Cubbins, she should give him a call. And though he knew that she probably wouldn't call him the very next time she was going, he knew that she would think about it. And at this stage of the rope-a-dope, that was all that mattered.

## WINTER BREAK 1983 – 84

The snow was coming down hard on I-80 when Larry Rovner pulled his Ford Country Squire off the highway into the parking lot of the Howard Johnson's in Lake Harmony, Pennsylvania. Larry didn't like driving in even slightly inclement weather for fear that he might wind up in some tragic, disfiguring accident that would compromise his performing career. But Michelle Wasserstrom, who was returning to Chicago for the *Godfathers of Soul* shoot, enjoyed driving fast in bad weather. She called Larry a pussy for driving with his hazard lights going, and had insisted that they drive until they found a Howard Johnson's. "Johnson Howard! Johnson Howard!" she kept chanting and slapping the dashboard, imitating a cartoon that she had once seen in *MAD* magazine. "We must find Johnson Howard!" Finally, in Lake Harmony, when the slanted, orange sherbet roof became visible, she had sung, imitating Jim Morrison, "There's a HoJo risin'!"

When Larry turned into the HoJo's lot, he was explaining to Michelle that he had begun reassessing his musical career in November when Bob Dylan had returned to his Jewish roots and released *Infidels,* featuring the song "Neighborhood Bully," a blistering defense of Israel that Larry wished he had written himself. Larry had been planning to borrow money from his fiancée's parents to record his breakout album, *Haifa Hi-Fi,* featuring such songs as "(Have You Ever Been) Circumcised?," "Hadassah Woman," and "Can I Get a Minyan?," but now knew that his record would be viewed as derivative. In truth, Larry explained, he had already been tiring of his Jerusarock-jock pose. In Chicago, with his assimilated parents and his impressionable sister, it had felt natural to adopt a belligerent Zionist attitude. But at Brandeis, where all members of Hillel were trying to out-Jew him, where Ira Schwartz saw Larry ordering a McRib in the McDonald's drive-thru in Somerville and said, "You are so busted," where Hannah would request cunnilingus by asking Larry to "take a little nosh," there was no need to pretend to be more Jewish than he actually was. The problem, Larry explained to Michelle, shouting over the wind as they stepped out of his station wagon—hailstones were ricocheting off of his guitar case—was that if he decided to turn his back on the Jewish content of his music, he might not have anything left to say.

Approaching the front desk, Larry told Michelle he was glad that they were road-tripping together to Chicago for winter break. Soon, he and Hannah would be choosing silverware. Soon, they would be devising seating charts. Soon, they would be unwrapping packages filled with crystal candy bowls and gravy boats. Larry was still waiting for someone to talk him out of the wedding, but nobody ever tried. His father and stepmom had offered to throw him an engagement party at the Sybaris. His mother told him that he probably wouldn't be able to do any better than Hannah. His sister Lana hadn't spoken to him since he had seen her last crappy report card and had informed her that she needed to get her grades up if she didn't want to wind up at a junior college. His grandma Rose loved Hannah, showed her pictures of Larry as a boy, and both of them would laugh at what a "fat butterball" he'd been.

Larry's old buddies from Ida Crown were hopeless; half of them were already engaged and planning their careers in law and medicine and their bourgeois lives in the suburbs. They now wore jackets and ties everywhere, even to Springsteen concerts. Ben Jacobs was planning to marry Charlene Rosen, whom he'd met at a frat party in Champaign; the moment she'd kicked his ass in Beer Boat Races, wagged her finger in his face, and chanted, "Drink beer! Drink beer, mother-fucker, drink beer!" he had known that he was in love. And at Brandeis, most of Larry's friends were really Hannah's friends, save for Nate Yau, who claimed to loathe Hannah so much that Larry never consulted him.

When discussing Larry's imminent wedding, most everyone would mention the Goodman family's wealth. Larry's father habitually asked how much the Goodmans' condo was worth. And sure, Larry told Michelle, he wanted to make a lot of money, but not to buy things; rather, to have proof of his own talent. If his songs netted him millions, that would mean his talent was worth millions; if he represented clients in personal injury lawsuits, like Ben Jacobs's father did ("1-800-INJURED"), the cash would be meaningless. And yet, he said, no one understood him during the intermission of the Springsteen show, when he'd said that The Boss had probably been happiest playing small clubs. They'd all thought that Larry was jealous, especially Arik Levine, who said that Larry's assertion was just as absurd as saying you'd rather fuck an ugly chick than a pretty one, at which point everyone else got quiet, remembering an infamous party, when Randy Weinstock had declared that ugly chicks fucked better than hot chicks, and, as if to prove this point, had danced, Budweiser in hand, behind Bettina Wright, pretending to penetrate her as she boogied to "Safety Dance." But ever since he and Bettina had gotten engaged, the topic of ugly versus hot chicks had not been raised. No, no one could understand Larry, except for two people: Rabbi Jeff Meltzer (who'd played with Larry during some of the earliest incarnations of Rovner! and who'd quit the rabbinical racket to pursue music shortly before his wife left him and took up with her gardener, Ray Kilbourn), and Michelle, whom, Larry said, he should have been dating all along.

When the HoJo's desk clerk asked Larry and Michelle whether they would require a king-size bed, Michelle quickly requested separate beds, and when they got to the room, Michelle asked Larry, "So, which bed do you want, Isro-boy?" Larry just smirked, but Michelle said that she'd take the bed nearest the door so that she could run and seek refuge by the ice machine if Larry "tried anything funny."

Larry tried putting his arm around Michelle and kissing her, but when

Michelle told him that if he tried that shit one more time, she'd beat the crap out of him, Larry got pissed. Why was she taunting him by pretending to be some prudish, Orthodox bitch when she knew that he would be married in six months and they might not have another chance to screw? Where was her *schmatta,* he kept asking, *where's your fucking babushka and your* schmatta? He suddenly remembered something that she'd said to him the last time they'd had sex, in his Amtrak roomette—that she would try anything once. Maybe they should do something they'd never done before, he suggested—anal sex, for example. Michelle said that anal sex was a splendid idea; she told him to bend over. Well, for crying out loud, Larry said, he just didn't get what her problem was.

"The problem," Michelle said, "is I'm in love, Yeshiva Boy."

For a full half-minute, Larry said nothing. Through the window, he could see the snow swirling past the lights in the motel parking lot, tiny hailstones pinging against snow-dusted cars. He felt stupid, like a little kid who'd tried to kiss his big brother's girlfriend and she'd been too nice to laugh. He asked Michelle if she was serious. Michelle nodded and frowned. Larry then said it was really great that she was in love; he asked her what it felt like—did it feel really cool? Come on, Michelle said, he knew what being in love felt like. Oh sure, Larry said, every other day he fell in love with somebody else, but he wondered if this was different. Michelle shrugged. "It's like how you felt when you were first with that Hannah chick with the big tits," she told him. Larry said he hadn't remembered feeling much of anything his first night with Hannah save for a sense of relief that he had lost his virginity; being a virgin had really started to piss him off. He took off his coat, draped it over the back of a chair, then asked Michelle if she would marry the guy. Michelle said she doubted it. Larry said then he guessed that she was just in it for the sex. No, Michelle said, not that either—they hadn't even kissed yet; in fact, ever since she'd fallen for this guy, she hadn't had sex with anybody.

Larry asked Michelle if she at least "whacked off" thinking about the guy. No, Michelle said, not really. Wow, Larry said, that was pretty intense—he'd never heard of anybody not whacking about someone they were really into; Michelle must really be in love, had she met the guy in school? No, Michelle said, he was older, maybe forty. She had taken off her boots and was sitting cross-legged on her bed while Larry sat at the edge of the other bed. The word *forty* came as yet another baseball bat to the solar plexus of Larry's self-confidence. Wouldn't that feel kind of weird, he asked—going out with someone that much older. Michelle said that the whole thing was weird, the whole enterprise was, frankly, doomed—the guy was older, they didn't live in the same city, plus he already had a serious girlfriend. She half-wondered if she was only pursuing the relationship because she knew it wouldn't work out. If she didn't know the people involved, she would have said that it was all some cheesy Hollywood flick: Cicely Tyson and Paul Winfield would play the happy couple; her part—"Miss Happy Home-wrecker"—would be played by Sissy Spacek.

Wait a minute, Larry said, it was a *black guy*? Yes, Michelle said, rolling her eyes, it was indeed a *black gentleman*, did he have a problem with that? Of course he didn't, Larry said, he didn't believe in discrimination—he was a registered Democrat and voted the straight party ticket, except in the most recent mayoral race, when he'd voted absentee for Bernard Epton, but that wasn't because Harold Washington was black; that was because he hadn't liked Washington's racially divisive rhetoric. No, Larry said, he didn't have a problem with her dating anybody as long as she was happy, but what would happen if they got married? Would he convert?

Michelle gave Larry the finger. She said that she and "Tyrone" had not discussed marriage, because, as she'd explained earlier, she and "Leroy" weren't dating yet, and since her relationship with "Cleophus" was doomed, there was no point in discussing their future. Far out, Larry said, the guy certainly seemed to have a lot of names, but if the relationship wouldn't work, why bother? He tried to push his next thought back down the moment it asserted itself, but he couldn't help himself—he wondered if the guy had a really big *schmeckel*. But Michelle only repeated her initial assertion—she was in love. How did she know for sure, Larry asked.

Michelle said that it was because she'd never had this sensation before, this feeling that washed over everything. It was more than physical attraction; it was the sense of ease she felt around him, the fact that she could discuss anything with him—it had nothing to do with his ambitions or his so-called artistry, both of which she found suspect. In fact, it was in spite of all that. Sometimes, she'd be studying for a final or rehearsing lines for a play and an image of him would float before her and she'd wonder what he was doing at that very moment. She'd been playing Queen Elizabeth in the worst production of *Richard III* of all time and, for the first time ever, she had blown a line. "Ah! He is young," she had said, "and his minority is put unto the trust of Melvin Coleman, a man that loves not me, nor none of you." And because director Destry Valance thought that there were no such things as mistakes, only challenges to overcome, the cast, following upon Michelle's error, changed the name of Richard, Duke of Gloucester, to Melvin, Duke of Coleman. "Where is my lord, the Duke of Coleman? I have sent for these strawberries," the Bishop of Ely said. And in his penultimate scene, Richard trembled—"What do I fear? Myself? There's none else by. Melvin Coleman loves Melvin Coleman."

Larry thought for a moment. Was that the Melvin of Coleman he knew? The Melvin of Coleman who'd produced his first demo tape? Yes, Michelle said, assaying a Basil Rathbone accent, Mel Coleman and Melvin of Coleman were one and the same. Hell, fuck it, she said, by which she meant love, life, and everything that they had just discussed. She undressed, stood in her underwear, and daintily picked up her thick maroon bedspread as if handling a bag of toxic waste, then let it fall to the floor, pausing for a moment to wonder aloud how many layers of dried sperm were collected on that particular bedspread, and to theorize that if one could salvage all the sperm from all the motel bedspreads in America, there would be no need for men; the human race could be propagated in perpetuity via dried spunk courtesy of Howard Johnson's, Super 8, and TraveLodge. She took off her bra, flung it onto the dresser, rummaged in her backpack for her *Candide* T-shirt, then noticed that Larry was still sitting on the edge of his bed.

Shit, Michelle said, why did he look so depressed—because he couldn't date Mel? Larry said no, but being gay wouldn't be the worst thing; at least he wouldn't have all this pressure to get married and have kids. He'd even contemplated having his tubes tied, but had heard that men with tied tubes couldn't be buried in Jewish cemeteries, the same reason he'd chickened out of getting a Led Zeppelin "Zoso" tattoo on his ass. He didn't know which he dreaded more—the marriage in June or the musical in May. But if *The New Jazz Singer* was a hit, his future was pretty much decided. Hannah had already started compiling his newest songs and outlining a musical based on *Romeo and Juliet: West Bank Story*. Every time Larry returned from class, Hannah would suggest new lyrics for songs with titles such as "A Goy Like That"—*"A goy like that who killed your brother / Forget that goy—go find another."* And because she gave such boss handjobs, Larry kept his sarcastic remarks to himself about her plans for more Jewish musicals: *A Funny Thing Happened on the Way to the Mikva, Golda Meir Superstar!, Do I Hear a Valtz?, Little Shop of Horas, Aviva, Semitic Overtures,*

*Katz.* Now, Larry said, he was reluctant to finish writing songs for fear that Hannah would find them and change them; there were a handful that he'd never sung aloud. Michelle asked him to play one.

Larry took out his guitar and began to strum. Michelle sat on her bed and rolled a cigarette. She was thinking of Mel, thinking of all that mattered to her and all that didn't. She was thinking of how excited she would have been just a few months earlier to have a part in a movie, any movie. She would have been aching to sit in a makeup chair with someone powdering her face, to hear someone bark out "Fifteen minutes till action," then bark back "Thank you, fifteen!" But now, she was most concerned about whether Deirdre would be watching on the set. She lit her cigarette and took a drag. She knew that she spent too much time thinking about what her life could be, not what it actually was. She suddenly thought that everything she had ever done was wrong. And then she realized that no, she'd never done anything wrong; in fact, every decision she'd ever made was right. Now she was free, and if her love for Mel would be requited, hallelujah for that, and if not, then it would be shalom to love. She then wondered why such a retarded phrase had insinuated itself into her mind. It could have been because love had a tendency to render profound emotion in banality, but more probably it was because that was the title of Larry's new song.

"*Say* Yahrtzeit *for me, baby,*" he sang, "*I'm saying kaddish for my love.*" And as was always the case with Larry's music, Michelle stopped just short of laughing, just short of finding it absurd. Soon, she was singing harmony on the chorus: "*I'm saying shalom to you, babe / And shalom to love.*" And as always when she sang, she started getting aroused, even though—and this was something that she wouldn't even tell Larry for fear of depressing him more—it sounded more like a show tune than anything he'd previously written.

Several hours later, when the snow had stopped, Michelle, wide-awake, heard a rustling sound coming from Larry's bed. What was that, she yawned. What was what, Larry asked quickly. That sound like a cat licking itself, she said, was he "whacking"? Larry admitted that he'd been trying. "Trying?" Michelle asked—she said she didn't realize that guys *tried;* once they started trying, they were basically done. Yeah, Larry said, that was usually the case; he asked if Michelle had been masturbating too. No, Michelle said, but it probably would have been more constructive than what she'd actually been doing. Which was what, Larry asked. Brooding about Mel, Michelle said. Well, this was great, she added, here they were,

two people at the height of their sexual potencies, and they couldn't even mastur-
bate successfully. She asked Larry what he'd been thinking about. Girls, Larry said.
Wearing stewardess uniforms? Michelle asked. No, Larry said, boots and Israeli
army jackets. Michelle said that sounded hot; she asked why it wasn't working.
Larry said it was because whenever he started getting into it, he'd think about
Broadway musicals. Michelle suggested that they keep their minds occupied by
singing one of his songs. And just a few minutes later, when they had finished,
Michelle and Larry both wondered whether you could call something a simultane-
ous orgasm if the two parties involved had climaxed six feet apart from each other.

B y the time she arrived on the set of *Godfathers of Soul,* Michelle had spent
two days in West Rogers Park at the former Funny House, where she slept
on a fold-out couch in the living room since Gail had converted her bedroom
into a home office for her PR firm, GSW Communications. She'd felt irritable
the whole while, and it seemed as if she had spent all her time getting into
arguments—with Gail, who said that she was practicing her lines too loudly and
keeping Rachel awake; with Myra Tuchbaum, who had told Michelle to forget
about a serious relationship with Mel, because "mixies"—the word she used for
children of mixed-race parents—"looked kinda funny."

On her first night back in Chicago, she'd fought with Gareth shortly after
he'd introduced her to his new boyfriend, Blair Hayden, a slim South African
Philosophy major in expensive glasses and a black turtleneck, who spent most of
Michelle's truncated visit to Gareth's parents' basement cutting up lines of cocaine, exhaling sharply whenever Michelle said anything, and making proprietary
remarks.

"Help yourself," he'd said with a smirk when Michelle grabbed a beer out of
Gareth's cube refrigerator. When she'd turned off Blair's Simple Minds *Sparkle
in the Rain* cassette, replacing it with Patti Smith's *Wave,* he sarcastically suggested that she turn the volume all the way up—that way he could be sure not to
hear anything she said. When Gareth offered Michelle a line, and Michelle shook
her head, saying that she'd never done coke fearing she'd like it too much and
would want to keep doing it, Blair had said, "I guess someone's a little uptight,"
at which point Michelle had called him a "pud-knocking apartheid ponce," and
Gareth had told her to leave.

Michelle kept waiting for Mel to call and rescue her, but he didn't. At home, when she wasn't trying to stop Rachel from crying the moment that anybody left her room, Michelle would have frustratingly circular discussions with Jill, who had loudly proclaimed that she would not be going to her prom, least of all with Muley, since the two of them did not even have the same sexual orientation. Michelle had told Jill that, much as she might like to be one, she was not, in fact, a lesbian. Jill curtly responded that Michelle was out of touch; she'd been speaking of Muley. Michelle said that she wasn't exactly out of touch with gayness, seeing as she was studying theater in Greenwich fricking Village. Jill said that all guys in theater weren't gay; that was just a stereotype. Michelle said no, actually all guys in theater *were* gay. And on top of that, all guys who *weren't* in theater were gay, too. There wasn't really a question of which guys were gay and which weren't; it was just a question of how gay they were, and, given that information, Muley was on the low end of the gayness spectrum; had Jill ever considered the possibility that Muley had lied about being gay so that she wouldn't act like such a tight-ass anytime he got close to her? Jill said no, she hadn't considered that, and furthermore, it was time for her to walk the dog. Michelle asked Jill how many times she'd already walked the dog; she'd barely been home a day and Jill had walked Fidel a dozen times. Give her the damn leash, Michelle said, she'd walk the fucking dog.

What aggravated Michelle most about these arguments was that she thought that she and Jill had moved past having them. During the summer when they had lived together in New York, they had argued only once, after Jill had started running the vacuum cleaner at eight o'clock on a Sunday morning and had awakened everyone, including Bert Liu, who'd exited his room naked, squinted at Jill, and groaned, "Man, be cool." Here in West Rogers Park, they always fell into their old roles. In New York, Michelle would feel twenty years old going on twenty-five; here in Chicago, she would look up at the green and white California Avenue street sign, the *eruv* strung from the lampposts above her, and she would feel fifteen all over again, with a learner's permit instead of a driver's license, her lonely, widowed father asleep on the couch in his clothes, her precocious sister still in grade school. Sometimes, she'd awaken from a dream about an exam for which she'd forgotten to study, and she would remember everything—where she was, all that had happened.

Michelle took Fidel's red leash and latched it to his collar. Jill had reminded Michelle that the dog was trained to eliminate on the curb and warned her not to let the animal soil the neighbors' lawns, while, when she walked outside, Michelle—dressed in a denim jacket and sneakers despite the bracing subzero temperatures—contemplated which lawn Fidel should soil. Perhaps the Sternbergs' residence on Sacramento, perhaps the Rovners' next door, perhaps the Eisenstaedts' on Whipple, or maybe twerpy-ass Sarah Silver's on Mozart Street. But then she realized that none of them lived here anymore. Douglas Sternberg, her lecherous Mather High teacher who had failed her in Public Speaking and whom she partially blamed for the fact that she didn't get into Yale, had finally moved out of his parents' house and was working as a teacher and drama director at Mather and the Warren Park Fieldhouse, where he self-produced coolly received musical adaptations of American novels, such as *Liver of No Return,* based on *Portnoy's Complaint.* The Rovners were divided among Waltham, Massachusetts, Lake Geneva, Wisconsin, and Evanston. The Eisenstaedts now lived in Northbrook. And as for Sarah Silver, following the end of her affair with Douglas Sternberg, she had gone to Oberlin, where she was sporting a sea-green Mohawk and working at a record store.

Emerging from the alley west of Mozart Street, Michelle walked past K.I.N.S., where she and Jill had both been Bat Mitzvahed—Jill had quoted Kwame Nkrumah in her Bat Mitzvah speech ("I speak of freedom"); Michelle had quoted Boston ("Don't look back"). The *shul* was no longer Conservative; it was Orthodox. At the corner of California and North Shore, there were two newspaper boxes—the *Tribune*'s was empty, but the *Sun Times*'s was visible: BRRRR! declared the headline. The K.I.N.S. announcement board was barely readable through its fogged-up glass case: "Sermon, Rabbi Shmulevits: Beware the Savage Jaw of 1984!"

The Wills apartment was just across California and Michelle felt oddly unprotected, knowing that Mel's lady friend lived there; she always felt vulnerable when her dreams and reality stood in close proximity and one threatened to contradict the other. Nevertheless, she crossed the street with Fidel, bravely facing the possibility that the door would open to reveal Mel, smelling strongly of latex and lubricant, while Deirdre would beckon him to "come back to bed, honeybunch."

Instead, Connie was standing in the doorway of the Wills apartment; she looked tired, pasty; there were shadows under her eyes and she looked heavier than when Michelle had last seen her with the late Britt Hurd and his hooligan friends. She wore flared, stonewashed blue jeans frayed at the cuffs, and a man's paint-splattered, black corduroy shirt. She knelt down to greet Fidel; the animal licked her nose and her ears. Michelle asked Connie how she was doing. *Whatever,* Connie said, as she walked through the apartment toward the kitchen. *Fine,* she guessed. She said that she was considering moving to New Mexico once she'd graduated from high school. "*If* I graduate from high school," she added with a caustic laugh, then grabbed a thin metal Museum of Science and Industry ashtray from a drawer.

Muley's room was now devoid of furniture save for the bed and a ladder, which leaned against the closet door. Every inch of wall was covered with sketches on squares of heavy white paper. Suspended from the ceiling was a hockey net filled with plastic orange pucks. Muley was lying on his stomach, fiddling with a small wooden model of an open-air movie theater mounted on a Styrofoam cube. Seated on the floor was Ephraim Tekulve, who had broken off his engagement to Irit Ben-Amar and had moved Connie's belongings to his Angel Guardian shed. Connie sat down between Ephraim's legs; Ephraim locked his hands across her stomach.

Michelle crouched beside Muley's bed. "Hey, gay boy," she said. Muley exhaled briefly, somewhere between a laugh and a snort, kissed her on the cheek, then returned to studying his model. Fidel patrolled the room before settling beside Connie. Michelle asked if she could bum a cigarette from Connie, who looked up to Ephraim; he nodded his assent, unzipped Connie's purse, and handed the pack to Michelle without looking at her. Michelle took a cigarette and asked Connie a series of questions, which Ephraim answered using the pronoun *she* ("*She*'s doing quite well even though the grades don't reflect it"); while Connie began her sentences with *we*—"*We*'re gonna find a really big ranch out in Taos," and, ten minutes later, "*We*'re gonna head home; take care of yourself, Mules." They sauntered out, their hands tightly clutching each other's. Connie winked at Michelle—"Don't try to convert him," she said, referring to Muley, "I've already failed"—at which point Ephraim stopped holding Connie's hand and whispered something to her. "It was just a joke," Connie said. *"God."*

When Connie and Ephraim were gone, Michelle lay down on the floor, her left ear beside Fidel's snoot. She took a drag on her cigarette and blew the smoke up toward the net of hockey pucks overhead. Muley stood and circled his wooden model, studying it from all angles, while Michelle asked Muley what was all this crap about him being gay—she said she assumed that it was an "Overgaardian scheme" devised to get him back into Jill's good graces and to get that skank Connie out of his face. Muley smiled. Something like that, he said, adding that he was following her advice too; she herself had told him that the best way to win Jill was to make himself seem less attainable. Less attainable didn't mean more gay, Michelle said. She rolled her eyes and swatted him, at which point Muley asked Michelle what the deal was with her and Mel.

Michelle blanched. What made Muley think there was a deal, she asked, had Mel told him there was one? Muley said he hadn't talked to Mel about it, but his mother had recently asked him whether the Michelle Wasserstrom who'd attended Mather was the same Michelle appearing in Mel's film. And, he said, he'd just assumed that Mel had seen Michelle when he'd been in New York. Well, Michelle wanted to know, why did all that constitute a "deal"? Muley shrugged and said if that didn't sound like a deal, he didn't know what did.

Michelle suddenly felt exposed, discovered, guilty, then irritated for feeling guilty about something that she hadn't done yet. She had done many things in her life for which she could have felt guilty but didn't, such as pretending to stick her finger down her throat and gag after she read the beginning of the first chapter of *In Her Footsteps: A Father's Journey,* her father's book manuscript. And yet, she still felt uneasy, as if she'd been keeping a secret that everyone had known all along. Well, she asked Muley, what had he been doing for "poontang" lately? Not much, said Muley. *"Mees-tah Sohn?"* she asked, sounding out the Korean words for *Mister Hand,* the one piece of useful knowledge she'd gained from a roommate at U of I.

"Not lately," Muley said with a short laugh.

Michelle asked Muley if he knew that he could have basically any chick he wanted between the ages of fifteen and twenty-one and possibly some horny housewives over the age of forty who wore "big burgundy-colored underwear." Muley said he doubted that, adding that most girls at Lane tended to find him nerdy and obsessive. And you wanna know why, Michelle said, ignoring his remark, it was because Muley was so fricking unassuming. She leaned over him and kissed him hard on the lips. Muley looked at her, startled. Michelle explained that she just wanted to see how kissing him would feel; she hadn't made out with anyone in more than a year and her sudden loss of libido was bugging her. Well, Muley asked, how did it feel? Fucking sick, Michelle said, like kissing a kid brother. How about for him, she asked. Like kissing Jill's big sister,

Muley said, and Michelle laughed and threw her head back, ran her hand through her hair, lazily flopping the hand downward where she accidentally crushed Muley's miniature theater with a snapping of balsa wood and a crackling of Styrofoam.

"My fault," she said. She asked if Muley was mad. No, said Muley, it was just a model. He picked up the two halves and walked to his closet in search of a bottle of glue. Michelle asked Muley if he ever got mad. Sure, Muley said. Bullshit, Michelle said, *when*? Muley said he couldn't remember any times offhand— did Michelle actually remember specific incidents when she'd been mad? Yeah, Michelle said, about a million. She asked if there was anything she could do to make him mad. "You mean like if you started dating Mel?" Muley asked.

"For example," Michelle said, too disarmed by Muley's pinpointedly accurate question to pretend to have been hinting at anything else. As he began to glue the two halves of his theater back together, Muley said he didn't see why that should make him angry. Well, maybe because he had feelings for his mother, Michelle said. Muley observed that he'd spent the first sixteen years of his life fretting about his mother and he couldn't do it full-time anymore. Well, Michelle said, then maybe Muley had feelings for her. Or for Mel. Muley said that he had feelings for just about everybody, but still, just about every time you felt glad about somebody's success, you were feeling glad about someone else's loss. So, Michelle asked, what did you do when you hoped that everyone would be happy, but realized that happiness came so often at someone else's expense.

"I don't know. Maybe draw pictures," Muley said. He placed the miniature theater, now whole again, back on the ground.

"What do *you* do?" he asked Michelle.

*"Meestah Sohn,"* she said.

M el Coleman loved the feeling of being on a movie set. And he loved it most of all at five o'clock in the morning, an hour before his crew was scheduled to arrive, three hours before the cast. It was December 18, 1983, the coldest December day in the history of Chicago. Elsewhere, the mayor was Harold Washington, but on this, the first day of shooting for *Godfathers of Soul,* Mel surveyed the streets as if they belonged to him. *Mel Coleman, Mayor of Bronzeville,* he thought, as he strode past beaters and flivvers, past Plymouth Furies and Model Ts, in the glow of streetlights and gas lamps, over asphalt and cobblestone, underneath an elevated train platform, over streetcar tracks, past gang graffiti—the Corsairs, the Blue Demons, the El Rukns, the Vice Lords. He wished that his parents had lived to see this day, how proud his mother would have felt seeing him sitting in his yellow director's chair on South Michigan Avenue. And then he realized that, most probably, if his parents were alive, he would not be here now; he would be attending to his mother, doing his father's bidding, trying to live up to his siblings' financial successes.

During Richard J. Daley's twenty-two-year tenure as mayor of Chicago, moviemaking in the city had been virtually nonexistent. Now, more than seven years after his death, it had returned with a vengeance. When Mel had been working as an engineer at WBOE radio, he'd taken a long lunch to watch a police car drive through a cloud of pigeons in Daley Center Plaza for *The Blues Brothers.* Late one night, he'd walked from his apartment to Budlong Woods and stayed up past dawn waiting for the façade of a house to blow up in *Thief.* He had even played an extra walking west on Wacker Drive as a car broke through an embankment in the Marina Towers parking lot in *The Hunter.*

Now, south of the Loop, Mel's designers and construction workers had built, in and among burnt-out and shuttered liquor stores and chop suey joints, the façades of a bustling nightclub district for *Godfathers.* There was the Domino Club, the jazz and dance hall where Tiny Walker commanded Table 1; the Two Gents cocktail lounge, where Walker got his start running numbers; the New Zanzibar Hotel, where Jasmine Huggins worked as a high-class hooker before finally taking down both Al Capone and Tiny Walker.

The irony of all this activity was that only the devastation of the neighborhood could have created so much cheap, available land for a movie set. Nearby, a handful of buildings from Bronzeville's heyday remained—the long-shuttered offices of the *Chicago Bee* newspaper, the Overton Hygienic Building. But there were no more nightclubs, movie theaters, or legitimate stages. Immediately surrounding the soundstages of Bronzeville Studios were fast-food restaurants, tire shops, public aid offices, Rogers Pontiac, housing projects, DuSable Hospital.

Mel had barely slept the previous night—a fitful two hours at most. He had awoken in his apartment at 3:30 in the morning, showered, dressed, then drove all the way south through the city, passing as many movie theaters as he could find. He started at Clark Street by the Adelphi, cut over to Southport past the

Music Box, southeast on Lincoln past the Three Penny and the Biograph, then he drove by the decaying palaces of the Loop—the State-Lake, the Roosevelt, the Woods. And though each theater he passed was showing a different movie—*Uncommon Valor, Scarface, Never Say Never Again*—on each marquee he could see *Godfathers of Soul: A Film by Melvin Coleman.* He drove until he reached Bronzeville Studios, where this side of Cermak Road, there were no movie theaters whatsoever.

Three blocks of Michigan Avenue were blocked off and Mel now sat perched on his director's chair in the middle of the street and looked across Cermak at the remnants of the New Michigan Hotel, once Al Capone's headquarters. On its brick façade, a chipped blue sign: HOME OF THE BLUES. Delivery trucks smoked down Cermak—Gonnella Bread, Canfield's Sodas, *The Chicago Defender.* This would be a landmark too, he thought—Bronzeville Studios, where Mel Coleman got his start. He hopped down from his chair and walked south toward the studio, the air so cold that it felt as though a thin layer of frost was jelling over his pupils. And as he looked up at the sky, the city streets still cast in the early blue glow of dawn, he wondered if this moment would be the one he would remember most of all—before the day's shoot had begun, before he would wrap at eight o'clock at night and wonder whether to return to Deirdre's apartment or his own, before he would have to choose between Deirdre and Michelle, among Chicago, New York, and Los Angeles—this moment, when everything still seemed possible, and his film could be the greatest that anyone had ever made.

When Mel pushed open the front door to the studios, Michelle was already standing in the lobby.

"Hey," she said.

"Hey," said Mel. He moved toward her, then stopped.

"All right," he said. "Let's get to work."

Mel had always been a decent athlete. He'd run junior varsity track at Evanston High and still occasionally played pickup basketball with the old-timers at Emmerson Park on Granville. But little could have prepared him for the physically grueling nature of life as a filmmaker, particularly in the dead of a Chicago winter. With the exception of his trip to audition Michelle, every day of Mel's past six months had been a dizzying whirl of meetings, auditions, video shoots. He'd interviewed makeup artists, viewed audition reels, scouted college campuses for extras and grips. He'd applied for permits from the Chicago Film

Commission, shot test rolls, all the while writing and rewriting every damn scene. As he approached the shoot, he had viewed it as an opportunity to relax, but once he had plotted the shooting schedule—only two days off: one on Christmas, the other on New Year's Day, when the Fighting Illini would play USC in the Rose Bowl—he realized that he would have to kick himself into an even higher gear.

Director of photography Ron Claxton was first to arrive on set. And soon, the rest of the crew came with their gear and their armloads of track—Irit Ben-Amar, focus puller; "Grendel" Tate, boom operator; Sid "Hippo" Steinberg and Narc Davis, the grips; Angela Giudice, head of craft services, who could make bologna sandwiches at a rate of ten per minute. It was a crew of a dozen in all, plus volunteers from the Columbia College film department whom Claxton had rounded up by promising extra credit.

Then came the actors with dance bags over their shoulders, coffees in Dunkin' Donuts cups as they shimmied off parkas and leather jackets and settled into makeup chairs or paced the floors of the studios performing vocal exercises ("Heeeeey! That's my caaaaaar!"), rolling their heads, shaking out their arms and hands, smirking with studied disbelief when they read the day's shooting schedule and contemplated the inefficiency of film—how little time they would spend acting and how long they'd hang around waiting, wondering aloud when they would be fed and whether it would just be bologna sandwiches like the last film they'd worked on.

Carl Slappit Silverman had said that he would keep out of sight during the shoot, partly because he wanted to demonstrate faith in Mel, partly because he would be driving to the Joliet Correctional Center with Deirdre, who had called him the previous night to ask for a ride. Nevertheless, early that first morning, he too was slouching about Bronzeville, nodding perfunctorily or looking down at the ground when he saw white actors and crew members, greeting their black counterparts with his own hipster jive, slapping Vance Coffey, the actor playing Tiny Walker, on the back and telling him to "keep it smooth," asking Narc Davis where the "fly-looking bitches was at," giving Mel a soul handshake and telling him, "This is on time, Brotherman, on time" before he headed for the door.

The first scene of the day was shot from a crane nearly one hundred feet above the ground. The year: 1918. The camera descended slowly to focus on one particular abandoned lot where two kids were playing fast-pitch. A twelve-year-old Tiny fired two fastballs past the batter, his best friend Buddy Bradford, who swung at the third pitch and launched the ball onto Cermak. The ball rolled across the street, then stopped under the shoe of a young man wearing knicker-bockers and a newsboy's cap. Tiny ran across Cermak and came face-to-face with the man holding the ball.

"Ain't youse a little far from home?" the man asked.

"Who the fuck are you?" asked Tiny.

"Al Capone," said the man.

"That's a stupid fucking name," Tiny said and grabbed the ball out of the young Capone's hand.

By lunch break, the shoot was already behind schedule; by dinner, Mel had caught up, but only by forfeiting the perfectionism he'd spent months cultivating. He had insisted on repeating the opening crane shot fourteen times. But for the key early scene where Al Capone murders Buddy Bradford behind Big Jim Colossimo's cocktail lounge, after the first take, Ron Claxton had said, "I think we got it," and Mel said, "Cool, let's break for some of those young bologna sandwiches."

Cliques had already asserted themselves during rehearsals before Michelle had arrived in Chicago. The white actors hung out with the white actors; the blacks with the blacks; Mel—eager to preserve his image—with himself; every-one avoided the crew. Michelle, on the other hand, after Mel had told her that he couldn't socialize with any actors because it would be bad for morale, ate with the crew, in no small part because she sought to maintain as much distance as possible between herself and actor Lennie Kidd, who had pursued her when she'd acted on a kids' radio show he'd hosted and had not relented until he'd had a nervous breakdown, from which he'd more or less recovered, a fact attested to by his glazed facial expression and by the books about meditation that he read during downtimes.

As for her other fellow actors, Michelle relished neither their competitiveness nor their false intimacies. She shuddered at some of their "method techniques," such as Malynie Singer's insistence on having a tub filled with ice water in the dressing room so that she could have the "sense memory" of coldness for the scene in which her brothel radiator breaks down. When Michelle first met Vance Coffey, she enjoyed the R-rated stories he spun about housewives who hit on him while he was working his regular gig for a diaper delivery service. But after din-ner, when they had rehearsed their first scene together, he had grabbed her forearm hard. She had told him to lay off, but he'd justified himself by saying that the script said "Tiny grabs her hard." Michelle observed that in a later scene, the script also said "Jasmine grabs gun and fires it at Tiny" and she wasn't going to actually do that, so why didn't he try acting for once? When they shot the scene, Vance grabbed Michelle harder than ever and Michelle, not breaking character, grabbed his arm with her free hand, flipped him to the pavement, and told him, "I thought I told you not to grab me, you tiny piece of shit." Mel laughed loudly, and said, "Damn," that was the best thing he'd seen anyone do so far.

It was the last scene Michelle would perform that day, because at 8 P.M., when Ron Claxton muttered the word *overtime,* they were behind schedule again, and Mel knew that they'd be playing catch-up in the morning. He waited until the cast and crew had left the set before he offered to drive Michelle home. But during the ride, he talked only about how the shoot had gone, and how much work he had to do before the next day. Before they reached North Shore, Michelle asked Mel if he would mind stopping at the 7-Eleven on Western; she bought Creamsicles and a bottle of wine, thinking that she and Mel might stay out late. But when she got back to the car, Mel's seat was tilted all the way back, and he was snoring.

On the first day off from the shoot, Mel threw a Christmas party at his apartment on Clarendon Avenue. He had hoped that he might steal a kiss from Michelle under the mistletoe, perhaps in full view of Deirdre, which would make his romantic decision-making process significantly less complicated. But Michelle, already weary of hanging around the *Godfathers* set as if she were some sort of Mel Coleman groupie, figured that Deirdre would attend the party and chose to make other plans.

Instead, Mel spent much of the night glugging eggnog and discussing the poor quality of Christmas films with Carl—the only one he liked was *How the Grinch Stole Christmas*; the rest belonged "back in the 'Cracker Barrel,'" particularly the aptly named *White Christmas.* Mel drunkenly hoped that, if he could keep Carl engaged in conversation, he would eventually lead the man back to Deirdre, who would kiss him under the mistletoe out of pity, after which Mel would feel perfectly justified in pursuing his relationship with Michelle; while Carl, who was uncomfortable with the idea of attending a Christmas party with

Mel and Deirdre who, he assumed, would soon kiss under the mistletoe like all goyish couples, tried to make his escape, but was intercepted by Lennie Kidd.

Lennie sat with Carl on a sofa and reminisced about the time he'd worked as an unpaid intern at Slappit Records, when it was a penny-ante operation in Old Town, then proceeded to try to recruit Carl for the neo-Buddhist sect he'd joined. Chanting, he told Carl, rewarded one with not only world peace but also material gains; he had chanted for a new air conditioner, a regular slot at Zanies comedy club, and a better relationship with his mother, and he had gotten everything within three months, leaving out the fact that the improved relationship with his mother—who had spent much of the first forty years of his life telling him that he looked *puchky* and how come everything he touched "turned to *dreck*"?—resulted from the fact that she had stopped speaking to him when he had installed a *gohonzon* in his childhood bedroom.

Lennie told Carl that he could get anything he wanted by chanting. Carl said that, in his life, he'd gotten most everything he wanted while being an atheist. Yeah, Lennie said, but think of how much more he would have gotten if he'd chanted. Carl thought that his rope-a-dope effort to woo Deirdre could benefit from some spiritual assistance, and agreed to attend a meeting. He scurried out of the party just as he saw half of the *Godfathers* cast leading Mel and Deirdre toward the mistletoe.

Michelle, meanwhile, was sitting in the passenger seat of Gareth Overgaard's sputtering brown police cruiser, bound for Larry Rovner's mother's house in Lake Geneva. Larry had called Michelle from Wisconsin to ask if she wanted to spend her day off "checking out something really cool." Michelle had asked if he was referring to his schlong, and if so, she'd already seen it. No, Larry had said, he was sick of thinking about his schlong—he'd done that for the first two decades of his life; it was time to start thinking about something else.

Larry had said that he hadn't been able to stomach the idea of staying at his dad and stepmom's house in Evanston after he'd gotten into an argument with his stepmother, Dr. Cheryl Mandell, whom he'd confronted about the noise that she and his father made while having sex. He'd tried to talk to his father about it, but the moment Larry brought it up, Michael Rovner had tried to look concerned but couldn't conceal his proud grins. When Larry spoke with Cheryl in her study, she informed him that sometimes mommies and daddies got tired of each other and divorce was nobody's fault. Larry said that he didn't give a shit what she and his father did; his concern was for his sister, who could hear every sound Michael and Cheryl made, especially when they engaged in role-playing games, in which Michael pretended to be a sailor and Cheryl a Filipino prostitute beckoning him ashore with the entreaty, "Fuckee suckee ten buckee; I *ruv* you *Amellican sairuh* boy."

"She can't even do the accent right," Lana had complained to Larry.

Cheryl asked Larry what she was supposed to do. Stop doing her kegel exercises because "little Lana" was frightened by the sounds of her father making love? Larry said it was obvious that their actions were directly affecting Lana—why did they think that she was drinking all night with her friends, why had she totaled the Renault Le Car that they had bought for her sixteenth birthday? Cheryl said that she was willing to help Lana, but not until she wanted to be helped.

"It's you who needs help, lady," Larry had said and called his mother; she had laughed caustically at Larry's report and told him that she would be vacationing in Grand Lahou; he was welcome to use her house in Lake Geneva, as long as he didn't invite Lana and her "thieving suburban friends."

During the first part of the Wisconsin drive, Michelle unleashed some of her frustration at how little time she'd been able to spend with Mel. She censured Gareth for listening to a Heaven 17 cassette, saying that he was trying too hard to seem gay and it was "just not working." But she relented when Gareth told her that he and Blair had broken up. He said he had spent so much time being antisocial that he found it difficult to accurately judge others' characters; it never seemed clear to him if someone was an asshole when he'd already decided that all people were assholes. Michelle said that was a really excellent attitude for someone joining the Peace Corps. Gareth said that this attitude was called "humanism," which made him a fine candidate for the Peace Corps—he respected humanity; he only found individual people to be assholes. Michelle asked if he thought Larry Rovner was an asshole. No, Gareth said, he was just an idiot.

In Lake Geneva, Gareth parked behind Larry's station wagon and a rusty brown Datsun with a new green bumper sticker—"Moshiach Is Coming!"—and a faded blue one—"My Son Is an Honor Student at Solomon Schechter Day School." A handwritten sign tacked to the front door of the house advised, "If you can't see us, follow your ears." And as they walked around the dark house, Gareth and Michelle could hear drums. A half-moon illuminated a snow-covered path to the lake and a little wooden landing where Larry's mother tied her rowboat during the summer. Black cords led from the rear of the house all the way to the center of the lake, where a pair of shadows was silhouetted in front of a distant orange flame. They now heard the thump of a bass drum, the occasional crash of cymbals, the wail of an electric guitar, muffled, indistinct singing. Gareth stopped, then sat on the boat landing, his arms folded, his gym shoes dangling down. Michelle asked Gareth why he wasn't moving. Gareth said that he wasn't about to walk on the ice, then drown. Michelle said that it was about a billion degrees below zero outside and this "pissant lake" wouldn't melt anytime soon. Gareth told her to go ahead; he was staying. He removed a scrunched-up joint from the pocket of his black parka and rolled it between his fingers. Oh, Michelle said, so it was fine for her to drown, but he wouldn't risk it, just like that time when they had planned to break into Soldier Field and dance naked on the 50-yard line, and he'd pretended that he'd sprained his ankle, so she and Myra had done it by themselves "like a couple of militant dykes." Gareth lit his joint, inhaled, coughed, and made a face. Michelle told him that he did too many drugs. Gareth told her that she bossed too many people around. *Fine, be that way,* she said, and started running toward the center of the ice, only stopping when she reached the chairs.

There were ten rows of black metal folding chairs, five in each row; in front of them, lit by a fire burning in a trash can, Larry was attacking his drum kit and erstwhile rabbi Jeff Meltzer, former *heh* instructor at K.I.N.S. Hebrew school, dressed in a black overcoat and a black ski cap, was playing an electric guitar plugged into an amp. Larry was singing a cover version of John Lennon's "God," for which he improvised new lyrics—*"Don't believe in Torah; don't believe in Hannah—just believe in me: Rovner! and me."* Upon seeing Michelle, Larry stopped, then leaned into his mike and said that he and the band would take a short break, but they'd be back soon with some surprise guests.

Michelle greeted Meltzer, who, she noted, had shaved off his beard and looked significantly less mature than when she'd last seen him, officiating at her father and Gail's wedding. She asked Larry if he'd finally lost his mind. No, Larry said, stepping down from his drum kit, he'd finally found it. When he'd arrived in Lake Geneva, he'd used the "ungodly sum of Chanukah money" that the Goodmans had given him to purchase a stack of videos, including *The Song Remains the Same, The Last Waltz,* and *Let It Be,* hoping to learn some moves. Robert Plant's outfit had given him some pointers about how to best show off his *pupik,* but the Beatles' movie had given him this idea. He'd been inspired by the rooftop concert scene where the band played an impromptu gig, solely for the love of the music. Just a couple years ago, he said, he would have been crushed if he'd set up fifty chairs for an exclusive, unannounced concert and no one had come. But performing in front of these empty seats had reunited him with his music, reminding him why he'd wanted to be a songwriter.

Jeffrey Meltzer asked Michelle if she'd come with her friend Gareth, then asked Larry if they were taking a break. Larry regarded Meltzer with slight irritation, but consented, saying that Jeff could "take fifteen," but afterward, when Larry started playing his new material, he'd want Meltzer to be right there with some power chords. Meltzer made a longhorn's gesture with his index and little finger and said he could rock all night, man, but he needed to get some hot cider and warm up his hands.

Once Meltzer was gone, Larry asked Michelle to promise him something. They were standing by the fire, warming their hands over it, stamping their feet to try to get some feeling back in their legs. Larry said he knew that Michelle didn't love him, but it would always be difficult for creative people such as themselves to find partners who understood them. Probably a year from now, he would be married to Hannah and living in New York, and Michelle would soon be in Hollywood with Mel. But if that didn't turn out to be the case, one year from today, why didn't they meet back here and get married? Married to whom, Michelle asked. To each other, Larry said. Michelle asked if Larry had been doing 'shrooms with Rabbi Meltzer. Larry told Michelle that she was right—how would either of them know anything in a year? What about two years, he proposed.

Absolutely not, Michelle said. Even if her relationship with Mel ended the grisly way she anticipated but she wanted children anyway, she wouldn't ask Larry for his sperm. But didn't she see, Larry asked—the fact that Michelle could talk that way to him and he didn't take it personally showed how compatible they were. Michelle said that if Larry wasn't taking her remarks personally, he was missing the point. All right, Larry said, what if they just got a place together to "see how it goes." No, Michelle said, no marriage in one or two years, no "living together to see how it goes."

O.K., Larry said, what about this promise. Spring would mark the most critical period of his life: graduation, the backers' audition for *Jazz Singer,* marriage, and then the honeymoon—one week on a cruise ship, one week in Israel, which, Larry said, given that he had "OD'd on Judaism" at Brandeis, was the "last fucking place" he wanted to go now. The one way he could make it through these next six months was to believe that another destiny awaited him. Part of him wanted to show up at that backers' audition, listen to his emasculated songs, then hear the audience shout, "Composer! Composer!" He would jump onstage, bow, then leap off, walk through the aisle to the back of the auditorium, keep walking until he found a cab, say "JFK and step on it," then get on the next plane to L.A. All that he was asking Michelle was not to join him, not to marry him, just to walk off-stage with him, out of the auditorium, into the taxi, see that he got on that plane.

Michelle took Larry's glove in her mitten. Not only would she agree to Larry's proposal, she said, if Larry wanted, she would walk out right during intermission just so she wouldn't have to hear the Hannah Goodman–penned rhyme *"Go to shul, boy / Shul's cool."* No, Larry said, if he found the guts, he would walk out right when it was all over. Then he told Michelle to grab a mike and check her voice level; it was time to rock out for the second set.

Michelle leaned into a mike. "Hello, Lake Geneva," she said, her voice travel-ing the entire circumference of the lake, "Rock on, Wisconsin!" Larry strapped on a guitar and strummed with fingerless gloves as he played "For Those About to *Daven* (We Salute You)," "Instant Torah's (Gonna Get You)," and "Goys in the Attic" before he and Michelle performed an a cappella duet of "Oh My Mordecai," the first song they had ever sung together back in K.I.N.S. Hebrew school, one that had been cut from the Purim musical when Larry's voice had started changing.

That last number was so saccharine that Larry started to launch into his most recent and arguably angriest song ever, *"Shtup* the World (We All Wanna Get Off)," for which he wanted Meltzer to play lead. Except Meltzer was not back yet. Larry asked Michelle how long Meltzer had been gone, and where the hell was that "lazy rabbinical mofo anyway?" He bellowed into his mike—"Rabbi Meltzer, Rabbi Jeffrey Meltzer, please return to the stage area." Come on, Michelle said, leave him alone. No, Larry said. He shouted into the mike again to remind Rabbi Meltzer that he was wanted on the stage. Michelle told Larry to stop being such a dick—Meltzer was probably cold and had gone into the house to defrost. Larry admitted that he was a dick, but observed that being a dick was the only way to accomplish anything.

When Michelle made it back to the house, Meltzer wasn't there. And Gareth was gone too; Michelle saw only a big rump-shaped impression in the snow. She walked through the house, shouting, "Rabbi J! Rabbi J!" then "Wake up, gay boy," but no answer came. Jeff Meltzer's Datsun and Gareth's police cruiser were still parked in front of the house, but their doors were locked. She returned to the stage to see if Jeff and Gareth were there, but all Michelle could see in the flickering glow of the trash can fire were rows of empty chairs, two guitars on stands, the microphones, the drum kit, and Larry crouched in front of his amplifier, turning it all the way up.

Larry suggested that he and Michelle perform another set, but Michelle said it was "beyond bizarre" that Gareth who, to her knowledge, had never exercised in his life would be out taking a nature walk. She suggested that she and Larry split up and "case the area." Larry snorted. Meltzer was always pulling shit like this, he said. Ever since his wife had left him, Jeff would call and leave rambling, self-pitying messages, or he'd get Hannah on the phone, and the two of them would talk for hours. If Jeff was off on some "crying jag," Larry wouldn't beg him to come back; he'd play the last set solo. He wiped the ice crystals off the chair behind his drum kit, took a pair of sticks out of his back pocket, sat down, and pumped the bass drum. Michelle went off in search of Gareth.

As Michelle slid across the smooth, dark ice, she imagined herself starring in a movie version of a Jack London book, searching for her lost sled dog, Gareth. She pictured lumbering yetis dragging Gareth's and Jeff Meltzer's bodies to igloos, pictured herself luring the abominable snowpeople back to the trash can fire, where they would surely melt. She imagined Gareth, lying frozen, snow swirling over him, then collecting on his cheeks and his beard until there was nothing more than an impression of his body beneath the layer of white, like someone lying underneath a white sheet, like her mother when she had seen her for the last time in 1976 in the apartment on Fairfield Avenue.

Michelle always had an hour between her last period of grade school at Boone and evening prayers at Hebrew school, a time during which she would start her homework while watching the 3:30 movie on Channel 7, usually a Neil Simon comedy. But when she arrived home that day, an ambulance was double-parked outside, its back doors open, motor running, nobody inside but the driver listening to John Cody on WBBM talking about tall ships arriving at Navy Pier for the Bicentennial. The front door to the apartment building was propped open with a full trash can; out front, two paramedics were smoking cigarettes. She ran past them, up the stairs, two steps at a time, and when she reached the third floor, the doors were open to both her apartment and Mrs. Vaysberg's next door. Mrs.

Vaysberg was standing in the hallway. This was bizarre—the only glimpses Michelle usually caught of the woman were of eyes peeping through a slim space in the doorway, followed by a slam and the sound of locks being turned. Now her door was wide open, there were silver candleholders on her dining room table; she asked Michelle if she wanted some Boston cream pie from her bakery.

Michelle said no, she wanted to know why an ambulance was outside. Yes, Mrs. Vaysberg said, but "Mr. Wasserstrom" had told her to invite Michelle in for pie. Michelle burst into her own apartment, where Rabbi Mortimer Shmulevits was conferring with Charlie Wasserstrom, who was pale, whiter than the short-sleeved oxford through which he was sweating; he shut the door to his and Becky's bedroom. And when Michelle asked why she couldn't go in, he yelled at her for the first and only time in her life, tears racing down his cheeks as he told her not to question him, he was her father, damn it, and didn't Mrs. Vaysberg tell her to eat cream pie with her.

But in the split second before Charlie shut the bedroom door, Michelle saw the white sheet on the bed, the impression of a body underneath. She walked dutifully across the hall to Mrs. Vaysberg's apartment. Once Mrs. Vaysberg had cut a slice of pie and placed it on a Mary Poppins "Happy Birthday" plate, Michelle thanked her and sat on the radiator by the window, eating tiny morsels until she saw Jill walking home from Boone, at which point Michelle, plate in hand, tore downstairs and outside where the paramedics were still smoking. Jill was already gone—she had seen the ambulance and had run as fast as she could south, then east for the lake, so Michelle asked the paramedics if they wanted to finish the pie. And while they ate, they asked her whether she was the girl from upstairs. No, she told them, that girl, Michelle, was at Hebrew school; her name was Henrietta and she was the daughter of the British ambassador and she would soon be moving to Peking. She maintained this fiction, speaking in an English accent, even as the stretcher was carried downstairs, even as her father told her that she could stay home from Hebrew school if she wanted; she had already been Bat Mitzvahed and her attendance was no longer mandatory anyway. But Michelle, who had no desire to stay home, no desire to be inside anyone's home ever again, said, "No, Father," his offer was "quite kind," but she was "chuffed up" about attending Hebrew school, and besides, she was late for the blessing over high tea. She thanked the paramedics for sharing her cake, then strolled north toward K.I.N.S.

As Michelle now walked across Lake Geneva, she passed snow-covered boat landings, squinted into the frosted back windows of mansions. She kept calling Gareth's name, but all she could hear in response was her own voice echoing back to her underneath the insistent beats of Larry's drums, the drums that were resounding with such force that, even if Gareth's flabby frame were buried in an ice floe, his lips so frozen that he could barely speak above a whisper, Michelle would not be able to hear him. She ran back toward the trashcan and the source of all that noise.

While performing the greatest drum solo of his life, Larry could not keep his eyes off of his hands and his drumsticks as they moved in the orange glow of the flames. It seemed as if the hands belonged to another person altogether, moving in slow motion, and, at the same time, faster than humanly possible. The echoes sounded like a second drummer out there in the wilderness, answering every beat with a resounding yes, yes, this was good. With his right foot still thumping the bass drum, Larry leaned over and reached for a guitar. But the moment his fingers had formed a chord, the night was shattered with the sound of one raucous, contemptuous laugh, and, instantly, Larry recognized the laughter of Jeff Meltzer, Rabbi Jeff Meltzer, who had single-handedly sabotaged the success of Rovner!'s debut album by writing down every note of his guitar solo on the flyleaf of a *Machzor* and consulting it every two seconds; Rabbi Jeff Meltzer, who wasn't really even a rabbi anymore, thus destroying the only stageworthy gimmick he had. Larry kicked over his cymbal assembly, leapt down from his seat, and ran for the woods, song titles like "The Rabbi Done Died" darting in and out of his mind; he was too possessed by the desire to kick Meltzer's ass to notice the hand reaching out to grab his sleeve, causing him to spin and fall onto the ice, after which Michelle stood over him and quietly posed the question, "Walk much?"

Moments before Larry fell, Michelle had finally spotted Gareth. He was standing in a clearing, his arms around Jeffrey Meltzer. Michelle had made as if to shout something snide, but stopped and watched Meltzer leaning in to kiss Gareth, heard the sound of their coats rubbing against each other. She tried to picture herself in such a pose with Mel, but couldn't.

That was fucking sick, Larry said when Michelle pointed the two men out to him. "Cheese it, Torah Boy," Michelle said. Why was it sick, she wanted to know; this was the eighties, studies had shown that ten percent of the population and forty percent of the military happened to be "ho-mo-sex-shoo-ull," and gays were no different from anyone else leaving aside what Larry thought was written in the *Chumash:* "Thou shalt not covet someone of the same sex because it's 'fucking sick.'" Larry said he didn't care about that. As long as there were gay men, that meant there were more women to go around for everyone else, he hypothesized. The sick thing was that someone would give up everything just for the sake of a cheap feel. He started running back to his drum kit, the guitars, and the fire as Michelle watched Gareth and Jeff kiss, wondering why—when she had always been the one who had never had any trouble getting dates, when she was the one who had had to fend off phone calls from dozens of unsuitable suitors, when she was the one who could have sex with whomever she pleased—she was practically the only person she knew who was alone.

And at this precise moment, as Gareth and Jeffrey embraced in the woods, as Larry ran back toward his instruments, as Michelle continued watching, wondering why the hell Gareth was getting more action than she was, there was a crack, a bang, and a *kersploosh,* and Larry yelled, "Fuck me." That "fuck me" echoed back to him as he watched the trash can fire melt the ice of his makeshift Lake Geneva stage. The guitars and amplifiers sparked and the ice beneath them gave way. The instruments, the equipment, and the folding chairs sank below the surface of Lake Geneva until nothing was left save for two guitar necks, a cymbal, a trash can, and the half-moons of chair backs bobbing gently on the surface of the water until they too sank into the all-encompassing blackness.

Larry, standing on a firm patch of ice a good distance away from the wreckage, gaped at the black hole; an aching cold savaged his thighs and his ankles. He couldn't believe it, he kept saying as Michelle, hands in the pockets of her parka, walked back toward him. This was symbolic of life, Larry opined—performing a concert for an invisible audience, and *Hashem* wouldn't even allow you an encore.

On the final day of the *Godfathers* shoot, Deirdre Wills was seated at a table in the visiting area of the Joliet Correctional Center, observing a surprisingly animated discussion between Tiny Cubbins and Carl Slappit Silverman. It was the third time that Carl had driven Deirdre to Joliet in the past three weeks, but only the first time that he had accompanied her inside. For Deirdre's two previous visits, Carl had dropped her off in the prison parking lot, then drove down the road to White Fence Farm, where he attempted to balance his checkbook and consumed corn fritters and three-bean salad. Deirdre would meet Cubbins in the visiting area—she'd hand him a book and ask him if he had read the one she'd brought the previous week. No matter what the book— Deirdre usually gave him some of her favorites: *An Outcast of the Islands, Murder in the Cathedral*—Cubbins would only say, "I read that book you gave me," hand it back to her, take the new one, and say nothing else about it.

Cubbins was serving a twenty-year sentence for possession, racketeering, and attempted armed robbery. It was said that, even in jail, he kept a stranglehold on the south side heroin business through emissaries to whom he'd issue orders via coded telephone conversations. Deirdre had never felt at ease during their conversations, but she visited him nonetheless—when she'd started teaching at Marshall High, she had hoped to return the favor of all the time Muley had spent in his childhood trying to cheer her, but now that Muley worked late virtually every evening at Angel Guardian, she sought out the people who seemed to need her most: her students, Carl Silverman, Tiny Cubbins.

Deirdre's car was running smoothly and she had no great need for Carl's chauffeuring services, but since Mel spent his days on the set and his nights at his own apartment, she appreciated Carl's company. And though Carl's discussion of his growing interest in neo-Buddhism did not move her—she had not set foot in a church since she was fifteen—they amused her nonetheless, particularly when he favorably compared the new sect he had discovered to the Jewish tradition in which he had been raised.

On the ride to Joliet, Carl had told Deirdre that he had never really had much appreciation for religion except as a show. He enjoyed clapping his hands at gospel churches, observing the antics of faith-healing evangelists, but to his tastes, Judaism was far too somber and subdued—the colors were too dull: too much black and white, too many dark suits, too many black beards. He didn't enjoy the Torah as a work of literature: too much repetition, too many names. Though he wasn't sure that chanting *nam myoho renge kyo* would bring the world any closer to peace or get Lennie Kidd the red Jaguar XKE for which he was chanting, he did find the show immensely entertaining, loved the smell of incense and the intricately designed prayer mats and scrolls, loved the way the faithful addressed each other with military titles—"What did you chant for today, Corporal?"—and above all, he loved the chanting: hundreds of people filling the rec room of the Chippewa Park Fieldhouse with a muttering, mumbling, buzzing sound that brought locusts to mind. He wondered, he proposed to

Deirdre, what would happen if someone could introduce a meditative yet goal-oriented religion to the prison system. Maybe, he said, Deirdre could give Tiny Cubbins some neo-Buddhist literature and he could convert his fellow prisoners. Deirdre told Carl that if he was so interested in getting prisoners to chant, he was welcome to try it himself.

Walking through the metal detector, then up the stairs of the main prison building, Carl felt at home—among his people. When he saw the men in their orange jumpsuits or their prison blues, he saw his brothers. If he hadn't discovered music, he could have wound up here, he thought, doing hard time for dealing dope, even though he'd never actually touched the stuff. As he walked with Deirdre to a circular table in the cafeteria where Cubbins was seated alone, he greeted prisoners as if he were a celebrity musician or athlete from the 'hood who'd been hired to motivate his brothers to stay straight. "Right on, right on," he kept saying as he flashed peace signs. He gave a soul shake to Cubbins, asked him how much of his sentence he had left to serve, whether he was being treated well.

With Tiny, Deirdre usually did all of the talking—when she was done summarizing the books she had given to him, she would discuss the progress of her writing students, and when that failed to interest him, she would discuss her own fiction that she submitted to children's magazines, using the anagram Drew Sillreid as her pseudonym, stories that reimagined fairy tales with new, grim endings: sleeping beauties who didn't wake up, princes who never found their Cinderellas and married her evil stepsisters instead—stories that magazine editors always found too disturbing to publish. Tiny would grunt or nod, unable, it seemed, to find any way in which Deirdre could be of use to him. With Carl, the conversation was more convivial. There were throaty chuckles, enthusiastic handshakes. Tiny paid scant attention to the book that Deirdre had brought him—*Great Expectations*. Deirdre had thought that Tiny might learn something from the story of a convict, a "mere varmint," who becomes a young man's benefactor, but Tiny only seemed interested in Carl's soliloquies about great thinkers who had found themselves behind prison bars: Jack Henry Abbott, for example.

When their time was nearly up, Carl finally asked Tiny if he'd heard of *nam myoho renge kyo*. He took some crumpled pamphlets out of a pocket and placed them on the table. Tiny laughed and asked if this was some kind of religious bullshit. Carl said that he too had been suspicious, but chanting really focused your thoughts on something larger than yourself, and that's what everyone needed.

Carl had his business; Deirdre had her students and her son. That's what made you human, Carl said—the ability to see beyond yourself.

Tiny blinked once; he appeared surprised for the first time. He looked over to Deirdre. "You never said you had a son," he said. Well, sure she did, Carl said, Deirdre was mother to one of the sharpest brothers in the public school system. Carl proceeded to enumerate Muley's accomplishments, omitting the fact that he was the boy's father. He mentioned Muley's stint as a youth correspondent on NPR, his floor hockey skill, his plans to apply to art and design schools. Deirdre, who had had no idea that Muley would be applying to art school instead of a liberal arts college, asked Carl how he knew so much. Carl said that word got around.

Cubbins smiled at Deirdre, adding that a son was the one "worldly possession" he still wanted but hadn't gotten yet. He hadn't liked how harshly his father had treated him, how leniently he had treated his brother, and if he wasn't behind bars, he said, he would have a son and try to raise him right. Carl said that Tiny should consider chanting for a son, or perhaps for Governor Thompson to commute his sentence—if he demonstrated he'd converted to a new religion, maybe he could win his freedom earlier. Carl had been planning a major fall premiere for *Godfathers of Soul,* and now he wondered whether it could be more than that; why not a benefit screening for the Tiny Cubbins Legal Defense Fund, a not-for-profit whose proceeds could go toward securing Cubbins a new trial? Carl raised his hand. "Can I get some skin for that, my brother?" he asked Tiny. He didn't notice that Deirdre had stood up and was already waiting at the door. Tiny nodded, then shook Carl's hand, took the copy of *Great Expectations* that Deirdre had brought, and told Carl that he had to make a few phone calls.

All through the drive home, Carl continued to plot his benefit premiere. Deirdre said that Tiny didn't seem interested ("Them cats, they don't wanna get their hopes up," Carl countered), and that Tiny's innocence wasn't really in question. Carl said that guilt or innocence didn't matter much to the movement. Deirdre asked to what movement he was referring. Carl said that she had identified the precise problem; he didn't like the idea of Muley growing up in a society that didn't know what "the movement" meant. With the slate gray landscape of I-55 blurring past her window, Deirdre asked Carl why he was suddenly so interested in Muley. On the one hand, she still distrusted Carl; on the other, she believed that people could change their circumstances—if she hadn't been able to change, she would still be living above a Laundromat on Devon, addicted to sweets, blaming Carl and herself for her plight; if she didn't believe that people could change, there would have been no point to visiting Tiny in Joliet.

"There's lotsa jive y'all don't know about me," Carl said. "This brother's a changed man." He said that his schedule was wide open for the next month; he'd be happy to drive Deirdre to Joliet whenever she wanted. But Deirdre suggested that he go alone next time.

"He needs you more than me," she said.

Bright lights were on in Muley's bedroom when Deirdre arrived home. She had invited Carl inside, but Carl said that he couldn't accept her invitation if Muley wasn't inviting him too. Deirdre said that Muley didn't ask her to approve his guests. Even so, Carl said, he didn't feel "righteous"—he understood Muley's position; Muley was well within his rights to never forgive him for leaving Chicago.

Muley was holding the stop-action clicker of a movie camera pointed down toward a scale model of a space shuttle when Deirdre entered his bedroom. Deirdre asked what he was doing and when Muley said that he was experimenting with a film project, she asked him if this was the sort of project he would need to submit with his art school applications. She expected Muley to say something evasive, to deny the fact that he was ignoring her advice. Instead, he said no, he'd already sent in his applications. He began to adjust a spotlight that he'd trained on the shuttle. Muley's response was so insubordinate and dismissive of her wishes but at the same time so self-confident that rather than angering Deirdre, it made her less sure of herself. She thought of how difficult it was for her to write a good sentence, how many rejection slips she'd received from *Highlights* and *Cricket* magazines, and then she looked at Muley, watched him gaze through the viewfinder of his camera, thought of how much she'd needed him, how little he seemed to need her now. Deirdre asked Muley if he knew how she'd learned of his plans. Muley said he presumed that she'd heard the news from Mel, and when she shook her head, he said that perhaps Mel had been talking to "Slappit." Deirdre said that Muley had a father and his name was not "Slappit." She asked Muley why he couldn't forgive Carl when she herself had done so.

"Because that's your life, Ma, not mine," Muley said. He turned off his spotlight and gathered the camera and the shuttle, then placed them in a black canvas bag.

Deirdre was about to counter Muley's statement, but stopped. For what Muley said, though hurtful, was also accurate. This time next year, Muley would be gone—at a university or an art school; the decision would ultimately be his, just as all other decisions would be. Having started teaching full-time only two years earlier, Deirdre had had the sense that her life was just beginning, but now she saw that another part of it was nearly over. As Muley zipped up his bag and said that he'd be at Angel Guardian until late again, Deirdre immediately felt within the pit of her stomach her apartment growing larger and emptier, the walls and her son seeming to move away from her. When she heard the front door shut behind Muley, she took a breath, then walked into her dining room with a pen and a notebook. The first words she wrote were *In an empty house.*

As Deirdre wrote, Carl was driving south on Lake Shore Drive, the black, silver-tipped waves of Lake Michigan more than a foot high as he neared Cermak, a vision of Deirdre dancing just in front of his windshield, the words *nam myoho renge kyo* buzzing through his brain. When he pulled up in front of Bronzeville Studios, he saw a delivery truck parked in a loading zone. Two men were unloading tables and trays of appetizers for the wrap party. Carl had expected to see the cast and crew already milling about, but the only person inside the building was Mel; he was chewing on a cigar. Carl asked how the final scene with Michelle had gone. "It's done," Mel said. He added nothing more.

That morning, Michelle had arrived at Bronzeville shortly after her eight o'clock call, but she doubted that anyone would notice: the first few hours on the set always consisted of her studying lines, getting into makeup and costume, then sitting on her ass, reading, and occasionally leaving long messages on Gareth's answering machine, which usually began with Michelle singing, *"I'm booooored, so fucking boooored,"* or grunting, "Tell Rabbi Meltzer to roll over and hand you the phone." But at 8:15, the cast was not there and neither was the crew.

Michelle had not given much more than a passing thought to the fact that the last scene on the shooting schedule—Scene 28A—was one in which Tiny Walker watched her while she sang in the shower. She had even found amusing and titillating, if somewhat pathetic, the possibility that Mel had added the scene after he had cast her. She had the sense that almost every actress's first film role was as a hooker, a stripper, a murder victim in a Brian De Palma film, or a Woody

Allen girlfriend. The idea of doing an R-rated film that featured lurid violence but was prissy about nudity didn't make sense; if you were going to say that some chick had seduced Al Capone and caused his downfall, you damn well better show the audience what the fuss was about. Her only trepidation had been what her father might say—she would have to endure not only his terrified visage at the premiere, but also the column he'd write ("It was at *Godfathers of Soul* that I realized my little girl had become a woman . . ."). She had decided to assure Charlie that the nude scene had been performed by a stunt double.

Once she had put on her maroon kimono, which had gotten fairly rank four weeks into the shoot, and applied her blush and eyeliner, she sat alone in the dressing room with a foot up on the makeup table, rereading *Politics and the Law* for a class she'd be taking the follow semester; Mel, dressed in a pale yellow suit and spats, entered and asked Michelle why she was late. Michelle, not bothering to tie her kimono, just letting it hang down in a manner more lazy than provocative, advised Mel to have this conversation with the cast and crew members who hadn't arrived yet. Mel said actually, no one else was due back before the wrap party; he thought she'd be more comfortable shooting the final scene privately. Michelle suddenly got a good glimpse of Mel; he looked clean-shaven and suave in his suit. Michelle said she knew that this was Mel's first film, but the casting couch was generally used before the first day of filming, not on the last—it was bad strategy.

"Just a word to the wise," Michelle added, but this was a bit much for Mel this early in the morning. He excused himself, saying that he had to put the finishing touches on his set. "Put the finishing touches on your what?" Michelle asked, but he was already out of the room. Michelle couldn't decide whether she found Mel's apparent discomfort with her sexually charged speech adorably modest or irritatingly prudish. She had grown weary of men who, at first, thought that they had stumbled upon a soul mate when they had found a young woman who cursed like a sailor, only to realize, weeks or months later, that they really wanted a meek, virginal lass sufficiently ashamed of sex so that she would over-look their sexual inadequacies.

For one of the first times in her life, Michelle was worried about being hurt—sure, people had hurt her during the first twenty years of her life. She had felt tears coming when acting instructor Geoffrey Woshner pointed out that her Cockney accent sounded Bavarian, had to swallow hard when a letter from Yale had informed her that many other qualified applicants had also been rejected because they hadn't gone down on the dean of students or proved their blood relationship to Yale cofounder Arthur T. Dongpuller III. But she didn't cry about guys. If she ever liked one too much, she would either bone him early to destroy his mystique (Exhibit A: erstwhile Mather sophomore Eddie Pinkstaff), or avoid him at all costs (Exhibit B: K.I.N.S. and U of I student Avi Sherman), which was why she'd spent most of her time with guys who amused but didn't challenge her (Exhibit C: Lawrence Elliot Rovner).

In his final production meeting, Mel had said that he only wanted the smallest possible crew on hand for Scene 28A. Ron Claxton said that they could "probably get away with a crew of three," if Mel was willing to "pick up the slack." Mel promptly fired Claxton for challenging his authority and said that he'd light and shoot the damn scene himself, thank you very little. Mel had already adjusted Jasmine Huggins's bathroom set twice before Michelle had arrived. Nevertheless, he once again checked his light levels, then studied his shooting script; he changed an *isn't* to an *ain't,* then back again.

Shortly after casting Michelle, Mel had considered removing the nude scene since it would assure him of an R rating, thus limiting his film's marketability. But then, every Saturday, he had religiously watched critics Roger Ebert and Gene Siskel on *Sneak Previews,* and it seemed to Mel that the critics rarely agreed on films, save for ones that prominently featured swearing and tits. Movies with swearing and tits always got two thumbs up and were described with adjectives such as *gritty, authentic,* and *uncompromising.* In Siskel and Ebert's print reviews, swearing-and-tits movies always got three and a half stars.

Mel himself didn't particularly enjoy nude scenes in movies. Whenever he saw one, he felt the indelible presence of his deacon father seated beside him, not admonishing him for watching filth, rather elbowing him in the ribs and narrating the action, as he had during Mel's brother-in-law James Carruthers's bachelor party, which Mel counted as one of the worst nights of his life. Carruthers's buddies from his firehouse had hired two limousines and ridden downtown to Jimmy Wong's. Then, drunk on mai tais, they headed north, and, even though Mel was only fourteen, he wasn't carded when they attended a stag film at the Rialto.

Once the movie was over, the party had spent nearly an hour in the adjacent "book and novelty store." Mel had never been able to erase one particular image from his brain—his father in a black suit and overcoat, turning to a wall of girlie magazines and greeting them with a playful wave of his fingers. "Hiya, ladies," Deacon Coleman had said. Mel had returned to the limo and chatted with the driver until the bachelor party returned, whereupon James Carruthers mocked Mel until they arrived at the Essex Inn, where a stripper was waiting.

The experience might have turned Mel off sex forever but for an incident later that evening at the Essex. A supercilious bouncer with the word *Tiny* tattooed on the knuckles of his left hand was positioned outside the hotel suite while a woman who called herself Sunshine danced to Drifters songs playing on a portable radio tuned to WVON and deejay Herb "The Cool Gent" Kent. As Sunshine danced, Deacon Coleman kept waving his wallet, pulling out bills, and asking her how much money it would cost for him to "get a taste." At the end of Sunshine's half hour, Deacon Coleman once again asked her how much "a taste" would cost. Sunshine collected her tips, put on her skirt, her blouse, and her heels, then gave Mel's father a long, nauseated stare. "You'll never taste nothing, you fat, dirty, ugly old man," she said.

James Carruthers laughed loudly at this, and after one shocked moment, Deacon Coleman laughed as well. And down the hall, Mel could hear Sunshine's bouncer laughing too. But Mel hadn't laughed, and at that moment, he resolved never to be a "fat, dirty, ugly old man." One month later, he lost his virginity to Lavonne Curtis, whom he'd met at a track meet. By the time that he entered Roosevelt, he had already notched five sexual partners and declared himself "an ace." Now he no longer felt the same need for validation, but he still did feel some satisfaction at the idea that Michelle, fifteen years his junior, might not consider him a "fat, dirty, ugly old man."

Michelle arrived on the set wearing navy blue tennis shoes and a fake shearling coat over her kimono. Mel took her by the shoulder and led her through the scene. She was to enter the bathroom, disgustedly throw off her kimono, step into the tub, turn on the water, then sing *"I'm gonna wash Al Capone right out of my hair."* Mel said that Vance Coffey had already performed his reaction shots, so they only needed to shoot her today.

This was going better than expected, Mel thought. They were both professionals. If the rest of the cast had been this businesslike about their clothed scenes, he would feel that much more confident about this film's prospects. Michelle's dutiful and conscientious approach was refreshing. She always hit her marks, always got what you asked for in the first take. He needn't have fretted about this scene. They'd be done in a half hour, and it would be one of the best scenes in the film. Mel saw himself as a demanding yet inspiring director, one who did not blush at nudity. He began to tell Michelle that he was ready, but instead, as Michelle started to undo the knot of her sash, he told her that if she didn't want to do the scene, she didn't have to.

"What the hell?" Michelle asked. Her face flushed. She hoped that he was joking.

Mel said that the scene was important for the film, but if she felt uncomfortable doing it, they could work around it. Michelle's jaw dropped. She stared at him blankly as if he were some sort of pervert. Her nostrils twitched. Whenever she felt nervous, she relied on anger to overcome it. He'd been avoiding her during the shoot, and now that they were alone, he was turning into some lascivious prude. She said that Mel was right—she didn't feel comfortable doing this scene and, in fact, she would only be comfortable if the cameraman was buck naked. Come to think of it, she said, she would only be comfortable if the entire cast and crew returned to the set buck naked too. Mel told Michelle that there was no need to be a smart-ass; he was trying to put her at ease. Oh, Michelle said, that's why he had given the whole cast and crew the day off—so she would be at ease, not so he could get a "private little nudie show"? She told him to just get back behind the camera, they'd shoot the fucking scene, then he could put it in the movie, jerk off to it, or do whatever the hell else he wanted. She dropped her kimono and walked stark naked toward the bathtub. "Are you ready, Hitchcock?" she asked.

Mel, his cheeks and earlobes aflame, his heart beating fast, didn't look at Michelle's body—he had a close-up lens on the camera and, through it, all he could see was Michelle's face and, after her little tirade, he had half a mind to just let her stand there, cold and naked. You didn't talk to a director like that. More important, you didn't talk to *him* like that. All he had done was to try to act the part of a gentleman. But apparently she wasn't that kind of chick; she didn't want a gentleman. Fine, he thought. He'd film Michelle naked, but he'd never sleep with her, didn't even want to, he told himself as he felt himself getting hard, then felt guilty about getting hard, guilty for filming this scene at all. And though he didn't have an inch of fat on him, though he was only thirty-six years old, he felt a little like a fat, dirty, ugly old man.

"I'm ready for my close-up, Mr. DeMille," Michelle hissed. She wondered if Mel truly thought that he was being a gentleman by offering to eighty-six the nude scene. It was always stunning to her how misinformed people were about themselves, how they were usually coolest at their most clueless hours, sexiest at their ugliest, most perverted at their purest. She liked the Mel Coleman who joked with her, who laughed with her during bad movies and in Chinese restaurants; Mel Coleman the overcompensating film director who ignored her on the movie set, who pretended to be slick when he was uncomfortable, was just a gigantic pain in her ass. She wondered, as Mel adjusted his focus, if he knew that the least sexy thing in the universe was a guy who didn't know what he wanted. She didn't like asking or being asked; she liked telling or being told. In *heh,* Arik Levine had had a crush on her, a crush so obvious that he was the only one who didn't know that everyone else knew. Finally, he had acquired the nerve to ask her to study with him at the Nortown Library. And, because she was bored or because she was a masochist or because she was curious or because of a combination of all three of these reasons, a condition that she called "Robitussin"—a cough syrup brand that offered an expectorant, a cough suppressant, a decongestant, or a *combination of all three*—she had consented. They had sat at a rear table, and while she crapped out a book report about Mesopotamia, he spent two hours staring at the same page in *The Martian Chronicles,* occasionally stealing glances at her.

After Arik walked her home, he lingered on her doorstep. Michelle asked if he wanted to kiss her. Arik blushed and stammered out a yes. Then Michelle asked how long he had known that he wanted to. For about six months, Arik said. Michelle asked if he knew when she would have said yes. Arik said no. Six fricking months ago, loverboy, Michelle said. She had never liked how Larry Rovner stared at her greedily, like a yarmulke-clad big bad wolf with a big red tongue lolling out of his mouth. But at least his intentions were clear. This "Yes, do the nude scene," "No, don't do the nude scene" *mishigoss* was painful, all the more so because she actually liked Mel, even thought that she was in love with him, and the possibility that he might not be different from a dozen other mopes she'd dated was devastating. Now she was angry with herself for wasting precious hours thinking about Mel. But mostly she was angry with Mel for being so much less than the man that she had created in her mind; she was angry with him for being uptight, angry with herself for not seeing it earlier, angry with him for making her fall in love, angry with herself for ever falling in love at all, angry that Mel had made her shoot this nudie scene, angry that he had the close-up lens on the camera, which meant that he probably couldn't see anything below her neck.

Christ, was that the *close-up lens,* Michelle asked. Never mind what lens it was, Mel said. But, Michelle said, the way that he had set up the shot, he'd be just as well off filming the whole fricking thing with her in a kimono. Mel said that he was starting with a close shot, moving to a medium, then a wide. All right, Michelle said, but he'd better get a full-body shot if he wanted his movie to get three and a half stars; only movies with swearing and tits got three and a half stars. Mel stared at her, silent for a moment. Yeah, he said, as if he had awoken from a dream to find a great truth revealed, why was that, why did they always get three and a half stars? Michelle said that it was one of the divine laws governing cinema—not only did they get three and a half stars, their reviews were always accompanied by adjectives such as *gritty* and *uncompromising*. Man, Mel said, it was like he was talking to himself.

They sat together on the edge of the bathtub, him in his yellow suit, Michelle with her kimono back on, discussing movies and critics and acting and college, and once again it seemed to Mel that he could discuss anything with her. With Deirdre, every conversation felt like cramming for a test, one he felt proud and lucky to pass; he sensed that if he wasn't discussing *To the Lighthouse* or Hans Robert Jauss, Deirdre didn't feel that his opinions were worth consideration. He asked Michelle if he could have one of her cigarettes. And after she laughed at the way he smoked and told him that you weren't supposed to gum the damn thing, Mel told her that he was sorry that he had made such a big deal about the scene. Michelle told Mel that the one thing worse than someone who wasn't clear about his intentions was someone who apologized for his behavior; the apology was far less telling than the action for which one had to apologize. Yeah, Mel said—he turned philosophical now—that was his problem with religion, the idea that you could apologize and be absolved for what you'd done. That's the one thing Michelle liked about Judaism, she said—there was no talk of absolution or redemption, no afterlife as far as she remembered from Hebrew school; good deeds were performed for their own sake. Mel said that Judaism sounded all right to him, except if there wasn't some payoff, if this was all there was, life would be too depressing; his theory was that the universe was cyclical; it kept forming and re-forming, and everything you did you would get a chance to redo throughout eternity—the only question being whether you would always make the same decisions or whether you could try something different to see if you could get it right. Michelle asked Mel what he would do right now if he knew he could try it over again. Mel said that there was no limit to the sorts of things he might try.

He had thirty seconds to kiss her right now. She knew that he wanted to kiss her, knew the look that guys got when they wanted to kiss her, recognized that clear, filmy layer that interposed itself over their eyes. And she knew that feeling she got when she wanted to kiss somebody—that eager bounce in her knees and her thighs, that feeling that her neck was made of rubber. Mel was thinking of a previous life he may or may not have had, a moment when he may or may not have sat next to Michelle on the edge of a pale yellow porcelain bathtub on the set of *Godfathers of Soul,* his mind an infinite flowchart of actions and outcomes, of words he would or would not utter, of roles he would or would not play. He thought of a life in which he did or didn't kiss Michelle, in which she did or didn't reciprocate, in which he did or didn't tell Deirdre, in which Deirdre did or didn't care. He moved in toward her, but by then, the thirty seconds were up. Michelle stood and asked whether they would shoot this scene or not—it was cold as shit in here and she was losing sensation in her toes. Yeah, Mel said, O.K., why didn't he throw up the wide lens and they'd shoot the fucker.

The nude scene was shot from a wide, a medium, and a close angle, and each was completed in one take, which meant that they were through. There was no more script; it was all improvisation now. After Michelle changed back into her sweater and jeans, she sat with Mel on Jasmine Huggins's bed. Mel now thought of how young Michelle would still be when he was forty, thought of how old he would be when Michelle was thirty—strange, he thought, to feel old when he had always been the youngest: the youngest of four in the Coleman family, the youngest in his class at Roosevelt.

Michelle thought of how old Mel would be when she was thirty, thought of how he was one of those men who would only grow more handsome with age, imagined him becoming a virile, older man secure in the knowledge that she had no interest in the prepubescent fumblings of her male Hollywood costars.

"Shit," Mel said and shook his head.

"What?" asked Michelle.

"I don't know if I should say this shit, but I think I'm in love with you," he said.

Michelle began to feel a certain panic taking hold, a sense that she was in danger of losing control. Mel looked to Michelle, tried to catch her eye, then turned away. He had the uncomfortable sensation that he was ceding his fate to her. He had spent the better part of his twenties telling any woman he dated that he loved her, the first part of his thirties avoiding saying it at all. Michelle, for her part, had said "I love you" plenty of times, but never to anyone with whom she was in love—she said it to her father and her sisters; she said it to the dog. She said it to Gareth, but only because it made him squirm; she had said it to Larry, but only because she was joking.

"I think I'm in love with you too, Melvin," she said, then added, "but really, when it comes down to it, so what?"

Mel stared at her. What did she mean *so what,* he asked. So what was he going to do about it, she asked. Being in love and saying all kinds of lovey-dovey shit was an amusing way to spend one's morning, but come the following day, she'd be in New York, and he'd still have a girlfriend. Mel asked if she wanted wedding rings and prenuptial agreements and shit like that. No, Michelle said, not shit like that. Mel stroked her hair and leaned in to kiss her, but she swatted his hand away. Not shit like that either, she said.

And even though at that moment, Michelle wanted nothing more than to feel Mel's lips against hers, his hands on her legs and her tits, wanted, to be quite honest if she were forced to pass a lie-detector test on the topic, to feel his warm cock against her thigh, a finger upon her clitoris, she resisted. As she looked at Mel, it was almost as if she could see two of him—the man he was, the one he wanted to be; she was in love with the former, but he wanted her to love the latter.

Here's what she was saying, she said. He had to decide what he wanted, because she had no clue and she was getting nauseated trying to figure it out. Was he looking for a committed long-distance relationship, some saucy bit on the side, a sordid one-night stand, or some weird-ass platonic relationship based on delayed gratification? Only when he had decided, when his intentions were absolutely crystal fucking clear, should he find her. But until then, she wouldn't listen to any more "love" shit.

And then, because it seemed like the absolute wrong thing to do at the absolute wrong time, after she had zipped up her coat and put on her gloves, she put her lips to his, smelled the faint scent of his nasty-ass aftershave mingling with traces of her perfume. She looked into his eyes, felt an almost magnetic pull, wondered for a moment if she should say to hell with everything she had just said. But then he blinked, and in that split second she found the strength to walk quickly for the door. When she was outside, she started running, scampering all the way to the Cermak station, where she boarded a waiting train.

That night in the Bronzeville lobby, Carl Silverman approached Mel and told him that he had spent his day in Joliet, where he had had a "good, long rap" with "brother Tiny Cubbins." He said that he would be incorporating the Tiny Cubbins Legal Defense Fund, for which the *Godfathers* premiere would function as a benefit. Carl said he wanted to be sure that this wasn't just another movie; if it was to really capture the imagination of brothers and sisters in the 'hood, it would have to be somewhat revolutionary, somewhat dangerous to the honky establishment.

It was the wrong time to engage Mel in any discussion. He had spent his past hours alone, dismantling sets and brooding about his conversation with Michelle, making decisions, then changing his mind and making other ones. He proceeded to tell Carl exactly where he could shove his Cubbins defense fund. Why the hell would he want his picture to appear "dangerous" to the "honky establishment?" he asked. They needed the honky establishment to distribute this picture. No honky gave a shit about Tiny Cubbins, no brother either. They'd be better off incorporating a nonprofit dedicated to keeping Cubbins's sorry ass in jail. He pushed open the front door and marched out into the frigid Chicago night.

The streets were empty as Mel walked south down Michigan Avenue, all the way from Cermak to 63rd Street. The flivvers and the Model Ts were already gone, returned to the vintage car leasing company. The façades for the Domino Club and the Two Gents had been taken down as well, along with the rest of this Potemkin Bronzeville. What remained were housing projects, liquor stores, rusted cars. Mel didn't come from here; he came from Evanston—and though some of the blocks around the high school and his father's church could get a little rough, if you were observant, fast, and unassuming, you could keep out of trouble. Here, the farther south you walked, the bleaker it seemed. West was even worse. West was Bridgeport and the heart of the white Chicago Democrat machine. He thought about Klan rallies farther south in Marquette Park, recalled the anger in the faces of the white protesters who had lined the streets when Harold Washington had campaigned, the posters they carried—EPTON: BEFORE IT'S TOO LATE. Nothing changed in this city, he thought, the same hatreds were still here, the same boundaries. Sure, he could fool himself, make believe that he was out to change society or some shit like that, but the best you could hope for was to change your own circumstance.

As he stood on an overpass looking down on Lake Shore Drive, Mel watched the world pass below and beyond him as in a dream. He was fairly certain that he was in love with Michelle. If Michelle did not attend the wrap party tonight—and he knew she wouldn't—he would find the appropriate moment in which to confess to Deirdre. He would fly to New York; the moment Michelle saw him, he would say that he had made up his mind.

After he had downed Champale after Champale at the wrap party, Mel felt satisfied with his decision, all the more so given that Deirdre hadn't bothered to show up, choosing to stay home to write. He spent most of the party hugging people to whom he had never talked on the set, hugging people he didn't even like. He hugged Ron Claxton, told him no hard feelings. He caught Vance Coffey in a headlock and said that he wanted him to play JFK in one of his next films.

He found Carl upstairs in his office sorting through coffee-stained contracts for a boilerplate Articles of Incorporation form for the Cubbins Legal Defense Fund. Mel told Carl he was sorry that they'd argued and asked if Carl might come downstairs later to join the party. Nah, Carl said, he had a shitload of work to do. Well, Mel said, mussing up Carl's hair, saying he'd always heard that rubbing a honky's head would bring him good luck, he'd tell the gang downstairs to keep it down and to be sure not to wake Mel's main man. That was all right, Carl said, he didn't like to sleep, especially when it was quiet. Mel said he'd bet Carl a sawbuck that Carl would be asleep long before he would. But only fifteen minutes later, Mel crashed out in Jasmine Huggins's bedroom, his brain reeling with dreams of himself standing beside Michelle, watching lines of moviegoers extending all the way down State Street past the Carson Pirie Scott department store, across Van Buren, past the Pacific Garden Mission, past Cermak Road, the eager audience members not caring about the boundaries that separated them; they were all joined together by a movie that Mel had made. Harold Washington was walking toward him, offering him the key to the city.

## SPRING 1984

W hen Mel finally decided to inform Deirdre that he would be reordering his life and her place in it, he had just stopped watching the final rough cut of *Godfathers.* He and Deirdre were still dining and spending weekend nights together. But lately, it seemed as if they were always saying good-bye to each other—Mel would drive to the studio to edit, Deirdre to the library to write. Mel hadn't wanted to distract himself by dwelling on his romantic life until he had finished his preliminary edit; up until the last moment, he still allowed for the possibility that he might change his mind.

He had sat all day in the pitch-dark, top-floor Bronzeville screening room with a DO NOT DISTURB FOR ANY GODDAMN REASON! sign on the door and watched *Godfathers of Soul*—all four and a half hours of it—two times straight without interruption. The first time he watched it, he loved every second right from the moment he saw the words that he'd wanted to see on a screen ever since he'd been a boy: *Bronzeville Studios Presents: A Melvin Coleman Film.* He'd always despised long films, but he didn't see much to cut. If anything, Mel thought that scenes unfolded too quickly. He had cut one of his favorite scenes with Al Capone and Meyer Lansky playing snooker in a speakeasy; Tiny Walker enters and asks Capone if he feels like shooting pool. This isn't pool, Capone says, this is snooker, at which point Tiny shoots six holes in the snooker table.

"Now it's pool," he says.

The second time Mel watched the film, having taken only a five-minute break to relieve himself, then scrawl "M.C. #1" above a urinal, he had no idea how he could have deluded himself. Every cut seemed artificial, every transition clumsy, all the blood looked like corn syrup and food coloring. The only parts he liked were the music and the credits.

By nightfall, he tried watching a third time but couldn't stand it anymore. He had no concept of whether the film was good or bad. He imagined competing headlines—"Gritty, uncompromising, two thumbs way the hell up," "*Godfathers* has no *Soul.*" He thought it equally possible that he would be lauded by the black community as a trailblazer and reviled by the white community as a revolutionary or embraced by whites as a visionary and shunned by blacks as a traitor. He found it more likely that no one would give a damn. He no longer knew which of his self-images was accurate—the brash, young film director or the washed-up, self-deluded poseur; the only thing he knew was which one of those Mel Colemans would date Michelle and which would date Deirdre.

Mel stood at the sink in the Bronzeville washroom, splashed his face with water, and stared in the mirror. He studied the bloodshot eyes, the sparse stubble that had begun to form on his chin, two of the whiskers silver. He winced as he tweezed out the whiskers, then studied his scalp looking for any other signs of gray. His mother had gone gray early, his father bald. At his age, his parents had already had four children, already owned a house in Evanston. His father had died at sixty-eight, his mother at seventy, which meant that his life might already be half over. He closed his eyes and pictured Deirdre's hair, the gray at her temples—she had laughed when he asked her if she'd ever thought of dyeing it.

Mel returned to his editing suite and scanned his shelves until he found a videotape of raw footage that he had shot of Michelle, then brought the tape up to the screening room. He thought that by watching it, he might feel ashamed or indifferent. He hoped that she would look too skinny, too young, too pale. But as he watched, all he thought was how much he needed her youth, her talent, and her energy, how much he liked the idea of her standing by his side for his publicity shots. He rewound the tape, popped it out of the player, and stuffed it in his jacket pocket. He decided that he would drive to Deirdre's apartment and place the tape on top of her VCR with a note saying that he had fallen in love with someone else and he was leaving for New York. If she wanted to know anything more, Deirdre should watch the video. She would hate him for it, but that was O.K.; he preferred the end of a relationship to come when he was hated.

When Mel arrived at the Wills apartment with his videotape, Muley answered the door in a pair of denim overalls worn over a plain white T-shirt and said that his mother was still out writing at the library. That was O.K., Mel said, he was just leaving a package for her. He then walked slowly around the apartment, studying every inch as if to memorize it. He sat on the living room couch, walked into the kitchen, poured himself a glass of ice-cold milk, stirred two spoonfuls of sugar into it, knowing that each time he performed these activities might be the last— his last look out the window onto California and the announcement board of K.I.N.S. (ANDROPOV R.I.P., it read), his last look in Deirdre's mirror, his last conversation with Muley.

Muley's bedroom was nearly empty now; all that remained were his bed, his desk, a lamp, the hockey net on the ceiling, and two hockey sticks mounted on the bare white walls. As Mel drank his sugared milk, he sat on the floor opposite Muley and told him that he might not be coming around much anymore, but he'd always be there for Muley if he needed him. Mel felt honorable as he spoke, humble, but when Muley told Mel to say hi to Michelle if he was going to New York, Mel quickly said that he needed to head home.

Mel went to bed early, hoping to sleep before Deirdre's angry phone call. But no call came and Mel slept straight through the night and awoke to Luther Vandross on his clock radio. He packed a small suitcase, then got on the road, wondering whether Deirdre had watched the tape. But once he had pulled onto the Dan Ryan, heading south past Comiskey Park, the Chicago skyline in the rearview mirror, the Skyway turnoff just a few miles ahead, he began thinking about that less and less.

As it turned out, Deirdre had not watched much of the videotape. After Mel had closed the door to the Wills apartment, Muley had noticed the tape atop the VCR, and the note. He read the note, then inserted the tape in the machine and studied the footage of Michelle. Muley sighed and shook his head; there were definite problems with Mel's film, Muley thought—the camera work was jittery and amateurish. Muley noticed a glare against the tile wall of the shower that seemed to originate from an offscreen light source, and at one point, Muley caught a glimpse of Mel's camera in the bathroom mirror. Muley was about to make notes, but in the time that it took him to fetch a pad of paper, Deirdre returned from the library. She dropped her books on an armchair and noticed the TV on.

"Muley Scott Wills," Deirdre said, "get in here."

As Muley returned, Deirdre asked him where he had found this tape. Before Muley could explain, Deirdre led him to the couch and told him that she wasn't angry—she understood that young men sometimes liked looking at naked girls—but she also wanted him to know that watching this sort of material provided no intellectual benefit. If he returned his dirty movie to whomever had given it to him—she pushed Stop, then Eject, on the VCR, extracted the tape, and handed it to him—then she would pretend that she had not seen it. But if she caught him watching these movies again, she'd ground him. Muley took Mel's note and tape out to the trash.


A t the precise moment that Mel crossed over the George Washington Bridge into New York City in his rumbling Chevy Nova, Michelle was buying a cup of coffee from a roach coach in Washington Square, having just finished her midterm on *Politics and the Law*. From four to seven, she would be rehearsing for an NYU mainstage production of *Spring Awakening*, after which she would cab it to the backer's audition for *The New Jazz Singer*. She had been in

New York for less than two years and *Jizz Slinger,* as Michelle referred to it, would be her fourteenth theatrical production. She'd stage-managed *Count Oederland, An Enemy of the People,* and *Quartermaine's Terms,* operated the VCR for *Hamletmachine,* understudied every role in an all-female *Twelve Angry Men,* played a guard holding a stick in *Macbeth,* sang in the chorus in an experimental, clothed version of *Oh! Calcutta!,* assayed a pantomime Titania in *A Midsummer Night's Dream,* a butch queen in Destry Valance's *Richard III,* a tap-dancing sphinx in *Oedipus Rex,* and assistant-directed what she termed a "crap-out-of-the-ass production" of David Mamet's *The Disappearance of the Jews,* to say nothing of all the parts she'd played in readings of student-written dramas, most of which concerned young playwrights whose significant others didn't understand them.

She had not heard from Mel since she had left Chicago in January, and she had been too busy to think of him for more than an hour or three every night. It was amazing how much time she could save by committing herself to a man she never saw—it was like being engaged to a member of the Foreign Legion. Though she had not communicated with Mel, still she had gained from the possibility of a relationship with him, which allowed her to reject potential suitors using lines she'd memorized from books and movies. "*Ah'm* sorry, but *ah aim* promised to someone," she told Benedict Drake, who had played Oedipus; "All right, yes, but just for this night," she told her professor Geoffrey Woshner, with whom she had agreed to sleep only because he had once slept with Tennessee Williams and she thought that having that link to theatrical greatness would be (a) interesting and (b) good for her biography, even though Woshner ultimately just drank himself to sleep on his moth-eaten couch while Michelle swilled his brandy, smoked his clove cigarettes, and listened to his John Gielgud LPs before she got a good look at him in his yellowed jockey shorts, yacked in his bathroom, and left with the turntable still spinning.

During weekend rehearsals for *The New Jazz Singer,* Larry had taken an increasingly arrogant attitude toward the production, routinely arriving late from the Boston train, then telling various cast members, all of whom had Equity standing, that their performances were "laughably weak." On the night of the backers' audition, Michelle made quick work of her *Spring Awakening* rehearsal, suggesting a speed-through instead of a run-through. By the time the actors were assembling for the curtain call, Michelle was already in a taxi.

*The New Jazz Singer,* Hannah Goodman had written in her handsomely printed program notes, opened in a *shul.* Cantor Hiram Singer is concluding a Sabbath service, after which his son Yehuda belts out his first solo ("[I Wanna] Sing, Papa," slightly altered from Larry's original lyrics "[I Wanna] Soar"). At the family dinner table, Yehuda explains that he doesn't want to be a cantor, the job for which he is being groomed; he wants to be a star. In a flashback, Yehuda walks along 42nd Street, enters a theater, and is thrilled to see a musical being performed. He returns for seven consecutive nights, attending even on Shabbos. After the eighth show, he sees Christine, a chorus girl, exiting the stage door. They share a taxi, and during the ride, she inquires about his Jewish heritage ("What's That Beanie For?"), invites him to her apartment ("[Take Me to] Your Promised Land"), and pours him a drink ("My Milk, Your Honey"). After she has bedded him, she asks what he does for a living ("[I Wanna] Sing, Papa [reprise]"). Christine tells him that the musical is looking for replacements ("[You Can] Sing, Yehuda").

Back at the dinner table, Yehuda's father angrily says that his son will never sing on Broadway ("A Cantor Can't!") and sends Yehuda to his room, where he dreams of being a star (*"Baruch Atah* on Broadway") until his mother enters and asks him if he's still planning to marry that pretty little Zipporah down the street ("[There's Something about a] Synagogue Girl"). She advises him to stay within the faith ("Don't Mixa with a Shiksa"). The next night, Yehuda explains his Broadway dreams to Zipporah ("[My Lovin' Ain't] Always Orthodox"), then makes a vulgar pass at her ("[Show Me] All Your Hair"), which she rebuffs ("[I Won't Get Down] Before Sundown"). Yehuda packs a bag and meets Christine, with whom he sings a duet ("[I Wanna/You Can] Sing [Papa/Yehuda]"), ending the first act.

Act II finds Yehuda in the chorus of a Broadway show and living with Christine. He catches the eye of the show's director, Mr. Richman ("[You Could Be] A Big One," a slight variation on Larry's song "[I Don't Need] A Big One"), who says he needs someone to play opposite Christine in his next show. Yehuda doesn't get the role, but is cast as an understudy (here, Hannah had worked Larry's circumcision song, "The Unkindest Cut," into the libretto). But on opening night, the lead actor breaks his leg and Yehuda takes his part. As he sees his name on the Broadway marquee, he begins to sing, but Zipporah enters and interrupts him; his father is ill and no one can lead Sabbath prayers. Yehuda says he can't go, this is his big break ("Follow That Dream"). That evening at the synagogue, Yehuda appears glumly wearing his *tallis* and leads the Sabbath service. Afterward, he goes to his father's house, where the cantor is in a wheelchair. Yehuda tells his father that he is sorry to have turned his back on his faith ("Wailing at the Wall [Again]"). But when he is done singing, his father, his voice faltering, tells Yehuda to "Follow That Dream." Yehuda tells him that there's no time left; the show starts in fifteen minutes. "That gives us just enough time," Zipporah says; they start running for Broadway. Yehuda arrives for the opening number and receives a standing ovation. Backstage, Christine tells him that the two of them have a great future together ("Convert Yourself"). But Yehuda tells her that he loves someone else ("Zipporah's Waiting"). In the penultimate scene, after Zipporah has gone through the rituals necessary for marriage ("Let's All Go to the Mikva [And Get Ourselves Clean]"), Zipporah and Yehuda marry, but during the ceremony, the cantor collapses and dies, paving the way for the finale, in which Yehuda sings the Kaddish. The whole cast joins in, then reprises "(I Wanna) Sing, Papa."

The backers' audition was held at the Delancey Street Project, a 100-seat black-box theater with warped wooden floors and beat-up red-cushioned seats, most with signs affixed to them—RESERVED FOR MR. AND MRS. MAX GOODMAN JR.; RESERVED FOR MR. AND SOON-TO-BE MRS. LAWRENCE ROVNER. A red curtain was drawn in front of the stage. Behind it were black metal chairs and music stands; in front of it, a piano. At precisely 8:05, when the seats were full, the overture began—a pianist in a white tuxedo played a medley of songs that had influenced the musical—"Hatikvah" melded into "Hell's Bells," which segued into the Kaddish. The curtain opened. Michelle and seven other actors dressed in black stood behind music stands and faced the audience.

When it came time for her first song ("What's That Beanie For?"), Michelle felt the hot spotlight on her face and sang the lyrics (*"That hat looks funny on a fella / Does it come with a propell-a?"*) with an intensity and conviction light-years beyond any she had demonstrated in rehearsal. It was her philosophy as an actress to always commit fully to whatever part she was playing; the more ridiculous a role, the more effort she gave. She delivered her song directly to the audience, nearly attacking them with each syllable she sang. She stamped her feet, raised her hands up high, and gazed out into the crowd. In the first rows, the audience seemed almost to be wearing uniforms; save for Larry, who was wearing sunglasses, ripped jeans, and a turned-around Cubs cap, all the men wore blue blazers, tan slacks, white shirts, red ties; all the women wore black. Everyone had expensive hair. But then on the aisle of the second-to-last row, Michelle saw Mel. She froze.

Since arriving in New York, Mel had already missed Michelle twice. He had stopped by her apartment, where Destry informed him that she was at *Spring Awakening* rehearsal. He had waited at the front door of the theater, only to learn that Michelle was already at the backers' audition, where he talked his way past an usher. The usher had told him that the show had already begun, then asked Mel for his name, and Mel, who generally found it easy to slip past white ushers by pretending to be a celebrity or athlete, offered his response: "Williams, Billy Dee."

"Oh, I'm terribly sorry, Mr. Williams," the usher said, then asked if he was working on any new films. Mel said that he had been reading a couple of scripts, one of which was titled *Godfathers of Soul,* for which he'd lost out on the lead role to a "cocky unknown," the other a Western called *Billy the Brother,* the best damn script he'd read since *Lady Sings the Blues.* The usher said that he hadn't cared for that film. Yeah, Mel said, but he should have read Melvin Coleman's original script, in which Billie Holiday was a kung-fu expert who kicked the crap out of Doris Day.

All through the overture and the first songs of *The New Jazz Singer,* Mel's overall sensation was one of displacement. It was not merely the fact that this was a wealthier world than his (after he had sold *Godfathers,* he would be able to buy and sell half of these New York aristocrats), not merely that it was a white world (he was no longer surprised to find himself the one black man in the box seats at Comiskey Park, the one black guest at the Bar Mitzvah), not merely that it was a Jewish world either. Yes, it was all of these, but most of all, it was Michelle's world, a world that did not need him in order to be complete. He saw her there in her element, in the glare of the spotlights, singing "What's That Beanie For?" with such passion, such commitment. Only when her eyes met his did she seem to falter.

As she stood center stage behind her music stand, Michelle once again felt the power she could exert over a crowd. She had felt it before: When she played Anne Frank, she saw tears rolling down her father's cheeks; when she had played Russian immigrant Peachy Moskowitz on NPR's *Young Town,* she saw Lennie Kidd's glazed stare. But now, as she stopped dead, searching for her place in her script, none of it meant a damn to her. She wondered what she was doing up here, why all these people were watching her. She had the sense that every time she had stepped onstage, she had been searching for something that she no longer needed. More than an act and a half was left of the musical, but the moment Michelle was most eagerly awaiting was the final curtain call, the moment when she and Larry would grasp hands and walk together up the aisle and out of the theater. Larry would jump into a taxi to catch the next L.A. flight, and she would walk home with Mel.

It was a disorienting feeling. From the moment that she had stepped onto the stage of the K.I.N.S. auditorium and belted out her very first solo in Jeffrey Meltzer's rock opera *Einmal in a Purim,* she had thought that she had found her true life's calling. One of her prime motivations, she had often said, was to honor her mother, Becky Wasserstrom, who had given up her dreams of performing, trading chorus girl roles for life as a mother in walk-ups on Chicago's north side. Michelle enjoyed making this dramatic claim when people asked her about acting, the sense of mission inherent in completing something that her mother had started.

She remembered how Becky had often discussed abandoning the theater. She would sit on her and Charlie's bed looking through old, creased *Playbill*s. Michelle would peer over Becky's shoulder as she would point to pictures of actors and dancers, each more handsome than the next, and say that this one had brought her flowers and this one had taken her dancing at El Morocco. "Well," Becky would say as she put away her pictures, maybe she'd be an actress again in her "next life."

Michelle often heard her mother use this phrase, and it always filled her with fear and ambition. Becky and Charlie would return from a nightclub show, and after the babysitter had left, Becky would sing songs or perform dances that she had heard or seen. She'd stop in the middle, laugh, and say well, maybe she'd dance and sing again in her next life. The evening of the dinner when Charlie and Becky had announced that they had seen the doctor and that Michelle and Jill would have to be brave because their mother was sick and would have to work "real hard" to "make herself well again," Michelle had struggled desperately yet successfully to keep herself from crying. For, though the news was devastating, Michelle did not find it entirely surprising; whenever she had heard her mother talk about her "next life," she could not escape the thought that this life of her mother's was, in a sense, already over.

At the funeral, Becky's mother, Edna, brought a scrapbook of Becky's photos and newspaper articles. What struck Michelle was both how beautiful her mother looked but at the same time how unlike the mother she knew—there was a youth and a vitality that Michelle did not recognize. Michelle had sat with Edna in the greeting room of the Piser-Weinstein Chapel and studied each picture and review until she became conscious of shadows passing back and forth in front of her chair. The next thing she knew, Uncle Dave had grabbed hold of Edna's arm, taken her to a corner of the room, and berated her in a loud whisper, saying that she had had no business bringing pictures of Becky to the funeral and look what it was doing to Becky's husband—he gestured in the direction of a despondent Charlie seated in an armchair. Edna made a motion toward Michelle as if to proffer the scrapbook, but Dave Wasserstrom stepped between them and told Edna to "get that goddamn thing outta here," then bore down on Michelle, telling her to stand by her father, he needed her right now, and what kind of family was this where one daughter was looking through pictures like she was at a goddamn wedding and the other hadn't shown up at all. And though Michelle had cursed Dave in silence, she had nevertheless walked over to her father and brought him a glass of apple juice and a stale kosher cookie while she watched Edna, scrapbook in both arms, shuffling out the door, too self-involved and thin-skinned, Michelle thought even then, to bother saying good-bye. As she sat on the arm of her father's chair, Michelle decided that she would never speak of what she would do in her next life; she would have to do it all in this one.

And what that meant, she now realized as she looked out at Mel and the rest of the crowd, was that she could not retire from the stage just yet. She would have to win a Tony award or an Oscar, she would have to receive top billing in a major motion picture, command a million dollars a film. Only then could she quit, until, perhaps, decades later, someone would lure her out of retirement to appear in a movie based on *Heart of Darkness,* for which she could shave her head and mumble the whole time. As long as her mother's ambitions remained unfulfilled, Michelle's purpose remained clear. And if she wanted to do something else, like, say, go to law school or run away with Mel, she'd have to do all of it at once. No, you're wrong, Dr. Overgaard, not one, the other, or the third: *all three.*

"Line," Michelle heard a voice hissing at her, *"line."* The white-tuxedoed pianist was looking at her expectantly and pointing. "Line," he repeated. Michelle sighed. She found her place in her script and, with a sense of duty and regret, sang the final verse of Hannah and Larry's dumb song.

Once the curtain fell for Act I and the intermission began, Larry sprang from his seat between Hannah and her father. He found Michelle backstage and took her by the elbow. Michelle told him not to touch her, she wasn't his fricking wife, and punched him hard in the shoulder. Larry held his shoulder, said "Ow," then apologized. He flipped his sunglasses up on his head and held both of Michelle's hands in his. Michelle told him not to do that either and punched him hard in the other shoulder. They walked out onto a fire escape, where Michelle lit a cigarette, flicking the match two stories down into a ditch in the dark alley behind the theater, nearly hitting Mel, who was smoking a cigar below, contemplating the fact that Michelle had been performing so confidently until she had seen him. Larry asked Michelle if she'd ever had the sensation of watching her entire life pass before her eyes and realizing that it was a life she didn't want.

"Right now, Sondheim Boy," Michelle said. She asked Larry if he had seen who was in the audience. Larry mouthed the name "Mel" and Michelle nodded. He asked if she had known that he was coming. "Nope," she said. Larry asked Michelle once more if she would honor her promise to walk out with him after the curtain call. And though Michelle now wondered what Mel would think if he saw her and Larry walking hand in hand out of the theater, she told Larry that she would.

In Act II, Michelle regained some of the energy and enthusiasm she had lost upon seeing Mel and flubbing her opening song. She even got a laugh when she gleefully sang the praises of the Christian faith in "Convert Yourself" (*"Come a little closer to me / You know everything's kosher to me"*). She approached the finale with cool professionalism, as if she were offering her personal farewell to the stage. She saw the curtain fall, heard applause ripple through the theater, saw the curtain rise, heard the clapping growing louder. She looked out to see people rising to their feet, felt the actor on her left and the actor on her right grasp her hands. She could see Mr. and Mrs. Goodman standing. "Author! Author!" they yelled. The chant began to make its way through the rest of the audience. "Author! Author!" Then Mrs. Goodman shouted, "Composer! Composer!"

In the audience, Hannah reached for Larry's hand and led him onto the stage, and then the other members of the cast started applauding, too. Larry watched the actors applauding, watched Hannah applauding, one hundred and ninety-nine audience members applauding. Hannah clapped for Larry, then dropped her hands to her sides, expecting him to clap for her too. Rock stars don't clap for their fiancées, Larry thought, but though he didn't applaud for Hannah, Larry did take a bow, and as the audience kept clapping, he took another one.

Michelle reached for Larry's sleeve and tried to yank him down from the stage, but he kept smiling and bowing again and again, unwilling to stand anywhere but center stage. And then, as the applause and the shouting and the bowing persisted, it was only Michelle who stepped down from the stage and walked toward the back of the auditorium. She looked back and saw Larry walking backstage, then strapping on a guitar for an encore. As she walked, faster now, Michelle heard someone muttering, "Everyone was so wonderful except for that trampy blond girl who messed up her lines." And though Michelle had half a mind to smack Mr. Goodman after he had made that remark, she kept walking toward the exit, where Mel was waiting for her.

There were many things that Mel had rehearsed saying to Michelle as the two of them walked along Delancey Street, then halfway across the Williamsburg Bridge. He wanted to tell her how he had driven eight hundred miles in thirteen hours on I-80 just to see her. He wanted to tell her how he had left his videotape at Deirdre's apartment. But when he stood beside her, his hands gripping the railing of the bridge, all he said as he looked out through the fence at highways, bridges, and the water racing below was that, though he didn't like New York much, this view was "pretty fly." And though Michelle could think of a hundred statements to make in response, she merely agreed. Yeah, she said, the view wasn't bad.

Mel made as if to speak, but stopped when he realized that he had memorized everything he wanted to say from 1940s movies ("Deep in our hearts, we both know you belong to Yehuda"). He lit a cigarette, began to inhale; Michelle snatched it out of his mouth and threw it into the river. "You still don't know how to smoke," she said, reached into her bag, and pulled out a stick of Juicy Fruit. He unwrapped it and chewed. Damn, Mel said, how did she know that Juicy Fruit was his favorite flavor? "Great minds," Michelle started to say but Mel stopped her thought with a kiss.

It would have been stupid for Michelle to think that she felt sparks flying during that kiss, stupid for her to feel that her heart was fluttering just millimeters above her head, stupid to feel that her entire body had been swaddled in a soft blanket—true or not, these were stupid things to feel; true or not, they were just unspeakably queer. As she felt Mel's tongue upon hers, she stopped, pulling away from him slightly.

"No tongue while chewing gum, buster," she said. Immediately, Mel took the gum out of his mouth and flicked it through the fence toward the water. Michelle leaned in to return Mel's kiss, but then he turned away from her, thinking of how he might appear to anyone watching him, how selfish he was, how selfish he had been all his life, how everything he had done—even the most seemingly generous acts—had been for himself. He imagined Deirdre alone in her apartment, watching his video. And he thought about how Michelle had stumbled when she had seen him in the crowd, and what did it matter that he had literally felt sparks as he had kissed her, and what did it matter how fast his heart was beating. He could either do the selfish thing—follow his passions and ruin two people's lives—or be noble, do the right thing by two fine women, both of whom he now realized that he loved. Which is what he finally told Michelle, but not until after he had gotten to kiss her once more, not until after he had gotten to hold her hand, not until after she had asked him how long they were going to be standing up here because it was getting cold as a bastard and she had to take a wicked piss, not until after they had walked back to Delancey Street and taken a taxi back to her apartment.

Mel was sitting on Michelle's bed when she returned from her washroom, having put in her depressingly dusty diaphragm just in case. While she'd been out of the room, Mel had assessed the apartment—the crushed containers of Tab, the boom box and the hand-labeled cassettes of Patti Smith and Joni Mitchell, the trash can filled with crumpled Marlboro packages, the bookcase topped with ramen noodles and Cup-of-Soups. Again, he couldn't escape the sensation that this life was complete, and had no need for him.

Michelle opened a warm Tab, took a swig, and asked if Mel wanted any. No, he said. He took a deep breath, then said that he shouldn't have come here, and he thought that he'd better get going before anything more happened between them. Michelle choked on her Tab, then swallowed hard. *Get going,* Michelle repeated. *Where?* Listen up, Mel said. Over the past twenty-four hours, he'd been doing a lot of thinking. *No,* Michelle said, no way, she wouldn't listen to any speech that began with "I've been doing a lot of thinking," she wouldn't listen to any speech that he had *rehearsed.* Mel said that what he was about to tell her was as much for her benefit as for his; he was thinking of her needs now. "Needs?" Michelle asked. Mel asked Michelle if she knew how old he was, then asked her to guess. Michelle said that she didn't know, maybe forty? Mel flinched, then told her to guess again. Forty-five? Michelle asked. Shit, Mel said, did he look that old? He said that he was thirty-six and he was an old-ass man, and old-ass men had different needs than young-ass girls. The fact was that, as far as he could see, she didn't need him and there was someone in Chicago who probably needed him a whole lot more.

What the hell was this, Michelle wanted to know, a need competition? She didn't realize that he was distributing needs-based grants. If he was looking for needy cases, she could give him a slew of cases *needier* than hers. Why didn't he call up Larry Rovner—there was a special needs case. The best relationships, she said, were between two people who had no need for each other whatsoever, but wanted to be together nonetheless. If she had based her life on finding the guy who needed her most, she would be busily boffing Arik Levine right now. But as long as she had a brain, she would make her decisions on the basis of who she wanted to be with, not who needed her more—that's how she'd choose her boyfriends and how he should choose his girlfriend.

That was the thing, Mel said—he didn't want a girlfriend anymore; he wanted a wife. "A what?" Michelle asked. "A *wife?*" She said that she didn't even know what that word meant. That's because she wasn't thirty-six, Mel said. What the fuck difference did that make, Michelle said, thirty-six was just a number. Mel said if she were thirty-six, she wouldn't say that. Fine, Michelle said, why didn't he just go home to his wife now. Mel said that he didn't want to leave on a bad note. Michelle said that she didn't much care what note he left on just as long as he left. Damn, Mel said, didn't she realize that this wasn't what he wanted to do; it was what he felt he needed to do. He couldn't spend his life chasing girls around like some kid. He had a reputation to uphold, an image. He was trying his best to be a decent, upstanding man. No he wasn't, Michelle said, he never gave a damn about anyone's needs but his own. A line from Destry Valance's production of *Richard III* came to mind: *There's none else by,* she thought, *Melvin Coleman loves Melvin Coleman.*

"You know what you are?" she asked Mel—she searched her arsenal of epithets for the worst insult she could find, a word that she had never seen fit to call anyone else.

"You're a fucking *ac-tor,*" she said, then asked him to give her regards to his wife.

After Mel left, attempting to appear as if leaving had been his idea yet slamming the door hard anyway, Michelle tried to sleep in her clothes but kept staring at the ceiling; the room was too bright even though the blinds were drawn and the door was shut. She tried to read, she tried to masturbate, she tried doing jumping jacks. She tried turning on one of her Patti Smith tapes and playing air guitar, but now she hated every cassette she owned. At a quarter to three, she knocked on Bert Liu's door.

Destry had dubbed Bert's room The Sex Room because everything in it was devoted to sex. On his dresser were rows of colognes and aphrodisiacs—ginseng roots in bottles of urine-colored liquid, a large mason jar filled three-quarters of the way up with a hard, lox-colored substance labeled "Sex Wax." On the floor was a gigantic boom box, which played mood-setting "sex music," and Bert's "love light," a rotating lamp that cast multicolored speckles on his wall.

As Michelle entered Bert's room, her nostrils were infused with a stale, vaguely medicinal odor—three parts Polo cologne, one part semen. Bert was sleeping diagonally on his waterbed. "Move over, lard-ass," Michelle said and sat beside Bert, turned on a Kitaro tape, and switched on the love light. She vowed that from this moment forward, she would have sex only in two circumstances— only if she were completely in love or if the sex was completely instrumental. Which was why her face was now freckled with the pox of Bert Liu's love light, and why she was absentmindedly fingering one of Bert's condom tins and telling him to wake the hell up. But after five minutes, all she could rouse out of Bert was "Ma-an, be cool." So, Michelle switched off the light, unrolled a condom, blew it up into a balloon, then went to take a shower.

Michelle didn't know how long she'd been in the shower—long enough at least for her to cry for what she determined to be a reasonable amount of time (three minutes), then sing Side 1 of *Court and Spark.* But when she stepped out of the shower in a towel and walked toward her room in Bert's shower clogs, she espied Mel crashed out on her couch. He had taken a taxi to his car, but he could barely keep his eyes open and he had not liked the thoughts swirling through his head. He had wished that he had never cast Michelle in his film, wished that he had never driven all the way out here, wished that he had at least fucked her so that his trip would have had some purpose. But then, as he felt guilty for all those thoughts, he asked the driver to turn around. Destry, who was returning from Limelight, had let Mel in, observing that he was glad to see at least one person who'd had a worse night than he had. Mel had taken the couch and listened to the sounds of the shower and Michelle singing some of the worst white-people music he'd ever heard; soon, the shower and Michelle's singing had insinuated themselves into his dreams.

Michelle awoke to find Mel at her living room table—a bag of bagels, a block of cream cheese, a pitcher of orange juice, and a pot of coffee in front of him. She blew away the strands of hair that had fallen into her eyes, stood in front of him in an inside-out *Merrily We Roll Along* T-shirt and blue Mather High shorts, and asked Mel if this was a Friendship Breakfast, a Lovers' Breakfast, or an Apology Breakfast. Mel said that he'd had enough of lovers' breakfasts and enough of apologies, so he guessed that it was a friendship breakfast. Michelle asked if an engagement ring was hidden in the cream cheese. Mel asked why, did she want there to be one? Nope, Michelle said as Destry entered in his pajamas en route to the refrigerator singing, *"Lovers in the night. Exchanging rubbers in the night."* Michelle told Destry to fuck off and he slunk to his room with a fistful of granola bars and a glass of Tang.

And now that it seemed a foregone conclusion that Mel would return to Chicago, where he would seek out a "wife" instead of a "girlfriend," the ease in their rapport returned. They spent breakfast trading lines from classic movies ("Where you goin', Shaft?" Mel asked. "Goin' downtown; get laid," said Michelle). Mel told Michelle that he would cast her in every film he ever made, that he wanted to be one of those directors who always worked with the same actors—Scorsese and De Niro, Parks and Roundtree, Coleman and Wasserstrom. And though Michelle felt that Scorsese and Wasserstrom seemed a lot more likely than Coleman and Wasserstrom, particularly since Mel seemed incapable of sticking with any decision he'd made, saying so seemed cruel, so Michelle said that sounded fine to her, but now she really had to get dressed for class; why didn't he call her once he was back in Chicago and he could tell her all about the bridesmaids' dresses and the napkin designs? And then she kissed him—a kiss that to Mel felt like a promise of what still could be and that to Michelle felt only like a fond suggestion of what was never meant to happen, at which point a bleary-eyed Bert Liu emerged from his room and asked Michelle if she'd been in his bed last night.

"Dream on, Sex Boy," Michelle said.

Mel arrived back in West Rogers Park at eight that night, just as Deirdre was returning home from a meeting with Rattigan Glumphoboo, the student writers' group she had formed at Marshall High. Catching her on the way to the door, Mel asked if she'd join him for dinner. They ate at Yenching on Western, where Mel asked Deirdre if she'd missed him while he'd been gone.

Deirdre said that she didn't realize he'd been away. Mel asked if she'd seen the videotape, but Deirdre said that she didn't know what he was referring to. Mel couldn't tell if Deirdre was testing him, if she genuinely didn't know, or if she was giving him another chance so that they could both live as if the last forty-eight hours had never happened. Mel said it didn't matter; he wanted to discuss something more important.

Deirdre smiled, but tentatively, as if she already knew what was next. What did he want to discuss? "Marriage," Mel said. Deirdre laughed breezily, as if Mel's proposal was not something he had agonized over but rather had invented on the spot to pass the time between garlic chicken and glazed bananas. She said that she found it sweet that Mel wanted to get married, but she really wasn't a marriage person.

Mel claimed that he wasn't a marriage person either, but he wanted to marry her. He wanted to sleep and wake up beside her, take a honeymoon, do everything married couples did, didn't that sound good? Sure, Deirdre said, but they could do all those things without being married—she didn't want to state her personal business in front of a whole bunch of strangers and some corrupt judge. As far as she was concerned, she was as married as she would ever be.

Damn, Mel said, then why didn't she at least move into his apartment? Deirdre said that her place was bigger than his. All right, Mel said, why didn't he move into hers? Deirdre asked what was wrong with keeping things just as they were? Because nothing was decided, Mel said—everything was in flux. But that's how life was, Deirdre said; marriage was about pretending things were permanent and had happy endings when, in fact, everything was precarious. Still, she would be happy to have Mel's company whenever he wanted to stay over. And what if someday he met someone else, Mel asked. Then that's what would happen, Deirdre said.

The following day, when Mel returned to Bronzeville Studios exhausted and ill-tempered, he stopped at Carl's office to ask him if he'd watched the rough cut of *Godfathers*. Carl, who had no patience for the two-dimensionality of movies and had stopped watching at the end of the opening credit sequence, told Mel that he'd only watched the first ten minutes and found them "fly." In fact, he'd found them so "fly" that he'd had to shut the flick off because he hadn't been in the right frame of mind to watch something so "fly." Carl told Mel that he looked "pretty fagged out" and asked if he'd been eating righteously. Mel said that he'd just been going through a lot of "personal shit." Carl asked if everything was "coolage" with Deirdre. Mel shook his head, then revealed that he had proposed to Deirdre, but she had turned him down cold.

"That's ice," said Carl, who, not wanting to seem too eager, waited until Mel had been in his editing suite for a half hour before he called Deirdre at Marshall High; when he didn't find her, he tried again at 3:31, right after the school bell, after which he called her at home every half hour, hanging up each time Muley answered. He finally reached Deirdre at six, and invited her to dinner that night. And when she said no, he asked about Tuesday, and when she said no to Tuesday, he went through all the days of the week until the following Thursday; what was so important that they couldn't discuss it over the phone? Deirdre asked.

Carl made reservations at a half-dozen restaurants and canceled all of them, unable to settle upon the appropriate venue for a proposal. All the restaurants where Deirdre and Carl had eaten on their first dates had closed—Fritzel's, Don the Beachcomber, Shangri-La. He finally reserved a table at the Cape Cod Room at the Drake Hotel, where he had once shared a plate of oysters with Big Mama Cole, an early performer on the Slappit label, and gone Dutch on the bill. It was not only the most expensive restaurant he knew, but also the darkest, which he thought might play in his favor. Before arriving at the Cape Cod, he picked up a jewelry catalogue at C. D. Peacock, thinking that if all went well at dinner, he could whip it out and Deirdre could choose a ring.

Deirdre arrived at the Drake a half hour late, and because she wore slacks, she and Carl were ushered to a table by the oyster bar where rust-colored lobsters crawled resignedly at the bottom of a brownish-green tank. She hadn't recognized Carl at first because he had gotten a shave and a haircut, and put on a suit that he had only worn twice before—to Big Mama Cole's funeral and to the Grammys. And when Deirdre spotted Carl, she didn't know whether to be amused or appalled. His former scraggly, unkempt look always left hope for the possibility that there was a handsome, sweet-faced gentleman underneath. But now Carl looked awkward, like an ape in a suit, the lack of hair on the face and the head calling attention to the hair on the knuckles and wrists, the dandruff on his shoulders. His suit smelled like an old cardboard box full of records and newspapers. During dinner, Deirdre drank only ice water, despite the fact that Carl had offered to drive her home if she wanted to order a stinger—he remembered that this was her favorite drink. Instead, Carl did the drinking, though he had never held his liquor well.

Once the dinners had been cleared away, Carl's place had been cleaned, and the maître d' had taken Carl's order for a slice of frozen strawberry pie, Carl finally told Deirdre that he had heard about Deirdre and Mel's discussion. After a long silence, interrupted only by a waiter who brought Carl his pie and coffee, Carl said that he felt badly for Mel, but he understood why she had rejected him—if you weren't in love, it was best to be direct.

Carl removed his lobster bib and took a bite of pie. He asked Deirdre about Mel's reaction. Deirdre said that this was getting a bit personal. Carl agreed, adding that their conversations were always far too impersonal. Deirdre looked away from Carl and stared at the pie he was slowly consuming, the unfinished pie a constant mocking reminder of the questions Carl would continue to ask until the dessert was gone, until the check arrived. Carl asked Deirdre if she ever thought of the future. "Rarely," she responded. She didn't ask if he thought about the future; still, he allowed that he did. The problem, he said, was that when he looked at the future, he saw two paths. There was the path of economic success, the path he had taken when he had left Deirdre and Muley. But that path wasn't "really on time," because he had taken it alone. And then, he said, there was the other path; it didn't lead to wealth or fame, but it was still "pretty much on time" because you took it with your "old lady." He finished his pie, reached in a pocket for his jewelry catalogue, and asked whether Deirdre would consider being that old lady.

Deirdre had spent much of her life gladly avoiding marriage proposals. She had now received two such offers in the space of a week and a half. Ever since she had taken her teaching job, she had learned to control her anger, to channel it into her writing, to always take a breath whenever she felt her cheeks getting hot, her nose twitching with rage. She took a deep breath. Carl said that when he learned that Deirdre had refused Mel's proposal, he had suddenly started to think about how much the two of them had in common, not just the child they had made—they shared the same politics, dug the same tunes, felt the same inner drive. There was no logical reason why they shouldn't be together.

"Except," Deirdre said, "Mel needs me more."

In an instant, Carl felt as if he had been hit with a powerful punch that had turned him around so quickly that no one could even notice he'd been touched. Why had she told Mel that she wouldn't marry him, Carl asked. Deirdre could have said that she didn't believe in marriage, that she found it to be an outdated institution, one that compromised the privacy of all who entered into it. Instead, she told Carl that she hadn't rejected Mel at all, that Mel must have misunderstood her.

The more Deirdre studied Carl's face, which looked as if it were made of wax held close to an open flame, the more she began to reassess her views of marriage, not just as an act of love, but as one of self-defense too. For if she had been married to Mel, this conversation would never have taken place. And if she had been married to someone else, her previous conversation with Mel would not have taken place either. She was further convinced that these two discussions were not isolated incidents; they were harbingers. Soon, her fellow unmarried teachers at Marshall would seek her out—recently hired and newly divorced Marshall High journalism teacher Louis Benson had already made a habit of sitting at her table at lunch and asking if she wanted to swig from his flask of hooch; Algebra instructor Benny Grabowitz (nicknamed "Benny Grabanything" by his colleagues) had told her that she could share his season tickets to the Body Politic Theater, even though he usually took his mother; and career counselor Sonny Dickinson often ogled her as she passed through the metal detector and remarked that it had to be jelly because jam sure didn't shake like that. Given the right occasion, they would tell her that they were good men looking for a good woman. If she were married, she wouldn't have to adapt her responses to each candidate; "Sorry, I'm married" would suffice for all.

Carl could not conceal his disappointment or his fury. He began by saying that he had chanted for both his and Deirdre's happiness and he was glad to see that God or whoever had granted Deirdre hers. He called out to the maître d' and asked him to fetch two glasses of the Cape Cod Room's finest champagne ("under five bucks a glass, brother," he said *sotto voce*), but before the champagne arrived, he was out the door, leaving Deirdre to pay the bill, after which she drove home alone.

The following morning, Carl awoke with a hangover, dropped to his knees for his morning chants, then realized that he wouldn't be performing them anymore. He now wondered whether he had been too indulgent with Mel, hoping that word of his generosity would reach Deirdre. It was foolish to woo a woman by pretending to be a person you were not—if he had succeeded in capturing Deirdre's heart, he would have had to keep wearing suits, shaving, cutting his hair, chanting *nam myoho renge kyo* all the fucking time. When Deirdre had first fallen for him, he had been unkempt, ill-mannered, arrogant. He preferred that particular Carl Silverman and hoped that one day soon, she would, too. Someday—whether a month from now, a year, even on his deathbed—if he knew that Deirdre loved him and that Muley cared for him, that was all that would matter. But for now, he decided that he would tell Mel exactly what he thought of his movie.

Later that day, Mel found Carl in the screening room, where he was forcing himself to watch *Godfathers of Soul.* Carl had written pages of furious, illegible notes in a spiral notebook. He was wearing the same suit that he had worn to dinner with Deirdre and now it smelled vaguely of shellfish and showed stains of drawn butter. Mel started at the sight of him as if he had caught a glimpse of a werewolf a few moments before midnight.

"Congratulations, brother," Carl said with a disquieting grin and turned off the projector.

Mel smiled, assuming that Carl was complimenting his movie. He asked Carl whether he liked that twelve-minute drag race between Tiny Walker's Trans Am and Al Capone's Model T, the one that ended with Capone at the side of King Drive, beating his driver with a tire iron while smoke billowed from the hood of the Ford and Tiny circled back around, leaned out his window, and asked, "Need a ride, muthafucka?" Carl said that he was only half-through with the movie and he wanted to finish before he gave Mel all his notes. Then why was Carl congratulating him? Mel asked. Carl said that last night at the Drake, Deirdre had told him that she hadn't rejected Mel's proposal after all.

Mel was about to tell Carl that he was full of shit, but stopped. He didn't know whether or not to be angry with Carl for trying to move in on his action right after he had confided in him. He looked at the slender Jewish man in his butter-stained, dandruff-flecked suit and saw little more than loneliness, the wayward, wandering Jew of the sermons he'd heard at his father's church; he wanted to laugh but also to cry. Then, later that same day, Carl asked Mel to join him in the editing suite; even after Mel reminded Carl that he, Melvin Coleman, had complete creative control over the film, Carl enumerated all the problems he saw in the movie, and all the cuts that Mel needed to make. At that point, Mel no longer pitied Carl; he wanted to kick the shit out of him.

When Mel opened the door to Deirdre's apartment that night, he saw a half-finished fudge cake on the table. Deirdre was at the sink rinsing off plates. Mel kissed her cheek, then flopped down in a chair by the kitchen table. He asked if he had forgotten someone's birthday. No, Deirdre said, she'd made the cake for Muley and his friend Jill—they had both been accepted into college, and now they were downtown seeing *This Is Spiñal Tap* at the Fine Arts to celebrate. Muley, Deirdre said, would be attending the Art Institute of Chicago and Jill would be going to a small liberal arts college in New York. Mel said he thought that she didn't want Muley going to art school. Yes, Deirdre admitted, but she was done fighting. Me too, said Mel, cutting himself a slice of cake; he'd fought enough today. Why, Deirdre asked—she stopped washing dishes and sat at the table across from Mel—was Carl still angry after what she had told him?

Then it was true, Mel said—now she wanted to marry him? Deirdre said she had told Carl something like that. Shit, Mel said, why did she tell Carl something that wasn't true? Deirdre told Mel she wasn't sure that what she had told Carl wasn't true. Mel was about to ask Deirdre what had changed, but did not, for fear that he already knew—that Carl had pounced upon her the moment he heard that she would not be marrying Mel, and now she realized that getting married would provide the best defense against more indecent advances. He assumed that this was the case, in large part because the motivation was not dissimilar from his own—marrying Deirdre could provide a defense against Michelle and all the future temptations she represented.

Mel laughed and said all right, he'd marry Deirdre, but only because she'd asked him. In his mind, he began composing guest lists. He wanted a big wedding, liked the idea of tuxedos and dresses, a jazz combo, everyone shaking his hand. He asked Deirdre where they would hold the reception: the South Shore Country Club? Deirdre said that City Hall was good enough; they weren't in their twenties anymore. All right, Mel said with a sigh, City Hall was all right with him too. Though, in bed that night, Mel did tell Deirdre that he wouldn't marry her unless there was a honeymoon. Deirdre said that as long as they didn't have to call it a honeymoon, that would be fine. And as he saw Deirdre smile, Mel took her in his arms, thinking of how happy he could make her, how much she needed him.

T hough Deirdre and Mel's Jamaican non-honeymoon—two weeks of writing, lovemaking, and in-depth discussions of Victorian literature—went
well, the premiere of *Godfathers of Soul* did not. Throughout the summer and the
early autumn, Mel had begun to doubt his film and accept some of Carl's criti-
cisms. He had worked hard to cut the movie down to a reasonable length. Carl
had hired Gail as a publicist for the premiere and Cubbins benefit at the Chicago
Theater. Now that Gail had enrolled Rachel in the Kiddie Kollege day-care
program, she thought that she would have more time for her clients, but with so
much work to do for the Peas Be with You vegetarian restaurant and her husband Charlie's interview schedule for his forthcoming book, she had even less.

Gail had advised Carl during their first conversation not to hold the benefit
during the High Holidays. "If the Jews don't get behind this, no one will," she
said. Carl insisted that Jews weren't his target audience; he wanted to tap the
Buddhist community. Gail had advised Carl to downplay Cubbins's name; she
couldn't think of a less eligible candidate for a charity. Carl informed Gail that
this movie was for brothers from the street, not sisters from the suburbs. Matters
were further complicated when the Chicago Cubs won their division for the first
time since 1945; a play-off game was slated for the same date on which Carl had
scheduled the premiere.

Despite the fact that the Chicago Theater boasted a capacity of five thousand
and Carl had purchased advertising in all local newspapers and magazines, a
grand total of seventy-five tickets were sold, most of them to followers of a
neo-Buddhist sect who had been intrigued by the flyer Gail had designed:
"Bronzeville Pictures is proud to present *Godfathers of Soul,* a uniquely Buddhist
entertainment." There was a picture of Tiny Walker with a gun pointed at Al
Capone's head. Above Walker's head, a thought balloon: "I chanted for this day,
muthafucka!" The rest of the audience was composed of members of the cast
and crew and their families, who had to fight their way past picketers protesting
the Cubbins benefit. Even Charlie Wasserstrom, on the advice of his eldest
daughter, who had chosen to stay in New York and skip the premiere, instead at-

tended High Holiday services, listening to the Cubs game broadcast on the transistor radio that Rabbi Shmulevits had conveniently left in the men's room.

At the premiere, Deirdre sat alone in a box seat while Mel spent the first part of the evening hidden away in the empty second balcony, nervously wolfing down a bucket of plain popcorn. But a half hour into the movie, Mel took cover in the lobby. For the first moments, he had been ecstatic to see his work on an enormous screen. He remembered coming here after midterms at Roosevelt, taking girls up to the balcony and making out underneath blinking electric stars during Bruce Lee flicks. Now it was his name, not Lee's, twenty feet high. He felt elated when the audience burst into applause upon seeing his name. As the opening credits faded to black, Mel wished that he had performed a Hitchcockian cameo in the film; he would have liked to see himself that big.

But the moment the first scene started, Mel heard whispering and muttering, people shifting their weight. He spent the next twenty minutes looking over the railing, trying to decipher the reactions of individual spectators. When he heard laughter, he wondered why people were laughing. When the audience was silent, he wondered why no one was laughing. When someone got up and walked down the aisle, he wondered if they were buying popcorn or walking out for good. On one hand, he was furious with Carl for scaring off spectators with the Cubbins benefit; on the other, he was glad that hardly anyone was here.

When the muttering from the audience became even louder, Mel exited the balcony and walked along the theater's threadbare crimson carpet, underneath the cobwebbed candelabras and down a curved staircase to the lobby, where Lennie Kidd sat behind a card table with stacks of Xeroxed flyers announcing upcoming neo-Buddhist meetings. Mel walked out of the theater, then south on State Street, through Chicago's ghostly downtown with its darkened office buildings, half-full hotels, hamburger restaurants, lunch counters, and empty lots. He walked by green lampposts on which were affixed the detritus of political campaigns past, a palimpsest of the names of those remembered and those forgotten—Daley for Mayor, Byrne, Hanrahan, Bakalis, Washington. Only chugging green buses and rumbling el cars interrupted the silence of the night. Mel was gazing into the dark window of Woolworth's when he heard footsteps and then a familiar voice calling out, "Brotherman."

Carl Silverman, his gray-black hair wavy, his multicolored beard fuller than ever, was dashing south across Madison Street against the red light when Mel saw him; the tails of his wrinkled suitjacket flapped as he ran. These days at Bronzeville, they greeted each other gruffly if at all; if circumstances required it, they shook hands. But now Carl wrapped Mel in a hug and Mel felt obliged to hug the man back. Carl said that he had been looking everywhere for Mel; why wasn't he watching the flick? It was getting some pretty fly reactions from the crowd. Mel forced a smile and said that he wasn't so sure about that; he supposed that they'd like it better once he'd done a cleaner edit and had a sweeter sound mix. Carl said he didn't like to hear that defeatist talk from Mel; he'd been sending out video copies of the edit and had been very encouraged by the response of a distributor out in L.A. Mel was dubious, but Carl said that this was the dope shit; within a week, he was confident that they would have a sale.

Once Mel and Carl were back in the theater lobby, both of them walking swiftly past Lennie Kidd's booth, Mel asked Carl which distributors he would be meeting, but Carl told him not to sweat those details—he was the businessman; he'd cut the deals. Carl knew that this was hardly the time to mention that the edits the distributor had in mind were rather more drastic than Mel might have imagined. For the one man who had responded somewhat positively to the video Carl had sent, as opposed to returning it, said that it was too disjointed, too choppy, too long, too controversial, too black. But he had also said that the film's episodic structure did lend itself to a shorter format—say, a series of four- to five-minute segments. As cinema, it wasn't much, but as raw material for music videos that could be used by rock and rap groups, it could be "killer."

As Mel reentered the auditorium, he felt a new lightness in his stride. As he thought of Carl's promise of a distribution deal, he glided, nearly floated up the first flight of steps to Deirdre's box. He sat beside her, took her hand, and watched the movie, *his* movie, now delighting in each shot. And even if no laughter was heard for Mel's best jokes, Mel laughed loudly enough for everyone in the auditorium. He felt his heart racing as Tiny Walker ran after Capone's gang, felt a lump in his trousers when he saw Jasmine Huggins in the shower. He stayed rooted to his seat until the final credits rolled, and smiled with pride when he read that any similarities between these fictional characters and actual living beings was completely coincidental. When the lights came up and scattered applause was heard from the few remaining cast and crew members and their families, Mel was kissing his wife, and he felt so proud that he did not even think to ask whether she had liked his film.

— — — —

The following day, Michelle Wasserstrom was seated on the floor of the Main Hall of Grand Central Terminal, consoling Rabbi Jeffrey Meltzer as the two of them waited for Gareth Overgaard to arrive. Gareth had completed an orientation session in Philadelphia for the Peace Corps, and now he and Jeffrey would be spending two nights in Michelle's 350-square-foot studio apartment in Alphabet City. Afterward, Gareth would fly from JFK for a two-year stint in Port-au-Prince, Haiti.

Mel had sent Michelle two invitations to the *Godfathers* premiere, and one letter with a Jamaican honeymoon picture; he had also left a sheepish message on her answering machine. Michelle had not responded; she had sent Mel and Deirdre a gravy boat for their wedding, but hadn't bothered to include a card.

Jeffrey Meltzer had arrived the previous morning, and Michelle was already eager for him to depart. Though he had professed his desire to be treated "like any other guest," he had acted surprised when Michelle revealed that she didn't keep separate cabinets for meat and dairy—hardly likely, given that she only owned three plates, Michelle had said. He had then rummaged through Michelle's drawer in a futile search for a *machzor*, and today insisted that they walk all the way from her apartment to Grand Central because they shouldn't ride the subway on *yontiff*. Worst of all, once they arrived at the train station, every five minutes or so, Jeffrey would send Michelle off to find a TV to check the score of the final game of the National League Division Series between the Chicago Cubs and the San Diego Padres, which Jeffrey wasn't allowed to watch during the holidays. It was Game 5, he had explained, the Cubs had been up two-zip, but the Padres had evened the series, and now it was the Cubs' last chance.

Michelle had more than five hundred pages to read for her History of Legal Systems class, a half-dozen pages to memorize for an audition for a cameo in a Woody Allen film—Allen had apparently caught a glimpse of her shower scene in a video that had been sent to his production office—and she would have much preferred working to running down the Grand Central stairs and asking a busboy in the Oyster Bar to update her on the Cubs score. She hadn't attended a sporting event since she'd left Chicago; the last time she'd gone to Wrigley Field had been on Take-a-Photo-with-a-Cub Day. Myra Tuchbaum had asked Michelle to take her picture with three hirsute Cubs stars: Bruce Sutter, Bill Buckner, and Dave

Kingman. Michelle had stood there with her camera and pleaded with Myra, "Can't you pose with someone else? They all look like fricking porn stars."

The final time Michelle asked the Oyster Bar busboy for the score, he told her that the Cubs had lost. They had been leading, but a grounder had squirted through Leon Durham's legs, and Tony Gwynn had knocked home what would become the winning run. And now Harold Washington was on TV wearing a Cubs cap—"Maybe next year," he was saying. Michelle thanked the busboy, told him for the third time that she wouldn't give him her phone number because she was "experimenting with celibacy," then returned to report the news to a despondent Jeffrey Meltzer.

"Aww man," Meltzer kept saying, "Aww *man.*" The previous year, he said, he'd had a gentleman's bet with his childhood buddy, Gabe Goldstein—a singer-songwriter who had recently self-produced the album *Love over Goldstein.* Goldstein was a Sox fan, and Meltzer had bet him that his team wouldn't make it to the World Series; this year, Gabe had made the same bet. Jeff couldn't believe that one year later, the same thing was happening. He wondered if Chicago was cursed. He loved the Cubs, he hated the Sox, but what difference did it make when both of them lost? Michelle put her arm around him and his head dropped to her shoulder.

When Gareth finally arrived at Grand Central, a bag in each hand and one on his back, Jeffrey Meltzer wiped his eyes and jumped to his feet. As Jeffrey ran toward Gareth, Michelle thought of what he had just said to her. She shook her head and smiled as she rummaged in her bag for a cigarette and began to consider her life philosophy. The point, she thought as she lit a cigarette, was not to root for the Cubs or the Sox; the point was to have better things to do than to give a damn about sports. She took a drag on her cigarette and stood alone, watching the two men embrace.

# III

# *Yetziyat Mitzrayim*

*Jill and Becky's Book of Exodus*

*(1984–85)*

━ ━ ━

(A STORY OF WEST ROGERS PARK, CHICAGO,
AND THE REST OF AMERICA)

*Hope is starting to rise again . . .*
—MAYOR HAROLD WASHINGTON, 1984

# FALL SEMESTER 1984

J ill Wasserstrom had been gone from Chicago for all of six hours when a massive four-poster bed came clunking through the doorway of her Vassar College dormitory room in Poughkeepsie, New York, carried by Marty and Angela Eiser staedt. Their daughter Bibi was trailing behind, instructing them to set the bed d own gently because she'd get in trouble if they scratched the floor. Up until that moment, Jill—who had already hung up her clothes, unpacked her typewriter, sticky-taped posters of Harold Washington and Che Guevara to her wall, plugged in her miniature boom box, and placed a shoebox of cassettes next to it—had enjoyed a peace and solitude that she had never known before.

At m any points during the summer, Jill's father had asked her if she would prefer for him to drive her to Poughkeepsie or accompany her on the plane to New York. Driving east with Michelle and Larry, as she had the previous summer, was n o longer an option, since Michelle, now a senior at NYU, had not returned to C hicago in eight months. Furthermore, Michelle had called Jill's choice of college "morbid" and avowed, quoting Popeye Doyle from *The French Connection,* that she wouldn't even deign to "pick her feet in Poughkeepsie." Ultimately, ove r dinner on North Shore Avenue, Jill said that she would prefer traveling to Poughkeepsie alone. Charlie was deeply saddened; this was obvious to Jill because he wouldn't stop smiling.

While Jill w as in school in New York, her dog, Fidel, would stay with Muley. Charlie had said that he and Gail would take good care of the dog, but Jill didn't believe him for a n instant. If she left the animal in Charlie and Gail's care, she was certain that it wo uld drag Charlie into a ditch, at which point Charlie would let go the leash and l Fidel, finally free, would madly dash into oncoming traffic; or, the dog would get a whiff of Rachel's diaper, lunge toward the child, and Gail would insist the animal be euthanized. Muley would be attending the Art Institute and living in a loft midway between the Loop and Chinatown. The loft was owned by Muley's old Nortown Theater boss, Ajay Patel. In exchange for free rent, Muley was helping Ajay with rehab work; he said that there would be plenty of room for Fidel to romp in the loft, the lake would only be a few blocks away, and he would be happy for the company.

The night before Jill was to fly to New York, the Wasserstroms held a going-away dinner at Myron & Phil's restaurant. Charlie gave an inspirational speech, warning Jill not to drink, try drugs, or "hang around strange boys," then told her to "go off and be somebody." Gail presented Jill with a Frederick's of Hollywood gift certificate ("in case you meet someone special"), and Rachel punched Jill hard in the thigh. Afterward, Jill walked with Fidel to the house on Mozart Street where Muley had been living with his mother and Mel since the beginning of the summer. At Jill's suggestion, she and Muley then walked to the lake, Fidel trotting between the two of them as they held hands, even though their relationship had been declared platonic more than a year earlier.

They spent the entire night at Lunt Avenue Beach, eating Levinson's cupcakes and drinking Asti Spumante out of Styrofoam cups, swimming with Fidel in the ice-cold lake, then drying off and waiting for the sunrise. It was still Jill's favorite place in the world, the place where she always came when she needed solace or rejuvenation, the place where her mother had taken her in her stroller, where the two of them had walked for hours collecting seashells and shards of glass made smooth by the water, where Jill had sat alone on the day of her mother's funeral, knowing that her mother's spirit wouldn't be at the cemetery; it would always be here at the beach.

Muley and Jill lay hand in hand, their heads cushioned by their crumpled summer jackets, looking up at a sky too cloudy for them to make out constellations or the path of space shuttle *Discovery,* which Muley said was passing above them. After the darkest part of the night had passed and a thin hula hoop of midnight blue was emerging at the horizon, they sat up, brushed the sand off of their clothes, and Muley talked about all he would do in the future, while Jill spoke of all she hadn't done in the past. Jill complained that she would be going to college in less than twelve hours and she hadn't done anything that she was supposed to have done—she hadn't had sex, hadn't smoked pot or Marlboros, hadn't even learned to drive. She said that she didn't like being the good girl, the one in whom all the smart guys confided their lust for Devorah Kerbis, didn't like being the girl whom guys kissed before apologizing, then going off to sleep with their girlfriends. She had eschewed all of her older sister's bad behavior—smoking weed at Boston concerts, doing 'shrooms, sleeping with everybody, even Larry Rovner—yet saw no overall benefits.

Jill told Muley that maybe she would become an entirely different person in college. Maybe she would wear miniskirts, cut her hair short and streak it blond, wear makeup, smoke cigarettes, have sex with burnouts, preppies, and jocks. She didn't like that people thought she was a virgin—she didn't mind being one, only that everybody automatically assumed that she was. After a *Lane Leader* party, she had walked to the drainage canal with Hillel Levy, made out with him, and he had remarked that kissing her was "like kissing Toucan Sam."

The whole situation was unfair, Jill told Muley; she estimated that Muley had probably made out with a dozen girls and had sex with three or four, and he wasn't even straight. Muley said he didn't know about that. Which part, Jill asked—the having sex with three or four girls part or the straight part. Both, he said. He had only had sex with two people—Connie Sherman, now three months pregnant and living in New Mexico with Ephraim; and his Lane film teacher, Irit Ben-Amar, shortly after Connie had moved in with Ephraim. So, Jill asked, was he gay or not? Not really, Muley said, finally admitting that he'd only told her that he might be gay to make their relationship seem less complicated. Jill briefly considered whether she should be angry that Muley had lied to her, then decided to be glad that he was telling her the truth now. Well, if he wasn't gay, Jill said, then they could have sex on the beach and she wouldn't have to go to college as a virgin, and since they'd be eight hundred miles away from each other in twelve hours, there would be no uncomfortable morning-after since it already was morning. True, Muley said.

For Muley, who still loved Jill deeply, there could be no moment better than this one. They were alone on the beach, the temperature just below seventy degrees, a warm summer breeze blowing, and the sky resembling layers of colored sand—a thin stripe of pink beneath thicker stripes of navy blue and indigo. The dog was asleep. It was the last night before college.

While Jill did not so much want to make love to Muley as to be able to say to herself twenty-four hours later that she had done it, to cross one more item off

her "To Do Before College" list between smoke a joint and see an X-rated film—
*Midnight Cowboy* and *Last Tango in Paris* had been rated X, but they were art
films and therefore didn't count. She wanted to feel the swooning of which she
had read in *Night and Day,* gasp with ecstasy like Rebecca De Mornay in *Risky
Business.* The closest she had felt to that sensation had been in Wes Sullivan's
bedroom the day he had left Chicago, but then she had felt him stop, heard his
patronizing words: "I just can't do it." Whenever she knew that she should sur-
render to a moment, she could feel her consciousness slipping out of her body,
looking down with an amused yet distant smile. When she had kissed Rae-Ann
Warner—who wrote Jill every so often from Indiana University to boast about
which sorority event she had chaired, which alum would help her to find a sports-
writing job covering the Ladies' Professional Golf Association tour—she was not
excited by the kiss so much as by the idea of making out with a girl. The previous
summer, on the night of her sixteenth birthday, after she had seen *Risky Business*
at the Lincoln Village with Muley, she had lain back in bed and attempted to masturbate. She had never had much interest in performing this activity, yet again felt
that it was something she should have done. But the moment that she began to
experience something approaching pleasure, she asked herself why she was wasting time with such a pointless, selfish activity when she could be writing letters
for Amnesty International. Jill now wondered whether, if she and Muley made
love as she had somewhat facetiously suggested, she would finally succumb to
passion or whether she would remain fluttering above, watching the two of them
below in the sand.

And since there was nothing Muley would have preferred to do than make
love to Jill at that moment, and since he knew that if the experience lived up to
his dreams, then he would not be able to forget it, that it would consume his
thoughts while he waited with Fidel for Jill to return home for Chanukah, he
didn't know how to respond. But by then, morning had arrived—a squad car was
cruising the boardwalk, a bulldozer was tamping down the sand, and in the distance, a garbage collector was spearing dead alewives and dropping them into a
black trash bag.

Jill's ride to O'Hare with Charlie, Gail, and Rachel was interminable. There
was bumper-to-bumper traffic all the way west down Devon, which Charlie took
both to avoid construction on the Kennedy and to make the farewell last as long
as possible. Charlie kept smiling the whole way, assuring Jill that four months

wasn't really that long; if Jill ever got lonesome, she could call collect—the truth, he said, was that she was embarking upon a new, exciting part of her life. He envied her because he had never gone to college, and it was O.K. to cry, crying was good, if people didn't know how to cry, they didn't know how to laugh. As the aphorisms mounted, Jill wondered how many would work their way into Charlie's next column or book. Charlie and Gail both hugged Jill at the airport, but the only moment she had truly enjoyed was when Gail had asked Rachel, "Don't you want to give your big sister a kiss?" and Rachel had spat out her answer: *"No!"*

Though, at seventeen, Jill had not yet experienced the all-encompassing pleasure associated with love and sex, she presumed that the rush she felt as her plane—the first she'd ever taken—took off into the clouds over Chicago had to be somewhat comparable. When the plane leveled off, she could no longer see the city below her, and she could already feel herself entering a new realm filled with people like her, people who read nonfiction in their spare time, liked black-and-white movies, and sported incendiary political buttons. Her friends would be the children of professors and politicians, social workers and activists; they would already be members of the American Civil Liberties Union, grudging volunteers for Walter Mondale's presidential campaign.

Which was why it had shocked Jill when she had been sitting at her desk in her second-floor dorm room in Cushing Hall, where it was rumored that both Edna St. Vincent Millay and Jane Fonda had once lived, reading Simone de Beauvoir's *The Second Sex* and blasting *Purple Rain,* one of only a dozen cassettes she owned and played incessantly, and in had stumbled Marty, Angela, and Bibi. Bibi *Eisenstaedt.* Bibi Eisenstaedt with whom Jill had attended K.I.N.S. Bibi Eisenstaedt whose older sister Missy was now majoring in Judaic Studies at Barnard. Bibi Eisenstaedt whom Jill had often seen from a distance walking toward Ida Crown Jewish Academy with the other girls in long denim skirts and tennis shoes until the Eisenstaedts had moved to Northbrook. Bibi Eisenstaedt who was now mauling Jill with a hug that sent both of them tumbling onto Jill's bed. Bibi Eisenstaedt who was now showing Jill her posters of Sting. Bibi Eisenstaedt whose father, Marty, had once worked with Jill's father in the advertising department of Schiffler Newspapers before the papers had shut down and Marty had found a job working as a real estate agent for Marum-Kagan Realtors, while Charlie Wasserstrom had become a best-selling nonfiction author. Bibi Eisenstaedt whose mother was now shaking Jill's hand, telling her that Bibi had been so happy to learn that Jill would be attending Vassar; hadn't Jill gotten Bibi's phone messages and her letter? "My dad's really bad at that sort of thing," Jill said quickly, at which Marty piped up, "That's old Scatterbrain Charlie for you," then asked Jill if she wanted to join them for lunch at the Nickel Inn.

Jill hadn't intended to ignore Bibi's two effusive phone messages and even more effusive postcard littered with capital letters, exclamation points, and smiley faces ("Wouldn't it be GREAT to be ROOMIES???!!!"). At the same time, Jill had had no idea how to respond. When the campus housing department had asked her to indicate her roommate preference, Jill had written, "someone from a different background, culture, and/or country," while Bibi had written, "I want to be roomies with Jill Wasserstrom!"

At lunch, Bibi asked Jill if she was still dating Muley ("He's *black,* but he's really smart and nice," she said), then filled Jill in about the lives of their Hebrew school classmates: Avi Small was a senior at Mather with Shoshana Levine, whose brother Arik's band, Weinstock!—composed of first-year law and medical students—was getting airplay on WLUP. Moshe Cardash was at Ida Crown and would be attending the Yeshiva the following year ("That's just a little intense for me," Bibi opined). Connie Sherman was living with some farmer out in New Mexico. Devorah Kerbis and David Singer were still attending Lane and working at Long John Silver's and Walgreens, respectively. Aaron Mermelstein—who hadn't been the same since he'd hit his head against a desk to see if it would hurt—was planning to join the Israeli army. Lana Rovner was at prep school in Connecticut; her brother Larry and his wife, Hannah, had written a new musical called *Gotta Sing!,* which would premiere off-Broadway in January; its original title, *The New Jazz Singer,* had triggered rumors of lawsuits. Shmuel Weinberg, whom Bibi had dated sporadically during her senior year before telling him that they should "just be friends," was attending Syracuse and would, most probably, visit Poughkeepsie to take her to the "Weird Al" Yankovic concert in Kingston, and Hillel Levy had won a scholarship to the Art Institute.

After lunch, Jill and the Eisenstaedts drove through Poughkeepsie to look at the sights—"That's where we'll be getting pizza!" Bibi said when they passed Napoli's Pizzeria; "That's where we'll be seeing movies!" Bibi called out when they passed the Juliet Theater, which was showing *The Jigsaw Man.* "That's where we'll get cones!" Bibi shouted when they passed Sweet Blondie's ice cream parlor. Then Marty Eisenstaedt drove back to the dorm. He got out of the U-Haul truck, hugged his daughter for what seemed to Jill like five full minutes; Angela shook Bibi's hand, then Bibi's parents got back in the truck and drove out of the parking lot while Bibi waved and cried. Once they were back in their dorm room, Bibi asked Jill to sit on her bed—she said she wanted Jill to feel how firm the mattress was, how soft the sheets were, wasn't it the best bed in the whole wide world?

For a moment, Jill thought that things might be getting interesting. For a moment, she thought that Bibi might be a lesbian, which would force Jill to regard her with new perspective, to reassess her predilection for holding hands with girls while doing the hora. Jill agreed that the mattress was, yes, quite firm and the sheets were certainly smooth, then asked why Bibi's parents had bothered lugging a bed from Northbrook—did Bibi perhaps have some spinal condition? No, Bibi said; she had just thought that she might miss her own bedroom so much that her father had suggested they drive her bed to Poughkeepsie so that she would feel at home there.

During the first weeks of college, Jill's euphoria at having escaped West Rogers Park did not abate. Every morning when she awoke at 6:30, she wondered why she had slept so long, she had already missed her favorite part of the morning. She would sneak past Bibi still asleep in pajamas, one arm over a stuffed goose, the watchful eyes of Sting looking down upon her with amused indifference, take her shower, get dressed, then walk to the nearly empty dining center where she would review the day's reading over black coffee and oatmeal. She had registered for five classes, attended lectures by Susan Sontag and Jesse Jackson, readings by James Salter and Jamaica Kincaid, screenings of *Last Year at Marienbad* and *Things to Come.* She had Xeroxed flyers for Students for Mondale, walked out of concerts by Urban Blight and the Butthole Surfers, and taken a part-time campus job filing tapes in the foreign languages department. She had written a paper on George Bernard Shaw's capitalist critique in *Mrs. Warren's Profession,* aced three German vocabulary quizzes, studied pictures of Greek pottery on flash cards, and camped out in the all-night reading room, poring over articles about Aristotle's theories of the elements. She had gone to a keg party on her floor, watched Bibi drink too much Genesee Cream Ale, and helped her throw up in the hall bathroom. She had attended a Gay People's Alliance party, received an edible condom as a door prize, and danced all night on tabletops with her dorm mates to "Pulling Mussels from a Shell" and "Let's Go Crazy," even timidly singing, *"Oh no, let's go!"* on the chorus of the latter.

She typed long letters to Muley and to her sister and brief notes to other friends from Hebrew school and high school, thanking Shmuel Weinberg for sending her his "Syracuse Update" and a stuffed kitty cat, which she said she'd donated to Goodwill; telling Moshe Cardash that she couldn't share his enthusiasm for the Talmud passages he had sent her; and informing Hillel Levy that she didn't appreciate his drawings of smiling penis people sodomizing Disney characters, and she'd thank him to not draw his cartoons on the envelope where Bibi could see them, although Bibi loved Hillel's cartoons, effusing, "Look at all the happy mushroom people!"

Jill had attended the orientation meeting of the college newspaper, *The Miscellany News,* and, though she had requested assignments covering campus news or national politics, editor Rob Rubinstein had told her that most freshman writers began their careers at *"The Misc."* by reviewing records. He handed her three albums—Lou Reed's *New Sensations,* The Replacements' *Let It Be,* and Fonzi Thornton's *Pumpin'* (*Let Me Show U How to Do It*)—and asked her to submit reviews the following day, and though Rubinstein later told her that she "didn't know dick" about music, her writing was "decent enough," and why didn't she work on news stories when there were ones that he and the other editors didn't want to cover themselves?

Every day in the hallways, in the laundry room, in the dining center, on the college's pine needle–strewn paths, she met dozens of people, half of whose names she'd forget before their conversations had concluded. She discussed her hometown, she discussed what her father did for a living (many people seemed interested in this), and she answered the question, the one question that seemed more important than all others: *What groups do you like?* It was the only question that she was unable to answer correctly, for when she answered honestly that she liked Lionel Richie, Billy Joel, Prince, and Madonna, women stifled laughs and men viewed her suspiciously. And when she tried to supply the answers that others provided (e.g., The Smiths, The Cure), she would inadvertently make some error that revealed her ignorance ("Oh yeah, Morrissey—they're cool"), so that she finally learned to make her tastes deliberately obscure ("a lot of early Gil Scott-Heron and Jim Pepper"), which had the unintended side effect of making her the object of desire for several gaunt males who deejayed for the campus radio station.

In her dorm, she befriended Matthew Chen, a gifted break-dancer and the son of a former advisor to Chiang Kai-shek, who rode his ten-speed fast up and down the hallways and boasted that D.M.C. and Jam Master Jay shopped at his family's jewelry store; Andrea Fleischman, a gum-snapping Memphis girl who stalked the hallways in her bathrobe and talked loudly about yeast infections on the hall phone; Tom Dunne, a tall, lanky basketball player and horse-racing enthusiast from Montana who drove a pickup truck with an "I Can't Drive 55" bumper sticker; Ford Graham, son of a South African diamond family, who sold hash brownies at college-wide bake sales; and Kenny Melnick, an ardent Knicks fan and lifelong New Yorker who challenged Jill to a racquetball match and, afterward, bought her a rack of Genesee, even though he'd defeated her six games to none.

During Jill's first three weeks, five guys asked her out on dates—Ezra Wiltz, a pale, weedy medievalist and member of the Society for Creative Anachronism; Stanley Barnes, a tennis-playing, African-American Republican who supplied her with books by William F. Buckley and assumed that when Jill called him a fascist they were enjoying a witty and sexy repartee; Sidney Florio, a Filipino premed student who routinely worked until four in the morning, at which point he blasted arena rock bands, such as Def Leppard and Zebra; Raj Stein, a half-Indian, half-Jewish aristocrat who stopped speaking to Jill when he discovered that she had gotten higher SAT scores than he had; and Horace Greenstein, a Chicago-born Econ major and part-time deejay who referred to himself as "The Horace," and often flapped his arms and squawked like a bird while imitating Morris Day of The Time—he had given himself the deejay moniker Killah-G ("Thinks he's a killa, but he's white like vanilla," Matthew Chen had opined). Horace had run afoul of Jill when he had danced in his room to Grandmaster Flash records, and said see, he was blacker than the blacks on this campus. Jill had made out with two of them, gone to Blodgett Hall to see movies with two others, had ice cream with another and always told them about her "boyfriend back home" toward the end of the evening when she realized that they weren't satisfied with just holding hands, kissing, or eating ice cream.

Sometimes, Jill came home early; usually, she came home late. Either way, nights ended with a discussion with Bibi, and discussions with Bibi nearly always involved Bibi's analyses of the "Meat Book." The Meat Book was about the size of a magazine and, in addition to an overview of the campus, its history, and its rules, it contained passport-sized, black-and-white photos of every member of the Class of 1988, their intended majors, and their hometowns. The summer before college, every student had received a Meat Book. Bibi's father had circled the nice-looking guys with Jewish surnames and written notes underneath them, such as "What does his father do?" or "A nice doctor for you."

Sitting on her bed, Bibi would point at a picture of a guy, then ask whether Jill had met him and, if so, was he nice and smart, and would he be a good date for her or did Jill "call dibs" on him? And then she'd ask Jill lots of personal questions. She would ask Jill how she liked to be kissed and what kinds of bodies she liked and whether she'd ever given a guy a blow job and when Jill said no, Bibi would laugh hysterically and say that she didn't see why anyone would do that, it sounded so gross, who wanted all that in their mouth? Who was Jill's ideal husband, she would ask, and when Jill would say that she planned to be a spinster and live on a ranch where she would wear her gray hair long and feed and milk goats, Bibi would sigh and say that unmarried women and widows were the saddest people on earth. But when Jill would invent some dream man to satisfy Bibi—say, a Marxist revolutionary from El Salvador imprisoned for teaching Gramsci in the classroom—Bibi would interrupt to once again discuss her ideal mate: Jewish, of course; financially successful (but not from family money, because that bred indolence); handsome (like Sting); family-oriented (she wanted at least three kids, because she had only one sibling and had always felt lonely); and supportive of her career (she was going to be a pediatrician, but would take time off after the kids were born).

Then Bibi would instruct Jill to recite her evening prayers and, afterward, to pray for a perfect boyfriend. And in bed, with the door closed between her room and Bibi's, Jill would lie in the dark and pray, for she did pray every night before she went to bed, not so much because she believed in prayer, but rather because she had made a vow to herself long ago that she would do so and she did not retract her vows. And she would, in fact, pray for the perfect boyfriend; she prayed that Bibi would get one.

＿＿ ＿＿ ＿＿ ＿＿

One October night, after she had turned in a story to *Miscellany News* editor Rob Rubinstein accusing the college of holding investments in companies that did business in South Africa ("People really aren't interested in this shit," Rob said and asked her to cut the article down to a 75-word brief to make room for Alec Savage's Kinks concert review), Jill returned to her dorm, where she heard Bibi talking with her mother. Jill always knew who Bibi was talking to—if it was her father, she'd giggle and talk about boys; if it was her mother, she'd just say "Mm-hm," "Uh-huh," and "I already *did*." And if Shmuel Weinberg was on the line, she'd remain silent for long stretches, hiss, "Do we have to talk about this now?" after which she'd say, "Yeah, she's here," and tell Jill, "It's for you." Jill would take Bibi's phone and talk to Shmuel about the wretched quality of the college paper, which devoted six pages to arts coverage, but only two to opinion and editorial, half of which was taken up by Rob Rubinstein's "From the Editor's Desk" column (Jill had nicknamed it FETID), in which Rob discussed such topics as how underclassmen wore too much cologne and mousse and listened to too much Duran Duran, how men shouldn't have to wear ties, or how there was no need for Martin Luther King Day to be a national holiday. Then Shmuel would ask Jill whether Bibi was dating anybody and Jill would respond, "You should ask *her.*"

On this night, as Bibi "mm-hmmed" her mother, Jill changed into a sweatshirt, sweatpants, and sneakers, tied her hair into a ponytail, and slipped *Purple Rain* into a salvaged Walkman that Muley had sent her. She was three-quarters of the way out the door when Bibi said, "Just hang on a second, Mom," then asked Jill where she was going. Out for a jog, Jill said. Bibi yelped that Jill was crazy, it was too late to go by herself, why didn't she wait for her to finish her conversation and the two of them could go? Jill said sure, but Bibi might not want to jog where she was going. Where, Bibi asked, around campus? No, Jill said, she was going into the city. "The city?" Bibi cringed. She asked Jill if she was serious; that wasn't safe. She again asked Jill to wait, but at the next "Mm-hm," Jill was out the door, skipping down the steps, then jogging through the TV room where male premeds in T-shirts, boxers, and flip-flops were eating tortilla chips and watching David Letterman, then out the front door and into the Poughkeepsie night.

Actually, there were two Poughkeepsies—immediately surrounding the college was the town, a quaint, vaguely suburban expanse dotted by professors' homes, chain restaurants, a 7-Eleven, a sports bar, a video store, and shopping malls; and then there was the City of Poughkeepsie, where Jill was headed. For the first three-quarters of the twentieth century, the city had been both an industrial center and a travel destination. It was the last stop on New York's Metro-North train line; honeymooners would stay here before venturing into Manhattan for dinner and a show or driving around Hyde Park to see where the Vanderbilts and the Roosevelts had lived. But by the 1970s, the textile mills closed, industrial jobs dwindled, and the city became mired in a depression from which it had not yet emerged. A block from campus, Jill jogged past white clapboard Collegeview Avenue dwellings and businesses that catered to students and their parents—a soap and stationery store, Angelina's restaurant, Silent Pictures posters, Pete's Pub. She then hooked a right onto Raymond Avenue, which led to Main Street and an ever more dingy and depressed downtown—Oasis Discount Liquor, the Pickwick Pub, the Grand Union supermarket. She jogged past head shops and cocktail lounges, nail salons and pawnbrokers, boarded-up storefront churches, and a fried-fish shack that made its money in the numbers racket. She jogged past the Salvation Army, through the center of the city and the nearly deserted pedestrian mall where homeless men and women and stray dogs slept in front of darkened discount stores, until she reached the locked train station.

Jill had wanted to see the Poughkeepsie station at night. In general, she liked train stations, liked the idea of people in transit, the sound of spinning wheels, liked train tracks, liked kicking stones as she walked across them. But she had wanted to see this station in particular. She had been here in the summer of 1974, when her parents had taken her and Michelle to visit Becky's parents, who lived in Poughkeepsie. Which was why, Jill presumed, Michelle had called Jill's choice of college "morbid," and why Jill, even though she had scored nearly perfect SATs and was ranked twelfth in her Lane graduating class, had immediately chosen Vassar once she had been accepted, never mind that this small liberal arts college, which had turned coed in 1969, was known far more for its English and Art History programs than the Journalism and Political Science studies Jill sought to pursue.

It was not so much that Jill wanted to track down any remaining relatives from her mother's side of the family. When Becky's cousins had responded to her Bat Mitzvah invitations with curt notes and her grandmother Edna Schulman had not written at all, Jill assumed that Edna was dead ("She's either dead or a bitch or both," Michelle had said). As for any of the other relatives on Becky's side of the family, Jill could not recall having met any of them more than once. Before her mother had died, Jill had already found it remarkable how uneven the distribution of family contacts had been between Charlie and Becky, how every Sunday morning, Charlie's aunt Beileh would call Charlie and complain about her lazy son Teddy, how every Sunday night they would all go over to Uncle Dave and Aunt Peppy's house for veal or chicken parmesan, how Charlie would chatter on at length with his car dealer cousins about the next Manley High reunion.

Becky, meanwhile, called her parents once a month at most, and after they had talked for five minutes, she would ask Michelle if she wanted to talk to Grandma. Michelle would grunt and pass the phone to Jill, and when Jill was done talking, she'd pass the phone to her father, who would effusively "chew the fat" with Edna and Sam Schulman until Becky would call out, "It's enough already, Charlie."

After Becky's father died of emphysema, Becky spoke to her mother even less. While Charlie and Becky went to Poughkeepsie for Sam Schulman's funeral, Jill and Michelle stayed in Elmhurst with Uncle Dave and Aunt Peppy, who said that children shouldn't attend school when they were in mourning, especially when their school was an hour's drive away. The first day, Peppy took them for root beer floats, then shopping for slacks at Marshall Field's in Oak Park, and afterward to a matinée of *A Boy Named Charlie Brown* at the Lake Theater. The second day, she brought them along for her chores—to the Jewel, the meat market, the eye doctor. "Treat it like a vacation," Uncle Dave told them over a dinner of take-out meatball sandwiches and strawberry Nehi.

That night in bed, Michelle said, "Prison break?" and Jill immediately agreed. In the morning, once they heard Uncle Dave's Lincoln pull out of the carport and onto Butterfield Road, they packed their bags and crept downstairs while Peppy and her sons were sleeping. Michelle snatched a ten-dollar bill from the stash that Peppy kept underneath the couch cushions, and the two of them slipped out the front door and began running for the train station. "Free at last, free at last, thank God almighty we're free at last," Michelle cried, then asked Jill what she wanted to do. Jill, who felt deprived of a trip to see her grandmother, and who felt guilty for playing hooky, said that the only place she wanted to go was school. At first, Michelle called Jill a "freak," but then said that she was a genius; school was the last place anyone would look for them. But they had been back at Boone for only an hour when they were each called out of their classes and sent to Principal Loretta Wharram's office. Even though Michelle had cried, "Please, don't make us go back to Uncle Dave and Aunt Peppy; they're creeps," Mrs. Wharram had told them to stop their nonsense and go home with their aunt.

Jill vividly remembered the night that Charlie and Becky returned from Poughkeepsie. Her mother's face was so cold and stern that Jill felt that it would turn her to stone. Becky grabbed Jill's shoulder, then gripped Michelle's hand hard. "Don't you *ever*," she said, fixing Jill with a hard stare then training her gaze on Michelle. "Don't you *ever* make me worry about where you are." Jill had felt so ashamed that she thought that she should do something to hurt herself—catch her hand in a door, skin her knee, or break her arm—but once they were in the back of Charlie's Ford, Becky turned around to face them with a big grin. She apologized for having made a scene in front of Dave and Peppy, but said that she had to; she didn't want to hear their lectures about how she was supposed to discipline her children. She asked Jill if she had scared her. Jill nodded, then laughed, wiping her eyes. "Sorry, kiddo," she said, adding, "See, your mother could have been a great actress." On the ride home, Becky pretended to violently change her mood, laughing hysterically, then whipping her head back toward them, her face cold, hollow, and terrifying again before winking and laughing even more. Jill laughed so hard that her stomach hurt, even though, after that evening, whenever her mother said something serious, she wondered if she was joking, and whenever she was laughing, she wondered if her mother was really mad. So much so that even when her mother could barely stand up and needed Charlie to help her in and out of the bathroom, Jill always hoped to see Becky wink and laugh, to say it had all been one grand joke.

Occasionally, after Becky's father's funeral, Jill would ask about Sam Schulman. But Becky's answers were rarely longer than a sentence. Jill asked her mother if they would be seeing more of Grandma. Probably not, Becky had said. And when Jill asked why, Becky said, "Because she lives in Poughkeepsie and we live here." Most of what Jill learned of her mother's family was related to her by Charlie after Becky had died. Sam had been a pianist and, during high school outside Cleveland, had supported his family by playing in speakeasies. He hadn't attended college, but had moved to New York to try to make it in vaudeville, but couldn't earn a living and took a job as a salesman, traveling up and down the

Hudson River selling sheet music. Sam first saw Edna working behind the counter at Grinberg's Bakery in Poughkeepsie, where he purchased a cup of coffee and an almond crescent before an appointment with a customer at the Bardavon Opera House. At least once a week, Sam would enter the bakery, greet Edna Grinberg, and place the same order. Edna didn't speak to him until Sam's fourth visit. "You actually like those *chaloushes* almond crescents?" she asked. Five months later, they were married, and Sam had secured a loan from his older brother—a tanner in New Jersey—and opened Schulman's Sheet Music on Market Street.

The sheet music store never turned much of a profit, but when Edna's father died and she took over the bakery, Sam and Edna moved into a bigger apartment on Main Street. Born in 1938, Becky was the Schulmans' only child. Beyond this, Charlie's version of events became sketchy; Becky had had a "nice childhood" and had been "happy." Her father had taught her to sing and accompanied her on piano while she sang songs and invented dances in the front room. After she graduated high school, she moved with a girlfriend to New York, then to L.A., where she stayed for only two weeks after her roommate found a boyfriend. Becky decided to move back east, taking a waitressing gig in Chicago, where she met Charlie, and Sam and Edna moved into a little white house with green shutters on Mack Road. "And that's the whole story," Charlie would always say.

Charlie's version seemed incomplete. Jill still didn't know, for example, why her mother had stayed in Chicago instead of going straight home, didn't know why her mother could be so happy one moment, so sullen the next, didn't know why she often referred to herself as "old and washed up," didn't know why she loved Charlie so much, why she always insisted on kissing him on the lips and mussing his hair, didn't know why, on her family's last trip to Poughkeepsie, once they were on the departing train and had waved good-bye to Edna, Becky had let out a huge sigh, laughed, then hugged Charlie and said, "Well, let's not do that again anytime soon."

Though Jill knew that being in Poughkeepsie couldn't answer all of her questions, she still felt that she was in the right place. Even though she had checked the White Pages for an Edna Schulman and the Yellow Pages for a Grinberg's Bakery and couldn't find them. Even though, as she jogged back from the train station, she noted that the white house on Mack Road had the wrong name on the mailbox and the door buzzer; they both said FERRANTE.

When Jill returned to her dorm, she saw Bibi flanked by a phalanx of young men, all walking toward the TV room. Kenny Melnick was wielding a flashlight like a club; Matthew Chen was brandishing nunchaku; Tom Dunne had a baseball bat; the others—Sidney Florio and Horace Greenstein—were unarmed yet still strutting, chests out. Jill smiled and nodded at Bibi, but Bibi grabbed her wrist and asked where Jill had gone; she'd been "worried sick." At first, Bibi's "worried sick" line irked Jill; Bibi was acting more protective than Jill's own father. But then she determined that Bibi was probably less concerned with Jill's welfare than with devising a common cause for which she could recruit a search party composed of guys she wanted to date. Jill thanked Bibi for her concern, said that she really hadn't been in any danger but next time she wouldn't come back quite so late, then added that she was taking a shower because she felt sweaty and gross.

Once Jill returned from her shower, she saw all of the guys whom Bibi had rounded up. They were smoking cigarettes in Bibi's room, dancing, laughing, listening to Run-D.M.C. on Bibi's boom box. Horace Greenstein and Matthew Chen were trading break-dancing moves as they rapped along with the tape; Sidney Florio was reciting Eddie Murphy comedy routines; meanwhile, Tom Dunne kept bugging the others to go driving in his pickup truck so that they might steal road signs. "Actually, that's felonious," said Kenny Melnick, whose father was a professor of criminal justice at John Jay College in New York.

Jill said good night to Bibi and her harem, entered her room, shut her door, and put on her pajamas—Lane Tech sweatpants and a white Greenpeace "Rainbow Warrior" jersey. She then sat in bed with her covers up to her knees, reading a book about behavioral imprinting by Konrad Lorenz. But then a knock came upon the door and Jill uneasily said, "Come in," assuming that Bibi wanted to scold her further for her jogging habits.

Instead, in walked Matthew Chen, nunchaku in hand. He shut the door behind him, asked if he was interrupting anything, then, after loudly quoting some Run-D.M.C. lyrics out of context (*"I got a big long* Caddy, *not like a* Seville"), he asked Jill what she was reading, and when she showed him the Lorenz book, he said that it looked like "some pretty serious stuff." Jill said yes, and although she didn't like that Lorenz had demonstrated behavioral imprinting on a family of geese, she found his writings thought-provoking. Matthew asked if Jill had been scared during her jog; he offered that whenever she wanted to jog, she should knock on his door because he needed to exercise since he was getting to be a "fat tubba shit"— he pulled up his shirt and thumped his stomach—plus he had nunchaku and he wanted to see the "townie" who would mess with him. After he left and Jill had returned to her reading, she heard another knock, this time from Tom Dunne, who sat beside Jill on her bed and asked what she was reading and when she showed him, he said it looked like "some serious shit," after which he stretched out his legs and opined that Jill was lucky to have returned safely, because in Poughkeepsie, the police would not be sympathetic to her. Where he came from, "Johnny Law" was on your side, but in Poughkeepsie, he just cared about protecting his own skin. If Jill ever went jogging again, she should knock on his door.

After Tom had left, Kenny Melnick entered and asked Jill what she was reading and when she showed him the book, he said that Konrad Lorenz was an asshole. And when Jill asked Kenny why, he said that Lorenz had "fucked up a lot of ducks." Then he sat down next to Jill and said he didn't understand why Bibi was so freaked out by the fact that Jill had gone jogging in Poughkeepsie. Speaking with a thick New York accent, he observed that the idea of black urban crime and a white edenic campus was a myth propagated by the white *"powuh struct-chuh"*— the only real crime in Poughkeepsie was property crime born of poverty directly related to Reaganomics, and that's where *"fuckuhs"* such as Ed Koch had it all wrong, because he failed to recognize that violent crimes were generally perpetrated not by some "scary black guy with a gun" but some "drunk asshole on campus." They were lucky that there wasn't more crime because if he were a black guy, he'd buy himself a rifle and take *"pawtshawts"* at white boys all day long.

Charmed and intrigued by Kenny's diatribe, Jill was about to ask if he wanted to have dinner with her some night, but then another knock was heard, Bibi entered, and Kenny sprang up from Jill's bed. Before Jill could tell Kenny that he didn't have to leave, Kenny was out the door, at which point Bibi pretended to swoon onto Jill's bed. Then she popped up and scurried into her room, returning with the Meat Book. Wasn't he just the dreamiest thing, Bibi asked as she turned to a page and folded it back to show the black-and-white photograph of Kenneth R. Melnick from New York, NY, projected major, criminal justice. "See, *Jewish,*" she said. "See, *Lawyer.*" She pointed out that her father had circled his picture and written underneath his name, "What does his pop do?" She thought that Kenny would probably ask her to the fall formal; the only question was who would ask Jill so that they could double-date. Jill said that she didn't have any interest in attending the formal; she would be too consumed by her classes, her newspaper assignments, and her work for Students for Mondale to bother with guys. Though, she allowed, if Bibi hadn't "called dibs" on him first, exploring Poughkeepsie with Kenny wouldn't have been the worst thing she could have done.

On three successive nights, Bibi asked Jill how she might get Kenny to ask her to the formal; afterward, she would enumerate all that she would and would not let Kenny do with her following said formal. And when Kenny finally invited Bibi to dinner, Bibi asked Jill if she should act surprised when Kenny popped the question. The night of the dinner, Kenny wore wrinkled jeans and an untucked, olive-green corduroy shirt that had once belonged to his grandfather, while Bibi wore contacts even though they hurt her eyes, and the black leather miniskirt and fishnets that her father had bought her for her high school graduation. Jill was dining at the cafeteria with a few junior editors of the *Miscellany News* when Bibi emerged from out of nowhere, then whispered loudly in Jill's ear, "Fine, he's yours; happy now?" Moments later, she was gone.

When Jill returned home, Bibi was at her desk, memorizing terms in her Anatomy textbook. She apologized for having "lashed out" at Jill; she hoped that Jill wasn't mad. No, Jill said, but what had happened? Bibi said that she and Kenny had been having a perfectly nice dinner. But halfway through, she had innocently mentioned the formal, at which point Kenny asked her if she thought that Jill might go with him or whether she was opposed to that "poseur bullshit" in which teenagers got "gussied up" to "imitate a class society to which they hadn't even fuckin' productively contributed yet" ("I can't believe how much he swears," Bibi remarked). Bibi told Kenny that yes, Jill was available and just waiting for him to ask her. Jill said that she didn't intend to go to the formal with Kenny or anyone else, particularly since she knew how much Bibi had wanted to go with him. Bibi said that she could find her own dates and didn't need Jill's *tzedakah*. She again apologized to Jill, this time for being "PMS-y," and gave her a good-night hug. Shortly thereafter, Jill heard Bibi talking on the phone to her father. "But he doesn't like me; he likes *her*," she said.

Not long after this conversation, Jill began seeing less of her dorm mate. Bibi would cut conversations short and only invite Jill along to activities in which Jill was certain to not have much interest—Hillel Society orientation, study sessions with other premeds, meetings of Jesters with Bells, the college madrigal group. Still, Jill tried to avoid Kenny so that she would not have to accept his invitation to the formal and risk upsetting Bibi. But whether she went to breakfast right when the dining center opened or after her first class, she nearly always saw him, usually yakking with members of the college service personnel, chatting up the servers behind the cafeteria counter about the Knicks, complimenting the groundskeepers on the state of the lawns, taking a security guard aside and advising him of a hazardous situation involving broken glass. In her first dorm orientation meeting, Jill had heard Kenny say that he preferred talking to campus workers over his professors; they were the only "real people" around who weren't "livin' in fuckin' Fantasyland"—he had learned a helluva lot more from his *grandfathuh* than from "any liberal *ahts professuh.*"

Kenny finally caught up to Jill in the 24-hour reading room and asked if she'd walk with him to the Retreat for a cup of coffee—he needed a break from reading this George Gilder book that was driving him "up a fuckin' wall." They walked together toward Main Hall, Kenny talking and gesticulating the whole way. With an apparent lack of self-consciousness, Kenny deprecated himself, his looks and his intellect, and discussed the difficulty he had in finding dates. "*Befaw*" he had "*discuhvuh-ed* ladies," he said, he would borrow "*paw-nahg-raphy*" from his buddies, read it in his room, and "*mastuhbate* like a chimpanzee in the fuckin' zoo." His fascination had lasted until he had come home from a summer working as a camp counselor in Nyack and discovered that his "*enti-yuh paw-nahg-raphy* stash" had "*disappee-yuhed*" from his "*puh-fect* hiding *spawt,*" and since then, he couldn't "read *paw-nahg-raphy*" or "*mastuhbate*" in his folks' place, though, he allowed, he did "*mastuhbate*" in the "*dawm show-uh,*" particularly when he had "blue *boo-alls,*" which, he said, was why Jill should wear a pair of "flip-*flawps*" if she ever showered on his hall.

After Kenny had purchased two coffees (one for himself, another for Mitch, the night security guard at the library) and they had started back on the path to the library, Kenny mentioned the formal. He had had a "really *uncomftable dinnuh*" with "*Baah-bruh* Eisenstaedt" (Bibi had invited him to call her by her full name). She'd been hinting around for him to ask her to the "*fawmuhl,*" which was "kinda flattering but also kinda *wee-yuhd.*" It would be like going with your "baby *sis-tuh,*" he said, then asked if Bibi had told Jill about the aforementioned "*dinnuh.*" When Jill said yes, Bibi had said that Kenny wanted to ask her to the formal, Kenny's face turned red. Well, yeah, he finally blurted out, but he'd just said that to get Bibi off his ass. He objected to formals—his parents had "*maw-ghidged*" their lives so he could attend "*Vass-uh*" and he was supposed to cough up forty-five bucks and pretend he was some "rich fuck" when the truth was that he and his folks would be in debt to this place until he was "soakin' his teeth in a *jaah*." Unless of course, he said, Jill wanted to go with him.

It was perhaps the most inelegant invitation that Jill had ever received. Even so, if Jill could have said yes to attending the formal with Kenny and left it at that, she might have agreed, but going with Kenny would entail getting dolled up in some "slut-suit," as Michelle referred to evening wear, having dinner before-hand, going to the Main ballroom, and either revealing that she didn't know how to dance or pretending that she did, and then he would ask her to go drinking with him and his buddies, all of whom would be silently betting on whether the two of them would have sex later, and she too would be wondering whether they would have sex, and either she wouldn't and he'd think that she was uptight or she would, and she would either enjoy it or not, but either way it would be too bizarre the next time she saw him walking down the hallway in his grandfather's old flannel bathrobe with his razor and his shaving mug. And since she really wasn't sure whether she wanted a one-night stand or a fully committed sexual re-lationship with Kenny, she said that there had to be better ways to ask a woman to the formal than the one that he had chosen.

At this, Kenny's tongue seemed to inflate to twice its natural size. He stam-mered, saying that just because he had asked Jill to the "*fawmuhl*" didn't mean that it was a date or anything; he was "totally cool" if she just wanted to be friends. Jill said fine, why didn't they just stay friends? The remainder of the walk back to the library was conducted in nearly complete silence as Jill sensed that Kenny resented the fact that she had said that they should just be friends, even though he'd made the suggestion. Once they reached the library and Jill held the door open, Kenny handed a coffee to Mitch, and began lecturing him about how he needed to register to vote, since this would be the most "*impaw-tant*" election in the past "*twenty-faw yee-uhs.*" Jill stood behind the two men, wondering whether she should wait for Kenny to finish talking, ultimately deciding to walk back to the reading room without him. Kenny, who had been ignoring Jill, repri-manded her for "leavin' without sayin' *good-boy.*"

The next night, when Jill came home, she found a note from Kenny in her message box; he apologized for "pressuring her," then asked if she wanted to get dinner soon and debate Marxism. Several nights later, a yellow rose was sticky-taped to her door; attached to it was a Hallmark card, which had originally read "Thinking of You." Kenny had crossed out "of You" and scribbled, "Thinking You Must Think I'm an Asshole." Once, Jill opened her door and found a pint of melted Rum Raisin ice cream on her desk with two plastic spoons swimming in it. Bibi informed her that Kenny had wanted to split the ice cream with Jill, but when he had found out that she wasn't home, he'd given it to Bibi, who hadn't eaten any of it; she certainly wouldn't clog her veins for a guy who didn't even like her. Jill was no longer intentionally avoiding Kenny, but midterms were approaching, the presidential election too, and any spare time that she didn't spend studying for the former or stuffing envelopes for the latter, she was spending in the city of Poughkeepsie, reporting for the *Miscellany News*.

Every week, she had attended *Misc.* editorial meetings, suggesting dozens of story ideas—a "Point-Counterpoint" about José Napoleón Duarte, a compare-and-contrast essay about Ronald Reagan's America and George Orwell's Oceania, an excoriation of the bikini contests held at Bogie's Nightclub on Route 9—but nearly always getting shot down by Rob Rubinstein, who would tell her to "keep comin' back with those good ideas, 'cause we need 'em." This had gone on until one meeting when Jill complained that the newspaper was too insular; an entire city existed just outside the college—wouldn't occasional reports on Poughkeepsie better link the college to the community? Rob Rubinstein said yes, if anyone *wanted* to be "better linked to the community," which was unlikely since it was a "godforsaken dump." But on this night, Rubinstein seemed to be in the minority; opinion editor Ronelle Leeds said that she would rather read six hundred words about "godforsaken dumps" than yet another "eighteen hundred masturbatory words" about Lou Reed, to which music editor Alec Savage said that he hadn't intended to write so much about Lou Reed, except that there hadn't been anything else worth publishing. After which, Rubinstein allowed that maybe something could be gained from more Poughkeepsie coverage; interviews with "jobless white trash" would make for better reading than the "bloated think pieces" about unemployment that Ronelle published. Ronelle said that she didn't see how Rob could use the word *bloated* after having taken up an entire page of the previous week's issue with a column that blithely dismissed the Vassar Republican Club's complicity in the destruction of a shanty built to encourage divestment from South Africa ("Come on, guys, the shanty was ugly anyway," he had written). To which sports editor Joe Rossi made a "T" with his hands and said, "Time out, guys"—the question on the table was whether they wanted Poughkeepsie coverage or not.

"If Wasserstrom wants the Poughkeepsie beat, it's hers," Rubinstein said, adding that Jill's reports should be no longer than five hundred words each.

"Six hundred," Ronelle Leeds said.

"Done," said Rob.

Venturing out into the city of Poughkeepsie on weekends and after classes with her reporter's notebook, Jill would visit typical neighborhood establishments—diners, offices, stores, the train station—gathering her impressions, listening intently to conversations, staying long enough that people started talking to her. Afterward, she would write concise, sober, yet atmospheric articles about the people of the city, allowing them to talk and letting readers draw their own conclusions without providing any Charlie Wasserstromian feel-good moralizing. She didn't criticize the racist epithets uttered by Giovanni Pisco, proprietor of Gio's Pizzeria, who said that "the Main Street coloreds" were destroying his business; she did not respond to Buster Biggs, owner of My Biggs Brothers' Barbecue, who said that 1970s inflation hadn't been Poughkeepsie's major problem; only when blacks started becoming the majority did industry start moving out. And as for Ian Graff, longtime owner of Sunshine Superman's Record Store and Head Shop, who said that being stoned was the only way to face living in Ronald Reagan's America, Jill ran his interview verbatim.

Toward the end of her interviews, Jill would often mention that her mother had been born in Poughkeepsie, that her grandparents had owned businesses here. But Jill's statement yielded little more than shrugs. Ian Graff didn't remember a sheet music business, and Giovanni Pisco found it unlikely that a Jewish bakery could have ever survived in Poughkeepsie. The lone Italian bakery hadn't made it, and Italians made better pastries than Jews. After more than a dozen interviews, Jill still had learned nothing more about Edna or Sam Schulman.

On election night, Jill returned home early from a Students for Mondale "Election Wake" at the College Center, where a conference room and TV had been reserved so that Mondale supporters could watch election returns, eat

Napoli's pizza, and do Jell-O shots. But when Jill saw the projections that Ronald Reagan would carry every state with the possible exception of Minnesota, she lost all sense of mirth and grew irritated with the postures of amused indifference and studied anger among her peers. Back at her dorm, she was infuriated to see the TV room occupied by Matthew Chen and a handful of other guys in basketball jerseys, who weren't even watching the election but, instead, *Scarface,* laughing as they imitated Al Pacino's Cuban accent ("*Fokk* you!" they cackled, "no, fokk *you!*").

Jill was typing the second single-spaced page of a rant to Muley when Kenny knocked on her door and asked if he was *distuhbing* her. Jill rolled her letter out of the typewriter and turned it facedown. No, she said, she was just doodling. Kenny was carrying a full U.S. postal sack over his shoulder; it contained his laundry and a six-pack of Rolling Rock. Kenny said that the election had ticked him off so much that he'd shut off his radio and decided to do something constructive—wash all of his laundry, then drink a six-pack. Kenny flicked open a beer, handed it to Jill, then opened one for himself. "*Hee-yuh's* to *faw maw yee-uhs unduh* the threat of *nuclee-uh wah-fayuh,*" he said. He asked Jill if he could fold his laundry in her room.

An hour later, Jill and Kenny were sitting on her floor, five empty Rolling Rock bottles in Jill's wastebasket, *New Morning* playing for the third time on the boom box (unable to find a single tape in her collection that he could listen to without wanting to "fuckin' strangle himself," Kenny had retrieved some tapes of his own). Once Kenny had finished off his last bottle and grimaced ("Even when *yer* drunk, backwash is nasty," he observed), he carried out his sack of folded laundry, ran down the hall, and returned moments later with two King Kans of warm Miller, a wax packet of crackers, and a squeeze bottle of cheddar and bacon Easy Cheese. As Kenny swirled cheese onto crackers, he and Jill discussed politics, their classes, and Woody Allen movies; they talked about their parents, their friends back home, and Kenny's future as a civil rights lawyer.

The beer and crackers ran out at two in the morning, moments before Bibi returned, dumped her Anatomy textbook onto her bed, and said that she'd had a long night, so would they mind if she closed the door between their bedrooms. Kenny said that he was leaving anyway and thanked Jill for the "*convuhsation.*" Once he was gone, Jill waited for Bibi to remark upon Kenny's presence in their room, but instead, Bibi just kissed Jill on the forehead, said, "Don't go too fast," then went directly to bed without calling her parents to say that she had gotten home safely.

Over the next days, Bibi continued to exhibit similarly aberrant behavior. She dyed her hair with henna, put her stuffed animals and her old ballet slippers in the closet, removed the family pictures from her dresser, replacing them with perfumes, lipsticks, nail polish, eyeliner. She played only classical music now, dumping all her old cassettes in a crate outside their dorm room. On the phone, she spoke to her father in clipped tones that reminded Jill of her own conversations with Charlie. She even took down her Sting posters. Bibi's phone conversations with Shmuel took on a new tone too; where she had once been curt, she was now flirtatious and knowing, telling him that there were some things you just never knew about a person until you woke up next to them. She made a big show of seeming tired, yawning, rubbing her eyes, and saying, "I am wiped out." One week before Thanksgiving, Bibi invited Jill to dinner with her for five o'clock on a Saturday. "Wear something nice," Bibi said. "No sweats or overalls."

Shortly before five on that Saturday, Jill's door swung open and Kenny was there. He looked at Jill's black slacks and turtleneck, said, "Ooh, look at the *covuh guhl*," then asked if Jill was going on "some *hawt* date." "No, no *hawt* date," Jill said. Kenny asked if she'd be his "*hawt* date *faw dinnuh*." Jill said she already had plans with Bibi, to which Kenny remarked, "*Guhl on guhl* action," and said he wouldn't mind checking some of that out, but then Bibi entered the room wearing a belted black trench coat and a pink broad-brimmed hat with a black bow.

Kenny exited, stifling a chuckle at Bibi's outfit. Bibi asked Jill if she had told Kenny where they were going. Jill said no, especially since she didn't actually know. But when they were out the front door, Bibi turned around to make sure that Kenny wasn't following them, then quickly click-clacked her way down a leaf-strewn path. Bibi said she really hoped that Jill would like Soren—she had developed a habit of mentioning names that Jill hadn't heard before with a studied familiarity.

"Who's Soren?" Jill asked.

"Oh," Bibi said, "didn't I tell you?"

Bibi said that she kept forgetting that nobody knew. She said that she had met Soren Davidson in Jesters with Bells, with whom he played harpsichord. He'd actually graduated from Vassar in 1977, studied briefly at Brandeis, and was currently finishing up his doctorate from McGill University while he worked as an archivist in the Skinner Music Library, and lived in Rhinebeck in a house that his father had bought for him. Though there were no official regulations about members of the college staff dating students, Soren thought it best that they keep the relationship quiet. "He is so dreamy," she said, adding that his hair was the same color as Sting's. She told Jill not to say anything to anybody, particularly not to Kenny, who was a "*kochleffel.*" Jill consented, saying that she wouldn't tell Kenny nor would she mention anything to Shmuel Weinberg if he called. "Oh, don't worry about Shmuel," Bibi said, "he already knows." Jill followed Bibi out the main gates, where a silver Volvo 242 GT with an orange racing stripe was waiting.

"There he is," Bibi exclaimed. She opened the car door, threw her arms around Soren Davidson, and said, "Hello, lover." Soren tossed his hair out of his eyes, then leaned across Bibi's lap to offer his hand to Jill; his smile was broad and toothy and his hand was warm and damp.

Soren drove, leaning back in his seat with one hand on the steering wheel and one on Bibi's back, every so often caressing her ear with his fingers, once in a while using the same hand either to conduct *The New World Symphony* on his cassette player or to dig into the can of mixed nuts wedged between the parking brake and his seat. It was to Bibi's credit, Jill thought, that she could consider "dreamy" a person whose smile resembled that of an exhumed skeleton in *King Solomon's Mines.*

Soren, his voice soft, barely audible above the wind and the Dvořák, quickly negotiated the curves of Route 9 with the windows open, the cool wind buffeting his pageboy haircut and ruffling his shirt. As Soren steered, Bibi took off her bonnet and turned around in her seat, her shoes off, one foot tucked under her skirt, and doled out tidbits of information about Soren's life, yelling over the wind and the stereo. Now and then, Soren would fix Bibi with a glance and she would playfully cover her mouth, realizing that she had revealed a secret. "Moving right along now," she would say. Soren's father was a diplomat, Bibi yelled, adding that Emile Davidson had been stationed at the U.S. Embassy in France and had met Soren's mother, the heir to a textile fortune. Soren had been named for Emile Davidson's favorite philosopher, Kierkegaard. His ancestors were French and Swiss, and he and his sisters had been raised mostly by a governess, spending their lives moving from country to country—a tour of duty in Costa Rica, another in Spain, another in West Africa, before Mr. Davidson abruptly resigned from the diplomatic corps, divorced Soren's mother, and moved back to

France to paint. Soren hadn't spoken to his father since, Bibi said as Soren turned quickly to face Bibi, his right nostril flared.

"Moving right along now," Bibi said. She held Soren's hand tightly.

As Soren drove on into the ever-darkening purple evening, Jill saw a ghostly manor rising in the distance. Soren turned onto a private drive, and Jill could hear Joan Fontaine's voice from the film *Rebecca* echoing in her brain: "Last night, I dreamt I went to Manderley again." Soren parked the car behind the house, which, Bibi explained, was absolutely spectacular; there was even a bowling alley in the basement. But after Soren emerged from the driver's seat and popped the trunk, from which he extracted two bags of groceries—fennel and leek stalks poked out of the tops of the bags—he walked away from the house toward a log cabin at the end of a path of rubble and grass.

"Servant's quarters," Bibi explained, adding that Soren preferred to live in the cabin because it didn't remind him of his parents' arguments; it was also easier to heat, which was important since she and Soren often cooked in the nude.

"Moving right along now," said Jill.

The inside of the cabin was stark yet tastefully decorated; the kitchen was twice the size of the Wasserstroms'. In the main room, illuminated by track lighting, there was an unfinished wooden table with benches instead of chairs. Pages from original scores by Samuel Barber, Aaron Copland, and John Cage were framed on the walls. An antique grandfather clock ticktocked away. Gleaming musical instruments were everywhere: an upright piano, a harpsichord, a lute.

While Soren and Bibi worked in the kitchen, Jill swirled and sipped from a glass of red wine and studied Soren's record collection, which took up one full wall of the cabin. Every so often, Soren would emerge and hand Jill an appetizer—a square of Brie on toasted French bread, a dish of olives—then return to the kitchen, leaving Jill alone; she could hear Bibi giggle then playfully admonish Soren with squeals of "Not now" and "But she's *out there.*"

Dinner was served in four hour-long courses: an asparagus and truffle-oil soup, a pear and Stilton salad, steamed kale and fennel risotto, tarragon sorbet. Bibi and Soren sat on one bench, Jill opposite them. Soren dissertated on such topics as classical music—how Mendelssohn had written music for *A Midsummer Night's Dream,* but Handel was far closer to that play's spirit; modern fiction—how Anthony Burgess's *A Clockwork Orange* was seen as predictive, but his more obscure works, such as *The End of the World News,* were the truly prophetic ones; and the cost of the ingredients he had used to prepare this evening's repast—the vial of truffle oil alone had cost nine dollars.

After they had finished eating, and Soren and Bibi had washed the dishes, and Jill had drunk another glass of wine, Soren asked Bibi to make espresso (he assured Jill that he was not "a chauvinist"; he just wanted "this one"—the words he used to refer to Bibi—to feel as comfortable as possible because she would be spending a lot of time here). Jill briefly imagined Bibi and Soren naked sipping espresso and to squelch that thought, asked if the harpsichord was an antique. Why, Soren asked, did she play? No, Jill said, she had no facility for music—she remembered three years of violin, an instrument she had taken up at her mother's insistence and quit shortly after Becky became ill, convinced that her squeaky and mechanical playing had caused her mother's headaches. Soren said nonsense, everyone had a facility for music. He proceeded to play several songs by Schubert. Bibi entered, carrying a tray of espresso cups, which she placed on the table. She put a hand on Soren's damp back and sang "Du Bist die Ruh," explaining that if Soren's father hadn't been Jewish, she didn't think that her father would have forgiven her for singing in German.

After the espresso, Soren asked Jill if she wanted to watch a movie. He pointed to a shelf of videos and asked Jill to pick one. Jill looked at the clock; it was 1:30 in the morning. She scanned Soren's shelf and chose the shortest film— *La Jetée*. Soren applauded the choice ("Good," he said, "smart girl"), but added that since that particular film was so short, they should have a double feature. He asked Bibi to choose a movie too, and when she uttered her choice (*Breakfast at Tiffany's*), Soren rolled his eyes ("But I love that movie so much," Bibi said). Fifteen minutes into the second feature, Bibi was asleep in Soren's arms.

Near dawn, Soren suggested that Jill sleep over, but Jill said that she really had to go home. Soren's nostrils flared, but he offered to drive her. He jostled Bibi slightly, and she slumped over on the couch. It was her typical routine, he said, lifting Bibi in his arms, this was how their nights always ended—she liked to be carried. He lifted the covers of his bed, plopped Bibi down, and put her stuffed goose in her arms. He asked Jill if she was ready to go.

Soren drove with his window rolled all the way down, and as he careened around now-deserted Route 9, he did not modulate his voice to compensate for the wind. He spoke in a confessional tone with blunt self-reflection. He said that he was nearly thirty and by all reasonable measures, he was a failure. He despised his father, yet could not live without the checks that Emile Davidson sent to him. He had sent the most recent draft chapter of his "rarified and ultimately inconsequential" dissertation about Dvořák to his committee chair and hadn't received even a note or phone call in response. After one particularly silent stretch of road, Soren asked Jill if she thought that he was a creepy lecher. Jill did not know how to respond and felt lucky that he hadn't asked her about adjectives that came more readily to mind—ugly or solipsistic, for example. She wasn't opposed to women her age dating thirty-year-old men; eighteen-year-old guys, Kenny and occasionally Muley excepted, could barely keep up their ends of conversations. Her problem was more related to a thirty-year-old man dating Bibi, who, to Jill, seemed too young to be attending college altogether. Why did Soren care what she thought of him, Jill asked.

"Because you seem like someone I could respect," he said, then assured Jill that he had only the best intentions toward "that one," and would never hurt her. He observed that it was funny and rather sad as well, but whenever he had tried not to hurt someone, he wound up being injured. "Conversely . . ." he began, but did not finish the thought—these were old men's problems, he said, not for young girls' ears. He said that he remembered being a college freshman here and thinking that seniors looked old; he couldn't begin to imagine how old he seemed to Jill. The only thing that made him feel any differently about himself was Bibi; was that shameful, he asked. Jill said that it wasn't up to her to say when other people should or shouldn't be ashamed. Soren smiled broadly. Jill understood him, he said as Jill espied a banner looming before them: POUGHKEEPSIE—QUEEN OF THE HUDSON.

"Ahh, Poughkeepsie," Soren said wistfully as he stopped at a traffic light. He remembered how popular he'd been here his first two years—he'd been one of the only students in his dorm who owned a car. He and his friends would cruise downtown Poughkeepsie in his Dodge Comet; sometimes they'd drive to Marist or SUNY New Paltz for parties, see if they could hit 120 miles per hour on the Taconic. He gestured to an empty lot beside the Crispy Wok Buffet Cantonese restaurant. "See," Soren said, "this used to be the red-light district." And over here, he said, this cocktail lounge was once a great diner. This new Subway sandwich shop had been vacant for years, but before that it had been a little sheet music store with interesting 78 rpm records. And right next to it, in the currency exchange, Ferrante's, an Italian bakery, had sold good coffee and cannolis.

At Ferrante's, Soren said, a little old Italian man worked in the back of the bakery and his flirty wife Edna worked the register. Edna Ferrante, Jill asked. Soren nodded and continued to point out businesses that were either no longer there or that had been significantly more appealing when he had been a student, for example, Sunshine Superman's, once the most important counterculture establishment in town, but now little more than a gigantic petri dish. Jill tried to jog Soren's memory about Edna from Ferrante's, but Soren said that he knew no more than he had initially revealed.

Still, in the days after she returned from Soren's house, Jill was not quite moved to ring the doorbell of the house on 5 Mack Road; she would just walk a little bit out of her way when she was researching her Poughkeepsie stories. She would pass the house with its yellowed lawn and gnarled maple trees out front, a dirt-spattered, black Buick Skylark parked outside. But walking up the three brick steps of the little white house to see if E. Ferrante was, in fact, her grandmother who had remarried or changed her name proved daunting.

As Jill passed the house, she would try to cast glances through the window. Usually the shades were drawn, but even when they were up, Jill rarely saw more than a few houseplants in a sparsely furnished room; once she caught a glimpse of a walker, but never an actual human being. She walked slowly, but never stopped and never passed the house more than once per day. Her ancestry interested her, but she did not want to be obsessive or, as Michelle had suggested, morbid. She had spent her middle school years skulking around in dark moods, haunted by images of her mother's last days, listening over and over to her sister's copy of the Beatles' *Revolver,* particularly "She Said, She Said (I know what it's like to be dead")". She had vowed to never return to those days; she would never be that gloomy, pale-faced adolescent again.

Thanksgiving supper was celebrated at the noisy, cluttered Melnick high-rise apartment on Third Street in Manhattan, where Kenny had invited Jill to spend the weekend with his family. Inviting Michelle had been Jill's idea, but when Michelle had arrived in a thrift store fur coat that looked as though it were made out of porcupines, bearing cigarillos for Kenny's father and a six-pack of Schlitz for Mrs. Melnick, Jill regretted the suggestion. Throughout the afternoon and the evening, Michelle's presence completely eclipsed her own. Jill always found herself off to one side, while Michelle puttered in the kitchen with Mrs. Melnick and criticized her condiments ("a true New Yorker wouldn't have this nasty Miracle Whip in her refrigerator, Mrs. M") and charmed Kenny's uncles, cousins, and aunts with her harsh assessment of Mr. Melnick's Ethel Merman records.

It was amazing to Jill how Michelle could say the rudest things with a smile and people would love her, while Jill, even when she was being polite, was viewed as arrogant and sarcastic. At one point, Michelle whispered loudly in Jill's ear, "This is torture; when are we gonna fuckin' get *out of here*?" but then bounced off to flirt with Mrs. Melnick's father, Mr. Popko, a World War I veteran who kept asking Michelle to dance ("You're too fast for me, Grandpa; I can't keep up," she repeatedly told him, and each time she said it, he roared with laughter). But whenever Mr. Popko would look at Jill, he'd make some cutting remark. "Does she talk?" he asked Michelle, pointing a finger at Jill before issuing military commands—"At ease, Private," he would say. When Kenny and a trio of his cousins went out to buy ice, and Michelle and Mrs. Melnick worked in the kitchen, Jill found herself on the couch with Mr. Popko, who was watching football. Searching for a conversation topic, Jill told him that she was glad to be spending this holiday with him; she had never really known her grandparents and Kenny was lucky to have such a close relationship with him. "You bet," Mr. Popko said, and asked her to turn up the volume on the TV.

At supper, Jill sat at a sharp corner of the dining room table on a cold metal folding chair. To her right sat Kenny; to her left, at the foot of the table, his father. The two of them kept whispering to each other about whether it would be safe for Mr. Popko to continue living on his own, while Jill leaned back as far as she could in her seat, pretending to listen intently to the other conversations around the table ("At ease, Private Wasserstrom, at ease," Mr. Popko said). Everyone else seemed to be having a grand time—Mrs. Melnick doled out portions of stuffing; her younger sister, Rudi Popko, made elaborate gestures that jangled her bracelets as she discussed the history textbook her principal was making her teach even though it skipped the Vietnam War; Kenny broke from his hushed conversation with his father, pointed at his aunt, and told her, "You do the right thing, Rudi, you teach what's gotta be taught," then continued whispering to his father while his cousins, uncles, and aunts heaped on stuffing and cranberry sauce. Michelle sliced turkey and asked, "Who wants more bird?" then regaled the crowd with tales of her acting career—how she'd spent four weeks on the set of an epic film that had been edited into a three-minute music video—that sent the assembled multitude into spasms of laughter. Rudi Popko said that she wanted Michelle to write her name on a slip of paper so that she would remember it when she saw it on Broadway. Meanwhile, Jill counted seconds in her head, wondering how long it had been since she had said a single word, thinking that she had to say something sometime, but whenever she lobbed forth a question, she would feel all eyes upon her. At her first opportunity, Jill slipped out to the kitchen to wash dishes, happy for the occupation and the solitude, interrupted only once by Mr. Popko, who entered and, with a mischievous smile, asked if Jill also did laundry and, if so, he liked light starch in his shirts.

Once she had finished the dishes, Jill stood in the kitchen doorway, wiping her hands on a dishtowel. She could see Michelle sitting cross-legged on the floor, taking a drag off Mrs. Melnick's cigarette, then getting up to put a record on the turntable and dancing with Mr. Popko to "Moonlight Becomes You," the old man surprisingly limber and quick on his feet as he described the times when he had gone out dancing with "showgirls." Kenny, red-faced and laughing, clapped wildly, then cut in to dance with his grandfather until Mr. Popko said, "What the hell's the *mattuh* with you; you think you're a girl all of a sudden?"

That night, Jill, Michelle, and Kenny went to the Peculier Pub and drank pints of Guinness. Kenny chatted up the portly silver-haired bartender, whom he greeted as Steve-O, telling Jill and Michelle that he'd been coming here ever since he was fourteen and Steve-O had never carded him. Here, Jill felt as if she had even less to say, and found herself inching away from the table, watching Kenny's face turn red as Michelle imitated him (*"Wheyah's* the *guhl* with my *bee-yuh?"* she demanded, pointing at Kenny, then readjusting pantomime glasses). Jill wondered if the two of them would spend the night together, if they'd all go back to Michelle's apartment and she'd be on the floor in a sleeping bag while Kenny and Michelle were screwing. After Kenny excused himself to "take a mean dump," Michelle asked Jill if she would be spending the night at Kenny's place. Why, Jill asked, because she wanted to fuck him? Michelle looked startled, took a sip of beer, then told Jill that she didn't sound authentic swearing and that she needed to practice before she tried those words out in public. Come on, Michelle said, give her some credit; she would not screw some guy who looked fifteen and acted seventy-five—the guy probably masturbated to the AARP magazine and ate schmaltz herring and halvah, Christ, his fricking grandfather acted younger than he did. Besides, she said, she was focusing on her career and had sworn off sex save for one-night stands pursued solely for tension release and aerobic exercise. Why did any of this make a difference anyway, she asked, did Jill actually *like* this pud? When Jill said nothing, Michelle stammered out a purportedly charitable remark about how everyone was entitled to their own sense of taste. After which, Kenny returned from the washroom ("Everything came out just fine, thanks *fer askin'*") and Michelle—not wanting to stand between Jill and Kenny—said it was time for her to "get running." She told Jill that they should see a movie the next day, kissed Kenny on the cheek, and asked him to tell his grandfather that she was saving herself for him. She skipped out of the bar, purse over her shoulder, singing "Everybody Wants You."

Kenny asked Jill if she wanted to get another round. And Jill, sensing a precipitous drop in the energy level now that her sister had departed, said that maybe they should just return to Kenny's apartment. Kenny said that he wanted to say good-bye to Steve-O first. Jill stood by the door while patrons shoved past her; she watched Kenny in his grandfather's weather-beaten peacoat leaning across the bar and shaking hands with Steve-O, who set up a shot. Kenny waved his hands as if to say that he didn't have time, but Steve-O pushed the shot toward him. Jill watched Kenny laughing and raising his index finger as if to say "Just this one," downing the shot and laughing harder, then gesturing toward Jill at the door. Steve-O grinned and set up two more shots. And as she watched, Jill couldn't escape the thought that everyone was more interesting than she was, particularly in Kenny's eyes—Steve-O was more interesting, his father, his grandfather, her sister, security guards, night watchmen. She considered getting on the next train back to Poughkeepsie, but after Kenny finally zipped up his coat, pointed at Steve-O, and yelled, "I'm gonna hold you to that," he asked Jill why she hadn't come over for shots; Steve-O was a good guy. They could come back the next day and Steve-O would buy them both shots; Jill's sister could join them.

Or, Jill proposed with studied indifference as they walked out of the bar, she could go by herself to see *The Killing Fields* at Cinema I, and Kenny and Michelle could hang out with Steve-O—she could give Kenny her sister's number. Kenny adjusted his glasses. Why would he want to do that, he asked. Jill said it really didn't bother her that whenever she and her sister hung out with guys, they would always ask only for Michelle's phone number. Why, Kenny asked, confused, were the guys masochists? Jill asked what he meant, and Kenny quickly apologized; he hadn't meant to suggest that anybody who would date Michelle would have to suffer from intense self-loathing ("which I do, by the way," he said). But Michelle was just too "*bittuh*" for him and he was already too "*bittuh*" for his own good. Once they approached Kenny's apartment building, Jill asked Kenny why he thought Michelle was too "*bittuh.*"

"Maybe it's just 'cause you're *prettiuh* than *huh,*" Kenny said.

The statement might have been offensive to Jill if it hadn't been so bizarre. *Prettiuh* than Michelle? Was he out of his mind? she asked herself as Kenny opened the front door and greeted Vince Peditto, the night watchman, and offered to make him a Thanksgiving sandwich ("We got tons o' *leftovuhs;* you like a lotta mayo or a little?"). As she stood in the Melnick kitchen watching Kenny slather mayonnaise onto two slices of rye bread to make a turkey sandwich for Vince ("I've known him since I was that *boy,*" Kenny said), Jill wondered if she could ask Kenny if he really thought that she was prettier than Michelle. Not that she really cared about being pretty; she mostly cared about not being ugly.

Before Kenny headed downstairs with the sandwich and a can of Diet Pepsi ("I'm tryin' to get Vince to watch his weight," he said), he rummaged through a drawer in his bedroom and found an old yellow T-shirt and a pair of dark brown boxer shorts, tossed them to Jill, and told her that she could wear them as pajamas. And once Jill had gotten ready for bed, she lay down on the bottom bunk with a copy of Goran Hyden's *No Shortcuts to Progress,* and waited for Kenny. Every so often, she could hear Mr. Popko in the guest bedroom clearing his throat.

Kenny returned, smelling slightly of pickle brine and cigarettes. He was shirtless and wore a pair of white pajama bottoms and dark brown socks. He entered his bedroom brushing his teeth and discussing Vince's marital problems before he told Jill, his mouth full of toothpaste, "I'll be back in a sec; I *gawta* spit." He returned wearing a white undershirt and told Jill that he *nawmally* slept in the *bawtum* bunk, because when he slept on *tawp* and had bad dreams, he'd sit up too suddenly and smack his head on the ceiling. Jill, consumed with a sudden boldness, asked if he wanted to sleep beside her.

For a moment, Kenny's face registered panic, which he quickly masked with self-assurance. He climbed in beside Jill, immediately putting an arm around her as if they had slept together many times before. Kenny stroked Jill's cheek and told her that she was the prettiest *guhl* to ever sleep in his bed, and when Jill asked if numerous others had slept here, he pretended to contemplate the matter and said uh yeah, *Bahbruh* Bach had slept here when she'd appeared in *Playboy*. Oh, he said, did she mean actual people?

As she and Kenny kissed, Jill was surprised that he tasted like mint toothpaste and not like herring or halvah. And as he slipped a hand underneath her T-shirt, she was surprised at how easy this all felt. Kenny took off his undershirt and she removed her T-shirt and she could feel his chest against hers and the warmth of his penis through his pajama bottoms against her thigh; she was thankful that she felt completely in sync with this moment, that she didn't feel herself slipping out of her body and watching from a safe distance. And it was at this precise instant, when this thought occurred to her, that she felt it happening again, felt herself drifting away.

Kenny now wore only a pair of pale-yellow bikini briefs. He leapt out of bed, opened a dresser drawer, pulled out a weather-beaten condom package that he'd received after a Vassar Gay People's Alliance party, grasped it in his fist, got under the covers, and asked Jill if she wanted to do this. And all Jill could think was that she didn't want to do this so much as she wanted it to be done already, that there was something strange about her since she hadn't done this, something that reminded her of walking past E. Ferrante's door but not stopping, something that reminded her of standing in the Melnicks' kitchen and watching her sister and the Melnicks laughing, something that reminded her of standing in the Peculier Pub watching Kenny trade shots with Steve-O. Yes, she wanted to do this, she said.

But once Kenny had taken off his briefs and rolled the condom down the shaft of his penis, in the next room, Mr. Popko cleared his throat. Kenny froze and put a finger to Jill's lips as he lay on his side waiting for his grandfather to go back to sleep. Once a minute had passed, Kenny kissed Jill again and stroked her leg and Jill felt herself drifting even farther away. And though she would say that she was sorry it had happened, she couldn't help but feel that fate was once again intervening when Mr. Popko cleared his throat and bellowed, "Don't you think it's time for people to get some sleep around here?" at which point Kenny rolled onto his back; his stomach was quaking with laughter.

— — — —

When Kenny and Jill finally did have sex, if that's what one could accurately call a single instance of insertion, followed by two and a half thrusting motions, a panicked and mistaken announcement from Kenny that his condom might have broken, and then a loss of desire and interest on both Kenny and Jill's parts, it was nearly a month after Thanksgiving, a few hours after Jill's Political Theory final, and about twelve hours before she would board the Hudson Valley Transporter van to La Guardia. As she had negotiated the last weeks of her first semester, she had the gnawing sense that the next time she and Kenny were alone, they would have to perform the act that they had not completed on Thanksgiving. Consequently, she had taken on more projects than ever— Poughkeepsie columns, extra-credit research papers, letters home to Muley, postcards to Michelle—anything that would keep her from time with Kenny, whom she would always greet with smiles and waves as she buzzed past him.

On the fifteenth of December, 1984, Jill was sitting at her desk, reading an article in the *Poughkeepsie Journal* about Mikhail Gorbachev touring Britain as the heir apparent to an ailing Konstantin Chernenko. Her bags were packed. Bibi had already left for a long weekend with Soren before she would return to her parents' home in Northbrook. When Jill heard Kenny's signature knock, she tensed. She could picture him in front of her door in one of his grandfather's old flannel shirts and a pair of corduroy slacks; she wondered what sort of snack he would be carrying—some processed cheese food? Smoked sable? Jill took a breath, said, "Come in," and was surprised to find Kenny, not in flannel and corduroy, but in a winter coat, boots, ski pants, and a green New York Jets ski cap. He was holding a red plastic sled. "Feel like sleddin'?" he asked.

Jill instantly agreed, now remembering everything that she liked about Kenny; she didn't even roll her eyes when he said that her sweater wasn't heavy enough. When they reached Sunset Lake, the snow reflected the light of the moon and illuminated the branches of bare trees encircling the lake. Kenny held Jill's gloved hand in his as they climbed to the top of a snow-covered hill. Jill sat down in the front of the sled and Kenny sat behind her, his legs against hers, his arms around her body as they pushed off and began to slide toward the frozen lake. Jill had never ridden a sled before—the only toboggan hill she had known was Mount Warren, but people never sledded on it, they just got wasted. She let out a joyful scream as they accelerated downward, then fell onto the lake, which they slid across before skidding then slamming into an embankment that sent them sprawling, giddy with laughter. They grabbed for the sled and ran up the hill, dashing faster until they reached the top and rode down again, rode on their backs, face-forward, backward, laughing and panting the whole way.

Back in the Cushing dormitory, they stripped off their clothes and wrapped themselves in towels, then walked barefoot down the hall until they reached a second-floor bathtub, which they filled with warm water. They stepped out of their towels and into the tub, teeth chattering as they held hands under the water. At one point, Kenny finished soaping up his torso and said, "You know what would make this fuckin' *puhfect*? A coupla plastic ducks." And after the water had swirled down to the last drop and they had stepped out and dried each other, they returned to Kenny's room and sailed underneath his covers. And Jill was ready for this now; she asked Kenny if he had condoms. Kenny turned out his bedside lamp, caressed Jill's body, then rolled on top of her, his knees between her legs. He bent down to kiss her, still touching her with one hand, clumsily unrolling his condom with the other, kissing her neck as he lowered his body onto hers and Jill felt something sharp that made her inhale suddenly and Kenny asked her if everything was O.K., if they should stop. Jill told him it was all right and then, the same sharp feeling as Kenny began to thrust inside her, once, twice, then almost a third time before he suddenly shouted "Aww fuck" and rolled off and turned on the light and said he thought that his condom had broken. And even though it hadn't, Kenny nevertheless lost his erection and ten minutes later, when Kenny was asleep, Jill started to get dressed.

After Jill walked out of Kenny's room and put on her coat, she ran down the stairs, then out a side door. She jogged past the cemetery and out the north gate, wondering as she ran how to describe what she had just done with Kenny, whether she was a virgin who had had sex or whether she was someone who hadn't had sex but wasn't a virgin either. She ran until she reached Mack Road, and when she got to number 5, she stopped. The shades were drawn, but in an upstairs window, she could see the light from a TV, and could vaguely hear the theme music to *Chariots of Fire*. She walked up the front steps and looked at the buzzer and its red label with raised white lettering: FERRANTE. She pressed the buzzer, but nobody came to the door.

On her first day back in Chicago, Jill had a stiff phone conversation with Kenny, who spoke too loudly and consistently asked her to repeat herself, as if he were an old man who had been born before the invention of the telephone. Kenny said that he had thought a lot about what the two of them had done that last night at *"Vassuh."* Though he didn't regret it, he thought maybe they had gone too fast—it was too early to start thinking about kids and a family. Just think about it, he said, one broken *"kwaandum"* and a thimbleful of "spilled *spuhm"* and soon, they'd be "pushin' a *strolluh* in the *welfayuh loine."* Maybe when they were next *"togethuh,"* they should take it *"slowuh"*—why didn't they discuss it after break? Jill leapt on this last thought, as if it were the one passage she'd understood in a foreign-language novel. Why didn't they discuss it after break, she agreed, thinking how small and distant Poughkeepsie seemed right now, just as small as West Rogers Park seemed now that she was here.

When Charlie had driven Jill from O'Hare Airport to North Shore Avenue, Jill no longer sensed that she was returning home. On Devon, there were businesses she didn't recognize—Friends of Refugees from Eastern Europe, Globus Groceries. Everywhere were men with black overcoats, long beards, *streimels,* young boys in suits, *kippot,* and *payess.* Russian signs were displayed in the windows of Rosen's Drugs, Sinai Kosher, Nagilah Israel, and the Schwartz-Rosenblum Judaica Bookstore. Once Jill arrived at the North Shore house, she noted that her room had changed too. Faded radical posters and a photo gallery of Harold Washington still hung on the wall. But now the toys that Rachel hadn't broken or eaten were all over the carpet. On either side of Jill's bed, stacks of file boxes from Gail's PR firm were piled; there were too many to fit only in Michelle's old bedroom.

Soon, Jill's room would probably be converted into another office for Gail's business. Yet, as she wandered about the house nibbling on a peanut butter and banana sandwich that Charlie had insisted on fixing for her, Jill sensed that as she was vanishing here, she was emerging elsewhere. Soon, her trips to Chicago would become even shorter. Wherever she lived—West Berlin, Montreal, El

Salvador—she would say that she was going home to Chicago to *visit*. She now felt as if she were in the transitory portion of something permanent, that her father, Gail, and Rachel were settled in their lives and that she was somehow in between, living here but not here, in Poughkeepsie but not really there either; she was a virgin and yet she wasn't. She thought that there must be a time—one that lasted for years but seemed like only an instant—between what you had been and what you became. For now, she was living in a great in-between. The next night, even her father seemed to acknowledge this fact. He just nodded and shrugged sadly when Jill told him that she wouldn't be staying home with him, Gail, and Rachel to watch videos of *The Goodbye Girl* and *California Suite,* and would be visiting Muley instead. He didn't tell her to take a jacket, to "watch herself," or to call if she would be late. He just shook her hand and said, "See ya, kid," when she walked out the door.

"Come back and bring the dog," Rachel called out.

As Jill took the southbound Howard–Dan Ryan el, she had the impression that the entire city was under construction; strip malls were emerging in the shadow of demolished motion picture palaces, the Granada Theater was boarded up, the Riviera vacant; Wieboldt's was having a going-out-of-business sale. In the skyline, Jill could see cranes and steel girders, half-finished skyscrapers rising alongside the Sears Tower and the John Hancock. As the train rumbled underground, the city disappeared, and pale yellow dome lights flickered. Jill wondered whether she should tell Muley about the Kenny Melnick virgin/non-virgin conundrum; she regretted the fact that she had no one else to tell or ask, as she now saw the world divided between those too experienced to bother and those too immature to understand.

After Jill emerged from the el train at Roosevelt Road, she walked south on Michigan toward 20th Street. The area was still rather desolate, an eerily silent expanse marking the transition from downtown to the south side. And yet, it seemed as if the neighborhood was emerging from decades of dormancy. There were art galleries, nightclubs—the Cotton Club, the Velvet Lounge, the Strictly Business Cocktail Room—once-condemned brick buildings with FOR RENT: ARTISTS LOFTS signs in their first floor windows.

In the nine-story building on Michigan and 20th where Muley was living, a naked lightbulb hung in the vestibule, sawdust covered the floor, and a row of unmarked, dusty, and dented green mailboxes looked as though someone had punched them. The elevator had an uncovered panel of buttons with bunched green, red, and yellow wires hanging out of it; when it stopped on nine, its doors opened onto a dimly lit, airy, and spacious room. The eastern wall was all exposed brick; mounted on it were artifacts suggestive of films that Muley loved: a giant propeller as in *Blow-Up,* a teeter-tottering wave machine as in *Diva,* a pair of wings like Trevor Howard's in *Light Years Away.* Hoagy Carmichael music played softly—"Baltimore Oriole"—but as Muley walked toward Jill, Fidel bounded toward her, interposing himself between the two humans, licking each at the moment they tried to kiss hello. Hillel Levy, currently rooming with Muley, was wearing a crash helmet and knee pads and roller-skating around the loft. He slapped five with Jill as he rode past her.

At the south end of the apartment were two small bedrooms: one was cluttered with magazines, sketchpads, pencils, pastels, and charcoal sticks, and on the walls, someone had pasted collages of vulvas, breasts, and cartoon characters. The other bedroom was pure white—white walls, sheets, and pillowcases, a white mattress on the floor beside a white dog bed. A white sketchpad rested against a white easel, a white film projector pointed toward a white movie screen. A white-framed window faced south toward the black roof of Bronzeville Studios. Guess whose room was whose, Muley asked.

That night, as Jill and Muley lay on his mattress, Jill told him about Poughkeepsie. She told him about college, about the people on her floor. She told him about the house on 5 Mack Road, and then she told him about Kenny. She described the sledding, bathtub, and seemingly broken condom scenario and felt surprised as the words tumbled out of her. She had never discussed such intimate details about herself, had only listened to Michelle's stories, never provided her own. She had heard conversations about boys and sex in the Lane bathroom, that "his was really big and it hurt" and "his was really small and I couldn't feel *anything.*" She had listened to Andrea Fleischman announce that she would never have sex in the wheelbarrow position again because she had sprained both of her wrists. Jill didn't mind hearing the stories—anything that educated her about an aspect of the human condition with which she was unfamiliar was knowledge worth possessing. But for her, discussing such experiences, if she had had them, would have felt exhibitionistic. Once, Rae-Ann Warner had played a "lights-out" game with her. Touching Jill and kissing her, Rae-Ann said that she was imagining that she was on a desert island with Loni Anderson. "Tell me who you're thinking of," Rae-Ann ordered Jill, who was dumbfounded; all she could finally say was, "Jean-Paul Sartre?"

"You don't even know how to play the game," Rae-Ann had snapped.

Jill concluded her discussion with Muley by asking him whether he thought that she was still a virgin. Muley thought for a while, then said that it didn't matter much, and the answer was whatever she thought it was. But that was just it, Jill said, she didn't know—that's why she wanted him to tell her. At this, Hillel, who had been eavesdropping, popped his head in the doorway. He pivoted back and forth on a roller skate. If you stick your dick in someone or someone sticks his dick in you even for an instant, that means you aren't a virgin, he proclaimed. Then he tightened his chin strap and skated away.

A week before her return to Poughkeepsie, Jill had settled comfortably into a life of reading, dog-walking, journal-writing, and traveling between West Rogers Park and the near south side. She had grown so used to this existence that when a call came from Bibi saying that she was borrowing her mother's car to buy a birthday present for Soren, Jill needed a split second to remind herself who Bibi was. So rattled by hearing Bibi's voice in an unfamiliar context, she instantly agreed to spend an afternoon downtown with her.

Bibi, her hair newly frizzed, drove her mother's white Cadillac Seville down Lake Shore Drive with Dvořák blaring until she tired of the music, ejected the tape, and put in *Vanity Six* instead. She bounced her shoulders and sang along as Vanity advised, "Bite it till you're satisfied," then parked underground in the Grant Park garage, leading the way to Marshall Field's. Jill trailed behind, uncertain why she was here and not playing with her dog, chatting with Muley, or reading Piven and Cloward. In the Field's Men's Store, Jill stifled a scream as Bibi stood for ten minutes at the necktie counter debating the pros and cons of spending fifty dollars on Soren for a navy blue silk tie with a pattern of treble clefs on it. But it was only when they were seated at a window table in the Walnut Room restaurant that Bibi revealed her agenda.

"Awful" was how Bibi described the three weeks that she had spent thus far at home in Northbrook; today was the only day that she hadn't cried. She had kept her whole relationship with Soren secret because she knew that her parents would "get all weird" about it. The moment she met her father at O'Hare, she knew that something was wrong, especially after Marty Eisenstaedt said that they would "have to talk, young lady." The last time he'd called her "young lady" was when she'd gotten a B in Calculus at Ida Crown. When she got home, where her father had purchased a new bed for her, exactly like the one in her dorm room, Marty finally asked what the story was with "this Soren individual."

At first, Bibi had no idea how her father had even heard of Soren, merely said that she'd met Soren through Jesters with Bells and hoped that would be the end of it. But when her father asked her whether it was true that she spent nights at Soren's house, that Soren was thirty, that he was some loser who was still in school and wasn't even Jewish, Bibi suddenly understood that this was the work of Shmuel Weinberg, to whom she referred as "That Darn Shmuel." She had made the mistake of confiding in That Darn Shmuel, and rather than act like an adult and accept the fact that he and Bibi would never be boyfriend and girl-friend again, he had behaved like "a big baby" and "blabbed" to her father, and not only that, Shmuel had started calling Domino's Pizza, pretending to be Soren, and sending extra-large sausage and pepperoni pies to his house.

Bibi said that she didn't want to lie to her father—she occasionally lied to her mom, but never to her dad—but she didn't want to tell him the whole truth, ei-ther. Rather than address That Darn Shmuel's allegations directly, she asked her father why he didn't trust her and why he immediately believed Shmuel's story, which was obviously colored by the fact that she had broken up with him, and had sent back the tickets that he had bought her for the "Weird Al" Yankovic concert. She told her father that Shmuel was a liar, and that Soren's father was Jewish. Marty Eisenstaedt apologized for doubting his "little girl"—he just wanted to make sure that she was being careful.

"Dad," Bibi told her father, "you're acting like you don't even know me," even though as she said this, she felt a small burst of pride—what she said was true, she thought; her father didn't know her at all anymore.

The next night, after her parents had gone to bed, Bibi called Soren from the basement phone to tell him what had happened. Soren was not amused. He said that he was too old to be dealing with teenage girls, their parents, and their old boyfriends. And how was it that she was telling people about their relationship when they had vowed to keep it quiet; now her father knew and this guy Shmuel knew, and why, by the way, were anonymous pizzas being delivered to him? Bibi tried to laugh off That Darn Shmuel's antics, but Soren got even angrier and said that he didn't play games and if Bibi wanted to play games, she should play with someone her own age. Bibi didn't know whether to laugh or cry, but she must have been crying because soon her father came downstairs in his T-shirt and underpants and asked Bibi who she was talking to. Nobody, she said, and told him to go back upstairs. But Marty grabbed the phone out of Bibi's hands. Who was this, he asked, was this Soren? This was Bibi's father, he said, and did Soren know how old Bibi was, and what kind of perverted layabout who was thirty and *still in school* would prey on some innocent kid? If Soren went near his daughter again, he would break him in two.

For the next week, Bibi barely spoke to her father, and he didn't even look at her at the dinner table, except when he repeatedly dispensed the same advice— how he knew that she was "angry as hell" at him, but someday she would know that he was right. As for Soren, Bibi couldn't reach him. The night of her father's blowup, she'd called him again, but his phone had kept ringing. And later, every time she called, she got a busy signal. The phone stayed busy even when she called at odd times when she wasn't supposed to. She even dialed the Skinner Music Library, but the man who answered the phone said that Soren wasn't taking calls.

Finally, Bibi was resigning herself to the fact that her relationship with Soren was over and she wasn't entirely blaming her father. She even said yes when he asked if she wanted to see *Oh God! You Devil* at the Highland Park, then go out for ice cream at Peacock's, just the two of them. But when she was getting dressed, the phone rang and she picked it up—Soren was on the other end. He instructed her to call him back collect from a pay phone. It was snowing outside and the movie started in fifteen minutes, so she asked her father if they could see a later show. She then trudged in her sneakers to the White Hen Pantry and called Soren. He was crying and he told her that he'd been a fool and he loved her; could she come back to New York now? Bibi said that she couldn't, but she'd be there soon and she loved him too. Every night since then, she'd spent an hour in the White Hen parking lot laughing and crying and talking to Soren, with whom she felt closer than ever. But now she had to tell her father the truth because it broke her heart that she couldn't tell him her secrets.

So, she told Jill, she was now going to her father's office to confess. All she asked was for Jill to accompany her and "back her up." What was she supposed to say? Jill asked. Bibi said that Jill wasn't supposed to say anything; she just wanted Jill there for moral support. Jill said that she actually didn't think this was any of her business ("I know it's not," Bibi said) and that she didn't really know Soren ("I know you don't," Bibi said) and that she had no particular opinion about Soren. "That's why I want you to come," said Bibi.

In the Marum-Kagan real estate office, Jill sat silently on a black leather arm-chair and fiddled with its gold buttons as Bibi honestly and straightforwardly presented her case before Marty Eisenstaedt, who leaned back in his desk chair with his hands folded and his eyes half-closed in contemplation. Bibi told her father that she did not want to lie, but she was an adult, and she wanted the right to make her own mistakes. To Jill, the conversation was so unfathomable that it was initially interesting from a sociological perspective, suggestive perhaps of what her life might have been like had she been raised in the shtetl. But as Bibi continually made the same points and drew on the same examples ("How old was Mom when you met her?"), Jill stared out the window at the el tracks, wondering how long it would be before she was sitting on a train, bound for Muley's loft.

Bibi did not ask Jill to speak at all, but when Marty finally broke his silence, he addressed his remarks to Jill, as if she had vociferously argued Bibi's case. He told Jill that he knew she didn't like him much right now. He told Jill that he respected her father, and he knew of her family's integrity; if Jill was vouching for Soren's character, he would have to consider her opinion very seriously. And when Jill said that she didn't know Soren well enough to vouch for him, he thanked Jill for her honesty and said that Bibi was lucky to have a friend like her. Then he gave Jill a somewhat damp handshake and thanked her for having made him realize "some things about himself." He said that he should give "old Charlie-boy" a call and they all could have dinner sometime soon.

Moments later, Jill and Bibi were headed down in the elevator. Bibi gave Jill a smooch on the cheek and thanked her for being so reasonable and articulate. But she hadn't said anything, Jill said. Yes, said Bibi, but it was the *way* she had said it. She asked Jill if there was anything else she needed to do because she had an hour to kill before she could call Soren. Jill said that she had to go; Fidel needed a walk and she was off to see Muley.

"Say hi," Bibi said, after which Jill exited the elevator, then made a quick call to Muley from a pay phone to say that she was on her way. She walked across Daley Center Plaza, past the eternal flame memorial, then toward the Washington Street subway as quickly as she could.

When Jill emerged from the train station at Roosevelt Road, Muley was waiting for her, Fidel seated patiently at his side. Jill felt so elated to see them that, without thinking, she kissed Muley on the lips, startling him. Muley asked what that was for. But just as Jill was about to kiss him again, she felt someone else's presence beside her. She turned her head and saw a man in a wrinkled dark suit with a salt-and-pepper brush mustache walking briskly past her toward a waiting limousine, a beat-up brown leather briefcase in his hand.

"Don't let me stop you," the man said to Jill, then opened the rear limo door, and stepped into the backseat.

"Wait," Jill said, then dashed toward the curb where Harold Washington's limo was pulling away. But the windows were tinted, and soon all Jill could see of it were red taillights speeding out of view into the swirling snow.

## SPRING  SEMESTER  1985

Jill's January O'Hare–to–La Guardia flight did not possess the same exhilarative quality of her first plane ride. She could not watch the city of Chicago roll away from her; seconds after takeoff, the plane was enveloped in fog. Chicago had once seemed to be all about expectation while Poughkeepsie was all about possibility, but now Poughkeepsie had its own set of expectations, and though Jill was eager to return to her work at the newspaper and another full slate of classes, she was also dreading the fact that Bibi would continue to involve her in her entanglement with Soren, that Kenny would want to hash out their relationship, that she would have to find out once and for all who lived at 5 Mack Road.

Upon entering her room, Jill saw Bibi seated on her four-poster bed, her head down as she studied what appeared to be an illustrated letter from Muley. Peculiar. Why would Bibi have a letter from Muley? Bibi hardly even knew him—had she been rummaging through Jill's desk? That didn't seem like something Bibi Eisenstaedt would do. And come to think of it, that overpoweringly toxic scent didn't smell like Bibi's perfume. That wasn't Bibi's hairstyle either. And Jill realized, as the young woman seated on Bibi's bed looked up with a guilty glance that she soon replaced with an enthusiastic grin, that wasn't Bibi Eisenstaedt at all; that was Lana Rovner.

Jill had not spoken to her Hebrew school classmate Lana since the night of Ronald Reagan's 1981 inauguration when Lana had spun some improbable tale to Jill and Muley, which necessitated Muley's helping Lana to break into her own house. Like all of Lana's stories, its downfall had been in its details. In Hebrew school, it had never been enough for Lana to tell Rabbi Meltzer that she hadn't finished her *Chumash* homework; there was always a dead grandparent or a doctor's appointment. Just as now, after Lana had thrown open her arms and exclaimed, "How *aare* you?" she couldn't merely say that she had been bored and started reading Jill's letters; she had to present the letter from Muley and say that she had found it on the floor. And Jill, who remembered how furious Lana would become whenever anyone challenged her fictions—how she had flung a *machzor* at Hillel Levy when he said that he didn't believe she'd ever Frenched with Todd Bridges—chose not to question Lana's story. If she actually thought for more than a moment that Lana had been snooping through her belongings, Jill—who had never been in a fight—might just have had to smack her.

Lana said that she was visiting "Beebeep" (she imitated the cartoon character the Roadrunner when she said Bibi's nickname), who was out with "some mysterious man." On Sunday, she would head into the city with her father and stepmom for the premiere of her brother and sister-in-law's musical, *Gotta Sing!* As Jill took all of Muley's letters out of her desk and placed them in a taped box, Lana told Jill about the "wild time" she had had in the years since they had last seen each other. For the first years of high school, she had attended Roycemore and "partied too much." Her behavior had gotten so bad that her mother, Ellen Leventhal, whom she had barely seen at all in years, had reentered her life. After Ellen had called her ex-husband to inquire about some overlooked paperwork regarding their divorce, she asked about her children. Michael revealed with a chuckle that Larry was doing well at Brandeis, and Lana was "doing what girls her age do." Ellen asked what it was that girls Lana's age did and he had told her that Lana was spending a lot of time shopping and crashing cars, but he was confident that she could get her grade point average back up to a solid C.

Ellen Leventhal flew into a rage. She called her lawyer and then she called the Lake Geneva school board. One day later, she called her ex-husband back and told him that she was prepared to pull Lana out of Roycemore and cart her off to Wisconsin. And then she had talked to Lana who, after she had yelled at her mother "for about an hour," agreed that her situation in Evanston was less than optimal; maybe a fresh start in Wisconsin wasn't the worst idea. What had really terrified her, Lana said, was when her mother had said that she might have to attend a "community college." Lana didn't like the word *community;* only minorities and poor people lived in communities. But one week later, she called her mother to veto the Wisconsin plan; Michael and Cheryl had offered a better proposal—instead of sending Lana to Lake Geneva, they would ship her off to Cheever Academy, and though it was important that she do well, even if she didn't, the school's prestige would help secure her admission into a good college. And since she had started attending Cheever, life had improved immeasurably— "a really different class of people" attended boarding school. She had dated one boy who was trying to get into Yale and had already secured recommendations from George Bush and William F. Buckley Jr.; another boy's father had worked as Chico Marx's accountant; and there was a girl on her floor whose father had a Learjet, which he flew down to Colombia on business every other weekend. She had done less work than ever in her first semester, but had gotten straight As.

"So," she asked Jill, "what have you been up to?" At which point Kenny entered in red sweatpants, black buckle shoes with no socks, and a brown corduroy shirt. He kissed Jill on the cheek and introduced himself to Lana, who said that she was an old friend of Bibi's and Jill's and was a senior at Cheever Academy. Kenny adjusted his glasses, pointed at Lana, and said he thought that "*only buhnouts and rich ayussholes*" went there.

Jill had never felt happier to see Kenny. All her anxiety about their night together evaporated instantly; now he could provide the simple, polite reason for why she couldn't sit here and listen to Lana. She told Lana that she and Kenny were going out for a snack. Kenny, however, suggested that the three of them "pull a diner" at the "*Acrawpalis*"; he asked "*Lawna*" if she wanted to get a "*buhguh*" with them. Lana said sure, they could take her car; she'd leave a note for Bibi, who could catch up with them after her date. "Date?" Kenny asked. Did she mean that "gnarly old *puh-vuht*" who'd been "skulking" around the "*dawmitory*" looking like "a hyena stalking fresh meat"?

Lana laughed sharply at this, crinkling her nose—Jill remembered this look of Lana's, the display of sharp incisors, the glint and sparkle in the eyes, the laugh that began way back in the throat, worked its way to the nose, and concluded with a sound that was half snort, half sneeze. Jill remembered that laugh that always seemed to come at the expense of others—Aaron Mermelstein when he slammed his head against his desk, Hillel Levy when Rabbi Einstein had grabbed him roughly by the collar after Hillel had asked if there was a kosher way to urinate. And even though some of those laughs had come at Jill's expense, the only time Jill ever felt sorry for Lana was when she saw her laughing, when she saw what seemed to make her happiest.

The three of them rode to the Acropolis Diner in Lana's new Renault 5. Lana drove just a little too fast on the slick streets, the car swerving slightly whenever she switched the radio station, while Kenny pointed out *shawtcuts,* and offered driving tips, telling Lana to keep her hands between ten o'clock and two o'clock and to toot the horn in anticipation of "potential *hazuhds,*" even though he had lived his entire life in Manhattan and had never driven a car. As Lana drove past fast-food restaurants, pizzerias, and ramshackle houses, she kept saying, aghast, "Look at how these people live," remarking that some of the houses were no bigger than her garage, and why were those poor people walking into Wendy's so fat if they didn't have money to buy food? Would her car be O.K. if she parked in the Acropolis lot? There certainly seemed to be a lot of *schwarzers* shuffling about.

Jill didn't know which was worse—that she had to endure Lana's rants or that Kenny laughed at everything Lana said, apparently not knowing that she was serious. At the Acropolis, Kenny and Lana gobbled cheeseburgers, while Jill sipped peppermint tea and flipped through the tableside jukebox, listening to Lana and Kenny whoop it up. Lana crinkled her nose and laughed as Kenny played along with her by parodying the attitudes and vocal patterns of a stereotypical racist, joking that Chinese people had slanty eyes and that's why they couldn't "*droive*" and *schwarzers* ought to pull themselves up by their bootstraps and stop drinking Wild Irish Rose and Native Americans gambled and drank too much "*Budweisuh*" and Hispanics drove Firebirds with flames painted on them, and Jews were stingy sons-of-bitches who'd crucified Christ—"Wait a minute," Lana said, "that's not funny," but she laughed anyway and Kenny laughed harder, taking off his glasses and wiping his eyes, asking Jill why she wasn't laughing. Didn't he get it, Jill asked, Lana meant everything that she was saying.

After they left the diner, Kenny sat in the front seat of Lana's car and continued his routine, suggesting that they drive downtown to make fun of "*poo-uh*" people. Jill said that they could keep driving, but she was going home. Kenny, sensing Jill's offense, said come on, you had to laugh at this stuff, if you couldn't laugh at it, you were letting the enemy "get the *bettuh* of you." "*Laughtuh,*" his father had always told him, was the best weapon Jews had. At a red light on the corner of Raymond and Main, Lana fixed her eyes on Jill in the rearview mirror and said yeah, why had Jill always been such a Communist anyway? Kenny tried to keep a straight face, but couldn't contain himself—he burst out with a sudden laugh. Jill opened her door, got out, slammed the door shut, and walked away, her hands in her pockets as she trudged through hail and slush. Kenny jumped out of the car and tried to catch up—why didn't she get back in the "*cah*," it was cold outside, and she wasn't dressed "*wahm*" enough. Lana drove slowly alongside them, the muffled sounds of "Missing You" on WPDH underscoring the honks of her horn.

As Lana kept honking, Kenny asked Jill where her "sense of *hyoo-mah*" had gone. Jill said she could ask him the same thing, adding that only people who had a little bit of racism in them could make those jokes; pretending to mock prejudice was a handy way to be offensive while maintaining an aura of liberalism. Kenny said that you had to "*unduhstand* the language of oppression" to overcome it. Well, *she* didn't see it that way, Jill said, gesturing toward Lana's car; *she* thought Kenny was serious. Kenny said "Bah," Jill didn't give people enough credit. He kept pace as hail fell down harder. You know what, he finally said, he knew what this was all about; this had nothing to do with "*pawlitics*" or principles. Jill was just jealous.

Jill stopped dead. "Jealous?" she asked. Sure, that's what it was, Kenny said— he stumbled slightly at first, but gained confidence as his thoughts coalesced. He pointed out that he'd been "enjoying *Lawna*," and Jill was feeling left out. He remembered when he'd been dating a "*guhl*" at "*Brawnx Soyence*" and when they'd gone out with his buddies Irv and Hanif, she'd spent the whole night talking to them and he "*fig-yuhed*" that she liked them better than him and he wanted to make sure Jill knew that just because he'd been talking more to Lana didn't mean he liked her more.

Jill stared at him dumbstruck, shook her head, then walked away. She heard Kenny say "Shit" and then the door to a car opened and closed as Jill started walking toward Mack Road. She could hear the Renault accelerating and then the night returning to silence, the only sound that of the hail slapping her jacket, her cheeks, and the Buick parked outside number 5. She pulled up the hood of her coat and tied it tightly as she walked past the house. She stepped nimbly over the icy sidewalk, gazed at the front walkway and the three snowy front steps.

Though she could hear music coming from inside the house—it sounded like the theme to *Spartacus*—the shades were down, and Jill had a sensation akin to walking through a cemetery as she often had in grade school when she had sought solitude. She drew a "J" in the snow on the Buick's windshield, then wiped it off, wishing that someone in the house would invite her in for coffee or cocoa.

Instead, she walked on, hood up, hands in her pockets, around and around the block, thoughts of Kenny Melnick, Lana Rovner, and E. Ferrante whirling about in her brain. She circled the block until she became aware of the Renault honking at her again. Now Bibi emerged from Lana's backseat, cautiously negotiated her way over a snowbank in high-heeled shoes, and called out to Jill. It was freezing, she said. Bibi grabbed Jill's hand and said that she had returned from Soren's and found Lana and Kenny chatting in the dorm room. When they told her that they had left Jill, she had gotten "so darn mad"— she told them that if they didn't drive back and find Jill, she would never speak to either of them again. And Jill, who was tired of walking in cold, wet sneakers and, frankly, too tired to argue, followed Bibi into Lana's car.

Lana and Kenny were seated up front; Kenny was holding three bottles of Genesee—he offered one to Jill, saying that his *fawthuh* had always taught him to admit when he'd been "an *ayusshole,*" so why didn't Jill just call him one and they'd forget about it. Jill said that she didn't want to call him an asshole. Come on, Kenny said, why didn't she just come out and say it? And though Jill wondered why Kenny had to set the terms even for his own apology, she called him an asshole. Kenny popped a beer and handed it to her.

Then it was Lana's turn to apologize. In the rearview mirror, Jill could see her eyes shifting from side to side, looking at Jill, then away. The windshield wipers were going fast as Lana turned the volume up on the radio, which was playing "Hot Girls in Love." Bibi asked Lana, didn't she have something to say? Lana's nose crinkled. Please, Jill said, couldn't they just go home—she was tired and wet. Why didn't they forget about saying they were sorry and go to sleep? No, Lana said, she did owe Jill an apology; she turned down the radio volume, swerving slightly then righting herself as Kenny advised her to "aim high in steering" and watch the road. Lana said she had forgotten that she was a guest, and it wasn't right to impose her beliefs on Bibi and Jill so long as they were her hosts. Politics was the last thing that one should discuss among friends. It wasn't like politics meant anything anyway; she just liked Republicans because they wanted her father to pay lower taxes and they dressed better. *I mean,* she said, how could anyone have voted for Walter Mondale—his suits looked like they'd been purchased at JCPenney and he used Grecian Formula.

For a moment, the car was silent. Lana smiled, satisfied with herself, and turned the volume of the radio back up. Jill shrugged—she always preferred an honest statement of evil to a counterfeit declaration of purportedly good intentions. She thought that this would be the end of it—the main gate of Vassar was just ahead. The sleet was coming down harder and it would be a good night to curl up in bed with a cup of tea and a copy of *Orientalism* by Edward Said. Kenny put down his beer. He squinted, adjusted his glasses, and looked at Lana bopping to Loverboy. He took another swig. It was true? he asked; she believed everything she had said? Of course, she told Kenny—didn't he believe it? Didn't he believe *what,* Kenny asked, that *poo-uh* people *desuhved* to be *poo-uh* and presidents had to have good haircuts? Lana nodded and smiled.

"You've got no fuckin' *haht,*" Kenny said, thumping his chest, then added under his breath, "fuckin' Republican bitch."

Lana's face went pale, and her eyes grew large. She gripped the steering wheel tightly and looked to Kenny to see if maybe he was joking, not noticing that she had crossed over the median and two headlights were bearing down hard on her car. The next thing Jill knew, she was lying across the backseat of Lana's Renault, a cold wind blowing through shattered windows.

It all happened too quickly for Jill to say for certain what had happened. She had seen headlights practically up against the windshield, sensed a sudden swerve that had thrown her back against her seat, heard brakes, felt the side of the car hitting something hard. She saw Bibi's door swing open, then heard glass breaking and a hiss like a balloon deflating. The radio switched off, and then she heard a long, low blare of car horn. Glass in her lap and on the seat, she looked to her left and noticed that Bibi was no longer sitting there. Jill swept the glass away with a mitten and opened her car door at the same moment as she heard Kenny expel a nervous-yet-relieved laugh.

Lana was already walking toward the security guard, a hulking man in a black slicker with trashbags tied over his boots. Bibi was sitting on the wet ground at the side of the totaled Renault, her arms around her knees, her fingers tightly interlaced as the guard asked if she was O.K. (she nodded) and if she thought that she'd broken anything (she shook her head). While steam billowed out of the hood of the car, the guard suggested that they get out of the cold while he called the police. Bibi stood up slowly. Her skirt was soaked, and there were gray streaks across her forehead. Kenny pushed his hand toward her face—"How many *fing-uhs*?" he kept asking. Bibi said that she was fine, but in the tiny security booth, when the guard asked her where she lived, she gave her address in Northbrook and when he asked how she'd wound up on the ground, she couldn't remember.

Out the window of the security booth, under the pink glow of the streetlight whose pole had bent all the way over the body of the Renault, Jill could see sleet falling down fast and the red and orange lights of an approaching squad car and tow truck. As Lana explained her version of the accident to the guard, Jill crouched beside Bibi, who was seated in the guard's chair, and asked if she was sure she wasn't hurt. Yes, Bibi said curtly, she was just scared, that's all; now she wanted to go back to the dorm and call Soren—it was almost eleven and she wasn't supposed to call him any later. Kenny, who was jockeying back and forth between Lana and the guard and Bibi and Jill, said that no one was going anywhere because they'd all have to give statements, in the event of any future litigation associated with the accident.

Lana was telling the guard that she had been driving well below the speed limit and had signaled a left turn when a salt truck had veered into her lane; the truck's shovel had clipped her bumper. Kenny interrupted; that's not how he had seen it, he said, it was "*drivuh's errah* plain and simple." Lana glared fiercely at Kenny but calmly said that that had not been her "recollection." Kenny asked whether that was not what she "recalled" or not what she wanted to tell the insurance company, while the guard opined that insurance companies had enough money and he didn't care what people told them. Kenny countered that the reason insurance companies' rates were so high was because people lied to them, but why didn't they discuss all this with the policeman who was getting out of his squad car? Lana sprinted outside to intercept the officer.

Kenny was about to follow Lana out to the police car, but as he put his hand on the doorknob, Bibi stood and announced that she was going home. Kenny started to say that no one could go home until their statements had been signed in the presence of a notary public, but before he could finish, Bibi stumbled. Jill grabbed hold of her and eased her back into her chair, at which point Kenny declared that Bibi was going to the "*hawspital.*"

In the back of an ambulance, Kenny chattered about the evening's traumatic events, while Jill held Bibi's hand and asked if she was all right, thinking that once she had made sure that Bibi was healthy, she would begin her new semester by being less tolerant and more proactive, less willing to get into cars driven by people she didn't like. Meanwhile, Bibi nervously eyed her watch, smiled cheerfully, and said that this was really an overreaction, though every so often, she scrunched her eyes tightly and gripped Jill's hand so hard that it hurt.

When they reached the intake room of Vassar Brothers Hospital at a quarter past eleven, Jill, Kenny, and Bibi approached the front desk and received a clipboard with a form to fill out. Jill and Kenny began walking toward a bank of plastic pumpkin-colored chairs, but Bibi ran down the hallway to a pay phone. Jill then followed Bibi, who had just finished dialing a number; she told an operator that her name was Bibi and she was calling collect. A moment later, she scrunched her eyes again, and asked the operator why the charges had been refused, did she say that "Bee-Bee" was calling from the *ho-spi-tal*? She hung up the phone hard. Jill invited her to sit down and fill out her forms, but Bibi said that she was calling Soren again. The next phone call produced the same result; Bibi told Jill that she knew Soren had specific hours when she was allowed to call, but this was an emergency. She unzipped her purse, extracted a dollar bill, walked to the reception desk, and asked for change.

As Jill sat back down beside Kenny, Bibi was dialing again. Jill started filling out Bibi's medical form, while Kenny dictated Bibi's symptoms in what he perceived to be accurate medical jargon—"acute complaints of dizziness," "symptoms of dislocation," "possible evidence of internal hemorrhage"—but then Jill heard a loud bang followed by three short ones. She looked up to see Bibi slam down the telephone receiver, pick it up, then bang it down again. Jill ran to Bibi, clipboard in hand. Kenny followed behind, his life having taken on new purpose. Bibi's eyes were red and wet as she held Jill tightly.

"She said that Soren wouldn't come to the phone," Bibi sobbed.

"Who?" Jill asked.

"His wife," said Bibi.

"Bastard," Jill said under her breath, while Kenny observed with a point of a finger that marriage was "*fawmed*" by a "legal, *boinding cawntract,*" and if Bibi was interfering with the execution of said *cawntract,* she could be subject to "*fyootchuh* litigation."

With Bibi in her arms, Jill asked Kenny if he couldn't do something more useful than moralize. Kenny responded that little was more useful than a lesson in morality.

On Sunday morning, Jill stopped at the hospital to check on Bibi for the second time that weekend. Jill had declined Lana's offer to accompany her before she would head off to the city for the *Gotta Sing!* premiere—it had turned out, Lana said, that her father was far less angry about the car accident than she had anticipated; he only asked her to promise not to tell her mother.

The day following the accident, Jill had brought Bibi's books to the hospital. The official diagnosis was a mild concussion, but Bibi was to remain for another twenty-four hours for observation. As she sat up in her bed, Bibi seemed surprisingly cheerful, laughing about what a wreck she had been the previous evening, joking that she now knew what it was like to be "the other woman." She suddenly understood why she had never seen the inside of Soren's house and, well, it had been fun while it had lasted, but at least she knew how to make espresso now.

On Sunday, Jill brought Bibi a bouquet of irises and lilies, but when she entered Bibi's room, there were already three bouquets—two dozen pink roses and a dozen red ones. Still, Bibi, dressed in a pink sweatshirt, matching sweats, and leggings, had squealed when she saw Jill's bouquet. She said that her parents had sent those pink roses and her sister Missy had sent these pink roses. Jill was about to ask about the red roses, but there was no need, for Soren entered the room.

Soren stood with his hands in the pockets of his drooping blue jeans, his yellow button-down shirt untucked, his slick hair parted at the side. "This one" had brought the red ones, Bibi said. Soren grinned and offered his hand to Jill. Bibi nodded to Jill as if to say that shaking his hand was O.K. Jill moved her hand toward his, but stopped when she saw the palm glistening. Soren said that his name was Soren and did Jill remember him from that night at his house? No, Jill said, stuffing her hands in her jacket pockets, she didn't remember him from his house because she hadn't been in his house; she'd only been allowed in the servants' quarters. Soren looked momentarily stunned, but he smiled nonetheless. Right, he said with a chuckle, then added that soon, he and "that one" would give Jill a full house tour. Yes, Jill said, she'd look forward to that, particularly after Bibi had gotten a chance to see the house first. "Good luck, Bibi," Jill said, then left.

As she trudged through the snow on Montgomery Street, Jill briefly felt that she'd acted in a petty manner by deliberately snubbing Soren's handshake. But at the same time, she had survived a harrowing car accident, and she wanted it to mean something. She wanted it to be a message from fate, telling her to take charge of her life. The previous evening, while Lana had used Bibi's phone to call her father's insurance company, Jill had typed a five-page-long, single-spaced letter to Muley about adopting a new take-charge attitude, but it hadn't been enough to stem her enthusiasm; she longed to talk with someone immediately, and decided to call Michelle, who, she thought, would appreciate her newfound strength—Michelle had always done exactly what she wanted.

But when Jill called her sister from the hall phone, Michelle was neither as excited nor as supportive as Jill had anticipated. When Jill told Michelle that she was taking charge of her life, Michelle pointed out that taking charge had little to do with talking about it; it was just something that you did, a fact that she demonstrated by monopolizing the discussion, enumerating the different plays she'd been asked to star in or direct, then letting slip the fact that she had "just for the hell of it" taken the LSATs and someone must have "fucked up" and "given her the retard's version" of the exam because she'd finished in half the time allotted, checked her answers "a bazillion times," then spent the last hour staring at everyone else in the exam room, trying to imagine them naked. "Not a pretty sight," she added. She asked Jill how life was in "Poo-fuckin'-keepsie" and whether she was still a virgin, and when Jill said that she wasn't, Michelle hooted, then yelled elatedly, "The Queen is dead! Long live the Queen," adding that she sincerely hoped that her "cherry picker" hadn't been Kenny Melnick, who, she theorized, either had "the world's tiniest dick" or was "hung like Milton Berle," but either way was probably one of those guys who stuck his dick in a girl once, then got nervous, which you couldn't exactly call having sex. Well, she said, at least one of the Wasserstrom gals was "out bonin'"; as for herself, she was about as sexually fulfilled as Mother Teresa. She asked Jill to fill her in on "all the disgusting details." Jill said that she was out of change.

When Jill reached 5 Mack Road that Sunday morning, the sidewalk was shoveled and so were the stairs. Jill pushed the buzzer, and when no one came to the door, she knocked until she heard rustling inside the house. She stood rocking back and forth, wondering why she was nervous; she was a journalist, after all, this was her job, what she might well be doing for the rest of her life. The door opened slowly and in the dim glow of a low-watt hallway light, Jill saw a slightly stooped, gray-haired woman leaning on a metal cane, squinting at her. She was wearing a gray velour sweatsuit and thick gray socks. Her knees were bent slightly and her feet pointed inward. A pair of thick glasses on a chain dangled from her neck. "Grandmother?" Jill asked.

In one swift motion, the former Edna Schulman née Grinberg lifted her spectacles and held them in front of her eyes, peering suspiciously before letting them drop. "Lois?" she asked. Jill shook her head. "Vicki?" asked Edna. Jill said no. And when Edna proposed "Bettina," Jill said, "Becky's daughter." Edna's mouth formed an "O" and she reached out her hands and hugged Jill. "Michelle," she said, "Michelle, Michelle, Michelle." And it was only after her grandmother had let go that Jill corrected her. "Not Michelle," she said, "Jill." Edna pursed her lips—a series of thin vertical lines formed below her nose as she lifted her glasses again and looked through a lens. "But you were just a baby," she said curtly.

Jill stood in her wet hiking boots on Edna's frayed, green plastic welcome mat. She explained that she was attending Vassar now and asked if this was a bad time. Why, Edna asked, did she look like she was busy? Jill said no, but she had come unannounced and Edna might have someplace to go. Did she look like she had someplace to go, Edna asked. Jill observed the drawn shades in the living room, the drooping plants. Probably not, she said. Well, Edna asked, then why did she ask if she had someplace to go? She led the way to the kitchen. Jill took off her boots, placed them on the floormat, and followed. Edna switched on the fluorescent kitchen light; one bulb was out, the others flickered briefly, then illuminated an empty sink and an olive-green dish rack, a Formica counter, white cabinets, a whirring Frigidaire, and a lopsided electric stove. No, Edna sighed, she had no place to go, the only places she went were doctors' appointments; they wanted her to have an operation on this hip—she slapped her right side—but she'd be in a wheelchair for at least two months afterward and what was she supposed to do, sit in a wheelchair in an empty house? *Nisht far mir,* she said. She opened a kitchen cabinet, revealing rows of pill containers. See, she said, she had a pill for this, a pill for that, she couldn't keep track anymore, but she didn't want to tell Jill her problems, who wanted to listen to people's problems?

Well, Jill said as she leaned against the stove, at least she had people to talk to. Who, Edna asked, who did she talk to? Jill said it seemed as if someone had been kind enough to shovel her walk. Who shoveled her walk, Edna asked. Me, she said, a seventy-nine-year-old lady with a cane and a babushka. There was some *schmuck* down the street who'd offered to do it, but he charged ten bucks and did a *vercockte* job. So, she asked Jill, what was new in her young life—did she want something to eat? She walked to the kitchen cabinet. Jill stood to help, but Edna told her to sit down ("What am I? A helpless person?" she asked). She tried to flick down a can of soup, then said that maybe Jill could help her. Jill climbed on a chair and took down a can. What did it say, Edna said, squinting through a lens of her glasses, did it say vegetable? Yes, Jill said. Did she like vegetable soup, Edna asked. Sure, Jill said, but Edna didn't need to bother making soup. Edna said that she wasn't crippled, but the can opener was in that drawer and the pots were over there. And as Jill poured the soup into a pot, Edna asked her if she had ever been to this house; she couldn't remember Jill being here.

Like her sister, Jill had a memory that could nearly have been called photographic. But unlike Michelle, who had been born with hers, Jill had developed her memory over time. Not until she realized that her mother was ill and that her world was disappearing with each passing day did she train herself to focus in on details and sear them into her brain, so that now, nearly a decade after her mother's death, she suffered from an imbalanced memory. From 1976 on, there was a journalistic precision to her recollections, pre-1976, only a patchwork of sensations—the dank smell of the Boone school library, the sting of a bee on Lunt Avenue Beach, the taste of licorice Chuckles at her fifth birthday party. She had expected that entering this house would trigger a series of repressed memories, but even in Edna's kitchen, all that she remembered were the green shutters outside, the view of the Hudson River out the window of a railcar, the Poughkeepsie train station. Her mother's words upon departing: "Let's not do that again anytime soon."

As she stirred the soup, Jill asked Edna what she had been doing for the past decade. Edna asked what difference it made, who wanted to listen to old people's stories, old people's stories were all about death and if they weren't about death, they were about surviving, and when it came down to it, there wasn't much difference. Jill said that she liked listening to people's stories, but Edna said that she didn't have any; her first husband, Jill's grandfather, he had stories; her second husband, George Ferrante, had stories for every one of his recipes, but not Edna; she'd lived her entire adult life in Poughkeepsie and she would die right here too. Maybe in her next life she'd have stories, she said.

After they'd eaten the soup and Jill had made coffee—Edna had said that she didn't want anyone to "wait on her hand and foot," but if Jill was making coffee, she didn't like it too strong—Edna did provide some details about her recent life. She showed her pictures of George's children—Lois, Vicki, and Bettina, and their children—George saved everything, she said. Once she had saved things, but now she just threw everything out.

At four in the afternoon, Edna said that she was sure Jill had places to go and that anyway, she needed to go to the drugstore to refill a prescription. Jill said that she could run to the drugstore, but Edna waved her off; she wasn't a corpse just yet. Still, it had been lovely of Jill to stop by. She told her to say hello to her father ("if he wants to hear about me") and her sister ("if she remembers me at all"). Jill hugged her grandmother and said that it wouldn't be hard for them to see each other again; she only lived a mile away now, and would be happy to visit. "Visit the old people's home?" Edna asked. Well, if Jill wanted to, that was fine, but Sunday afternoons were no good. Saturday, then, Jill said. Saturday was O.K., said Edna, and she'd be sure to have enough soup. Jill put on her boots, thinking how lonely her grandmother must be in this dark house with all the shades down, both of her husbands and her only daughter gone. She told Edna to call her hall phone if she ever needed anything.

That night, Bibi returned from the hospital. She said that she and Soren had worked everything out. They had talked about Soren's wife, Deenie—when she'd gotten pregnant, Soren had told her that she wasn't ready to be a mother and she'd agreed to put the child up for adoption. But midway through the pregnancy, "that manipulative Deenie" changed her mind and decided to keep the child, even though Soren's money would be supporting it. Soren had generously relented, but said that Deenie would be responsible for taking care of it and if it ever made too much noise, he'd sleep out in the cabin. But then the child had died six days after its birth, and his wife had blamed Soren, saying that the baby had died because he hadn't wanted it, and ever since then, Deenie hadn't let him touch her, yet still wouldn't give him a divorce because she was after his money. But thankfully, Deenie had met "some weirdo" who wanted to marry her and she was now hounding Soren for a divorce, and the only reason why he had been slow to agree was that he wanted to "give her a little taste of her own medicine." Now Soren had agreed not to delay anymore; once Deenie had removed the belongings she needed and Soren had burned the rest, Bibi could move into the house with Soren. Bibi told Jill that that they should all have dinner together "real soon."

"I don't think that will be happening," said Jill.

Jill's second encounter with her grandmother the following Saturday began even more uncomfortably than the first. Initially, Edna had asked Jill at the door if she was a representative from the senior center. Jill could not tell if she was joking or just didn't recognize Jill because she wasn't wearing her glasses, which Edna said she wore only sporadically because the prescription wasn't strong enough. But after a few moments, Jill noted that two places had been set at the kitchen table and a pot of vegetable soup was heating on the stove—Edna said that she had bought vegetable because she knew Jill liked it; she, however, found it *chaloushes*. After soup, Jill made coffee and she and her grandmother sat in the living room facing the windows. Jill asked Edna if she wouldn't prefer the shades up. Why, Edna asked, what was there to see? She didn't want people looking in and pitying the old lady. Still, she shuffled to the windows and pulled up the shades. See, Jill said, that was better with a little more light, wasn't it? Edna said that it was all the same to her—she had pulled up the shades only because Jill had wanted her to.

Over the course of the next weeks, when Jill would visit Edna, their interactions would follow a similar pattern. Edna would suggest an activity ("Do you want to watch a television program?" "Do you want to eat a sandwich?"). Jill would agree, thinking that this was what her grandmother wanted to do. Soon, Edna would reveal her lack of interest in whatever she had suggested. "I don't understand how a person can waste their life watching TV," she said after Jill had endured an hour's worth of men's diving competitions on *Wide World of Sports*. Still, what Jill liked about visiting Edna was that the experience usually presented tangible problems with obvious solutions. There was a checkbook to balance, there were drawers to organize, prescriptions to fill at the drugstore. Plus, there was the simple matter of providing help and company to a woman too proud or self-effacing to request it.

During the course of her seventeen and a half years, Jill had had little contact with people of Edna's generation. She felt cheated by the fact that her father's parents had died before she was born. Occasionally, she saw her great-aunt Beileh, but since the woman was quite wealthy, her son Teddy, a Jaguar-driving, jeweled-bracelet–wearing writer for underfunded Chicago periodicals, such as *Nit & Wit,* always tried to keep his mother at a distance from relatives. Edna was Jill's only remaining connection to a mysterious ancient culture with its roots in Eastern Europe. When Jill visited her grandmother, she would press Edna for details about her childhood and her only daughter. Edna would always say that she couldn't remember; they oughta make a law, she said—those with good memories are the only ones who survive.

Edna soon came to expect Jill's visits, pulled up the shades the moment Jill arrived, put on the Culture Club and Queen cassettes that she thought Jill liked, fixed Jill her "favorite" soup. But Jill did not learn more than she already knew. She listened to the same George Ferrante stories ("A genius, the man could fix anything"), the same Sam Schulman stories ("The women loved him; why he chose me, I'll never know"), and received the same pinched reply to questions about Becky ("Your father talked to her more than I did; he'd know"). So that, even after a month of soup, crackers, and chores, Jill knew all about her grandmother's life, save for the thirty-seven years when her mother had been alive. An effort to turn Edna's memories of early Poughkeepsie into an article met with a chilly reception—when Jill brought a portable tape recorder to interview her grandmother, Edna suspiciously eyed the spindles as Jill asked questions, addressed the recorder as "Hello, Machine," and provided terse answers. If Jill pressed for more detail, she'd say, "I didn't think I was talking to you; I thought I was talking to a machine."

On the last Saturday in February, after Jill and Edna had finished consuming their soup and sandwiches and retired to the living room to watch men's water polo, Jill suggested that one night she could invite a friend or two or maybe Michelle to Edna's for dinner. At first, Edna said that she didn't "want a whole *tararam.*" But when Jill resolved not to mention the idea further, Edna kept asking questions—when did Jill have in mind, whom did Jill plan to invite, what was she supposed to make, would young people like stew or hamburgers? When Jill said that she didn't know because she hadn't asked anyone yet, Edna became sullen—oh, she said, so Jill didn't even know whether anybody wanted to come or not. Jill explained that she hadn't asked anyone because she didn't know if Edna would want her to. "Ah, you're just makin' up stories," Edna said, why didn't they just forget the whole thing. Though, before Jill left, Edna told Jill that Friday nights were best and asked whom she would bring, a nice-lookin' fella?

After Jill had invited her to dinner at Edna's, Bibi said that she would absolutely love to meet Jill's grandma; her grandmother had sent her an applesauce coffee-cake recipe and they could make it together. And Kenny excitedly told Jill that she didn't need to ask him twice. Michelle, deep in rehearsals and law school interviews, reminded Jill that she would not "pick her feet in Poughkeepsie." She said that she had little interest in interacting with a person who'd blown off the two of them for a decade, and if her grandmother wanted to see her so badly, she could "pick up a fucking phone" or "get off her lazy, octogenarian ass," and take a train into the city. Jill said that Michelle didn't understand—it was a big deal that Grandma had said yes to having company; it had taken all of Jill's energy to start getting her to pull up her shades and take her medicine. Michelle said that it sounded like Edna had Jill "trained pretty well," after which Jill hung up on her sister, then moments later, felt guilty and called her back, whereupon Michelle, laughing, told Jill that she should never apologize for hanging up; it ruined the entire effect. So Jill hung up on her again.

D inner was scheduled for six at Edna's house on the third Friday in March, precisely two hours after Rob Rubinstein had deep-sixed Jill's think piece about the death of Konstantin Chernenko, replacing it with Alec Savage's review of a Krokus concert. The plan had been for Kenny to meet Jill and Bibi in their room at 5:30. He arrived punctually, wearing a tan corduroy sportcoat, a dark brown necktie, and black slacks. He carried a six-pack of "really good *bee-yuh*" (Leinenkugel's). When he saw Jill's black overalls and workboots, Kenny asked her if that was what she was *"gonna weah-yuh"* and when Jill said yes, he said that old people *desuhved* a little *maw* respect; his *grand-fathuh* had retired more than twenty *yeauhs* ago and he still wore a coat and tie every day. Before Jill could respond, Bibi's phone rang and Jill picked up.

"Jill Wasserstrom?" asked a voice at once formal and uneasy. "It's Mr. Davidson, I mean Soren." He said that Bibi was on her way to his house in a taxi. Soren said that she had asked him to call Jill and say how sorry she was that she wouldn't be able to have dinner with her grandmother, but there was a coffee cake in the refrigerator downstairs. Soren added that if anyone asked, Jill should not say that Bibi was with him. Jill asked why Bibi wasn't coming. "I'll have to let her tell you that," Soren said.

Kenny and Jill retrieved Bibi's coffee cake from the refrigerator, then walked through the TV room where a Napoli's deliveryman was clutching a large pizza box. They walked under Kenny's clear plastic umbrella through a thin rain that gathered in the potholes of Raymond Avenue. Jill explained that Kenny shouldn't expect Edna to be friendly; she wasn't "your typical, cuddly, loving grandma." She had insisted that Edna not make anything elaborate for dinner, but even if it turned out that she had only warmed up Campbell's soup, Kenny should say how much he liked it and then afterward, they could go to the Acropolis.

But when Edna opened her door, Jill barely recognized her or her house. She had had her hair coiffed and colored a golden-blond and she was wearing a cheerful yellow blouse with parrots on it, and panty hose. She was walking without her cane. The house was brighter, too; Edna had replaced all the lightbulbs, and there were tall orange candles on the table. Jill instructed Kenny to remove his boots, but Edna dismissed this with a "pish-posh" gesture and said that this wasn't Japan. Thanks, Kenny said, he didn't want anyone to know that he was wearing mismatched socks. That was all right, Edna said, squeezing Kenny's shoulder, men couldn't be expected to match their socks. As they walked through the hallway, Jill in socks, Kenny in wet boots, Edna apologized for being behind schedule; PBS had been rebroadcasting one of her favorite films— *Chariots of Fire*—and she had had to wait for the locker room scene before she could start cooking. She asked Kenny if he wanted a cocktail. No thanks, he said; he'd just take one of his *bee-yuhs*.

"A beer man," Edna said, taking the six-pack, and telling Kenny to help himself. She added that her first husband had been a beer man, while her second husband had been a "wine man"—what a pity it had been that for the last year of his life, he hadn't been able to drink it and would ask her to tell him how it tasted, even though she preferred beer. She took a Leinenkugel's, opened it, and swigged; there, she said, that's what she liked. Jill placed the coffee cake on the kitchen counter and conveyed Bibi's regrets. "Ahh, who needs her; there'll be more cake for us," Edna said; two women were already enough for "poor Kenneth."

For dinner, Edna made chopped liver, schmaltz herring, and flanken in the pot. She refused to let Kenny help Jill serve ("Men should relax and let the women wait on them," she said). Edna's transformation puzzled Jill, but she was glad of it nonetheless. She was happy to see her grandmother laugh and smile, even if, as a vegetarian, she hadn't been able to eat most of the food that Edna had prepared. But during dessert, after Edna sliced cherry pie, supplying Kenny but not Jill with a scoop of vanilla ice cream ("Men have to eat; you've had *genug*," she said), Jill became uncomfortable, sensing that her grandmother was flirting with Kenny. Yes, she welcomed the idea that Edna could feel youthful enough to ask Kenny to make a muscle then pretend to fan herself, but Edna was far more forthcoming with Kenny than she had ever been with Jill. Now she was full of Becky stories— she knew the songs that Becky had sung in her living room, the names of high school musicals in which she'd performed. She talked about Becky's brief fling with Broadway composer and producer Max Goodman, and her marriage to Charles Wasserstrom ("Soft in the head, thick around the middle," Edna said).

After dinner, they sat at the dining room table, and Edna passed around handfuls of photos. There was a black-and-white one of Becky in a one-piece swimsuit on the beach and beside her, a young Charlie, shirtless, in long swimming trucks, his arm around Becky's waist. There was a color snapshot of Becky and Charlie walking through Caldwell Woods amid the autumn foliage. And there was a family portrait taken on the front lawn of 5 Mack Road. All the photos had one thing in common: Jill had never seen any of them. She asked Edna why she'd never shown them to her. Why, Edna asked, didn't she know what she looked like? Edna made it sound like a joke, but Jill felt as if she'd been slapped, and the tears rose to her eyes so fast that she had to run to the bathroom. She returned blowing her nose and forcing a smile. She told Edna that she needed to put the photos into an album. Why, Edna asked, who would look at them? She'd had an album once and no one was interested then, so why would anyone be interested now? Kenny pointed at Edna—Jill was right, he said; these were "*wundahful pictchuhs*" and they had to be "*presuhved.*" Edna said that she didn't want to be preserved; *preserved* sounded like *pickled,* and though she was "no spring chicken," she wasn't ready to be put in pickle brine.

Kenny laughed hysterically, then told Edna that she would get along tremendously with his grandfather. Edna said that she didn't like spending time with old people, listening to them kvetch about this aching and that aching. Kenny said that his grandfather was eighty-nine, he still walked three miles every day, and his memory was *shahp.* His parents would sure "enjoy" her, too; she should come down to Manhattan sometime, his folks had a spare room, and she could have her own key. Surely, Kenny's parents wouldn't want "a strange old lady" in their house, Edna said. Of course they would, said Kenny, they were constantly meeting people and offering them the spare room. Before Jill could respond to Kenny's invitation, Edna was paging through a datebook and saying that this weekend looked bad, but that weekend looked O.K., and what weekend was good for him? Kenny said he'd check with his parents but was certain that any time would be fine. Later, when Edna walked Jill and Kenny to her door, she said good-bye to Jill, gave Kenny a hug and a kiss, then said that she was sorry to rush them out, but *Lifeguard* was on TV and she hadn't seen it in years.

Outside, the rain had stopped. Kenny asked if Jill thought that her grandmother had liked him or if he had been too overbearing. Had Edna liked him, Jill asked incredulously, she was ready to adopt him. Jill knew it was selfish to be upset by the obvious fact that her grandmother preferred Kenny to her. But what was with her grandmother's obsession with young men—every program Edna had ever watched always prominently featured hunks in togas or Speedos. As they walked, Jill tried to raise this topic, suggesting that they buy Edna a videocassette player so she could watch all the gladiator movies she wanted. Kenny pointed at Jill and asked what was wrong with *olduh* people havin' sexual thoughts; when he was *ovuh* seventy, he sure was gonna have sexual thoughts.

When they were back on campus, Jill told Kenny that he had been generous to suggest the weekend at his parents' apartment in New York, but he didn't really have to follow through. Kenny wouldn't hear of it; he wasn't one of those "phony rich fucks" who gave those "phony invitations," such as that asshole Stanley Barnes, who'd invited him to his parents' vacation house in Southampton and when he'd asked which weekend, Stanley had gotten all vague. No, he said, if Edna wanted to come, she was coming.

As they reentered the dormitory, Jill was considering the words that her mother had spoken upon leaving Edna Schulman's house for the last time: "Let's not do that again anytime soon." She wondered if Edna had embarrassed Becky by flirting with Charlie, if she had been paying attention to everyone except Becky. Jill turned to say good night to Kenny, but then she looked ahead to the Cushing Parlor, behind whose glass doors was a bearded young man at the piano bench, waving frantically and mouthing her name. "Uh-oh," said Jill, now realizing why Bibi had escaped to Soren's house. Kenny asked if she knew "that guy from *Fiddler on the Roof.*" Yep, Jill said, that was Shmuel Weinberg.

If Jill had seen Shmuel since Hebrew school, she couldn't remember. His presence had always been unremarkable; spending time with him was much like spending time alone, only less so somehow. He had informed Jill and Bibi that he might visit, via personal notes attached to his Xeroxed monthly updates—crudely produced double-sided mini-newsletters titled *Shmuel's Syracuse Summary,* which was printed in a banner headline beside a caricature of Shmuel that Hillel Levy had drawn with a penis for a nose. There were continuing columns: "From the Wings" (a summary of shows he'd stage-managed), "Weinberg's Women" (a largely fictional list of his dates), and "Valley of the Shmuel" (random observations and pleas usually written in code to Bibi ["Let it BE that B.E. will BE with ME!"], to which Bibi responded with friendly but curt letters, all of which concluded with a chilly closing line: "Regards, Bibi," "With Fondness, Bibi," or, worst of all, "Your *friend,* Bibi").

Shmuel was taller than Jill remembered, also skinnier, as if he'd spent the years between Hebrew school and college in a stretching machine. He stood nearly a foot taller than Jill and about ten inches taller than Kenny. The nervous twitch in his left eye and the black-framed glasses held together with Scotch tape were familiar; the beard and the deep, gravelly voice were new. Shmuel now had a habit of saying the phrase twice in a row, nodding as he did so. "You look good, look good," he told Jill after they had sat down. "It's goin' real well, real well," he said when Jill asked him about Syracuse. And during a lull in the conversation, he looked around the parlor and said, "This is nice, real nice." Kenny pointed at him and said that he had heard him the first time.

Shmuel told Kenny and Jill that he had "grown up a lot" at Syracuse. He spoke of his and Jill's childhoods with an affected nostalgia, as if the events of just a few years earlier had actually transpired decades ago. Did Jill remember riding around on bikes because you weren't old enough to drive a car? Did Jill remember Big Wheels and tricycles? Did she remember when Rabbi Grossman had gotten so mad that he had broken his *tzedakah* box? Did she remember when Hillel Levy said that he wouldn't read Maimonides because Maimonides liked little boys? Did she remember spin-the-bottle and champagne snowballs and *Dynamite!* magazine and CB radios and concert jerseys and jeans with patches on them and chisanbop and Marshall Brodien and Intellivisions and laser light shows and dancing the "time warp" and guys with big afros and Beverly Cleary books and Kristy McNichol and Peter Frampton and Bo Derek and *The White Shadow* and Rubik's Cubes and Caravelle candy bars and iron-on T-shirts? Did she remember when McDonald's sign had read MORE THAN 8 MILLION SERVED? Those had been "good days, good days."

Jill hoped that Bibi had not invited Shmuel to stay with them, yet wondered where else he could possibly be sleeping. She didn't know how to ask gracefully without sounding as if she were kicking Shmuel out. Kenny was less diplomatic—he asked whether Shmuel was sleeping in his *cah* or heading back to Syracuse, 'cause there was a *dawmitory* policy against last-minute *visituhs*. Oh, it was "sweet" of Kenny to ask, Shmuel said, but he had rented a room at the Alumnae House. At this point, Kenny identified Shmuel as the enemy, someone with money for a car and a hotel room. Kenny said that he thought those rooms cost at least fifty *dollahs* a night. Yes, Shmuel said, fifty-five, but his parents were paying.

Kenny adjusted his glasses. That was bullshit, he said. He hated when eighteen-year-old kids spent their parents' money on bullshit like *cahs* and hotels. Shmuel smiled and said he agreed with Kenny. There were lots of rich kids at Syracuse, but he was working his way through school designing sets and lights at a community theater. The only reason why his parents were paying for his trip was that they knew why he was coming.

Why was that, asked Kenny.

"Because they're worried about Bibi," said Shmuel.

Jill said that she knew all about Soren, knew that he was married, but Bibi was an adult; sending pizzas and crank-calling Soren was not the most constructive way to show concern. "You shouldn't send pizzas," Kenny said, pointing a finger at Shmuel, adding that if you *awduhed* pizzas for people who hadn't *awhduhed* them, the deliveryman would get stuck with the bill, and that was unethical.

But the new tall bearded Shmuel seemed invulnerable to criticism. In Rabbi Meltzer's *heh* class, Shmuel had apologized for everything, even things that he hadn't done: David Singer's plot to stuff toilets with gefilte fish, Lana Rovner's inability to remember the aleph-beth, Hillel Levy's insertion of the word "V.D." into the song "Quando El Rey Nimrod." Now, when Kenny scolded him for the pizza deliveries, Shmuel just grinned, shook his head, then acknowledged, "that was real bad, real bad" and said that he was more mature now; he had done a lot of thinking about himself lately and what was important to him. Kenny said that he thought a lot about himself and what was important to him too, but he usually had to wipe off the sheets when he was done. Shmuel laughed and said yes, there had been a time when he had thought that way about Bibi, but not since he'd learned that she wasn't a virgin. Kenny said that Shmuel was "fucked up"—other people's relationships were none of Shmuel's business; if Jill wanted to date some "*shawt* New *Yawk* guy" who "points at people and beats his dick too much," that was her business, and if Bibi wanted to date some "ugly, married jagoff," it wasn't Shmuel's place to judge her. Yes, Shmuel said, but he had discovered something about Soren that Bibi didn't know.

So, what was this Soren guy's deal, Kenny finally asked, was he "a *vampiyuh* or what?"

"No," Shmuel said, "his deal is he's poor."

Kenny erupted. So that's what this was all about, he said. What his father had told him was right; the only thing that *mattuhed* was class. You could be a "low-down rat *bastuhd,*" but as long as you *wuh* rich, it didn't *mattuh*. He said he was sick of Shmuel's shit and now he was "*goin' upstazz.*" He exited the parlor with a kick to the door.

Shmuel told Jill that Kenny was "a good guy, a real good guy," but Kenny had missed his point—Jill knew that his own family wasn't rich, that his father managed a photo store, and his mother was a secretary at Northeastern Illinois. Whether Soren was rich or poor wasn't the issue; Soren was misrepresenting himself. He told Jill that he would be honest; he had crank-called Soren a lot, not just pizzas—sometimes he'd ask if he had "Prince Albert in a can" and if he did to let him out. Sometimes he'd just breathe heavily, or ask Soren in a Jimmy Stewart voice, *"What have you done with herrrrrrrrrrr?"*

Shmuel said that he had outgrown this sort of behavior, but recently, he had had "a relapse" and called Soren, pretending to be a warlock. When a woman answered the phone, Shmuel asked in his warlock voice if Soren was there. No, the woman said, this was Paige, the real estate agent; was Shmuel calling about the property? Shmuel panicked and hung up, waited ten minutes, then called back and said that he was "inquiring after the property." After establishing that Shmuel wasn't "that strange man who had called before," Paige said that there was a six-bedroom house for sale, and a cabin: sum total—a quarter-million dollars. Shmuel knew nothing about real estate, but on a hunch, he said that the price sounded too low; was there something wrong with the property? No, Paige said, the seller was "cash poor" right now and was trying to "regain some liquidity." Shmuel then said that he would have to talk with the seller directly because something wasn't sitting right with him. Paige said that she was handling all of Mr. Davidson's business, but she would take down Shmuel's name. "I'm Sammy Wine, Syracuse Developers," Shmuel said.

Shmuel and his roommates had been routinely answering their phone "Syracuse Developers, Sammy Wine's Office," when a "Mr. Davidson" called. Shmuel told Soren that he was suspicious about the price of his house, but Soren revealed that he was willing to take a loss, if he could unload the property by the end of the month. "Where's the fire, partner?" Shmuel asked. No fire, Soren said, he was just having "some cash-flow problems," and there was a relationship from which he needed to extricate himself. And then because Shmuel had already run out of things to say, he asked if Soren had Prince Albert in the can and when Soren asked him what he meant, Shmuel said that Soren had better let him out. Soren started swearing at Shmuel, who adopted a mock-Asian accent and said, *"Fuck you velly much,"* then slammed down the phone. And when Soren called back, Shmuel pretended not to speak English, yelling *"Hong Kong Gai-WAH!!!!"* over and over until Soren hung up. Shmuel told Jill that Soren was up to "something nefarious," and Bibi needed to know. Bibi might not listen to him, but she'd listen to Jill.

Jill said that she didn't know what to think. She felt sorry for Bibi, but still, whatever Shmuel had discovered had been through lying, and who knew if even Soren had been telling the truth—she said she had a hard time believing anybody anymore. She told Shmuel that she would have to "sleep on it." All right, Shmuel said, and proposed that they have breakfast the next morning to discuss strategy. He asked Jill to lead him to Kenny's room, because he didn't want Kenny to think that he was "some rich prick." Jill told Shmuel to follow her upstairs.

Kenny was on the hall phone when Jill told Shmuel that she would see him at breakfast, but Kenny made a "Stop" sign with his hands, while he laughed loudly at whatever he was hearing on the other end of the line. "No, here she is," Kenny finally said, still laughing, then handed the phone to Jill. She picked up the phone and heard Edna's voice. "Hi, Grandma, what's wrong?" Jill asked—her grandmother had made a point of saying that she never called anybody. Nothing was wrong, Edna said. She just wanted to say what a "lovely time" she had had and how much she had enjoyed her and Kenneth's company. She knew that sometimes she could act like she didn't care about people, but she wanted Jill to know how happy they had made her, and how excited she was about their trip to New York.

Late that night, while Kenny and Shmuel shot eight ball in the Cushing basement, Jill lay awake in her bed and stared at the ceiling. Her initial instinct regarding Shmuel's proposal had been to let the situation sort itself out on its own. So what if Bibi continued to pursue a relationship with a mendacious older grad student; this was the sort of experience that built character. And yet, Edna's uncharacteristically gleeful call made Jill wonder if there wasn't something to be said for taking control and insinuating oneself into other people's lives.

The next morning at breakfast, Jill sat with Shmuel and Kenny in the cafeteria. Both had shadows under their eyes and were drinking black coffee. Kenny said that after "this guy" had had some beer, he was a "fuckin' wild man." They had stayed up until four, dancing at The Mug to Frankie Goes to Hollywood, and Shmuel had muscled his way to the center of the dance floor and started break-dancing and doing head-spins ("That was real bad, real bad," Shmuel said with an ashamed laugh). Then, at Pete's Place, they were carded by the bouncer, who, Kenny said, was "a real dick." Kenny distracted the bouncer while Shmuel dropped his pants and "took a dump right there on the front steps," which, Kenny allowed, was "kinda unethical," but also "kinda hilarious."

"I shouldn't drink, shouldn't drink," Shmuel said, then asked if Jill had thought any more about the previous evening's discussion. Jill said that she had decided to talk to Soren and Bibi, recount everything that Shmuel had told her, then let them discuss the matter among themselves. And what else, Shmuel asked. And that's it, said Jill. Shmuel seemed disappointed that Jill was proposing such a reasonable course of action and suggested that if Soren denied any of the charges, he and Kenny would "give him a swirly."

That night, Jill sat in the front seat of Shmuel's rented chartreuse Chevy Vega and Kenny sat in back beside a twelve-pack of toilet paper and told both Jill and Shmuel that they were "doin' the right thing." Shmuel drove slowly along Route 9, his seat all the way forward, nose a half-inch from the glass. Kenny said that he liked "*cayuhful drivuhs*," but drivin' too slow was a *hazuhd* too.

The lights were on in Soren's cabin. And while Shmuel and Kenny sat in the

Chevy with the heat and the radio on, Jill walked up to the front door and knocked. Soren answered wearing shower clogs and a black, short-sleeved bathrobe that fell just below his knees. At the sight of Jill, he grinned broadly and motioned her in. Well, this was a lovely surprise, he said, adding that Bibi was in the shower and he was preparing a late Shabbos dinner—they would be serving shad roe and Bibi would be lighting candles and making dessert—why didn't he set an extra place? Jill said no, thanks; she just needed to talk briefly to both him and Bibi. She heard the sound of a faucet turning off, then Bibi asking if Soren was coming in to dry her off. Not right now, dear, Soren said, they had company. He asked Jill if she wanted some olives and when she declined, he led her to his couch by a roaring fireplace. Bibi exited the bathroom, wrapped in a pink towel. She kissed Jill on the forehead.

Jill didn't know which was worse—that Soren had lured Bibi into this world of temporary domestic bliss before he would rip it out from under her by selling his house and leaving her behind, or that she would deny Bibi even a few weeks of happiness. She told Bibi that she couldn't stay long; Kenny and Shmuel were in the car. Bibi covered her mouth with her hands. "I'm so sorry," she said, and apologized for leaving Jill to deal with Shmuel alone. She asked Jill if she wanted to invite "the boys" in. No, Jill said, she just needed Bibi and Soren to listen.

Jill calmly presented the facts of the previous night's discussion with Shmuel, pretending that she was an expert witness giving testimony. Soren didn't interrupt, just kept his head down, his hands folded. As Jill spoke, she could see Bibi's facial expression changing bit by bit, the smile getting smaller and smaller until it was no longer a smile, the dry eyes growing larger and larger until they were no longer dry. She felt as if she were punching Bibi in the stomach in very slow motion.

When she was through, Jill told Bibi and Soren that she would leave them to discuss the matter. She stood, but then Soren, still looking down, told her to wait. He turned to Bibi, who was staring at him; he asked if she wanted to "leave with her friend." But Bibi shook her head, her wet hair slapping her cheeks as she did so. She mouthed "I'm sorry" and "Thank you" to Jill, then ran to the bathroom and shut the door. Jill heard the faucet being turned on, then water rushing out of a tap; above it, she could hear Bibi crying. Soren walked Jill to the door; he said that Jill probably thought that he was "angry as hell," but she might have just made his whole life easier. The one thing she should never forget, no matter what she heard, was that he loved Bibi dearly.

Back in the car, Shmuel asked Jill what had happened. Jill said that she had done as she had said, but wouldn't provide more details. "Good *faw* you," Kenny said, then asked if they could drive to Oasis for beer. No, Shmuel said, he was going home now. He had a look of fierce disapproval on his face; his left eye was twitching madly. Come on, Kenny said, why didn't they grab a case; if Shmuel started driving now, he wouldn't get back to Syracuse until dawn anyway. No, Shmuel snapped, nearly shouting, he was leaving now and that was "fucking final" and Kenny should "fucking stop bossing people around." Shmuel dropped Kenny and Jill off at the Main gate, his right foot on the brake but the car still in Drive. Jill thought that she should offer, if not a hug, a handshake good-bye, but Shmuel kept both of his hands on the steering wheel and his eyes focused straight ahead. And when Jill and Kenny were out of the car, he floored the accelerator.

After a cup of coffee at the Retreat, Jill and Kenny returned to their dorm. At the front desk, Ralph the security guard, who was also a recreational hunter, was smiling; a half-finished venison sandwich was on his desk. "What are you grinnin' about, you Bambi-killin' fuck?" Kenny asked. Ralph handed Kenny a receipt on which was written "$45.20, C.O.D." Kenny grabbed the receipt, stuffed it in his pocket, then mounted the stairs and invited Jill to his room. When Kenny opened his door, he saw a roomful of people; he and Jill entered, and everyone started applauding.

Sidney Florio's boom box was blasting "It's Like That"; Matthew Chen and Horace Greenstein were trading raps; Tom Dunne was lying on Kenny's bed reading *National Lampoon.* Everywhere were empty pizza boxes. That had been "so fuckin' cool" of Kenny, a drunk Sidney Florio said, putting an arm around him. According to Sidney, the Napoli's deliveryman had said that Kenny was picking up the check for the pizzas. Before Kenny could speak, he heard someone down the hall calling his name; did he know anything about toilet-papering some Soren guy's house in Rhinebeck?

Jill had just spoken with Edna and confirmed that they would spend the first weekend of spring break in the Melnicks' New York apartment when Bibi returned to their dorm room in a surprisingly cheerful mood. Jill was sitting at her desk, underlining a copy of Plato's *Apology* as Bibi told her how thankful she was that Jill had come to Soren's house the other night. For a short while, she said, she had been furious, but after she had spent an hour in the bathroom and Soren had finally broken down the door because he was worried that she had done something to herself ("Like I would ever do that; that's *his* trick," she said), she realized that she was angry at the wrong person. Over the past forty-eight hours, she had cried more than ever, but now she was done letting Soren make her cry.

In the weeks preceding spring break, Jill saw more of Bibi than she had since September. A wonderful energy radiated from her, a newly self-aware, bawdy, and surprisingly caustic sense of humor, too. Whenever Jill and Bibi had dinner and Bibi spotted a woman who looked particularly distressed, she would ask what the matter was with that person—perhaps she was dating someone who was selling his house without telling her. And though, frankly, Jill could have done without Bibi's new assessments of men in the Meat Book ("Craig C. Chilton from Yonkers, New York, looks like he would come in about five seconds"), Jill now enjoyed spending time with Bibi, who would occasionally join Jill at Edna's house. And Jill hardly minded when Edna would go into ecstatic convulsions after tasting Bibi's coffee cake, then sneer at whatever Jill cooked.

Jill had asked Bibi if she wanted to join her, Kenny, and Edna at the Melnick residence in New York. The invitation had been less an act of generosity than one of self-preservation. Jill thought that Bibi's sunny presence would offset that of Michelle, who consented to meet her grandmother for dinner and a show, but informed Jill that if Edna "acted like a cunt," then she would call her one to her face. Bibi, however, said that she would be back in Northbrook to "surprise her parents," whom she hadn't seen since January.

On the Friday that she was to travel to New York with her grandmother and Kenny, Jill packed lightly, knowing that she would be carrying both her and Edna's bags. But when Jill hopped out of the taxi that she and Kenny had hired to pick up Edna, then let herself into her grandmother's house, the house was dark, the shades were down, and the whole place smelled stale. "Grandma?" Jill called out. She turned on a hallway light, ran through the rooms on the first floor, then mounted the steps to Edna's bedroom.

Edna was wearing a plain white T-shirt and gray sweatpants, and she didn't have her shoes on. She was holding a bottle of Windex and when Jill asked if she was ready, Edna told her that she wasn't going. What would she do in New York in an apartment filled with strangers, she asked, the whole thing sounded peculiar. But Kenny was waiting outside in the cab, Jill said. "So go," said Edna. Jill said that she wouldn't be going if it weren't for her. "So stay," Edna said, what was it to her whether Jill stayed or went? Arrangements had already been made, Jill said ("So they can make other arrangements," said Edna), tickets had been purchased ("So I'll pay for the tickets"), Mr. and Mrs. Melnick had been looking forward to meeting her ("So let them come to Poughkeepsie if they're looking forward so much"). Not going was downright rude, Jill finally said. Edna flushed and her lips seemed to quickly contract as if she'd tasted something bitter. So she was rude, Edna said. Let people think she was rude; she'd be dead soon and then it wouldn't matter what people thought.

Edna sat silently at the foot of her bed. Jill wondered whether she should just walk out the door and acknowledge that her efforts to lift her grandmother's spirits had failed, but then she heard a door open downstairs, and footsteps ascending. Kenny entered the bedroom and asked what was "holdin' up the show." Jill said that her grandmother wasn't going.

Kenny cocked his head toward Jill. Then he looked at Edna. With one hand, he held on to his glasses. With the index finger of his other hand, he pointed at her. "Yer goin'," he said. He asked where her suitcase was, "in the *clawset*?" Edna nodded. Kenny darted into the closet and extracted a red plastic suitcase on wheels. He asked Edna where she kept her *unduhwayuh* and her *sawks*. Edna said that they were in the dresser, but she didn't want him packing just anything; some clothes she liked, some she didn't. She used her cane to lift herself off her bed and walked over to Kenny, who was rummaging through an open dresser drawer. She said that she liked this nightgown, not that one; this underwear was nice, those made her look schlumpy. Kenny said that he was tired of women saying they were schlumpy; if there was one thing Edna was not, it was schlumpy. Well, Edna said, didn't he always know what to say to a lady? Jill said that she'd wait in the cab.

During the train ride, Jill sat by a window beside her grandmother and Kenny sat opposite them, quizzing Edna about what New York had been like when she'd been a girl. Edna said that she had always loved the city whenever she had traveled down from Poughkeepsie—the neon, the traffic. She loved the Automat—all those delicious meals, she could never decide what she wanted. She loved the sailors, too, every one of them in white. She had danced with so many, broken so many hearts. Her daughter had always hated Manhattan, she said. How ironic it was that Becky moved to New York the moment she was old enough.

That must have been *hahsh,* having *yer* only *daughtuh* move out, Kenny said; how had Edna felt? Edna said that she couldn't remember that far back. But she had let Becky know that if she moved, it was final; there wouldn't be any coming back home to live anymore. That's what she told Becky when she walked out, and that's what she told Becky when she called crying from the L.A. bus station years later and said she wanted to come back. This sounded callous to Jill, but Kenny told Edna that she had done the right thing. "That builds *charactuh,*" he said. And he added, thumbing to Jill, if Edna hadn't taken that stand, Jill wouldn't be *heeyuh* today.

It was a terrifying statement. And Jill could not say whether this reality—that the only reason why she was on this earth, the only reason why her mother had taken a job where she had met Charlie Wasserstrom, was because of a phone call in which her grandmother had told her mother that she couldn't come home— was proof of the power of randomness and luck that had consistently bedeviled her as a child or of the inescapability of fate that she had embraced ever since.

As Edna and Kenny continued to speak, Jill watched the ripples in the gray-blue Hudson and dreamed up what-if scenarios: What if her grandmother had said yes, what if Becky had returned to Poughkeepsie, what if Becky had never met Charlie in Chicago, what if she had never been born, what if the earth had never been created, what if all the gases and particles in the universe had never collided? What if her existence and everyone else's for that matter was the result not of an accident or a misunderstanding, but of a callous act or choice. If her grandmother had been kinder, then where would they be now? If Edna had known that by telling her daughter she couldn't come home, that Becky would marry and have two children whom she loved, would she have acted differently? Would she have welcomed Becky home with open arms? Would that have been a better punishment?

The train arrived at Grand Central at 5:10 in the evening and Jill, wearing her backpack and pulling her grandmother's suitcase, tried to keep pace with Kenny and Edna as they headed for the subway. Jill felt lucky that Kenny was so eager to engage her grandmother in conversation. But when they arrived at the Melnicks' apartment, Kenny took a key out of a kitchen drawer and handed it to Edna; over there was the guest bedroom, he said, they'd find fresh sheets in the closet, milk and cereal in the fridge, and maybe he'd see them for breakfast the following morning. Jill asked where he was going. Kenny said that he was meeting some old buddies from *Brawnx Soyence*. Upon exiting, he pointed a finger at Jill and Edna. "You two have a good time," he said, "now that's an *awduh*."

Edna looked dourly at the door that had just shut behind Kenny. Well, Edna said, he certainly couldn't get away fast enough. She asked what Jill had said to him. Nothing, said Jill. Well, Edna said, maybe that's why he'd left, because Jill hadn't spoken to him. Jill ignored Edna's accusation and said that she would call Michelle to see where they were meeting. Edna said that she wasn't hungry. Jill said that Michelle hadn't seen her grandmother in nine years; they had already made plans and weren't changing them. "Well, aye, aye, Captain," Edna said, mockingly saluting her granddaughter. When Jill later reported that they would meet Michelle at six at the Kiev diner before they would go to a show, Edna saluted with another "aye, aye" and said that if she passed out from exhaustion, she hoped that Jill would know how to revive her. As they walked east toward Second Avenue, Edna kept asking Jill why they had come to New York, what would they be doing for the whole weekend? What would they discuss with Michelle, what did three women have to talk about when she was too old to discuss men?

Michelle was seated in a booth by a window. She was wearing an off-white thrift shop dress with red polka dots on it, her hair in a bun. A pair of glasses rested on her head as she smoked a cigarette and studied a script. Jill was struck by how much Michelle resembled their mother—the golden hair, the long, slender fingers gripping the cigarette, the dress of the sort that Becky wore when she was depressed and wanted to wear something to make herself feel "young and charming." But when Jill pointed Michelle out to their grandmother, Edna said that she "wouldn't have recognized her in a hundred years." Jill wondered if Edna and Michelle would hug, but all Michelle did when they arrived was transfer her cigarette from her right hand to her left, then sweep her books and ashtray out of the way.

As they ate, Michelle discussed auditions and law schools while Edna yawned and looked at her watch. Whenever Jill asked Edna to talk about her childhood, Edna would say that Jill could tell the stories better than she could. And whenever Edna did offer information or ask questions, Jill would wish that Edna hadn't spoken. At one point, Edna asked Michelle what fellas liked to do on dates these days. Michelle fixed her grandmother with an icy stare. "Well, Edna," she said, mostly they liked to screw. Edna smiled and said well, she was glad that some things never changed. Jill excused herself and went to the bathroom. Upon her return, she sensed that Edna was trying to draw Michelle into an argument, while Michelle enjoyed treating her grandmother as if she were the fifteenth journalist on a press junket asking her about her new film.

Michelle rushed through the meal, then called for the check, saying that they had to leave early if they wanted to get a good seat for the eight o'clock show. Edna said that she didn't know if she had the energy. Jill pleaded with her grandmother; they had already purchased tickets, she said. Michelle interrupted. Fine, she said, did Edna know the way back to the Melnicks' apartment or did she want them to hail a cab for her? Edna said that she could find her own way and didn't need "Girl Scouts" leading her by the arm. Good, Michelle said, well, it had been great catching up, but now she and Jill would have a girls' night out.

Michelle pulled Jill up from the table by a sleeve and led her out the front door. What was she doing, Jill asked. Michelle said that she wanted Jill to see something. They crossed Second Avenue, and Michelle positioned herself at a corner pay phone. Edna exited the diner, at first moving slowly with her cane, then picking up speed as she walked down the sidewalk. She then lifted her cane in the air. A taxi screeched to a halt, then zoomed off with Edna inside.

"There," Michelle said, assaying her British detective's accent, "just as I deduced."

You see, she added, that was the way to treat someone who took advantage of others' magnanimity; you kicked them off the diving board to see if they really couldn't swim. That Edna, Michelle said, could swim like a grouper. Jill began to propose that they return to the apartment to make sure that Edna would find her way back, but Michelle's next statement stopped her: "Let's not do that again anytime soon, O.K.?" Michelle said. Jill asked if Michelle remembered when their mother had made that statement. Absolutely, said Michelle. Jill said that she had recently gained new insight into Becky's words. She said that when their mother was leaving L.A., she had called Edna to see if she would take her back and Edna refused; that's why Becky had wound up in Chicago.

Michelle pondered this for a moment. Then she asked Jill if that's what Edna had told her, and when Jill said yes, she asked if Jill believed that shit. Michelle advised her sister not to apply to law school because she was too fricking gullible.

As for herself, she didn't believe a word that came out of her grandmother's yap; the whole story sounded like self-serving BS designed to make Jill feel indebted to her. Michelle said that it was obvious why Becky had left Poo-fucking-keepsie and why she had said, "Let's not do that again anytime soon." Why, Jill asked. One, Michelle said, because there was nothing to do in Poo-fucking-keepsie. And two, because Edna was a pain in the ass. Now, she asked, was Jill ready to do something fun? Where were they going, asked Jill. To a concert, Michelle said. Who were they seeing, Jill asked. Larry Elliot, said Michelle.

The Grotto was a dark, malodorous café located downstairs from Sushi Gucci on Sullivan Street. It had a poorly stocked bar, stools with ripped black cushions in front of it, and about fifteen wobbly tables crowded before a stage that could barely fit the drum kit, microphone, guitar stand, amp, and folding chair atop it. A makeshift lighting system—six bulbs in coffee cans—illuminated the empty stage while Larry Rovner, sporting a five-o'clock shadow and dressed in an embroidered red cowboy shirt, black boots, and sunglasses, sat at the bar sipping ginger ale. Michelle asked if Larry remembered her sister.

"Sure, sure," Larry said, shook Jill's hand, said, "Glad you could make it, Jane," then asked her how it was hanging, loose?

Jill associated Larry with growing up in West Rogers Park, where being allowed to socialize with her older sister's friends seemed a quick path toward the adulthood she craved. She had felt privileged when Michelle and Gareth had treated her to almond-flavored sodas at the Medici in Hyde Park or when she had seen Rovner! perform at the Thirsty Whale. But shortly after entering high school, she grew irritated with her sister's sexual banter, and began to view these outings more as impositions than escapes.

Michelle asked Larry how his music was going. "Shitty," Larry said, adding that four A&R reps from national record companies had checked out his act, and even though he'd told everyone that he wasn't interested, they were still sniffing around. Rejecting their money was suicide, he said, but so was accepting it. This Friday night gig at the Grotto had been designed as a way to let off steam after he'd been fired from *Gotta Sing!* It had never been intended as anything more.

Ever since Michelle had been canned for flubbing her lines during the backers' audition, *Gotta Sing!* had been one of the most eye-opening experiences of Larry's life. All through rehearsals, everyone had kissed his ass. Actresses flirted with him, even Hannah's best friend from the Brandeis Hillel Society, Amelia

Grossbacher, who had replaced Michelle in the role of Christine. They greeted him with hugs and cheek kisses, their bodies exuding so much perfume that Larry got hard just smelling them; actors shook his hand and told him that he was "the shit"; the rehearsal pianist said that he looked like a young Elliott Gould. At the opening night party, everyone toasted him, and when he and Hannah returned home, she opened their bedroom door and said that she had a surprise for him; Amelia Grossbacher was lying under their covers. Hannah said that a threesome would settle all of their nerves. And even though Larry ejaculated after two minutes and spent the next half hour watching his wife and Amelia going at it before he grew bored and made himself a Swiss cheese sandwich, he still felt confident that his life was moving in the right direction.

But then the reviews came out and everyone's tone changed overnight; it seemed to Larry that everyone blamed him. Mr. and Mrs. Goodman, who had raised the money, kept calling the show *aroys geverfeneh gelt;* Al Jolson's estate filed a lawsuit; Amelia Grossbacher said that he was a lousy lay. Every day, Larry would write new songs, while Hannah would change the plot, add characters; the changes only made the show worse, until the Goodmans fired the director, fired Larry, and made Hannah replace all of Larry's songs with classic ditties by Jewish tunesmiths such as Billy Joel and Neil Sedaka. Two weeks later, the show reopened and received raves from *Jewish Theater World* and the *Forward,* Jewish singles groups lined up around the block, and the Goodmans were looking for a Broadway house to which they could transfer the show.

The night after he'd been sacked, Larry had walked the streets of Greenwich Village, guitar on his back, contemplating business school. He stumbled upon the chalkboard sign outside the Grotto advertising Open Mike Night. And even though Larry felt that he had long since passed the point of playing open mikes, he wandered in and saw the empty stage; only two people were in the bar. He asked if there was a waiting list. "You're it," the bartender had said.

Larry stepped onstage and strummed a chord, preparing to sing one of his early tunes—"And She Stoned Me (West Bank Rhapsody)." But then he felt his fingers shift, producing a chord that he wasn't sure he had ever heard (actually, it was a B-flat, but he had never known how to play it). And instead of singing his intended opening line ("She's got Yasser Arafat's eyes"), he started ad-libbing a song; the chorus was "(My Girlfriend Likes) Big Girls." And after that song, he made up another: "(My Dad Reads) *Hustler.*" And before he knew what had happened, he had sung "My Sister (Crashed the Car Again)," and the audience of three had given him a standing ovation. The bartender asked Larry for his name. "Larry Elliot," he said.

Every night when he claimed to be taking a GMAT review class, Larry would return to the Grotto, where he had now stashed a guitar and a drum machine. He would never write songs before he showed up; he would improvise based on whatever happened to be bothering him that day. His choruses were not as carefully textured as his signature material; they merely repeated the song title over and over, growing louder as Larry became more confident, as in "My sister crashed the car, yeah she crashed the car, I said she crashed the car again, oh yeah," or "My wife caught me jerkin', yeah she caught me jerkin', I said she caught me jerkin' in the john, oh yeah." But the songs were so personal and so nakedly performed that they began to attract an audience. Soon, there were lines out the door to see Larry perform "(Nate Yau Can't) Sing for Shit" and "Hannah's Sister (Is Prettier)." Now the deals that these A&R snakes were offering were "too fucking insane" to pass up, but Larry didn't know how long he could keep performing his songs incognito. Hannah had stopped taking the pill because she wanted kids and Larry thought that she might react poorly to his latest song, "(I'll Bet You'd Be) A Crappy Mom."

Jill had seen enough Rovner! shows to know that she had little patience for Larry Rovner's music, but "Larry Elliot" was something altogether different. Watching him felt invasive, voyeuristic, and yet hypnotically so. The songs mesmerized her. She laughed at Larry's discomfort with his sister's newest boyfriend during "(Too Many) Pizzas from Shmuel," felt his anguish during "(Hope I See Hannah's Sister) Naked Again." And when the performance was over and Larry had sneaked out the back to avoid the A&R reps, Jill thanked her sister for taking her to "an amazing show." Michelle told her to take it easy; this was still Larry Rovner, and if she ever so much as thought about fucking Larry, she would have both of them flogged. And though Jill said that she hadn't been thinking anything of the sort, the idea had, in fact, crossed her mind. And it crossed her mind later that night after Michelle had returned home. Jill was walking back to the Melnicks' when she espied Larry sitting on a park bench blowing on his hands, and told him how much she had enjoyed his performance.

Larry, still wearing his shades, gruffly muttered that he couldn't relate to people saying that they "enjoyed" his music—what sadist would enjoy listening to someone else's pain, man? Jill apologized for disturbing Larry, but when she started to leave, he said shit, he was sorry, he didn't realize that he was talking to Michelle's sister, Jane; he was just sick of all these strangers complimenting him when he knew that he was just a hunk of meat to them.

For the next hour, Jill and Larry sat on the bench and talked about honesty and integrity. Larry said that he never realized how cool Jill was. He then tapped out a rhythm on her knee, and sang, "Michelle's sister is cool, yeah she's cool, I said she's cool, she's cool, her sister is cool, oh yeah." And though the song might have embarrassed Jill, Larry's performance seemed so honest that Jill felt touched, though she added that her name was Jill, not Jane, at which point Larry performed a drum solo on Jill's thigh, then sang, "I fucked up her name, yeah I fucked up her name, I'm such a raging asshole 'cause I fucked up her name, oh yeah." Larry asked Jill if she thought that he should sign with a record company and fuck up his marriage. Jill responded that he should do what felt right; that was probably what he was fated to do. How long did people live, really, and how much time would they spend regretting what they hadn't done or said? Larry looked into Jill's eyes and said man, she was deep; how right she was. Why was it that he only met cool chicks after he was married?

Larry grasped Jill's knee and said thank you, for now he knew just what to do; he asked if Michelle was still living in her little shitbox studio in Alphabet City, and when Jill nodded, he said that's where he was going. He would tell Michelle that they were meant to be together and then he would sign one of the record contracts and never conceal his true feelings. He held Jill close and asked how she'd like being his little sister and getting good seats to his shows, taking her boyfriends backstage and enjoying all the sandwiches, beer, and green M&M's. He ran off, singing, "Michelle's sister is cool, I said her sister is cool, yeah she's cool, she's cool, oh yeah."

While Michelle was busy booting Larry out of her apartment and telling him that until he had learned to be alone he would never have a successful relationship, Jill was entering the Melnicks' building and greeting night watchman Vince Peditto. And while Michelle was telling Larry that if he didn't sign with a record company, she would act as his agent and fricking do it for him, Jill was riding the elevator up to the seventh floor. And while Michelle was telling Larry not to let her door hit him where the good Lord had seen fit to split him, Jill was exiting the elevator and walking toward the Melnicks' apartment when she realized that Edna

had the key. And while Michelle was fast asleep, dreaming about prosecuting cor-
porate polluters before stripping off her business suit to reveal her *Cat on a Hot Tin
Roof* costume underneath, and while Larry was sneaking back into his apartment,
where the scent of Lysol mingled with that of Amelia Grossbacher's perfume, Jill
was ringing the Melnicks' buzzer. But Edna did not come to the door no matter
how many times Jill rang or knocked, so she took the elevator back down.

As she stood in the lobby of the Melnicks' apartment building, watching
Vince Peditto rummage through his desk for the master key, Jill felt an overwhelming sense of dread. She wondered where the taxicab had taken Edna, if the
driver had really brought her back here, or if he had had to rush her to the hospital; how could she have been so stupid as to listen to her sister, who had been
more concerned with proving a point than with the welfare of an eighty-year-old
woman? This evening would be forever etched into her mind—she had lost her
mother and had spent much of her childhood wondering if it had been her fault
when of course it hadn't been, but if she had now lost her grandmother, then it
truly would be her fault.

And it was at just this moment, when Jill was imagining her grandmother and
the Melnicks all slain in their beds, and wondering whether to call the police, that
Jill heard the front door open, bringing in with it a gust of wind, laughter, and
vodka. Seven people were staggering through the doorway—Mr. and Mrs. Melnick, Kenny, his arms on the shoulders of two male friends, and behind them,
Edna and Mr. Joseph Popko. Upon seeing Jill, Kenny broke from his buddies. So
there she was, he said, there was the girl who stuck her *grandmutha* in a cab, then
went out for a night on the town. Jill began to say that Edna had refused to go out
with her and her sister, but as they waited for the elevator, Kenny insisted that
*seenyuh* citizens were the boss and if they wanted to stay home, you stayed home,
and if they wanted to go out, you took them where they wanted to go. Edna had
wanted to go to the Rainbow Room, so that's where they had taken her. While
they all rode the elevator up, Edna said that she hadn't minded being left alone,
but Kenny interrupted. "Don't you defend *huh;* she knows *bettuh* than that," he
said. "It's enough," Mr. Melnick finally said. "She knows she's done wrong."

In the apartment, Mr. Melnick played an Yma Sumac record and Mr. Popko
and Edna danced, while an ebullient Kenny cried out, "Don't dip *huh,* Grand-
paw, *remembuh yuh* back." Kenny didn't speak to Jill, just glowered in her direction, then acted overly solicitous of Edna, telling her, "You look like a million

bucks." Jill talked to Kenny's buddies Hanif and Irv, students at Wesleyan and Boston College respectively, and asked if she could accompany them when they said that they were going out for falafels. But Hanif pointed to Kenny and said that "he" wouldn't like that and Irv said, "Yeah, you *bettuh* stay with *yuh grandmuthuh.*" Jill excused herself to the guest bedroom, changed into a T-shirt and sweatpants, and got into bed with a copy of *The Culture of Narcissism.*

Jill became so immersed in her reading that she didn't know Kenny had walked into her room until he was standing over her. He asked if she was awake, and when Jill said yes, he asked if she'd been crying. And before Jill could say no, Kenny sat beside her and asked if she was angry with him. Yes, Jill said. Kenny asked if she wanted to punch him. No, said Jill. Kenny said that sometimes people didn't like that he spoke his mind. Jill said the problem wasn't that he spoke his mind; the problem was that whenever he spoke his mind, he never considered that he might be wrong.

Look, Jill said. She sat up in bed and faced him directly. She told Kenny that she liked him; he was funny and smart. She respected his politics, his humanity. But once in a while, he was too convinced of his own opinion. Some people held their convictions as strongly as he did and that didn't make him right or them right, probably no one was ever completely right. And she wanted to say that, even if she disagreed with him, it didn't mean that she liked him any less; it only meant that she had a different view.

Kenny considered this for a moment, then stared into Jill's eyes. "Jesus," he said, "I don't understand you for one fricking second." He said that his father had been right about her. Why, Jill asked, what had Mr. Melnick said? Kenny said that his father had said that Jill was one of those girls who liked hearing herself talk and that during the whole broken condom incident, she had been leading Kenny on. While Jill was his guest, he would act civil to her, but that was only for Edna's benefit. And Jill, who couldn't begin to respond, merely said, "Good night, Kenny," and shut off the bedside light. She wondered whether she should feel deeply insulted by Kenny's assertion that she liked to lead men on or whether she should take it as a perverse compliment; she had never considered herself capable of leading men on.

On Saturday, Jill accompanied her grandmother, Kenny, and his parents on their sightseeing excursions, taking a separate elevator to the top of the Empire State when Kenny had said that there wasn't enough room for everyone, exploring exhibits in the Metropolitan Museum alone while Edna and Mr. Melnick studied statues of Greek athletes. And at Grand Central Terminal on Sunday morning, she watched each of the Melnicks and Mr. Popko hug Edna and tell her that she had to call as soon as she got home. Jill tried to thank the Melnicks and Mr. Popko for their hospitality, but before she could finish her sentence, Joseph Popko cut her off. "You bet," he snapped.

Still, Edna spent much of the train ride home saying how unpleasant she had found the Melnicks, how "Jewish" they were. Spending a day with them was *genug*; three was just too much. It was like her mother had always told her in Yiddish: "Once is nice, twice is all right, but the third time's a hit in the head." Kenny "meant well," but was "too unattractive" for her tastes. Mrs. Melnick was a *yuchna* who used too much schmaltz in her *pasgudna* cooking, but if her husband couldn't stand up for himself, then that's what he deserved. And that Mr. Popko—what was it with old men who always wanted to natter on about the past?

After they had taken a taxi back to 5 Mack Road and Jill had lugged Edna's suitcase into her dark, musty home, Edna said that the one highlight of the weekend had been seeing Michelle. Now, there was a girl who knew how to stand up for herself. My, what she wouldn't do to have her twenty-one-year-old body back for only a night; she could show people what to do with it. Jill asked Edna if she would call the Melnicks to tell them that she had arrived safely. Why, Edna asked, she just saw them two hours ago; the idea was peculiar.

Jill was contemplating the debasing act of calling the Melnicks to alert them of her grandmother's safe arrival when the phone rang. Jill picked up and heard Kenny's voice. *"Yuhgrandmuthuhome?"* he asked.

"Sure," Jill said tersely. Edna asked in a loud whisper who it was and when Jill said that it was Kenny, Edna hissed that she didn't want to talk to him. But when Edna finally took the phone, she said, "Well, hello there, my handsome boy." Ten minutes later, she was still on the phone; she had taken off her shoes and put her feet up on her kitchen table.

After spending spring break at Michelle's apartment and sharing the floor with Larry, who had signed a contract with Pico Records just hours before Hannah would kick him out of their apartment, Jill returned to her Cushing dorm room to find that both Bibi and her bed were gone. Not only was there no four-poster bed, there was nothing on the dresser or in her closets. The only items that remained were the bare wooden desk, chair, and twin bed with which the room had been initially equipped. On the unsheeted mattress lay a sealed envelope addressed to "The Best Friend Any Girl Could Have in the Whole Wide World." The return address was marked Bibi and Soren.

Jill sat down on Bibi's mattress and opened the letter. It was written in purple ink on lined paper. In the letter, Bibi apologized for misleading and, "in a sense, using" Jill by not revealing that she knew more than she did. She wrote that she had confronted Soren about his plans to sell his house, threatened to never speak to him again because he'd lied to her. She told him that she didn't care if he cried anymore, didn't care how many times he went down on her—she had heard it all before. Soren had taken a long while to speak ("I don't think I've ever been *that mad*!!!" Bibi wrote). The truth, he finally said, was that his wife ("that manipulating *b-i-t-blank-blank*!!!") had finally agreed to a divorce, but Soren didn't want to spend months haggling over money. He'd decided to sell the house ("His father bought it for him *anyway*") and everything in it, and give Deenie a third of the money, which was really more than she was entitled to. Meanwhile, Soren would take his two-thirds and buy a house in Fishkill for himself and Bibi. Bibi had wanted to keep the plan secret until spring break, when she could move all her belongings including her bed out of Cushing without "*kochleffels* asking a whole lot of *kochleffely* questions." She would take the semester off to travel with Soren and return to school in the fall, when the new house would be ready. She closed her letter telling Jill to "take good care, kiddo."

Jill hoped that having both her and Bibi's rooms to herself would give her more space and solitude, but this hope vanished as others learned of her newfound luxury. After Kenny's call to the Campus Housing department went unheeded (Kenny had complained that it was *inequitabuhl* for one freshman to live in a single while everyone else was "packed like *sahdines*" into doubles and triples), Bibi's former room became one of the dorm's most popular hangouts. Horace Greenstein set up his deejay equipment in the room; Matthew Chen practiced dance moves; and Andrea Fleischman conducted late-night trysts after her boyfriend Tom Dunne had fallen asleep. Every night, the room was the locus of political debate, stoned revelation, naïve discovery, and lurid confession.

Now Jill felt so consumed by opportunities—social, academic, and extracurricular—that visiting Edna seemed like more of an imposition. Yet Edna's calls on the hall phone became more frequent. She would always say that she didn't want anything in particular, but a few minutes into the conversation, she would suggest a task—"If you happen to be passing Grand Union . . ." she'd say, or "If the post office isn't out of your way . . ."

For the week when Jill was to interview for the assistant opinion editor position at the *Miscellany News,* Jill had told Edna that she wouldn't be able to visit her—she'd be writing papers, studying, applying for summer internships, and compiling a portfolio of her articles in preparation for her *Misc.* interview. Nonetheless, Edna called every night. On Monday, she told Jill that she hadn't seen a movie in ages and there was a new one at the Juliet starring "that handsome Patrick Swayze." On Tuesday night, Edna told Jill that her right hand felt numb, and though she didn't think that it was a serious problem, she wanted someone to stay with her just in case. On Wednesday, when Jill picked up the phone, Edna's voice was gruff. Well, she said, she guessed she'd throw it all out. Throw what out, asked Jill. Dinner, Edna said. What dinner, asked Jill. Edna said that the previous evening they had discussed Jill's coming over for dinner and she guessed that it hadn't been that important. Jill was certain that there had been no discussion of dinner the previous evening—the entire time had been spent discussing Edna's numbness, which miraculously disappeared once Jill tried to call an ambulance. But when she told Edna that they hadn't spoken of dinner, Edna grew disconsolate. Had she dreamed the whole thing, she asked. She sounded so sad that Jill immediately jogged over to Mack Road.

On the Thursday evening of her interview, when Edna called to ask Jill to pick up medicine at the drugstore, Jill could no longer contain her frustration. Damn it, Grandma, she said, she was not a 24-hour hotline, she could not be on call every minute to cater to Edna's whims. Edna turned quiet. Fine, she said, she'd never ask her for another thing. That's not what she meant, Jill said; she just needed some room to breathe. Well, Edna said, she would never call Jill and then Jill could breathe all she wanted. Grandma, Jill said. Don't "Grandma" her, Edna said. Jiminy H. Christ, she added, Jill and her mother were two peas out of a pod.

As she walked along the path to the *Misc.* office, a binder of her best articles in one hand, Jill could not stop replaying the conversation in her mind, wondering if she'd spoken too harshly, if it was wrong that the first time in her life when she'd truly yelled at someone, she had been arguing with an eighty-year-old woman whose two husbands and only daughter were dead. She wondered what sort of medication Edna needed, if the drugstore would still be open when she finished her interview.

She hoped that the *Misc.* interview would be short and productive. But the editorial board made her wait outside for forty-five minutes before granting her entrance. And when she walked into Rob Rubinstein's office, she saw an empty pizza box and two six-packs of Genesee on Rob's desk. As Jill sat politely, with her hands folded, the members of the editorial board laughed, drank, and debated such topics as Dwight Gooden and the Mets' pitching rotation and the trial of Bernhard Goetz. Ronelle Leeds finally reminded Rob that they were an hour behind schedule, but Rob said that part of editing was getting used to delays, and if people didn't want to wait, then they wouldn't be "good fits" for the paper. Anyway, official business couldn't begin without Alec Savage, who was out getting more pizza and beer.

Once Alec returned with provisions, Rob, feet up on his desk, suggested that they begin the interview. Jill said that she had prepared some remarks; Rob said that he would be glad to hear them, but they were running behind. He then talked about the history of the paper and the importance of upholding not only its reputation but that of journalism itself, even though he had been rejected by the journalism schools to which he had applied and would be beginning an MBA program in the fall. About twenty minutes into Rob's soliloquy, Ronelle told him that this was an interview, not a hazing ritual, and why didn't he shut up and "give Jill the floor"? Rob said that there was something Ronelle needed to learn about "the floor"—no one gave it to anyone; the floor was something you *took*. Ronelle said that the following year's editorial board would be more democratic since the editor would be a woman, though Rob said that "remained to be seen," alluding to the fact that both Ronelle and Joe Rossi were vying for the job. Joe, his mouth full of pizza, said that he too favored a democratic approach. Well, Rob asked Jill, did she favor a democratic approach too?

Jill eyed the clock. It was already half past nine. There was no way that the drugstore would stay open after ten, no way that she could get to Mack Road in time, no way that her grandmother would still be awake if and when she reached her house. She felt her insides constricting, and she felt anger taking hold again, at her grandmother for manipulating her, at herself for being manipulated, at Rob and his staff of pizza-eating, beer-swilling cronies for wasting her time. No, she said, she didn't favor a democratic approach, not if it meant people wasting each other's time. She had papers to write, exams to study for, a sick grandmother who needed medicine; in high school, she'd run a newspaper, and her meetings had always started and ended punctually because she respected people's schedules. The board knew her commitment; they knew her work. If they wanted to hire her, great; if not, they could waste someone else's time. As she walked to the door, Joe Rossi said, now there was someone who knew how to take the floor. As she rushed downstairs, Jill could hear the hearty laughter of male editors and the clinking of beer bottles.

Once she was outside in the cool, fragrant spring air, Jill headed directly for Edna's house, not knowing whether to run or walk. Running meant ceding her autonomy to bald manipulation, yet walking suggested indifference to her grandmother's needs. She walked at different speeds—slow, then fast, running, creeping, jogging, stopping to turn back, then dashing at full speed to make up for the time she had lost until she reached the house. Jill wondered how long she would have to knock before Edna answered. But it only took one knock for the door to open and Kenny to appear. He was wearing his grandfather's old denim jacket as a shirt.

"It's been handled," Kenny said. Apparently, Jill hadn't found it in her *baht* to bring her *grandmutha* the refill for her prescription, so she had called him and he had run right *ovuh* and saved Edna from having a *cawnary*. So, nothin' to worry about, he said as Jill heard Edna calling out his name.

"Stay there," Kenny said, then went back to the kitchen. A minute later, he returned. "She wants to know if you want soup," he said.

Jill thought for a moment. No, she said, she didn't want any soup. She walked quickly down the front steps, then jogged north without looking back.

I t wasn't until final exam week that Jill heard from her grandmother again. Jill had received mixed news from the *Miscellany News* editorial board; she would not receive the assistant opinion editor position; a new position had been created for her—city editor. She would continue to function as liaison between the newspaper and Poughkeepsie, despite the fact that Jill had written in her application essay that she was eager to stop covering local issues.

Later that day, Edna resurfaced; a note was in Jill's message box—"I called to say good-bye," it said. Jill assumed that the note was intended to make her think the worst; she would arrive at 5 Mack Road, see the shades down, the kitchen dark. But when Jill reached the house, the door was propped open and a SOLD sign was stuck in the front lawn. A moving truck was parked outside and workmen were humping boxes down the stairs and onto the truck. Edna was sitting on her steps with a clipboard, counting boxes and studying the movers' physiques.

Well, Edna said, look what the *ketzeleh* had dragged in. Jill asked her grandmother where she was moving. The senior center, Edna said—she supposed that she had Jill to thank or blame for the fact that she was moving, and Kenny Melnick for the fact that she was paying so much since he hadn't been able to help her move because he had two exams; besides, he was a "scrawny little dweeb" anyway and couldn't lift much. Well, Jill said, trying to sound cheerful, a senior center sounded preferable to an empty house; was she moving somewhere nearby? No, Edna said, far away: Manhattan. Jill asked what the center was called. The Popko Center, Edna said, at which point Mr. Joseph Popko stepped out of the house and onto the landing and, seeing Jill, tipped his cap, skipped nimbly down the stairs, and told Jill that he had asked this young lady to marry him. Jill said that she was very happy for both of them. "Why?" Mr. Popko asked, a twinkle in his eyes. Well, Jill said, it was nice that they were getting married. What was nice about it, he asked. What was she supposed to say, Jill asked, that she was unhappy? "At ease, Private," Mr. Popko said, then told Edna that he would see if anything was left in the upstairs closets.

Once Mr. Popko had gone back inside, Edna revealed that she hadn't agreed to marry him, only that she would move in. She wasn't sure that she liked the idea of getting married, she didn't want a whole big *tararam*. Plus, she didn't know how much "gas" he had left in his "tank." Sure, he moved around all right, but he had a list of pills to take every night, and she refused to play "nursemaid to some old crank."

Jill sat on the steps beside her grandmother and asked if she felt sad to leave. Why, Edna asked, because she was marrying an *alte cocker*? No, Jill said, she just thought that something would be sad about leaving a house with so many memories; so much had happened while Edna had lived in this house, in Poughkeepsie too—she had seen a century of history, industrialization, motorcars, airplanes, two world wars, then television, now computers, the rise and fall of a city. Maybe, Edna said, but she didn't "go in for reminiscing." What difference did it make anyway—it was all *nuchum*. Maybe someday she'd sit in the senior center and think great thoughts about her life, but now all she could think about was that she was moving in with a ninety-year-old man and not this boy right here—she pointed at a long-haired, wiry young mover in a black AC/DC tank top. He carried two boxes; one was marked SHOES, the other NOSTALGIA.

Edna told the young man to put the boxes down; he was working too hard. She asked him for his name. Reggie, ma'am, he said. Edna mentioned that she had once known a sailor named Reggie, then asked him if he thought this was ridiculous—a woman her age with so many things. Wouldn't it be better, she asked, to load everything onto the truck and drive it into the Hudson? How much would she need in the next world? She asked Reggie how much his crew had already loaded onto the truck. About half the house, Reggie said. Good, said Edna, take the rest of it to the alley. "Excuse me, ma'am?" Reggie asked. Take it away, she repeated, dump it all in the alley. But a lot of nice items were still in the house, he said, a dining room table, nice chairs too. Edna said that she didn't want any of it crowding up her life anymore; why didn't he start by dumping the two boxes beside him? Reggie shrugged and crouched, ready to lift the boxes onto his back again, but then Jill asked what was inside. Edna said that she didn't know; it said SHOES on the box. Yes, Jill said, one did say SHOES, but the other said NOSTALGIA. Well, if Jill already knew, why was she asking; what was this obsession with things that were gone?

At first, as Jill sat on the front steps and looked through the box, she was disappointed. It was full of photo albums and scrapbooks, but the first two contained pictures of George Ferrante's family. Only after she got to the bottom did she find what she was looking for. Here were the photos of Becky Schulman's eighth-grade graduation; the picture of Becky in the cast of the Poughkeepsie High production of *Twentieth Century;* the program for Becky's first Broadway chorus role in *Girls-A-Million!* And letters and postcards from New York City were signed "Love, Becky"—Jill could not remember when she had last seen her mother's handwriting. Below it all was another scrapbook, one that Edna had brought to Becky's funeral but Jill had never seen.

Well, Edna finally asked, had Jill finished traveling down memory lane? Jill said that she guessed so, and asked if Edna would mind if she took the box; there were some old pictures of her mother, letters too. Edna said she had no idea why she had bothered saving them. Jill said that she was glad; though it was unlikely, she might find answers to the questions that she had always had. "Such as?" Edna asked. Such as why Becky had married Charlie Wasserstrom, Jill said, such as why she had left Poughkeepsie. There was no mystery to that, Edna said. Then why did she leave, asked Jill. "She left," Edna said, "because she didn't want to stay," and that was enough with the questions.

Jill sat on the stoop of the house on Mack Road, scrapbooks and photographs in front of her, as the last of the other boxes was carted away. Before Reggie left with his crew, Edna asked for his phone number, because she had a grand-daughter in the city whom he might like. Reggie said that he was married; that had never stopped her when she'd been younger, Edna said.

Mr. Popko declared that the house was empty. He skipped down the front steps, saluted, clicked his heels in front of Jill, and said, "You are dismissed, Private," then took Edna by the arm as the moving truck drove off. Jill walked with her grandmother and Mr. Popko to Edna's Buick. Jill hugged her grandmother, then Edna opened her passenger-side door, got in, and slammed it shut. As Mr. Popko started the Buick, he gave Jill another salute. Jill waved, but Edna did not look up, just fumbled with her handbag. The car drove away and Jill returned to the stoop of the empty house and the box of scrapbooks and photographs. She briefly wondered if Becky Wasserstrom had left this house because of Edna's behavior, or if Edna had been a different person before her daughter had left home. And since there was no real way of knowing, she picked up the box, which was far heavier than she had expected, and began walking slowly back to campus.

Two nights later, to her surprise, lying on Muley's mattress on South Michigan Avenue, Jill did not once feel that she was ever floating outside or above herself. She felt Muley's arms around her, his breath upon her, his body underneath, above, and beside her—until the morning came and Fidel licked her awake. She opened her eyes to see Muley staring out his window; he was gazing south toward Cermak Road, where a bearded man with long gray hair was getting into a white Cadillac.

IV

# *Kaddish*

*Muley and Hillel's Book of Mourning*

*(1985–87)*

━ ━━ ━

(A STORY OF WEST ROGERS PARK,
CHICAGO, AMERICA, AND
THE REST OF THE MILKY WAY)

*The sad part of it is the crescent reaches its zenith . . .*
—MAYOR HAROLD WASHINGTON, 1986

*I truly do not have any fears; I'm looking forward to the trip . . .*
—CHRISTA MCAULIFFE, SCHOOLTEACHER AND
SPACE SHUTTLE *CHALLENGER* ASTRONAUT

On a clear, late September evening, as Halley's Comet hurtled toward Earth's orbit at a speed of nearly one million miles per hour, Muley Scott Wills was standing alone in his loft in front of a blank, white screen, contemplating his first solo exhibition at Larmer Galleries, when Mel Coleman knocked on his door, then entered before Muley had a chance to invite him in.

"You alone, Copernicus?" Mel asked. Muley nodded, chuckled, then shook Mel's hand.

Muley hadn't seen Mel much lately; he'd only visited Mel and Deirdre's West Rogers Park house once since the fall semester at the Art Institute had begun. When he wasn't filming, he was sketching, when he wasn't sketching, he was sanding or grouting, and when he wasn't sanding or grouting, he was walking Fidel to 31st Street Beach and gazing up at the night sky, making sure that the astronomers' predictions were correct, that the comet was still not yet visible.

For the past year, Muley had been studying the progress of various celestial phenomena. Not because he was particularly interested in astronomy. It had been one of his passions back when he'd been a student at Boone Elementary, where he had perused as many books and magazines as he could find on the topic, voraciously reading Carl Sagan and *Omni* magazine in the library; he would watch *Nova* on PBS, scan the skies for evidence of UFOs, speak with authority on the temperature of Mercury's surface, the composition of Venus's amosphere, the prescience of *Close Encounters of the Third Kind*.

But now, nearing the age of twenty, he knew less about interstellar travel than when he was twelve. What still interested him about the sky, though, was the idea that it, like the art he sought to create, was a seemingly static canvas that was nevertheless constantly changing, being destroyed, then reborn. The sky was not a film that remained the same every time it was threaded through a projector, no mere screen reflecting only what was projected upon it. Every second, stars were forming, exploding, planets were moving, changing shape. The story of everyone's life, he theorized, could be told as a reflection of events in the heavens above. He had been born when the U.S. *Surveyor* had landed on the moon; his father had left him and his mother when *Soyuz 1* had been launched; he had lost his virginity to Connie Sherman while the space shuttle *Columbia* was preparing for liftoff, made love to Jill Wasserstrom while the space shuttle *Challenger* was orbiting Earth.

In April, just a few short hours after the space shuttle *Discovery* had touched down at Cape Canaveral, he had met Calliope Larmer at an Art Institute student show held at the Randolph Street Gallery. Calliope, who had been born in Wausau, Wisconsin, with the same decidedly unartistic name as her great-aunt, "Brenda Sue," and had changed her name upon her 1977 arrival in Chicago, had discovered Muley's work in a corner of the gallery. She had been looking for a quiet place to smoke. The exhibit had exhausted her; she had seen one too many nude self-portraits, one too many LED displays of ironic slogans, and about a dozen too many smiling penis people sodomizing naked cartoon characters. When she saw Muley sitting on a paint can in front of a row of mason jars, she asked if he would split a cigarette with her. At first, she hadn't realized that he too was an artist, and she appreciated that he didn't change his tone once he learned that she owned and managed a gallery; most students turned either solicitous or dismissive, and invariably, in conversation, they would denigrate their fellow classmates' work. And when that didn't convince her to exhibit their art, they would compliment her spiky blond hair and ask where she had purchased her funky boots.

At the exhibition, Muley displayed no completed artwork. He had been continuing to pursue an art of ephemera and planned obsolescence. Perhaps because of his peripatetic youth, perhaps because he had always sensed the certainty of his life slipping away from him, perhaps because his art never fully satisfied him anymore, he embraced the idea of an art that could destroy itself, that could be seen once or for a limited period of time, then disintegrate. In his introductory drawing classes, he was never satisfied with a simple nude form; it didn't look right unless he had sketched the body with some part of it—a hand, a finger—

disappearing off the page. He would mount a sketch on flash paper, light a match to it, watch it flare up, pop, then resolve itself into ashes that he would collect in a small jar and present to his professor. For the exhibition, he had tacked blue-prints, storyboards, and Polaroid photos of his exploding screen projects to the wall, and arranged jars of ash on the floor. On a small screen, he projected a short animated film about his old neighborhood, running it on a loop, hoping that the film would eventually melt.

After they had finished the cigarette, Calliope looked at Muley's sketches and asked when he would attempt to realize his projects. When Muley said that he already had and pointed to the ash jars, Calliope asked if he wanted to go out for drinks at the Vu. There, after two rounds of Ricard and root beer, she asked if he wanted to see her own work—whimsical sculptures and photographs that mocked her midwestern upbringing: a kitchen installation that resembled a Bob's Big Boy hamburger restaurant, an enormous map of Wisconsin made out of Laughing Cow cheese wrappers. And when Muley stood in her apartment and told her how much he admired her art, particularly her grinning, bow tie–clad bowling pins that danced to "On, Wisconsin!" she asked if he wanted to sleep with her ("Just joking; not really," she said). And when he declined, she asked if he would consider letting her exhibit his work.

Mel Coleman had little patience for Muley's fanciful art projects. Art and film were incompatible, he had often told Muley: film was a commercial medium; art was about getting "your mama's friends to pony up money for shit you scrawl on a wall." Mel had become increasingly bitter ever since *Godfathers of Soul* had been edited beyond recognition for a series of music videos, an evisceration to which Mel had grudgingly agreed, largely because he liked being able to say that he had sold his first film, and the money that Carl had paid him out of his cut of the distribution deal was significant enough to give him a head start on financing his next film project—*Son of a Preacher Man:* as Mel described it, a somewhat fic-tionalized, coming-of-age gangster flick about a neglected clergyman's kid named Mel who grew up on Chicago's mean streets and witnessed a crime perpetrated by a stripper's bouncer that made him go straight.

Even though Mel had yet to get past page ten in his first draft of *Preacher Man,* his music video business was thriving. Music videos seemed to work better than feature films for Mel's attention span, and he was getting so much work that he had developed a coded, three-tier system of production, which created videos of varying quality for various price levels. At the S-level (S stood for *shit*), Mel would cobble together a volunteer crew and production team of art students, who would produce videos for local-access cable programs, such as *Lennie Kidd's Video Jukebox.* H-level (H for *hack*) allowed Mel to employ journeyman directors, such as Ron Claxton, to produce serviceable if trite concert videos for up-and-coming bands. Only at Mel's highest-priced C-level (C for Coleman) did a band get an expertly produced project with the potential for MTV airplay.

Mel had stopped by Muley's loft this evening because he had a difficult "C-Level project," and thought that Muley might be able to help. Pico Records had just signed Mel to direct a video for "Her Sister (Is Cool)," a single by Larry Elliot, who had bristled at the prospect of a weeklong video shoot and said that he would only allow his song to be used if he didn't have to appear in the video himself. Contacts with the artist were now handled only via his manager, "Clara Moskowitz," who said that she "*vas studink cuntwreck* law at *zee* New York *Univairsity,*" and asserted that *Meester* Elliot would "*nyet* be *doink* any of *thees sheety* promotional *bowlsheet.*" Knowing Larry's argumentative nature, Michelle Wasserstrom had offered to represent him, and knowing how easy it would be to cut a good deal with Mel if she flirted with him over the phone, disguising her voice and using a seductive foreign accent, Michelle had acted the role of one of her favorite characters—a slutty Russian émigrée—to talk Mel into producing a top-flight video at half price.

Mel, who was struggling with the Larry Elliot assignment, said to Muley that the only way to produce a video for a performer who would not be photographed was to take an "art shit" approach, and Muley was the only artist he knew who didn't give him a pain in his ass. Muley said that the assignment did pose some intriguing artistic challenges, but the Larmer Galleries' exhibition was taking up all his time, and he wanted to finish as much preliminary work as possible before Jill came back into town for her winter break. Why didn't Mel ask his roommate Hillel Levy, Muley proposed—Hillel was better at animation than he was. Mel asked if, by Hillel, Muley meant that guy who "drew dicks all over everything." Yeah, that was the guy, Muley said, adding that Salvador Dalí had made quite a career of drawing dicks all over everything, but Mel didn't have to worry about Hillel—if he had a specific assignment, he would follow it to the letter; Hillel needed money since his father wasn't paying for art school. Mel was dubious, but said that he'd give "dutiful consideration" to Muley's suggestion. He asked if Muley was certain that he didn't have a few days to "bullshit around" on some storyboards. Maybe after January, Muley said, but no sooner. Why January, Mel asked. Muley said because that's when Jill's break would be over, Halley's Comet would be reaching perihelion, and the exhibition would be opening.

"Damn," Mel said and added that Muley was a nut, did he know that? Yeah, Muley said and smiled; he had thought the same thing about himself many times before. He asked if Mel wanted to walk to the beach with him and Fidel to determine whether they could see any trace of the comet in the eastern sky.

On the same day that space shuttle *Atlantis* began its maiden voyage and Mel gave his "Coleman Seal of Approval" to Hillel's preliminary sketches for the "Her Sister (Is Cool)" video, Hillel returned from Bronzeville Studios and burst into the Michigan Avenue loft where Muley was at his easel, sketching Halley's Comet.

"Let me whip something out for you, big guy," Hillel announced with a cackle as he reached into the pocket of his overcoat, pulled out a folded check, and slapped it atop Muley's easel. Muley looked at the check and smiled, then tried to hand it back to Hillel. No, Hillel said as he kicked off his loafers, then slipped on a pair of roller skates, he wanted Muley to hold on to it.

As he skated around the loft, Hillel told Muley that he initially hadn't thought that he would be able to complete the job that Mel had offered him, since he had had such a negative initial reaction to the Larry Elliot cassette. The songs barely had melodies and the chorus of the single was little more than "Her sister is cool" repeated ad nauseam with only a couple "oh yeah's" and "I said's." Hillel said that he had never cared for folk or rock music; his favorite bands were Bronski Beat, Alphaville, and a-ha, bands whose music he could dance to and burn off aggression. But after a few listens, Hillel had seen the humor and honesty in the song, and soon he was snapping his fingers as Elliot sang, "So now you divorced me and you're diggin' Nate Yau and sleepin' with Amelia after breakin' your vows." The night before he was to deliver his initial storyboards to Mel, he had found inspiration and sketched Elliot as a two-legged cat in a dark black raincoat and sunglasses, his tail swinging out from under his overcoat as he watched his feline wife sleeping with the proprietor of a falafel restaurant. That was some funny shit, Mel said, shook Hillel's hand, and gave him his first payment.

Once he was done skating, a sweaty Hillel sat down on the floor of the loft and thanked Muley for the gig. He said that Muley had two choices—he could take Mel's check to cover all the rent he owed Muley, or Muley could collect a "prize blow job" now and they could "call it even-Steven." Muley held out Hillel's check and told him that he didn't have to worry about the money. Hillel opened his eyes wide and said *Gott im Himmel,* he never would have believed it; the man wanted a blow job. "No blow job right now, thank you very much, but no money either," Muley said; he only asked that Hillel not spend his first check on anything stupid. Hillel said that he'd spend it on junk food, drugs, alcohol, and cheap sex, but not on anything *stupid,* was that O.K.? Then Hillel sheepishly asked if Muley would mind keeping the money, just in case he had a moment of weakness and wanted to "buy coke or a hooker." Sure, Muley said. That was mighty white of him, Hillel said, Muley was a real *mensch,* he was doing a *mitzvah,* and if Muley wanted, they could play "hunt for the *afikoman*" in the shower later. Muley said that he'd keep the check in his room, and when Hillel needed it, he'd give it to him. But later that night, after Muley had returned from walking Fidel and photographing the comet, which appeared ever-so-dimly near the constellation of Taurus, Hillel was gone, and so was the check.

Ever since he had chosen to pursue art instead of medicine like his older brother Shimon, and his father had finally kicked him out of the Levy family house on Coyle Avenue, Hillel had been leading a life of self-abuse and hypochondria. He had exhibited self-destructive tendencies before at Lane Tech, which he had attended after intentionally failing the entrance exam at Ida Crown Jewish Academy, where his younger sister Leah was now a freshman—the first question had asked Hillel to state the current date and he had written "1980 in the Year of Our Lord." In high school, Hillel had habitually insulted the wrong people and gotten punched in the nose for his offenses. He had told a group of Led Zeppelin fans that Robert Plant sang like a girl; he asked football team trainer Reuben Sorkin if his job involved any responsibilities other than watching well-hung boys in the showers and guessing their waist sizes; one time, he had approached some gangbangers and showed them a sketch in which they were orally serviced by Ronald McDonald and Grimace. The gangbangers had laughed at the drawing, but they had beaten him up anyway. Sometimes, he'd get punched for no apparent reason; he was often told that it was because of his "shit-eating grin."

Hillel's fall from his father's favor coincided with two linked phenomena: the emergence of a rebellious irreverence on his part at the precise moment that his father had saddled him with adultlike expectations. Hillel's brother Shimon had also been a class clown, but the moment when Shimon had entered high school, he announced that he would stop parting his hair on the side and would instead part it down the middle, a change in behavior that also signaled a newfound seriousness. Shimon then dressed in clean, pressed shirts, color-coordinated his yarmulkes and socks, finished second in the race for student council president, and, as an upperclassman, counseled incoming freshmen, such as Ben Jacobs and Larry Rovner, on such topics as Onan and abstinence. Boaz and Shayndel Levy assumed that, upon entering high school, Hillel would follow Shimon's example, and when he didn't, Boaz responded with unprecedented disciplinary measures, which Hillel refused to take seriously.

Hillel's raucous if sometimes overzealous and inappropriate good humor in the high school classroom and in the *Lane Leader* office stood in stark contrast to the fierce chair- and pillow-throwing fits he threw whenever Boaz would ground him for swearing or illustrating the family's *Tanakh* (Hillel's drawing for Exodus 22:19—"Whoever lies with a beast shall be put to death"—had triggered a par-ticularly heated shouting match). The fits stopped only when Hillel lost his voice, when his sister started crying, or when his brother threw him against the wall and told him to repeat whatever he had said to their father, and to say it to his face. All this reached its climax during Hillel's last semester at Lane, when Boaz caught Hillel doodling in the *Tanakh* again ("The Lord said to him, 'What is that in your hand?' And he replied, 'A rod'"). Boaz chased Hillel around the house with a belt while Shayndel—whose favorite statement was "I can't hear anything; I'm in the kitchen"—emerged from said kitchen to tell Hillel to beware his fa-ther's temper. "Why? What's the worst he can do to me?" Hillel asked as he ran. "I'm already circumcised." Boaz Levy said that once Hillel was in college, he would no longer be allowed in the house until he had learned some respect for his parents and himself.

As of freshman year at the Art Institute, when Muley had invited him to share his loft, Hillel had begun to exhibit even less self-control. Routinely, he would spend the night dancing at Neo or Octagon, then cruise for one-night stands on Halsted Street and Montrose Beach or bargain with streetwalkers on North Avenue before Denny O'Toole, who had been dealing ever since his best friend had died in a car accident, would sell him a Baggie of coke in the Dunkin' Donuts parking lot on Belmont Avenue. Afterward, Hillel would return to Muley's loft and obsessively catalogue everything he had done, and ask Muley if he thought that he had any cause for concern. At the Oak Theater, he'd sucked the tit of a showgirl; did Muley think that he'd get herpes? He'd "smoked the pole" of a radiologist he'd met in Roscoe's; did Muley think that was an AIDS risk?

At first, Muley had thought that Hillel was inventing his stories to impress him, but he soon became convinced that they were all true. It was not so much the obsessively recounted details that convinced Muley of their veracity as much as Hillel's morning-after panics; often, Muley would espy him stuffing his nostrils with toilet paper, palpating his glands, checking his naked body for lesions, his genitals for open sores, studying a medical textbook and saying "Oh shit, oh shit" before declaring with evangelical fervor that he had "turned a corner" and was "goin' Orthodox, boys and girls." He would flush any remaining coke or pot down the toilet, perform an hour's worth of ablutions in the bathtub, then roller-skate fast around the loft, blasting "Dreidel Mine, Spin Spin Spin," and repeating a mantra out loud: "Gotta live clean, live clean." This would last for a week at most, after which Hillel would disappear for a day or two, then return with an even more harrowing story.

The few times that Muley tried to dissuade him from his behavior, Hillel always agreed with Muley—yes, he should seek counseling, yes, cocaine was addictive, yes, calling out "Hey, Leon Spinks!" to a gap-toothed bouncer at Dingbats' cocktail lounge wasn't smart. Once, Muley suggested that Hillel see a doctor, but Hillel shook his head; a doctor would only confirm what he feared all along. From then on, Muley, who had spent many years feeling responsible for others' behavior, merely tried to provide Hillel with a reasonable set of alternatives, such as taking a job animating a music video for Mel.

As Muley had hoped, Hillel was taking to the animation job with a zeal that he usually reserved for drawing pornographic cartoons or running from sex workers to whom he tried to pay significantly less than the amount upon which they had agreed. But when Muley returned home late with Fidel to find that Hillel and his check were gone, he shuddered at the amount of trouble that Hillel was probably getting into with a wallet full of money. When Hillel finally returned, Muley asked where he had been. Hillel said that he had gone back to work in Mel's editing suite, and Muley had trouble containing a smile.

Near the end of October, on the night before the space shuttle *Challenger* would lift off for its ninth mission, Hillel rapped loudly on the door to Muley's room. He had spent nearly a month working on the Larry Elliot video, and each night, he returned to tell Muley stories. But instead of lurid sex or drug stories, he would describe the work he'd done for Mel, how Mel had sternly ordered him to redo an entire animation sequence and to "get that penis-looking thing out of my frame," how Larry's manager, "some crazy Russian chick," told Hillel to hurry *heez ess opp end feenish hees preleeminary drawinks*. On this particular evening, Hillel boasted that he had drawn a hilarious nude caricature of this one guy he had met, who claimed to run Bronzeville Studios, this one "white guy who thinks he's black" and wanted everyone to call him "Slappit." You could just tell that this Slappit guy had never gotten laid in his life, because no self-respecting chick would ever listen to his jive; Hillel asked if Muley wanted to see the caricature. No, Muley said, he didn't need to—Slappit was his father. Hillel told Muley to "get the fuck out of town."

After Muley explained, Hillel apologized; though he might have drawn Slappit on his knees performing a "teabag" on Fearless Fosdick, he hadn't meant anything personal by it. But when Hillel pressed Muley for further information, Muley said that he didn't know his father, and he would say nothing more. Hillel said that he didn't understand why Muley didn't associate with his pop—the guy always seemed to be throwing his money around. Who knew—there might be a big payoff for Muley somewhere down the line. Maybe so, Muley said, but he really didn't want to talk about Slappit; he'd barely ever seen the man. He attached a leash to Fidel's collar and walked out of the loft, bound for the lake.

Moments later, Hillel, imagining the desolation of not talking to his parents—well, at least his mother—for twenty years, called home. He intended to assure Shayndel Levy that he was doing well in his studies, that he had found a legitimate, part-time job. But Shayndel whispered that she wasn't supposed to talk to him and handed the phone to Boaz, who asked who it was, and when Hillel said that it was his youngest son, Mr. Levy said that he had only one son; the other was buried in Waldheim Cemetery. That night, as Hillel lay in bed unable to sleep as always, he wondered if any father could be as unpleasant as his own.

Throughout his life, Hillel had created numerous alternative father figures to substitute for the Nagilah Israel proprietor with whom he had spent his first seventeen years. While other teens postered their walls with Christie Brinkley, Bruce Springsteen, and Tom Cruise, Hillel slept beneath pictures of avuncular men clipped out of magazines. He would gaze up into the watchful eyes of the actor John Houseman. He would wonder how Orson Welles's beard would feel against his cheek, imagine Burl Ives wrapping his furry arms around him. He did not understand how he could have the same father as his siblings, how Shimon could scratch his father's back, how Leah could lavish Boaz Levy with handmade Father's Day cards. Often, Hillel would quiz his mother for clues that might confirm his hopeful hypothesis that he had been adopted. Now, as Hillel lay awake in the loft, he thought of Carl Slappit Silverman—that slender man muttering into his telephone, slouching about Bronzeville Studios in baggy jeans, his gray hair flying, dust particles clinging to his multicolored beard. Carl didn't seem so terrible.

For Hillel, getting to Carl was easy; getting noticed by him was harder. Carl, who spent all his days on the phone, barely realizing that his staff had dwindled, that most of the offices and editing suites in Bronzeville Studios had been vacant ever since *Godfathers of Soul* had wrapped, had the general impression that all white people, particularly all white males, looked the same. He was never sure whom he had met before and under what circumstance and, hence, assumed that Hillel had legitimate reasons for hanging around his office or sitting in on the poorly attended meetings for the Tiny Cubbins Legal Defense Fund. He would assign Hillel such tasks as making phone trees, distributing pamphlets, or, when Hillel said that Carl's flyers were corny, designing new ones, then redrawing them when Carl said that he didn't like that mushroom in the lower right-hand corner.

For much of November, Hillel spent his mornings and afternoons at the Art Institute, his evenings at Bronzeville working for Mel, then doing odd jobs for Carl. He grew to like the man. He liked Carl's sense of mission, which combined strangely with his utter obliviousness, his ability to focus on one task so intently that he forgot even the most obvious things, such as shaving or paying his bills. "Jeez, man," Hillel heard Carl say to himself once, "have I gone to the bathroom today?" On the night that Hillel watched the rough cut of the Larry Elliot video before Mel would send it out for Pico Records' approval, Hillel asked Mel what was so bad about Carl; why wouldn't Muley even speak to him? Mel answered by asking Hillel whose side he was on—the side of The People or the side of The Man? Hillel said that he was on the side of The People. Well, then don't ask dumb questions about what The People had against The Man, Mel said; if he were on the side of The People, he'd know.

Nevertheless, Hillel continued to work for Carl. He'd meander his way into his office, and though Carl never remembered his name, he usually did remember that the kid could draw pretty well, and asked Hillel to design new fund-raising brochures for the Cubbins defense fund. "You know," Hillel told Carl one night after he had finished his work, "we have someone in common." And when Carl shrugged, but said nothing, Hillel added, "Your son, Muley." Hillel expected Carl to display, if not outright shock, at least some curiosity, but all Carl said was, "Yeah, yeah, right, Muley," as if he couldn't quite place the name.

The next night, when Hillel entered Carl's office, Carl was alone, swearing to himself as he flipped through the creased and coffee-stained documents atop his desk. He barely looked up when Hillel entered and told him that he had finished his job for Mel and would be happy to do anything that Carl needed. Carl said that his lawyer had told him to cut down his costs, and he couldn't pay much, but Hillel said that he didn't mind. Carl grumbled something about coming by the next day, then scratched his neck with a plastic fork, said hold on a second, and began rummaging through drawers. "You said you see Muley, right?" he asked; when Hillel said yes, Carl produced an envelope from the desk, opened his wallet, counted out some bills, and placed them inside. He asked Hillel to deliver the envelope to Muley, but not to say where the money had come from; Hillel could keep a fifty for himself.

When he returned to the loft, Hillel tried to be nonchalant about handing over the envelope. "I just wanted to give you that, big guy," he told Muley before putting on his roller skates with the hope of exhausting himself to the point that he would lack the energy to go out and spend the fifty-dollar bill that Carl had given him. But before Hillel had put on his second roller skate, Muley, envelope in hand, said that it seemed like too much money. Yeah, well, Hillel stammered, he was paying Muley back with interest; Mel had paid him today and he thought that Muley deserved the money for getting him the job. Mel paid him in cash? Muley asked. That didn't sound like Mel. No, no, Hillel said, Mel had given him a check and he'd just cashed it. For how much, asked Muley. Hillel's eyes shifted away from Muley's.

"Give it back to him," Muley said.

The next day, after Hillel ran out at the end of his Figure Drawing class, where his professor told him that his work showed vivid imagination, but the assignment had been to sketch the model and the model had been clothed, he walked into Carl's office, holding the envelope that Carl had given him the previous day. Hillel told him that Muley hadn't accepted his money. Carl took the envelope as if it looked vaguely familiar. He counted the money inside it and seemed impressed by how much was there. He took out his wallet, added some bills to the stack in the envelope, and handed the envelope back to Hillel. But that night, when Hillel handed Muley the thicker envelope, Muley pushed it away.

Over the next weeks, as November led into December, the pattern continued. After classes, Hillel would run to Bronzeville, where he would perform menial tasks for Carl, who would hand Hillel money that Muley would refuse to take and Carl would refuse to take back. Once the sum that Muley and Carl were passing back and forth grew to nearly a thousand dollars, Hillel came to a realization; he should neither upset Muley by offering him the money nor upset Carl by telling him that Muley hadn't wanted it.

Knowing that having too much money could be dangerous, Hillel spent it as quickly as possible. He would go to Marshall Field's and buy suits, power ties, shoes, sheer socks with patterns on them. He'd spend money on haircuts, mousses, gels, colognes. He paid back the small-time dealers, such as Denny O'Toole, who had long ago given up on collecting the piddling sums that Hillel owed them. There was a new vibrancy to the city. West of the Loop, galleries were rising on long-deserted industrial sites. There were new shops and boutiques on the Magnificent Mile, funky new nightclubs west of the Loop, a sense that more than two years of political stagnation were finally coming to a close, thanks in part to the egalitarian policies of Harold Washington's administration, in part to the fact that during blizzards the streets in every neighborhood were now being shoveled, but mostly to the success of the as-yet-undefeated Chicago Bears, who had an ability beyond the capacities of mere politicians to unite the city. The team's fortunes were on the lips of all its residents, who would greet each other on the el with smiles, impromptu raps from "The Super Bowl Shuffle," and "How 'bout dem Bears," a phrase as rich in meaning and goodwill as "Shalom."

Hillel immersed himself completely in the city's new spirit. He would use his fake ID, on which he had named himself Hugh Janus, to get into *Miami Vice*

Night at P.S. Chicago, then hit Medusa's juice bar, where he would dance to Ministry or DJ Joe Smooth's house mixes all night long. And when he had only enough money left for a few groceries and bus fare, he would stroll down North Avenue and turn down the advances of prostitutes, telling them that much as he'd like to oblige them, he only had five bucks left in his wallet.

C arl Silverman had known all along that Muley lived a mere three blocks away from his studios, had sensed it even before he had caught a glimpse of the young man staring out the window of a loft on South Michigan Avenue. Many times he had considered crossing Cermak, ringing the bell if there was one, knocking on the door if that's all there was. Muley would answer or he would not, he would invite him in or he wouldn't, but to Carl, it all seemed beside the point if he were the one making the first move. Often, he had envisioned the scene— Muley holding one of his hands, Deirdre the other. At one time, the image had represented the entire object of his actions; now, whenever it reasserted itself, the only purpose it served was to remind him of what he could have had if he had only had a little more foresight.

These days, Carl operated more by reflex than by inspiration, each action accompanied by a sense that whatever he was doing he had done better in the past. On the advice of his attorney Lou Eisenstaedt, after selling off Slappit Records, he also sold its offshoot businesses, such as The Penny Lane Foundation, which organized charity concerts for deceased musicians. There were no new feature-film projects for Bronzeville Studios. Ever since Deirdre had rejected him, ever since the subsequent failure of the *Godfathers* premiere and Cubbins benefit, Carl found his ambition steadily evaporating. Every night, he vowed to visit the Checkerboard Lounge or Wise Fools Pub to sign new talent, but he always wound up staying home. Now forty-three, he sensed that he would not live another forty-three years, never mind that his parents were in their eighties and, save for his father's rapidly fading memory and his mother's arthritis, had nary a health complaint, never mind that, despite a lack of sleep, a diet of Dock's fried catfish, Leon's hot links, and Soul Queen's collard greens, his doctor Mary Mitchum, who had recently transferred to DuSable Hospital, had pronounced him as fit as a man of twenty-five.

Though there was no evidence to support it, still Carl had a feeling that one day, his body would simply give out. With the aid of his attorney, he had made out a will, discussed its terms at Joliet with Tiny Cubbins, who turned out to be the shrewdest financial mind that Carl knew. He created a trust for his parents so that they would be provided for in the event of his absence. He had started giving things away—gold albums, original acetate recordings. A journalist would interview him and state admiration for some item hanging on the wall, and Carl would immediately hand it over. Money, too. He gave it to people on the streets, handed it to Girl Scouts selling cookies and didn't ask for change, pledged it to representatives of liberal causes when they got him on the phone, shoved it into Hillel Levy's fist.

Throughout November and December, each of Carl's actions was accompanied by a certain fatalism. When he made a plane reservation to see his parents at Bridlewood Village, their retirement community in Miami Beach, he felt strongly that he might not make the same journey again. Though his 1985 calendar had been crammed full of events, 1986 was nearly all blank squares.

Therefore, when Carl arrived at Bridlewood Village for Chanukah, he was stunned when his mother, who was always telling him how skinny he looked, greeted him with a bright smile, and said well, Chicago weather must really agree with him, he was "glowing." His father, whose eternal greeting was "You've lost some weight," now asked if he'd gained some. Briefly, Carl had questioned his parents' lucidity, wondered if he needed to take his mother back to her ophthalmologist, if his father's senility had gotten worse. But that night, when he entered his hotel bathroom and looked in the mirror, something he rarely did, he realized that his parents were right. There were no shadows under his eyes, his hair looked wavy and full, his eyes bright, alive. He wondered if it was just the warm Florida air or the fact that he was giving so much away that made him feel so light.

## WINTER BREAK 1985-86

On the night before Chanukah, the envelope that Carl handed to Hillel contained a good deal more money than usual, but Hillel read little significance into this fact. There never seemed to be much logic to the amount of cash Carl gave him; it seemed dependent only upon how much happened to be in his wallet at the time. On that December evening, Carl had given him a thousand dollars in new bills, and instead of telling Hillel to give it to Muley, he had just said, "Take it easy, but take it." Hillel had smiled and thanked Carl, not noticing the battered suitcases in his office.

The following evening, when Hillel returned to Bronzeville, he sensed an eerie, atypical calm. The lights were off in the foyer, and the only sign of life was in the editing suite, where Mel was eating a seitan and alfalfa sprout sandwich and still struggling with his first draft of *Son of a Preacher Man,* which had now stalled on page twelve. Mel was sitting in the dark, his face illuminated by the screen of his personal word processor, when he dropped his sandwich, swiveled around in his chair, and said *God damn,* Hillel had scared the living shit out of him; he thought that everyone else was gone. Gone where, Hillel asked. Mel flicked on a fluorescent overhead lamp and asked Hillel if he'd ever heard of holidays. Hillel said yeah, but Christmas was more than a week away. Mel said that in the entertainment business, nothing ever got done between the fifteenth of December and the fifteenth of January.

Hillel asked Mel if Carl had left for the holidays. Mel responded by asking Hillel if he looked like some sort of vassal who walked around fanning Carl, serving him mint juleps, saying "Yes, Bwana," and making his schedule; Carl was probably visiting his folks, and shouldn't Hillel be doing the same thing instead of fetching Carl hot toddies and shining his shoes? Sure, Hillel said, then asked if Mel needed anything. Mel said that he needed Hillel to stop asking him questions so he could finish his damn script. He reached into a drawer, pulled out a checkbook, and wrote out a check for $1,250. The final check from Pico Records would take a few days to clear, but Mel said that he would give Hillel his last payment in advance so that he would get out of his face. He handed over the check, said "Merry Fuckin' Kwanzaa," and asked Hillel if he had been hanging around him like Rochester just because he wanted to get paid. And Hillel, not wanting to admit that he just wanted the company and the conversation, and that the last thing he wanted was more money and free time, took the check and said yeah, he wanted the money. He asked if Mel would be here during the holidays. Not anymore he wouldn't, Mel said. He told Hillel to cash his check and buy himself some nappy, adding that if Hillel happened to pass a liquor store, his favorite brand was Glenfiddich.

Mel had been joking; nevertheless, the very next morning Hillel went straight to Bragno's Liquors and purchased a bottle of Scotch using his fake ID. But Bronzeville was completely dark when Hillel returned with the Scotch. Hillel placed the bottle in front of Mel's door and tried to avoid feeling the weight of the cash in his wallet, the check in his pocket. He saw the calendar of the next few weeks unfurling before him—Chanukah, Christmas, New Year's. The Art Institute dorms were already closed; students were home with their families, enjoying baked ham and roast beast. He thought of his family's Chanukah dinners—slippery latkes sliding around in an oily brown pan; brisket the color and texture of steel wool. He thought of how his mother would wash dishes while his father would recline in his living room TV chair, gather his children around him, and point two fingers at each of them, then ask them to tally up the *mitzvot* they had performed during the year, while he would write down all the mistakes they had made, after which he would issue a total score. If the *mitzvot* outweighed the mistakes, they would get a piece of Chanukah *gelt*. Every year, Hillel's sister and brother would receive their *gelt,* while Hillel would leave the room empty-handed, and even though his mother would slip him a piece of *gelt* afterward, he would only pretend to eat it, hurling it out the window when everyone else had gone to bed. In leaving his parents' house, Hillel had been happy that he would no longer have to endure Chanukah, but as he sat in Carl's empty office, he regretted the fact that he no longer had any option.

Hillel's first inclination was to take the bottle of Scotch from in front of Mel's door and guzzle as much of it as he could until he passed out or puked. But despite his penchant for cocaine, marijuana, and the occasional tab of acid, he had never had much of a taste for liquor. He didn't sip, he gulped, and when he gulped, the liquor burned his throat. To quell the temptation, he decided to occupy himself by cleaning Bronzeville Studios. He tried not to think of the rush that even a line or two of coke would bring, the rush that would send him flying onto the dance floor at Neo, talking and joking at warp speed, making girls laugh and getting guys hard. He tried to think of the aftermath, the waking up at four in the afternoon and wondering what day it was, the hours spent curled up on the refreshing cold tile of the bathroom floor, waking up only to puke, then wonder whether it was just the drugs that had made him feel so awful, looking up *vomiting* in the medical textbook that he had swiped from his brother Shimon and learning how many horrible things it could indicate before he would muster all his strength to get up, wipe off his face and shirt, and walk to the bus stop, take the bus to the el, ride it all the way to Belmont to find Denny O'Toole, if Denny wasn't home for the holidays; even dealers had families.

Hillel found a portable tape player in Mel's office and blasted the Larry Elliot demo as he mopped, vacuumed, buffed, and dusted, singing along on "Michelle, Ma Belle (*M'Appellait un Trou du Cul*)" and "(Don't Even Feel Like Touching Myself) No More." He swept the crumbs, dirt, and paper clips off of the floor, stuffed all the trash into big green bags. He scrubbed the toilets, polished the brass. He put on his roller skates and his helmet so he could move around the studios faster, crouched down low on his skates to inspect any stray bits of dirt he had missed. Many hours later, he sat down on the gleaming floor of the studio's empty lobby; by now, he had cleaned every last inch of Bronzeville Studios, and Mel's office was still dark. A full bottle of Scotch still stood in front of his door, Hillel still had more than two thousand dollars in his wallet, and he hadn't spent a cent of it yet.

O n Christmas Eve, Charlie Wasserstrom dropped Muley, Jill, and Fidel off at Muley's loft after a dinner at Mel and Deirdre's West Rogers Park house. During the drive south, Charlie had asked Jill and Muley how they would be spending the rest of their evening. And though Jill had hoped that she and Muley would finally have some time alone in his loft, Muley said that they would be going for a walk on 31st Street Beach to watch the comet—it was getting brighter now, he said, appearing for nearly four hours a night. Muley invited Charlie to join them, but Charlie said that he was sure that he would have other opportunities, and besides, Rachel would yell at him if he saw something so special without her. As Charlie drove off, Hillel was charging down the sidewalk, but when he saw Muley, Jill, and Fidel, he stopped, as if searching for someplace to run. He then walked toward them with a self-conscious calm to his gait, as if trying to pretend that he was sober. Jill glanced over at Muley; as he saw Hillel, he appeared strangely relieved.

In high school, whenever Muley had put an arm around Jill, she had often felt that his clutch was constricting her. But now, it often seemed as if Muley was drifting away. On most of her vacation nights in Chicago, Jill slept in Muley's bedroom, and she found it odd that lately, he would almost always wait for her to fall asleep before he came to bed, and no matter how early she woke, he'd already be up—sketching, taking pictures, walking the dog, or just staring out his window. In the summer, they had spent nearly every moment together, but lately, they were hardly ever alone. They were at Mel and Deirdre's house, at her father and Gail's, in the loft with Hillel next door knocking on their wall. "Enough chitterchatter; stick it in already!" Hillel would shout. Whenever Jill would ask Muley if something was wrong, he'd say no, everything was fine.

"Hey, boys and girls," Hillel said to Muley and Jill as they stood in front of the loft building. "Hey there, Cujo," Hillel said to Fidel. Muley asked if Hillel was on his way up. Hillel quickly asked why, were they hoping that the apartment would be empty so that they could make it their "private fuck pad?" If so, he could walk around the block a couple hundred times and they could stick a flag in a flowerpot in the window to let him know when they were done. No, Muley said, they were going to see the comet—did he want to join?

Jill shuddered. True, she now no longer felt as uneasy around Hillel as she had in Hebrew and high school when he was popular and made fun of her because, she assumed, she was ugly or not as smart as she wanted to be. She now viewed him as more pitiful than clever, now understood that when he made lewd jokes in her presence, told her about some girl who had "the most perfect, pouty blow-job lips," then asked Jill, "You know what a blow job is, right?" that her failure to find Hillel funny was not a result of her prudishness as much as of Hillel's hostility. Still, she wondered why Muley had to invite him along, especially to the beach, a place that was so sacred to her that she felt that walks by Lake Michigan should not be a right but a privilege granted only to those who had filled out detailed questionnaires.

Muley scampered upstairs to fetch his cameras; when he returned, camera bags over both shoulders, a tripod under his arm, Jill was touching Hillel's neck. Hillel had just asked Jill if he looked thinner than the last time she had seen him; he thought that he might have lost weight, but was too scared to weigh himself. He then asked if he looked bloated, asked if both sides of his neck looked the same, asked Jill to feel his lymph nodes. He took her hand and brought it to his neck, touched her fingers to one particular spot, and asked if she could feel anything round and raised. Jill saw Muley approaching and instinctively withdrew her hand. Muley smirked and asked if Hillel had been making people feel for his lymph nodes again.

As the three of them and Fidel walked east toward the beach, Jill—who had once been uncomfortable with public displays of affection—felt, in Hillel's presence, a need to demonstratively hold Muley's hand. And when Hillel remarked that he didn't know how he felt about all that "hand-holding stuff," she continued to hold hands with Muley. Hillel finally said that he was O.K. with the handholding, but if Muley and Jill started "doin' the wild thing," that was where he "checked out."

At the beach, Muley directed both Jill and Hillel to look up, and there it was. Halley's Comet shone above them, resembling the tail end of a firework. Muley set his tripod down upon a thin layer of ice that had collected on top of the sand; he reached into a camera bag, asking Jill didn't it look like fire from the mouth of a dragon, didn't she see how people would have thought that the comet was a harbinger of doom? Muley scanned the heavens with his cameras, one in each hand—the still camera and the Super 8 clicking and whirring away. But after a few minutes of watching the comet, Jill looked downward, to the ice and the water before her, to the Adler Planetarium, the Shedd Aquarium. She couldn't help but think that stargazing was a luxury for those who were not troubled by more pressing, earthly concerns. She asked Muley how long they would be standing here in the cold; she thought that she had already grasped the basic idea of the comet and didn't see what additional viewing might yield. But they had just gotten here, Muley said. Hillel said that he was bored, too, and told Jill that if she wanted to leave, he would walk her back to the loft, at which point Jill felt obligated to feign a greater interest in the comet.

Muley could not fathom Jill or Hillel's boredom, could not begin to understand why anyone would rather be anywhere else. Although he could physically hear and respond to Jill's questions about how long they would be standing there and could hear Hillel's remarks as he pointed out X-rated constellations—that wasn't really a sword in Orion's belt, he cackled—Muley barely registered them. He continued to photograph the comet, soon unaware of the passage of time or the meaning of any words spoken around him, at least not until he heard Jill shout, "Leave me the fuck alone."

Perhaps on a warmer night, perhaps at an earlier hour, perhaps if Muley hadn't been acting so distant of late, Jill could have tolerated more than the first dozen of what Hillel termed his "astronomically correct" jokes. But by the time that Hillel had said that he had had enough of the comet, then undid his belt, and said that it was time for everyone to get a good look at "the moon," Jill started to lose her patience. And when Hillel bent over and asked Jill if she wanted to see the "dark side of the moon," where he had a really big "telescope" that he always "waxed" to keep it from "waning," she had completely lost it. "Just give it a rest, Levy," she told him and walked away, but Hillel kept pursuing her.

Jill tried staring up at the sky, remembering how insignificant this conversation was to the vast universe above them, but soon Hillel's glinting eyes were no more than six inches from hers, so close that she could not keep his whole face in focus. Hillel suggested that the reason why she didn't want to study his moon carefully was because she was afraid of seeing all that manhood. He pranced about her, crouching low, hands on his knees as he swayed his hips back and forth, and sang "Hey, Big Spender."

"Leave me the fuck alone," Jill finally said. Muley stopped looking through the viewfinder of his movie camera, then turned to see Hillel take a step toward Jill and reach his hands out to tickle her. But as Hillel did so, Jill slapped him in the face. Hillel lost his balance and fell on the frozen sand.

What was going on, Muley asked. Hillel lay on his back; he saw the stars above him, Muley and Jill in between. "Oh, you asked for it," Hillel said to Jill. And when Jill began to grudgingly apologize and Muley offered Hillel his hand, Hillel jumped up on his own, pointed at Jill, and said, "Oh, you're gonna get it now, Leon Spinks. Just you wait." He beat his chest like a gorilla, then ran for the parking lot.

Muley looked skyward. He and Jill were alone on the beach now. The lake was icy and still, the darkest part of the night had passed, and the comet looked pale and diffuse against the blue-black sky; only a few more hours and it would fade into morning. Muley asked Jill to explain what had happened, and Jill recounted the dispute; it seemed trivial and petty to her when she described it. But when Muley asked Jill if she thought that Hillel would be O.K., she asked why Muley was so concerned about a drunken imbecile whose sole object had been to goad her.

Well, Muley said, Hillel had problems, his family wasn't talking to him, he didn't have any friends, he did too many drugs. Jill said that wasn't much of a surprise, and that the world was filled with countless lost souls in need of compassion; why waste it on people who didn't deserve it? Muley could see Jill steeling herself for an argument, her gaze intense, her face flushed by more than just the cold air. And he knew too that the argument, if they had it, wouldn't only be about Hillel—they would have to discuss why he now always felt himself pulling away from her, why whenever they touched, his mind always moved toward his art, the art that he was always most happy to see destroyed. Muley told Jill that she was right about Hillel, and apologized, while Jill felt just a bit deflated, for what frustrated her most about Muley was that he seemed so willing to concede her point of view. Her sensation of victory was hollow, like winning a match by forfeit.

They didn't speak much for the next few hours. Jill looked for shells and colored glass on the sand; Muley photographed the comet until it had disappeared from the sky. Jill had hoped that Hillel would have had ample time to clear out his belongings from the loft or fall asleep in a drug-induced haze, so that she and Muley would be able to spend the day alone. She didn't want any more of Hillel's abuse, didn't want any apologies either, just wanted him to be gone. But Hillel had been hard at work from the moment he had returned to the loft, and was now eagerly awaiting Jill and Muley's arrival.

Hillel was standing in front of a sketchpad upon which he had drawn a caricature of Jill. Working in a style rich with Asian motifs, he had depicted her as a pig-faced kung fu warrior, clad in a white jumpsuit and a white headband, dropkicking a line of grimacing penis people, while off to one side of the frame, a mule in an army jacket focused his camera on a school of crisscrossing spermatozoa shooting toward the full moon on which he had drawn Muley's face. He had covered his sketchpad with a bath towel, turned off the lights, then crouched down by the light switch. When Jill and Muley entered, Hillel flicked the lights back on, ripped the towel off the canvas, and shouted "Ta-da!" He doubled over with affected glee, slapped his thighs, then laughed louder when no one else did.

Jill, relieved that the punishment Hillel had devised consisted only of this immature artwork, smiled. "Very nice," she said, then rolled her eyes and walked to the bathroom to brush her teeth, wondering when to tell Muley that she would be spending the rest of her nights on North Shore Avenue. As Jill closed the bathroom door, Muley took one more look at the painting. Hillel grinned at him, raised his eyebrows, furrowed his brow, then pretended to stroke a pantomime beard. Muley told Hillel to pack his belongings and get out.

"Hey, easy there, slugger," Hillel said, but Muley shook his head. "Get out," he repeated. Hillel asked Muley why he was so sensitive about a cartoon; even "Kung Fu Mistress Wasserstrom" had a sense of humor about it. Well, Muley said, maybe he and Jill had different senses of humor. "Jeez, man," Hillel said—Muley had to lighten up; everything wasn't so serious. It was late, Hillel said, why didn't they just go to sleep, and when they woke up, he'd make latkes and applesauce for everyone. Now were they cool, he asked.

No, Muley said, they weren't cool. He had told Hillel to leave. "Now leave," he said as Jill exited the bathroom.

Oh, Hillel said, taking in the scene, he understood, now it was two against one; this was a conspiracy: "Little Leon Spinks" wanted him to leave so that they could have their own "private fuck pad." Muley could pretend that his stance was all about morality and being "Mr. Chivalrous Jesus Boy," but they all knew that Muley just wanted a place to "be alone with his bitch." Muley didn't care that it was zero degrees outside and that he had no place to stay; he didn't care that he was feeling feverish and that his glands felt swollen.

"Take your picture with you," Muley said, and walked toward his bedroom. As he passed Jill, he told her that Hillel was leaving.

Jill watched Hillel fetch a suitcase and start hurling his clothes into it. She began to ask him what had happened, but he said that she already knew; she had started this whole argument, and had gone into the bathroom to let her boyfriend do her dirty work. Muley had told him to go? Jill asked. Oh, what was this, Hillel wanted to know—good cop, bad cop? Jill walked into Muley's bedroom. He was lying shirtless on his bed, one hand beneath his head as he looked up at the glow-in-the-dark stars on his ceiling. What was wrong with Hillel's drawing, Jill asked him—of course it was offensive, but that's what Hillel had been doing ever since *aleph*. This one was different, Muley said—he told her to look at the sky.

But when Jill tried to take another look at the painting, Hillel was already standing before it in his winter coat and a knit navy blue hat. He had a piece of charcoal in his hand and was furiously drawing over the Muley-faced moon and the smiling, crisscrossed sperm shooting toward it. Why was he changing the sky, Jill asked—Muley had told her to look at it. Hillel stammered, then asked what stories Muley had been telling her. "Here," he said as he finished scribbling, then drew a smiling penis signature. "It's yours. Take it, you've earned it." He whipped his charcoal stick at the wall, picked up a suitcase, another case filled with drawings and sketchpads, his roller skates and his crash helmet, and walked out.

When Jill returned to Muley's bedroom, he was no longer in bed. He was looking out the window at the bluish haze that enveloped the south side, gazing down at a city that, at this hour, seemed entirely abandoned. Salt had left white and gray streaks upon the street. The windows in the New Michigan Hotel, where lately it had been rumored that Al Capone had left a vault filled with ill-gotten riches, were boarded up. The gates in front of the Soul Queen restaurant were locked, and to the immediate west, on the Dan Ryan Expressway, only an occasional truck rumbled by, bound for Indiana. Muley could see the black tarpaper roof of Bronzeville Studios.

Muley did not turn around when Jill entered the room and said that Hillel had left. As he watched Hillel on the sidewalk below walking south weighed down by bags, he wondered whether he had acted too harshly by telling him to leave, whether the fact that Hillel had concealed the words "Slappit Came Here" in the squiggles and crisscrosses of spermatozoa sailing toward a moon with Muley's face was sufficient offense to send Hillel onto the streets. He briefly considered calling down to Hillel, asking him to come back, but it was already too late, for he saw Hillel crossing Cermak. Jill was about to once again ask Muley what was wrong, but when she saw that he was staring down toward Bronzeville Studios, where she knew that his father lived and worked, she stopped, and then she put an arm around Muley's waist.

B y the time that he had reached Cermak Road, Hillel had already decided to embark upon a performance art project of sorts. In his application to the Art Institute, he had written that he wanted his work to look as if Jackson Pollock had retched on it, René Magritte had peed, and Andy Warhol had beat off. Hillel would approach his new project with the same intensity and humor, but in this case, the canvas would be his body. He had more than two thousand dollars, and before second semester began, he wanted to spend it all on hedonistic pursuits, every moment of which he would document in his second-semester paintings.

He dropped his bags in the Bronzeville lobby; this would be his base of operations. The idea was not to indulge all vices at once; he would be methodical, scientific. He would build up his stamina and tolerance, test his limits, push just to the very edge, look out over the precipice, and see what was there before pulling back. He would plot everything out on a calendar, budget his expenses, schedule his consumption of food, fluids, and hallucinogens, enumerate the sex acts in which he would attempt to engage. At the end of it all, he would return to class with a fresh set of ideas, and continue working odd jobs for Carl.

Alas, it was not long before Hillel strayed from his plan. The next night, in the front seat of a parked Oldsmobile at Montrose Beach, he paid a hustler twenty-five bucks for a handjob, but couldn't resist paying an extra fifteen dollars for a blow. Shopping at Gill's Liquors for a jug of beer, he learned that it was "Buy One, Get One Free" Day. When he met Denny O'Toole and asked to buy coke and a few tabs of LSD, Denny shook Hillel's hand, said it was good to see someone from the old 'hood, and asked if he wanted to do some lines for free.

Soon, Hillel was not gradually building his tolerance, but trying to reach a peak as quickly as possible to determine how long he could maintain it. For the first days, he felt a euphoric excitement and freedom, so much so that he had the sensation that he had inhaled a lifetime supply of laughing gas. He was looser when he was high, funnier, too. He lost that cynical edge that had caused his former best friend, Moshe Cardash, to tell him that he was "like chili dip" and that he could only have a little bit of him at a time. Now when Hillel walked through Neo, he felt everyone's eyes lock on to his; when he asked people to dance, they nearly always said yes, and when he said that he was throwing a New Year's Eve party at Bronzeville Studios, they said that they would be there.

Hillel had always been good at organizing parties, and he took steps to ensure that this one would be successful; he invited total strangers—deliverymen at Chinatown restaurants, checkout clerks at liquor stores, doctors, patients, and their families whom he had met in the DuSable Hospital parking lot. He left messages on the home answering machines of classmates with whom he had never spoken. He told them that there would be free liquor, munchies, and a "roll-your-own-joint buffet."

The only problem with the New Year's party was that it passed too quickly and too many people came. Not that there wasn't sufficient room in Bronzeville Studios. The lobby and reception area accommodated not only deejay Killah-G's turntables, strobe lights, and bubble machines, but more than seventy-five lavishly clad dancers, swaying and grinding as Hillel waltzed with a broomstick and led falsetto sing-alongs to "Cool It Now" and "Material Girl." There was intense conversation in the editing suites, vigorous foreplay atop Carl's desk, a twenty-minute wait outside the bathroom for lines of coke that Hillel had neatly arranged on slabs of mirrored glass laid atop the sinks. And Hillel—his mind and body overstimulated beyond reason—could not decide where to spend his time. Whenever he danced with one person, he would think that he should be dancing with another. Each time he talked to one group, he wondered if a more interesting conversation was taking place elsewhere. When he was drinking, he would think that he should be dancing, when he was dancing, he would think that he should be making out, and when he was making out, he would think that he should be making out with someone else. Even when he was standing with his pants around his ankles, two models sniffing coke off his *schwantz,* Hillel still wondered if he should be doing something even more hedonistic. At the break of dawn, Hillel couldn't decide which guest's postparty offer to accept—a walk to Promontory Point, breakfast at the Golden Apple, stoned foosball at Waveland Bowl. He said yes to every invitation, but arrived after each event was over.

When Hillel returned to Bronzeville Studios, he felt woozy, and cleared a space amid the beer bottles and the trash on the floor. He slept, using a brown leather couch cushion as a pillow. Which was where he spent the next three nights, subsisting on party remnants—beer and joints, snack foods and cigarettes. And soon, the mixture of alcohol, tortilla chips, Ho Hos, and three-day-old caviar began to blend in his stomach, swirling, churning, until Hillel could feel all of it rising slowly yet insistently, millimeter by millimeter, pinching his groin, rising into his gut, his chest, then his throat, and he would heave so hard that he would seem to be puking not just the contents of his stomach but his entire body as well.

Then came the medical textbook. Then came the chills, the fevers, and the fears. Then came the hour-long studies of the imperfections of his body. Then came the night sweats that left Hillel-shaped stains on the bathroom floor. Then came the walk to the YMCA, where he stood on a scale and wondered how he had lost so much weight. Then came the frightening questions: What was the difference between a lesion and a skin tag, between a wart and a blastoma? Why was he so skinny, why was he so pale? His mind swung back and forth between panic and self-mockery; he'd draw cartoons about his panicked state of mind to gain some feeling of control, then fear that his cartoons were prophetic. He'd wonder what the chances were that he had AIDS and figure them to be 50-50. His last tab of acid gave no respite as he cowered in the corner of Carl's office and fended off menacing orange dinosaurs wearing chartreuse yarmulkes.

Finally, he came to realize that there was no place for him to go other than home, and he vaguely relished the idea of implicating his family, his father in particular, in his current predicament. Although he had spent years keeping his family ignorant of the seedier aspects of his life—never mind that his brother Shimon had long made it a point to assert at the Levy dinner table that bisexuals were "people who couldn't make up their minds"—he now liked the idea of disclosing every aspect of his existence to his father.

Still, he could barely stay awake as he rode the A train north, beads of sweat forming at his temples, then sliding down his cheeks as the train curved through Lincoln Park, Lakeview, and Uptown. He got off at Morse Avenue, both hands clutching the railing to navigate the stairway down to the sidewalk. No part of his body seemed to experience the correct temperature—the forehead hot but the cheeks cold, the palms sweaty, the fingers numb, the toes icy and damp. He rode the Lunt bus west with his eyes closed, his head against the window. He bit the inside of his lip so hard that he tasted blood as he saw Indian Boundary Park approaching, the park where he'd gone to summer camp, where only Bibi Eisenstaedt would hold hands with him.

Once he'd struggled out of the bus at the corner of Lunt and California with his suitcase and artbooks, Hillel could barely keep his balance. He was only three blocks from home and yet he felt that he would never make it, that he would collapse face-first in the snow, that he would heave forth everything inside him, his blood, his organs, his bones; all that would be left would be the flimsy, pale, translucent shell of Hillel Levy frozen on the front lawn of 2740 W. Coyle Avenue. In his mind, he heard his mother wailing, saw the eyes of his sister, his brother, his father. But once he reached California, he stopped. The thought of seeing his triumphant father was now more than he could stomach. And instead of walking home, he stopped across the street from the Ezras Israel Synagogue. He waited for the Lunt bus to take him back east to the Morse el station, where he would board a southbound train that would take him all the way back to Bronzeville Studios.

After three weeks in Florida, Carl Slappit Silverman returned to Chicago. His skin was as pale as always, but to him, it felt warm and tan; and he was wearing a white golf shirt and white jeans, which did make his arms look just a wee bit darker than when he had departed. The visit to his parents had not been fraught with the usual anxiety. He had not had to make any late-night calls to their physicians; there had been no need to reassure his mother that it was unlikely that her octogenarian husband was having an affair. He had not had to warn his father to refrain from telling his wife that her *tuchus* was too big, to inform him that in many cultures, a sizeable posterior was a badge of pride. Now his parents actually seemed to get along—they watched movies together in the Bridlewood video lounge, took walks around the fountains and the reflecting pond outside, went *spaziering* in town. And even if Mendel Silverman's new acquiescence resulted in part from his memory loss, still their time together was more pleasant.

When Carl arrived in the Bronzeville lobby, a pungent stench was in the air, but he did not immediately notice anything amiss. He found squalor comfortingly familiar, for it was his natural state. It never took more than a few minutes of sorting through old newspaper clippings, fast-food wrappers, and demo cassettes to locate a contract that he had forgotten to sign; in an alphabetized file drawer, he could never track it down. Still, the chairs, couches, and tables were in different places than he had remembered, a carpet of beer bottles was on the floor, along with a row of kegs that he had initially mistaken for new furniture.

As Carl mounted the curved staircase en route to his office, the stench became stronger, the disorder more apparent. There were bottles, cups, paper plates, slips of paper with pornographic cartoons scribbled on them. He tried to avoid stepping on trash, but the detritus only mounted as he approached his office door. Now he could hear music, primal groaning, an insistent banging of drums and guitars, and a gruff voice singing, "She wants a divorce, yeah, a divorce, I said Hannah wants a divorce, oh yeah."

When he opened the office door, Carl saw that his desk was covered with Baggies, cigarette stubs, ash. Again, unusual, for Carl did not smoke; he had always thrived on the sharp edge that nicotine seemed only to dull. In a corner of the room, wedged between the radiator and a bookcase filled with record albums, lay a lump of white bedsheets, an army sleeping bag, and a threadbare Indian blanket with cigarette holes in it. The lump was moving. Carl studied the lump for a moment before removing a fistful of sheets, thus revealing a crouched Hillel Levy clad in a paint-splattered white T-shirt and boxer shorts.

Even with the covers gone, Hillel did not move. He remained with his arms around his knees. His bare feet were slender, pale; his teeth chattered. Carl stood over the young man, puzzled, as if in the presence of an animal he had accidentally hit with his car; he recognized him vaguely, but couldn't call his name to mind. He gently dropped the bedcovers over Hillel's knees. Hillel did not look up; his fingers, charcoal-black and pastel-pink, clutched the blankets tightly as he softly sang Larry Elliot lyrics to himself. Carl bent down to Hillel and asked if he wouldn't mind singing more quietly or in a different room. But before he had completed the sentence, Hillel stood and looked up at Carl with red eyes and pale, creased cheeks, then threw his arms around him and buried his face in Carl's shoulder.

Instinctively, Carl recoiled. He only liked when black people hugged him or clapped him on the shoulder. With pale Hillel's arms around him, Carl felt instantly uneasy. He had the sensation of standing in quicksand; if he did not move, Hillel remained stationary. But if he tried to pivot left or right, Hillel's clutch became tighter, his breaths quicker. The situation seemed to call for Carl to say or do something comforting, but the appropriate words sounded false, the appropriate gestures more so. Dimly, Carl remembered something that his mother would say to quiet him when he'd been a child. "Sha," she would tell him, "*sha,*" and then she would hold him close and pat him on the back. Turning his head to one side and breathing through his mouth, Carl held Hillel closer to him, one hand patting his back. "Sha," he told him, "*sha.*" And at that *sha,* the tears flowed freely from Hillel's eyes, and Carl could feel Hillel's chest against his own. Hillel said that he was sorry, said that what Carl was doing felt good; then he spilled forth all the stories of the past week, all his fevers, all his chills, all the weight he had lost, and he started crying even more. "Sha," Carl kept telling Hillel in a monotone. "*Sha sha sha.*"

After he had showered and put on fresh clothes, Hillel stood in Carl's office. He said that he felt better, but he still looked pale and gaunt and his hands were quivering. He assured Carl that he would take care of the mess, but Carl mumbled that Hillel didn't need to worry; he'd pay a junkie from the projects fifty bucks to clean up. Besides, they didn't have much time; they had to see three different doctors and he didn't want to kill the whole day at the hospital.

At the mention of doctors, Hillel grew paler; again he could feel perspiration on his forehead, under his arms. Hillel said that he didn't see any need for doctors. He was feeling better now; he had probably just had a bad reaction to some spoiled caviar, cocaine, and Fritos. Carl wasn't paying close enough attention to know or care whether Hillel was lying or not. He said that they needed to go to the hospital now, maybe they could get in early; he figured that Hillel had something serious, maybe AIDS. Get your coat, he said, it was time to "book."

As they walked west on Cermak, Carl felt no great affection for the young man. He saw his own actions as merely practical responses to a manageable crisis. In the entertainment industry, intimate knowledge of first-aid techniques and an ability to recognize the signs of overdose were every bit as useful as a patience for the small print of contracts. He knew how to bully nurses to get better rooms for his artists, knew just enough about medicine to intimidate doctors into being more thorough.

As a phlebotomist drew Hillel's blood, as Hillel was X-rayed, as an internist examined Hillel's ears, his nose, his throat, took his temperature, weighed his testicles, instructed him to fill a urinalysis cup and to present a stool sample, procedures that all seemed so harrowing that Hillel could not even joke about them, Carl followed the patient from to room, asking questions of the medical staff: Wasn't a TB test part of the standard checkup? How about a rectal exam? Wasn't she going to use gloves? Here, why didn't he hand the doctor a pair? At one point, a nurse asked Carl who he was, Hillel's father? Hillel looked hopeful when the question was posed, but Carl shook his head. "He's my brother, man," Carl said. "How old do you think I is?"

Over the course of the day, Hillel would prop himself up on examining tables in his hospital gown and his socks and glimpse Carl engaged in intense, hushed discussions with doctors and nurses, but he could never hear enough to understand what was being said, and though at one point he thought that he saw Carl's lips form the word *terminal,* he began to feel as if he were ceding control of his fate to others; it was up to them to save him or not. He answered questions quietly, succinctly, asked none of his own. He didn't look directly at the doctors; he gazed out the window at the branches of an oak tree. He listened to the sounds but not the meanings of words; they seemed to describe the condition of a stranger. When Dr. Mitchum told Carl and Hillel to return the following Monday so that they could discuss the test results, it took Hillel a moment to figure out whose test results they would be discussing.

The days in which Hillel awaited those results, swallowing aspirins and antibiotics to bring down his fever, he slept in Carl's bedroom while Carl slept on the couch in his office. For Carl, Hillel's care became just another chore, and he approached it with as much passion and distance as he had ever approached any aspect of his business. During these days, Carl ate pastrami sandwiches, coleslaw, and marble halvah. But he served Hillel toast, eggs, and chicken soup. At night, Carl would check in on Hillel, then read aloud to him from his favorite books: *Soul on Ice, Beneath the Underdog, The Spook Who Sat by the Door.* Carl would turn off Hillel's night-light, and Hillel would ask Carl to sing him a Larry Elliot song, but that's where Carl would draw the line.

Despite the fact that the antibiotics turned Hillel's stomach, he soon felt his appetite improve. He ate his soup and his rainbow sherbet. And though he still felt weak, his fever went down and he no longer woke up in pools of sweat. On the night before he was to return to the hospital, he even began to draw again, a series of wild, Rabelaisian panels about his descent into illness, in which he depicted himself as a tiny Fay Wray and Carl Silverman as King Kong delivering him to a hospital staffed by baboons.

On the drive back to the hospital, Carl asked Hillel whether his folks were still alive and when Hillel said yes, he asked when he had last spoken to them. Hillel said that he didn't think that it mattered much; his father didn't want to hear from him. Carl said he doubted that; he was sure that Hillel's old man got angry sometimes, but deep down, what every old man wanted more than anything was to have his family around him, his old lady on one side, his young 'uns on the other. Hillel told Carl that he didn't know his old man.

This time at the hospital, Dr. Mitchum, exhausted by Carl's behavior at Hillel's last visit, had taken the day off, and Carl's assurances to her colleague, Dr. Sheldon Silver, that he was Hillel's brother weren't sufficient to allow him into the examination rooms. He stood in the waiting room while Hillel met with Silver alone. And when Carl saw Hillel's knees shake as he walked down a long white hallway lit by fluorescents, he thought that it would have been better if he could have gone in Hillel's place, not because he cared so much about Hillel, not because he didn't value his own life, but simply because he thought that he was better equipped to handle such matters.

Nevertheless, Carl couldn't stand in one place. He tried watching the episode of *All My Children* upon which everyone else in the waiting room seemed to be focusing, but couldn't bear it; he didn't understand how everyone in the room, even the blacks, could be interested in these pampered whiteys. How come they never made soap operas about *bruthas* downtown, he asked a black nurse who told him to "hush up or leave." He introduced himself to strangers and commiserated with them as they waited for loved ones—"Keep the faith, my *brutha,*" he would say. "Be strong, *sistuh.*" Every five minutes or so, he would collar a doctor or nurse, slap the desk of a receptionist and ask what the holdup was. "Don't crowd me, Grandma," he said to an elderly lady in the waiting room who asked if he had *spilkes,* "y'all remember that."

As Carl paced the hospital floors, he contemplated two immediate futures— one in which Hillel would be diagnosed with a fatal illness, and one in which Hillel would be issued a clean bill of health. Although the initial scenario would be more complicated, dealing with it would only entail reorganizing his schedule to allow for an hour or two of daily soup-making plus bedtime readings of radical black manifestos. And yet, as he saw Hillel walking down a hallway toward him, talking to Dr. Sheldon Silver, Carl felt a sudden increase in the intensity of his heartbeat. He tried to find meaning in the speed at which Hillel and the doctor were walking, the pitch at which they were speaking. He presumed that they were discussing additional tests; doctors never gave concrete answers—to do so would run counter to their profit motive.

In reality, Hillel and Dr. Silver weren't discussing anything of the sort. Hillel was telling Catskills doctor jokes ("The patient died, but the surgery went great"). When the two of them reached Carl, Dr. Silver greeted him as "Mr. Levy," and told him that his "partner" would be O.K.; every test had come up negative. Carl breathed a deep sigh of relief. Man, that was "on time," he said. And, Hillel added with a smile, Dr. Silver had given him some sound advice, most notably that he was unlikely to get AIDS from someone snorting cocaine off his cock. However, Silver added, he did think that Hillel should "see someone fairly regularly," and wrote down the names of three psychologists. He said that Hillel seemed to have an unusually open attitude toward psychotherapy for someone his age. Hillel said that it sounded fun—he could spend an hour every week telling lurid stories about his life, and the doctor wouldn't tell his dad about it.

Over lunch at Manny's Deli, Hillel told Carl that he felt ready to start his therapy and his second semester at the Art Institute; all the experiences of the past weeks would work their way into the most intense paintings he had ever created, and he could work for Carl on weekends and on days when he didn't have class. But as Carl sipped a black cherry soda, Hillel's words made no impact, not even when Hillel promised to live his life in a "cleaner, more Orthodox" manner. Carl had already moved on; the brief period of his life in which he had dedicated himself to improving Hillel's health was over. He was glad that the young man was healthy, mostly because it cleared up his schedule. Briefly, he had felt what it would be like to be a parent; he couldn't imagine doing it for real—feeling responsible for someone all the damn time. He told Hillel that he was welcome to crash out in his crib as long as he needed to, and he'd give him bread for food and the shrink, if it didn't cost too much, but he couldn't promise much steady work.

Hillel immediately felt nauseated. He could now see all too clearly that Carl's efforts on his behalf had nothing to do with him personally, that he would have done the same for any stranger; he felt like a fool. For, even when Hillel had felt deathly ill, he had maintained some of his strength by imagining a future in which Carl would continue to be part of his life; that he would await Carl's return from business trips, tidy up his office when he was away, design his stationery, remodel his studios, take the place of Muley, who had turned his back on his father. Carl might even groom him to take over Bronzeville Studios, just as Boaz Levy had once said that Hillel, his brother, and his sister could each get their very own Nagilah Israel restaurant, and Hillel had laughed until his sides hurt and said that he wouldn't run any crap-ass restaurant; he was going to be a gigolo.

Hillel now felt disappointed that he was healthy, for at least when he'd been sick, his existence had mattered. He contemplated telling Carl to drive back to the hospital; he was sure that the doctors had missed something. But after that thought had passed, Hillel wanted only to finish his meal, drive back, gather his belongings, and leave as quickly as possible. In Carl's car, Hillel kept telling Carl to drive faster, that he drove "like a girl," and why did they have to listen to those same blues and jazz tapes; that music all sounded the freaking same. The second after Carl pulled up in front of Bronzeville, Hillel jumped out of the car and walked briskly to the front door; it was already half open, and Hillel was surprised to find that someone was waiting inside.

That same Monday, the day after the Chicago Bears defeated the New England Patriots to win the Super Bowl and the city erupted into euphoria, the day before the space shuttle *Challenger* would explode shortly after takeoff, killing all crew members aboard, that same Monday when Halley's Comet was now passing too close to the sun and would not be visible again until February, the opening event of Muley's art exhibition ("*Ephemeral!* The Art of Muley Scott Wills") was held outside the Adler Planetarium, followed by a reception at Larmer Galleries.

The generators were already chugging away when Muley and Calliope emerged from her white Volkswagen Vanagon (ART CHICK was painted on the side in magenta) into the cold, still planetarium parking lot. Muley wore a thin black suit, a white shirt, and a skinny black tie loosened at the neck; Calliope wore a black cocktail dress and unlaced black shit-kickers. Muley unloaded a movie projector and a film canister and carried them toward the screens, which were set up like great white dominoes on the sloped planetarium lawn. Illuminated by klieg lights, there were a dozen screens in all, one behind the other, leading down to the frozen docks. Before them were tiers of bleachers, a few people sitting in them already—Charlie and Gail, Mel and Deirdre, Muley's professors and classmates from the Art Institute.

Alongside the generators powering the klieg lights, an electrical cord ran over the grass leading to a projector stand and a creaky old spotlight. From each screen, a length of string led to one of a dozen giant spools that were lined up beside the projectors. Red lights were blinking on and off on the Meigs Field runway. As the crowd swelled to nearly one hundred, Muley inspected the projector, the spools, and the screens, while Calliope distributed business cards and directions to her gallery for the postshow wine reception.

At precisely 7 P.M., Muley stood by a spinning weathercock. The screens fluttered; the string on the spools grew taut, and Muley loaded a reel of film onto the projector. He was about to switch off the klieg lights and turn the dial on the projector to FORWARD when Calliope advised him to wait for stragglers. But Muley said no, the wind was just right—they only had a few minutes before the next plane would take off from Meigs, and the weathercock was really twirling now; he was worried that the screens might blow down. He asked Calliope to take her place behind the spotlight. He extinguished the lights, turned the projector dial, lit a fuse, then knelt behind the spools.

A tube of light burst from the projector onto a screen, first white light, then the countdown from 10, but when the number onscreen changed from 2 to 1, the screen did not fade to black; instead, it erupted in a shock of bluish-white flame and the entire screen was reduced instantly to ash, save for the metal frame around it. Muley pulled the string from the first spool, and the metal frame attached to it tumbled to the grass. The film kept rolling. On the second screen, a cartoon lion appeared, roaring inside a ring that caught fire. Muley pulled the string from the second spool; the frame and ring of fire tumbled downward. An image of the night sky was projected on the third screen. Stars rotated, at first imperceptibly, then faster. Halley's Comet appeared at the left side of the screen, sliced across it, and the screen split in half before flashing, then exploding to reveal the next screen. The comet grew larger; it sliced one screen diagonally from left to right, the next from right to left, then top to bottom, then zigzags, the screens exploding one by one. On each successive screen, Muley's stars took on more discernible shapes—dragons, archers, animals. The comet continued to grow, burning through screen after screen, one tumbling down after the other, until the final image: the blazing comet occupied nearly two-thirds of the last screen; it moved from left to right in superslow motion.

The wind was gathering strength, ruffling the image of the comet. The weathercock turned faster; it whirred as it whipped around. The black sky that surrounded the comet burned slowly; small sections of it fell away and swirled in the projector light like black snow until all that was left was the comet blazing in the center of the screen. Then the wind got hold of what remained of the screen and Muley lifted the last spool. Calliope turned on the spotlight and pivoted, shining it onto this comet-shaped screen, which fluttered just a few feet above the ground. Muley ran with the spool, letting the wind grab the comet-screen like a kite as it rose above the bleachers and the planetarium. He ran away from the docks and the generators, away from the spotlight, which followed the kite as it rose; soon, the kite appeared to be no bigger than the moon, then no bigger than a star. When there was no string left on the spool and Calliope had shut off the spotlight, Muley stopped running. He held on to the string and dropped the spool to the ground. He stood alone before the black lake with his arm above his head, the wind in his face, and the scent of smoldering flame in his nostrils. He felt the strong resistance of the kite; even though he could no longer see it, he could still feel it above him, darting left, then right, swooping down before leaping up higher. And then he let it go.

At the postshow reception, a slowly rotating film projector cast images of stars and planets onto the walls and the faces of the guests, who sipped wine, sampled Camembert, and viewed Muley's sketches, storyboards, and jars of ash. Muley walked slowly through Calliope's gallery, occasionally fielding questions from the attendees: Gail, who wanted to know how Muley expected to make a living from this; an art critic from the *Chicago Reader,* who asked for Muley's opinion of the Fluxus movement; Mel, who wondered aloud what all this shit was supposed to mean. Every so often, Calliope would track Muley down and blurt out that a curator wanted to offer him a commission, or that two men were bidding for ash jars. But Muley sensed that the work was no longer his, that everyone in the gallery felt a greater connection to it than he did. The art had been the film and the kite, but they no longer existed. Muley was just getting ready to walk out the door to contemplate his next project when he saw Calliope walking briskly toward him again with her broad, heavy, flat-footed, combat-boot stride. She made a telephone with her little finger and thumb, then pointed to her office in the back of the gallery; she said that there was a call for him.

Muley walked into Calliope's tiny office and picked up the phone. With the gallery still noisy and full, it was difficult for Muley to clearly identify the voice on the other end, but there was only one simple message that the other party wanted to convey: he was calling from DuSable Hospital; Carl Silverman had been shot. But when Muley asked who was calling, was this Hillel, and was this a joke, the line went dead.

Muley stood in the office holding the telephone receiver, even as the low, sustained dial tone resolved itself into an insistent, quacking busy signal. He leaned against the desk, held the receiver against his chest, and looked out upon the stark white gallery and the speckled black lobby beyond it. After standing and staring blankly into space for nearly a quarter of an hour, trying to make sense of what he had just heard, he called DuSable Hospital, where he had been born some twenty years earlier. He asked if the hospital had any record of a patient by the name of Carl Silverman. And moments later, when he learned that his birth father had been admitted to the emergency room, he asked about the man's condition. The attendant asked if Muley was related to Mr. Silverman. Muley began to say yes, but stopped. No, he said, he wasn't.

C arl Slappit Silverman, who had often thought of his legacy, might have appreciated the romance of being shot dead in a moment of heroism, saving the life of a young man with no thought of personal gain. But there was nothing so gratifyingly simple about the way that Carl wound up in the DuSable Hospital emergency room with two bullet wounds, one to the skull, one to the chest. After Hillel had gotten out of his car, Carl had followed him into Bronzeville Studios. He turned on the lobby lights and saw a man wearing a ski mask, pointing a gun at Hillel. Carl said, "Hey, brother," and told the gunman that there was no reason to "mess," because everything was "righteous." Carl walked toward the man, two shots rang out, Carl fell, the gunman ran, and Hillel rushed to Carl's side. Before Carl closed his eyes, his last word was *motherfucker.*

And when Carl said "Motherfucker," he spoke neither in anger nor in pain. His tone was that of an old prospector who had hit gold when he had no more use for it. "So this is it," he seemed to be saying, "so this is what it's like—mother*fucker.*" He had dreamt often of his own demise. And yet, he had thought that it would come differently—perhaps after one fried shrimp too many. He had been so convinced that his death would, on some level, be self-willed that he had never considered a violent end, had rarely bothered locking his doors. The worse the neighborhood, the safer he felt; what would anyone ever want from him save for his money, and he was now all too happy to give it away.

There would have been a poetic beauty to that sort of death for Carl Silverman—like something out of a western, a jazz opera, or a Mel Coleman script—but the following morning when Muley entered the hospital, Carl, who had survived surgery but had lapsed into a coma, was still breathing with the aid of a life-support system. And when Muley saw his father lying flat, pale feet peeking out from under a thin white sheet and a sea-green blanket, IV in his arm, tube in his mouth, Muley had trouble believing that this shell of a human being could have ever caused his mother so much pain. He watched the chest rise and fall under the sheet, and listened to the sounds of labored breathing, the whirring and humming of machines, disembodied voices over intercoms.

A bouquet of irises and daffodils in a white ceramic vase stood on Carl's bedside table; outside the window, a tall, gnarled oak tree cast a crisscross of shadows upon the floor and the wall. Muley studied the slim, sheeted body, the gray, black, white, and red beard, the gray hair wrapped by bandages, the creased, sallow cheeks, the hairy wrists, and the thin, yellowed fingers. He tried to recognize anything of himself, tried to make sense of any of the emotions that this man had once engendered—his mother's anguish, his own numb indifference. He felt a need to apologize, but had no idea for what or to whom.

Muley stood over his father and made a move as if to touch the man's hand, but stopped when Hillel entered the room, carrying a bouquet of daisies. His face was pale, he hadn't shaved, and he was wearing Carl's clothes—a faded denim jacket, loose-fitting jeans, scuffed brown shoes. Hillel took the flowers in the vase beside the bed, tossed them into the trash, replaced them with the new bouquet, then offered his hand to Muley. "So," he said, "you finally made it."

As Hillel spoke, his tone was businesslike and perfunctory, as if he were relaying information out of obligation rather than desire. He recounted the previous evening's incidents, making only fleeting eye contact with Muley. He played up Carl's heroism and his own unworthiness, and made a point of detailing all that he had done since the shooting—the newspaper interviews, the police questionings, the call to Carl's parents—and all that was left to do: the cleanup, the bookkeeping, the preparations for Carl's eventual return. Muley told Hillel that he was on his way out. "You're leaving already?" Hillel asked.

Muley took the stairs down to the first floor, then walked briskly through the lobby, where a group of doctors and hospital staff members were gathered watching a television screen. Muley looked up at the TV and saw an image of the space shuttle *Challenger*. White smoke billowed out from under the body of the ship, and for a brief moment, Muley forgot where he was, and what had happened. He felt a sudden jolt of joy, an ever-so-brief sense of endless possibility. And then he watched the shuttle as it began to rise.

That night, long past visiting hours, Muley returned to DuSable Hospital. He was carrying his sound recorder and his movie camera, but he never removed the lens cap. He just sat in Carl's dark room in a chair beside the bed. He inhaled the sharp scent of cleanser, heard the occasional roll of gurneys along the hospital floor, every so often the piercing voice of a woman down the hall, crying for a nurse, all of the sounds underscored by Carl's mechanical breathing—in then out, in then out. The room was thick with Carl's breaths, and yet, even with his father steps away from him, all Muley could feel was his absence; when he tried to picture the shooting, his mind kept circling back to the image he had seen of the space shuttle that afternoon—the ship lurching slowly upward, the billows of smoke, and then the shuttle bursting into streaks of cloud and light. Mayor Washington had announced that the lights of the city would stay on all night, and all flags would fly at half-mast. Muley looked out the window at the flags and at the bare branches of the oak tree, then back at the man in the bed beside him.

Muley briefly recorded the sounds of his father's breathing, then strapped on his camera case and walked into the empty hallway, silent save for the low hum of fluorescents and the sound of the woman calling out for a nurse. Muley followed that voice and entered another dark hospital room, where he saw the face of a woman aglow in the haze of a streetlight shining in through the window. He watched the woman's mouth open, about to call for the nurse again. Muley reached out and held her hand, and then her breaths came more easily; she eased gracefully into sleep. But when Muley returned to Carl's room and touched his father's hand, nothing happened at all.

As Muley stared out the hospital window once again, he contemplated the world that existed beyond that window and the one that existed behind each of the hospital windows. And he contemplated the world that existed within Carl's hospital room and the one that existed inside Silverman himself. He thought of a world that encompassed each of those worlds. And he thought of that seemingly limitless world up above and the one that had existed inside the space shuttle. He thought of just how quickly those two worlds had become one.

News of the shooting and Carl Silverman's stabilized but unimproved condition spread quickly. Already a suspect had been taken into custody—a young lieutenant of Tiny Cubbins named Keldrick Burden. In the mainstream and alternative press, theories about Burden's motives were legion: Burden had shot

Silverman on Cubbins's order because Carl's efforts on his behalf had become embarrassing, because they interfered with Cubbins's ability to conduct his operations from the Joliet correctional facility, because Carl had been planning to dissolve the Cubbins defense fund altogether, or simply because Burden was insane.

Deirdre was not only shocked but devastated, as if by learning of Carl's mortality, she was also being reminded of her own. Though she was an atheist, she whispered the phrase "Jesus God" over and over at Marshall High, canceled her last class, and spent the afternoon crying in the faculty cafeteria before visiting DuSable Hospital and bursting into tears again, unable to focus her thoughts, unable to write, unable to shake the feeling that somehow she was responsible. She drove to the Joliet Correctional Center, for she had read that Tiny Cubbins might have ordered Carl's shooting, but she learned that Cubbins was not accepting visitors. Mel Coleman took a more pragmatic approach; he moved all of his editing equipment out of Bronzeville Studios and into his Mozart Street basement.

While Carl lay in his hospital room, daily newspapers published lengthy stories paying tribute to his career, lauding his vision for having produced *Godfathers of Soul,* even though none of them had deigned to send a critic to review it. Jill heard the news about Carl from Bibi Eisenstaedt. Bibi, who hadn't spoken to Jill since she had announced her engagement to Soren Davidson, said that she had learned of Carl's condition from Lana Rovner, who had heard about it from Shmuel Weinberg, who had heard about it from Hillel. But whenever Jill tried to call Muley, nobody answered, and though she longed to talk with him, she knew that he would call her only when he was ready.

Muley began to visit Carl late at night, sneaking upstairs to the third floor after visiting hours. In the week following the shooting, he had stopped by three times, but each time ran into Hillel, who would obsessively detail all that he was doing to keep Carl's affairs in order, intimating that he was compensating for work that Muley was unwilling to do. He also once espied Mendel and Sadie Silverman, who had arrived in Chicago to keep a daily vigil for their son. When Muley introduced himself and neither Mendel nor Sadie showed any recognition of him or his name, he understood that they had never known of his existence, and this seemed hardly the occasion to correct that oversight.

Wherever Muley was—in class, at the hospital, on the beach—he spent his days thinking about what had been taken away from his life when, in 1967, Carl chose not to dispute Deirdre's decision to banish him from her and Muley's lives.

Muley had not spent countless hours bemoaning his father's absence, the childhood he had lost. And yet he now felt an unquenchable desire to make a film that would explore how his life might have turned out had Carl not fled to L.A. He would hole up in his loft for hours, reimagining his life, drawing and redrawing it frame by frame, never sure whether he was drawing the life he would have wanted to have or the one he was glad to have escaped.

He worked feverishly at his easel, drawing through the nights; he would only know that it was morning at the sound of his alarm clock, only know that it was time to eat or go out when Fidel would whine or paw an empty food bowl. Every so often, the phone would ring, but he wouldn't answer; he would feel a need to return to his drawing. He drew on the bus, drew on the train, drew at night on the beach, where Fidel would run until the sun started to rise. Sheets of sketch paper mounted so quickly that within a few weeks, the pile of sketches was a foot high.

He began with the house. If he had lived with both his mother and father, it would have been a house, not an apartment, and it wouldn't have been east of Western Avenue; it would have been west of California. Or, it wouldn't have been in West Rogers Park at all, maybe not even in Chicago. He drew the house large—a Victorian mansion with ivy-covered walls and statues of muses around a fountain out front. He drew it small—a two-bedroom, white clapboard shack beside an empty lot with a tiny garden and a doghouse. He drew it as a bungalow, a teepee, a houseboat docked on the Chicago River. He drew it with extra bedrooms for brothers and sisters; with each additional sibling, he drew a larger house. He drew family vacations in Wisconsin's North Woods, campouts by the Indiana Dunes, road trips to visit his mother's family in Atlanta and Carl's in Florida. He drew Sunday drives to Caldwell Woods for picnics, leaf collecting, arrowhead hunts. He drew party hats, chocolate cake. He drew his own Bar Mitzvah at K.I.N.S. and his own confirmation at Angel Guardian; he drew himself lighting Chanukah candles and decorating the Christmas tree, trying on costumes for Halloween and Purim, setting the table for Easter and Passover. He drew the moment when he walked into his house and saw his mother and father kissing and pretended that he hadn't noticed. He drew the moment when he had decided not to become a filmmaker or an artist. He drew himself having never met Jill. He told the stories of a dozen alternative lives. And then he drew Carl lying in his hospital bed, his breathing perfectly regulated—in then out, in then out.

Muley then drew scenes from his own life, in which there were no brothers or sisters, no family trips or Sunday drives, in which the table had only ever been set for two. He drew his mother, her body stooped. He drew her reading alone. He drew unfurnished apartments and empty refrigerators. He drew bare cabinets and drawers, freezers filled with cheap sweets. He drew himself typing his mother's résumé. He drew himself rooting through alleys and construction sites, searching for wire, metal, wood. He drew himself riding the el downtown on weekends to make extra money for his mother by working at WBOE-FM. He drew himself drawing pictures and making movies that were destined to be destroyed, just as this one would be. He drew himself and Jill climbing the jungle gym during recess at Boone, where they found a bond in their isolation. He drew the two of them walking by the beach, listening to records, watching movies, slow-dancing, kissing, gazing up at the stars on Muley's bedroom ceiling. He drew them holding hands beneath Halley's Comet. He drew himself in Chicago and Jill in New York. He drew the telephone ringing and ringing. He drew himself wanting to answer, but feeling unable to do so just yet. And then he drew the space shuttle exploding in the sky, its light reflected in the eyes of Carl Silverman lying in his bed, breathing in then out.

When Muley's hand would grow too tired to draw, he would load up a duffel bag with a hammer, nails, and wood and ride his bike west, Fidel galloping alongside him. They would speed down the sidewalks of the city until they reached the lawn outside the hospital. Here, Muley began to construct a spiral stairway that curved around the oak tree. When he was through for the night, he would gaze up to Carl's hospital window to see if it was still dark. It always was.

Early one morning, he and Fidel returned from DuSable Hospital to his loft to find Calliope Larmer standing outside his door. He shrugged when she asked why he never answered his phone. She then conveyed her best wishes for Muley's father, and informed him that she had good news—she had sold all the artifacts from his *Ephemeral!* exhibition. She asked if he was working on any new installations. Yes, Muley said, the next one would be called *Without,* but it would be a private showing; some works weren't meant to be seen.

Toward the end of February, with Halley's Comet now just beginning to peep over the eastern horizon each dawn, the press coverage of Carl's shooting had died down. Though he technically remained alive, reporters had begun to treat him as if he were already gone. Keldrick Burden had already admitted his guilt, said that Tiny Cubbins had told him to shoot Silverman for reasons that Cubbins had not specified. The obituaries had already been written; they would be published the moment word came from the hospital.

While Muley continued to work, shooting his film frame by frame, building his staircase step by step, Mendel and Sadie Silverman spent every day at DuSable Hospital, but Sadie had told Dr. Mary Mitchum that she now agreed that keeping Carl alive with machines was expensive and futile. Still, as she and Mendel would sit alone at their son's bedside, Sadie couldn't help but feel emptier and more distraught than ever—to outlive her only child was more than she could bear. Early in Sadie and Mendel's marriage death had seemed omnipresent. Every month brought letters with tragic news. The war had been followed by a long, ominous silence, and then there had been the stillbirth. But when Carl was born, there was a bittersweet sense that the worst had passed, that they were their families' only survivors; it was their destiny to persevere. And now, to have their long journey end here on the third floor of a hospital in a white room filled with machines seemed not to be the triumphal coda that all such American stories promised. There should have been scores of grandchildren, easing the thought of their imminent passage from this world into the next. But as with their journey to America, it seemed as if they would undertake the next chapter of their lives alone.

When Hillel walked into Carl's room with his daily bouquet of flowers and saw Mendel and Sadie huddled, Sadie speaking to her husband in a hushed voice, and muttering Yiddish words rich with grim portents, he intuitively understood that Sadie had decided to take Carl off life support. After he had thrown out the old bouquet, filled the vase with fresh water, and inserted the new flowers, he said that he hoped Mendel and Sadie would not abandon their faith. For, though Carl's parents had adopted the resigned attitude toward death that came from much exposure to it, Hillel had not yet experienced their losses. All but one of his grandparents had died before he was born and he'd staved off depression by assuring himself that Carl would survive.

Sadie told Hillel that she could see where this was all leading. This life was not a life, it was hard on her, on her husband too, and "for what?" So they could keep coming here and having doctors tell them the same thing? Hillel asked if money was the issue. "*An* issue," but not "*the* issue," Sadie said. Because, Hillel said, it would be a shame to make such a decision when more money would soon become available; he said that he had been planning a benefit concert to defray the cost of Carl's medical care. In fact, Hillel had given only vague consideration to such a concert, but the conversation with Sadie contributed a new sense of urgency. He spoke of the possible venues for the event, which would feature a mixture of high-profile acts who had performed on Slappit Records and up-and-coming artists, such as Larry Elliot, never mind that Silverman had once offered to sign Larry to a contract only if he didn't have to actually release his band's record. There would be tributes and testimonials from actors, dignitaries, and politicians, Hillel said. The concert wouldn't be a memorial; it would be a celebration of the man's life. He asked Sadie if she would consider delaying her decision. And with a sigh, Sadie said that she would.

Working late every night at Bronzeville, wearing Carl's clothes, speaking pseudo-jive on the telephone, drinking the same sugary sodas and eating the fried shrimp that Carl favored, Hillel met with more success than he had anticipated in planning a Slappit celebration. The Aragon Ballroom would donate its space; too many city council members had already agreed to speak; and most performers were willing to waive their fees. The only resistance came from Larry Elliot, but since his music had comforted Hillel in his darkest hours, Hillel acceded to all of the obscure demands issued via telephone by Elliot's manager, Clara Moskowitz.

In the days that followed, the Silvermans would still visit the hospital in the afternoons, but they would spend less time in Carl's room. They dined in the cafeteria, watched TV in the waiting room, browsed through the gift shop. At the end of the day, they would take the elevator back up to three to see if anything had changed. By the first Monday in March, Sadie had grown so weary of the hospital that she suggested to Mendel that they take the Roosevelt Road bus west to look at their old neighborhood, and Mendel agreed; the older he became, the more he deferred to Sadie's judgment. Sadie had heard that the Old West Side wasn't what it used to be; Mitzi Schiffler, their friend at Bridlewood Village, who had grown up on Homan Avenue, said that any white would be "murdered, then raped" the minute they walked through Garfield Park. But Sadie was too old for fears, or rather, now every moment possessed equal doses of terror. Yet, as she rode the Roosevelt bus, she was gripped not with fright but with an inestimable sadness. It was not so much that the neighborhood had once been white but now was black, not so much that synagogues were now churches. Rather, it seemed as if the entire world she had known had been erased.

There were no longer any vendors hawking homemade potato chips on Roosevelt Road; men with *pushkis* no longer sold rags and old iron or called out, "Rags-a-lion." The halls where she had danced with Mendel, the apartments where they had lived—practically all of it had been razed: The Jewish People's Institute, the Boys' Brotherhood Republic, the Marcey Center. The theaters were gone. Electronics shops and fast-food restaurants stood in place of the Marboro and the Paradise; a vacant lot was all that remained of the old Yiddish theater. The streets were cracked, pocked with potholes, occasionally revealing old streetcar tracks beneath. As a girl in Chernovtsy, when she'd been hospitalized for pneumonia and the rabbis had given her a new name in order to fool the dybbuk, Sadie had lain in bed and was struck by the notion that the world could go on just as easily without her. But as she rode west through the old neighborhood, it was no longer a matter of acknowledging that one day the world would go about its business without Sadie Sadkowsky; the truth was that it was already doing so. When she and Mendel returned to the hospital, Sadie sat with her husband at their son's side, waiting with guilty anticipation for the day when they could go back to Florida.

On the sixth of March, not long after the Soviet Vega probe would make its nearest pass of the comet, Muley's installation *Without* would have its first and only screening, attended by an audience that Muley had said would consist only of himself, his mother, and an unconscious Carl Silverman. Calliope had asked Muley if she could attend, but he had said no, maybe next time. He had spent the previous week working under cover of darkness to complete his exhibit, hammering and sanding the last steps of the stairway, bolting 8 mm movie projectors on the branches of the oak tree outside his father's window at DuSable Hospital, assuring members of the building security staff that yes, this was an approved construction project.

The night of the sixth, Muley dined with his mother on Mozart Street before they drove south to the hospital. It had been months since Muley had spent any time alone with Deirdre. On the occasions when he would visit the house in West Rogers Park, if Deirdre was alone, she would always find an errand to run; if Mel was home, she'd excuse herself and retire to her room, where she would spend hours alone trying to write *In an Empty House,* a short story that now seemed to be growing into a novel. It was as if by spending more than an hour together, both Muley and Deirdre would recall too clearly the days they had spent in his childhood when no one else was there but them. Back then, their years of solitude, with Deirdre voraciously reading to prevent herself from descending further into sorrow, with Muley desperately trying to cheer her, hadn't seemed so awful. But now, when they looked back on that period, it seemed so impossibly dreary that both wondered how they had managed to survive; every time they thought of it, Muley would feel cold and numb, and Deirdre would feel overwhelmingly guilty.

As a child, by necessity Muley had grown up so quickly that it seemed to Deirdre that he almost hadn't grown up at all, that, because of her depression, she had squandered the time for games and picnics, for sledding, hide-and-seek, and peekaboo. She now felt as if she had awoken from a deep sleep to find that everyone around her had grown old. She barely recognized the young man sitting in her car, so tall that he had to sit with the passenger seat pushed all the way back.

On the third floor of DuSable Hospital, Carl lay in his dark room. Save for the life-support machine, the only sounds were those of the clunking radiator, the hum of fluorescent hallway lights, and the buzz of intercom boxes. When Carl breathed, it looked as though only the white sheet atop him was moving, not the man himself. While Muley placed chairs on either side of his father's bed facing the wall, Deirdre contemplated the man lying before her. His peaceful expression didn't suit him. The hair was too neat, the beard trimmed too close. His sleep seemed too restful, not that of a man who had only ever slept four hours a night, snoring, grabbing at covers, kicking away imaginary dogs in bad dreams. This was the face of a man who could have been a good father and husband. Deirdre reached out to hold one of Carl's hands, and it felt different from what she had remembered as well; now it was dry and cool. She wanted to see his eyes, the only part of him in which she could ever recognize her son, but they were closed.

With Carl's hand in hers, Deirdre could see her son looking out the window at the oak tree. Upon its branches were mounted thirteen Super 8 projectors all pointed toward this room, resembling fruit in outstretched hands. As Muley walked out of the room toward the stairs, ready to start the private screening,

Deirdre let Carl's hand fall gently back on his bed, and walked to the window to get a closer look, her eyes following the spiral stairway down to the ground.

Dangling down from the oak tree like vines were projector cords, which were bunched together with black tape, all of them plugged into one central cord at the base of the tree. Muley unbundled and carried that cord over his shoulder to a set of stone steps and into a side entrance of the hospital, then plugged it into a socket below a series of fuse boxes. From thirteen projectors, a low hum reverberated like more than a dozen mechanical crickets; a flock of crows flew upward in search of a quieter tree.

Beside the tree trunk, a large glass garbage drum was filled with dry sticks that had been doused with lighter fluid. Muley reached into his pocket and pulled out a book of matches. He lit one, tossed it in the can, and a whitish flame rose up. Inside the glass drum, the flame glowed like a candle behind a foggy window. As Muley quickly mounted the steps, he sensed that he wasn't rising so much as feeling the ground falling away from him. He looked below and saw the empty expanse of dead grass. But once he reached the top step, he only saw branches, projectors, and the window directly in front of him; he cupped his hands to look inside and saw the back of his mother's head. Deirdre sat facing the wall; Muley's father was lying beside her.

Muley had memorized the positions of each of his film projectors. He took a breath, checked his watch, and started projector 1. It whirred to life; its lamp sent a thin beam of light through the hospital window. He waited a second before starting the next, another second before starting the third, used both hands to start the fourth and fifth. Moments later, thirteen film reels slowly twirled, thirteen projector lamps burned, thirteen sabers of light crisscrossed each other through the window, so that from a distance, the window too looked as if it were the illuminated lens of a projector. From each projector, film cascaded down toward the fire. Muley watched the film fall, watched the projectors on the branches, looked at the light in the window, listened to the crackle of burning twigs in the trash can below, then walked quickly down the stairs. As he reentered the hospital, he thought that he heard heavy footsteps passing behind him, but he did not let the sound deter his progress.

When Muley entered his father's room, light was blazing through the window, almost as if the tree outside had caught fire. His mother sat haloed by the light, transfixed by the succession of images projected upon the wall. Thirteen brief films were screening at once, one beside the other, like a series of doors, opening onto twelve alternative lives that Muley, Deirdre, and Carl could have led; and in the center, images of the life they had. Deirdre watched the films. Muley watched his mother; her face flickered in the light. The sheet covering Carl's body was illuminated as well, as if it too were a film screen.

There were too many images for Deirdre to process at any one time. Her eyes shifted from square to square, never settling on any one for more than a second before turning her attention to another. She watched images of families, picnics, games; embraces and hearts and scenes of flight. And in the center of it all, she saw a drawing of Carl lying in his bed, the tree, the sky and its comets and constellations visible through the window behind him. As she watched, Deirdre began to think of the lives she could have lived and the lives she had, the places where she could have gone and the places where she'd been. She thought of empty rooms and rooms that were full, thought of families and of being alone. She thought of her own father, who had died at the age of fifty-four. Instinctively, she reached a hand out to Carl's and as she did so, Muley did the same.

As the films continued threading through the projectors, the images accelerated as in the finale of a fireworks display, one flashing after the other after the other. Here was a mansion and there a bungalow, here an ocean filled with porpoises, there a sky filled with birds. Colors swirled and danced before becoming individual squares of color—a red square, a yellow, a purple, a blue, a white, and a black; then every single square turned black, and in the center of each square, a tiny pinpoint of light appeared. The lights transformed into comets streaking up, down, and across the squares, moving so fast that they seemed to describe shapes as they flew—stars, lilies, planets, a dozen faces, two dozen, three. But then they became smaller bit by bit, until once again there were only thirteen pinpoints of light, which darted about as they wrote on thirteen squares upon the hospital wall, the words THE END. Those words hung in the air before exploding and shimmering, then falling to the bottom of each square like snow.

At that moment, Muley's film was supposed to fade to black, the last length of it was to fall from each of the projectors, then enter the trash can, where all of it would melt and burn until nothing would be left of Muley's films save for smoke, ashes, and the sounds of thirteen projector motors humming, thirteen film reels twirling. But the film did not go black; it went white. Not just the dull white of a screen when a projector has run out of film, but a much brighter white that bathed the entire hospital room in light.

Down below, on the hospital lawn, the cord that ran from the basement socket to the projectors sparked. Each projector was jolted with a sudden surge, bursting forth for just a few moments with hot white light before the fuse was blown. The fluorescents on the third floor hallway made a zapping sound, the intercom boxes popped, and then the hospital room was silent. Muley made as if to get up and run down to the fuse boxes, but in that brief moment when everything was bright, he felt a slight pressure against his right hand and, when he turned to look at Carl lying on the hospital bed, he saw that his father's eyes were open; he saw that the man was breathing on his own, even as the life-support machine had gone dead.

And in that moment of brightness and silence, Carl looked up to see Deirdre Wills and his son on either side of his bed, Deirdre holding his left hand, Muley holding his right, saw the two of them as if in a dream, distantly remembered this as the one moment he had long sought but never dared believe could ever happen. His lips formed words, barely audible at first, but when Deirdre and Muley leaned closer, they could hear him. "Heeey, man," he whispered, "this shit is *onnnn tiiime.*"

Then the hallway lights flickered, the room went dark, the projectors were extinguished, and the emergency electrical system kicked in. The hum of the life-support machine returned. Carl's hand went limp, and his eyes closed. The intercom boxes began to hum again, and so did the fluorescent lights in the hallway. The life-support machine started whirring, and once more Muley could hear the sounds of his father's breathing. Muley shivered. But then he began to feel an odd new sense of clarity, as if a screen that had always stood in front of his eyes was lifting. He looked up to see a shadow passing before the window outside the room, but a moment later, it was gone. Muley held his mother close to him; she was still holding Carl's hand.

After Muley had run down to the basement to flip the switches in the fuse boxes, he sat beside his mother in Carl's hospital room, waiting to see if the man's eyes might open again, if he might speak. Deirdre touched Carl's cheek, Muley felt his wrist, but neither said a word. When morning began to break and a light rain started to fall outside, Muley and Deirdre took an elevator down to the first floor, and on the lawn of DuSable Hospital, Muley kissed his mother on the cheek, and then they said good-bye beside the oak tree. As Deirdre drove quickly west on Cermak, bound once again for the Joliet Correctional Center, she could see her son with a wrench in his hand, preparing to take down his projectors and dismantle the stairway encircling the tree. Over the lake, in her rearview mirror, she saw the faint hints of a pair of rainbows.

When she arrived at the waiting room of the Joliet prison, Deirdre asked once more if she could be admitted to see Tiny Cubbins. But the receptionist told Deirdre that Cubbins had been moved to solitary confinement. However, she did say that Cubbins had left something for her in case she ever visited again. She opened her desk drawer and took out a book—the last Dickens novel that Deirdre had loaned him—and a note written on a square of pink paper. If he couldn't have a son of his own while he was incarcerated, Cubbins wrote, at least he could do something to benefit the son of the woman who had been kind enough to visit him and give him books. Cubbins had not signed his name; he had merely written, "Sincerely, a mere varmint." As tears began to form in her eyes, Deirdre crumpled the note into a ball.

When Muley had unbolted the projectors and carried the last of them down to the lawn below, he walked to his glass trash can. He expected to find a jungle of burnt film inside, but the trash can was empty. Later that morning, when he returned to his loft building, he saw Calliope. She was standing on South Michigan Avenue with a cardboard box filled with 8 mm film. She admitted that she had climbed his stairway and watched the movies on the hospital room wall; she couldn't believe that he wanted his work to be destroyed. She handed him the box and told him to call her if he ever changed his mind.


When Hillel arrived at the hospital the next afternoon with his bouquet and discovered Carl's room empty, a man at the nurses' station told Hillel that he could not learn of a patient's status unless he was an immediate family member. But when Hillel threw a fit and said goddamn it, that wasn't righteous, and did he have to "put a foot halfway up y'all's ass," the nurse relented and told Hillel that Mr. Carl Silverman had died during the night. The circumstances of the death were hazy, he said, for the life-support machine had apparently continued to function all the while. The man's heart had simply stopped beating, and his personal theory was that the death had been willed by the patient himself, as if Mr. Silverman had fought against the machines and intentionally stopped breathing, stopped his heart.

For Hillel, this answer was both unbelievable and unacceptable. When he was done berating the nurse, he berated the physicians, and when he was done with the physicians, he returned to Carl's hospital room, where the floor was still wet, the sheets were heaped in a corner, and everything smelled like lemons. He sat in a wheelchair, rolling back and forth over the wet floor, practicing pivots, turns, and sudden stops. He held his breath to see if he too could will himself to stop breathing, but invariably, after thirty seconds, he would cough out a breath and his heart would race faster, trying to make up for the beats it had lost.

Hillel sat by the empty bed with his right thumb and forefinger digging into the corners of his eyes, two rivulets of tears trickling down either side of his nose before coming to rest in his mustache, which tasted of salt when he licked it. A custodian gathered up the sheets, attempting to ignore the thin, bearded man in another man's ill-fitting denim jacket and jeans, softly crying by the window, and asking over and over in a voice that he thought was inaudible what he would do now. And then, as Hillel sat, his fingers now as wet as the tip of his nose and his mustache, a phrase popped into his mind. A rich and powerful phrase. "What would Slappit do?" he asked himself.

In the hospital room, Hillel thought of all the unsatisfactory father figures he'd created for himself in the past. And once again, his mind settled upon Carl Silverman, who had been the first to understand Hillel, the first to hold Hillel in his arms. He began to construct a Slappit to replace the one who had passed away, an infallible Slappit, an infinitely wise, patient, and understanding Slappit, a Slappit to show him the way. What would Slappit do at this moment, he asked himself. Would he sit in a hospital room overcome with grief? No, he would not; Slappit did not dwell in despair. And so, after Hillel had recited the kaddish three times, bending his knees and bowing just as his father and brother always did at services, he stood and wiped his eyes. He pulled up the window shades and looked out on the day. The stairway and the projectors were gone, and both the rain and rainbows had cleared. He left the hospital and headed for Bronzeville Studios to help Mendel and Sadie prepare for the funeral. For that was the practical thing to do, and whatever was practical was what Slappit would have done.

Carl's demise received scant attention in the press. The newspapers that had reported his shooting on page two relegated news of his passing to the obituary section, where a picture ten years out-of-date—when Carl had favored wide-collared, Calypso-style shirts worn underneath open leather vests—was printed in a tiny square. His funeral was poorly attended. When Carl had made out his will—the contents of which were known only to his attorney, Lou Eisenstaedt, and to Tiny Cubbins, with whom Carl had discussed the will at Joliet—he had also made specific arrangements for the funeral. Carl had little patience for mourning rituals, believed neither in an afterlife nor in wasting good money on coffins and burial plots. He hated the solitude of cemeteries, thought each head-stone should come equipped with a built-in jukebox. But for his parents, he would have liked to have one of those funerals that he imagined old-time Delta blues musicians to have—with good vittles, with corrupt preachers razzing each other and guffawing while the bereaved said wise, soulful things and bonnet-clad ladies nodded and said "Mm-hm." Carl had given Lou two sets of instructions—one to be used in the event that he outlived his parents, in which case, after his cremation, a funeral would be held at the Church of the Holy Nazarene with a gospel choir and a fire-and-brimstone preacher, and another, which instructed that Carl was to be buried at Waldheim Cemetery, reception to follow at Harold's Chicken Shack. There, Sadie and Mendel sat politely as Rabbi Jeffrey Meltzer—who had recently written to Haiti to tell Gareth Overgaard that he had recon-ciled with his wife—sang Jewish versions of Slappit artists' hit songs and blues standards, punctuated by "eye-yi-yi's" and "die-dee-die's" ("One leg to the east, *eye-yi-yi,* one leg to the west, *eye-die-die,* me in the middle, *die-dee-die,* tryin' to do my best, oy!"). Hillel said the *brachas* over the wine, the chicken, and the white bread, said that it was such a blessing from the Lord to be presented with this soft bread, so good for sopping up sauce. Neither Muley nor Deirdre at-tended, not wanting to intrude upon the Silvermans' grief. Muley worked alone in his South Michigan loft; Deirdre, who had told no one of the note that she had received from Tiny Cubbins, taught class, then went to the school library to write—she had found an ending for her novel.

On the day following the funeral, Hillel chauffeured Mendel and Sadie to Lou Eisenstaedt's office on Wacker Drive in the Jewelers' Building, where they were to discuss the contents of Carl's will before Hillel would drive them to Bronzeville Studios to pack, then on to O'Hare for their return flight to Florida. As Hillel drove Carl's Cadillac, the passenger seat was empty; Sadie and Mendel sat in the back talking in Yiddish, while Hillel strained to make out any words; he listened particularly for the word *boychik* so that he could know that they were speaking favorably of him. He dropped them off in front of the building, put the car in park in a loading zone, and switched on the flashers; he told Sadie and Mendel that he would wait for them here. He sat in the car for five minutes with the motor running; then, when a police officer urged him on into traffic, he drove east on Wacker, then circled the block.

As Hillel circled, he remembered riding in the back of his father's Plymouth Duster to look at parade floats on these streets, but Boaz Levy had always driven so fast that Hillel would get carsick and keep his eyes closed, never seeing more than one or two floats before Boaz got back on Lake Shore Drive. And as Hillel thought of his father, he began to blame him for everything that he'd ever done wrong. He blamed him for having smoked too much pot and snorted too much coke, blamed him for having sucked too many tits and smoked too much pole, blamed him for the fevers, the chills, and the nosebleeds, blamed him for the love that he had sought from Carl, the love that had, he thought, somehow set off the chain of events leading to Carl's death. After a half hour of circling, Hillel finally saw Mendel and Sadie coming back into view in front of the Jewelers' Building. He slowed the car and reached for the flashers. But the moment when he leaned over to disengage the passenger lock, he saw something that made him shiver, gulp, then slam on the accelerator and drive fast past Mendel and Sadie, screech onto Wabash and underneath the el tracks, running yellow and red lights until he slammed on the brakes at Washington Street. He took a breath and lay his forehead against the steering wheel. For when he had seen Mendel and Sadie walking toward the loading zone, he had also seen that Muley was walking between them.

Lou Eisenstaedt had called Muley to ask if he would meet him at his office to discuss Carl's estate. Muley had felt uneasy about the meeting; he had told Lou over the phone that if he stood to inherit money from his father, he didn't feel entitled to it, but Eisenstaedt had assured him that the meeting wasn't really about money, and anyway, it wouldn't take long. After his sculpture class, Muley had taken the el to Washington Street, then walked to the Jewelers' Building, riding the elevator up to the 27th floor, where he entered one of the smallest offices he had ever seen, one with barely enough room for one receptionist and one lawyer, Eisenstaedt, who had only ever had one steady client, Carl Silverman. Eisenstaedt had never been much of a lawyer—Carl had ghostwritten most of Lou's contracts—and during Carl's off-years, Lou made most of his money transcribing depositions or helping out his older brother's ad sales and real-estate businesses. Yet Carl maintained his loyalty, and always acted as if Lou were a top-notch advocate; Lou was the best in the business, Carl always said.

Lou was sitting behind his paper-strewn desk when Muley entered the dim, brown office. Lou was a short, balding man who looked as if every one of his forty-two years had been a Herculean labor. He wore a thin beige shirt opened one button to reveal the white T-shirt underneath, and his thinning, pomaded hair was combed over his scalp from a jagged part just above his left ear. Behind him, a sooty window looked out onto an airshaft. In front of him, Mendel and Sadie were seated on metal chairs that seemed too short for them. Muley stood in the doorway and asked if Lou wanted to finish up with his clients before meeting with him, but Lou waved Muley in. As Muley warily approached Lou's desk, he could detect the scent of mothballs on Mendel's dandruff-speckled navy blue peacoat. Muley felt a sudden urge to hide, but the office was so small that he had no idea where he could go.

Lou shook Muley's hand, and asked if he and the Silvermans had met. Muley said not exactly, but they had seen each other in the hospital. He shook Mendel's and Sadie's hands and they smiled, but if they had any recollection of having seen Muley before, their vacant expressions showed no evidence. Lou indicated a rickety wooden chair for Muley to sit in, then produced a legal-sized envelope, tore it open, and put on his bifocals. He unfolded a document that appeared to be about a dozen pages long, licking his index finger and thumb as he paged quickly through it, then took off the bifocals and chewed on one end.

What he had before him, Lou said, was the last will and testament of Carl Silverman. He said that he and Carl had spent many hours refining the language, but Carl had never wavered about its main substance. Eisenstaedt said that when Carl had asked him to draw up this will, his first concern had been to make sure that his parents would be well provided for, and, with the trust that he and Carl had created, he could say with confidence that Mendel and Sadie would be able to live comfortably, given all reasonable eventualities. Carl had left all his remaining collections and personal effects to Lou—his records, his reel-to-reel tapes, his preferred customer card from Leon's Barbecue. But as far as the remainder of Carl's estate, he had left it all to his one and only son, Muley Scott Wills.

Eisenstaedt held the document in place on his desk with the middle finger of one hand and flipped it around with the fingers of the other so that Mendel, Sadie, and Muley could read it, but none of them did. Sadie whispered to Mendel, cast quick glances at Muley, then whispered some more while Muley took a quick, deep breath, turned away, and stared out Lou's window. His palms were perspiring. He now wished that he had never agreed to come here. He felt as if Lou had tricked him. He had told Lou that he could never accept Carl's fortune; he felt as though he had done nothing to earn it. The whole idea was absurd. He had barely ever seen the man awake, and he could already feel Mendel and Sadie's resentment; they whispered to each other in Yiddish, while Eisenstaedt briefly narrated the story of Carl's ill-fated relationship with Deirdre, one of many stories that Carl had apparently never told his parents.

When Lou had finished and Muley finally spoke, he did so slowly and softly. He said that he was grateful, not only to Carl, whom he had never known, but also to Lou, for having asked him to meet, and finally to Mendel and Sadie, who, he said, were probably shocked by what they had just learned; he was sorry that they had to be introduced under these circumstances. He supposed that he should have said something at the hospital, but he had felt that it wasn't his place to do so. He told them that he understood their confusion, even perhaps their anger. But he wanted to reassure them that he could not accept the terms of the will; he had explained to Lou that he did not feel entitled to Carl's millions, and he would sign any document that would relinquish his rights to the money. Clearly, it was theirs, not his.

Lou grinned broadly. He nodded at Mendel and Sadie as if to say, Wasn't this a decent young man. Lou said that the money Carl had left belonged to Muley, and he could, in fact, give it to Carl's parents, donate it to charity, or do whatever he wished with it. He pulled a sealed envelope out of the center drawer of his desk. Then he asked Mendel and Sadie if they would mind excusing the two of them. He shook Mendel's hand, hugged Sadie and kissed her on the cheek, offered his condolences, and told them how glad he was to have seen them after so many years. And then he walked the Silvermans to the door; Muley felt too ashamed to even look at them, despite the fact that Sadie kept glancing back at Muley as she walked out of Lou's office.

When the Silvermans had left and Lou had closed his door and sat back down behind his desk, Muley said that he did not want to seem ungrateful, but quite honestly, he didn't care about how many millions he was supposed to inherit; he had survived this long without his father's generosity; it would be distasteful and dishonest to start profiting from it now. Carl's parents deserved it, perhaps his mother deserved it; he did not. Well, Lou repeated, Muley could do whatever he wanted with his inheritance. He took the envelope and pushed it toward Muley.

Muley's head was reeling, his stomach felt tight, he was dizzy, nauseated. He shook his head, let out a breath. He reached across the desk and took the envelope. He slid his index finger under the flap and carefully ripped it open. Inside were a key and a check. He pulled out the check. "Pay to the order of Muley Scott Wills," it said, "the amount of three hundred thirty dollars and thirty-seven cents."

Muley stared at the check for a long time, trying to determine if, perhaps, a decimal point had been misplaced, if he was reading it wrong. Then he looked back up at Lou. Was it a joke, he asked. Lou shook his head. Unfortunately, it wasn't, he said. Ever since Carl had come back to Chicago, Lou said, he seemed to have lost whatever business acumen he once had, perhaps intentionally so. He had become profligate in his spending, made one bad investment after another— *Godfathers of Soul,* the Cubbins defense fund. On Lou's advice, he had sold off Slappit Records and his other companies. Convinced that he had cheated the artists on his label on their contracts, he'd sold the contracts back to them for far less than they were worth. He'd spent millions on rehabbing Bronzeville Studios, but that hadn't helped him either, because the city still owned the property. Lou said that he would have explained this to Muley when he had first walked in, but Carl had been very devoted to his parents, and would never have wanted them to know that he wasn't as rich as they had assumed.

Muley looked at Lou, then down to the check once more. For the first time, his father's life was beginning to make sense to him. Not complete sense, but some. A smile formed on his lips. Then he asked Lou why a key was in the envelope. Lou said that it was the key to Bronzeville Studios.

When Muley left Lou's office, he had thought that Mendel and Sadie would be gone, but they were still in the hallway, standing by the elevators; an elevator arrived, and the three of them stepped onto it. Mendel took off his hat and held it in his quivering hands as the doors closed and the elevator crept downward. Muley watched the numbers flashing above him: So many floors to go, he thought. He stared at Mendel's dusty peacoat, at Sadie's pink babushka. He watched the numbers—26, 25, 24. He wondered if the Silvermans were angry and fantasized briefly about an elevator that could rocket through the roof of the building and sail over the city, the doors opening only to let in the light of the moon and the stars.

Sadie finally turned around and fixed Muley with a stare at once curious and uneasy. Then she turned to her husband and whispered a question to which Mendel did not respond. At the 22nd floor, she turned around again. *Muley,* she said, that was a funny name. Muley shrugged and smiled. Yes, he said, he supposed it was. At the 21st floor, she turned back to her husband and whispered something else, but at 19, she turned around again. The name was just so strange, she said, she had never heard it before, had he? In *The Grapes of Wrath,* Muley said, but Sadie did not hear. That was right, she said, she'd never heard of anyone with that name either. She asked Muley who his mother was and how she had met Carl—she hadn't quite understood what Mr. Eisenstaedt had said. Muley said that his mother's father had recorded one of the first albums on Slappit Records, *Wills's Ways.* Oh, those poor people, Sadie said, by which she meant blacks and musicians in general, black musicians in particular, and even more specifically, black musicians who had recorded on Carl's label—they worked so hard, were paid so little. She asked Muley what his mother did. She taught high school English, Muley said. Oh, those poor people, Sadie said again.

The elevator opened onto the lobby. As Muley walked alongside Mendel and Sadie, passing the newsstand and the confectionery, Sadie asked further questions, then provided Mendel with Muley's answers, as if she were an interpreter—"He says he goes to an art institute," "Not a house painter, he draws pictures." The questioning continued as the trio emerged into the windy afternoon and began walking east on Wacker. They took no notice of the Cadillac with its Playboy air freshener and its fuzzy dice, swerving wildly onto Wabash Avenue.

Muley walked between his grandparents, and as they turned south on State Street toward the el, Sadie continued asking questions. At first, Muley had the sensation that he was being tested; for what purpose, he was initially unsure. Mel always spoke of the members of the "white interrogation squad," who, whenever they found "an affable Negro," quizzed him or her about every aspect of black culture—what did they really think of Harold Washington, and wasn't Larry Bird just as great a ballplayer as Magic Johnson, and where were all the good barbecue joints, the real down-home ones where only brothers ate? Mel would always try to trap these people in their stereotypes, tell them that their questions reminded him of what he and his barefoot buddies discussed back in Jackson, Mississippi, while they were sitting on fences consuming large watermelons; when the interlocutors would ask, "Really? You ate watermelons on a fence?" he'd tell them to fuck off.

But in the barrage of Sadie's questions, Muley detected something other than mere anthropological interest. And as Sadie looked at Muley with her cloudy blue eyes, it struck Muley that just as Carl Silverman had been absent from his life, so too had he himself been absent from Mendel and Sadie's, the difference being that Muley had been aware on some level of this absence forever, while Mendel and Sadie had only learned of it now. As they stood on the el platform, waiting for a southbound train that would take them back to Bronzeville Studios, Sadie held Muley's face in both of her hands, tapping his cheeks lightly with rough fingers as if she were holding something precious that she had lost and now had found long after she had given up hope of ever seeing it again.

"Your father was a very rich man, wasn't he?" Sadie asked Muley, who began to feel his eyes water. He thought about the check that Lou had given him. He thought of his mother, how he had always worried about her, how he had always assured her not to fret about him.

"Yes," Muley said with a smile, "he was."

And then Sadie told Muley, *sha*. "Sha," she said again. "Sha sha sha." She brought his head close to hers and kissed his eyes, first the right, then the left, and again and again. And then she covered her own eyes, which sparkled with tiny rainbows, and said the *Sh'ma Yisroel*. She looked through the spaces between her fingers to make sure that Muley was still there.

And as Muley and his grandparents rode south on the train, Muley began to envision a new art project; for the first time in his adult life, he wanted to create one that would last. After he returned from escorting Mendel and Sadie first to Bronzeville to retrieve their luggage, then to the airport, where he had promised Sadie that he would visit soon, he sat on the floor of his loft with a sketchpad beside the cardboard box of film that Calliope had salvaged for him. He began to draw the exterior of Bronzeville Studios. When the next dawn arrived, he was still drawing.

— — — —

Hillel was drawing too. Shortly after Muley, Sadie, and Mendel had started heading south, Hillel had burst into Lou Eisenstaedt's office, demanding to know the identity of Carl's heirs, and when he learned that he was not among them, he had spent hours driving around and around the city. All the while, Hillel the Id had struggled with Slappit the Superego. He cruised by each of his old haunts, asking himself what Slappit would do. Would he go to the Dunkin' Donuts parking lot in search of a packet of hash? Slappit would not. Would he buy a blow job from a hooker on Lake Street? He would not. Would he cruise Montrose Harbor, flashing his lights at johns? Slappit would not. Finally, he returned to Bronzeville Studios, where Mendel and Sadie's belongings were already gone.

Hillel wondered how soon it would be before Muley took over Carl's business and sent him packing once again. He put on his helmet and his skates, rode around and around the studios, and when he was so exhausted that his knees were quivering, his thighs stiff, his jeans and jacket damp with sweat, he stood before an easel with a hunk of charcoal; he sketched one line and then another. And when he finished his sketch, he stood back and laughed; he had drawn a mule.

By week's end, Hillel had drawn more than a hundred mules in a variety of styles, media, and periods. In his studio drawing class, he was assigned to copy a painting in the Art Institute; he chose Caillebotte's *Rainy Day in Paris,* and drew a rain-soaked Parisian boulevard populated by umbrella-toting mules. He drew Grant Wood's *American Gothic* with a pitchfork-wielding mule and his four-legged Wasserstrom-faced wife. He drew Whistler's mother with gray ears flopping down from underneath her snood. He painted a nude, bearded Hillel bent over a table spread with cocaine while a mule humped him from behind. He painted a mule robbing a bank, his body weighed down by the pieces of silver he had stolen. He painted a mule photographing comets, a mule kicking a shivering and bearded Hillel out of his loft. He titled his works with references to biblical passages (Genesis 22:5—"Then Abraham said to his servant, 'You shall stay with the ass'"; Leviticus 15:2—"When any man has a discharge issuing from his member, he is unclean"). And when he signed his work, he no longer used his smiling penis signature; he signed his full name, Hillel Eliezer Levy, or simply his initials: H.E.L.

Hillel's work would soon win accolades from the Art Institute faculty. While professors had called his depictions of cartoon character sodomy sophomoric, his use of the icons of the mule and the bearded Hillel was interpreted variously as the struggle between a humanistic and an animalistic society, between classical culture and modernity, Judaism and Christianity. It was not long before professors and classmates were suggesting that he seek a gallery to represent him.

Calliope Larmer had seen Hillel's work only once before, when she had toured an Art Institute student show. But even if she had recalled his smiling penis-people paintings, it was unlikely that, when Hillel entered her gallery, she would have recognized the man standing before her. His hair was long and wavy, his beard unkempt, his denim jacket and jeans splattered with paint and smeared with charcoal, his fingertips black. His clothes had the smell of a diner about them—cigarettes and eggs fried in too much butter. Despite his poorly affected pimp walk and his unearned familiarity as he greeted Calliope as "Sister Calliope," she still thought that she had found someone else whom she could sell. And when Hillel laid out his portfolio, Calliope knew that she was right.


Hillel's solo show, *The Mule Series,* was to open toward the end of May, on the same day as the nationwide celebration of community, "Hands Across America." He had already stored a series of canvases in the basement of Larmer Galleries, where he was now spending his nights. But before he could devote his full attention to the exhibit, he was hosting the Carl Slappit Silverman tribute concert. Even though he was not among Carl's heirs, he knew that Slappit would never have reneged on such a commitment. After he had moved out of Bronzeville Studios, he had maintained his enthusiasm for and dedication to the tribute, even as tour manager after tour manager called to cancel their acts' appearances at the Aragon. But three acts had not canceled, and one of those acts was Larry Elliot.

Only a month had passed since Pico Records had released Elliot's self-titled professional debut album, and though the record hadn't screamed up the charts as quickly as Scritti Politti's debut, it was selling respectably, and Larry knew that thinking man's artists, such as himself, took longer to catch on. There had been a brief, on-the-cheap national tour where Larry had opened for more popular acts and gotten heckled off the stage. He carried his own bags, loaded in his gear, got two free tickets for friends and acquaintances and a twenty percent discount for anyone else. He traveled by bus or flew coach, and slept in Budget Hosts with bad television reception, no room service, and vending machines down the hall where the ice cubes tasted like skunk. He would sit alone at roadside Ponderosas, where he would eat chili and pretend to read Jack Kerouac, hoping that the books would lead to conversations with sexually adventurous, denim-clad girls who would take him for rides on their Harley-Davidsons, though when he would return to his motel room alone, he would put down *The Dharma Bums* and pick up the GMAT study guide. On Friday nights and Saturday mornings, he would put on a baseball cap and sunglasses and sit in the back of makeshift synagogues for services organized by college town Hillel organizations. He would *daven* quietly, hoping that he would not be recognized and, at the same time, getting irritated because he never was.

And yet, when Larry arrived for the Silverman memorial, Hillel accorded him the treatment of a true rock star. The Aragon's green room, despite its peeling paint and its stained and speckled mirrors, was appointed to the specifications set by Larry and his manager, Clara Moskowitz (who had told Hillel over the phone that she would not be accompanying Elliot "because of Chernobyl"). There was a waterbed and a copy of the *Tanakh,* fresh fruit juices and cold borscht, six bottles of Jim Beam and a case of assorted Dr. Brown's sodas, two cases of Maccabee and two cases of Budweiser, a dish of green M&M's and a box of Barton's chocolates, smoked sable, bialys, Muenster cheese, lambskin condoms, Tylenol, K-Y jelly, and kosher edible strawberry underwear.

Larry had been sitting at his makeup table, reading a copy of *City Times* magazine and daubing white greasepaint on his face to give his performance a sense of an old-time traveling medicine show, when Hillel entered, carrying a copy of Larry's album. He explained to Larry that he had organized the tribute concert, and had drawn the animation for his video. Larry immediately recognized Hillel, remembered him as the wiseass from his sister's graduating class at K.I.N.S. who'd inserted swear words in "Cuando el Rey Nimrod." Larry often felt lonely on the road, and was delighted to see someone from the old neighborhood. He shook Hillel's hand energetically, asked him how his family was doing, whether his dad's business was thriving, if his brother still played hoops.

Hillel regarded Larry quizzically. He did not make the connection between Larry Elliot and Larry Elliot Rovner, the older brother of his Hebrew school classmate Lana. Elliot was a rock star, and there was no way that he could ever have associated with any member of his miserable family. Hillel said that Larry must have confused him with someone else, then proffered his album and asked if he could have an autograph. And suddenly, Larry could see that Hillel didn't really want to know him at all. He sighed, then began to take on the role that he played when he was being interviewed by college newspapers, the role he understood that Hillel wanted him to play. He shook his head and gave Hillel a disapproving glance—he didn't give autographs, man, he said gruffly. The whole concept creeped him out; it was like people were trying to get a piece of you. This, from the same Larry Elliot Rovner who, at age twelve, had hung out for hours by the players' entrance of Chicago Stadium waiting for Bulls star Chet Walker to sign his program, ultimately settling for the autograph of Superfan, the beer-bellied mascot who ran laps around the court during halftime. Larry told Hillel that he wouldn't sign his album, but he'd have a drink with him, how would that be?

As Larry and Hillel sat on a couch drinking Cel-Ray tonics, Larry practiced his rock 'n' roll spiel, most of which he had adapted from Bob Dylan interviews. He told Hillel that the rock 'n' roll lifestyle was a drag, it was so fuckin' empty, man, he kept saying. He said that, if he had it to do all over again, he would have done something small with his life, something small but meaningful. He would have been a teacher or a construction worker, known what it was like to work with his hands. He would have stayed married to his first wife and had a house and a couple of kids. What he was doing, man, when you thought about it, was really only one step up from being a pimp. All the fashion shoots, all the glamour girls, all the hotel suites, all this, he said, gesturing to the green room, didn't mean shit. He now saw Hillel looking at him with awestruck eyes; Larry finally said that he didn't mean to be rude, man, but he didn't like anyone in his room when he was doing his vocal exercises.

After Larry walked Hillel to his door, he slapped five with him, then asked him to hand over his record album. Larry signed his name big across the front, and told Hillel not to tell a soul that he'd given him the autograph, because if he did, then everyone would want one. And as Hillel left the green room with the album under his arm, Larry spewed forth a litany of wise sayings, each of which he had just read in Charlie Wasserstrom's most recent *City Times* column. He advised Hillel to lead by example, to touch people's lives, to honor his mother and father, to take time every day to tell someone that he loved them. And "This above all," he told Hillel, "always be a *mensch*."

When Larry took the stage, Hillel stood near the back of the Aragon. He watched Larry slash his guitar, kick at his drums, howl into his microphone. At the end of Larry's set, he watched men raising lighters, *tsitsis* in their fists, women flinging brassieres and *ch'ais* onto the stage. He couldn't help but feel sorry for Larry; he knew how sad and lonely he must have been feeling up there onstage, how much he must have hated the sound of the applause. When Larry was called back for his first encore, Hillel couldn't believe that the audience wouldn't allow the man his privacy. When the audience called Larry back a second time, Hillel couldn't stand it anymore. Even though he had planned to stay at the Aragon well after the concert had ended, to supervise the cleanup and tally the receipts, he couldn't bear watching Larry for another minute, knowing how empty he must be feeling inside. Larry emerged for his second encore, fired up and shirtless, *mezuzah* bouncing against his bare chest as he threw his arms out and proudly bellowed, "Fuck 'Hands Across America'—how about some hands across Larry Elliot?" Hillel ran out a side entrance of the Aragon and into the alley before he had the chance to see Larry lead the closing sing-along of "We Are the World."

Mindful of the hour and of the fact that he would have to return to the Aragon before the night was through, Hillel proceeded briskly. The air was warm and the wind had a hint of the imminent summer about it as he entered the Lawrence el station, paid his fare, walked up to the platform, and took a southbound train. As he rode, he thought about what Larry Elliot had said, how he had told him to live an honest, decent life, to be a *mensch*. And as he thought about Elliot's words, he became convinced that this was not really Elliot who had spoken to him, but Carl Slappit Silverman, whose spirit had a message to impart that was so important that he had taken human form. He had seen the direction that Hillel's life was taking and disapproved so strongly that he had sent Larry as his messenger. For the first time since Carl had found him shivering in the corner of his office and taken him in his arms, Hillel felt completely secure.

Hillel got off the train at Chicago Avenue and jogged west until he reached Larmer Galleries. He switched on the lights and walked through the lobby, then down to the basement, where he found a stack of his paintings. He had always been his own greatest admirer, even in *dalet* had signed his works with a smiling penis inscribed with H.T.G. (Hillel The Great). But now his art angered him. He shrank at its bitterness, shivered at its self-obsession, wondered why he had put so much energy into mocking another human being, mocking Slappit's only son. He looked at his H.E.L. signatures and wondered what it all amounted to, when he knew perfectly well that he wasn't touching anyone's life but his own. From this point on, he would follow Larry Elliot's advice; he would be a *mensch*. He collected all his paintings, then carried them out to the dumpster, knowing that this was what Slappit would have told him to do.

Hillel then packed his clothes, his sketchpads, and his skates, and wrote a note to "Sister Calliope," saying that he was sorry to be canceling his exhibition, and walked back to the el. Now he felt so full of love that he wanted to hug everyone he saw. He told the station attendant seated behind bulletproof glass at the Chicago Avenue subway stop that she was so lovely that he felt like crying, told his fellow passengers on the northbound train that *Hashem* was with them, tipped the Aragon bartenders and said that the job they had done had been a *mitzvah*. And when the lights were off in the Aragon and he had padlocked the doors, he took the train back south to Roosevelt Road, hoping to find Muley at his loft to apologize to him, but when he knocked on the door of the loft and no one answered, he decided to go to his parents' home on Coyle Avenue instead. He wondered where he might find a picture of Larry Elliot to tape to the wall of his room.

# 1 9 8 6 – 8 7

While Hillel had been knocking on Muley's door, Muley was sitting on board a Greyhound bus, bound for Miami. He had left Fidel at his mother and Mel's house, then taken the el to the bus station with two suitcases; one contained his cameras and a set of clothes, the other a set of tools, a book of matches, an orange-and-black canister labeled BUTCHER'S WAX, thirteen reels of Super 8 film that he had once projected onto the wall of Carl Silverman's hospital room, and a small white model rocket ship. Muley had paid for the rocket, the tools, and the bus ticket with the three-hundred-odd dollars that Carl had willed him. He had called his grandmother from the bus station pay phone to tell her that he was on his way.

As the bus sped down Highway 9, Muley read books on the stages of rockets, on aerodynamics, on thrust-to-weight ratios. He studied maps and took notes about ocean currents and wind patterns. And when he wasn't reading, he was writing shopping lists. Once he arrived in Florida, he stayed with Mendel and Sadie, who soon took to calling him by his middle name, Scott, because she found his first name too difficult to explain to her friends at Bridlewood. Muley ate breakfast, lunch, and dinner with his grandparents, taking notes as he listened to Sadie's stories of Chernovtsy, their Atlantic crossing, Ellis Island, and Chicago's Old West Side. At breakfast, one day before Halley's Comet would attain its maximum brightness, Muley asked Sadie whether she and Mendel would consider joining him for a short road trip to Cape Canaveral. Though Mendel only grunted in response to Muley's question, Sadie said that she would be delighted, and insisted that she do the driving; Mendel's license had expired more than ten years earlier and Muley, she said, was far too young to drive a car.

Leaving aside the time that they had spent in Chicago during the last month and a half of their son's life, their grand voyage to New York, and the train ride from Grand Central Terminal to Chicago when they had been barely more than teenagers, Mendel and Sadie had seldom taken trips longer than twenty miles. And as they had grown older, it seemed as if their world shrank with each passing year, until it was now no larger than the one they had each known in Chernovtsy. Once, the world had expanded to the point where it was as large as the ocean, America, and Europe combined; until the moment that Muley had arrived, it seemed to be only the size of the tiny sphere of Bridlewood Village.

For decades, Sadie had prided herself on her perfect vision, but by now, she had lost fifty percent of her eyesight, and when she drove, she insisted on staying in the rightmost lane; thus, it took nearly eight hours to complete the 180-mile trip to Cape Canaveral. During the ride in the rented Ford Fairmont, Mendel, who had spent most of his adult life complaining about Sadie's driving, sat in the passenger seat with a beatific smile on his face, watching the signs that they passed on the highway, the palm trees, the orange groves. Muley sat in the backseat, his movie camera next to him, his rocket ship on the floor.

It had been nearly four years since Muley had first arrived at the Space Coast Inn with Dr. Sam Singer and Connie Sherman, who was still living in Taos, New Mexico, running an organic farm with her husband, Ephraim, and taking care of her son, Christopher Muley. Since Muley had last visited Cape Canaveral, the surrounding towns had become eerily quiet. While NASA searched for an adequate explanation for the *Challenger* tragedy, the space program remained dormant, and the tourist industry had dwindled. The bars and restaurants were three-quarters empty; the souvenir shops closed early; every motel had vacancies.

They arrived at the Space Coast Inn just after midnight on the eleventh of April, and drove to Playalinda Beach shortly before dawn. As Muley stood with Mendel and Sadie on the deserted beach, a lighthouse to their immediate north, Halley's Comet was visible over the ocean, brighter than Muley had ever seen it. In a few days, it would disappear entirely, not to return for another seventy-six years. Muley unloaded the rocket ship, the metal cases, his movie camera, and his tools, laying them down on the white sand. He worked quickly in the dim, metallic blue light, and when he was through, he stepped back to look at his creation. The rocket ship, whiter than the sand, stood waist-high; and at its widest, its circumference was that of a reel of film. He had based its design on numerous objects, he told his grandparents: the space shuttle, a piñata, a barber pole, a Pez dispenser. It stood on the base of a music stand; beneath it was the canister of Butcher's Wax, which was filled with Sterno.

Muley used a wrench to loosen the bolts that connected the metal cone at the top of the rocket to its body, took off the cone, then placed his thirteen reels of 8 mm film in the body of the rocket, one on top of the other. He then replaced the cone, tightened its bolts, and waited until he felt the hint of a southerly wind. He told Mendel and Sadie to stand back, then reached into his pocket for matches. He struck one and dropped it into the Butcher's Wax canister, which glowed with a circle of blue flame. Muley lifted his camera and filmed Mendel and Sadie watching, silhouetted against the dawn sky. White smoke billowed from the base of the rocket, which crept slowly, then shot straight up, describing a vertical trail of white smoke before, one hundred feet in the air, the wind got hold of it and sent it flying over the Atlantic Ocean. Soon, the rocket was merely a white pinpoint of light slicing through the sky; it faded from view only moments before the comet did.

As he stood on the beach, Mendel Silverman could feel the cold salt spray of the ocean on his cheeks; he remembered this sensation from long ago, but could not place from when or where. *Now,* he asked Muley, *exactly why had they driven all this way to look at a rocket?* Muley packed up his tools and his camera, then walked back to the car with his grandparents. When they returned to the motel and had settled back into their rooms, the first thing that Muley did was to call Jill. And then he called Calliope. He had the key to Bronzeville Studios in his pocket.

One week before the first anniversary of the space shuttle *Challenger* explosion, one week before Muley would unveil his newest installation, titled *Five Spheres,* Muley stood hand in hand with Jill beside a whirring film projector in the center of the lobby of Bronzeville Studios, Fidel between them. The following day, Jill would be returning to Poughkeepsie, where she planned to spend a good deal of the final semester of her junior year working diligently to assume the mantle of editor in chief of the *Miscellany News.*

Though he hadn't entirely completed his exhibit yet, Muley wanted Jill to see it before she left. Each floor, he explained, was dedicated to a different period of his family's evolution. The rear wall of the lobby had been painted white and on it, Muley was projecting a short, animated film that tracked Mendel and Sadie's childhoods, their journey to America, their early years in Chicago. The ground-floor rooms that had once housed studios and editing suites contained artifacts of their youth—passports, a model of an ocean liner, a bottle from the pop factory where Sadie had worked.

As the film continued to roll, Fidel followed Muley and Jill up to the second floor; the film projected against the white back wall depicted images from Deirdre's youth—the apartment on the South Side where she had lived with her father, her first meeting with Carl, their first date, their final argument. Muley had built bookcases and filled them with the novels she loved and the stories she had written; on the floor were piles of record albums. The third floor was devoted to Muley's own childhood—a movie depicted him walking with Jill, his mother alone in their apartment, his father in Malibu, thousands of miles away. Scattered about were reels of film, sketchpads, a hockey net, sticks, pucks, electronic equipment, wood, wire, radios. In the fourth floor screening room, a rocket ship stood on the sandy floor, and on a screen, a film loop played over and over—Mendel and Sadie Silverman watching a rocket rise into the sky, then streak toward Halley's Comet.

In one corner of the room, there was an illuminated red-and-white exit sign. Jill followed Muley through the doorway underneath the sign, then up a set of concrete steps to a fire door. This was his favorite part of the installation, Muley said as he pushed open the door and stepped onto the tar-paper roof; he had painted it white. Muley held Jill as they gazed east and Fidel stretched out beside them. The streets and sidewalks were white with snow; beyond them, Jill and Muley could see the black lake.

What did this represent, Jill asked.

What happens next, said Muley.

He pressed his lips to hers. She felt the wind ruffling her hair.

V

# Aliyah

*Jill and Rachel's Book of Homecoming*

*(November 25, 1987)*

— — —

(A TALE OF THE MILKY WAY,
THE WORLD, AMERICA, CHICAGO,
AND WEST ROGERS PARK)

*We are seeing a coming together of two trends:*
*one encouraging and one ominous.*
—MAYOR HAROLD WASHINGTON, 1987

*We parted with the old world, rejecting it once and for all.*
*We are working toward a new world.*
—MIKHAIL GORBACHEV, 1987

*The Lord will scatter you among the people,*
*and only a scant few of you shall remain . . .*
—DEUTERONOMY 4:27

O ne day before Thanksgiving, five-year-old Rachel Wasserstrom was
standing on the lawn of her parents' West Rogers Park home waiting im-
patiently for her sister Jill to come home when a pale orange BMW 2002 with a
broken muffler and a dangerously low tailpipe came to a stop on North Shore
Avenue. Jill had been due home from Europe several hours earlier, and Rachel
was looking forward to her arrival, in part because she liked her sister, but more
because she liked when the house was full and the fact that Jill often arrived
with a dog.

During the first years of Rachel's life, it had seemed as if the house had always
been abuzz with activity. And before Jill had left for college, Rachel had delighted
in the precious little time she was able to spend alone with her parents—going
to lunch at What's Cooking with her dad, accompanying her mom on trips to
Rosel's Stylists or Crawford's Department Store, always bringing along a plastic
bag filled with pretzel rods, butter cookies, and rye bread and margarine sandwiches. But when they all returned from driving Jill to O'Hare, Rachel immediately felt the immensity of her house, the emptiness of its rooms. Now when
Michelle or Jill returned for a day or a week, Rachel would start to feel their absence long before they actually left.

The previous year, Rachel had eagerly anticipated nursery school; she had
picked out her Crayola box two months in advance. During orientation in the
Boone Elementary School auditorium, the evening before the first day of classes,
she sat with her parents while Principal Aviva Bernstein described what to expect
during their first weeks; afterward, Rachel joined the other kids in the gymnasium for Hi-C and Mystic Mint cookies. And though most children clung to their

parents' hands or hid in their mothers' skirts, Rachel had walked proudly and confidently up to the other children, declaring that her name was Rachel and she lived on North Shore and she had two sisters, one of whom had a dog.

While Charlie and Gail shook hands with the other parents and sipped punch and ate cookies, Rachel met a boy named Gershom Globus who lived on Washtenaw and a boy named Brendan O'Hara who lived on Artesian and a girl named Ava Brodkey who lived on Coyle. Gershom had pointed out his parents and Brendan had pointed out his parents and Ava had pointed out her mom and then Rachel had pointed out Gail and Charlie, and Ava laughed and asked whether those were her parents or her grandparents—they looked *so old*—at which point Rachel made a fist just as Jill had taught her, and swung, felling Ava Brodkey with a right cross to the chin followed by a judo kick to the shoulder. Gail swooped in and carried Rachel out the gymnasium door.

The memory of that orientation lingered on—not so much for Rachel's classmates, who routinely forgot that she was a skilled playground grappler, an oversight that frequently resulted in the knockdowns of the occasional foe who dared to ask Rachel why her mother wore slacks or why her father didn't wear a yarmulke—but rather for Rachel herself, who couldn't shake the idea that her parents were old. This thought consumed her whenever her father said that he was too tired to play, whenever her mother said that her back would hurt too much if Rachel sat on her shoulders. On the rare occasions when she would take walks through the neighborhood with Michelle, passersby would assume that they were mother and daughter, a misconception that Michelle did nothing to dispel, frequently gossiping with neighbors, saying that she was amazed that she had kept her figure after the pregnancy.

Rachel sensed that her parents did the things that old people did—they didn't play Pinners or Wiffle ball; they went to restaurants and concerts. Wolfy's hot dogs were bad for her father's heart; her mother couldn't keep up when they played tag. On one occasion, Rachel had asked Charlie why he was so much older than all the other fathers, and he had said that it was because he and Gail had loved her so much that they wanted to let her take her time before she entered the world. This didn't make sense to Rachel—if they had loved her so much, why had they waited so long?

Once Rachel had entered kindergarten, she lost many friends, particularly on her parents' block, where the Orthodox Jewish children with whom she had attended nursery school were now at parochial institutions. Some of the children were no longer allowed to play with Rachel, because, Gershom Globus explained, she was a *shiksa,* a word that Gershom and his Big Wheel–riding, Nerf-football–playing friends would shout at her as she rode her tricycle past their houses.

One day after dinner, Rachel had asked her mother what *shiksa* meant and Gail had told her that it was a bad word for a girl who wasn't Jewish. When Rachel said that she thought that she was, in fact, Jewish, Gail explained that there were three kinds of Jews: Orthodox Jews, who had separate plates for milk and meat, went to *shul* all day, and made their wives walk six paces behind their husbands; Reform Jews, who weren't really Jews at all except during holidays and funerals; she and Rachel's father, Gail explained, were Conservative Jews, which was somewhere in between.

But it was getting harder to be a Conservative Jew in West Rogers Park, Gail said. When she had moved into the neighborhood with her first husband, nearly everyone had been Conservative; now the neighborhood was almost exclusively Orthodox. The children of the Conservatives had either married gentiles or turned Reform and moved to the northern suburbs. On the west side of California, there were klezmer music shops and social service agencies catering to newly arrived Russian Jews. A Chabad House stood in place of the Bagel Deli; every day, the Mitzvah Mobile would park on the corner of Devon and Sacramento with its motor running and its back door open as Lubavitcher Jews would ask male passersby if they were Jewish. Banged-up station wagons were ubiquitous, usually sporting Orthodox Jewish bumper stickers—"I Listen to Torah Radio Network" or "Let Them Call Me Rebbe"—while on the east side of California, the working-class Jews, the ones who worked in the restaurant business, as salesmen, as contractors, had moved to the suburbs, paving the way for a new wave of East Asian and Middle Eastern immigration. The Orthodox Jews stayed on the west side of California, the Middle Easterners and Asians on the east, all of them still encircled by the *eruv* strung from the lampposts of West Rogers Park.

But it was only when Gershom Globus arrived on the Schiffler-Wasserstrom doorstep with a present for Rachel that Gail suggested to Charlie that they move out of West Rogers Park altogether. Gershom had rung the doorbell and Gail had invited him in, but Gershom said that he wasn't allowed in unkosher houses. Gail then asked him to show her his present for Rachel; he removed the top of a shoebox, revealing a half-dozen toy soldiers lying on white tissue paper. He held up one of the soldiers—a Crusader with a red cross on its uniform—and said that he had received them for his birthday; his father wouldn't let him keep soldiers with crosses on them, but since Rachel wasn't Jewish, she would probably like them. Once Gail had sent Gershom back home with his soldiers, she walked directly into her husband's office. "We're moving," she said.

Moving out of West Rogers Park seemed traumatic enough, particularly to Charlie, who associated change with death, but after Gail had spent a few weeks researching real estate, it seemed inevitable that they would move not only out of their neighborhood but out of Chicago entirely. Each neighborhood was either too rich or too poor, too black or too white; the gulf in the city that editorial writers attributed to the economic policies of the Reagan administration and that Gail blamed on the divisive agenda of the Washington administration seemed to have erased the middle in which Gail had lived for most of her life. The Jewish families that remained within the city limits were scattered all about, living in small outposts near the Koreans in Albany Park, the Yuppies in Lincoln Park, the academics in Hyde Park, the Reagan Republicans on the Magnificent Mile. The neighborhood in which they were living was really the only Jewish one left in the city, and yet they no longer felt welcome. Evanston, the first town beyond Chicago's northern border, seemed to be the most logical choice, and by October, Gail had found a three-bedroom house on Orrington Street and a buyer for the house on North Shore—a family of Russian Jews who would pay cash and would build an addition over the garage to accommodate their eight children.

At any rate, it was settled: on January 31, 1988, the Rosows would move into the house that Charlie and Becky had once called The Funny House, and Charlie, Gail, and Rachel would move to Evanston. The intervening months would be a celebration of sorts, a "farewell tour," as Michelle had said when she first learned of it. Charlie, Rachel, and Gail would celebrate their last West Rogers Park Halloween—which was just as well, seeing that during the previous year's Halloween, no one came to the door, save for Yoav Mermelstein, who drove the Mitzvah Mobile and asked Charlie if he had put on *tefillin* that day. And on the twenty-sixth of November, the Wasserstroms would celebrate their last Thanksgiving on North Shore.

Michelle, now in her final year of law school at NYU, had agreed to attend. She would allow her understudy to take her role that weekend in a "shitty new play" titled *Almost Twenty,* in which she was appearing under her stage name, Clara Moskowitz, to avoid raising any suspicions among her classmates and professors that she was not committed to the legal profession. She would be bringing Gareth Overgaard, who, after returning from the Peace Corps, had begun work on his dissertation in Education, which he referred to as "forty-two pounds of edible fungus"; Larry Elliot Rovner, now touring small clubs to support his second album and new single, "My Dad (Likes to Watch Hillel)," would be coming, if only to avoid his "dad's fucking family," all of whom had taken umbrage with a number of his songs, particularly Lana, now a junior majoring in Communications at Lake Forest College, where her sorority had been put on probation for unpaid pizza deliveries. Deirdre would be coming with Mel, who had finally abandoned his screenplay for *Son of a Preacher Man* and was working on adapting an anonymous, unpublished novel that Deirdre had shown him, titled *In an Empty House,* which Mel thought might have an excellent role for Michelle. Marty and Angela Eisenstaedt were coming along with their youngest daughter, Bibi Davidson. And though Jill had planned to spend the entire first semester of her senior year traveling in Europe, she shocked Gail by agreeing to come home for Thanksgiving. "Why the hell not?" she had said, adding that Muley would probably accompany her.

On the Tuesday before Thanksgiving, Rachel had asked Gail eight times when Jill would be coming home. Gail assured her that she would be there the next day by the time that Rachel got home from Boone. But on Wednesday, when Rachel returned from morning kindergarten—where she had fought with Sammy Chung after she had told him that Santa Claus was fake—Jill wasn't there. Every few minutes or so, Rachel, who was watching *3-2-1 Contact* on TV, would jump up from the couch to see if a taxi was pulling up, hopefully with Jill in it, and even more hopefully with Jill and a dog. But when her television program was interrupted by a Special Report, Rachel went to the kitchen, where Charlie was cutting celery and Gail was toasting challah for turkey stuffing. She asked her mother whether she could wait outside for Jill.

Rachel had been playing football with herself for nearly an hour, pretending that fallen ginkgo leaves were her pursuers, when the orange BMW appeared. Rachel jumped up, thinking that this might be a taxicab—she knew taxis to be yellow, but orange was fairly close to yellow. She could not decide whether to run toward the car or inside the house to tell her parents that Jill was here. But then she heard the motor being turned off and saw the driver's door open, at which point a tall, bearded man in a ripped white T-shirt and paint-stained khaki work-pants emerged. As the man walked toward her, he asked if she remembered him.

Another young girl might have been frightened by the approaching figure of William Eamon Sullivan Jr., pale, haggard, and somewhat emaciated, but though Rachel was given to nightmares, which occasionally made her stay awake playing electronic football long after her parents thought that she was asleep, she was rarely ever afraid of anyone she met in real life, save for Mr. Boaz Levy, who hadn't gotten over the fact that his youngest son was still studying art, like some kind of *faygeleh*. Boaz scowled at Rachel whenever her father bought falafels at his restaurant, and had once remarked to Charlie that having one girl was unfor-tunate, two was bad luck, but three meant that Charlie had been cursed.

Rachel told Wes no, she didn't remember him. Perhaps it was the long hair, he said, or perhaps it was the fact that the last time he'd seen Rachel when he had visited Jill, she'd been a baby. Oh, he was a friend of Jill's, Rachel deduced aloud. More than a friend, said Wes—he thought that he was in love with her. He had come here on this very day to tell her, and he thought that she'd be here by now. Yeah, Rachel said, she thought so too. Wes asked if Rachel would mind if he waited for her; they could blow soap bubbles or play hopscotch, just like he used to do with his little brother, who hated him now and had head-butted him the moment he had returned from West Berlin. Blowing bubbles was for babies, Rachel opined; she liked football. Good, Wes said, why didn't they throw the football around while they waited?

At first, Rachel enjoyed playing with Wes, particularly since her mother didn't know how to throw a football right and her father never played for more than ten minutes. But after a half hour, Rachel's arm had grown weary from flinging the little plastic ball back and forth with Wes, and she wondered why Jill still hadn't arrived.

J ill had planned to spend her junior year in either El Salvador or Budapest, but when she learned that studying abroad would disqualify her from considera-tion for the editor-in-chief position of the *Miscellany News* her senior year, she changed her plans. She was aware that the college paper was not particularly important in the grand scheme of things; still, she could not abandon it in a time of growing campus conservatism. One of the papers at Dartmouth was making national headlines for its anti–South Africa divestment stance, and even Vassar's own conservative periodical, *The Spectator,* once little more than a satirical rag, was gaining attention. *The Spectator*'s outspoken editor, Stanley Barnes, had recently debated the efficacy of affirmative action with the Reverend Al Sharpton before a hooting live audience on the *Morton Downey Jr. Show.* Meanwhile, the *Misc.,* despite Jill's columns decrying the bombing of Libya, the invasion of Grenada, and the corruption of the Contras, focused nearly all its coverage on arts and culture so that editor in chief Alec Savage could devote two-page spreads to his reviews of Smithereens, Feelies, and Larry Elliot albums, all of which he entered into college journalism competitions in the hopes of nabbing a summer internship with *Rolling Stone.*

Jill had begun her junior year as opinion page editor, but once Alec had secured his internship at *Rolling Stone,* he ceded his "From the Editor's Desk" column to Jill and promoted her to deputy editor, letting her lead editorial meetings while he played CDs in his dorm room and had sex with his girlfriend, Andrea Fleischman. At the end of March, not long after Jill had published a column about the pleasures of having voted in her first election, casting her absentee ballot for Harold Washington, who handily defeated Mayor Jane Byrne in Chicago's Democratic mayoral primary—a column that was viciously lampooned in a subsequent issue of *The Spectator*—it seemed so obvious that Jill would win the position of editor in chief for her senior year that no *Misc.* staffer opposed her. Her job interview was a joke; Alec only asked if she had a driver's license and whether she would hire a deputy editor with a car to get to the printer in Wappingers Falls.

The morning that the 1987–88 editorial staff was posted on a sheet of paper tacked to the door of the *Misc.* office, Jill at first did not even bother to look at the list, thinking it too self-involved to take a special trip to see her name—one of the first policies that she would institute at the paper would be to eliminate bylines, so that the paper would concern itself with the news, not with the egos of the writers reporting it. She was sitting alone in the dining center, nibbling on a bowl of bulgur wheat, raisins, and dried apples, when Kenny Melnick—with whom Jill had not spoken since her grandmother's wedding—slowed but did not stop at Jill's table, observing that he thought that what the *Misc.* had done to her was *hahsh* and that if she wanted to *staht* a petition, he'd be *fuhst* in line to sign. Jill dashed across campus to the newspaper office. On the door was the list of the following year's editorial staff; at the top of the list was Stanley Barnes.

Jill opened the door to find Alec in a haze of pot smoke, his feet up on his desk. He was smoking a joint and listening to "Tell Hannah (I Ain't Home)" on a boom box. When Jill entered, he turned down the boom box volume. He'd expected that she might be stopping by, he said, adding that he had strongly supported Jill's candidacy for the editorship. But at the last minute, Stan Barnes had submitted his résumé and had shown a great deal of talent and, in the end, it had been a toss-up between the two applicants. Jill and Stan were so evenly matched that he had written all their attributes on a dry-erase board and they had canceled each other out, until he recalled that Stan had two things that Jill didn't: a driver's license and a car. He told Jill that he hoped that they could remain friends, and that he might be able to help her out with an internship at *Rolling Stone* once she graduated.

Jill spent the summer before her senior year living with Muley above Larmer Galleries' new location in the Bronzeville Studios building, where the *Five Spheres* installation was still being exhibited. The loft where Muley had lived for his first three years of college had been sold as a condo. Jill worked for minimum wage as an intern at the City News Bureau, reporting ten hours a day about murders, robberies, and meetings of the City Council, where Mayor Washington now held a majority. And at the end of the summer, she had saved enough money to spend the first semester of her senior year traveling through Europe, far away from the sordid politics of Vassar College's newspaper.

On the late August day that Jill was to take a flight to Luxembourg to begin her European journey, she and Muley had awoken early and stayed in bed chatting past noon, both agreeing that they would not make love for fear that the act would imbue Jill's departure with too much significance. Neither Jill nor Muley questioned whether they would be together when she returned; they were now planning their future with sentences that concluded with periods instead of question marks. Jill still ached over the loss of her mother, but it no longer consumed her. Muley no longer felt the weight of his father's absence, or the sole responsibility for his mother's happiness. Jill no longer compared herself to Connie Sherman or Calliope Larmer or any of the women who attended Muley's installations; Muley no longer flushed when he thought of Wes Sullivan or Kenny Melnick.

And if Jill and Muley did not tell each other everything, if Jill did not confess that she had slow-danced with "The Horace" Greenstein to "Sledgehammer" while tipsy at a party at the Vassar Terrace Apartments or that she had made out with Ronelle Leeds on Founder's Day, if she did not reveal that she had kissed Larry Rovner when she was visiting her sister in Manhattan until Larry had said that they had to stop because what they were doing was a *shandeh,* if Muley did not confess that he had spent the better part of a night and a morning in Calliope's apartment drinking Scotch and root beer, or that he had slept with Connie one final time when she had been visiting her family and her husband was in Wisconsin buying ginseng, it was not because Jill and Muley were keeping secrets so much as that each thought that giving voice to the aforementioned incidents would have granted them too much importance.

It was this deep confidence in her relationship with Muley that would lead Jill to seek out Wes Sullivan when her European travels would bring her to West Berlin; allowing herself to stand in the presence of the first person who had inspired a feeling of passion unlike any she had known before would, she theorized, demonstrate not only how strong her relationship with Muley was but how strong she herself was. She had copied down the return address in West Germany that Wes had scrawled on his last letter, the only letter he had written with any return address at all.

Wes might have been attempting to appear self-effacing by not including his return address on previous letters, Jill thought, but she had found his omission to be further evidence of his arrogance; he seemed interested only in having a one-sided correspondence. And yet, when Wes's letters started arriving every month or so on North Shore Avenue, or in Jill's Vassar mailbox, they held an undeniable fascination. With the pacing and keen eye for detail of an adventure novelist, he wrote of befriending gunrunners and contracting malaria in Pakistan, of continually being ignored by a girl named Sabine at the *Damenwahl* in a Bremerhaven dancehall, of having dinner at the home of a diplomat in Abidjan and falling victim to the charms of the diplomat's American girlfriend. He wrote of stalemating Bobby Fischer in Budapest, doing shots with IRA members in Belfast, smoking dope with skinheads in West Berlin. And though Jill sometimes doubted Wes's accounts, he pointed out that he'd been stringing for wire services, where fact-checking was rigorous. "But I wouldn't believe me if I were you either," he wrote.

Before she left Chicago for Luxembourg, Jill had plotted her itinerary in a black notebook purchased especially for her trip. She wrote down the names of museums with free days, of highways considered safe for hitchhiking, made reservations at youth hostels. She planned exactly how long she would spend in each city—four days in Brussels, two in Ghent, five in Amsterdam, three in West Berlin. She had arranged for visas so that she could travel into Eastern Europe to explore Budapest, Warsaw, and Prague.

She arrived at the Zoologische Garten train station in West Berlin on a warm, gray October afternoon following her stay in Amsterdam, where she met a group of American students, including Dartmouth student Prescott Connor Pendleton, who tried without success to get her high. She did not seek Wes out on her first day; she would have despised the idea of his thinking that, to her, he was the most important German tourist attraction. Instead, she checked into the Jugendgasthaus am Zoo, walked all the way to the Berlin Wall, and took a tram into the Eastern Bloc, spending hours strolling through the East before returning to the hostel just before the 10 P.M. curfew. On the second day, she visited the library and spent most of the afternoon in the Tiergarten reading English translations of Christa Wolf essays before riding the U-Bahn to the Prenzlauer Berg stop.

She had expected Wes's address to lead her to an apartment building, but the further she walked, the fewer apartments she saw. There weren't any businesses in this section of West Berlin: no *Konditorei,* no *Lebensmittelgeschaft,* only a cemetery, then graffiti-covered walls, abandoned buildings, empty lots, and rubble. In the distance, the East Berlin TV tower loomed, and in its foreground, Jill saw a complex of tan, windowless brick buildings blocked off from the street with a thick metal fence and razor wire. On the wall of a seemingly abandoned factory across the pothole-pocked road, someone had spray-painted AUSLÄNDER RAUS.

Through the fenced-off driveway, Jill could see the grounds—four low, rectangular, tan brick windowless buildings clustered around a small green space, a playground at its center with a rusty swing set, a seesaw, and a sandbox. In and around the playground, children were chasing each other, playing jump rope while two adults kept a close watch. One of the adults was a slim woman with a black braid that descended all the way to her blue jeans; the other was Wes. Even though Jill was more than fifty yards away from the playground, and even though his back was turned, Jill recognized him instantly. He was wearing army pants, an untucked white shirt, sleeves rolled up, and black boots; his hair reached just past his shoulders. Jill watched him as he held the hand of a small boy, then proceeded to let go and chase a little girl around the playground. The girl giggled as Wes pursued her then grabbed her under her arms and swept her into the air, lifting her above his head then down again, then up, then down, the little girl laughing all the way until he put her back on the ground and she chased him through the sandbox, around one building then another, then out onto the cracked roadway toward the front gates where Wes saw Jill through the fence.

Sheepishly, Jill gave Wes half a wave. Wes stopped dead. Then he bent down to the little girl, put his hands on his knees, and said something to her in a voice just loud enough for Jill to understand how fluently he spoke German. He stood with his hands in his pockets, slouching like someone who has always had to compensate for his height, gazing at Jill with those familiar black eyes, grinning his same dopey, dimpled grin. He looked youthful, carefree, as if he had been relieved of some great burden.

Wes pressed a button on his side of the fence, the metal gate slid open. He wore a necklace with a cross, which Jill did not recall seeing before. Wow, he said, it was so amazing to see her. He said nothing for nearly a minute, gaping at her; his eyes were twinkling. He said he was hoping that someday she might come. He stepped forward, as if he wanted to embrace her, but then he held out his hand. Did she have time for a tour, he asked.

As they walked around the playground, Wes explained that for the past year, he had been working at this camp, which had once been an armaments factory but now served as temporary quarters for asylum seekers, mostly from Sri Lanka, Eritrea, and Lebanon, while the West German government reviewed their cases. He helped the asylum seekers fill out documents, he played with their children, he recruited volunteers. He was a babysitter, a counselor, a tour guide, a friend, an administrator, and, he added with a wry smile, an unlicensed bodyguard; one time, when skinheads had thrown Molotov cocktails into the barracks, he'd put out the blaze before chasing the thugs down with a bat, the same bat with which he had taught a group of refugee children to play baseball. He received free room and board and, as long as he gave notice to his supervisors, they were cool about letting him take time off to pursue journalistic assignments.

The pay was poor, Wes said, the hours brutal, but the work was more satisfying than any he had ever done. For the first time, he felt as if he was doing something that mattered. The only downside was that it was too easy to become attached to people—you'd fall in love with parents, with their children, become part of their families, and then, weeks later, they were gone; sometimes he would see them on the street, they'd invite him to their first apartments, but he always felt as if he were intruding. All this may have sounded corny, he said, and he wouldn't be surprised if Jill thought that he was full of beans, but he swore that he was being truthful. Then again, he said, he had told Jill much the same thing at least once before; he guessed that this was his penance.

Wes showed Jill the playground, the cafeteria where the refugees cooked their meals, the medical facilities, the indoor activities center. He showed her the cramped living quarters—cheerfully decorated little white rooms that could house families of four on bunk beds and roll-away mattresses. He knocked on one door, then opened it to reveal a black-haired girl in a lime green jumper and chartreuse socks. This was his best buddy, Wes told Jill, picking the girl up and placing her on his shoulders. Her name was Amal and she was from Palestine and he had taught her some words in English. Amal asked Wes, "Is that your wife?" Wes laughed, and shook his head.

"I wish," he said.

The tour continued with Amal on Wes's shoulders. Jill wondered how Wes could be so comfortable around children; they always made her uneasy. She had no idea how to speak to them, always worried that they found her boring, fretted the few times she'd babysat that the child would suffer some mortal wound in her care. There had been times when she'd offered to play with Rachel, who had run out of the room screaming, and Jill couldn't blame her. Some people like Wes could just walk around lifting kids up, but Jill had never liked being lifted; could tickle children with abandon, but Jill had always hated being tickled: whenever Artie Schumer had tried to tickle her, she'd wanted to smack him. Her relationship with Rachel had improved only when she had taught her some self-defense moves; until then, Jill had the impression that Rachel tolerated her presence only so that she could play with her dog.

Nevertheless, Jill felt totally at ease with Wes, so much so that before she had the chance to say that it was time for her to head back to her hostel, Wes had asked her to stay for dinner and she had said yes. And at dinner, which was consumed upon long metal tables in an echoing hall, the people she met were so fascinating that she lost track of time there as well, spending more than an hour discussing her hopes of a new era arising from the policies of Mikhail Gorbachev with a teenage girl from Romania. By then it was past nine o'clock, and Jill had less than an hour to get back to the hostel before it locked its doors for the evening. She fumbled with her backpack and motioned to Wes, who asked where she was going—he'd made baklava, and everyone would be having after-dinner drinks and cigarettes. Yes, Jill said, but if she didn't return to the hostel by ten, she wouldn't have anywhere to sleep. No worries, Wes said nonchalantly, she could sleep here. Unless, of course, she wanted to leave.

Jill had the nagging sensation that Wes had been planning all along to casually ask her to stay overnight. And yet, she wanted to. Not just for the night, but for a week, months even. She thought about how petty, self-centered, and hedonistic her American life was, how much it paled when compared to Wes Sullivan's. Yes, she had volunteered for Greenpeace, had doors slammed in her face; yes, she'd exposed the ravages that Reaganomics had wreaked upon urban America in the *Miscellany News,* reported on Chicago politics for the City News Bureau. But everything she had accomplished seemed so small when she looked at Wes's existence, how committed he was to the plights of people who had no one else to care for them; perhaps there was something self-aggrandizing about it, but what did that matter if he was actually accomplishing something?

Jill considered whether Muley would wonder why she'd neglected to write him today as she had on every other day of her trip. She considered the same question the next day too. She would spend her next thirty-six hours with Wes, playing left field and making three errors in Wes's baseball game, riding the U-Bahn to the *Krankenhaus* where Wes chatted up nurses and asked if they could give him some of their overstocked supplies, spending the night in Wes's room, in Wes's bed, in fact, though not with Wes in it. He had insisted on taking the floor; it didn't matter to him, he said—his neurons fired more rapidly than most people's, and he usually stayed up most of the night thinking.

While Jill lay in bed, Wes curled up with a pillow on the cold concrete floor, refusing to take any blankets. He didn't need them, he said, he had a very high internal body temperature. The two of them would talk until Jill could stay awake no longer, and willed herself to fall asleep if only so she wouldn't embarrass herself by sleeptalking, something she vehemently denied whenever Muley accused her of doing it. Conversations moved freely from Gorbachev to Jack Kerouac to Elvis Costello to Erich Honecker, who had recently traveled to West Germany and who, Wes said, would someday soon bring about a united

Germany. Jill said she wasn't sure whether that would be such a good idea; the last time Germany had been united, things hadn't turned out so well. Times were different now, Wes opined, Germans were cool—it was the United States that the world really needed to fear.

Jill only became uneasy around Wes when he stopped talking about current events and instead talked about her, how smart she was, how gifted. Any time he mentioned some book or political movement with which she was unfamiliar, he would take for granted that she knew more about it than he did, and Jill would find herself playing along, feigning a detailed knowledge of the Baader-Meinhof gang or Walter Benjamin's writings on barbarism. Wes made a habit of saying how natural he felt around her, looked at her wistfully, and said damn, he really could have had something with Jill, but he had fucked it up, and man, what he wouldn't give to have 1983 to do over again.

The morning that she was to leave West Berlin and catch a noon train to Hamburg, Jill stood under the shower for a full fifteen minutes, for once in her life not caring about the water she was wasting, not caring about the fact that a dozen people were probably waiting to use the shower, not caring that the water got colder with each additional minute she remained. All her thoughts urged her to stay, which was why she knew that she had to leave. She had to follow the schedule in her black datebook, or else she would lose all bearings.

The previous morning, Wes had already showered and dressed by the time that Jill had awoken, but on this day, even when she had returned from her shower, Wes was still on the floor, barely awake when she reentered the room in the monogrammed bathrobe that he had lent her. She stood for a moment over her backpack, wondering whether to wait until he left before she dressed, then thought no, that was stupid, they were both adults, there was nothing shameful in nudity, this was Germany, this wasn't a body-obsessed culture like America; here, everybody got naked and lazed in the sauna together, then ate vegetarian hamburgers and protested nuclear weapons. She reached into her backpack, past her open datebook, and found a pair of underwear. But as soon as she had begun untying her robe, Wes stood up, asked how late it was, grabbed a towel, and dashed out of the room. Jill was left to dress alone, which, given her newly casual approach to nudity, was disappointing.

As she dressed, slower than usual, she wondered whether Wes would ask her to stay longer and if so, how to respond without sounding ridiculous. Her schedule was a fantasy; her next two months were totally free. There were sights that she wanted to see, historical monuments, museums, but all that was egotism; there was no social value in it, no refugees inviting her to dinner, no wire service editors publishing her stories. She felt bourgeois and useless. If Wes asked her to stay, Jill would not be able to refuse. The only question would be what she would tell Muley. But Wes did not ask. When he returned from his shower, fully dressed in jeans and an open, pale green button-down shirt with the sleeves rolled up, his cross tucked behind a scoop-necked white undershirt, he said that he was sorry that Jill was leaving, but would she mind if he didn't accompany her to the train station? He had asked to take the morning off, but it was short notice and the center was understaffed.

Once Jill had finished packing and her hair was dry, she found Wes in the cafeteria, cooking an omelet for Amal and her mother, Hanan. Jill had imagined what Wes might do or say upon her departure, how he might say that he wished that they could have had more time together, but all Wes did was ask if she was "cruisin' out already," and when she said yes, he told her to "be safe," and flashed a peace sign. Instead, Jill said all that she had envisioned Wes saying, told him that it was a drag that she wouldn't see him again anytime soon. Wes patted her shoulder twice. Well, you never knew what might happen, he said with a smile, and if they were destined to meet again, he was "sure the fates would decree it." And with that, he returned to his skillet, shaking it over the burner, humming "Auf der Flucht," while Jill walked quickly out of the asylum center and into the gray, misty autumn afternoon.

As Jill rode the train to Hamburg, gazing out the windows at endless brown and yellow fields, Wes's words upon her departure kept returning to her. For though she did not subscribe to the tenets of any major religion, had not entered a synagogue since her father and Gail's wedding, she still was a great believer in fate; she had some sense that events did not transpire randomly, that there were larger patterns at work. Jill no longer believed in a philosophy of accidents, the way she had during her adolescence shortly after her mother had died, when everything—the universe, the earth, her life—seemed to have resulted from the chance intersection of molecules, chemicals, and bad luck. She now believed that what appeared to be accidental usually served some greater purpose. Whenever something unusual or seemingly random happened, she tried to determine an overall reason for it, to make out the hidden pattern. The world seemed full of possibilities—the Chicago Democratic machine had disintegrated; there were rents in the fabric of the Iron Curtain; Ronald Reagan's administration was on the way out, and here she was, once again thinking about Wes.

Thus, it was not entirely surprising to Jill that, during her travels, she would see Wes again. Yet the regularity with which he reappeared became disconcerting. For over the course of the next three weeks, it seemed to her that Europe was hardly larger than West Rogers Park. There Wes was, chowing down on a currywurst in the square in front of the Köln cathedral, then there he was again, clinking beer steins with a trio of female backpackers in an open-air bar along Düsseldorf's Königsallee. Whenever their eyes met, Wes would smile, but in a sad, nostalgic way. He was always on his way somewhere else, just leaving whenever Jill was arriving, just coming into town when Jill was running to catch a train.

Until Jill arrived in Prague.

Jill had been strolling by the Vltava River when Hradčany Castle came into view. Wes was sitting on the steps, scribbling madly in a notebook, stubbing out a cigarette on the cement, an open copy of a Kundera novel on his knee. When he looked up, Jill was already sitting beside him. The last time Jill had seen Wes—in Vienna as he was walking out of the Tirolerhof Café—he had been rushed; he had said that he was late for an appointment to interview a group of "neo-Nazi assholes." But this time, as Jill took off her backpack and sat down on the steps, he smiled calmly, and when Jill asked why he was here, he merely said that he was doing some sightseeing. Sightseeing, Jill said, foreign correspondents didn't sightsee, did they? No, Wes said with a smile, maybe they didn't, but it seemed like a better answer than the real one. Which was what, Jill asked. She wouldn't believe it, said Wes—he reached in the pocket of his black Chicago Police Department jacket, pulled out a pack of Gauloises, and slapped it nervously against his palm. He said that the last thing he wanted was for Jill to think that he was still a liar; that was the worst thing that had happened those four years ago, not that Louis Benson had written letters to the colleges that had accepted him, not that he had let down his family, not that he had lied to Rae-Ann—after all, he said, he thought that Rae-Ann had spent most of her life lying to herself, denying her innermost desires when he alone understood that she was a closeted lesbian. No, he continued, the worst part was losing Jill's respect. And he knew that if he told Jill why he was sitting right here, he would risk losing it again. Why, asked Jill. Christ, Wes said, would she really make him tell her?

Here it was, he said. He pulled a cigarette out of his pack and lit it. He said that the reason why he was sitting here was because he knew that Jill would be coming. He'd had a vision of this very moment. He had imagined her walking up the steps of the castle. He had never been to Prague before, had not been certain that his West German passport would allow him entrance, did not even know which castle he was imagining, but when he saw it rising in front of him, he knew that he was in the right place. He had spent the day on the steps reading and writing. The first time he looked up, Jill was there. Jill said that Wes had to be joking.

"I wish I was," said Wes. He asked Jill where she was staying, and when she told him the name of the hostel, Wes laughed; he was staying there too. And despite the fact that Jill had made a reservation two months in advance, all the rooms were filled when she and Wes arrived at the Strahov Hostel. Marina, the pony-tailed desk clerk, winked at Wes when he turned to Jill and offered that she might share his room for the night. Then he carried Jill's backpack up all six flights of stairs.

That night, as cold, damp air seeped in through a cracked gray window behind a rusted grate, Wes lay on a pillow on the floor, a drain branding its impression into his back. Down the hall, German backpackers were carousing in their rooms. Beer bottles clinked. *"Zwei Männer und eine Frau; das ist ganz richtig,"* someone said with a cackle. A distant boom box was blaring out the Armed Forces Radio Top 40—"I Want Your Sex," "I Still Haven't Found What I'm Looking For," "My Sister (Crashed the Car Again)."

In the glow of a streetlight shining through the window, Jill took off her shoes and socks. Then she slipped off her jeans and sat down on the bed in her faded *Rainbow Warrior* T-shirt and her underwear. She folded the jeans, placed them in her backpack, took out her datebook, then climbed under the thin, frayed covers. The bed was big enough for two if they squeezed, she told Wes; it was silly for them to be so puritanical in Europe. Wes said nothing for a moment, then he nodded nonchalantly and stood. He carried his pillow toward her, and for a split second, he looked unsure of himself, perhaps even afraid.

As the two of them lay side by side, Jill paged through her datebook. Wes stared at the ceiling, his long arms stiff at his sides as he discussed politics, expressing his outrage at the moral poverty of the America he had left, where an ethically bankrupt man such as Robert Bork could be considered for the Supreme Court while a petty and dubious accusation of plagiarism could jettison

Joseph Biden from the presidential race. Jill was studying the names of the cities that she had visited—West Berlin, Düsseldorf, Vienna, Prague. She did not think of museums, libraries, or cafés; she thought of Wes—Wes at the café, Wes at the train station, Wes on the steps of the castle. Now she was lying beside him in the only remaining bed in the hostel. She thought of the next cities on her itinerary—Warsaw, Kraków, Budapest. Then she closed her datebook and began moving her hand under the covers toward him. A year from now, she thought, she would look back at this moment and everything would seem preordained. "If the fates decree it," Wes had said, and fate was clearly at work here.

Either that, or Wes had read her datebook.

Jesus, she thought. She stopped moving her hand toward Wes and picked up her datebook again. She glanced over to Wes and felt her body suddenly suffused with nausea. Her stomach churned, her body felt cold. He hadn't changed—not a bit. She must have been the stupidest person in the world. When had it happened, she wondered, when had he stolen a look at her book—when she'd been sleeping in the asylum center? When she'd taken a shower? Was this hostel really full? Marina the desk clerk had winked at Wes when she'd said it. *Fate,* he had said—she wondered if he'd remembered her using the word back in high school. She had no idea whether to pity Wes or despise him—still inventing stories, still snooping through other people's belongings, still trying to make her believe lies since he knew that he couldn't woo her with the truth.

Three loud raps sounded against the door, and when neither Jill nor Wes said a word, three more were heard, followed by some words in Czech. As Jill lay in bed, her mind swirling with anger, despair, and just a pinch of mordant humor, Wes rose and walked barefoot to the door, opening it to reveal Marina in her navy blue suit and sooty white, backless high-heeled shoes, one with a broken strap. "Phone," she said. Wes stepped into a pair of flip-flops and told Jill that there was a call for him, probably one of his editors. But Marina shook her head, said "Phone" twice more, and pointed at Jill. "Me?" Jill asked. Marina nodded, pointing down the hall to a wall-mounted phone.

As Jill stood in the hallway, her datebook in her hand, she picked up the phone and heard her voice echoing back to her before the line crackled. Gail was on the other end. She told Jill that she was sorry to track her down so late, but this was the only time when she knew that she'd be able to find her and the sooner they talked, the better. Jill was about to ask if someone had died, but Gail instead informed Jill of her and Charlie's imminent move out of Chicago and the final Thanksgiving dinner to be held at the former Funny House. And though Jill had not once thought of going home early to Chicago, though cutting her trip short was quite possibly the last thing she would have ever considered, she wondered what difference it made; Chicago, New York, Prague, outer space—it all seemed the same to her now. Sure, she told Gail, she'd come home for Thanksgiving: "Why the hell not?" And she'd bring Muley too, she said. Gail sighed, then asked Jill if she wanted to talk to her father. After Jill had spoken to Charlie for ten minutes, then Rachel for less than one, she returned to the hostel room. Wes was asleep in bed; though he was alone, the air was thick with the scent of Marina's lilac perfume.

Jill stood for a minute in the dark, gazing down at Wes—one of his arms was draped across the mattress; a hand was tightly clutching her pillow. She scribbled a note in a page of her datebook, placed the book on Wes's pillow, then tiptoed across the floor. She reached around for her jeans, and when she had put them back on, she put her socks in her shoes, zipped up her backpack, grabbed her coat, and walked barefoot out the door.

The next morning, when Wes awoke, he opened his eyes and saw Jill's note in the datebook on the pillow beside him: "This should save you the trouble," she had written. Wes studied the note, flipped through Jill's book, then read the note again. He felt his eyes burn; he knew that he never should have told her the truth.

Midway through the afternoon of November twenty-fifth, with the sun sinking quickly in the gray Chicago sky, Gail Schiffler-Wasserstrom, her eyes and nose red, leaned out the front door of her house and called out to Wes, interrupting the football game that he was playing with Rachel. It had been a long game of football. The part that Rachel had most enjoyed was when Gershom Globus had skipped by and said that girls didn't know how to throw footballs; Wes had curtly asked Gershom if he could throw a football and when Gershom had said yes, of course he could, Wes had said that was funny, because he had thought that Gershom was a girl.

After Gail and Wes had whispered to each other for a half-minute—"He was such a good man, wasn't he? I was just beginning to like him," Rachel heard her mother say—Gail went back inside the house, and Wes handed Rachel's football

back to her. He said that he had to go. Rachel was disappointed but not surprised; her entire life seemed to be composed of brief moments of happiness separated from the grim anticipation of people leaving—leaving for college, for
Europe, for work, for ever. Her parents were old, she thought, so old that they
said they couldn't have a little brother for her, even if they wanted one; when they
left her with babysitter Leah Levy, she would sometimes wonder if they would return. From the moment when she and Wes had started playing football, she had
wondered when he too would say that he was leaving. And when he said it, she
had the sensation that she had heard him say it before. She asked him if he would
be coming back the next day or some time afterward. He kissed her on the head,
told her that he hoped so, but he really wasn't sure. She walked back inside the
house and sat on the living room couch with her mother and father, who were
staring blankly at the TV screen, watching the news, waiting for Jill to come
home, waiting for her to leave.

Wes started up his car and drove fast through West Rogers Park, speeding
south on California, underneath the *eruv,* then east until he got to Lake Shore
Drive. All the while, he kept the windows shut and WBBM Newsradio 78 up
loud as John Cody reported the news that Gail had just told Wes, that official
word had come from Northwestern Memorial Hospital—Mayor Harold Washington had died of a heart attack at the age of sixty-five; a vigil was being held
downtown at Daley Center Plaza. Wes pushed his foot down harder on the gas;
he knew that if Jill was in Chicago, he would find her there.

When she had arrived at O'Hare Airport that afternoon, Jill had appeared so
happy to see Muley standing outside the customs hall with a bouquet of white
roses that he had waited until they had boarded an eastbound subway car before
he told her the news. By the time that they reached Daley Center, hundreds of
mourners had already gathered. Jill had her backpack over her shoulders and
Muley's bouquet in her hands as they walked through the swelling crowd: some
people were crying, holding on to each other for support. A preacher in a White
Sox cap was delivering an impromptu sermon in front of the plaza's unnamed
Picasso sculpture, quoting the last passages of Deuteronomy. But mostly, the
plaza was silent—people were milling about, nodding at each other, biting
their lips, shaking their heads, dazed, standing with their hands in their jacket
pockets, waiting for someone else to once again tell them something that they
already knew.

Jill was thinking of the great hopes that she had had just five years earlier when she had listened to Washington speak in Hyde Park. Muley was thinking of the joy he had felt in Florida when he had first seen the space shuttle rising into the sky; now *Challenger* was gone, Harold Washington and Halley's Comet too, but, he thought, at least he and Jill were standing together. Jill and Muley saw lines of police cars and limousines stalled in front of City Hall; purple and black bunting was hanging from the County Building, and all downtown flags were already at half-mast.

In front of the eternal flame memorial, Jill laid her flowers on the ground. She turned to Muley, smiled through her tears, kissed him, then asked if he wanted to go home now. He nodded and took her hand, briefly wondering if she meant West Rogers Park. But when Wes Sullivan finally arrived at Daley Center, Jill and Muley were heading south toward Bronzeville Studios. Wes did not cross to follow them; it looked as if they knew exactly where they were going.

# Glossary of Selected Terms

**Abbott, Jack Henry.** Convicted murderer and author of *In the Belly of the Beast,* a work that grew out of a correspondence with Norman Mailer.

*afikoman.* A piece of matzo that is hidden for children to find on Passover. Literally: dessert. Vulgar alternative uses: "Hey, do you want to hide the *afikoman* with me tonight?"

**a-ha.** 1980s band, perhaps best known for the lavishly animated video of the 1985 hit single "Take on Me."

*aleph.* First letter of the Hebrew alphabet; first grade of Hebrew school.

**Alphaville.** Quintessential 1980s band named after Jean-Luc Godard's sci-fi film. Best known, if at all, for the 1984 single "Big in Japan."

*alte cocker.* Old fart. Literally: old shitter (Yiddish).

**"American Pie."** Ubiquitous 1971 Don McLean song.

**Anderson, John.** Republican U.S. Congressman from Illinois. Ran unsuccessfully as an independent candidate for the presidency in 1980.

**Andropov, Yuri.** Former head of the KGB and general secretary of the Communist Party (1982–84).

*aroys geverfeneh gelt.* A waste of money (Yiddish).

*ash'rai.* Hebrew prayer. Literally: blessed.

*Aliyah.* Ascent. Moving to Israel (Hebrew).

**"Auf der Flucht."** Catchy song by Austrian pop artist Falco. Literally: "On the Run" (German).

*Ausländer raus.* "Foreigners, out" (German).

**Babilonia, Tai.** Figure skater whose dreams of Olympic glory ended when partner Randy Gardner suffered a groin injury.

*babka.* A coffee cake.

**babushka.** A scarf or headcovering; a Russian grandmother who might wear this sort of scarf or head covering.

**Bakalis, Michael.** 1978 Democratic candidate for Illinois governor.

**Balsam, Martin.** Film and television actor. Best known either for winning Oscar for *A Thousand Clowns* or for meeting an unfortunate end in Alfred Hitchcock's *Psycho.*

**Barber, Samuel.** Twentieth-century American composer. Known for operas and his *Adagio for Strings.*

*Baruch Atah.* Praised be Thou (Hebrew).

*Battle of Algiers, The.* Seminal 1965 cinéma verité account of the French-Algerian war.

*Bebe Le Strange.* 1980 Heart album featuring the title song as well as hit singles "Down on Me" and "Even It Up."

*Beit ha Knesset.* A house of prayer or community (Hebrew).

*Beneath the Underdog.* Occasionally lurid, often manic, always compelling autobiography of jazz legend Charles Mingus.

**Berle, Milton.** Actor and entertainer known for both his comedic and, umm, physical endowments; aka "Mr. Television" and "Uncle Miltie."

**Biden, Joseph, Jr.** Democratic senator (from Delaware) who, in 1987, dropped out of the race for the presidential nomination amid allegations that he had plagiarized a speech of British Labour Party leader Neil Kinnock.

**Big Bopper, The.** Born Jiles Perry Richardson Jr., the singer who passed away in the same 1959 plane crash that took the lives of Buddy Holly and Ritchie Valens.

*Big Chill, The.* 1983 Lawrence Kasdan film whose ubiquitous soundtrack triggered a Motown music revival.

**Bleier, Rocky.** Legendary Pittsburgh Steelers running back and Vietnam vet.

*Blow-Up.* Michelangelo Antonioni's existential 1966 thriller.

*Blues Brothers, The.* Classic 1980 John Landis feature film, which helped to revitalize the Chicago film industry.

**Boomtown Rats, The.** Seminal 1970s and '80s New Wave band fronted by future Live Aid organizer Bob Geldof.

**Bork, Robert.** Conservative judge who was nominated to serve on the U.S. Supreme Court by Ronald Reagan but did not survive Senate confirmation hearings.

**Boss, The.** Dorky nickname for Bruce Springsteen.

*boychik.* Boy (Yiddish diminutive).

**Boy Named Charlie Brown, A.** 1969 animated feature concerning the titular character's trip to the spelling bee.

*bracha.* Blessing (Hebrew).

**Bradford, Buddy.** Three-time outfielder for the Chicago White Sox, with a strange ability to launch baseballs onto the roof of Chicago's Comiskey Park.

*breirot.* Choices (Hebrew).

**Brezhnev, Leonid.** General secretary of the Communist Party (1966–1982).

**Bridges, Todd.** Actor best known for playing the role of Willis Jackson on TV's *Diff'rent Strokes.*

**Brinkley, Christie.** Quintessential 1980s supermodel.

**Brodien, Marshall.** Longtime Chicago-based magician and entertainer, best known for advertising magic playing cards on television.

**Bronski Beat.** UK pop band that attained worldwide fame in the 1980s with "Smalltown Boy" and "Hit That Perfect Beat."

**Bronson, Charles.** Tough-guy actor with limited emotional range; best known for playing Paul Kersey in *Death Wish* and its numerous sequels.

**Buckner, Bill.** Droopy-mustached sex symbol who played first base for the Chicago Cubs (1977–84).

**Butthole Surfers.** Rock band founded in 1981 in Texas by Gibby Haynes and Paul Leary.

**Byrne, Jane.** Chicago's first woman mayor (1979–83), perhaps best known for her citywide music and food festivals and her singing voice.

**Caravelle.** Crispy, chocolate-covered candy bar.

**Carew, Rod.** Hall of Fame Minnesota Twins and California Angels infielder.

*Chabad.* A form of Chasidic Judaism.

*ch'ai.* A pendant featuring the Hebrew word for "alive."

*chaloushes.* Nauseating, foul-tasting (Yiddish).

**Champale.** A fizzy malt-liquor beverage with a purportedly classy-sounding name.

***Chariots of Fire.*** Academy Award–winning 1981 film about British runners Harold Abrahams and Eric Liddell.

**Chernenko, Konstantin.** General secretary of the Communist Party (1984).

***Chicago Bee.*** Weekly black-owned Chicago newspaper headquartered on South State Street during the first half of the twentieth century.

***Chicago Defender, The.*** Founded in 1905, the oldest black-owned newspaper in Chicago.

**chisanbop.** A method of calculation using one's digits.

***Chorus Line, A.*** Long-running Broadway musical, originally directed by Michael Bennett.

***Chumash.*** The Five Books of Moses (Hebrew).

***Civic Culture, The.*** Seminal political science text edited by Gabriel A. Almond and Sidney Verba.

**Cleary, Beverly.** Beloved children's author and creator of such characters as Henry Huggins, Ramona Quimby, and Ribsy the dog.

**"Cool It Now."** 1984 song by New Edition.

**Copland, Aaron.** American composer of *Rodeo, Billy the Kid,* and *Fanfare for the Common Man,* whose music has been frequently used to introduce Bob Dylan concerts.

***Count Oederland.*** 1951 theatrical parable by Swiss playwright Max Frisch.

***Court and Spark.*** 1974 Joni Mitchell album and soundtrack to the lives of hundreds of thousands of college students.

***Cujo.*** Stephen King novel about an unpleasant dog.

**Culture Club.** UK-based New Wave band fronted by Boy George.

***dalet.*** Fourth letter of the Hebrew alphabet; fourth grade in Hebrew school.

**Daley, Richard J.** Blustery Chicago mayor (1955–76) and subject of books such as *Boss* by Mike Royko.

**Daley, Richard M.** Former Cook County State's Attorney, unsuccessful 1983 mayoral candidate, and son of former mayor RICHARD J. DALEY.

***Damenwahl.*** A Sadie Hawkins–style dance. Literally: ladie's choice (German).

**Danceteria.** Popular New York City dance club.

***daven.*** To pray (Yiddish).

**Day, Doris.** Singer and actress known for her film roles in *The Pajama Game, The Man Who Knew Too Much,* and *Pillow Talk.* No relation to MORRIS DAY (see below).

**Day, Morris.** Leader of the band The Time. No relation to DORIS DAY (see above).

**Def Leppard.** Hard-rock band that made the musical request "Pour Some Sugar on Me."

**De Palma, Brian.** Film director whose 1980s work, e.g., *Dressed to Kill,* spawned several excellent parodies in *MAD* magazine.

**Derek, Bo.** Noted thespian, featured in such films as *10, Bolero,* and *Tarzan, the Ape Man.*

***Dharma Bums, The.*** 1958 novel by Jack Kerouac.

***Dick Deterred.*** 1974 play by British playwright David Edgar.

***Disappearance of the Jews, The.*** 1982 playlet by Chicago playwright David Mamet.

***Diva.*** Atmospheric 1981 French flick directed by Jean-Jacques Beineix.

**Dohrn, Bernardine.** Chicago-based political radical, onetime member of Students for a Democratic Society and the Weathermen.

**Downey, Morton, Jr.** Host of the eponymous *Morton Downey Jr. Show.*

***dreck.*** Shit (Yiddish).

***dreidel.*** A spinning toy used primarily on Chanukah.

**Duarte, José Napoleón.** U.S.-supported president of El Salvador.

**"Du Bist die Ruh."** Song composed by Franz Schubert to a text by Friedrich Ruckert. Literally: "You are the Calm" (German).

**Duran, Roberto.** Panamanian-born boxer who immortalized the phrase *"No más"* in a 1980 match against Sugar Ray Leonard.

***Dynamite* magazine.** Classic 1970s children's periodical popular among fans of John Travolta, Shaun Cassidy, et al.

**Effigies, The.** Influential 1980s Chicago punk band.

***einmal in a Purim.*** Once in a long while (Yiddish). Literally: one time in a Purim.

**Ellerbee, Linda.** 1980s NBC television journalist.

***Emmanuelle.*** 1974 X-rated film starring Sylvia Kristel. To date, the only pornographic film to play in mainstream movie houses in West Rogers Park.

***End of the World News, The.*** 1982 novel by Anthony Burgess.

**Epton, Bernard.** Moderate Republican congressman from Illinois and unsuccessful 1983 Chicago mayoral candidate.

**eruv.** A border usually made of twine or fishing wire used to encircle Orthodox Jewish neighborhoods (Hebrew).

**E.T.** 1982 Steven Spielberg weeper about the titular marooned extraterrestrial.

**Evert, Chris.** 1970s and '80s tennis star.

**"Everybody Wants You."** 1982 pop single from the album *Emotions in Motion,* performed by Billy Squier, a man able to do a killer Robert Plant imitation.

**FALN.** Radical Puerto Rican independence group; acronym for *Fuerzas Armadas de Liberácion Nacional.*

**Fanny and Alexander.** Comparatively cheerful 1982 Ingmar Bergman film.

**"Far from Over."** Theme song from STAYING ALIVE, performed by the brother of the film's director, Sylvester Stallone.

**faygeleh.** Disparaging term for homosexual. Literally: little bird (Yiddish).

**Flash, Grandmaster.** Leader of the seminal hip-hop outfit Grandmaster Flash and the Furious Five.

**Flirtin' with Disaster.** Album by southern rock group Molly Hatchet.

**Fontaine, Joan.** American film actress, winner of Academy Award for Best Actress for the Alfred Hitchcock film *Suspicion.*

**Fool for Love.** 1983 Sam Shepard play.

**Fosdick, Fearless.** Bumbling detective from classic Al Capp comic strip *Li'l Abner.*

**Frampton, Peter.** British guitar legend and cofounder of the band Humble Pie; best known for the 1976 double album *Frampton Comes Alive!*

**Frankie Goes to Hollywood.** Momentarily huge 1980s UK pop band that urged its fans to relax.

**Fratianne, Linda.** 1980 U.S. Olympic figure-skating silver medalist.

**Garfield.** Cartoon cat created by Jim Davis; ubiquitous in college dorm rooms circa 1984.

**gedempte fleisch.** Pot roast (Yiddish).

**gelt.** Money (Yiddish).

**genug.** Enough (Yiddish).

**Gielgud, Sir John.** Shakespearean actor who won an Academy Award, not for playing Hamlet, not for playing Richard III, but for playing the wisecracking butler in the 1981 film *Arthur.*

**Gilder, George.** An architect of Reaganomics and author of the 1981 book *Wealth and Poverty.*

**Ginsu.** A brand of knife advertised frequently on late-night television.

**"Go Down Fighting."** Hooliganish love song by the band Nazareth.

**Goetz, Bernhard.** Aka "the Subway vigilante." Achieved notoriety after shooting four young men who'd allegedly asked him for change on board a Manhattan subway in December 1984.

*gohonzon.* A prayer scroll. Literally: object of worship (Japanese).

**Gonzalez, Speedy.** Fleet-footed, large-eared Warner Brothers cartoon character.

**Gooden, Dwight.** New York Mets fireball pitcher, 1984 National League Rookie of the Year.

*Gott im himmel.* God in heaven (Yiddish).

**Gould, Elliott.** 1970s Semitic heartthrob and movie star.

**Grant, Amy.** Christian pop songstress.

**Grecian Formula.** A hair-care product designed to eliminate unsightly grayness.

**Greene, Shecky.** Jewish stand-up comedian.

**Grimace.** A strange purple creature who advertises McDonald's restaurants.

**Grosbard, Ulu.** New York stage director who also directed the 1981 film *True Confessions* and the 1984 film *Falling in Love.*

**Guardian Angels.** Founded by Curtis Sliwa in New York City, a red-bereted patrolling security force.

**Hadassah.** Jewish women's Zionist organization.

**"Hair of the Dog."** Pugnacious song by the band Nazareth.

*Hamletmachine.* 1978 play by Heiner Müller.

*Hashem.* Hebrew word used in place of *God.* Literally: The Name.

*Havdalah.* Ritual performed at the end of the Jewish Sabbath.

**Heaven 17.** 1980s pop band that took its name from Anthony Burgess's *A Clockwork Orange;* best known song: "(We Don't Need This) Fascist Groove Thang."

*heh.* Fifth grade in Hebrew school; fifth letter of Hebrew alphabet.

**hell's bells.** An exclamation of astonishment; also a song by AC/DC.

**Herman, Jerry.** Composer and lyricist for such Broadway musicals as *Hello, Dolly!* and *Mame.*

**"Hey, Big Spender."** Relatively suggestive (by Broadway standards) ditty from the musical *Sweet Charity,* featuring lyrics that address the topic of cork-popping.

**Honecker, Erich.** East German Communist Party leader.

**"Hot Girls in Love."** Cautionary tale of romance by Loverboy.

**Houseman, John.** Actor, director, and producer who gained fame in the 1970s and '80s for his role as Professor Kingsfield in the movie and TV show *The Paper Chase;* also as pitchman for Smith Barney.

**Hunter, The.** 1980 film partly shot in Chicago and starring Steve McQueen and Eli Wallach.

**Infidels.** Classic 1983 album by Bob Dylan, produced by Dire Straits guitarist Mark Knopfler; hailed as Dylan's return to his Jewish roots.

**Intellivision.** Home video game system popular in the 1980s.

**"It's Like That."** Hit hip-hop song by Run-D.M.C., espousing a rather passive life philosophy.

**Ives, Burl.** Burly actor and singer known for his roles in *Cat on a Hot Tin Roof* and *White Dog,* and as a narrator for *Rudolph, the Red-Nosed Reindeer;* also for the album *The Lollipop Tree.*

**"I Want Your Sex."** George Michael song featuring the titular plea.

**Jackson, Jesse.** Civil rights leader, president of Operation PUSH, and unsuccessful 1984 candidate for the Democratic presidential nomination.

**Jauss, Hans Robert.** Noted literary critic and author of *Toward an Aesthetic of Reception.*

**Jigsaw Man, The.** Spy thriller that reunited *Sleuth* stars Michael Caine and Laurence Olivier.

**jizz.** Semen (vulgar).

**Johnson, Earvin "Magic."** Star member of Los Angeles Lakers' championship teams.

**Jolson, Al.** Legendary song-and-dance man and star of the first sound movie, *The Jazz Singer.*

**Jordan, Barbara.** The first African-American woman since Reconstruction to be elected to the U.S. Congress from the South. Famous for her keynote speech at the 1976 Democratic National Convention.

**Journey.** Rock band responsible for "Open Arms" as the ubiquitous high school prom song of the 1980s.

**Juba.** A traditional West African group dance.

**Judas Priest.** Seminal British heavy-metal band.

**Juggs.** A pornographic periodical with a mammary focus.

**Just Say No.** 1980s motto opposing drug use popularized by First Lady Nancy Reagan.

**Kaddish.** A prayer of mourning (Aramaic).

**Kent, Herb.** Legendary Chicago disk jockey, nicknamed "The Cool Gent."

*ketzeleh.* A kitten (Yiddish).

*kichel.* A Jewish sugar-coated cookie.

*kiddush.* A blessing said over wine.

**Kihn, Greg.** Leader of the Greg Kihn Band.

**Kingman, Dave.** Heavy-slugging Chicago Cubs outfielder and first baseman (1978–80).

*King Solomon's Mines.* Oft-adapted Sir H. Rider Haggard adventure.

**K.I.N.S.** A West Rogers Park synagogue.

*kippah.* A head covering (Hebrew).

**Kitaro.** One of the earliest "New Age" music artists.

**Koch, Ed.** Mayor of New York (1977–89).

*kochleffel.* A busybody. Literally: cooking spoon (Yiddish).

*kugel.* Traditional Jewish side dish generally made with noodles or potatoes.

**Kupcinet, Irv.** Former Chicago *Sun-Times* gossip columnist, sports announcer, and host of local PBS program *Kup's Show.*

**Kuti, Fela.** Controversial political activist and Nigerian musician fond of evocative titles, such as "Confusion Break Bones."

*Lady Sings the Blues.* 1972 Billie Holiday biopic starring Diana Ross and Billy Dee Williams.

*La Jetée.* Influential 1962 short film directed by Chris Marker.

**Landers, Ann.** Famed Chicago advice columnist, born Esther "Eppie" Friedman.

*Last Waltz, The.* Classic 1978 documentary featuring The Band and numerous guest musicians, and credulous interviews performed by director Martin Scorsese.

*Last Year at Marienbad.* Classic 1961 mind-screw directed by Alain Resnais from a script by *nouveau roman* pioneer Alain Robbe-Grillet.

**Law, Johnny.** A police officer (colloquial).

**Le Pew, Pepé.** A debonair French cartoon skunk.

*Let It Be.* Classic 1984 album by The Replacements.

**"Let's Go Crazy."** Opening track of *Purple Rain.*

**"Lido Shuffle."** Hit single from the 1976 Boz Scaggs album *Silk Degrees.*

*Lifeguard.* 1976 film featuring Sam Elliott as an aging lifeguard.

**Light Years Away.** 1981 Alain Tanner film starring Trevor Howard; winner of the 1981 Cannes Grand Jury prize.

**Lorenz, Konrad.** Austrian-born behaviorist, notorious for fucking up a lot of ducks.

**"Love Hurts."** 1976 Nazareth power ballad.

**Loverboy.** 1980s rock band.

**McCarthy, Eugene.** Liberal Minnesota senator and unsuccessful presidential candidate in 1968 and 1976.

**McDade's.** A defunct Chicagoland department store.

**McDonald, Ronald.** Clown mascot for McDonald's hamburger restaurants.

**McGee, Fibber.** Character on the long-running radio comedy *Fibber McGee and Molly.*

**machzor.** Jewish prayer book.

**McNichol, Kristy.** Actress best known for her roles on TV's *Family* and in such movies as *Little Darlings* and *White Dog.*

**Maimonides, Moses.** Twelfth-century rabbi noted for his biblical commentaries.

**Manero, Tony.** Disco dancer and Broadway star of the classic show *Satan's Alley;* portrayed by John Travolta in *Saturday Night Fever* and *Staying Alive.*

**mensch.** A decent, upstanding individual (Yiddish).

**Merrily We Roll Along.** 1981 Stephen Sondheim musical.

**mezuzah.** A small scroll inscribed with passages from the Bible.

**Micheaux, Oscar.** Early-twentieth-century African-American filmmaker.

**mikvah.** Jewish ritual bath.

**Ministry.** Seminal industrial Chicago band formed by Al Jourgensen and fronted for a time by Chris Connelly.

**minyan.** The required number of men for prayer services.

**mishigoss.** Craziness (Yiddish).

**"Missing You."** 1984 hit single by John Waite.

**mitzvah.** A good deed (Hebrew).

**Mondale, Walter "Fritz."** U.S. senator from Minnesota, vice president under Jimmy Carter, and unsuccessful 1984 presidential candidate.

**Moose Murders.** Not particularly successful 1983 Broadway play by Arthur Bicknell.

**Moral Majority.** Right-wing fringe group founded in 1979 by Reverend Jerry Falwell.

***Moshiach.*** The Messiah (Hebrew).

***Mrs. Warren's Profession.*** Provocative George Bernard Shaw play noteworthy for its consideration of prostitution.

***Murder in the Cathedral.*** Play by T. S. Eliot, concerning the murder of Thomas à Becket.

**MX missile.** A mobile intercontinental ballistic missile, nicknamed "The Peacekeeper" by Ronald Reagan.

**Myron & Phil's.** Classic Lincolnwood restaurant known for its steaks and relish trays.

***Nam myoho renge kyo.*** A chant that reportedly produces enlightenment upon repetition.

**Nappy.** Fuzzy (adj.); pubic hair (vulgar).

**Nazareth.** Popular 1970s hard rock band. (See also "LOVE HURTS" and "HAIR OF THE DOG").

***Never Say Never Again.*** 1983 James Bond flick featuring Sean Connery.

***Nisht far mir.*** Not for me (Yiddish).

***Night and Day.*** Early Virginia Woolf novel.

**Nkrumah, Kwame.** President of Ghana (1960–1966).

*nosh.* Snack (Yiddish).

*nuchum.* In the past (Yiddish).

**Odetta.** Folksinger often featured on Chicago radio show *The Midnight Special.*

***Officer and a Gentleman, An.*** 1982 date movie starring Richard Gere and Debra Winger.

***Oh! Calcutta!*** Mid-1970s revue of theatrical sketches penned by John Lennon, Sam Shepard, and others, and featuring a cast of nude actors.

***Omni Magazine.*** Popular 1980s magazine blending science and science fiction.

**on time.** An optimal situation (colloquial), e.g., "Man, that is on time."

*oy gevalt.* Oh God (Yiddish).

***Paint Your Wagon.*** 1969 movie based on the Broadway musical and featuring unlikely singing performances by Clint Eastwood and Lee Marvin.

**Parker, Dave.** Right fielder for Pittsburgh Pirates, among other major league baseball teams.

*pasgudna.* Disgusting (Yiddish).

*payess.* Sidelocks (Hebrew).

**perihelion.** The point in which a celestial body is closest to the sun.

***Pesach.*** Passover (Hebrew).

**Pez.** Pastel-colored small candies most noteworthy for their amusing dispensers.

**Pinners.** A game involving whipping a rubber ball at the stoop of a house and attempting to catch it.

**Piven, Frances Fox, and Richard Cloward.** Political scientists and authors of seminal text *Poor People's Movements.*

**Plant, Robert.** Lead singer of Led Zeppelin, fond of showing off his PUPIK.

***puchky.*** Chubby (Yiddish).

**"Pulling Mussels (From the Shell)."** Danceable song from hyperliterate pop band Squeeze.

***pupik.*** Belly button (see PLANT, ROBERT).

***Purple Rain.*** Classic 1984 Prince album and not-so-classic 1984 Prince film.

***pushki.*** A pushcart (Yiddish; colloquial).

***Quartermaine's Terms.*** 1981 play by British author Simon Gray.

***Quest for Fire.*** 1981 caveman flick directed by Jean-Jacques Annaud.

**Rathbone, Basil.** South Africa–born actor who played Sherlock Holmes in numerous films.

***Risky Business.*** Classic 1983 critique of 1980s greed and prostitution (see also MRS. WARREN'S PROFESSION), starring Tom Cruise, Rebecca DeMornay, and featuring Wayne Kneeland. Filmed in and around Chicago.

**Rob Roy.** Alcoholic drink containing whisky and vermouth.

**Rochester.** Gravelly voiced valet on radio and television's *The Jack Benny Show.*

**"Rocket Man."** Hit song from Elton John album *Honky Château.*

**Romeo Void.** Pop group best known for "Girl in Trouble (Is a Temporary Thing)."

**Rossman, Mike.** Jewish light-heavyweight boxing champion.

**Rubik's Cube.** Maddening multicolored puzzle cube.

**Run-D.M.C.** Groundbreaking 1980s hip-hop group hailing from Queens.

**"Safety Dance."** Hit single by Men Without Hats.

**Sagan, Carl.** PBS television host and author of books such as *Cosmos.*

**Salter, James.** American author perhaps best known for 1975's *Light Years.*

**Saura, Carlos.** Stylish Spanish-born director of such films as *Blood Wedding, Carmen,* and *A Love Bewitched.*

***schlafen.*** To sleep (German).

*schmatta.* A rag or babushka (Yiddish).

*schmeckel.* Penis (Yiddish).

*schwantz.* See SCHMECKEL.

**Scritti Politti.** UK pop band that achieved worldwide fame with the album *Songs to Remember.*

**Sedaka, Neil.** Semitic pop singer-songwriter of such ditties as "Calendar Girl."

**Seeger, Pete.** Founding member of The Weavers, singer-songwriter, and political activist.

*Sh'ma Yisroel.* Hebrew prayer ("Hear, O Israel").

**Sha Na Na.** 1950s retro band, which also spawned a late-night television show of the same name.

**Shaft.** Lead detective character in the novels of Ernest Tidyman and their cinematic adaptations.

*shandeh.* A shameful act.

**Sharpton, Al.** Prominent African-American reverend and activist who gained notoriety in the 1980s.

*shiksa.* A non-Jewish woman (derogatory).

*shtup.* To engage in the act of coitus (vulgar).

*shul.* Synagogue.

**skank.** A woman of questionable repute. Adjectival form: skanky.

**Smith, Patti.** The godmother of American punk rock.

**Smithereens, The.** New Jersey–bred rock band that emerged onto the national scene with the 1986 album *Especially for You.*

**Smiths, The.** Angst-ridden 1980s Brit band led by Morrissey and Johnny Marr.

**"Snatch It Back and Hold It."** Blues song written and performed by Chicago blues harpist Junior Wells.

**Sondheim, Stephen.** Groundbreaking lyricist and composer of *Company, Pacific Overtures,* and *Sunday in the Park with Gershom.*

*Song Remains the Same, The.* 1976 Led Zeppelin concert film featuring bizarre fantasy sequences. A favorite of burnouts everywhere.

*Soul on Ice.* Memoir of Black Panther Eldridge Cleaver.

*Soul Train.* Long-running dance, music, and variety show hosted by Don Cornelius.

***Soyuz.*** Name given to spacecraft in the Soviet space program. Literally: union.

**Spacek, Sissy.** American actress who achieved fame in 1970s films such as *Badlands* and *Carrie,* in which she uttered the immortal lines "They're all gonna laugh at you" and "I can move thangs."

***spazier.*** To walk around and browse.

***spilkes.*** Visible anxiety; ants in one's pants.

**Spinks, Leon.** Briefly world heavyweight boxing champion.

***Spook Who Sat by the Door, The.*** Classic African-American revolutionary novel by Sam Greenlee.

***Spring Awakening.*** Late-nineteenth-century play by Frank Wedekind.

***State of Things, The.*** 1982 Wim Wenders film shot in Los Angeles and Portugal.

**Staying Alive.** 1983 sequel to *Saturday Night Fever.* See also MANERO, TONY and "FAR FROM OVER."

**Stevenson, Adlai.** Governor of Illinois and twice-unsuccessful Democratic candidate for the presidency; father to Illinois Senator Adlai Stevenson III.

***streimel.*** A particularly furry hat.

**Sumac, Yma.** Peruvian singer who attained cult status in the 1950s.

**"Super Bowl Shuffle, The."** Unlikely hit single sung by the musically challenged Super Bowl champion Chicago Bears, including "Speedy Willie" Gault, William "Refrigerator" Perry, and Walter "Sweetness" Payton.

**Sutter, Bruce.** Chicago Cubs relief pitcher (1976–1980) who maintained a scruffy appearance for good luck.

**Swayze, Patrick.** Mulleted 1980s heartthrob.

**swirly.** A bizarre form of grade school torture involving the dunking of one's foe's head into a toilet.

***Tanakh.*** The sacred book of Judaism.

***tararam.*** A big fuss (Yiddish).

***tefillin.*** Phylacteries (Hebrew).

**Theus, Reggie.** Guard for the Chicago Bulls (1978–84).

***Thief.*** 1981 Michael Mann movie filmed on the north side of Chicago, featuring James Caan, Tuesday Weld, and Dennis Farina.

***Things to Come.*** Fanciful 1936 sci-fi flick scripted by H. G. Wells.

**Thompson, James.** Governor of Illinois in the 1980s, nicknamed "Big Jim."

**Thompson Twins.** New Wave, somewhat synthetic 1980s band, best known for the 1984 album *Into the Gap*.

**Thornton, Fonzi.** Noted R&B performer.

*Timerider.* 1982 sci-fi flick with a script cowritten by former Monkee Michael Nesmith.

*Time Stands Still.* 1982 Hungarian coming-of-age film set in 1950s Hungary, directed by Péter Gothár.

**Tommy Tutone.** Band best known for the disturbingly catchy song "867–5309."

*trou du cul.* Asshole (French).

*tsitsis.* Fringes worn on the corners of garments (Hebrew).

**tubular.** Cool, desirable (slang); adjective featured in the song "VALLEY GIRL" (see below).

*tuchus.* Rear end (Yiddish, informal).

*tuchus auf den tisch.* Rude and unsubtle. Literally: ass on the table (Yiddish).

*tzedakah.* Charity (Hebrew).

*Uncommon Valor.* 1983 MIA drama featuring Gene Hackman and PATRICK SWAYZE (see above).

**"Valley Girl."** 1982 Frank Zappa song featuring the vocal stylings of daughter Moon Unit.

*vercockte.* Shitty (Yiddish).

**Vrdolyak, Ed.** Former Cook County Democratic chairman and unsuccessful 1987 Illinois Solidarity Party candidate for mayor.

**Washington, Harold.** Forty-second mayor of Chicago. Born April 15, 1922; died November 25, 1987.

**Wenders, Wim.** Seminal figure in German cinema. Director of *Kings of the Road, Hammett,* and *Paris, Texas*.

*White Shadow, The.* Television series about Coach Ken Reeves's efforts to turn around the fortunes of an inner city high school basketball team.

**Williams, Billy Dee.** Devilishly handsome actor in such films as *Star Wars* and *Lady Sings the Blues*.

*yahrtzeit.* Anniversary of a relative's death.

**Yankovic, "Weird Al."** Kinky-haired comedian who made a career of song parodies.

*Yetziyat Mitzrayim.* The Exodus (Hebrew).

*yontiff.* Holiday (Yiddish).

**Youngman, Henny.** Comedian known as the "King of One-Liners."

*yuchna.* An unpleasant woman (Yiddish).

**Zebra.** Rock band that received 1980s airplay with songs such as "Who's Behind the Door?" and "Tell Me What You Want."

*Zelig.* 1983 mockumentary directed by Woody Allen.

# *Appendix I. Eruv*

| 1983 DEMOCRATIC MAYORAL PRIMARY | |
|---|---|
| **Candidate** | **Votes** |
| Harold Washington | 424,146 (36.5%) |
| Jane Byrne | 388,250 (33.4%) |
| Richard M. Daley | 344,721 (30%) |
| Frank Ranallo | 2,366 (less than 1%) |
| William Murkowski | 1,417 (less than 1%) |
| Total | 1,160,900 |

| 1983 GENERAL ELECTION | |
|---|---|
| **Candidate** | **Votes** |
| Harold Washington (D) | 668,176 (52%) |
| Bernard Epton (R) | 619,926 (48%) |
| Ed Warren (Socialist) | 3,756 (less than 1%) |
| Total | 1,291,858 |

# Appendix II. Breirot

| | | | | | | | | | | | |
|---|---|---|---|---|---|---|---|---|---|---|---|
| FIGURE 1.1 |
| *October 8, 1983* |
| *Comiskey Park (Chicago, IL)* |
| *Game 4* |

| | 1 | 2 | 3 | 4 | 5 | 6 | 7 | 8 | 9 | 10 | Total |
|---|---|---|---|---|---|---|---|---|---|---|---|
| Baltimore Orioles | 0 | 0 | 0 | 0 | 0 | 0 | 0 | 0 | 0 | 3 | 3 |
| Chicago White Sox | 0 | 0 | 0 | 0 | 0 | 0 | 0 | 0 | 0 | 0 | 0 |

| | | | | | | | | | | |
|---|---|---|---|---|---|---|---|---|---|---|
| FIGURE 1.2 |
| *October 7, 1984* |
| *Jack Murphy Stadium (San Diego, CA)* |
| *Game 5* |

| | 1 | 2 | 3 | 4 | 5 | 6 | 7 | 8 | 9 | Total |
|---|---|---|---|---|---|---|---|---|---|---|
| Chicago Cubs | 2 | 1 | 0 | 0 | 0 | 0 | 0 | 0 | 0 | 3 |
| San Diego Padres | 0 | 0 | 0 | 0 | 0 | 2 | 4 | 0 | — | 6 |

# *Appendix III. Yetziyat Mitzrayim*

| 1984 PRESIDENTIAL ELECTION | | |
|---|---|---|
| **Candidate** | **Total Votes in Chicago** | **Total Votes in USA** |
| Ronald Reagan (R) | 387,719 (37%) | 53,354,037 (58%) |
| Walter Mondale (D) | 669,227 (63%) | 37,573,671 (41%) |
| Total | 1,056,946 | 92,628,458 |

# *Appendix IV. Kaddish*

| HISTORY OF SPACE SHUTTLE CHALLENGER MISSIONS | |
|---|---|
| **Date of Takeoff** | **Date of Return** |
| April 4, 1983 | April 9, 1983 |
| June 18, 1983 | June 24, 1983 |
| August 30, 1983 | September 5, 1983 |
| February 3, 1984 | February 11, 1984 |
| April 6, 1984 | April 13, 1984 |
| October 5, 1984 | October 13, 1984 |
| April 29, 1985 | May 6, 1985 |
| July 29, 1985 | August 6, 1985 |
| October 30, 1985 | November 6, 1985 |
| January 28, 1986 | — |

# *Appendix V. Aliyah*

| 1987 DEMOCRATIC MAYORAL PRIMARY | |
|---|---|
| **Candidate** | **Votes** |
| Harold Washington | 587,594 (53%) |
| Jane Byrne | 509,436 (46%) |
| Sheila Jones | 2,557 (less than 1%) |
| Total | 1,099,587 |

| 1987 GENERAL ELECTION | |
|---|---|
| **Candidate** | **Votes** |
| Harold Washington (D) | 600,290 (54%) |
| Ed Vrdolyak (Illinois Solidarity Party) | 468,493 (42%) |
| Donald Haider (R) | 47,652 (4%) |
| Total | 1,116,435 |

# Acknowledgments

Thanks for reasons too numerous to mention to: Joan Afton, Susan Ambler, LyleBenedict of the Municipal Reference Library, Beth Blickers, Christopher Cartmill, Mih-Ho Cha, Robin Chaplik, Paul Creamer, Mary Jo Doyle and the West Ridge Historical Society, Alexander Fest, Jennifer Gilmore, Anne Gleason, Mark Gleason, Rabbi Niles Goldstein, Dorian Hastings, Don Humbertson, Anne Jackson, Kazoo, Kristin Kloberdanz, Jerome Kramer, the Langer and Sissenich families, Belinda Lanks, Gadi Levanon and Amber Seligson-Levanon, Douglas Lynch and Neri DeKraemer, Tatiana Nell, Hemmendy Nelson, Mihai Radelescu, Stephanie Sorenson, Alison True and the *Chicago Reader,* Gary Tuber, Thomas Ueberhoff, Evaristo Urbaez and the Diego Rivera Building, and Eli Wallach. And also many special thanks to Beate Sissenich, Cindy Spiegel, and Marly Rusoff, without whom you would, most probably, have never had a chance to read this book.